Fire of the Covenant

Book 1
of the Dragon-Called Legend

PETER CRUIKSHANK

To Jared,
I hope you find this
little tale fun.

Peter
Cruikshank

'Be True to Your Fire Within!'

WICKED WOLF
━ B O O K S ━

Publisher

Wicked Wolf Books

1499 The Wilds,

Pretoria, Gauteng 0081

www.wickedwolfbooks.com

Editor

Ethan James Clarke

Silver Jay Media

Artist / Book Cover

Aidana WillowRaven

WillowRaven Illustration & Design

Maps

Peter Cruikshank

Hans-Peter Schöni

First Edition, 2013

ISBN 978-0-620-58399-2

DEDICATION

To my lovely wife Carol, who has supported and encouraged me through the many long hours of revision and the erratic bouts of frustration that it took to create this novel and fulfill a forty year dream. I love you for all you are and all you have done for me.

To my kids for always believing that Dad really was a writer.

To my Uncle Frank whom I used to humor when he told me someday I would be a writer, I know he is looking down on me now and saying, "I told you so."

ACKNOWLEDGMENTS

My thanks to Kirsten Bolda for reading the rough first draft, then providing constructive critiques and encouraging me through the turbulent times; to Ethan James Clarke, my editor, for taking me by the hand and guiding me through the publishing process without making too much fun of my grammatically-challenged abilities; to the Valley Center Writer's Group for providing invaluable feedback and making Saturday mornings a delight; to Frauke Nonnenmacher, Liz Schroeder, Jasmine Lee, Megan Eccles, and Watson Davis for taking the time to beta read this extremely long novel and providing insightful feedback; Hans-Peter Schöni for making sure my maps look like maps; Aidana WillowRaven for providing the gorgeous book cover; and my friends in Holly Lisle's forums who kept me on track, when I was going crazy, and reminded me that it is only a book and, most importantly, that the first draft is supposed to be torturous!

CONTENTS

MAPS

Prologue

Dark Messenger

The boy, tonight's Messenger, sat there, his long, drenched blond hair slapping against his cheeks as he quickly turned from one yellow-robed priest to the other, gibbering away in the local language. "Mi sain ham yo."

The sound was ugly and without any of the beauty of Chuluun-Uul's native tongue. The Uul imagined that, as with all the previous ones, the boy wanted to know what he had done wrong. He cried, and from what few words Chuluun-Uul could make out, the boy insisted he would not do it again.

"Mi bahn gung han yo."

The pleas barely registered on Chuluun-Uul's mind as his thoughts drifted to his homeland on the far eastern shores of Kieran. The ignorant cries only served to remind him that he was a great distance from home. Yet he never regretted the time, over twenty years traveling for the Master, overseeing the conversion of kingdoms to the Shin-il Way.

Chuluun-Uul wiped his bare forehead with a finely decorated cloth that matched his blood-red silk robes. The humid air of the cell added weight to the twisted hair that ran down to his waist and his floor-length robes stuck to his body. He decided he would need another bath before the night was out. He thought about what that meant.

I will have to wake Mei-Yin and Jun.

A smile crossed his lips as his mind turned to the two adolescent girls that he had acquired. He had been sure they had only recently had their first bleeding and he had confirmed for himself, just the other night, that they had not been spoiled by another man. He shook his head and pushed the thought to the back of his mind as he considered tonight's events. Even though the king and his nobles were firmly under the will of the Shin-il

1

priests, what was going to transpire tonight was not something he wished readily exposed to anyone outside of the small chamber. The musty smell of the dank cell and sulfur from the sconces on the wall made Chuluun-Uul wrinkle his nose. Even so, he thought he could almost smell the fear of the boy chained to the bench through the odor of mold and smoke.

The flickering light from the sconces cast an eerie glow over the child and Obeah priests. Both of the lower caste priests began chanting in their island tongue, one that Chuluun-Uul had never bothered to learn. After all, it was not necessary to speak the language of those whom you used any more than one talked to a mule or a desert death worm. You simply used them.

"Mi dain lam ko!" The boy yelled and pleaded for mercy, the sound bouncing off the thick cell walls. His tears flowed and he strained against his chains as he tried to turn his head toward Chuluun-Uul. The frightened boy promised he would do whatever the Uul wanted. Anything! Chuluun-Uul smiled. If only the boy could comprehend his contribution to the Way.

There was a glint of hope in the boy's eyes until one of the priests grabbed the blond hair and pulled the captive's head back. The second priest forced open the struggling boy's mouth and poured in an elixir of ground herbs doused with some liquid that smelled worse than the cell it-self. The Messenger sputtered for a few moments, a brown foam forming on his lips and streaming out of his nose.

Chuluun-Uul left while the priests began to insert small needles, coated with more of their toxins, under the boy's skin, causing him to jerk so hard it threatened to rip him from the bench. The sand would drain for a full turn of the hourglass before the Messenger would be ready. Chuluun-Uul would have time for a relaxing supper.

When Chuluun-Uul returned the Messenger sat unmoving, still connect-ed to the bench but his chains hanging limp. The black center of the eyes had grown, obliterating the bright blue they once were, until the entirety of them was nothing but a dark void. His mouth hung open, a yawning cavern, and the rest of his carcass a puppet suspended on loose strings.

Chuluun-Uul looked to the Obeah priest on either side of the Messen-ger. Their yellow robes covered every inch of their body except for their ebony hands. Even their faces were hidden behind the folds of their hoods. They were the very best at spells and herbs. And he hated them.

The magic of *il fennore* allowed a man to communicate with the Spirits and to bend the fabric of the world to his will... this was natural and as the Master commanded. What the Obeah did with their potions and talismans was an abomination. Chuluun-Uul had never understood the reason behind allowing the fanatical southern islanders into the priesthood, yet he truly believed the Master had reasons for everything he did.

Chuluun-Uul wrinkled his nose again as he stared at the necromancers.

The dead should be left to the Spirits, yet he could not argue with their success. The Messenger was needed and Chuluun-Uul had no qualms about the boy's fate. It was necessary.

"Is the Messenger ready?"

The priest on the left took out a small needle-thin blade. He stepped behind the Messenger, who never flinched as the blade point jutted out from his chest. Chuluun-Uul was surprised, as in past times, by the little amount of blood that stained the Messenger's tunic.

Chuluun-Uul never asked where the children came from. He assumed an outlying village or taken in some dark alley down in the poorer regions of the city, if that is what you could call it.

Even though it was the center of the kingdom, compared to the sprawling city of Tsagaan it felt like nothing more than a mud village. Chuluun-Uul chastised himself for such thoughts. He should be used to it after having been away from home for more than four hands of years. He had arrived in this kingdom over a year ago and hated the place almost as much as he did the Obeah priests.

The priest pulled the blade out, again leaving little blood to mark the tiny hole. As usual, the priest said nothing, but his hood nodded his response.

"Good. It is time." Chuluun-Uul moved over to stand in front of the Messenger.

A momentary feeling of compassion came over him as he stared at the flaccid boy, but Chuluun-Uul drove the thought from his mind as he had with the two young girls waiting for him. He reminded himself that the Messenger was just a tool, like the Obeah and the girls. Tsagaan was a great distance away and a message could take months depending upon weather conditions in this cursed northern wasteland. A few days around each full moon the Obeah priests were employed, another child was found, and Chuluun-Uul would be able to communicate with his Master. Once again he would receive the inspiration he needed to continue until the next full moon.

The priest resumed their chanting, and the one with the blade sprinkled a fine powder over corpse until it jerked upright. The once-limp frame became solid and the head lifted of its own accord. The black eyes stared directly at the waiting Uul. Lowering himself to his knees, Chuluun-Uul bowed his head, but kept his eyes on the Messenger. He waited for the Messenger to speak first.

"Chuluun-Uul." The voice sounded nothing like the pleading squeal from earlier. Though still a child's voice it contained all the authority and power Chuluun-Uul had grown up with.

"Master." The Uul bowed a little deeper. He knew that the Messenger's body would be a true conduit reflecting everything Chuluun-Uul said and did back to his Master at the temple in faraway Tsagaan.

"Rise," he was commanded.

Standing, Chuluun-Uul kept his head bent in a respectful posture. "Thank you, Master. May the spirit of your life and the Shin-il Way be entwined forever." His traditional response was no less heartfelt after all these years. "How can this servant serve the Master?"

"You have done well," the child gave voice to the words of the distant master. "May I be assured the Kingdom of Rorterin is on the Shin-il Path?" It was a challenge as much as a question.

Chuluun-Uul lifted his head to stare into the eyes of the Master's vessel and did not flinch in his response. "Whatever you wish you may expect the king and his court to fulfill."

The momentary silence was unusual, but the Shin-il priest waited patiently, and would as long as was required.

"Can you leave Rorterin to the Kiyati-Uul?" The question caught Chuluun-Uul by surprise and his eyes popped, but he smoothed over his features quickly. *Could I possibly be going home?* His thoughts turned joyfully to the possibility.

"The king is very familiar with Kiyati-Uul. He has been at the king's side day and night." Once the defiant king had been converted, his kingdom had fallen in line. Chuluun-Uul had remained in the background while a subordinate functioned as the king's personal advisor to ensure his loyalty. "I have complete faith in his abilities."

"We have need of your special talents once again. This will be a long trip." The monotone voice did not lend itself to such news. Chuluun-Uul allowed himself to feel a quick sense of disappointment, but only for a moment. His life was that of the Shin-il Way and to serve his distant Master. The Messenger spoke again. "I have felt the Dragon-Called."

An excitement filled Chuluun-Uul's body. His disappointment at not returning to the temple was a far memory as he realized that all his previous service to the Master would be as nothing compared to this task. Chuluun-Uul fought to keep the emotion out of his voice, but still he asked bluntly, "Where?" He remembered his courtesies and added, "Honorable Master."

As a member of the Master's inner circle, the Gai-Ten, Chuluun-Uul was one of the few given the greatest task of all… to find the Dragon-Called.

"To the Far West. To the shores of Kieran and possibly beyond." The Messenger's lips moved but the face showed no expression other than the blank stare of those dead eyes.

The western shores of Kieran, Chuluun-Uul thought as he tried to estimate the distance. Over four thousand miles. With the poor conditions between the Kingdom of Rorterin and the Central Lands, it could take him more than a year, possibly two, to reach his goal. A stray thought jumped into his mind and as quickly jumped out, but gave him a tingle in his stomach all the same. *It will give Mei-Yin and Jun time to hone their skills.* "Master, the distance is great, it will take time."

"I have considered this. Know, my Gai-Ten that it will take even longer. They were lost to me after they were born – their mother – and I have searched long to find them. They are still young and their power is weak, but I can sense their presence, as yet faint, too faint to tell you exactly where, though their power grows."

Chuluun-Uul put his hands together and bowed his head in acceptance of the mission.

"You are like a son to me. You are my greatest Uul. Foremost of the Gai-Ten. You will not let me down."

The Messenger's flat tone held no emotion, yet Chuluun-Uul took pride in his Master's words. The pride in his thoughts were contrary to the Shin-il Way, but Chuluun-Uul relished in them nonetheless.

The Master continued, and even though the tone was lifeless, the insistence in the warning was clear. "Beware the Burning Lady." The voice paused, then added slowly, "Her vile servants will oppose you. And they are many in the unclaimed lands to the west."

The child's voice began to crack as it tried to speak again. The weakened body began to fail much sooner than Chuluun-Uul expected and even with all their skills, it was evident that the necromancers would not be able to keep the conduit functioning much longer.

Chuluun-Uul glared at the priest. This was unacceptable. The Vessel was flawed. The priests should have discovered this before they started the *calling*. The Messenger's head started to fall forward and the priest had to hold the rest of the carcass upright. The solid black eyes were fading to a dull, lifeless gray. Chuluun-Uul moved closer and leaned forward.

"Make your way to the coast. As they grow and their abilities become evident I will lead you to them."

The voice faded to a bare whisper. Chuluun-Uul moved even closer as the Messenger's lips moved one more time before the hollow corpse passed completely.

"My Uul. My son. Bring them to me."

1

Cousins

Willoe peeked out from behind the corner of the weaver's shop. The rain had dwindled to just a trickle and she watched the street urchin struggle in the grasp of an overly-muscled trader's guard. The guard was a lot bigger than he had looked when Willoe was across the square, the leather and woolen jerkin stretched tight across his chest, the muscles in his arms bulging like cords of twisted rope. She named him Big Guard.

A man in a decorative doublet with a knee-length cape, whom Willoe imagined from his finery was the trader, walked up with another guard only two-thirds the size of Big Guard. Willoe smiled as she named him Little Guard. She had to hold back a giggle when the trader's stomach shook like the cook's pudding as he straightened the belt around his robust waist.

The trader balled his fists and put them on his hips as he stared at the bawling, grime-covered boy. Big Guard shook the boy to get him to quiet and settle down, without success. The trader laughed, his cheeks rippling, and said something to Little Guard, causing them both to laugh louder.

The humor disappeared in Willoe's mind as she remembered what had driven her and her younger cousin's hastily put together plan. Casandra would be waiting under the bridge, across the square, at this very moment.

She looked at the street urchin again and it was hard to tell, since the boy was so thin and she couldn't make out too many details, but she thought he might be around fourteen or fifteen – two or three years older than Willoe. Straight hair, uncommon among Cainwens; a dark brown and sheared so that it hung raggedly around his shoulders.

It was mid-day and the planked walkway reminded Willoe of when the scullery maids flushed out rats from the kitchen pantries. Workers and shoppers filled the walkway, scurrying from shop to shop. Willoe moved onto the muddy planks and edged along the front of the shops lining the square. She kept close to the slatted and rough stone walls, tugging the front of her hood a little farther forward to make sure it covered her hair and face as it might raise an alarm. Most people would burn her at a stake for the signs of evil she bore, though she could do nothing about the green eyes or flaming red hair. If not for her Grandfather… well, she just couldn't let herself be identified. She couldn't afford to embarrass her family. Again.

The trader and his guards stood near the back of a loaded wagon where the street urchin had been caught by Big Guard. The silver goblet the boy had stolen from the open wagon lay on the cobblestones at his feet. Willoe hadn't seen the goblet from across the street, but regardless, she thought Big Guard was being a bit rough with the boy.

She was now close enough to hear the clink of coins in the trader's purse as it swayed with his movements.

The street urchin's voice broke as he pleaded with the trader. "I beg, let me go! Da is dead. Ma and three sisters. I only want t'buy food!"

"I am sure you are caring for your mother and sisters." The trader smiled and spoke in a mocking tone as he winked at Little Guard beside him, then his expression hardened. He leaned forward, grabbing the boy by the neck of his shirt. "I doubt you knew your father, you base-born little thief. You probably do not even know your mother, or whatever whore pushed you out."

"No, no!" The boy tried to break free from the trader's grip and only earned another rough shake from Big Guard.

The trader let go of the boy and stood up, anger staining his face. "I should not even waste my time turning you over to the City Guard. Maybe I should just punish you myself." He looked at Little Guard, who just snickered, the smaller man's eyes gleaming in anticipation.

The boy surprised Willoe by trying to kick Big Guard, which only caused all three men to laugh harder. He showed a lot more courage than his frightened cries had led her to believe he possessed.

The discussion only reaffirmed Willoe's decision to help the boy. She spotted Casandra walking across the small square toward the trader's wagon. Even though her cousin was just a year younger, she was a good four fingers shorter than Willoe. Casandra moved closer, almost floating like a bird gliding on the wind. Even at this distance Willoe could see a boldness in her eyes that contrasted with the soft features of her cousin and closest friend. As Casandra approached, she pulled up the hood of the green cloak that matched Willoe's.

Working her way along the shops, Willoe stopped in front of a leather-smith that was directly across from the captive boy. She kept close against the wall while busy passersby went about their business, further concealing her so she could spy on the scene at the wagon unnoticed.

She was close enough to see more details about the boy. His face had sharp lines and he was not as thin as she had first thought. Yes, his skin was taut, but he didn't appear to be underfed. More like his body was hardened with developing muscles. She had thought his hair brown and wavy, but it just needed washing; which made his hair stick out in clumps and under the dirt it looked to be almost blond. The boy's face would have been handsome, at least from what she could tell through the layers of dirt, but a scar marred his young face, starting from the side of his left ear and curving down to the left side of his chin.

She looked back to the front of the wagon as Casandra headed toward the wagon's horse, which snorted and pawed the ground at her approach. She stopped where Willoe could see her, closed her eyes and put a hand on the horse's forehead. Even after the two years she had known her cousin, Willoe was still amazed at the effect Casandra had on animals. The horse immediately quieted and lowered its head, nudging gently at Casandra.

Once the horse settled, Casandra opened her eyes, looked over at Willoe and nodded her head.

With a deep breath Willoe moved away from the wall, stepped between two strangers and onto the worn and rounded stones of the square. With a final glance at Casandra, she then turned to face the trader and screamed hysterically.

"Help! Help me!" she shrieked as if in pain and dropped to her knees in tears on the wet stones. "Won't summ'on please help me?" She hoped she didn't sound like a noble.

With everyone focused on Willoe, Big Guard did not notice the wagon moving backwards until it was too late for him to jump out of the way, and it slammed into his back. He yelled in surprise and stumbled, putting both hands out to break his fall and letting go of the struggling street urchin in the process.

"Run." Willoe's tears ceased as she ordered the street urchin.

The boy held his ground and did not falter as she had been afraid he might, but instead stared at her, his eyes narrowed questioningly. Willoe commanded him again, louder this time, more urgently.

Instead of rushing away, the street urchin sneered and ran straight at the trader, pulling out a short knife. The trader had whipped his head around at Big Guard's cry and then back to Willoe with her last shout. Willoe started to yell a warning to the trader, afraid the boy might take his revenge on the unsuspecting man. Before she could get out the warning, the boy swept the short knife once and cut the purse hanging from the trader's belt. He grabbed the free-falling purse expertly with his other hand.

"Stop!" The trader jerked his head back toward the boy, but the young cutpurse was well away before the hefty man could grab him.

The boy darted between bewildered bystanders and reached a side street that ran into the square. He turned to face Willoe, bowed clumsily, held up the purse and gave her a big grin before disappearing down the street.

"You." The trader turned his face back to Willoe, his eyes burning into her as his face visibly reddened with anger. "You. You're with him. You're with the little whoreson thief. A misbegotten burning cutpurse." He pointed a finger, screaming each word and leaving no doubt as to whom he meant.

Willoe realized too late that she should have already fled. She stood to run, but Little Guard clamped a hand tightly on her left wrist. She struggled for a moment until she felt a fire light up deep inside that engulfed her heart. She stopped moving and gasped for air. Her breath came in hurried wheezes, then it slowed and she was able to catch her breath. With the breath came a warmth, like a simmering pot of water, which spread out to her limbs. As she stood, the warmth turned into a surging heat, as if her blood had begun to boil. She felt a burning sensation on her skin and she looked at her free arm to see her pale skin had indeed turned a rusty hue. Her head pounded to the beat of her heart and she imagined that her fiery hair had actually become a flaming halo.

Willoe's mind whirled.

Not again.

As she struggled with Little Guard the blaze continued to flood her veins and everything started to become hazy. She felt herself fade to the background and watched as she reached out with her free hand and grabbed Little Guard's wrist. She yanked up while trying to pull her captive hand free.

Amazingly, Little Guard released his grip and as if through a tunnel she could hear what sounded like an agonized scream. She faced Little Guard, her mind in shock, but her body, as if possessed by a stronger and angrier spirit, shoved him in the chest with her freed hand. The man, though shorter than his fellow guard, was much heavier than Willoe, yet when she struck him he flew backwards several feet to land on his back with a thud.

"Grab her, she is a cutpurse!" The trader's voice cut through the haze and she slammed back into her own skin feeling drained and soaking wet.

Big Guard had risen and started toward her. Her body felt exhausted but a burst of energy flowed through her and she spun toward the front of the wagon. Casandra raced over and almost collided with Willoe as they both stumbled and ran down the nearest side street.

They had gone past a couple of shops when Casandra grabbed Willoe's cloak and pulled her into a small alley that ran along the back of several other shops. Willoe slid on the damp and slippery cobblestones, but was able to keep up with her cousin. They ran a dozen feet down the alley and ducked into a doorway. They leaned back against the door trying to stay as flat as possible, both of them breathing heavily. Willoe felt like she had been running all day rather than just a few minutes. Above her own breathing she could hear the voices of the men that were chasing them fade away down the street. The pounding of her heart and head slowed and after a few moments she peeked out around the edge of the doorway. Seeing an empty street, she signaled for Casandra to come out.

"What happened back there?" Casandra asked, still trying to catch her breath.

Willoe could feel strength returning with every breath, but still needed a couple of deep breaths before answering. "I do not know. I was overcome by a… a fire."

Casandra's eyebrows narrowed. "A fever?"

"Ten times worse." Willoe's breath and body was finally starting to return to normal. "A hundred times." She sucked in another deep breath before adding. "It was… It only happened once before. It was a year before you came to live with me."

"But what you did to that guard—" Casandra frowned. "You threw him like he was nothing more than a pillow. And your face—"

When Casandra did not continue, Willoe was concerned her cousin had seen the change in Willoe's skin. "What about my face?" she asked hesitantly.

"It…" Casandra's lips pursed as she seemed to have trouble with finding the right words. "It was all hard and bulging. Your teeth were clenched so hard I thought they would shatter. I was scared."

Willoe was no less confused and upset than her cousin. "I do not know what happened. I mean, I could see what was happening, though I had no control over what I did."

"There they are!" A shout made them both turn to see the two guards, with several other men standing behind them, filling the end of the alley. Little Guard glared at them, his cheeks puffing in and out as he sneered and mashed his teeth.

Casandra grabbed Willoe's cloak again and pulled her into a run down the alley. They turned down another street heading toward the outskirts of the city, then cut randomly down several streets and alleys. Willoe fought to catch her breath, another burst of blistering fire and energy driving her forward. The men almost caught them once right before the two girls slid through a jagged hole in a wall too small for the men to follow. Willoe and her cousin continued shifting from one street to another until they reached the western stables near the outer wall and couldn't hear the men anymore.

They leaned up against the stable's wooden slats, Willoe's heart beating so hard she thought it would rip out of her chest at any moment. They bent over with hands on their knees, taking quick, shallow breaths. After a few moments they leaned back and slid down to a sitting position on the dirt-packed ground just outside one of the stable's doors. Willoe looked over at her cousin and Casandra turned her face to look back. They stared like that until Willoe raised her eyebrows to say, *That was close*. Casandra started to giggle, and Willoe soon joined her. They went on like that for a while until they heard Big Guard's voice.

"I tell you, I heard them this way."

Casandra put her hand over her mouth, as did Willoe. Willoe turned her gaze down the street and realized it ended against the city's wall with no place to hide. She pushed Casandra toward the open stable doors and the girls slipped inside just as Willoe caught sight of the two guards entering the street.

Once inside, Willoe quickly questioned her decision. There wasn't any back door and the stable was empty except for some buckets, a few empty wooden stands used to hold the horses' tack, and the stalls filled with straw and peat moss. Willoe could hear the guards' voices getting closer when Casandra pointed to one of the stalls. Both girls moved halfway into it, laid down, and pulled straw over their bodies. The smell of horse urine nearly choked Willoe and she jumped when little bugs started to crawl up her legs and arms, but the sound of the stable doors opening stilled her.

"They're here, I tell ya." Little Guard's voice filled the empty stable. "I saws a green cloak come in here."

"There's a lot of green cloaks in this here city," Big Guard argued.

"With a gold trim?"

Damn the Shadows, she thought. Her and Casandra's cloaks were custom-made in the distinctive green and gold pattern of the kingdom. Of course they would stand out.

It was silent and she couldn't hear any movement from the guards. She lay as still as possible for several more minutes and she hoped the guards had given up when Big Guard finally spoke.

"That is queer. What would a cutpurse be doing with a cloak like that?"

"The bitch of a whore stole it, I tell ya. That's what cutters do." Little Guard's anger was heavy in his words and Willoe was suddenly worried that a lecture from Grandfather might be the least of her problems.

She could hear the guards rummaging around in the stable with pails tossed about and wooden stands being turned over.

"Where'd they go?" Big Guard sounded as if he were getting frustrated.

"Aye, this bring them out." Little Guard laughed. The sickening sound of it sent shivers up Willoe's spine. "Just poke in the stalls. I wager they are hiding."

"If they're under the straw the prong will stick 'em." The concern in Big Guard's tone gave Willoe some hope.

"If it be the Burning Lady's will."

"You should not jest about the Burning Lady. Taunting the goddess never brings good on those that use it."

"Tell that to the bitch who nearly broke my wrist." Little Guard grunted and Willoe could hear the sound of metal striking the ground.

The same sound echoed across the stable several times and continued to move closer to Willoe's and Casandra's stall. Willoe couldn't see her cousin, but could feel a slight movement to her right. They would have to do something soon or be speared by the tine used to bale the straw. The next time it hit the ground it sounded really close and she could even feel the vibration as if it were just a few feet away. Willoe could feel her blood starting to simmer again.

She sat up pulling straw out of her face and yelled, "Stop!" She wasn't sure whether she was ordering the guard or her own body. Casandra sat up just a moment later.

"There be the little whore." The sharpened metal prongs were aimed at the floor just in front of Willoe. "I'll teach you to hurt ol' Brac." Little Guard raised the tip of the tine and pointed it directly at Willoe.

The determination in his eyes made her angry more than scared and she began to fade into the background once again as fire started to fill her body. Little Guard took a step toward her when Willoe heard the stable doors slam against the wall and a familiar voice come from behind the two guards.

"Put down the stick." The deep voice resonated with authority. "Now!"

Little Guard gripped the shaft tighter and both guards turned as Little Guard started to say "Who you think—" His voice dropped and the tine followed.

Both guards knelt and Big Guard said with deference, "Protector." With heads still bowed Big Guard started to explain. "These two worked with a cutpurse to rob our master. We was only—"

"Enough." The command cut the guard off. "Leave these to me." The Protector stood a good hand taller than even Big Guard and was broader in the chest and shoulders. A sleeveless leather studded jerkin with fur trimmings covered his upper body, highlighting the thick muscular arms that rested at his side. A pair of heavy leather pants fit well with the jerkin. An iron buckle in the shape of a dragon's head held the belt together. His strawberry blond hair was pulled back and hung over his left shoulder onto his chest. It was tied every few inches with leather straps to keep it from interfering with his ability to reach the sword handle that stuck up from over each shoulder.

"But he will want his money," Little Guard whined.

"I doubt your master will miss a few coins." The Protector turned his right arm slightly so that the inside of the forearm was visible. An old scar burned into the skin created an image of a dragon in flight from the wrist to the elbow.

Eyeing the dragon, the Big Guard's voice was tinged with awe as if he had finally come to some sort of realization. "You're Protector Dougal."

He turned back to look at the girls, his eyes grown wide. "Then this must be— Why would she—" His eyebrows knitted together in confusion, but he recovered and stood, grabbing Little Guard and pushing him toward the stable door. They kept facing the Protector, their eyes cast down as they edged their way past the imposing warrior. After they exited the stable Willoe could hear the pounding of their boots as they fled the stable yard.

With the arrival of the Protector, the fire rising under Willoe's skin subsided and the haze was kept at bay. When the flames retreated, they left her feeling odd in her own skin.

She rose, pulled back her hood and started to wipe the damp straw off her cloak while swatting at the few bugs that still clung to her. Casandra also stood and pulled back her hood, shaking out her thick hair.

Even at eleven years old, Casandra was one of the most beautiful girls Willoe had ever met. No, not a girl, but a woman almost grown. Casandra was already starting to blossom, the childhood fat gone, soft features forming with high cheek bones and full lips. Willoe loved her cousin, but she couldn't help feeling envious at times. Willoe knew no one would ever accuse *her* of being beautiful. In fact, she would settle for even just attractive. Casandra, on the other hand, had a natural beauty that captured the heart of every male – and female – that set eyes upon her. And even now, while Willoe had straw sticking out from every part of her body, Casandra flicked a few strands off her clothing, shook her hair again, and looked like she had just stepped out of her dressing chamber.

Willoe turned to the large Protector, but then heard someone clear their throat and a stranger, a young man, edged out from behind the stern warrior. Willoe's first thought was that he was beautiful. In fact, she thought, *He's so beautiful.* He was a good head taller than Willoe and it was obvious he kept himself physically in shape. Then her twin brother, Rowyn, stepped out next to the young man.

"Row." Willoe smiled at her twin. They were nearly identical. The same curly red hair, deep and bright, with luminous green eyes. She was a couple of fingers taller, but she knew that would change as they grew older. She loved her brother, though she couldn't say the same about her two older brothers, from a different mother. No one knew who Willoe and Rowyn's mother was, not even Willoe. It was even told that their father hadn't known about the two of them until Protector Dougal had appeared one day with the three-year-old twins on his saddle.

"Wil." Rowyn responded with a smile. He stepped toward her but then hung back, wrinkling his nose. "What have you been doing? You smell like horse piss."

Willoe inhaled deeply and coughed. "Shades or the Shadows."

Rowyn smiled at her reference to picking between two poor choices, but it quickly faded and he squinted as he questioned his twin. "Are you well?"

The way he asked the question made Willoe curious as to his meaning.

"Yes. I am fine now." She tilted her head, trying to figure out exactly what Rowyn had meant.

He nodded his head slightly with twisted lips. She knew there was something still troubling him.

The other young man cut off her train of thought and said with a wide grin, "So this is the ill-famed Willoe. Is it true that trouble covers her like an early morning mist in a mountain valley?" He looked to Casandra for an answer, the hint of a twinkle in his eyes.

"I am not—" Willoe started to protest, but Casandra spoke up.

"Yes."

Willoe looked at Casandra in shock, but her cousin only shrugged her shoulders and whispered, "It is true."

Willoe faced the young man again, set her chin and furrowed her brow.

Casandra gestured toward the young man. "Let me introduce my brother, Aeron Cadwal of Pembroke. The next First Duke of Cainwen."

Now that she knew the connection, Willoe could suddenly see the resemblance clearly; by his stance, Willoe could see that Aeron carried himself with the same refined grace and courtly charm - though with a manly bent – that Casandra exuded. How unfair that it came so naturally to her young cousin! Evidently it ran in their blood.

Aeron bowed just as courteously as his sister and stood back up with the grin still plastered on his face. Even though there had to be a three or four year difference between the brother and sister, both of her cousins had the same flowing golden bronze hair, smooth facial features, and a bearing that could only come from the children of the First Duke.

Willoe tried to curtsy, but knew it did not come off very gracefully. "Pleased to meet you, cousin."

He bowed once again.

"He is coming to live with us, Wil, and finish his training to be a Shield." Rowyn's voice was filled with the most excitement Willoe had seen in him in years. It was a nice change from his normal solemn demeanor. "Just like you and Casandra, I will finally have a friend." His mouth opened to say more, but he must have realized what he had said; Willoe smiled as her brother lowered his gaze, face flushed with embarrassment. He picked furiously at the seam of his cloak, confirming his mortification.

Aeron must have noticed the younger boy's embarrassment, and he reached out to put a hand on Rowyn's shoulder, then squeezed it. "That is right, cousin. We are going to be the best of friends. Just like our fathers." He bellowed out a big, hearty laugh and then slapped Rowyn on the shoulder, almost knocking the younger boy over. But when Rowyn regained his feet he had the biggest grin Willoe had ever seen and it made her smile that much more.

"We must go." Protector Dougal's deep, bottom-of-the-barrel voice stopped any further discussion. "We be expected back at the castle 'fore supper."

"I just wanted to thank you for saving me. Once again."

"Just like after your ninth naming day," Rowyn added.

Willoe's thoughts went back three years to when the kidnappers had nearly succeeded. If not for Protector Dougal–

He looked at her and his lips parted as if to speak, but instead they rested in a tight-lipped smile.

She thought of him as an uncle, not a Protector sworn to protect her and her brother. She also knew he would be hard to sway, yet she still had to try to convince him to keep this within their small group.

Before she could state her case, he fixed her with a disapproving gaze. "Did it nay occur to you that the boy be a cutpurse?"

"The trader was going to hurt the boy," Willoe exclaimed. "He said he was going to punish him and not turn him over to the City Guard."

Protector Dougal didn't answer immediately and his expression was hard for Willoe to read. "Did he harm the lad or was it just words floating through the air?"

Willoe started to answer, but then she bit her lip in thought. The trader never actually hit the boy.

Protector Dougal grunted and shook his head. "I'd thought as much." And as if her plan was known to him, he told her, "No, I be not saying a word to the King."

Willoe breathed a sigh of relief, until Protector Dougal added in a rigid voice, which contrasted with the thin smile that had returned, "I'm sure when their master," he pointed to the open stable door, "hears who you be, he be telling everyone who lend him an ear. Your grandfather be hearing all 'bout this by nightfall."

Willoe sighed and bent her head, resigning herself to her fate. She pushed it to the back of her mind as another thought struck her. "How did you know where to find us?"

Aeron, a smile still plastered across his face, answered. "We were looking for the both of you when we heard you screaming. We started in that direction when your brother here," he squeezed Rowyn's shoulder again, "almost collapsed right there in the street."

Rowyn hunched his shoulders and kept his gaze on the ground, seemingly embarrassed by the event.

"He recovered after just a moment and said he was fine, but that it was urgent we find you." Aeron turned back to Willoe with a quizzical look. "All he would tell us was that you were on fire. Though you seem fine now, if somewhat disheveled."

Willoe sucked in so hard she lost her breath for a moment. *How could*

Rowyn know about the fire? She started to say something to him when Rowyn looked up directly at her and shook his head ever so slightly. She almost didn't catch it, but something in his eyes told her to leave it.

"You can imagine how that worried us." Aeron nodded his head toward the large Protector. "By the time we reached the square, you were gone and we got the story out of witnesses to your— shall we say rescue of the boy. We tracked you to this area, but we were not sure where you were until Row turned as pale as a dove and pointed to this stable."

She kept her eyes on Rowyn, who barely shook his head again as their cousin finished the tale. Even as close as she was with her twin, there were some things he would not confide in anyone, even her. She knew how stubborn he could be and realized she might never find out what happened.

"But now you are safe." Aeron smiled again as if he had had something to do with it. Before she could point out that it had been Protector Dougal, Aeron waved his hand toward the stable door with a little tilt of his head. "Princess Willoe. Lady Casandra." The elegance of the courteous action was somewhat dimmed by the sarcastic smirk on his face. He turned to Rowyn. "What say, Row, we remove ourselves from this," he looked around the stable, "rather dull setting."

No one had ever called Willoe's twin Row other than herself, and she felt a momentary pang of jealousy. Protector Dougal indicated for her and Casandra to leave the stable. She pulled her hood back up, as the rain had picked up and was pelting the stable's roof and doors.

The jealous feeling subsided when she heard Aeron behind her. "So how do you like being the son of the Crown Prince?"

Rowyn surprised Willoe with his retort, as he rarely saw humor in anything. "I do not know. It has its advantages. How do you like being the son of the First Duke?"

Aeron burst out with another loud laugh. "Very good, Row. It does have its advantages. But yet there is also the other side of the coin."

The easy manner in which Rowyn conversed with their newly-met cousin cloaked her with a sense of relief. Mothering her twin had become second nature to Willoe, but maybe he would finally find a friend and companion, the first in his life other than Willoe and Casandra. A male friend.

"Yes cousin, there is the other side." Rowyn quieted for a moment and then added, "Much more than anyone should have to bear without fighting back."

Willoe was saddened by his words. He spoke of a shared burden, one that Willoe understood all too well. They lived in a culture that had not truly accepted them and even considered them evil.

She looked over her shoulder to see her twin and as their eyes connected, the boiling heat suddenly flared through her body, the same as when she had broken free from Small Guard's grasp. Her chest heaved and she inhaled quickly, then the sensation died.

Rowyn stumbled as the fire ran through her body, then regained his feet, continuing to walk behind her. He stared up at her, his eyes first wide, then narrowed and his lips twisted like when he was worrying over some mystery.

She snapped her head forward and kept walking. Had Rowyn also felt the strange fire? She drew in another deep breath and swallowed hard. Maybe it had something to do with them being twins? But that would not explain the fire itself.

As they exited the stable the fading fire left a warm feeling, but not a comforting one. She wanted to ask Rowyn, but she feared what he might answer. Willoe could only hope that Rowyn's words were not an omen of things to come.

2

Piglets

Willoe loved days like today. The sun in early autumn provided just the right amount of heat and the days were still long enough to provide reading light into the evening without the smoky smell of tallow candles. Her body moved as one with the horse and she looked up to enjoy the glimmer of sunlight filtering through the canopy of leaves. The forest picnic to celebrate her and Rowyn's sixteenth birthday was a wonderful idea and she reminded herself to thank Casandra again for suggesting it.

She turned back to see how the others were faring. The contrast made her smile. Just a few paces behind was the dainty Casandra, bubbly and beautiful, riding next to the quiet, always-somber Protector Dougal. Casandra chattered away and, in his usual sedate manner, the Protector listened politely, if not intently. Behind them rode Rowyn and Aeron who, like his sister Casandra, was extremely animated and doing most of the talking between bursts of laughter, Aeron's loud guffaws stood in sharp contrast to Rowyn's dour bearing; her brother was sparing with his laughter, so unlike the full-bodied laugher of his closest friend.

"Dear cousin," Aeron called out to her with a hint of humor in his voice. "Did you really dump an entire keg of Langford wine on Master Jonnes?"

So that was what he was laughing about. Willoe rolled her eyes. "It isn't that simple," she tried to defend herself. "I was only showing Casandra what to do if a brigand tried to grab her from behind." It was something she had learned from Protector Dougal's private training. "I only twisted away from her and—"

"You knocked the keg off the ledge, it broke apart, and splashed all over the wine master," Aeron finished for her, and slapped Rowyn heavily on the back of the shoulder, very amused with himself.

Shoved forward in his saddle by the friendly gesture, Rowyn sat back up and pushed his curly red hair out of his eyes. He only smiled at the joke, lips together.

"Who knew Master Jonnes would be standing right next to the ledge?" She had no desire to experience that ridicule once again and spurred her chestnut to trot slightly ahead of the others.

Aeron yelled out, "Don't get upset, cousin. You weren't the one that ended up wine-soaked." He laughed again as she rode a little faster ahead of them.

She slowed the horse to a walk and cut across the narrow forest path through a thicket, leaning forward to avoid the low-hanging branches, to finally emerge near the Great Crossway Road. She was grateful for the leather riding breeches and matching boots as she rode through the brambles and briers.

The Great Crossway would lead them directly to the East Gate of Castle Westhedge. She waited for the others to join her. They would ride back toward the castle on the hard-packed dirt and crushed seashell road. The others continued their conversations while Willoe lost herself in the waning summer afternoon, until she glimpsed a wagon off to the left side of the road. Actually it was more a cobbled-together cart than a wagon, even though it had four wheels.

As they rode toward the cart she could see an elderly farmer behind it and a young boy on the driver's bench. The farmer had his shoulder leveraged against one of the rear wheels while the young boy snapped the horse's rope reins. The man stopped and looked over his shoulder at the riders, then turned back and continued to push against the wheel.

It was obvious that the cart was properly stuck and not moving regardless of the farmer's efforts. As they rode up behind it Willoe could see that the left rear wheel had gone off the road, landed in a rut, and the horse was unable to pull it out.

Willoe pulled off the road a dozen paces behind the cart, dismounted and hobbled her horse. She turned to the others who had by now come up behind her. "We should help the old man."

Rowyn looked at the farmer still grunting against the wagon wheel, ignoring the riders. "I'm not sure if that is best, Wil. I think we should continue to the castle. It is getting late."

"He is one of Grandfather's subjects; we owe him our assistance." Willoe couldn't see how the farmer and boy would ever get the wagon free without help. "If you will not help then I will do it myself." She set her shoulders and spun toward the cart, stomping away.

She could hear Aeron mutter as she walked away. "If we don't help, do you think she will give up?"

"It would be the first time." Casandra's voice was clear and Willoe looked over her shoulder to see Casandra already standing on the ground with Aeron and Rowyn dismounting their own horses. Protector Dougal stayed in the saddle and took the reins from the other three.

Willoe continued to walk turning toward the old farmer. "Allow us to help you, ancient father." Willoe spoke in a kind voice with an intentionally friendly expression of respect.

"Your help is welcomed," the old farmer said with his back to her. "We got a sow to deliver for a castle merchant."

The boy was probably his grandson and from the sheepish look on his downcast face, he was the one that had driven the cart off the road.

The farmer stood. "I been flaming well at it for a bit now." He started to turn back to her while wiping sweat off his forehead with a rag. "Forgive my foul words. My wife says I n'ver should—" He choked on the apology. Stepping back several steps, he put his thumb, index and middle fingers together and touched his forehead. He then brought the fingers to his mouth kissed them and ended with them on his heart. As he touched his heart, he whispered, "Burning Lady protect us." He continued to step back until he was even with the boy, to whom he waved to jump down from the cart.

The boy just stared at Willoe, his eyes full of fear. "Are you gonna kill us?" His voice shook with the very same fear she could see in his eyes.

Willoe was stunned. *Why would they think such a thing?* Then she realized her hood was pulled back and her flaming red hair was hanging loose down around her face. Along with her vivid green eyes she must have appeared to the two as the culmination of every nightmare tale they had been told since being toddlers. She couldn't help that she and her twin shared the same hair and eye color as a dreaded, half-dead Shade. "I mean you no harm." She tried to use a soft, soothing voice.

The old farmer was not calmed and dragged the boy roughly from the cart, causing it to rock side to side. With the sharp motion the sow began to squeal and bang up against the side of the cart.

Casandra had come up next to Willoe and reached over the back slat. She closed her eyes for a moment and put a hand on the sow until it quieted, then pulled her arm back out.

Repeating the plea to the Goddess, the farmer dropped to one knee. "Take the sow, but have mercy on us and leave the piglets."

Piglets? A squalling noise made Willoe look into the cart, where she saw a half dozen piglets scurrying around behind their mother, a rather small sow. They were so little and kept bumping into each other; Willoe had to laugh at their antics. She realized too late that the farmer must have mistaken her reaction, because he bowed his head and began to whimper. Willoe needed to do something quickly before the old man collapsed. The boy was still staring at her as if she had two heads.

Willoe reached in for one of the piglets, hoping that if the boy saw how gentle she was with it they would know she was only trying to help. But the little pig squirmed and slipped from her grasp, kicking out at Willoe. "No!" She shrieked as she started to fall backward, trying to avoid the piglet's cloven hooves. She reached out and grabbed for the slats to steady herself, only to pull the restraining slat totally off and tilt the back of the cart downward. She fell on the ground and was nearly crushed when the sow jumped out the back, barely missing her. She wasn't as lucky when all six of the piglets followed their mother out of the cart and two of them landed on Willoe's leg. Willoe grunted and could feel a bruise already starting to form on her right leg.

"My pigs!" The farmer had raised his head and stood at the noise of the pigs squealing loudly as they ran randomly around the base of the cart. He started toward his pigs, but then stopped short and stepped back again when he saw Willoe lying on the ground.

"Grab them!" Aeron yelled as he chased after one of the piglets. Rowyn and Casandra each ran around the cart after one of the frightened animals. The farmer and his grandson pressed up against the cart, their eyes wide with terror, especially after seeing Rowyn's red hair fly past them.

Willoe took after one of the piglets and slipped on a grassy patch, falling into the loose dirt along the road's edge. She finally caught the piglet and looked around for the others. Aeron also had one as he hunted down another, while Casandra knelt with the sow and two of the piglets in front of her, while she calmly stroked them in turn. Rowyn was closing in on the last of the escaped piglets when Willoe heard the neigh of a horse behind her.

She turned and came face to face with a black warhorse, and looked to identify the rider. The cropped dark brown hair, gray at the temples, and the speckled beard were all too familiar to Willoe.

"Captain Harte. It is good to see you Ser." Willoe looked beyond the horse and saw two decorative carriages with a two score of mounted Shields and Guardsmen stationed behind it. Behind that there were other wagons and a number of servants. Ten of the mounted warriors wore the green cloak with a golden dragon over the left breast, the emblem of her own kingdom, Cainwen. What surprised her was that the remaining soldiers wore a dark gray surcoat emblazoned with the red lion of the Eastern Kingdom. "Is this an envoy from Franchon?" She had not heard of any expected mission from that part of the island. "What is this all about?" She quickly regretted her question as she knew it wasn't her place to question the head of the King's Guard.

"I would ask the same of you, Princess Willoe." He did nothing to hide the frustration and annoyance in his voice.

"Princess Willoe?" a voice came from the first carriage as the door opened. A servant riding on the back of the carriage jumped down and put a stool under the open door. A young woman stepped out. She was dressed in a brightly-colored dress with a red threaded design of a lion stitched on the breast and white fur trim around the hem.

Not the kind of dress I would have picked for traveling, Willoe thought as she watched the woman flow from the carriage. Instinctively, she tried to smooth out her own wrinkled dress and brush off what dirt she could. She realized she still had the piglet tucked under her arm as the woman approached her.

Willoe estimated the woman's age at a couple of years older than herself. She was slender in all the right places and not in all the other right places. Willoe suddenly felt very conscious of her own small breasts, and without thinking put her shoulders back a little more, though she doubted it emphasized what little she had.

The woman seemed to glide from the coach radiating an intoxicating animal magnetism. She walked past Captain Harte right up to Willoe, coming uncomfortably close. She curtsied flawlessly, much better than Willoe could ever achieve, and gave Willoe a smile that could have blinded the sun. "I have been waiting so long to meet you."

Willoe didn't know how to respond. The piglet began to squirm and Casandra walked up to take the little pig from her. Upon Casandra's touch the piglet immediately calmed.

"Ah, you must be the First Duke's daughter, the Lady Casandra. I had heard the two of you were inseparable."

Casandra stopped and looked from the woman to Willoe and back at the woman again. "I am the First Duke's daughter." Casandra didn't address the second comment, but did match the Franchon woman curtsy for curtsy, even while carrying the piglet. "May I inquire as to whom I am speaking with?"

Willoe wished she could switch to the formal speech of the court as easily as her cousin. She also did not think it was possible, but the newcomer's smile widened. Willoe couldn't help but be entranced by the contrast between the unbelievably white teeth and the raven hair. It was so black it was almost blue, which complemented the woman's deep blue eyes. Those reminded Willoe of the center of a bottomless lake.

"Forgive my manners," the Franchon woman exclaimed. "The trip has been long and I am not accustomed to such conditions."

Willoe had no doubt that this woman had never spent any real time on the road before this. The woman was exactly like all the other women Willoe knew — and resented — from court. A noble's wife or daughter who rarely knew anything about what was going on outside of their own small world.

"I am the Lady Emeline Jaquette Louvier Renier." The woman curtsied again and Willoe wished she would stop. It made her feel inadequate for some reason.

Casandra acknowledged the visiting woman with a nod, then excused herself and headed for the cart, stroking the head of the piglet she held under her arm to calm its renewed squirming.

"And this—" Lady Emeline turned slightly as Aeron walked up with a piglet under each arm.

Aeron put on a shining smile. "May I introduce myself, dear lady?" He bowed ever so elegantly, which should have been hard to do with a piglet under each arm, but he somehow managed it. "I am Lord Aeron Cadwal of Castle Mount Somerled, heir to the First Duke of Cainwen." He straightened and shook his head ever so slightly, causing his thick wavy hair to flip gently from side to side. "May I say it is a pleasure to meet you, Lady Emeline. Your appearance has brightened my day as surely as the warm sun on my skin after a refreshing swim." His smile broadened and his dimples still showed through the beginnings of a beard. Willoe felt like she would gag at his suggestive words.

"Yes, well—"

Willoe had to keep from smiling at the woman's discomfort with Aeron's mention of swimming and bare skin.

"And this must be Prince Rowyn." Changing the subject, the Franchon woman looked past Willoe toward the cart.

Rowyn just nodded shyly and started to put his piglet back into the cart along with the one Casandra had brought over.

Willoe didn't like the way this woman knew all about them and Willoe didn't know anything about her. "We are twins. Why are you here?" It came out more harshly than she had meant and she realized too late that her bluntness was inappropriate.

Emeline turned back to Willoe, the smile vanished. "The resemblance is remarkable." She studied Willoe from head to toe. "If not for the soiled dress, I would not be able to tell you apart".

She loosed the comment like an arrow and Willoe suddenly felt sure that Emeline had a full quiver.

The woman's smile quickly returned as if it had just slipped. "Again, forgive me for my lack of courtesy. I was asked to accompany the envoy to Castle Westhedge. I had never crossed the Saltrock River before now and relished the chance to see the West. I did not realize the trip would be so tiresome." She looked at Willoe for sympathy, but received none.

Turning from Willoe to look across the road, Emeline's eyes became wide as she spotted the Protector still mounted and still holding onto the other three horses. "This must be the famous Protector Dougal. I have never met a real Protector before." Her voice held an awe that Willoe had heard many times before.

"Lady Emeline." A strange yet firm voice called from the second carriage, making them all turn to look in that direction. The voice sounded foreign, which piqued Willoe's curiosity.

"Bat-Uul," Willoe heard Emeline say with a gasp. The woman's voice rose at the end of the name. When Willoe turned back to Emeline, the look on the woman's face took her by surprise. The shining smile was gone and the fear in the woman's eyes made Willoe's skin crawl. The change lasted only a moment then the bright smile and cheerful expression quickly returned. "Yes, yes," Emeline answered obediently to the voice.

"Who is Bat-erl?" Aeron asked, a little concerned, having evidently seen the quick change in Emeline's demeanor.

"Bat-Uul," Emeline corrected. "He is… Well, he and Dimah-Uul… It is hard to explain." She stumbled through her words. "They advise King Benoit. It is hard to explain." She gave up with a sigh.

Ah, Willoe thought, 'Uul' must be some type of title in Franchon.

"Lady Emeline. We are behind schedule," the foreign voice called once again from the carriage. It carried an air of command.

Emeline curtsied one more time and gave Willoe a thin-lipped smile; which Willoe thought difficult considering how full the woman's lips actually were. "I know I will enjoy spending time with each of you at Westhedge." That seemed to end the conversation and she turned abruptly to walk back to the carriage.

Once Emeline was back in the carriage, Captain Harte said to Willoe, "I do not understand how you manage to embroil yourself in these little adventures." He nodded to the cart where Aeron was putting the last of the pigs back in and securing the slat that had broken free. "I am sure when our guests arrive at the castle, word will spread of this incident, and the king will no doubt require an accounting." He nodded to Protector Dougal, who nodded back. Willoe didn't know the details, but both men had become close friends when Protector Dougal had brought Willoe and Rowyn to live at Castle Westhedge.

Before Captain Harte could signal the rest of the escort, the old farmer, forgotten in all the commotion, called out from the front of the cart that Aeron and Rowyn had moved out of the rut while Willoe had been talking with Emeline. "Kind Ser. Can'na make her give back our sow and piglets?" The emphasis on *her* was unmistakable.

Captain Harte looked up into the sky as if asking for divine guidance, then just shook his head with eyes closed. He opened them, gave Willoe one last glare, then signaled the escort to start again, spurring his own muscular destrier forward at a brisk walk.

As the carriage passed, Willoe could see Lady Emeline through the first window, sitting next to a much older nobleman. At the second window was another man who wore a blood red robe with the hood pulled back. He had ink black hair like a Franchon, but it was easy to tell he was a foreigner to their island country. His face and one hand, holding on to the window, showed his skin to be several shades darker than most Tarans, and rather than a beard he only had a mustache which hung down on either side of his chin. He stared at Willoe as they passed, his dark eyes piercing her as if she had been hit with a lance. She even took a step backward, it felt so real.

A burning sensation flooded her body, her senses keener and her field of view sharper as if everything had been a blur and now came into focus. It only flared momentarily in response to the robed foreigner and then settled back down just as swiftly, but a mild simmering remained. Her mind bolted back to the square and the street urchin of four years past. The trader and his guards all too real, and the burning sensation, remembered as though only a bad dream… yet evidently not. It wasn't just a child's wild imagination after all.

Finally Protector Dougal called out to them to remount and Willoe was brought back to the present. She was the last to mount, as she had to retrieve her horse and unhobble the animal. Before turning her horse to ride with the others she looked over at the cart. The old man had just helped his grandson up and stared back at Willoe. He quickly averted his eyes and slapped the reins to get the horse moving again.

Willoe spurred her horse to catch up with the others and in a short time they were riding slowly down the road behind the vanishing carriage and its escort.

The feeling of dread hung over Willoe even after the carriage had disappeared. They rode in silence until Aeron, riding in the rear, blurted out, "Does anyone know what an Uul is?" When no one commented, he added, "I am sure we will find out soon enough."

Willoe had an eerie feeling that her cousin's words were only too true, which did nothing for the dread she felt.

3

Assumptions

The Franchon envoy had been in Westhedge for a week and Aeron was glad the initial formalities had finished, though it meant that he and Rowyn would need to return to training in the Pell, starting that afternoon.

Aeron leaned his elbow on the castle's courtyard wall, the rough texture of the aged stone biting into his flesh, but his thoughts were elsewhere. He rested his chin on his balled fist and crossed his feet as he tried to think about where else he could look for Rowyn. They were both already late for training with Master Gwron, and the later they were the more intense – and subsequently, painful – the lesson would be.

He could hear the sounds from Master Gwron's domain, on the other side of the wall that separated the upper bailey from the Pell. The faint clatter of wood on wood only reminded Aeron of the sword and battle axe training that had been scheduled for that morning, which only heightened his anxiety.

He had checked Rowyn's rooms and also the library, Rowyn's favorite hiding place. Rather than sitting down for dinner, he'd spent his time rushing around checking all the likely places.

So, even though unlikely, he passed through the kitchen, hoping he might find his wayward cousin there. He could have commanded some of the cold leftovers from dinner, but a simple smile, a little charm, and a kind word ensured he left with something special. He finished the warm gingerbreade and wiped his hands together to remove any remaining pastry crumbs. The sharp sweet scent clung to his hands and he inhaled deeply before he started across the bailey to let Master Gwron know he could not find Rowyn. A horse nickering and the *rat-ta-tat-tat* of iron horseshoes clattering on stone pavers caught his attention. A boy leading a horse exited from one of the many archways to Aeron's right. In plain dark green pants and a matching jacket, it was obvious he worked in the royal stables.

"Boy," Aeron called out as he walked over to the stablehand. Aeron knew he was only putting off the inevitable.

The boy stopped and bowed his head, his eyes avoiding contact. "My Lord."

"I am searching for Prince Rowyn." Aeron used his best lordly voice, but had to choke back a laugh. He remembered it wasn't too long ago when he, even as the heir to the Duchy of Pembroke and First Duke of Cainwen, would be in total fear of anyone with a title.

The stable boy shrank back, but spoke up, as to do otherwise would be unthinkable. "I did see him, my Lord. He was walking up to the Middle Gallery. Protector Dougal and the Lady Casandra were with him."

Ah, finally a lead. "That will be all, lad." He dismissed the boy, and wondered what Casandra would be doing with Rowyn.

His feet pounded on the stone stairs as he hurried up to the second level and then he walked quickly past the carved columns lining the Gallery and several closed doors. He would have kept going if not for the clash of metal muffled by one of the doors he had just passed. He went back to the door, one he had never bothered with in the past. Considering the size of Castle Westhedge, there were a considerable number he had never opened.

He knocked once, but the sound on the other side of the door drowned it out like a dripping pipe in a rainstorm. He knocked again and then opened the door.

When he entered he saw Protector Dougal, the warrior's back to Aeron. The Protector wore his customary leather pants with the studded leather and fur vest. Casandra was sitting against the wall to the left, reading, and only glanced up quickly at her brother before returning to her book. Aeron kept his gaze on her for a moment. *I still don't understand. What is she doing here? Where is Willoe?*

Maybe she had developed an interest in Rowyn, but that was impossible. Even though they were distantly related cousins, they had all grown up together over the last several years, like brothers and sisters. Besides, even though she was only his little sister, and while he couldn't see it himself, others said that she was probably the most beautiful woman in the kingdom. Not quite the type of woman that Rowyn attracts. Smiling fondly, Aeron thought, *I can't actually remember him being interested in any woman.*

Protector Dougal stepped aside to set his great sword against a chair. All the furniture in the room had been moved aside, leaving the planked floor bare in the center. Directly across from Aeron and facing him was Rowyn, attired in a leather doublet, soft leather leggings, and over that a common guardsman's cloak. The Prince was leaning on the pommel of his sword – which Aeron noticed was much shorter than Protector Dougal's – and his cousin was breathing very heavily. Aeron realized he must have entered just after the two had finished a lesson. He was confused about why Rowyn wore a cloak, and especially a simple guardsman's. He was also puzzled by why Rowyn pulled the hood up when Aeron entered. *Maybe something Protector Dougal uses in his training.* He would have to ask the Protector about it later.

"Row, what are you doing here?" Aeron asked forcefully, unable to keep the frustration from his voice. "Master Gwron was expecting us two turns of the glass ago. Do you have any idea what sort of horrors he will inflict upon us for being late... again?" Aeron had always tried to cultivate a relaxed attitude about most everything. Bathing in the sorrow of misfortunes rarely gained him any advantage. The one exception was the misfortune Master Gwron would inflict.

"That's not going to be a problem." Rowyn paused for a moment. "Master Gwron was called away and delayed our time."

Protector Dougal looked from the Prince to Aeron and just shook his head.

"I wasn't told of this." Aeron frowned. *Have I been running around worrying for naught?*

"It was recent," Rowyn said. "I apologize for not sending you word." The Prince was still panting, causing his voice to sound strained. The Protector must have really been driving him hard during their training.

Casandra just snickered once, never looking up from her book.

Aeron shot a glare at his sister. *What is she up to?*

"What's going on with all this?" Aeron indicated the room. "You are going to be exhausted for Master Gwron. And he isn't going to retreat any just because you are a Prince."

"I thought I could use some extra time with the sword." Rowyn lowered his gaze and picked clumsily at the hem of his tunic.

Aeron smiled, feeling relieved, and chastised himself for being so worried. "That goes without saying. No offense intended." He gave an exaggerated bow.

"None taken. Let me finish up here and I will meet you at the Pell."

"Do not be late or we will both pay dearly." Aeron turned back to the door.

Before he could leave, Rowyn spoke up again. "Can you do me a favor and stop by Uncle Brom's room? He has something for me and if I stop I will be delayed."

"I can do that. Just don't be late." Aeron closed the door behind him, but before it shut completely he heard Casandra collapse into a fit of giggles. *Now what could be so humorous?* he thought, then shrugged and headed for the eccentric Uncle Brom's quarters.

It was a short walk back through the Gallery to the steps that led up the tower, on the southern corner of the castle, where the twins' uncle resided. Aeron's boots echoed off the walls as he wound his way up past the Upper Gallery, on the fifth level, to the top. Uncle Brom's apartment was the only living space among the many storage rooms, workshops, and unused room. It did not surprise Aeron when he didn't encounter another soul on his way to the eighth level. Aeron had asked Uncle Brom once why he lived in the smallest tower and so far from the King's Keep centered along the northern wall. The twins' uncle had just smiled and said 'Let us just say there are times when a little privacy has its rewards' before chuckling.

Stepping out onto the platform, Aeron walked across to the only door visible on the top level, an iron-bracketed wooden door. He was about to knock when he heard Uncle Brom talking to someone. Unbelievably, the voice that answered sounded like Rowyn's. Grasping the handle, Aeron began to pull the door open. "Row—" he began to call out.

Rowyn's uncle shouted, "Do not open the—"

He may have finished what he was saying, but Aeron never heard it. Instead, he was thrown sideways to the rough stone floor when the door slammed open. His eyes caught a white blur that streaked out of the room and past him.

Aeron quickly ran a hand over his chest – fully expecting to find claw marks – but other than a slight soreness in his left cheek and chest, he could not see or feel any major bodily damage. Hitting the stone floor had scraped his elbows and arms, but it didn't feel serious.

It only took a few seconds to complete the evaluation, and by then he realized that, as lucky as he was to have escaped serious injury, the animal could still be loose nearby.

Rising silently, he crouched and looked around the platform. He spotted it instantly across from the door: a white creature of some sort, whirling near the top of the stairs. He had seen a funnel cloud once from a distance. It wove a random path of destruction as it swept over the countryside and this looked exactly like that, though on a smaller scale. Twisting and spinning inside and on the outer edges of the whirlwind was something white that kept changing its shape.

Not sure what he faced, Aeron instinctively pulled out the small dagger at his waist, the only weapon he carried with him. He wished he had something a bit more substantial.

Before he could move toward the strange attacker, Uncle Brom ran from the room, raised his hands and said something unintelligible. The whirling monster began to slow and finally stopped, the white mass falling to the ground. Aeron walked across the platform and, using his dagger, lifted the white mass and looked back at Uncle Brom.

"A table cloth?" he asked in a state of mixed confusion and anger.

"It is fine," Uncle Brom stated simply as he walked over and took the cloth off of Aeron's dagger. He headed back into his combination apartment and laboratory, passing Rowyn, who had just come out of the room. Uncle Brom added nonchalantly, "Do not trouble yourself, you didn't ruin the experiment."

Aeron just stared, amazed, and he could feel the heat of anger rising with each step he took toward the room. "Your experiment? You could have killed me!" He yelled as he followed Uncle Brom into the room. "What were you doing?" His curiosity began to overcome the anger.

From the corner of the room came striding Uncle Brom's collaborator, the Tink, Drel Donlin. He was a short creature, topping no higher than Aeron's waist, and he wore his ever-present tan pants and black shirt under a black robe with strange green symbols embroidered along the edges.

Though the Tink was only half Aeron's height, he was otherwise quite human in appearance. He had short curly brown hair and an equally curly beard, worn close. The Tink also had a rather large nose and body proportioned like a man. Rowyn had told Aeron that this was one of the features that distinguished the Waljantinks from mountain dwarfs who had massive chests and short legs. Aeron had accepted Rowyn's explanation, seeing as Aeron had never met one of the legendary mountain dwarfs. Then again, he had never met another Tink.

The eyes glared at him from under bushy eyebrows and scanned him from foot to head. "You be fine." Uncle Brom's collaborator walked back over to the table and helped Uncle Brom right a table and three chairs. Then Uncle Brom laid the table cloth down on the table top. The little Tink pulled himself up onto the chair, his legs dangling over the front edge, while he and Uncle Brom inspected the cloth.

Aeron glanced around and noticed that the room had not changed since the last time he had been there. Old books and scrolls were scattered all over the chamber, taking up nearly every available surface. Besides the one Uncle Brom and Drel Donlin were using, there was another table in the corner covered with more books and scrolls. Strange-looking instruments sat on various stands. Rising from the floor, random stacks of books created a maze. He knew the door in the back led to a sleeping chamber and Aeron felt confident it was filled with even more books.

"I guess I should say thank you," Uncle Brom commented without looking up. "We would not have known if the Bone Fang would actually travel if you had not opened the door and created a cross-draft from the window."

The noise of castle activity came through the window across the room. Aeron maneuvered around several stacks of books to the open window. He stared down at the southern corner of Castle Westhedge and the surrounding capital city of Faywynne that stretched out on the other side of the wall. It was mid-day and the streets were full of people about their business, most having just finished their dinner. Aeron's stomach reminded him that he had missed the mid-day meal trying to find his cousin. He could feel a slight breeze against his face, confirming Uncle Brom's comment. Moving over to the table, Aeron put both hands flat on its surface. "What were you doing?"

Drel Donlin turned the fabric over while Uncle Brom continued to examine it. "I was showing my nephew here…" He nodded toward Rowyn who had reentered the room and had walked over to the table, "how to create a Bone Fang. Though just a little one. Call it a Baby Fang." Uncle Brom chuckled at his own joke.

"It seems like a useless pursuit." Aeron had little patience for such frivolous exploits.

"Imagine what you saw, except ten, twenty, fifty times larger".

"Why would you do that?" Aeron enjoyed a mental challenge, but he could not fathom the purpose.

Uncle Brom lifted his head and stared across the table at his collaborator, then went back to examining the table cloth while Drel Donlin tilted his head and answered as if the question did not really need answering.

"Because others cannot." The Tink shook his head, sighing, and went back to examining the cloth and quietly discussing some facet of the experiment with Uncle Brom.

Drel Donlin was still an enigma to Aeron. Outside of rumors about the Greenwald Forest, creatures like Tinks were seldom seen even as far south as the Open Lands. Except for men like Lord Brom Brynmor, few in Cainwen dabbled in the spirit world. Most common folk, and quite a few nobles, saw little difference between wizards and the dreaded Shades. Being labeled a Shade could easily get one burned at a stake, as could any sign of evil like the green eyes and red hair his cousins shared.

"And the table cloth?"

"It allowed us to see how the Bone Fang actually moved material," Rowyn chimed in.

"How would it–" Aeron's thoughts shifted and as if recognizing Rowyn for the first time he squinted one eye and twisted his lips, then asked a bit loudly, "What are you doing here?"

Rowyn responded, but with a baffled look that reflected Aeron's own confusion. "I already told you. I have been watching Uncle Brom create a

Bone Fang."

"You cannot have been here the whole time. I just left you in the Middle Gallery." He looked back at Uncle Brom for a moment to get confirmation, but the older man just sat and turned the table cloth over in his hand, pointing to a small rip in the cloth so Drel Donlin could see.

"Impossible," Rowyn countered. "I have been here for several turns of the glass."

Aeron turned his eyes back to Rowyn and wondered if he was the brunt of a joke. "Does this have something to do with the Spiros you have told me about? Did you wave your hands around, say a few of those strange words, and a Spiro moved you up here before I could run up the stairs?" His eyes narrowed, looking for some sign of lying on Rowyn's part. "You changed clothes also."

"No, no," Rowyn insisted. "As I've told you before, I do not have my uncle's gift. Besides, that would be impossible."

"Not impossible." Uncle Brom spoke, still inspecting the white fabric. The two young men stopped and looked at the wizard.

When Uncle Brom said nothing further, Aeron faced Rowyn, his temper rising. Was Rowyn lying to him? "Then how could you be in the Middle Gallery one minute and up here the next?" Aeron demanded, then waited for Rowyn to answer truthfully.

"Willoe." Uncle Brom sighed deeply.

"Willoe?" Aeron asked. He remembered he still held the dagger and put it back in its sheath.

"Have you and she not done similar in the past?" He addressed Rowyn with a slight tilt to his smile. "I believe, as a child, you sat for her in more than one study without my knowledge. A hood, a change in tone, little was required."

Rowyn cringed at the accusation, but did not say anything, then he also sighed and closed his eyes. "Willoe."

The truth finally dawned on Aeron. Now he knew why Casandra was giggling. He thought back and realized that the swordsman across from Protector Dougal had always faced Aeron, never turning their back to him. All he had seen was the hair pulled around to the back in a braid, a style worn by many fighters, he and Rowyn included, when they suited up for practice. And she had pulled up the hood as soon as Aeron had entered the room. If he had seen her longer hair and possibly the scar on her neck, he would have known immediately. He thought also of the small change in voice. How could he have been so easily fooled?

Aeron felt his face getting hot and his fist clenching. As he thought about it a bit more, his fist relaxed. He could appreciate a good jest as well as anyone. After all, he had quite the reputation himself for such folly, to his father's dismay. A few moments later he began to laugh quietly, and the more he considered what had happened, the louder his laughter became.

"What is so funny?" Rowyn was still fuming, his sense of humor not as finely tuned as his cousin's.

"Willoe," Aeron was able to get out in spurts between boisterous laughter. "I was fully convinced that she was you. And she didn't even have to do or say much of anything. I convinced myself."

Rowyn considered Aeron's words, a smile spreading on his face, and he joined Aeron in his merriment with a mild chuckle, actually making him look more like his outspoken sister than his usual sullen self.

Feeling better that he had not lost his senses, Aeron turned back to Uncle Brom and the Tink. "You were talking about the table cloth?"

"The speed and how the cloth rotated provided important knowledge," Drel Donlin added. "Something you have decided to forego." There was no love lost between the little Tink and Aeron. Drel Donlin never missed a chance to bring up the fact that Aeron had elected not to continue his studies as Rowyn had done. Aeron put up with the barbs only because Uncle Brom treasured his companion.

"How did you get it to twirl to begin with?" Aeron spun his finger in the air simulating the spinning table cloth. He didn't really understand Rowyn's obsession with the history of Cainwen, and he couldn't argue with the possible value of learning from the past. Yet this experimentation, as Uncle Brom called it, seemed somewhat foolish, though it did pique Aeron's interest.

Rowyn thought for a moment, then piped up. "You know that everything contains some of the Burning Lady's essence, what we call the Spirit?"

"Of course." Aeron didn't understand what that had to do with what had just happened.

Rowyn grinned and dove eagerly into an explanation. "Uncle Brom is able to reach across the barrier between the physical world and the Spirit world, the *il fennore*, and call out to a Spiro." Rowyn had explained about the creatures of the Spirit World to Aeron in the past.

Excited, Rowyn moved from side to side, his voice sped up as he continued to describe what Uncle Brom had accomplished. "When the Spiro merges with Uncle Brom he is able to control the Spirit that resides in all things created by the Burning Lady." Which, Aeron knew, was pretty much everything. He still held doubts about the merging concept even though Rowyn had explained it several times in the past. It just seemed so odd.

Rowyn, his Uncle, and the Tink all smiled. It was the first time Aeron had ever seen the little companion smile. At least, Aeron *thought* Drel Donlin was smiling, and that worried Aeron almost as much as the issue about merging with a Spiro. "A Spiro merged with Uncle Brom and he told it to spin the Spirit of the air above the table cloth. When the Spiro did as Uncle Brom requested, the air in the physical world spun, creating a whirlwind that lifted the table cloth. You know what happened after that."

Aeron nodded, but still thought it mostly an enchanter's trick.

"You mentioned something about Master Gwron?" Uncle Brom changed the subject, his smile broadening into a grin.

"Yes, thank the Burning Lady. Willoe told me that Master Gwron had delayed our morning training session." Aeron's shoulders relaxed and he smirked. "Master Gwron is not known for his charitable heart."

"It had slipped my mind." Rowyn sighed with relief and smiled as well. "I'm glad he did, but I wonder how she knew."

A sudden realization came to Aeron and he nearly choked. Why would Master Gwron tell Willoe? He would have been in the Pell all morning and Willoe, dressed as she was, would have avoided the training square at all cost. "No!" He ran a hand across his face, pulling the skin tight.

Rowyn stared at him, obviously concerned, but just as evidently confused.

"You're right, Rowyn. How *would* she know? She probably just said that to avoid my suspicions."

"But that means..." Rowyn began, realization dawning on his face.

Aeron nodded. "Master Gwron is going to work us to death," he said flatly. Master Gwron was a formidable warrior, and the Weapons Master; he was as hard as they came.

Uncle Brom looked back down at the white cloth probing it with a small wand. He just shook his head slightly and murmured to no one in particular, "Ah, the young and the old... half-witted."

The half-wits turned and stared at Uncle Brom.

The thought of what Master Gwron would do to them weighed on Aeron's mind. Aeron was sure whatever he could think of would not match the torture Master Gwron would actually inflict upon them.

4

Unexpected

Panting and wiping at the sweat that ran down his face, Rowyn leaned against the worn stone wall of the Pell. He looked down at Aeron sitting on the ground; his cousin had his head between his knees. With the afternoon sun on the opposite side of the training square, the coolness of the stone under his hand felt like a dip in the river. He took several deep breaths, the odor from both himself and Aeron nearly stifling as he tried to regain his voice.

He had hoped that when Master Gwron had told them the day before, after they had shown up late for training, to arrive early today, that he was not angry. His hopes had been dashed, however, when he and Aeron had stepped into the Pell that morning.

"Do you think Master Gwron is done with us?" he managed to ask between breaths.

Aeron lifted his face, beads of sweat soaking his face and his golden-bronze hair plastered to his back. He looked up at Rowyn and grinned. "I think about four turns of the glass, running us through every drill, should have him satisfied." Master Gwron had had them work through everything – including both sword and mace – against the Pell, the large wooden post that gave the training ground its name, and then hand to hand combat with the large wooden batons and shields.

That Aeron looked to be as worn as Rowyn himself, gave Rowyn a little comfort. Aeron was three years older and had filled out with a broader chest and thicker limbs. But Rowyn knew it wasn't just age. Even without the age difference, Aeron would have towered over Rowyn by at least a hand. Rowyn used to think he would someday match his older cousin, but had recently resigned himself to just rising a finger or two over his twin's height. He took some pride in that he was able to keep up physically with his older cousin during their training sessions. Aeron had received his induction into the Shield Order of Coel a year before, but today's intensive training session had exhausted Aeron no less than Rowyn. And worse, before they started the actual training, they'd had to endure a lecture from Master Gwron on the duty of young nobles to keep up with their training. The Weapons Master spent a full turn of the glass telling them stories of past battles where negligence in training on the part of some Shield had meant their demise. Gory demises that the Weapons Master happily described in great detail. Rowyn had to keep from smiling during the lecture when, strangely enough, the deceased negligent nobles all seemed to be Rowyn's or Aeron's age. It had been a tongue-lashing they had received more than once before. After the lecture, Master Gwron had worked them until they could barely stay on their feet. He did not distinguish one from the other. It didn't make any difference if you were a novice like Rowyn or already a Shield like Aeron. Tomorrow Master Gwron would treat both of them as if today never happened.

Using the wall to stand, Aeron rose, then stretched his back and legs. Rowyn started to lead the way out of the training area of the Pell when he saw Mael entering from the opposite archway, along with the three Shields that were his usual cohorts. One only needed to look at him to know that he was heir apparent. The way he walked – or rather, swaggered – into the training yard and called out to everyone by their first name announced his position clearly. Even the Weapons Master was not left out, he whom everyone else – Rowyn's father included – called 'Master Gwron' out of respect for the old warrior's skill and position.

Mael had their father's curly brown hair and the same piercing hazel eyes. Uncle Brom had explained to Rowyn a little how looks often passed from father to son in the blood, but Rowyn still felt like it was a constant reminder that Willoe's and Rowyn's red curly hair and green eyes marked them as outsiders. A different mother. *Whoever she was*, Rowyn thought sourly.

Rowyn heard a muffled voice above and looked up to see Lady Emeline, her raven hair hanging over the Middle Gallery rail as she peered down into the Pell. Turning back, he saw that Mael was still staring up at the Franchon beauty. Rowyn started to his left, hoping to exit through one of the other archways before Mael noticed them.

Yet, as life would have it, Mael called out, "Prince Rowyn, dear brother, are you in such a rush to leave Gwron's good instruction?"

Rowyn stopped and turned back to the inevitable. He caught the frown on Master Gwron's face from behind Mael, just before the Weapons Master left the training grounds. Few would invade Master Gwron's domain, but Mael treated everything in the castle as if it were his personal property.

"No, Mael, we have finished our drills," Rowyn explained.

Aeron had come up next to Rowyn and gave Mael the minimum bow without being disrespectful. Rowyn knew Aeron had no stomach for the older prince and his companions, but Mael would someday be king and Aeron someday the First Duke. Even tired as he was, Aeron put a smile on his face when he addressed Mael. "We were just off to the kitchens for pints of wine and then maybe a bath before supper."

"It cannot be that you are through for the day?" Mael feigned shock as he turned to look at his companions. They only smirked and laughed. Mael looked back up to the Gallery, and Rowyn followed his gaze for just a moment.

The woman was still looking over the rail, but now the foreigner to Taran stood next to her, his red robes contrasting with her brilliant blue dress. Mael smiled at her and then turned his attention back to Rowyn.

Mael indicated the rather large and overly muscled man behind him. "Ser Tanguy was so looking forward to a little exercise. There have been so few opportunities of late." The snicker turned into a full snort as he sneered at Rowyn. "As Gwron is so fond of reminding us, you should stretch out your muscles after intense exercise. What better way than a friendly trial." He looked at those few who had remained on the training ground. "We will make it simple. The first to score five points will be declared the winner."

"This is not a tournament, Mael," Aeron said as he stepped up to Rowyn's side. "We have just finished a rigorous session and we do not have a lot of time to rest before tonight." He added in a harsher tone, "Rowyn is no match for your man. Tanguy is a three-time champion of the tourneys."

Mael's demeanor shifted, his jaw tightening as he sucked in his breath deeply. But the change was only momentary and his ever-present smile returned. "Lord Aeron." There was no mistaking the emphasis on the word 'Lord.'

"Prince Mael." Aeron withdrew, and while the words were submissive, the voice that spoke them was anything but.

Ser Tanguy flexed his muscles and his sneer grew a little wider as his large forehead wrinkled. He pawed the dirt like a bull and Rowyn had no problem imagining the older and more experienced Shield with a set of horns.

"I am sorry, brother—" Rowyn began, trying to excuse himself.

"Good, very good. I am glad you agree, brother." Mael ignored the attempt and walked over to the weapons rack set up near the wall to select one of the training polearms. It was as tall as Rowyn, only a little over half the length of the ones used on the battlefield, and instead of the razor sharp blade inserted in the end, it had a small thin block of soft wood covered in several layers of goat skin to provide the weight of the blade without the associated lethality. He handed the polearm to Rowyn and grabbed a similar weapon, which he tossed to Ser Tanguy. The sneering man caught it in one hand and immediately flipped it back and forth, changing the upper hand each time and leaving little doubt as to his expertise with the weapon.

Rowyn hated the polearm; it was probably the weapon he had the least experience with, but, if he had to admit it, he had no love for any weapon. Given the opportunity he would never pick up a blade or lance again and spend all his time in study with Uncle Brom or reading one of his uncle's many tomes. But he was his father's third son and even though a bastard, still part of the royal family. So he spent his time in training along with all the other young nobles of the castle, but he had made it a habit to do just enough to keep Master Gwron satisfied, if not happy. Mael was, however, the oldest, and heir apparent, and it would not do to argue or disobey him, especially in public. Rowyn supposed he could take this to his father, but he would not do that. He may not be a great warrior, but he was not craven either.

Gripping the weapon, Rowyn shifted his feet and planted them in the dirt and straw of the training yard. He needed to defend himself — attack was out of the question. The polearm felt awkward and he couldn't remember if he had his hands placed as Master Gwron had taught him.

The other men moved back a suitable distance from Rowyn and the Shield. Before stepping away, Aeron whispered to Rowyn, "Stay away from the forward hand and keep low." Rowyn nodded and gripped the polearm even tighter, though he knew that was the opposite of what Master Gwron would have told him to do. Aeron whispered again before finally leaving Rowyn's side. "You might also want to go down quickly."

Mael stood between Rowyn and Ser Tanguy. He looked up to the Gallery above, and Rowyn assumed that the Franchon lady and her escort were still watching. Mael actually nodded to the Gallery, then looked back at Ser Tanguy and Rowyn. He moved back to join those in the circle that had formed around the two combatants.

Rowyn turned toward Aeron to ask about the placement of his hands when he heard Mael call out, "Begin."

Rowyn spun around just as the opposing Shield stepped forward and used the unencumbered end of the polearm to smack Rowyn on the wrist, causing Rowyn to drop his polearm. The Shield flipped the weapon and used the end with the padded wooden block to punch Rowyn in the stomach. Rowyn doubled over, trying to regain his breath, and did not see the cushioned end of the weapon as the Shield swung it upward again. It caught Rowyn on the chin and knocked him backward in the air to land on his back with a loud thud, kicking up a cloud of dust around him.

Lying there, dazed, Rowyn tried to focus as he slipped in and out of consciousness. Slowly his mind cleared and he rolled over on his side. He had no idea where his weapon was, and as badly bruised as his face felt, he didn't really care. He wasn't about to give Mael the satisfaction by bending a knee to his champion.

He felt a hand grasp his arm and help lift him to his feet. Rowyn glanced around, looking for his weapon and the deadly Shield, but instead he saw Mael and the others roaring with laughter as they walked back through the archway they had entered through. Ser Tanguy took one last look back at Rowyn, chuckled dismally, and tossed the polearm into the dirt at Rowyn's feet before he followed the others out.

"Is it over, then?" Rowyn asked, still a little woozy.

"Let's see." Aeron held up his fist. "Contact to the wrist." He held up one finger. "Contact to the body." He held up two more fingers. "And knocking you down." He held up all five fingers and his forefinger on the second hand. "Yes, it is over."

Aeron put an arm around Rowyn and moved them toward a different archway. "We will spend a little extra time in the baths with an ample supply of wine."

Rowyn turned to glance up at the Gallery, only to see Lady Emeline's blue dress disappear from the rail. The red remained, however, and the dark eyes of the foreigner stared down at Rowyn.

He turned away and gently rubbed his chin. While even the lightest touch caused some pain, it didn't feel as if any serious damage had been done. Rowyn wasn't one to hold a grudge, but as they left the Pell he swore to himself that some day it would be different. Some day they would need something from him and... He stopped the thought and frowned, because he knew his own character. He was incapable of holding back and would do whatever was needed. Rowyn almost despised himself as much as those that tormented him. If only he had the will to be like everyone else.

"Cleric Bat-Uul." The page came up behind the Shin-il priest as he was crossing an atrium between hallways.

Bat-Uul stopped, put a hand on Caspar-Jin's arm, and smiled at the page. "Yes, Tomos." Bat-Uul made it a habit of learning the names of everyone whom he had any dealings with, even if they were just a lowly page. Ever since his parents had died and he was delivered as an Initiate to the temple, Bat-Uul had followed the Shin-il Way, which recognizes that all people have value — no matter their station in life. He was rewarded with a smile from the page. "Cleric Yoan and I have followed different paths. I do not use the title 'Cleric.'" He tried to be as gentle in the correction as possible.

"My apologies, Lord Bat-Uul." The page nodded his head, accepting the correction.

"And I am also not a Lord." He did not lose his smile. "Bat-Uul is sufficient." He looked the boy in the eyes and spoke slowly to make himself understood. "Bat is my name. Uul is a title that I wear with pride."

Caspar-Jin next to him stifled a chuckle.

Bat-Uul frowned at the lower-ranking Jin priest, but Caspar-Jin just smiled back and Bat-Uul shook his head. Though close in age, the Jin priest was always a challenge to Bat-Uul. Caspar-Jin seemed to take his priestly duties a bit lax at times, a definite contrast to Bat-Uul's unyielding fealty to the canon of the Shin-il Way, but there were few whom Bat-Uul could confide in.

"Yes Lo— Bat-Uul." Tomos smiled again. Then he seemed to remember why he had been sent to find Bat-Uul. "A raven arrived from Castle White Cliffs with a message for you. Master Grafith, he is the Master of Birds, could not determine its importance."

Bat-Uul kept his silence, but thought that Tomos provided more detail than his master probably intended.

"He commanded me to find you and deliver this." The page held out the scroll.

Bat-Uul took the scroll and unrolled it. His smile widened into a grin and then he quickly brought it back to a thin smile. "Thank you, Tomos. And thank Master Grafith."

Page Tomos' eyes squinted and Bat-Uul could tell the young man was confused.

"The scroll is fine," Bat-Uul assured the young page.

The messenger didn't seem convinced, but when Bat-Uul didn't say anything else, Tomos just smiled, nodded, and headed back the way he had come.

After the page had left, Bat-Uul unrolled the scroll again. He could understand why Master Grafith had had problems reading the message. The markings on the scroll were in Bat-Uul's native language. Or, at least, the language he had grown up with, not the language of his parents. The Shin-il priest rolled the scroll back up, put it into the pocket of his sleeve and walked out of the atrium to a small courtyard he had found the other day.

He settled down on a bench under a Whisper Glen tree. Many of the white flowers had already fallen off to announce the end of summer, but the dipping branches still created a nice canopy over the bench. Caspar-Jin sat down next to him.

Bat-Uul pulled the scroll out, unrolled it and saw the signature at the bottom, then let the scroll drop into his lap.

"What is it, brother?" Caspar-Jin asked.

Bat-Uul looked over and could see the concern in Caspar-Jin's face. The man had become more than just Bat-Uul's attendant, but a companion and advisor Bat-Uul relied upon.

"It is a message from Dimah-Uul." As Bat-Uul had expected. His superior at Castle White Cliffs. The sight of the gnarled old priest's name on the scroll soured Bat-Uul's thoughts. The trip out from White Cliffs had let him nearly forget about the perverted older priest. Bat-Uul had no evidence that Dimah-Uul had fallen off the path of the Shin-il Way, but the man had given Bat-Uul little reason to trust his superior. It took Bat-Uul a moment to regain his inner composure before he was able to read the letter.

Caspar-Jin sat quietly, but Bat-Uul could see the tenseness in his body. Bat-Uul knew the priest was anxious to find out what was in the message, but would never ask.

Bat-Uul picked the scroll back up and he caught a smile on Caspar-Jin's face as he started to read aloud.

"Brother Bat-Uul, your message regarding Prince Mael was received and I am pleased that Lady Emeline is fulfilling her duty adequately."

"Though you have had success, it is imperative that you become aware of important changes in the mission. A certain Chuluun-Uul has arrived on the latest ship. He brings new directions directly from the Master."

"But the mission had not changed in over a hundred years," Caspar-Jin interrupted, his eyebrows raised and eyes wide. "And more than two Uuls on a single mission." He shook his head and crunched up his face.

He did not have any answers for his friend and instead just continued reading.

"It is necessary that your return to Castle White Cliffs include Crown Prince Beynon's bastard twins, Prince Rowyn and Princess Willoe. Initiating a marriage bond between Prince Mael and Lady Emeline remains an objective to be pursued, but it is secondary to the royal twins returning with your retinue.

"You will receive further instructions after Chuluun-Uul has settled and reviewed the current situation. Signed Dimah-Uul."

As he put the scroll back down he tried to comprehend the meaning behind the words. One thought kept going through his mind. *What is the importance of Prince Rowyn and Princess Willoe such that it would subvert the primary object of Prince Mael?* The marriage bond between Prince Mael and the Lady Emeline would take time to achieve the objectives necessary to bring the Shin-il Way to first Franchon and then all of Taran, but it was a plan that had worked consistently in the past, in many kingdoms. The new directions made no sense to Bat-Uul, but he was sure that if it was the Master's will then it was likely beyond his ability to understand. This new Uul, this Chuluun-Uul, would surely bring all in line with the Shin-il Way.

Rolling the scroll back up, Bat-Uul sat for a few moments, then stood and headed for the Franchon count's guest quarters, Caspar-Jin following. Bat-Uul could not make such a request of the king, but the count had been brought along for just such matters. As he strolled through the atrium and down the appropriate hallway, his thoughts kept returning to the question that troubled him the most. *Why are the twins important?*

He had not read to Caspar-Jin the additional note Dimah-Uul had written under his signature, as if an afterthought.

Eliminate differences and conflict is eliminated.

The line was from the canon of their faith, the Shin-il Way. It was meant to stress a path to brotherhood and peace, but from Dimah-Uul it seemed to hold a different meaning. A meaning Bat-Uul could not understand, but one that brought a sense of fear.

5

Hall of History

Rowyn was the first out of the room with Aeron closely behind. Rowyn rarely drank ale while the sun was up, if at all, but after spending all morning with Chancellor Liam, he was ready to take Aeron's suggestion of a tankard, even if the mid-day meal was still a turn away.

Mael exited the room with two young nobles in tow and walked up to Rowyn and Aeron. Rowyn had not spoken with his older sibling for almost two weeks – ever since the day in the Pell with Ser Tanguy.

"Ah, my dear brother, I have need of your service. The Franchon woman has requested a tour of the castle and our father advises that I escort her. Sadly I have little time for such frivolous endeavors." He snickered and the others joined in on the joke. "I am sure Father will understand that I find myself otherwise occupied and unable to satisfy her request. Therefore I know you will give my regrets to the lady and find an emissary to escort her."

Mael started to walk away without waiting for acknowledgment. He knew his younger brother could not refuse. He stopped and turned back for just a moment, wearing a smile. "Possibly Chancellor Liam? He knows the castle as well as anyone." He chuckled and the two noblemen laughed right along with him. Having discharged his responsibility, Mael turned to stroll away, but before that he pushed back the hair on his right side, a habit he had around Rowyn. It was something Rowyn was sure Mael did intentionally.

The movement was intended to highlight the hereditary mark proudly borne by all the Brynmor royal family… excepting Rowyn and his sister. It took the form of a blond streak that ran from the fringe to the hair that hung down the back of the neck, crossing along the right side and separating the dark brown hair on top from the side. It was attractive on the other men of the family, but with Mael's strutting it only reminded Rowyn of a peacock.

Rowyn let out a deep breath and looked back into the room. "I should inform Chancellor Liam of this new duty." He could not imagine anything more dreary than spending endless time with the dour, ancient Chancellor Liam.

Before Rowyn could step into the room, Aeron clasped him by the elbow and pulled him aside. Aeron lowered his voice. "Would you wish a day with Chancellor Liam on your worst enemy?"

Rowyn glanced at the retreating back of his older brother with a slight smile.

Aeron laughed. "Yes, there are some I would also." Then he turned serious. "But not this woman. What has she done that she should bear the pain of Chancellor Liam's instruction?"

Rowyn nodded in agreement. "Then whom shall I send?"

"Just find someone that can provide the lady with a tour of the gardens, stables, and whatever else she may find of interest. Someone who knows the castle well enough to answer the lady's questions." As if an afterthought, he added, "And make sure they are entertaining. No point in making the lady's tour any more boring than I imagine it will already be."

Rowyn thought for a moment, then patted Aeron on the shoulder. "Thank you, cousin. Please make sure to show her the gardens. I am sure she will find them most exciting." He turned away and strode off in a different direction than his older brother.

"Wait!" Aeron called after Rowyn. "I did not mean that *I* should. I have many a task today." He searched for an example, but nothing came to mind.

"Your sacrifice is duly noted, dear cousin." Rowyn didn't turn back but just kept walking and waved a hand in the air above his head, dismissing Aeron's attempts to avoid the task.

"I won't do it," Aeron called after Rowyn.

Aeron strolled alongside Lady Emeline as they entered an atrium from one of the many hallways that honeycombed the castle. He had had little to do with the Franchons since their arrival three weeks ago other than an official reception and a few suppers. He hadn't even talked with this woman since they met on the road. *Oh cousin, you really owe me*, Aeron thought as he smiled politely at a comment from the Franchon woman. He thought of what Mael had said earlier about marrying her and pitied the woman if she had to be Mael's queen.

His sister had told Aeron that the ladies' gossip told that the king had agreed to a marriage bond between Mael and the Franchon woman. King Benoit of Franchon had no living children. His only son had been killed in a riding accident. A niece, even one distantly related as Emeline was, would provide an alliance that could end the decades of skirmishes up and down the Saltrock River.

Aeron and Emeline had already visited dozens of locations, including the king's gardens and stables. He was impressed with the woman's knowledge of horses.

"Josiane, were not the stables just wonderful?" Emeline spoke to her maid walking several steps behind them.

"Yes, milady."

"Did you enjoy the gardens?"

"Yes, milady."

"I have tried for over a year to stifle her fear of the nobility," Emeline leaned toward Aeron and whispered, "but she is like a castle cat, scared of her own shadow. But seeing as she is my maid and chaperone, it does afford me a great deal of freedom."

Aeron was surprised at Emeline's confession, but it made him laugh nonetheless. He glanced over his shoulder at the maid Josiane. The young girl was small, her light brown hair identifying her position well below the raven-haired Franchon nobility. She rarely raised her head as they walked, and so Aeron had no idea what her face looked like.

They had just finished roaming through more than a dozen corridors, with a great number of sections still unexplored. The castle had been built well in the past, over fifteen hundred years ago, by early ancestors of the current King. Additions provided by subsequent lords and kings had turned Castle Westhedge into a hulking behemoth, looming over the valley. Having lived most of the last four years in Castle Westhedge as a ward of King Einion, Aeron had wandered through much of the castle, though Westhedge was so large there were still areas he was not familiar with.

The city that carried the same name as the castle had sprung up over the years, and now housed over eighty-five thousand souls, with extensive farmlands spreading throughout the valley and into the surrounding mountains.

They came to a stop and Lady Emeline seemed to be waiting patiently for directions from Aeron. He considered which places she might be interested in. "I thought you might find the royal weavers' chamber of interest. It is also where ladies of the royal family and other noble ladies weave the tapestries of the kingdom's history."

"Yes, please. I helped my mother finish a tapestry of my father at sea, in battle with pirates." She sounded excited, but then her gaze turned down and she said coyly, "I will do the same for my husband."

"Then just across the atrium." He pointed to a hallway on the other side. "Is your father still at sea often?"

"My parents and brother are—" Her breath caught in her throat and the full-lipped smile faded. "I have not seen them this last year."

"Do they not live in Castle White Cliffs?" Aeron asked as they started across.

Lady Emeline stopped and, as if she had not heard the question, she pointed to a hallway to their right. "What is down this hallway?"

Aeron thought it strange that she avoided such simple questions. He looked at the hallway she had indicated, his concerns fleeing to the back of his mind, but not forgotten. It was a long hallway decorated with tapestries that hung along the right-hand wall. It was shortly after mid-day, and the sunlight poured through dozens of large windows running down the left side of the hall, illuminating the hangings.

"It is called the Hall of History."

"It sounds ancient... and interesting. Can we look at it first?" Her tone was excited, as if she had discovered something new and wondrous.

They walked over into the hallway and Aeron started toward a painting, the nearest to them, but just a quarter of the way down the hallway. Lady Emeline came up next to him as Aeron stared at the first picture. It was the width and height of two men and covered the wall in front of them from floor to ceiling. "The hangings chronicle the history of Cainwen back to its beginning."

"Beautiful." She touched the hanging.

"It was created by King Einion's wife, Queen Wynnifred. Unfortunately, Crown Prince Beynon's wife passed on to the Burning Lady within a few months of Prince Hafgan's birth and Princess Willoe has not yet created one for her father." He thought that it was unlikely she ever would. He imagined the royal weavers would have to create one in her stead.

The tapestry's scene depicted a Cainwen army overwhelming Tonn warriors in a bloody confrontation along a shoreline. A Shield on a rearing horse was slashing at the barbarians in front of him with a blood-stained sword. The Shield wore a circlet and was surrounded by Guardsmen brandishing swords and polearms as they waded into the horde of fear-filled warriors. *At least, they look like they are scared in the tapestry,* Aeron thought. He knew better, though. The nomadic Tonn believed to die in battle was the greatest glory a warrior could hope to achieve.

"This is King Einion." Aeron indicated the Shield. "It was nearly forty winters ago. It was a long and hard winter that year. Several Tonn tribes banded together and trekked south along the edge of Crystal Bay, ravaging villages and creating havoc throughout the northern regions of Cainwen. King Einion pulled the entire garrison out of Fort Winterpass, along with what northern vassals he could muster, and pushed the Tonn back into the Open Lands. This was the battle of Athfort where the king broke the Tonn's back.

Lady Emeline stared at the painting and said with uncharacteristic compassion, "But they were just hungry, were they not? They had children that would starve if they stayed in the Open Lands."

Aeron had never thought about it from the Tonn's perspective. "The Tonn roam the Open Lands with their herds, bartering with traders for whatever they can't hunt or make themselves. But you may be right. I was told the long winter wiped out many of their herds. Lord Brom, the Crown Prince's brother—"

Emeline nodded that she knew who he meant.

"He used the tapestries to teach Prince Rowyn, Princess Willoe, my sister Casandra, and me about the kingdom's past. He said tribes farther north had come south, pushing the southern tribes in front of them. These southern tribes are the ones depicted in the tapestry." Every time Aeron had looked at the image, he had focused on the victorious Cainwens. Now, he turned his focus to the barbarians being speared and cut down in a bloodbath. "When facing a Tonn warrior, one does not normally ask about his family," Aeron said without humor in his voice.

"Why did the northern tribes come south?"

"Lord Brom would not say, other than a day would come when we would all find out. He seemed quite serious."

"An ill-boding prophecy." She continued to examine the scene.

Aeron had not seen it as such back then, but now wondered about Uncle Brom's explanation. He looked sideways at the Franchon woman. Her insight into the tapestry astounded him.

He skipped a couple of tapestries to one that showed an undaunted Shield, on foot with a handful of Guardsmen behind him, forcing a raging creature twice his size backward. The creature had features similar to a man, but its skin had a blue tint while its arms and legs were inappropriately thick for the body. The background clearly showed a rocky hill or mountain covered in ice and snow.

"Strange creature." Lady Emeline stepped closer to the painting.

Aeron smiled. "Lord Brom called it an ice giant. They are from the far north, even farther north than the Haldane capital and the Open Lands, somewhere in the Hoarfrost Mountains. I have never seen one myself, and I hope I never do. This fellow looks like he would not be a pleasant companion."

Her tittering laugh was cut short when she suddenly snorted. She quickly put a hand over her mouth and her eyes went wide. "Forgive me. I was envisioning you sitting around a fire sharing a tankard with this brute, telling the tales that men tell."

Aeron laughed himself. The unlady-like act was actually charming in his view. "That would be quite a thing to see." He found himself curious about this woman. Intelligent and with a sense of humor, not the pretentious lady of the court he had thought her to be. And beautiful. "I am not sure what tales we could share in common, but I would be most interested in what he has to say."

She laughed modestly, regaining her composure.

They moved on to more paintings as he explained each one in turn. They continued down the hall as Aeron explained some of the more interesting tapestries, most involving a battle, either small or large. All depicted past kings of Cainwen, and though the armor and uniforms changed to match the period of history, every hanging recounted a battle scene. Aeron was impressed with her knowledge of some of the more famous battles. Without consciously making the change, he realized his tone had become less formal and he was enjoying himself as he answered the woman's questions.

They came across one that made Emeline stop and catch her breath.

Aeron paused at her side to look up at the scene and understood her reaction. "This is the Battle of Legendre in the marshes of Greenmerrow."

"Yes, I know," she said softly.

Aeron could see a sorrow in her eyes that told of some past horror that had been brought alive by the tapestry.

"These are Franchons." She pointed to the soldiers being soundly beaten back by a Cainwen army.

He didn't want to respond – a knot had formed in his stomach – but he couldn't lie to her either. "The battle established the Saltrock River as the border between Cainwen and Franchon that has not changed in nearly seven hundred years."

She kept staring at the tapestry without saying a word. After several moments of consuming the colorful lines of the woven fabric with her eyes, she spoke, but her voice no longer contained the excitement of before. "Cainwen defeated Franchon, ending the expansion of the Franchons who would otherwise have spread all the way to the western shores, the shores of the Forever Waters." It was if she were simply reciting a well-known, but sad, history lesson.

"Yes."

Her eyes moved from top to bottom and side to side as she took in the entire tapestry. Then she smiled, as she had done most of the afternoon.

She took his arm, a bold gesture that stunned Aeron at first; his throat became dry and the knot in his stomach leaped at her touch, but he walked with her as she continued until they reached the second to last tapestry.

Aeron explained the historical significance of the scene. They had traveled almost two thousand years of Cainwen history in a matter of a couple of turns. Aeron felt a sense of pride as he reflected on all the heroes and leaders they had seen.

"What about this one? It is different than the rest." Emeline moved to the final tapestry hanging by itself on a wall at the end, facing back down the hall.

The tapestry was three times the size of the others. It was the only scene in the entire hall that did not show a battle. Most of the tapestry was taken up by a dragon that towered over a lone man. The tapestry was so large, the creature stood as high as three men, giving it an even more terrifying appearance. The dragon had a long boney snout with two horns that curved up like a wave. Spikes sprouted at the crown of its head, getting smaller as they ran down the spine to the end of the tail. Large wings splayed from just behind the front legs to just above the rear ones. The scales were layered over the entire body with the exception of the chest and underbelly. Yellowish-gold yarn had been used to recreate the scales, which reminded Aeron of a topaz gem his mother had worn several times.

He walked up and put his hand on the fabric. "It's very old. I'm not sure anyone knows its real age."

"Who is the man?" She stepped up and touched the image of the man in front of the dragon. He wasn't dressed in metal or leather as the subjects of the previous hangings, but in a colorful robe. Unlike the other subjects he didn't have brown or blond hair, but a bright red that more closely resembled Aeron's twin cousins.

"I don't really know. Prince Rowyn and I asked his uncle once. He just told us it was a king from ancient times, when Elfs and Men lived as one." He tried to remember the story, but he had not paid much attention when Uncle Brom had told the tale. "I think it's a King Korlac, or Cormac."

"And the dragon?" Emeline tilted her head back to look up at the creature.

"They say dragons are the messengers of the Burning Lady." He turned toward her. "The bard's songs are filled with such tales."

Her eyes became wider and her lips parted slightly. "Does that mean that a dragon will appear with a message from the Burning Lady?"

"Only stories the minstrels recount to entertain." He laughed harder. "If dragons ever existed, they passed with the ancients."

He was surprised when she lowered her head and seemed disappointed.

The sound of boots on the stone floor echoed down the hallway, causing both of them to turn back the way they had come. Approaching them was the Earl of Greenmerrow, and trailing behind was Rowyn's middle brother, Hafgan.

"Lady Emeline. Lord Aeron." The Earl nodded his head as he came to a halt in front of them.

Aeron nodded his head in response, then indicated the man behind the Earl. "Lady Emeline, I believe you have already met Prince Hafgan." Even though Hafgan was around Aeron's age and a member of the royal Brynmor family, a stranger would never believe Hafgan to be third in line to the crown. He looked disheveled, though Aeron knew this was his normal appearance despite the efforts of his servants and the Crown Prince. Hafgan had a perpetual slight bend to his body, not what one would call hunchbacked, but there was an obvious physical affliction that gave him a frail appearance.

"Prince Hafgan." Emeline curtsied with a friendly smile.

Hafgan nodded hesitantly in response, then edged his way back around the Earl.

Facing back toward the Earl, Aeron introduced the man. "May I introduce the Earl of Greenmerrow, Grioral Malbery."

Emeline curtsied. "It is a pleasure."

"The pleasure is mine." Malbery bowed.

Malbery looked up the wall and chuckled. "The long and glorious history of Cainwen."

"Lord Aeron was entertaining me with tales of Cainwen bravery." The way Emeline said it made Aeron feel as if he had been the hero in one of the hanging pieces of art. Emeline had a way of saying things that could charm a snake – which when he thought about it would be appropriate for Malbery.

"Yes, quite brave." The Earl, just under forty winters, returned to the tapestry displaying the Battle of Legendre. Hafgan kept close by.

"Did he tell you of this battle?" he asked, looking back at Aeron and Emeline.

"Yes, the battle is well known among Franchons." The lady walked up near Malbery, Aeron at her side, and he noticed her smile had faded once again. "We tell the tale from a somewhat different viewpoint, as you can imagine." She paused, staring at the tapestry again before continuing. "But the end result is the same no matter the perspective. The Cainwens led the Franchon army into the marches where they became mired and slaughtered. Hence the name Legendre's Folly." She turned to look at Malbery. "From your interest I would infer that you have more to tell?"

"As it so happens, I do. It was fought on the lands of Greenmerrow. It was the soldiers of Greenmerrow that led your... I believe ancestors, into the swamp. Were you aware that Greenmerrow was not part of Cainwen or Franchon at the outbreak of hostilities between the two kingdoms?"

"I was not," Emeline answered, her head tilting a little.

He stepped up to the tapestry and ran a finger over a group of warriors at the bottom of the scene. It contained several Shields and Guardsmen in dark blue, in sharp contrast to the green and gold of the Cainwen side of the tapestry. His face was reflective and serious. "Greenmerrow was a separate realm ruled over by my ancestor, King Roblin. But war came to our lands. Our misfortune was to be located along the southern end of the Saltrock River, where the Franchon army decided to cross in their conquest of Cainwen."

Neither Aeron nor Emeline said anything, and Aeron wondered where Malbery was headed with his story.

"King Roblin had a decision to make. A very difficult one." He turned back to face Aeron and Emeline, the smile returned. "Many with Franchon blood lived on the land, as did those of Cainwen. King Roblin himself was of Franchon blood, as were many of our ancestors."

Aeron had never noticed before, but the Franchon influence in Malbery's appearance was obvious, now that he looked for it. Straight, raven-colored hair, like Emeline's. Even in Malbery's mustache it was evident, as it ended in a small chin beard with the area between the chin and the ears clean-shaven similar to a fashion Aeron had heard was common among Franchon nobles.

"But war had come and the larger kingdoms would not leave Greenmerrow out of the fray. King Roblin had to make a decision as to whom to support." Malbery turned again to the tapestry. "He chose Cainwen." His voice lowered and held a strange tone to it.

"And Greenmerrow has been a loyal supporter of the Brynmor line ever since," Aeron added. "Your father, may his flame burn brightly with the Burning Lady, was renowned for his staunch support of King Einion and his father, King Gadnog, before him."

"Yes, he was." Malbery sighed once and stood for a few more heartbeats absorbing the tapestry, then turned back to Aeron and Emeline. "Pardon me. I did not mean to interrupt your tour. Please continue. We have other duties elsewhere." He bowed and started to walk away up the hall, with Hafgan left behind still staring up at the tapestry, evidently engrossed in the story Malbery had told. As the Earl strode away he called over his shoulder in a harsh voice, "Prince Hafgan."

The Prince shook his head as if coming out of sleep and hurried after the Earl.

Standing next to Emeline, their forearms touching, Aeron could feel her give a little shiver. He turned and grinned at her. "The Earl has that effect on everyone," he reassured her. "Like coming across a snake in the middle of a path."

She giggled and seemed to relax.

Aeron turned to gaze down the hall at the retreating back of the Earl, and couldn't help but frown a little as he wondered what it was about the Earl that made the man seem that way.

6

The Banquet

Willoe stood on the porch just outside the large archway entrance to the Great Hall, waiting for Casandra. She paced until she saw her cousin coming up the long set of stairs leading to the porch. Willoe hated banquets; they were nothing more than grand displays of power. She only suffered through them with Casandra's help.

Casandra finally came up the step to the porch.

"Another banquet." Willoe made no effort to hide her displeasure from her cousin, who had heard it often enough.

"Just keep smiling and try to avoid drawing attention to yourself," Casandra advised her with a hint of humor at the end.

They walked down the screened passageway and rinsed their hands in the basin outside the doors. A servant held out a towel for each of them to dry their hands. The two women entered through the iron-banded wooden doors of the Great Hall. Over the years she had been required to attend quite a few banquets in this Hall.

Willoe was always impressed with the thoroughness of the preparations. From past experience she knew that the servants, under the direction of Steward Robat, had been at it since before sunrise. They had cleaned and rehung the tapestries against the wood panels that rose as high as four men. Above that, wooden beams ran up daub walls, which doubled the height of the walls, allowing the smoke to rise above the nobles, castle staff, and city officials seated below. Banners and polished shields displaying the king's coat of arms and those of his nobles hung between the tapestries. Sconces were already lit and spaced evenly along the sides, with dozens of wooden wheel-shaped devises hanging from the ceiling. Each held twenty large candles. Additional groups of candles were placed on all the tables. When all lit, there wasn't a corner of the Hall where a shadow could be found.

The head table was standing on the raised dais at the end of the Great Hall. Two tables sat to either side and trestle tables five rows deep lined the sides of the room facing the center, for those of lesser birth. All the tables were covered in white linen.

"The king will be down shortly." Steward Robat approached them from the side and bowed. Even when bowing, he somehow managed to maintain a stiff posture and made Willoe feel somewhat lacking in the social graces. Only a few wisps of hair sat atop his head and he was as thin as a pole. He seemed so frail, but he had looked just as he did when Willoe was a child and, according to Uncle Brom, had always looked that way. The steward was a fixture around the castle, having served Willoe's great grandfather many years ago. Nothing of a social nature happened around the castle without Steward Robat's involvement. Standing as stiff as a board again, he indicated one of the tables to the side of the dais. "Princess Willoe. Lady Casandra."

Both nodded and followed two pages that led them toward the table on the right side of the dais, where Rowyn and Aeron were already seated.

Casandra stopped to talk with several people while Willoe continued on. Before reaching the table someone called out to her.

"You are looking well tonight, Princess." The elderly woman in a heavy velvet dress and adorned with a dozen gems around her neck, on her arms, and in her hair smiled warmly, as usual.

"Thank you, Dame Jestin." Willoe curtsied, but the Dame's smile was evidence enough that Willoe still needed more practice. Willoe also knew the woman would not say anything. Ser Jestin was well known for his fierceness on the battlefield, but Willoe had only seen his gentleness, especially with his wife and grandson. Not everyone was disposed to the tales of evil green-eyed, red-haired fiends. The few who weren't, like Dame Jestin and her husband, made an effort to show the twins kindness whenever possible. Willoe knew, however, that there were few who felt this way.

"And how are you, Cedrik?" Willoe looked at the older boy seated next to the Dame.

The boy only nodded and hunched down closer to the table.

Both Willoe and the Dame smothered their laughter, settling for a shared smile.

"Go check to see where your grandfather is and tell him that his wife misses his old scraggly gray beard and battered face." The Dame ruffled the boy's hair and sent him on his quest.

After the boy left, the old woman laughed out loud. "He is just like his father... was." A sadness crept into the woman's eyes, but cleared quickly with a smile.

"How is the king?" the Dame asked politely.

It was a common question of late. Her grandfather seemed to have aged a decade in the last few months. Rumors abounded, but no one, not even the healers, could explain why his health was failing.

Before Willoe could answer a gruff voice interrupted. "What is wrong with my beard?" A giant of a man stepped up, stroking his gray and white beard, grinning at them with a mouth mostly filled with teeth.

"I just missed you, my husband." The Dame put a hand on his arm as she looked up and Willoe could see the unyielding devotion in her eyes.

Ser Jestin leaned back and roared, his hands on his chest. "And I you, my love."

He turned toward Willoe. "My Princess." His lips closed over his teeth and he stared at her intently. "How is the king faring?"

Willoe didn't say anything, but looked down at her feet and took a deep breath. When she looked back up the Shield and his wife were watching her, their faces reflecting her own concerns.

"Hmmggg." Willoe turned to face Steward Robat, who was clearing his throat, with the page standing by his side. He bowed and swung his hand out toward the dais.

"Pardon me." Willoe turned back to Ser and Dame Jestin and nodded respectfully.

They both nodded deeply in return and Willoe continued to follow the page to her table.

She arrived at the table sooner than Casandra, as many of the feasters wanted to get her cousin's attention and have a few words with Casandra. Especially the young Shields and nobles. Casandra was not only the prettiest woman in the Hall, but she was also the daughter of the most powerful man next to the royal family, the First Duke. If not for the stigma that their bright red hair and radiant green eyes brought down upon them, she too would be surrounded by suitors. Everyone knew they were not really vile Shades – in fact, she doubted anyone in the room had ever seen one – but having the same eye and hair color, reportedly a trait associated with the creatures of the living dead, along with their questionable heritage, was enough of a deterrent for most people.

Willoe's stomach gurgled. The porridge she'd had to break her morning fast could not compare to the smokey aroma of roasted beef, along with salmon and pike from the king's own fish farm. The delicious smells floated up from the banquet tables against the walls.

As she approached her seat she nodded an acknowledgment to Protector Dougal, who was standing behind her table. Knowing his habits, she guessed he had eaten a simple meal earlier so he would not be distracted from his duties. A servant pulled out her chair and she sat.

"I've not seen you around the last three days, cousin." Willoe leaned forward to see past Rowyn.

"He has been busy with a certain raven-haired lady," Rowyn said with a sly smile.

"I took her on one tour of the castle and then the Franchon count requested that I take her on a ride through to a local village two days ago," Aeron argued passionately. "Then yesterday it was a visit to the market. Your father agreed. I had no choice."

"You should have seen him today, Wil, when no command came to escort the lady. He bemoaned his loss all day long."

"I did not!" Aeron insisted, sitting back heavily in his chair with arms crossed. Then he leaned forward again with a grin. "How is training going, dear cousin?" He picked up a knife from the table and pointed it toward her and waved it from side to side like a sword.

"Shush." Willoe hoped Aeron would keep her secret. She wouldn't be the first woman to train with weapons. Almost all Cainwen womenfolk learned how to use the shortbow, a lighter and smaller bow than what men used, but that could still kill at short distances. During war, everyone might be called upon to defend the realm. There were even a few women who had fought as men with sword and pike, but seldom a noble lady, and never a princess.

Casandra walked behind and past Aeron, pulling the back of his hair where no one could see. "Ow," he blurted out as his head jerked back. He quickly sat up straight as several minor nobles at one of the tables near them looked up at his outburst.

"Behave brother," Casandra said with an innocent smile as she took the seat next to Willoe. Anyone watching would think she had just complimented the young men, her delicate smile charming anyone nearby. Casandra's humor set Willoe at ease. She sometimes wished she, and especially Rowyn, could be as easygoing as their cousins.

Before Aeron could retort, Mael arrived with Lady Emeline on his arm. They proceeded slowly down the Hall between the trestle tables, with Steward Robat leading them the entire way. Only Casandra had drawn more attention with her entrance. When they reached the table, on the floor to the other side of the dais, Steward Robat sat Lady Emeline and then Mael. The Steward said a few words, bowed, and then left them.

Willoe noticed that Lady Emeline was looking over at their table, but not at Willoe or Casandra. Turning her head to the left Willoe saw Aeron staring back across the open space, in front of the dais, just as intently. She returned her gaze to Mael and Lady Emeline as Mael spoke to the lady, who turned to face him with a pleasant smile. Willoe shifted slightly toward Rowyn and caught Aeron staring for a moment longer before he turned away.

The next to arrive was the Franchon count, who was leading the envoy. Steward Robat seated the count directly to the king's left with two empty chairs next to the Count. A moment later, Willoe was surprised to see the red-robed Bat-Uul led to Mael's and Lady Emeline's table. That alone demonstrated the foreigner's importance.

A trio of horns blew and everyone's attention was drawn as Chancellor Liam, tall and stately, pounded his staff on the floor three times. A herald stepped forward and announced in a loud voice, "His Majesty, Protector of the Realm, First Son of Cainwen. King Einion of the House of Brynmor." The entire Hall stood as King Einion entered from a stairway near the Hall's door, followed by the twins' father, the Crown Prince Beynon Brynmor; and then Casandra's and Aeron's father, Duke Drem Cadwal, the First Duke of the Kingdom. A little further back came Grioral Malbery, the Earl of Greenmerrow; the kingdom's treasurer and one of King Einion's chief advisors, Morcar Priddy; and finally Cleric Yoan. Willoe's father, Duke Drem and Cleric Yoan sat to the king's right. Earl Malbery walked past the king's chair and sat down next to the Franchon count, with Morcar taking the last seat next to the Earl. The king stood in front of his chair and stared around the Hall as if taking in his domain, then sat. Everyone else sat in their chair, or, if they were eating at one of the trestle tables, sat down on the shared benches.

Steward Robat stood behind the king and gave a slight wave with his hand to the Minstrel's Gallery overlooking the Hall. The sounds of strings, pipe and flute quickly filled the room, accompanied by the tinkle of a triangle and the rumble of a small drum. Two jugglers appeared as if from nowhere and with another wave of the steward's hand, servants began arriving at the dais and other tables with rare Kreller meat stew and wheat bread, a delicacy. Other servants followed behind with ale and wine; not the watered-down kind that one often found at banquets, but a strong, full-bodied wine that one could savor.

Uncle Brom entered from a rear door and took a chair at the twins' table. It was an ever-telling sign of what their grandfather thought of their uncle.

With the banquet now firmly underway, the Hall erupted with conversation and good-natured laughter. The king divided his attention between Duke Drem and the Franchon Count. The twins' father was engaged with Cleric Yoan, while Bat-Uul talked with Mael and Lady Emeline. Willoe noticed the treasurer, Morcar, scanning the entire room as if taking a tally of the number of participants and weighing the cost of each one.

After a short while, Willoe finally relaxed and talked idly with Rowyn, her cousins, and Uncle Brom. Willoe turned from talking with Casandra to say something to Rowyn and was surprised to see Bat-Uul standing between and behind Rowyn and Aeron, talking with them.

The red-robed foreigner turned to face Willoe and smiled. "Princess Willoe. I am pleased to introduce myself. I am named Bat-Uul." He put his hands together in a fist and placed them on his head as he bowed slightly.

Willoe nodded, but didn't respond. Something about the man made her hackles rise.

Aeron leaned toward her and spoke a little loudly, as the Hall had become quite noisy. "He is like a Cleric in his homeland."

"Sorry if I misled." Bat-Uul shook his head at Aeron's comment. "Clerics, I believe talk with your Burning Lady, and also are the Healers of your sick. Is this not true?"

Aeron nodded, but seemed a bit confused. Willoe felt like there was something wrong, but she couldn't fathom what it was.

Casandra spoke from her chair on the other side of Willoe. "Do you not have the Burning Lady in your homeland?"

"We are aware of the Burning Lady. However, I follow the path of Shin-il." He smiled again. "I pray to Koke Tengri, lord of all things."

Uncle Brom spoke up from the end of the table, his tone full of mirth. "Your Koke Tengri must be the Burning Lady's husband."

Bat-Uul smiled in return, but answered seriously, "I cannot say as I do not know the Burning Lady. I will have to speak of this with my teacher Poojan-Uul. Surely the Master would know."

Rowyn's shoulders tensed like they did whenever he became intrigued with something new. "Is Poojan-Uul your master?"

"No, no. Poojan-Uul was my teacher and the presiding Uul at the temple in faraway Avanis, where I was raised." Bat-Uul's face lit up for just a moment and then settled back into a friendly, yet distant, expression. "The Master I... I have never met. But I hope to serve and spread his truth." He suddenly stopped talking and the smile faded.

Willoe wondered what he had said that had made him fall silent so suddenly.

A call from the Franchon count made Bat-Uul turn to look at the dais. The count was looking at Bat-Uul expectantly.

"Excuse my presence. I am needed."

He started to the dais and passed within a hand's breadth of Willoe. She gasped and suddenly could feel the stew coming back up in her throat. She turned away to face Casandra and took a couple of deep breaths to keep her food down. A thought raced through her mind. *That smell... The essence of it is the same. I could not mistake it.* The pungent scent reminded her of incense; nutty, but bitter. And the kidnapper.

Willoe spun her head around and looked over at Protector Dougal, whom Bat-Uul had just passed. The Protector stiffened as his eyes followed Bat-Uul up to the dais. Then he turned to look at Willoe, his eyes narrowed and his lips tight.

Willoe stood and Casandra put a hand on her arm.

"What is it, Wil?"

"I... I have to get out of here." Willoe started toward the door leading out the back of the Hall. Her mind was whirling and her heart beat rapidly. She felt suffocated and had to escape into the night air.

As she reached the door, she noticed that Casandra was right behind her. Willoe turned once to look back at Bat-Uul and then caught sight of Protector Dougal walking toward her. She held up a hand and shook her head. He stopped, nodded, then took his place back at the table.

She turned around briskly and exited the Hall, her red hair flipping back around into her face, while Casandra followed. As they walked down the rear steps, Willoe couldn't get any words out. She was so frustrated with the mystery surrounding the priest, and just about everything else that had happened to her in the last few weeks. It all combined to feel like a hammer beating her down. She balled her hands into fists, the nails biting into her palms as she held back a scream that only came out as a high-pitched squeal from her closed lips. The one thing she desired the most was to be in control, but it seemed like it was the one thing to be denied her.

Instead of heading directly for Willoe's room, they walked silently along the portico that ran under the Lower Gallery from the back of the Great Hall around several courtyards to the Pell. They stopped every so often for Willoe to pace back-and-forth and then just as suddenly start striding down the portico again. Most of the servants and staff were preoccupied at the Great Hall, so they ran into few others along their walk. They had wound their way around the portico until they neared the Pell when Willoe stopped and slapped a flat hand on one of the stone columns, the sound echoing through the empty courtyard. She had an eerie feeling that seemed to haunt her. She leaned her head against the cold stone; the coolness of the smooth column felt good against her skin.

Casandra had been following patiently as they walked, and stopped dutifully when Willoe paced, but now she stepped up and put a hand on Willoe's arm. "What's going on, Wil? Is there anything I can do?"

Willoe realized she was gritting her teeth to the point where her jaw hurt. She tried to relax. "I just know there is a connection between that Bat-Uul and what happened to me seven years ago."

"I know you have tried to forget it, but maybe if you told me about it..." Casandra rubbed Willoe's arm. "I never really heard the details. Maybe talking about it would help."

After that day she had never told the story to anyone, as she constantly fought against the vulnerability it had brought. She had never heard Protector Dougal, Cleric Yoan, or her father speak of it either. Willoe sat on a stone bench and Casandra sat next to her. She inhaled as she returned to that time. The time when she had almost died.

7

Visitation

"It was just after my ninth naming day. We were on our way back from one of the summer manors and stopped in a large village for the evening. Erwood." Willoe looked up at the moonlight filtered through wispy clouds.

"That's just a day's ride away," Casandra said.

"Yes, we arrived mid-day. I snuck away from Protector Dougal, Rowyn, and Father. For a while it had been fun going wherever I wanted in the village. There was this one tavern that had a bull and a barrel of wine on it. I think it was called the Beast and Barrel." She looked up, trying to remember exactly, but couldn't. "We had passed it when we first arrived in Erwood. There was a small goat, in the back, that Cleric Yoan said the tavernkeeper probably kept for fresh milk. I really wanted to play with the goat, so I headed down a little alley, between the tavern and the building next to it." She could still remember the aroma of meat cooking and the spicy, sweet smell of ale as she walked along the side of the tavern.

"Weren't you afraid to be wandering around without Protector Dougal?" Casandra put her hand back on Willoe's arm.

"I was nine. I had no idea." She patted Casandra's hand twice. "Just before I reached the back corner, a man stepped out from the building. He was small and wore a dark blue robe that hung to the ground. He had his hood pulled up so I couldn't see any of his features." As if it were yesterday, Willoe could hear the sound of footsteps behind her as they resounded in her memories. "I tried to get away but two more of the robed men were behind me. Before I could run away the first man grabbed me by the arm and pulled me close to his body."

"You must have been frightened to death." Casandra's grip tightened on Willoe's arm.

"The other two men came up and spoke to the first one in a language that sounded like crows calling out from the treetops. It was a higher pitch, but also sounded harsh, like it was coming from the back of the throat. It was different from priest Bat-Uul's, but the inflection was the same. I tried to break free, but the man held me tight and dragged me behind the tavern. I tried to scream, but he was holding a cloth over my mouth. So I screamed the only way I could... in my mind." She paused, not sure how to say what happened next.

Casandra looked at her expectantly.

Willoe stared across the small courtyard they found themselves in. "Something... answered. It felt raw and savage. It came at me... no, inside me. It told me that all would be well... if only I let it in."

The sound of Casandra's gasp made Willoe look at her. She asked her cousin, "Remember when I was twelve and we rescued that street urchin?"

"The cut-purse," Casandra answered.

"We don't know that for sure." Though there was little doubt in Willoe's mind, she didn't like to admit it, and preferred to hold onto the idea that the boy still might have been innocent. "Remember how I was able to break free from the smaller guard?"

"You threw him more than six paces through the air. I still don't how you did it."

"I was scared, I guess. When he clamped down on my arm, I got the same sensation, as if something wanted in. I gave myself over and then I felt a fire within. It spread out through my body and somehow I felt stronger than I thought was possible. It wasn't me, but the fire that threw the guard." Willoe sat quietly for a few moments.

Casandra just waited, watching her.

"It had happened once before, when I was nine. The kidnapper held me to his body as he started to drag me beyond the tavern toward the edge of the forest. The smell of bitter nuts clung to his blue robes. I could hear his labored breath and as he sucked in air and let it back out in quick spurts, I could feel his heartbeat as if it were my own, and the bitter aroma became overwhelming. The voice came to me again, inside my head, telling me all would be well. I could sense a warmth reaching out from my chest, through my limbs. It was slowly heating up."

Willoe had to pause again, then took a steadying breath before continuing. "I managed to twist my head and saw Protector Dougal running down the alley, his knife in hand, but it seemed to me as if in a dream." Willoe described it as she watched the scene play out in her mind. "I could see each of his feet leave the ground, moving slowly through the air, and landing again. It felt as if time had slowed down. My thoughts were directed and I was able to block out everything else around me. Protector Dougal's face appeared overly calm, but his eyes... his eyes were fixed and centered on me. There was no hesitation in his movements."

"What about the other men?" Casandra's eyes were wide as she followed Willoe's story.

"One stepped into Protector Dougal's path and he swung a curved sword that Protector Dougal easily deflected with his knife. Then the Protector brought the knife back up to slice across the man's throat. I remember blood spurting out and covering the front of Protector Dougal. The man spun sideways and dropped to the ground. The second man drew up short, still between Protector Dougal and me. The Protector drew one of his swords from over his shoulder, keeping the knife in his other hand, and they circled. The man holding me let go of my mouth and drew a sword similar to those of the other men, and held it out in front of me while he continued to drag me toward the forest. I could see Protector Dougal glance over at me and he took a step in my direction. The man facing him swung the sword back and forth to keep Protector Dougal from getting to me.

"'Stend back!' the man's rasping voice yelled while he swung his sword threateningly at Protector Dougal. His voice carried the same guttural accent in Taran as it did in the strange language they had used earlier. After one such slice of the sword, Protector Dougal dove forward and used his sword to ward off the back swing. He drove the knife into the man's arm and pushed the handle backwards, forcing the man to twist. I could hear the crack as a bone snapped under the heavy knife's blade, but the man never uttered a sound."

Casandra cringed at the description.

"Protector Dougal shifted his sword, spinning away from the man and brought it around to slice across just under the man's chest. The man crumpled; severed intestines spilled out." Willoe told the story without emotion as if she were telling someone else's tale.

"How did Protector Dougal get you free from the kidnapper?" Casandra's voice rose with excitement at the telling.

"The warmth grew until I felt as if my blood were boiling. My vision became blurry and I faded from my body. I was still conscious, but it was like watching someone else's movements from afar. Something in the back of my mind – not a conscious thought, but something more subtle – warned me, and without thinking I threw my arms up, breaking the man's hold on me. Like when I broke the grip of the trader's guard. But I fell to the ground, rolling over onto my back, staring up at the kidnapper. I still couldn't see his face, as it was hidden in the folds of his cowl, but his hands were bony and his skin was dark, almost gray, yet somehow murky; not a natural color."

As she recalled what happened next, Willoe continued through gritted teeth. "He planted a foot on my chest and raised his sword above his head with both hands. Even at nine I knew what he meant to do. As he brought the sword down, the fire helped me to turn to the side, wrenching my body free from under his foot. The tip of the sword caught the back of my neck, carving a gash angled across my neck to my right shoulder." She reached up and rubbed the spot. Just telling the story made it seem to burn with the memory.

"I've seen it and knew it happened when you were nine, but had no idea how you had received it." Casandra's voice was saddened as she stroked Willoe's other arm.

Willoe could only nod her head, the emotion starting to get to her. A tear rolled down her cheek. "I rolled back as he was raising the sword again, but something flew over my head and struck the shadow of the robe's hood. The man dropped the sword and grabbed for the handle of Protector Dougal's knife as he fell backward. He jerked twice and then his limbs went slack. The fire fell away and I felt more tired than I had ever felt before. Protector Dougal ran up and pulled the bloody knife out of the hood, then cut a piece of fabric from my dress and pressed it to the gash. It hurt." She smiled with a slight chuckle. "It hurt when he pressed the rag onto the cut."

Casandra smiled back, shaking her head. "You confound me cousin. You find humor in this?"

"I didn't feel anything else until then. It just seems... I don't know, somehow strange." Willoe tilted her head, wondering if it sounded as strange to her cousin as it did to her.

"Maybe the fire somehow protected you." Casandra looked thoughtful.

Willoe only nodded in response. That was what she had thought, when she considered it later, though she tried not to think about it if at all possible.

"He picked me up and started to run back up the alley to find Cleric Yoan. I remember feeling as if I had just taken a bath; I was dripping wet. My head was turned back toward the rear of the tavern and I could see Rowyn following close behind. He looked as ragged as I knew I should be, but I was just numb. What I never told anyone was that beyond Rowyn I saw two more of the robed men staring out from the forest. I think I thought if I talked about them they could find me somehow."

She finished the tale and stared at Casandra for her reaction. After a moment's silence she added, "This is why I have been training so hard with Protector Dougal. After the kidnapping attempt, and then again when the trader's guards threatened us, I swore to the Burning Lady that I would never let myself be that vulnerable again... ever."

Casandra only nodded. Willoe had appreciated Casandra's support for the last four years. She had never asked Willoe about the training, she just came along and carried whatever gear Protector Dougal and Willoe couldn't. She would sit there and read or go beg a flagon of wine from Master Jonnes, until they finished, and then she and Willoe would go off like normal, after Willoe had cleaned up.

Willoe waited for Casandra to speak, but as soon as her cousin opened her mouth, a bright light made both of them throw up their arms to protect their eyes as they stood, holding on to each other. Torches along the Gallery provided enough light for walking, but this was as if night had suddenly turned to day. It faded almost as quickly as it had come, but through blinking eyes Willoe could still see that the darkness in the courtyard had given up some of its cover, and centered in the small courtyard was a shining ball twice the size of a man. The brightness continued to fade and Willoe was finally able to lower her arm and look directly at the light.

Before her stood a dragon, with golden teardrop scales of different sizes that blended together to cover the entire body, except the neck and stomach. It stood on all fours, and seated on it, just behind the neck, was a woman encircled in a shimmering white light. She was naked as far as Willoe could tell, but her entire body – and the hair that hung down below her waist – was as white as new-fallen snow.

A shimmering light continued to flicker around the woman and dragon as Willoe heard a soft, but clearly audible voice say, "Willoe Brynmor." It was not a question, but a statement.

"Who... who are you?" Willoe asked hesitantly. Her body wanted to flee from this strange apparition, but her mind held her in place.

The woman ignored Willoe's question, but the dragon tilted its head, and its scales stood on end in a quick-moving ripple, spreading out then falling back into place. It took two steps toward Willoe and Casandra, the woman's body rocking with the movement.

Every nerve in Willoe's body wanted to flee, but as the dragon moved closer it brought the shimmering woman into better view. Willoe noticed that the only part of the woman's body that was not a shimmering white were the eyes. Where black should be, small flames of red and orange flickered. Willoe realized that Casandra gripped her arm, but still stood there nonetheless. It was enough to keep Willoe from running.

The woman's lips never moved, but Willoe could hear her words clearly. "Willoe Brynmor. Thou hast been called and thine ancestor's promise binds thee to respond."

Willoe wanted to say something but stood frozen. Her mind spun as she tried to comprehend what the specter's words meant. After a few moments she was finally able to speak, though she had to swallow first. "What ancestor? What promise?"

The shimmering light around the woman and dragon started to brighten. "The time has not come for thee to know. Prepare thyself, many trials await thee. The Darkness will try to consume thee and all that thou lovest."

"What Darkness? How do I prepare?" Willoe asked in confusion, but instead of an answer the light grew, filling the entire courtyard, making both her and Casandra throw their arms up as before. The voice came one more time before the light flickered and disappeared altogether. "Thou wilt know when the time is right; then thou must findest the Lady in the Woods."

With the woman's disappearance the night returned, but Willoe still had to blink several times to get rid of the residual brightness from her eyes. The light from the torches felt inadequate compared to what the two women had just experienced.

Casandra finally let go of Willoe's arm and turned toward Willoe, her face still frozen in shock. "I heard you talking. Did she say something to you?"

Willoe was amazed at her cousin. "Of course, you did not hear?"

"No. I heard you, but nothing from the–" The look on Casandra's face was nearly as white as the shimmering lady.

"She told me about a promise one of my ancestors made that I am somehow now responsible for."

"What was the promise?" Casandra sounded even more surprised by what Willoe reported than the appearance of the shining lady.

"I have no idea. But I am supposed to find 'the Lady in the Woods.'"

"I heard you ask about her. Who is—" Casandra started, but stopped as Willoe shrugged her shoulders before her cousin could finish.

They both stood there for a short time facing into the courtyard, staring at where the woman and dragon had been. Casandra turned back to Willoe and asked in a soft and reverent tone, "Do you think that was—" She let the question hang between them.

"I don't know."

"Wil, is that you? Are you well?" a voice called out from the dark and then Rowyn walked into the light of the sconces. A moment later Protector Dougal came into view behind him.

"Row." Willoe suddenly felt relieved, as if the two men brought a sense of reality back to what her life. "Yes we are fine."

"Someone said you had gone for a walk around the portico. We were following and from the other courtyard…" He pointed to the next courtyard over, "we saw a light like the sun had just risen," Rowyn said as he walked over to them while Protector Dougal walked around the courtyard as if looking for something.

Rowyn's words caught Willoe by surprise, but it also validated that what had just happened wasn't something Casandra and she had imagined. She struggled for the right words, then just said, "We saw a lightning bolt a few moments ago."

Rowyn looked up into the sky. It was a clear night. Then he stared down back to Willoe with a quizzical look.

"Row, could I get you to do something for me?" She moved closer to him so Protector Dougal couldn't hear.

"What do you need?" He leaned closer to her.

"Do you think you could ask Uncle Brom about someone called the Lady in the Woods, without raising too many questions?" She patted his shoulder as she smiled.

Rowyn straightened and looked at her, his eyes narrowing, then asked warily, "Who is the Lady in the Woods and why do you think Uncle Brom would know of her?"

"She doesn't know who it is," Casandra interrupted. "That is why she wants to find out about her."

Willoe nodded. "He has traveled extensively all over Taran. At least, that is what he has told us when he returns from his trips. And he is more knowledgeable of our history than anyone else we know. If he has not heard of this lady, then I imagine no one else has." She put a hand on his arm and squeezed it. "But don't tell him what we know. I just don't want anyone else to know just yet. I just need you to trust me right now."

Rowyn thought for a few moments, his head lowered; then he raised it and grinned. "If you think it is important, then I'll try." His grin widened. "It shouldn't be a problem telling him what I know, as I know nothing. But you need to tell me who this Lady in the Woods is when you figure it out."

"I promise." She returned his smile. "Oh, it might have something to do with the ancients or the Burning Lady."

Rowyn's eyes opened wider and he started to speak, but Willoe cut him off.

"I can't tell you right now."

His lips wrinkled and he stared at her for a moment, then nodded.

The three of them started back along the portico and as they came up to Protector Dougal, Willoe let the other two go a few paces ahead.

Protector Dougal fell in step next to her. She looked up at him and he looked back. "The same scent," she said softly.

The Protector only nodded and then stared forward as they started back to the Great Hall.

As they walked, Casandra looked over her shoulder at Willoe; her cousin was biting her lower lip. Willoe just nodded at their shared secret. She hoped she hadn't asked too much of her twin and wished she could tell him about the shining woman, but she wasn't even sure what to tell him. To recognize what both she and Casandra suspected was beyond comprehension, but she couldn't deny what they had both just seen. She wanted to find Cleric Yoan, but knew she couldn't talk about this, even with him. Among all the people she knew, he would know the answer, but she was already pretty sure that no one had ever actually described an image of the Burning Lady.

8

The King's Solar

The sunlight edged across the room and finally onto Willoe's bed, streaking across her face. Her eyelids opened to a slit and she peeked out at the world. Her body could not believe it was already daybreak; she felt like she had only slept for a turn of the glass, and she realized she had.

Rowyn and Aeron had come to her room last night and joined Casandra and her as they tried to unravel the mystery around the king's command. Neither woman mentioned the golden dragon and its shining rider from earlier in the evening. After the men left, Casandra and Willoe sat up most of the night talking, and the only thing they were able to develop was a headache from too much wine.

As she became more aware of the bright world filtering into the room, the conversation from the previous night continued in her mind. *Who is the Lady in the Woods and how can I find her?* But before any of that, she had to face her grandfather.

Willoe splashed water on her face, her mind still foggy from the previous night. She finished just as a knock sounded at the door, followed by an older female voice. "Princess Willoe?"

"Dilys." Willoe found herself smiling. "Come in," she said cheerfully.

The door opened and a short matronly woman ambled in, her gray hair and chubby face as familiar to Willoe as her own reflection in the mirror. The woman lay a tray on a small table in the middle of the room, removing a small platter and a goblet of wine from the tray. "It appears there was a gathering here late last night." Dilys placed the four dirty goblets and the empty flagon that had been left on the table onto the tray.

Willoe wiped her eyes and yawned. "We had a lot to talk about." She had few people she could confide in, Casandra and Dilys the only women.

"Do you remember when Casey came from Mount Somerled?"

"Aye. She be but a wisp of a thing. A shame only nine and had to leave her home." Dilys began to look through the clothes in the dressing chamber.

Willoe did not remember her life before being delivered to her father at three naming days, but could image how difficult it might be, being separated from your family at nine. But it was the way of the nobles to take each other's children in as wards and help train them in the ways of the court. It said a lot that the twins were never farmed out to any nobles, though she knew the First Duke had offered. *To be honest, I wouldn't have missed Mael and Grandfather all that much.* She nearly laughed as she realized she had forgotten all about Hafgan.

"After all the others I wondered if ye would ever find a companion," Dilys' faint voice added.

"It wasn't my fault," Willoe complained as she nibbled on pieces of an apple from the platter and stared at her reflection in the full-length mirror. "Those other girls were terrified even before they arrived." Willoe pulled at her hair and looked into her own luminous green eyes. "I just had to look at them and they flew home faster than a raven."

"Aye, they did. But she be full of the Spirit, that one." Dilys pulled out a tan dress, shook her head, and put it back into the dressing chamber.

Willoe smiled when she thought of all the times she and her cousin had gotten into trouble together, dragging Rowyn and sometimes Aeron into many of them. "I am so glad father and the First Duke were such close friends."

"Grew up together, those two did." Dilys' muffled voice came from deep within the dressing chamber. "And his wife, Lady Cadwal. A real lady, that one be."

Casandra's mother was the closest thing Willoe had to a mother, but with her responsibilities as the First Duke's wife, her visits to Casandra and Aeron were infrequent. And while Willoe looked forward to when Lady Cadwal could spend a month or so with them – almost as much as her cousins did – it did not truly satisfy Willoe's cravings.

"This one has always looked well on ye." Dilys stepped out of the chamber with a blue dress held up in her hands.

Willoe glanced away from the mirror and looked at the dress. "I think the green one with gold trim, Dilys," Willoe politely directed her. "That is Grandfather's favorite." It showed the colors of Cainwen. She would need every advantage she could get, and she had very few with her hardened grandfather.

"Now hold still, lassie, while I slide on the kirtel." Dilys put the white under-dress over Willoe's head and pulled it down, while Willoe took the hoops on the pointed sleeves and attached them over her middle fingers to keep the sleeves in place. She leaned over so Dilys could slip the silky over-skirt on and then, as she had done since Willoe and Rowyn first showed up at Westhedge, Dilys secured each of the buttons that ran up the back and tied a belt around Willoe's waist. As a final touch, Dilys pulled Willoe's hair back and held it in place with a barrette.

Willoe twisted from side to side, smiling. Dilys slapped her gently on the rear, getting Willoe to stand still while she adjusted the belt and pulled at the shoulders. Willoe continued to nibble on the cold meat and a hard roll.

"You know I love you, Dilys." Willoe reached a hand up and patted Di-lys' hand on her shoulder. She could see Dilys' face in the mirror as the woman looked from around Willoe's back. Dilys was the only caretaker Willoe had known since coming to her father. Willoe had to fight with her grandfather when she rejected offers of more servants, and he finally threw up his hands and sent her out of his presence.

"And I love ye, child." She gave Willoe a big grin, strands of gray hair hanging in her face. The king's wife – Willoe's grandmother – had passed away long before even Mael was born, and their father's wife had died a few years after Hafgan's birth, just a year before Willoe and Rowyn had arrived, leaving Willoe as the only woman in the family. Outside of visits from her cousins' mother, which she anxiously looked forward to, and a few older women like Dame Jestin, Dilys was the only adult woman Willoe could look up to for guidance. *Well, considering how peculiar Dilys is…* Willoe smiled affectionately at the old servant.

Dilys gave her a funny look, then said, "You be ready." With her stomach feeling a little better, Willoe brushed off her dress and left her room to make her way around the portico to the King's Tower.

After climbing three sets of steps, Willoe reached the door leading into the king's private apartments. One of the guardsmen on duty opened the door for her. As she entered, she glanced to the right and saw Rowyn seat-ed on a bench, leaning back against the polished wooden panels that lined the wall.

Upon seeing Willoe he stood and quickly walked over. "Wil." He smiled half-heartedly. "I wrestled with it all night and can't understand what Grandfather is planning." His drawn face showed the truth of his words.

Willoe laid a hand on her twin's shoulder and caressed it gently, as she did whenever he became anxious. "It's a mystery. We will just have to go in and see." She smiled confidently, though that was the last thing she felt. Instead, a coldness ran down her spine, causing her to shiver even though fall was still a week or more off and the air was warmed by the fires from the various rooms that lined the King's Hallway.

Rowyn smiled back, joining in their mutual reassurance.

She turned him toward the king's solar and they walked up to the door. At a knock, the king's page opened the door from within. He stepped back and bowed as they entered, then left and closed the door behind him. As Willoe followed Rowyn into the solar she noticed her grandfather and father seated in gold-trimmed chairs, handsomely carved, with purple velvet cushions. They were facing the small blaze in the hearth, each of them with a goblet in their hand.

She had expected to find both of them there, but to her surprise, Hafgan was seated in the corner and Mael was standing behind the king's chair, resting his hand on its back.

Even Uncle Brom was there. *He rarely leaves his cloistered apartment*, she thought as she nodded to her uncle. *Especially without Drel Donlin*. Rowyn was one of the few that had pierced the reclusive veil of their uncle's life. Their shared love of history was a strange bond. Yet even in the midst of the rest of the family, Uncle Brom still looked isolated. He stood next to the hearth, moving the burning logs around with a poker, his face turning to the fire and focusing as if divining something from the blaze.

With Uncle Brom present, Willoe noted that the entire Brynmor family was there, three generations of them in one room. Excepting official gatherings, like last night, seldom was the entire family together like this. A new worm of worry seemed to writhe in her stomach. This felt like a trap she had walked willingly, if unintentionally, into, and she found herself wondering how and when it would be sprung.

"Grandfather, Father, Uncle Brom, Hafgan," Willoe acknowledged each of them, intentionally leaving out Mael.

"Willoe. Rowyn," Hafgan smiled and mumbled as he nodded in their direction.

"You're looking well, brother." Willoe always tried to say something nice to Hafgan, as the poor man was nearly as despised as she and her twin were. His body was so twisted and hunched over that he could never wear armor or properly take up a sword. He was Aeron's age, but as opposite a person as could be imagined. He lacked the refinement of a noble and isolated himself by his unimpressive personality. The only one that seemed to give him any credence was Malbery, the Earl of Greenmerrow, who had taken Hafgan on as a ward.

Hafgan's smile widened as he replied, "I have been better. A week ago—"

"Spare us your constant troubles, brother," Mael shut his brother off.

The grin on Hafgan's face dropped like a stone and he glared at his older brother as he clamped his lips tightly. His body trembled.

Mael turned to Willoe with a smirk. "Ah, dear sister." He then turned his head sideways to glance at Rowyn. "I see you brought your shadow."

"Mael!" her father snapped. He turned to his eldest, his face stern with anger. "These are your siblings. Behave or do not speak at all."

"My apologies, Father. I meant no disrespect," Mael said apologetically, but his smile returned when Father turned back to the fire. "They know I was only jesting." His sincerity was in sharp contrast to his smug expression.

"Enough!" The king raised a hand to end any further discussion. "I have the Baron Fychan waiting to bend my ear over some foolish enterprise that will surely fail as before. But he still contributes handsomely to the treasury, so we need to get this over with." He gestured to Willoe and Rowyn. They came over and stood on either side of their father's chair.

The king stared up at Rowyn and said nothing, as if he were appraising his grandson. Then he sniffed. "I do not understand why you would challenge Ser Tanguy. What foolishness would cause you go up against one our best Shields? You know he has been champion of the Lifts three years in a row." He didn't wait for Rowyn to answer his question. "Was it some sort of attempt to impress your father and me?"

"I... I..." Rowyn stuttered, the look on his face reminded Willoe of how a rabbit must feel with a hawk circling overhead. He finally answered, "I was not trying to impress you, Grandfather."

The king shook his head and sighed. "A shame. I had had hopes." He sipped from his goblet and closed his eyes. "Mael will be returning to White Cliffs with the Franchons as our envoy to discuss recent skirmishes along the border."

Willoe looked over at her oldest brother, who stood a little straighter, the grin on his face contrasted with the scornful look in his eyes.

"Along with other important discussions," the king added with a look toward their father.

Mael's stance relaxed a little and his face became neutral.

Willoe assumed that the rumors of a marriage bond were true. She began to relax. If Mael's venture was what had required the entire family to gather, she would wish Mael well and be happy that she was not the subject of the king's concern. This time.

The king went on to explain. "Captain Harte will lead the escort and Cleric Yoan, along with Count Idwal, will advise Mael once there. Count Idwal will also be in attendance to discuss mining ventures that would be of interest to us."

Willoe just smiled and wondered how long the family meeting would go on. She had hoped to go riding with Casandra before the mid-day meal.

The king looked directly at Willoe. "I have had a request from the Franchon envoy for you and your twin to return with their party to Castle White Cliffs."

"Why?" Willoe blurted out and then put her hand over her mouth. She knew her abrupt manner easily irritated Grandfather, among many other things.

"Because I command it," the king roared and stiffened, glaring at Willoe. After a moment's silence his body relaxed slightly, as did his tone. "Rowyn will go as part of the escort, but you, my dear girl, will remain. I agree that he will be most likely useless."

Willoe's father cleared his throat.

"I am not insulting the boy, Beynon." The king turned his attention to his youngest son, but also the Crown Prince since Brom had given up his claim. "I am not stating anything that is not known throughout all of Westhedge." Mael's smirk turned into a wide grin. "The boy is not a man-of-arms and never will be. It is not in his blood like with you and Mael. He follows Brom's path."

Uncle Brom stopped playing with the poker and lifted his head up, smiling. "Well thank you, Father. Though I am not sure if I should be pleased or just pleasantly amused."

The king gave Uncle Brom a hard look until the oldest son went back to staring at the fire, though Uncle Brom's smile did not fade.

No one had ever explained to Willoe why her father, the youngest of the two brothers by a year, was the Crown Prince, and her uncle Brom, who should have been next in line behind her grandfather, sequestered himself in his apartment. Rumors had it that around twenty years ago, Uncle Brom walked into the throne room and announced, in front of the entire assembly, that he was renouncing his birthright. A commanding warrior, known for never losing a fight, his retirement to a quiet life of study came as a shock to all of Westhedge. From what Rowyn had told her of his experiments, however, their uncle's life was not as serene as everyone seemed to think.

Turning back to the hearth as if it provided some elementary foundation, the king spoke unemotionally. "Regardless, it will remove Rowyn from Brom's dusty hall of tomes and take him out into the world. The change can only improve the boy's perspective."

Willoe could tell by the tone of Grandfather's voice that he was starting to become annoyed. He was not used to explaining himself.

"A short trip to White Cliffs and back," the king continued. "Probably less than three moons. Not particularly exciting, but an improvement over being barricaded in Brom's solar with that impish Tink." He looked back at Uncle Brom again and snorted.

The king returned his gaze to the hearth and his disposition changed.

His eyes narrowed and the lines in his face creased around the edges of his white beard, as if an unpleasant task awaited him. "And you, Willoe."

"Yes, Grandfather." She would never be that personal in public, but when it was just the family, certain privileges were allowed. Even if her grandfather seemed barely to consider her family.

"I understand you managed to embarrass us once again a few weeks ago."

"If you mean the incident with the carriage, I only—"

He raised his hand to quiet her before she could explain.

"I have already heard a full account."

But not from me, Willoe thought, yet obeyed her grandfather's demand for silence.

"When are you going to learn what it is to be a lady?" It sounded more like a statement than a question.

Willoe took no blame for her lack of graces. Other than Casandra's mother, who could only visit infrequently, she had to rely on Casandra and Dilys for her induction into society. Even they could only do so much, since Willoe had little interest in courtly pleasantries.

"Since you were a child and your father claimed you and your brother as family, I have tried to accept his decision and to find a place for the both of you. But time and time again you have demonstrated a reluctance to fit into your proper role. You unceasingly find a way to create a disturbance among our loyal nobles and seem intent on hunting out another unique way to bring down contempt upon yourself and, consequently, the Brynmor name."

Contempt is probably a strong word to use, she wanted to blurt out, but held her tongue.

"You have managed to offend, antagonize, or horrify every suitor who has approached you over the last four years."

Regardless of what Grandfather thought, she wasn't a piece of meat to be bartered off to gain the loyalty of some retainer. And most of the so-called eligible young nobles – along with a few old ones – were more interested in furthering their own future than capturing Willoe's heart. This was an old argument and she still got the feeling that she could be blind, deaf, or have two heads, and the suitors would not have cared as long as it brought them closer to the royal line.

"I am not sending you with Mael and Rowyn." He paused and turned to face her. He gazed for a moment and she thought his eyes softened. Then his face squished up like he had just eaten a lemon or caught a whiff of some unpleasant odor. It was a look she recognized; Grandfather wore it whenever he was faced with an unpleasant decision. He shook his head at some thought, then spoke quickly. "I have been more than patient, at your father's request." He looked over at Willoe's father and inhaled before continuing. "However, at sixteen years it is improper for you to still be unwed. You have a duty to Us and Our people to find a husband that can strengthen Our kingdom."

She knew that when he used his royal persona, there was little room left for argument.

"We have had a list of suitable nobles drawn up and you *will* pick one for your husband." He held a paper out to her.

She grabbed it, probably too roughly, and scanned the list. "I just can't pick from—"

"Granddaughter!" His voice rose as he called her by a rarely used term.

She knew there was little she could say to change his mind at this moment. She had to find a way out of this or at least to delay it until she could come up with a better idea. She was trapped and wanted to scream that she was not a prize to be bartered off, but she knew it would do no good here. There had to be a way to avoid this destiny.

Delay, delay. I need time to think. "May I wait until Rowyn's return before making a decision?" she pleaded. "I will not be able to turn my mind to this matter as long as he is in danger."

"He is only going to White Cliffs." Mael's mocking voice made her grit her teeth.

"Mael," the king growled.

"Rowyn knows me better than anyone and can advise me on a suitable husband upon his return."

The king raised his hand and she was afraid he would dismiss her request, but her father put his hand on the king's arm, whispering something to his father.

She heard Grandfather say, "Very well," and then he turned back to Willoe. "You will have until Rowyn returns from White Cliffs, but there will be no delay from there. You will have one week after he returns. And then you will pick or I will pick for you."

He stood and started to leave for his meeting with Baron Fychan. Willoe could hear him mumble as he left but could only catch something about "family" and a big sigh.

As soon as the door closed, Willoe stepped in front of her father's chair, ready to launch into an entire list of reasons why this was insane. "Father!"

"Do not bother with your list of objections," he said, then stood and began to step around her. "I have made every argument you are about to give me. But you have ignored your Grandfather's warnings once too often. He will not be turned from this." He opened the door to leave, but turned back to look at Willoe. "Maybe this is for the best. You may finally find your place in the world... away from all this." He then turned to look at Rowyn. "I never have understood my brother." He glanced over to Uncle Brom, who rose up and stared back at his younger brother. "But I know he is a good man, and I for one would not lament if you followed in his foot-steps." Looking at his twins his voice saddened. "Your grandfather may not show it so that you can see, but he does have your best interests in mind at all times." He turned and exited; the room was painfully quiet after his leaving.

Finally the silence was broken by Mael's mocking tone. "So, Father's little girl will finally have to step up and do something for our family."

The last thing Willoe needed right now was Mael's incessant hounding.

Before she could respond Uncle Brom spoke up, the anger in his tone evident. "Mael, do you ever manage to open your mouth without something foul slithering out?"

"I only speak the truth, dear Uncle," Mael retorted smoothly.

"I believe the truth would find itself without a friend and very lonely inside your head." The anger faded from Uncle Brom's voice and his ever-present smile returned. "I also believe that Willoe and Rowyn will do more than their duty for this family and the Kingdom."

That caught Mael off-guard and the confused look on his face gave Willoe some comfort, and also a chance to escape.

"Row." Willoe grabbed his arm and they fled the king's solar, leaving Mael still questioning their uncle. As they made their way down the stairs Rowyn was quiet, but Willoe could tell he was upset. "It will be fine, Row. We will figure this out."

"You can't go against Grandfather's commands," he finally stated, his lips tight and his eyes fixed. "And an escort to Mael." He shook his head. "What about my books? My work with Uncle Brom? This is insane. You're a better warrior than I am."

Willoe's mind whirled, her thoughts racing. "Yes, I am." By the time they had reached the bottom of the stairs and headed away from the King's Tower, Willoe's smile had returned.

9

Runes of Fate

Rowyn knocked on his uncle's door a second time. It edged open slowly and a pair of bushy eyebrows stared up at him. "What do you want?" Drel Donlin asked brusquely.

"I wanted to talk with my uncle." He gave the Tink a friendly smile, though it was meager at best.

The hairy little man grunted and walked away from the door without a word. Drel Donlin went back to a corner table where he had evidently been deep in study, a book nearly as big as he himself spread out on the table. Still looking at the book, he twirled his hand above his head and a small ball of light appeared, illuminating the book. Many people would have fled at that moment, but little that Uncle Brom and his wizard comrade did disturbed Rowyn anymore.

"Uncle Brom." Rowyn scanned the all-too-familiar clutter of the room for his uncle. Uncle Brom rarely left his room, but when he did he would disappear for a moon or more and no one knew where to.

He called again, a little louder.

Drel Donlin looked up once then went back to his book, shaking his head and muttering to himself.

Just when Rowyn was about to leave, the door to one of the inner rooms opened and Uncle Brom came out, his eyes on a book in his hands, his eyebrows drawn together in concentration. He took several steps before he lifted his head and smiled at Rowyn. "Ah, my favorite nephew." The overstuffed wizard closed the book and strolled over to Rowyn. "To what do I owe this pleasant surprise?" His eyes narrowed. "Should you not be preparing?" He looked out the window to see whether it was still daylight. "I was under the impression that you and Mael were leaving in three days."

"Yes, we are." Rowyn hated to keep a secret from his uncle, but he'd promised Willoe. "I had to see you before I left." He became sullen as he thought of leaving the security and familiarity of this chaotic, muddled, comfortable room, and also his uncle, who was very much like the room he lived in. Rowyn would even miss the cranky old Tink.

They sat at the table in the middle of the room, the same table cloth used for the Bone Fang still spread out across it.

"I came across something in one of the old scrolls in the library and thought maybe you could help me understand what it meant." Rowyn crossed his arms as he rested them on the table. This might be his only chance, before leaving for White Cliffs, to try to get the information Willoe wanted.

"I would be pleased to help you in any way I can, dear Nephew." Uncle Brom grinned as he leaned back and clasped his hands together, resting them on his protruding stomach.

"I came across a story about a woman that lived in the forest."

Uncle Brom nodded politely.

This was going to be easier than Rowyn had thought. "Not just any woman, but I think a noble, as the story referred to her as a Lady."

Uncle Brom leaned forward the smile disappearing, his body seemingly tense. "Where did you find the scroll? What exactly did it say?"

This is not going well, Rowyn thought, as he fought to keep from jumping back.

"I can't remember." He had to think quickly. He hadn't expected this kind of reaction from what Willoe had said. "It was an old scroll stuffed behind a large tome in a back corner of the library. I didn't think much of it at the time and just left it out to be filed."

Rowyn's uncle just stared at him. Uncle Brom's continued fixed stare made Rowyn want to crawl under the table.

"No matter." Uncle Brom finally seemed to relax and leaned back in his chair again, his hands back on his stomach.

"Have you heard of this story?" Rowyn asked.

"No, no. Not at all. It just sounds like an interesting story." The stare returned, but more quizzical this time. "You are sure you do not remember where in the library you found it?"

"No, I don't. Sorry."

"If you come across it again, you will let me know." Uncle Brom reached across and patted Rowyn on the arm. "It sounds like something I would be interested in."

"I will be gone three moons. What about my studies?" Rowyn needed to change the topic and was also seriously concerned about missing his time with Uncle Brom.

"Do not worry. You will be back before the first snowfall."

Rowyn nodded, but he wasn't so sure. While the others had foregone further study, Rowyn had continued to delve into his uncle's endless supply of books and ancient tomes, especially the study of Taran's history. Rowyn was fascinated with the successes of those long dead and even more so with their mistakes. He knew he would never see sunlight if not for his sister and cousins. Now even this would snatched from him within a matter of days.

"You will be fine," Uncle Brom added after watching Rowyn sit lost in his thoughts for a few moments. Rowyn's expression must have betrayed his doubt.

"Just because we are not together does not mean you cannot continue your studies." Uncle Brom stood and went over to the nearest stack searching through the books, and then probed two other stacks before finding what he was looking for. Reaching down into the third stack, he pulled out a small book, blew the dust off it, and smiled as he walked back to the table and lay the book down. "This is a book of runes that I want you to read while on your travels." It had a tooled leather front and spine.

Rowyn had never seen leather binding like that which wrapped around the book, and wondered what kind of animal had produced the leather. The craftsmanship of the etched symbols and the elegant designs incised into the cover reminded Rowyn of the oldest tomes in Uncle Brom's library, yet it looked as if it were brand new.

"Runes?" Rowyn tilted his head to get a better look at the book cover.

"The language is little known, but I believe you will unravel it with some effort." Uncle Brom opened the book.

Rowyn slid his chair over closer to his uncle and looked at the runes, but he couldn't recognize any of them. Yet after a moment of focused attention, even looking at the book from the side, he thought he recognized some that at least looked similar to the older tomes he had been studying. His experience was that most current languages evolved from some earlier language. Thinking along those lines, he could see where the variations on existing languages could have been derived from these ancient runes. "Where did you get this?" Rowyn was intrigued.

"Ah, that is a good question." Uncle Brom smiled and leaned back again. "It goes back a long way. To when Elfs were new to the world."

That surprised Rowyn. He tried to remember from his studies what he knew about the elusive Elfs. They were more folklore than reality. Supposedly they still lived in Eahdun, deep in the Greenwald Forest, but Rowyn had never known a single person who admitted to meeting an Elf.

Rowyn realized that Uncle Brom was still talking.

"—when our people were the only men on Taran, before the Franchons or Haldanes came to this land." Uncle Brom was thumbing through the back of the book.

Rowyn understood that most common folk spent their time on daily survival, and those lucky enough to belong to the noble caste rarely found interest in the old days like Rowyn had under his uncle's tutelage.

Uncle Brom continued and Rowyn was sure his uncle was taking the opportunity to reinforce Rowyn's training. "This was before the seafaring Haldanes settled in the cold north and the Franchons invaded from the mainland."

A map of Taran appeared in Rowyn's mind with the Saltrock River separating east from west and the Blackburn Mountains providing a natural border separating Haldane from Franchon, while Crystal Bay did the same between Cainwen and the Tonn Tribes that roamed across the Open Lands. "I am familiar with our history, dear Uncle." Rowyn tried to smile, but he still felt uncomfortable with his uncle's reaction to the question about the Lady in the Woods.

"Yes, yes." Uncle Brom handed the book to Rowyn.

Rowyn turned it over in his hands and reverently flipped through some of the pages.

Uncle Brom pushed the chair out and stood, his voice somber. "You are sixteen now. It is time you began to grasp some of your history and I believe this book will help you to understand." Then he smiled, filling his wide cheeks. "Translate the runes as best you can and then when you get back we will see what you learned from the book." Uncle Brom's jolly disposition could put anyone at ease. Over the years, his love of food and a sedentary lifestyle had given Rowyn's uncle a rotund appearance. He was probably the least threatening person Rowyn knew and one of the few people Rowyn felt comfortable around. He stepped over to wrap his arms around his nephew again.

Rowyn laid the runes on a stack of books next to him so he could put his arms around his uncle.

Uncle Brom let him go and then shooed him out of the room. "Drel Donlin and I have work to do and you, my dear nephew, need to finish preparing for the escort. Your brother will not relent until you return."

As Rowyn crossed the room he called out to Drel Donlin a Tink blessing he had learned from their many interactions. "May your life be ordered and your feet never touch the ground." Upon glancing at the jumble of books and general disarray of the room, Rowyn very much thought it was a contradiction in terms.

Drel Donlin looked up at Rowyn, squinted and wrinkled his nose. "I be wishing you the same, but I don't believe it be in your future." Then he went back to his book, running his finger across the page as he read.

Uncle Brom closed the door in Rowyn's face. Rowyn started back down the stairs, wondering if he had time before going to Willoe's apartment for supper. She had said it was important. As he circled around the wall he wondered what the Tink had meant.

Brom stared at the closed door, his smile faded. This was a bit unexpected.

"Ye know he be talking 'bout the Lady in the Woods?" Drel Donlin said and Brom turned to see the Tink looking at him from across the room.

"Yes, I know." Brom walked over to the window and looked out. "Do you think he knows?"

"He be not asking if he did."

Brom nodded. He had no idea where his nephew had heard the name, but the question meant their time had grown short. It saddened him. Brom had thought he had another year or two to prepare them. He started to turn and stopped as he spotted the book of runes lying on one of the stacks. He picked it up, turning it as he thought how to proceed with this new opportunity. Brom smiled. He did not believe events happened randomly. There was purpose in all matters related to the Burning Lady. Then as if an answer to the thought, an idea came to him and he grabbed a piece of paper, ripped off a corner, and wrote down the words that had come to him.

Thumbing through the book he came to the page he wanted, where he placed the sliver of paper and closed the book. He looked up and whispered a silent thanks, then began to plan how to get the book to his nephew before the boy left for White Cliffs. It seemed that events were moving faster than desired and the time was upon them sooner than any of them had thought. He only hoped the twins were ready.

10

An Irrevocable Proposition

Aeron looked over at Rowyn and sipped on his wine, savoring the flavor, and thought, *Ah, grapes soaked in wormwood with a touch of honey. Excellent.* Dilys had made sure they had bread and cheese, placing it on the side table next to the wine Aeron had brought before she left them alone. A few kind words to Wine Master Jonnes and a couple jars of wine from the banquet had been delivered to Aeron's apartment this morning.

Fall hadn't fully blown in yet, but the evenings were already turning cool. The warmth of the fire roaring in the stone fireplace was welcomed and made the room toasty. A little smoke wafted over him with a sweet, rich odor that made him want to close his eyes. He hadn't felt so serene in a long time. *It would be truly serene if the girls were not late.* The thought interrupted his peace. It was a turn of the glass past supper and he was about to suggest to Rowyn that they go down to the kitchens when the door opened and Willoe entered with Casandra right behind.

"You are here," Willoe said and walked over to the side table to pour two goblets of wine. She handed one to Casandra and then took a large swig from her own. She nearly choked at the taste, evidently having expected diluted fruit wine. Sputtering ungracefully, she wiped her chin with a piece of fabric lying on the table, seeing as no servants were present to provide a towel.

A knock sounded and the door opened. Dilys led in two young male servants who brought in a metal platter of assorted vegetables and a wooden slab filled with meat. The two servants approached each of the cousins, one holding first the platter and then the wooden slab, while the other filled the cousins' plates with whatever meat and vegetables they indicated. After the cousins had been served, the servants moved toward the wall to wait until needed, but Dilys shooed them out, saying that she would ensure the nobles were served. Then she filled another plate for herself, poured a goblet of wine, and took a seat in the corner of the room.

After the servants were gone the four cousins dug into their meals. Aeron looked up from his plate at Willoe and Casandra. "So, where were you? We were about to leave."

"I wasn't," Rowyn countered.

"I am warmed by your support." Aeron shot Rowyn a look of betrayal, then smiled. Holding up a piece of meat on his knife, he waved it around as if to make a point. "I have been permitted to join Row in the escort," he quipped, before grinning and stuffing the food into his mouth.

"Good, that will fit nicely with my plan." Willoe grinned, though Aeron thought that it might be as much from the second goblet of wine she held as anything else.

A thought came to Aeron and he dropped his knife on the plate. "Oh no!" He shook his head in refusal. "The last time you had a plan we ended up scooping pig shit for a week." He grunted and stared back at Willoe. "If it was not for your father, the king would have us *still* knee deep in pig shit."

"This time it will be different," she countered, and before Aeron could argue she turned to face Rowyn, her lips strained as she dared him, "Do you want to go to White Cliffs as Mael's escort?"

Rowyn cleared his throat. Even among his sister and cousins he still did not want to seem the coward, but the truth won out. "No."

She whipped around to face the others, her voice dripping with disgust. "In three moons I will be traded to a relatively minor Baron, or maybe even a lowly baronet. Why? To guarantee some remote border is protected or to secure an interest in some mining venture. And what does the lucky man get in return for relieving Grandfather of a thorn in his side? A connection to the Brynmor line that he can claim for his children, which he will just as surely want me to pump out one after another like a hen in the chicken coop."

"Now Wil, you are exaggerating," Casandra said in a soothing voice.

Aeron nodded his head in agreement with his sister.

Willoe walked back over to the table and poured herself another measure of wine. In Aeron's mind she had had more than enough already.

"You think not, my cousin?" She turned to stare at Casandra as a sneer appeared on her lips. "You won't be far behind. You have already told me your father has implied most vigorously that you are well past marrying age."

"Yes, but he is not forcing anything upon me," she contended, though somewhat hesitantly.

"You say that now." Willoe continued her cause. "But once I am bartered off, the First Duke will have no excuse for not doing the same to you… It is his duty." This phrase was one they had all grown up with.

Willoe walked back and forth across the room as if on some mission, but without a true destination. "And you, Row." She turned her attention to her brother. "You're not going to have the freedom you have enjoyed." She waved her goblet in the air like a baton, spilling wine as she went. "Escorting Mael is just the beginning. Grandfather won't be happy until he transforms you into a replica of Mael." She stopped and gazed off in thought. "Though I imagine you should be honored, as he has given up on Hafgan." She returned to Rowyn. "Your time with Uncle Brom is going to be limited at first because of your other duties, and then eventually you will find that you have no time of your own. Grandfather considers his oldest son a bad influence."

"What I do is my—" he started to dispute her prediction, but Aeron knew she was telling the truth and cut him off.

"She is right, Row." Aeron reached over and put a hand on Rowyn's shoulder. "You knew it was coming. The increased training with Master Gwron and your presence at council meetings."

"Though kept to the back of the room and forced to be quiet," Rowyn added with a mix of sadness and anger.

"Yes, we took it as the king's way of increasing your knowledge of the kingdom and weapons skills, but I see now that it was also meant to keep you away from your uncle."

Aeron could see the reality sink in as a sour look descended on Rowyn. He must have known, but had refused to see it for what it was, as Aeron himself had.

"Yes." Willoe pointed her finger at Aeron and wagged it around as he proved her point. "If I'm going to sacrifice the rest of my life for the realm, I'm at least going to make the final days of freedom worth living."

They all looked at her a bit confused, but intrigued. She knelt down next to Rowyn and brought her face to just a hand's breadth from his. A bright grin spread across her face. "We are going to switch places."

Aeron stood up, his chair rattling behind him. He wondered whether his cousin had finally gone insane. He wanted to tell her how stupid it was, but he could only curse at the idea. "The Shadows take the Burning Lady."

Willoe stood and Casandra was just a heartbeat behind. Both yelled at Aeron together. "Don't you dare curse the Burning Lady!"

Then they both put fingers together and touched forehead, lips, then stomach.

Aeron knew neither was especially fanatical superstitious, so their outburst and devotional gestures took him by surprise.

He dropped back into his seat.

The two women stared across at each other, nodded, and then Casandra sat back down.

Willoe stayed standing and walked around the others' chairs. "I know you think this is insane, but it can work. I can pretend to be Row and go as part of the escort."

Aeron was the first to speak. "You're right. It *is* insane." He stood again and glared at her. "It will never work. You're... you're a woman."

"And better with a sword and bow than most of the soldiers in the escort. Protector Dougal says so," she spat back. "Plus, I can easily hide these." She put her hands over her small breasts and covered them to emphasize.

"Wil!" Rowyn gasped, stunned.

"Does the Protector know about this absurd plan?" Aeron demanded.

Willoe's eyes burrowed into Aeron's, mouth twisted in a sneer. "No, of course not. He would be the first to try to stop me."

"It will never work." Rowyn stayed seated, but he was as adamant as Aeron.

Casandra just shook her head. "How will you ever pass as Row? You will be amongst a troop of men. Traveling in the open."

"I have been mistaken for him in the past," Willoe pointed out. "It was only last week, Aeron, that you thought I was Row."

Aeron was not going to be swayed that easily. "You were wearing a gambeson, your hair was pulled back, and you had a sword in your hand. It was an easy mistake." He hoped she would see reason. "And you mimicked his voice! What else was I supposed to think?"

"Exactly!" She moved around the chairs again, stopping behind Rowyn, who seemed very uncomfortable and shifted restlessly in his chair. She looked across at Aeron. "You expected to find Row so that is who your mind told you I was. And that is exactly what the soldiers in the escort are going to see."

"The only thing that can give me away is my hair." She grabbed her hair and pulled it out and in front of herself. "If I cut my hair to the same length as Row's, no one will know."

Casandra's eyes widened. "Your hair? You wouldn't."

In response, Willoe reached down in front of Rowyn, grabbed the knife he had been using to eat, and pulled out her hair with the other.

"Stop!" Casandra shouted, and jumped up to grab Willoe's arm before she could cut her hair. "If you're going to do this, then do it right."

Casandra let go of Willoe's arm and looked over at Rowyn, pushing her hair back with both hands. "And what about Row?" The concern was evident in her voice. "What is he supposed to do while you are off running around the countryside pretending to be a warrior?" Her tone was becoming angry, which baffled Aeron.

"I talked with Father and he has agreed to allow me to go to Highkeep

Manor until Row returns. He believes I will take the time to meditate with the Burning Lady and her Spirits to reflect and prepare myself for my marriage bond." Willoe moved to the front of Rowyn's chair, her dress swaying across Rowyn's legs. "Only you, Casandra, Dilys, and a small escort. The manor has minimal staff right now and you would have near isolation."

"You still haven't said why Row should go along with this," Aeron demanded.

Willoe looked down at her twin and said firmly, "Apart from a chance to study in isolation before it is all taken away from him?" Then she knelt down in front of him, put the knife back on his plate, and took both his hands in hers. She looked deep into his eyes, pleading. "My brother. The one whom I have shared my entire life with. The one whom I have loved more than my own life. I have asked so little of you, but I must ask this one thing. I need it. I beg you. Go off with your books for a few moons and give me this one thing before I am condemned to an unwanted and woeful life."

Aeron could see tears in her eyes.

Rowyn frowned and Aeron could see he was definitely impacted by his sister's plea. Aeron had rarely seen this level of vulnerability from her. He was speechless. He had never understood what it meant for a young noblewoman, had never even thought about it. Men married or they didn't. And while they may have to bow to an arranged marriage, it did not necessarily restrict their activities as he now realized it would Willoe and his own sister. He had to restrain himself emotionally, thinking about the two free-spirited women – the closest friends he had next to Rowyn – becoming someone's property. Maybe someone twice their age. Sent away. Separated from those they love.

"So what is the plan?" Aeron heard himself say to Willoe. He was shocked by his own surrender to this insane idea.

She looked over at him and wiped away a tear with the back of her hand as a smile crept on to her face. "I will take Row's place in the escort. We are near the same size, and when wearing a doublet or gambeson no one will look too closely. And if you teach me how to act like a man I believe I can do it. Everyone will be expecting Prince Rowyn, so even if there are a few small differences they will ignore them." She turned back to look at Rowyn. "No offense, brother, but no one is going to spend much time talking with you."

Rowyn sadly nodded his agreement.

"I heard Protector Dougal is also going with the escort," Aeron added. "Evidently your father believes White Cliffs is more dangerous than Highkeep Manor." He laughed.

"I am not wearing a dress," Rowyn blurted out. "I would never get away with it."

His sister stood and moved next to Rowyn's chair, putting a hand on his shoulder and squeezing. "I have made arrangements for a carriage the day after the escort leaves to take you to Highkeep Manor. Casey and Dilys will be with you and they can help you deceive the escort until you arrive at Highkeep." She grinned broadly, and her eyes were bright with delight. "No one uses Highkeep in the fall, so it will be nearly deserted. Once you get there, no one would question Dilys taking over sole responsibility for your care. Just wear a cloak and you would even be able to walk the grounds without being bothered. There are only a few servants that will be in residence this time of year. You can spend the next three moons reading, practicing your studies, and, most importantly, *not* escorting Mael."

Aeron looked at Rowyn and Casandra to see what they thought. He could see Casandra's smile peeking through and knew she was sold.

Rowyn was still doubtful. "What if Father, or even worse, Grandfather, finds out?"

"They will not." Willoe walked around the chairs to stand in front of the one she had occupied during supper. "And what is the worst they could do if they did find out? Marry me off and make you a warrior?" She said sarcastically before plopping down in the chair. She reached for her goblet and took a large swig of the wine. This time she did not choke.

Aeron did not bother to mention that Casandra and he could also potentially face dire consequences, though they would only be accessories, a fact which might or might not make a difference. *Oh, what the four Shadows. If not this, it would be some other scheme.* "I am in," he said. "Providing Row is willing to do it." He drained his goblet in one swallow, walked over to the table, refilled it and sat back down.

"I also," Casandra added, a big smile on her face. Her motivation still eluded Aeron.

Willoe leaned forward, her hands on her knees, and stared right at Rowyn. Her lips were tight and she breathed deeply before asking, "What about you, brother?"

All of them stared at Rowyn as he squirmed in the chair. He looked her straight in the eyes, his lips twisted as if he were trying to make a decision. After a few moments the intense look turned into a big grin. "You really owe me this time, sister."

"Well then." Aeron stood and raised his goblet. They all stood and held out their goblets. "To Prince Rowyn." Aeron tipped his goblet toward Willoe, "And Princess Willoe." He turned the goblet toward Rowyn and nodded.

All four of them laughed.

"Dilys." Aeron was going to tell Dilys to get a goblet for herself, but he realized she had been sitting in the corner sipping from one for a while already. "Join us."

Holding his goblet out in front of him he quoted an old Cainwen blessing used by nobles and servants alike. "May the road be gentle, your baskets overflowing, and the Shades never cross your path." Then they all tossed down a large gulp from their goblets.

Aeron sat back down with a sly smile and put his goblet down. Leaning toward Willoe, he rested his elbows on his legs, wrung his hands gleefully and asked with a devious smile, "So where do we start? We have three days to turn you into a man."

11

Smiles and Laughter

"No, no, no!" Aeron shook his head as he told Willoe to stop walking across the room. The chamber was the one that she and Protector Dougal had been using for their weapons training, and it made a perfect location for Aeron to teach Willoe how to look and act like a man.

Willoe stomped a foot and gritted her teeth with fist clenched. What did he want? She was frustrated and quickly becoming angry. She had done everything Aeron had told her to do over the last two days. How to slouch the shoulders a little, how to lean up against a wall with ankles crossed, and dozens of other bodily acts that differed between men and women. Yet he still wasn't satisfied. "What was wrong with that?" Her stomach rumbled; they had worked right through supper.

Casandra and Rowyn sat along one wall, watching, while Dilys sat next to Rowyn, engrossed in her embroidery.

Casandra piped up. "I thought that was fine."

"I agree with Aeron. It doesn't feel right," Rowyn voiced. "There is something that just doesn't say... man. I still see a woman even though she is wearing my clothes, but I cannot tell you why."

"I am not sure either." Aeron walked over to Willoe and looked her over. He stepped back. "Can you walk across the room again?"

Willoe huffed in response. What else did he want from her? But she turned and walked back across the room to make him happy, trying not to stomp as she went. Once she reached the back wall she turned around to face Aeron, her fist on her hip.

"To start with, do not put your hands like that. Every man knows an angry woman's stance." Aeron laughed as he said it.

She dropped her hands and looked up at the ceiling. *Can I really do this?*

She wanted to cry, but Aeron had already warned her, repeatedly, against displaying such emotions.

"You almost have it. But there is still something missing." He rubbed his bearded cheek as if in thought.

Willoe started to jut her hip out, shifting her weight, then remembered what Aeron had told her and shifted back to standing normally, putting equal weight on both legs.

Dilys continued with her embroidery and spoke without looking up. "Bags."

Everyone turned to her as Aeron asked, "Bags?"

Dilys stayed focused on her needle and repeated. "Bags. She have no bags." Her frustration temporarily overcome by the mystery, Willoe asked, "What do you mean, 'no bags?'"

"No bollocks." Dilys put her embroidery down, made two fists next to each other, held a forefinger out between them and wiggled it. She folded the finger into the fist and held both fists up in front of her to emphasize what she meant. "Ye have no bollocks."

"Dilys!" Rowyn and Aeron said together.

Casandra, who didn't seem shocked at all, asked, "What does a lack of bollocks have to do with the way she walks?"

Now Rowyn and Aeron turned to Casandra, both frowning, which made Willoe smile. Why did men always think women never discussed topics like sexual organs, both their own and those of men? What would they think if they were ever to sit in a circle of ladies working on embroidery?

Dilys pointed at Willoe. "Dear, walk across the room again." She turned to Aeron. "Watch her feet."

Willoe walked across the room. She had already tried to correct the sway in her walk, as Aeron had pointed out earlier, and tried to stride rather than sway.

"Rowyn, ye walk across the room," Dilys politely directed Rowyn.

Rowyn looked to Aeron, who nodded. The prince stood and walked across the room as instructed.

Dilys nodded toward Willoe. "The woman's feet be close together and she walks almost one foot in front of the other, but not quite."

Aeron plopped down next to Dilys, taking Rowyn's seat. He sat with his mouth open for a few moments and, without looking at Dilys, said, "And Rowyn walks with his feet farther apart than Willoe."

Dilys picked up the embroidery again and looked back down as she pushed the needle through the fabric. "No bags."

Willoe walked up to Aeron and held out a hand with a big smile on her face. "I am glad to meet you, Lord Aeron."

"Wrong again." Aeron shook his head, frowning. "You're still doing it."

"I can't help it." She huffed again for the hundredth time in three days. "Are you sure that men do it that way?"

"Yes, I'm sure." He turned to Dilys, who was still working on the same embroidery from the day before. She had become Aeron's advisor in Willoe's training.

"He is sure," Dilys agreed.

Aeron twisted his lips, then told Willoe, "Go for a walk around the castle and watch the men and women you pass."

Willoe changed into her own clothing behind a screen and left the room with Casandra. *I don't see why this is necessary.* She stopped and took a deep breath, trying to calm herself before they continued. *I have to make this work.* They strolled down the Middle Gallery, walking slowly so they could run into as many people as possible.

As they passed other women, Willoe and Casandra would smile. In response, most of the girls' and women's lips would part, their teeth clearly visible, as they smiled in return, even among the castle staff.

She also noticed that if a man was in the vicinity, many of the older women kept their mouths tight-lipped, their teeth barely visible.

"Aeron was right, look at those men over there." Willoe pointed toward three men standing alone.

They talked vigorously, but their expressions were neutral, maybe with a thin smile, teeth hidden or barely visible. They seemed so much more serious and less social than the women they encountered.

After circling the castle once they walked several levels down to the Lower Gallery and completed the circuit once again, with the same result. They came across several men in a group who were all laughing.

"Look how open they are." Casandra said it as an accusation.

"I've heard *you* laugh like that." Willoe didn't see a difference.

"Not in public, and especially not around men."

"Oh no." It dawned on Willoe that she also would suppress her laughter if someone other than her brother or cousins were around. She wondered if this was as common a trait among women as Aeron had implied. It was confirmed a few moments later when they came across two women, alone along the walkway, who were both laughing similarly to the men they had just seen, but at a lower volume. Casandra grasped Willoe's arm and stopped her as several men came down the walkway. As the men approached, the women covered their mouths. They giggled politely through thin lips and nodded to the men as they passed.

"Damn the Shades." Willoe couldn't believe it. Something as simple as a smile or laughter could have exposed her on the first day of the escort.

When they returned to the training room, Willoe burst into the room and started to talk excitedly. "You were correct! I wouldn't—"

Aeron held up a hand, a frown spreading across his face. "You obviously did not learn anything."

Willoe clamped her hand over her mouth. She removed her hand, nodded at Aeron, then walked back to the door and left, closing the door behind her. She reentered the training room. She pulled her dress up enough to see her feet and strode over to Aeron, walking with her legs a little apart and a set expression on her face. She came straight up to Aeron, dropped the hem of the dress, bowed slightly, and addressed him with a thin-lipped yet polite smile. "It is a pleasure to meet you, Lord Aeron."

Aeron smiled back, and Willoe noticed that some of his teeth were visible. She did not, however, widen her own smile. He then bowed deeply in return. "It is my pleasure Prince Rowyn."

They both laughed out loud with mouths wide open and for the first time she thought, *This might actually work.*

12

When Fire Comes

Willoe and Aeron entered the Upper Ward and Willoe was amazed at the flurry of activity as stable boys and groomsmen hurried about saddling the remaining horses and servants finished loading the supply wagons. The smell of so many horses, people, and dogs crowded between the stables and the sixty foot high walls of the Inner Curtain was a bit overwhelming, yet at the same time she found it exciting. Willoe couldn't imagine what it would be like if the large square was at capacity with seven times as many bodies.

Her heart beat rapidly as she looked around. The noise assaulted her ears as everyone seemed to be yelling directions to one another, and with Supply Sergeant Trystan the loudest of them all as he harangued any servants that happened to be within his reach. He checked all five wagons to make sure food, the Shields' armor and miscellaneous weaponry, tents, and other supplies were secured and that none of the servants had absconded with something while everyone else was otherwise occupied. Squires looked after their Shields' horses, double-checking gear and personal belongings to ensure everything was in place.

"Quite a major undertaking for something so simple as a traveling envoy." Willoe scanned the yard, barely able to take in all the organized chaos.

"You forget, it's Mael," Aeron reminded her.

The two of them shared a good laugh.

"Mael has told Captain Harte he wants to cover the entire three hundred and forty miles, from Westhedge to White Cliffs, in two weeks," Willoe commented.

Aeron looked over at the wagons. "We will need to cover twenty-five miles a day. If not for the Great Crossway it would not be possible. Even so it will take everything Sergeant Trystan has to get all the wagons there intact."

It was turning into quite a large entourage. The Franchon count and Lady Emeline had originally arrived at Castle Westhedge with an escort of around forty, including a number of Shields, squires, mounted troops and a half-dozen various servants, in addition to the foreigner Bat-Uul.

Willoe couldn't imagine Mael's escort being anything less, and she wasn't disappointed. The returning party would be around one hundred, with the Cainwen green and gold outnumbering the dark gray and red of the Franchons.

She did not recognize most of the Cainwen escort, which was a blessing. She would need to rely on Aeron to help cover up any missteps she might make and run interference with some of the others that knew her, especially Captain Harte and Cleric Yoan. The one that worried her the most was Protector Dougal. Out of all the party he was the only one that knew her almost as well as she knew herself. Aeron was correct about the twins' Protector. Highkeep Manor would present little danger, making the escort to Castle White Cliffs his primary concern. She knew she couldn't avoid the Protector entirely, but if she and Aeron stayed together, Aeron could engage Protector Dougal whenever he approached them. At least, that was the plan.

While Willoe had been taking in the grand preparations Mael arrived with his three companion Shields in tow. Naturally, Tanguy was counted among them. Mael, along with Count Idwal, one of the king's most trusted and loyal advisors, would lead the column out of the city. Right behind them would come Captain Harte and his Franchon counterpart, then all the Shields and the two carriages containing the Franchon envoys and their aides. After that would come Aeron, Willoe, Protector Dougal, Master Gwron, and Cleric Yoan, with the pages not far behind. Bringing up the rear of the column would be the guardsmen, supply wagons, and servants.

A young boy, who looked to be around twelve, walked quickly up to Aeron and Willoe. He wore black tights with knee-high leather boots and a green shirt that hung down to below the waist. A yellow-gold dragon was emblazoned on the left chest, and a black belt secured the shirt around the waist. He did not need to tell Willoe he was a royal page; it was as evident as the sun above.

"I am Tomos. Along with Sion." He smiled as he pointed to another page being lectured by Mael. "Will provide service to you during your travel. Please follow me, my lords."

He had dimples that Willoe thought would do him well with the ladies in a few years. She was already taking a liking to this boy.

They made their way across the square, around wagons, horses and barking dogs. They approached a pair of horses, the bridles held by a groom. Tomos turned back to face Willoe, his brown locks draped across his eyes. He looked for a moment as if he wanted to say something, but then just indicated the two horses behind him. Aeron's mount was a courser, as befitted his station as a Shield and a future duke. In contrast, Willoe had been allotted one of Rowyn's personal horses. While a fine horse and probably more expensive than even the coursers, it was a much smaller animal, bred for speed and endurance rather than for the frenzied rush and violence of combat. Even the mounted guardsmen and squires rode the larger all-purpose rounceys.

"Prince Mael?" Willoe asked blandly.

Tomos just nodded in agreement, his eyes downcast.

Willoe sighed, pushed the hair back from her face and looked at Aeron.

He just shrugged with a twisted smile and said, "I can get Night Spirit." His palfrey would be similar to the one waiting for Willoe.

"No, no need." The insult was evident. The heir apparent was making a point that Rowyn was not fit to be in the escort. One of many insults over the years. But Willoe would be Shade-damned if she would let Mael get the better of her.

"It's fine, Tomos." Willoe stepped up and scratched under the bay's mane. "I'm very familiar with Row's Windsinger." Aeron cleared his throat and Willoe quickly corrected herself. "My Windsinger."

Tomos bowed again, somewhat relieved. Sion shuffled over, a lecture from the heir apparent evidently not sitting well with the boy. "This is Sion." Tomos put his hand on the other's shoulder.

Willoe tilted her head and looked intently at the boys. They had the same shoulder-length brown hair and brown eyes, strong chins and narrow noses. They looked like any other young aristocratic boys, but there was a definite resemblance. "Is there a relationship?"

"Yes, Prince Rowyn." Tomos' smile broadened. "Sion is my brother. Younger by a year."

"Your Family?" Aeron asked Tomos, his interest seemingly piqued now.

Willoe didn't think Tomos' smile could get any bigger, but it did. "Tybalt, my lord. Our sire is the Baron Glyn Tybalt," Tomos said, his pride evident.

"How long have you been at Castle Westhedge?" Willoe addressed Sion. Tomos answered instead. "A little over one year, my lord."

"Is Sion dumb?" Aeron asked, looking at Sion, his stare intent.

"No, Lord Aeron." He glanced at his brother, evidently a little embarrassed. "He is just a bit meek, Your Lordship."

"Makes it rather hard to be a page, doesn't it?" The boy's use of the formal court voice made Willoe want to giggle, but Aeron reached over and slapped her on the shoulder. Giggling is not very manly, she reminded herself.

"He does speak, Prince Rowyn, but only when necessary."

Willoe could only imagine what Sion would consider necessary. Yet she already liked both boys and was glad they did not show the fear or disdain shown to her and her brother by many others. It said a lot about how they were raised. "I guess that is all any of us can ask. Don't let us keep you from your duties. I believe we can handle any final preparations ourselves."

Both boys bowed and turned to continue preparations. Willoe watched after them, but they disappeared in the maze of people, horses, and wagons. She grasped the pommel and mounted her horse, then checked to make sure the canvas bags were secure. She took the extra small leather bag she had tied to her belt and placed it over the pommel. A smile crossed her face as she wondered what would be made of the contents if one of the men were to discover it. She ran her hands through her hair, pushing it off her face. It still felt strange to her ever since Casandra and Dilys had cut it that morning, but the color that condemned her would never change.

The groom reached up and handed Aeron the reins to his horse. Willoe noticed that the groom was heavily muscled under his shirt. She found it strange, however, that he had his head turned to the left, looking away. He had dirty blond hair cut short; not a common style, but not unseen. He had to turn his head back toward Willoe as he held the leather straps up for her to grab and she froze, the reins still a hand's breadth away. He had a handsome face, but what stopped her was the old scar that ran from the left ear and curved around to just under the left side of his lips. Her heart pounded so hard she found it difficult to draw breath.

He stood there and held the reins farther up so Willoe could easily grab them without leaning further out of her saddle. "Your reins, my lord." The groom's voice was deep and held a certain confidence, but his expression had a disquieted look about it.

It took her several moments before she could breathe again and take the reins. She inhaled deeply and regained her composure. "Your name, groom?"

"I am called Doy, my lord. I have been assigned to Your Lordship."

Willoe was still somewhat shocked, but knew that now was not the time to ask more questions. "That will be all for now, Doy. We look forward to your service."

He lifted his face, the concern on his faced turning into a grin... the same grin he had given her four years ago.

"What was that about?" Aeron asked her as Doy walked away to check on another rider's horse.

Willoe stared after the groom for a moment before answering. "That was the street urchin— I mean, the cutpurse that Casandra and I saved the day I met you."

"Are you sure?" Aeron looked after the retreating groom.

"I think so. He has the same scar."

"I cannot imagine the Marshall of Horses using a cutpurse as a groom."

The discussion was cut short when Aeron pointed across the Ward. Approaching them with a determined quickstep was Uncle Brom. His scraggly gray beard and hair was in total disarray as if he had just run out from his apartment. His robes flapped behind him as he rushed over. He sidestepped abruptly to avoid being run over by a wagon that had just moved into line.

"Are you a complete arse?" Sergeant Trystan yelled from the other side of the wagon. "Can't you see that—" He promptly changed his tone. "My apologies, Lord Brom".

Willoe's uncle just smiled and nodded to the sergeant then, continued toward Willoe and Aeron.

"Ah, Rowyn, I caught you before your leaving." His breath came in short bursts. He looked so out of place amongst the clamor of the warriors around them. He stopped, leaned forward, and his head hung for a moment as he caught his breath.

Willoe looked down at the older man and waited for him to lift his head. "Well, I am glad I got a chance to see you before we left, Uncle. I will surely miss you."

Uncle Brom began to speak but stopped and looked at Willoe, somewhat perplexed. Then he spoke with a curious undertone. "Are you feeling well, Nephew?"

"Why, yes." Willoe sat straighter, not sure what her uncle saw in her to make him ask a question like that. "I am perfectly fine."

"Your voice. You sound as if you are ill. Either that or you are wearing someone else's undergarments." He laughed at his own joke.

Willoe flinched at the comment and found herself worrying. Did Uncle Brom know Rowyn and she had switched places? She knew that was impossible. Maybe Uncle Brom had seen through her façade. She knew her imitation of Rowyn's voice was near perfect. It did not require much of a change, as Rowyn's voice had a somewhat higher pitch than Aeron's, more in a tenor's range. Yet someone who spent a lot of time with Rowyn might notice a difference, even the slightest change in tone. Someone who knew him intimately… like their uncle. "Yes, I had gristle caught in my throat last night. I am afraid it made my throat swell." She added quickly, "Though I'm fine now, just a little soreness that I'm sure will go away soon."

He stared up at her, absorbing her story, and finally grunted. "As it may be, I found the book of runes you left on a stack of other books in my apartments and wanted to bring it to you."

"The book?" Willoe said, trying to remember whether Rowyn had mentioned a book. She realized her head was cocked and one eye partially closed in a questioning look. She straightened her head and smiled at her uncle.

"Yes, yes. The ancient runes." Uncle Brom pulled a worn book out from an inside pocket of his robe. It had a leather tooled cover with faded colors and symbols that were unfamiliar to Willoe.

Why hasn't Rowyn mentioned this to me? she thought, and looked at Aeron for help. He just shrugged again. *That gesture really annoys me.*

Uncle Brom frowned. Willoe feared that her identity had been uncovered, and they had not even left the castle. "Oh yes, sorry. The ancient runes. Yes, I shouldn't have left them." She reached for the book.

Her uncle pulled his hand back slightly and stared hard at her, his eyebrows knitted. "Hmmm, yes. I am sure. Remember, the runes are from a Tonn tribe. You already know most of the words and you shouldn't take much effort for you to translate the rest. Just like we discussed."

She would have to speak with Rowyn when she returned, to come up with an excuse for why Rowyn hadn't been able to translate the book. "Yes, I remember. I will try to work on it as I find time." She smiled, hoping that it would satisfy him.

"Good," he said. "Very good." Then his expression changed and he smiled again, making Willoe breathe a sigh of relief. "Maybe it might be best if I hold onto the runes until you get back." He stuffed the book back into his robes. "You would probably be bored as you have already gone over them many times." His voice had a lightness to it.

"I think that would be best," Willoe agreed gladly, and thanked the Spirits her uncle was appeased.

Reaching out, he patted Willoe on the leg. "You have a safe trip, dear Nephew." He rounded on his toes to leave, but turned his face around to add, "Remember that what you can do and how you see yourself is more important than how others see you." After the unsolicited advice he spun back and headed back the way he had come.

"What a strange thing to say." Willoe looked at Aeron, who just shrugged his shoulders again and pursed his lips. She never realized that he did that so often. *I guess it doesn't bother Rowyn.*

The noise and energy level in the Ward continued to increase as wagons and horses fell in line. Willoe was anxious to get started. Her skin nearly tingled with excitement at the prospect of the journey. She couldn't believe she was getting the chance to experience life… life in the men's world, even if only for a short time. She would finally be free of the restrictions placed on her by her gender.

Like the Shields, she wore a long-sleeve linen shirt under a leather doublet that was comfortable for traveling. In one of the wagons would be a small chest of her personal belongings including her armor, the quilted gambeson to keep the armor from rubbing, and the green surcoat with the Brynmor coat of arms – a winged golden dragon – emblazoned on the left breast. She shifted the belt around her waist. She had worn similar clothing when practicing with Protector Dougal, but Rowyn's doublet and other gear was thicker and weighed more than what she had expected. She wondered if she would even be able to carry the weight of full armor when the time came. Willoe pulled the doublet back up so it sat properly on her shoulder. Rowyn was just a little broader than she was, and Dilys had been so busy hemming Rowyn's clothes, that were coming along on the trip, that the maidservant had not had time to modify the doublet.

Aeron reached over and touched Willoe on the shoulder, interrupting her adjustments. *What now?* He pointed again, another annoying habit she had not noticed before, but this time with a broad smile on his face. Willoe's excitement with starting out for White Cliffs was quickly subdued as she followed his finger and noticed the Lady Emeline and the Franchon count walking toward their carriage, with Emeline's maid trailing behind. The count stumbled like a drunkard as he tried to avoid the sea of horse droppings. He had his cape pulled up so it wouldn't touch anything on the ground.

Emeline said something to the count as they reached the first coach and then he stepped into the carriage. The Franchon woman said something to her maid, Josiane, who turned and joined the count's aide in the other carriage. She then turned around and headed toward Willoe and Aeron.

"I am pleased you are able to join us on our return." She addressed Willoe, but kept glancing over at Aeron.

"We're looking forward to seeing your home." Willoe answered politely, though she still had reservations about the woman.

"Lady Emeline." Bat-Uul had arrived and called to her politely, but firmly, from the count's carriage.

The fear that suddenly overcame the charming Emeline surprised Willoe. The alarmed expression was only momentary and then Emeline regained her composure. "I must go, but let us talk later." Then she stepped quickly to the carriage. Bat-Uul whispered something to her. She nodded her head a couple of times in acknowledgment, looked back at Willoe and Aeron, then stepped up into the carriage. Bat-Uul turned to look back at Willoe. He pulled the hood up over his head, nodded in her direction and then followed the Lady Emeline into the carriage.

Willoe wondered at whom Emeline's comment had been directed, seeing as Aeron had a large grin on his face.

Their focus was drawn away from the carriages when horns sounded, announcing the first movement of the column. Shortly thereafter Mael and Count Idwal rode to the front and led the way out the Upper Ward's main gate. After the Shields had started moving, the carriages behind them started up with a rumble as the drivers snapped the reins. Willoe and Aeron fell in behind the last carriage as they exited the gate.

The clacking of the wheels and the clip of the horses' hoofs on the castle's cobblestones echoed off the walls as they traveled down between the castle's Inner and Outer Curtain into the city proper. The dog handler let the mastiffs and hounds run with the front of the escort. They would be invaluable in hunting and add to the nightly guard. They wound their way down through the merchants' manors that filled the area just outside the Outer Curtain, and then the Craft Guild shops with masters and apprentices hard at work on their trades. The party made their way into the heart of the city where taverns, stores and street vendors offered a wide variety of goods and services among the houses of the common city dwellers. Along the way many people had lined the streets to see the procession. It wasn't as if they had not seen guardsmen and Shields before, or even one of the royal family, but gawking at such an ensemble, including the Franchons, helped to break up an otherwise ordinary day.

The procession rode slowly through the streets and after three turns of the glass they crossed the drawbridge and underneath the tower that guarded it. Finally, they were on the Great Crossway heading east from the castle. Another turn of the glass and they left the cobblestones behind. The outrunners took their position to the front and sides of the column. The slow-moving carriage and supply wagons kept them crawling along, but they were still able to more than triple the speed they had had to maintain on the sometimes narrow streets of the city.

If they could keep to Mael's plan, they would reach Castle White Cliffs in just a couple of weeks. Willoe tried not to think of what awaited her on her return. Instead, she would focus on the next few moons and enjoy the time she had. She was more resolved than ever to make the most of the circumstances that put her in this place at this time.

Looking about at the warriors around her, she felt free for the first time since being a child, but right then a sudden flash of heat, like a firebrand, ran up and down her spine. She sucked in her breath loudly enough that Aeron turned and leaned down toward her to whisper, "Something wrong?"

Willoe leaned forward over the neck of her horse and her breath came in short bursts as the burning sensation ran from her spine down her legs and arms. Her head felt like it would burst into flames as her mind swirled, and she had to fight to stay in the saddle. It was like when she was nine and again at twelve, but much worse this time. She was just about to scream out in pain and fear when the fire subsided.

Aeron pulled his horse closer. He reached over and grabbed her by the arm, pulling her back up, then whispered, "Willoe, what's wrong? Are you ill? Should I get Cleric Yoan…" He hesitated before finishing. "Or Protector Dougal?"

Willoe felt a warmth flood back through her body. Not like the fire that had assaulted her spine moments before, but a soothing heat that passed from her head down through all her limbs. With the emergence of the warmth the weight seemed to lift from her body and the bulky clothing became an easier burden to bear.

She took a couple of deep breaths and sat back up, turning in her saddle with a smile plastered on her face, and said quietly. "No... No, everything is fine." She lowered her voice enough that just the two of them could hear. "I just had a cramp. You know, it's that time..."

Aeron quickly leaned away and turned his attention to the road ahead. Even with the shock of the fire she was able to smile at his reaction.

She couldn't show any distress, even to Aeron, as he might tell Protector Dougal, and the large Protector would not hesitate to pull Willoe out of the escort if he knew the truth. Though the episode was disturbing, she was not going to let anything stop her at this point. Willoe looked out to the north, breathing slowly, trying to calm herself.

She was idly scanning the distant mountain range when she caught a glimpse of something just off the horizon. All she could make out from that distance was something that appeared to have wings. At that distance, and as large as it looked, it had to be bigger than any bird she had ever seen. She started to point it out to Aeron, but held her tongue when it circled once and disappeared beyond the horizon. Her mind whipped back to the other night and the dragon-mounted shining woman. What was going on with her? And what did this all have to do with the Burning Lady? She continued staring at the empty sky above the horizon and wondered if – no, when – the fire would return again.

13

Off to Highkeep

Rowyn snapped his head toward the door as the handle turned. Dilys had just left for the kitchen. She couldn't be returning so soon. He searched for a hiding place, then heard Casandra's voice call "I'm back, Willoe," as the door began to open. Casandra entered and he let out of sigh of relief. She started to giggle, but then stifled it with her hand over her mouth. She regained control and crossed over to a table under the window, where Dilys had left a decanter of spiced wine. Still smiling, Casandra poured a measure of the wine into two goblets and held one out to Rowyn. "Maybe this will calm your nerves."

With the goblet in hand, he swirled it before taking a sip, while Casandra sat down in one of the velvet-cushioned chairs near the table with a goblet of her own. He sat in the other chair and leaned against the elegantly carved wooden back, letting his muscles relax for the first time all day. The green crystal wine decanter glittered as it reflected the last rays of the setting sun. *Just make it through the night*, he told himself as he put the goblet up to his nose and sniffed, drawing in the aroma of pepper, cinnamon, and cloves. Dilys had done well. He reckoned he could barely handle a sword, but he knew his way around a wine cellar, thanks to Aeron. He finally sipped from the wine and let the smoothly blended spices roll over his tongue and down his throat.

They both sat there for a few moments, not speaking.

Casandra took a sip and then closed her eyes, leaning her head back as she recited the plan once again. "Right before daybreak we will make our way down to the carriage. It seems like the Burning Lady is with us. The escort is a unit that has just returned from the northern borders and is led by a recently inducted Shield. It's unlikely that they would have had any contact with you or Wil. It simplifies things a little."

Rowyn had never really paid much attention to his cousin in the past. Even though they had spent a lot of time in each other's company. She was Willoe's companion, and even though just a year younger he always thought of her as younger than that, when he thought of her at all. Sitting there, her head back, her hair hanging down and her slender neck exposed, he thought she looked different. Fair and elegant like a new-bloomed rose. His eyes followed her delicate chin to the curve of her neck down to her chest. He realized she had grown into a woman when he had been busy elsewhere.

He closed his eyes, hoping that when he reopened them the mischievous little girl that had been Willoe's accomplice would have returned. But when he reopened his eyes she still sat there. All grown up, her dress belted just above the waist, showing off her hips and highlighting the top of her bodice, causing Rowyn to turn his head so he wouldn't stare.

"Is anything wrong?" Casandra had opened her eyes and asked in a concerned voice, probably thinking that he might be crumbling under the stress of the plan.

"I am fine," he managed to get out before taking another sip. He looked back at her, keeping his eyes focused on her face. He forgot about everything as he thought, *She is beautiful.* She smiled and he surprised himself when he returned the smile. A knock at the door quickly shifted his thoughts. He looked at the door and then back at her. He could feel his eyes go wide like a rabbit at the sound of a hawk overhead.

She carefully put her goblet down.

The knock came again, followed by a familiar voice. "Willoe, it is Uncle Brom. I have come to talk with you." It was more of a statement than a request.

Casandra grabbed Rowyn's arm and pointed to the dressing chamber, at the end of the room, mouthing *in there* several times as she wiggled her finger in that direction. He stepped into the small room and pulled the door closed; leaving it opened just a hair so he could see into the main room.

He watched as Casandra straightened her dress, though it didn't seem ruffled. Probably more of a way to calm herself, he thought.

She took a deep breath and stepped over to the door to open it. "Please come in," Rowyn heard her say, and he could see Uncle Brom's smile in return.

Uncle Brom entered, nodding to Casandra, and looked around the room. "I had been told by the Lady Wilford that Willoe was secluded in her apartment." His brows narrowed as he questioned her.

"She is in the dressing chamber trying to finalize what wardrobe to take with her to Highkeep." As Casandra talked she guided Uncle Brom over to the table and held up the decanter, at which he waved his hand to decline politely.

He nodded at Casandra and then called out to the dressing chamber, "Willoe, could you step out here for a moment?"

Rowyn inhaled deeply as he leaned back from the door. *What now?* He took another deep breath and tried to remember how Willoe sounded and what she would say. He was usually so clear-minded and knew exactly what to do, but his mind now was like fog settling in on the moor during an early summer morning.

"Changing!" he called out in a clipped tone. He could feel sweat dripping and running down the curve of his neck.

Rowyn leaned forward and looked through the crack to see Uncle Brom cast a questioning look at Casandra.

She shifted uncomfortably and then told him, still with a courteous and calming smile, "I believe she just undressed and it will take some time to get properly dressed again. It might be quite a while before she can come out."

Uncle Brom looked at the dressing chamber and then back at Casandra, his brow furrowed in thought, then reached into his robe and pulled out a very old book. "Well, I must go, but if you could give this to Willoe? It is for Rowyn."

Casandra gave him a queer look as she took the book and turned it over in her hands. "It is a very rare and valuable book of runes," Uncle Brom explained to cure her curiosity. "I thought Willoe could hold onto it until Rowyn returns."

Rowyn realized that he had left the book in Uncle Brom's apartment. He smiled. He would now have it to study while at Highkeep. What luck! He almost stepped into the main room to thank his uncle when he remembered why he was hiding in the dressing chamber.

Casandra seemed a bit confused, but smiled back at Uncle Brom regardless. "I will make sure that Willoe gets it."

He thanked her and headed for the door. As he was about to leave, he called out to Rowyn. "Dear Niece. Remember that..." he paused to emphasize his words. "Remember that what you can do and how you see yourself is more important than how others see you." He smiled at Casandra, bowed slightly and left. She closed the door behind him and Rowyn saw her lean back against the wooden frame, letting out a puff of air.

"He's gone." She stood back up and moved toward her goblet while calling out to Rowyn. He came out of the dressing chamber and walked over to take the book from her. He opened it and looked over several pages.

"What is it?" She peered over his shoulder.

He looked at her in confusion. "These are ancient runes." He held up the book to show her.

She stared at him and the book for a few moments and said sweetly, "Nice."

He gaped at her and couldn't believe that that was the extent of her reaction. Didn't she understand how important a book of ancient runes was? He opened his mouth, but nothing came out.

She shook her head and walked toward the dressing room. "Let's finish packing. Dilys let this out a little so it would fit."

It was one of Willoe's riding outfits.

"Other than that you should just need a cloak to get you to and from the carriage, and around Highkeep. I packed three different ones." She stopped in a thoughtful gesture, tapped her finger on her lips, and turned back to Rowyn. "But we'll need some of her other clothes to keep up the charade, if someone looks in the travel chest." She dove back into the dressing chamber.

Rowyn picked up Willoe's riding outfit. *At least it has pants.* The garment was not too different from his own, but made from thinner material.

"We should take this in case you do need to wear it for some reason." Casandra pulled out a dress and held it up for him. "It is a little bigger than most of her others."

"No!" There were many things Rowyn was prepared to do for his sister – wasn't he proving that by going along with this whole charade? – but there were definite limits. He glared at Casandra, but she only laughed at him, and packed the dress anyway.

Rowyn lifted the curtain and peered out westward at the passing fields. This late in the year most of the fields had already been threshed and many had already had their final ploughing of the year. This left a largely brown landscape of turned soil and fallow fields. At least a scattering of fruit trees and a distant forest broke the monotony. He leaned back as the carriage rocked from side to side with an occasional bump.

"Do you know why Wil decided on Highkeep?" Rowyn asked his cousin.

"She said it was remote," she responded, putting down her book. "But I did wonder why not some other location... say by the Forever Waters?"

"Highkeep Manor is part of the royal estates, though more remote than most." He thought for a moment before adding, "The road we are on comes to an end at the manor and we would not have to worry about anyone stopping by on their way to Castle Westhedge. It is not very well maintained; which is one reason Highkeep is normally only used in spring and summer. This late in the year there will only be a cook, a stablehand, a couple of housekeepers, a few other servants and our escort, the twelve guardsmen and their Shield."

"Sounds like she has this well thought out." Casandra nodded.

"When has she not?" Rowyn responded with a smirk, though, from experience, he knew that thinking it through and it becoming reality were not the same thing.

Casandra leaned back to continue reading.

Rowyn had not added, but found himself thinking that most of Willoe's plans were well thought out, but more often than not they didn't go as planned.

They had left the castle at daybreak three days before per Casandra's request to the Shield. She had told Rowyn that the fewer people about when they had to board the carriage, the better. Ser Rhein, the leader of their escort, had originally planned a six day trip. With the early start, however, Casandra had convinced him to continue until shortly before dusk their first day and to have a late supper. They had followed the same plan for the next day, and the same plan was scheduled for today. With only a short break for mid-day dinner, and another to water the horses at one of the villages they would pass through, they would be able to make Highkeep late the fifth day.

"I will be glad when we stop tonight." Rowyn shifted in his seat trying to find a comfortable position, even though he had pretty much given up on that the first day out. Dilys sat dutifully knitting – something which she never seemed to tire of doing, though he never saw a finished product – and Casandra was still reading a book. The introduction of movable type from the mainland had quickly expanded the number of different manuscripts available. Still, even with King Einion's support, few villagers could read more than basic information and many none at all. Rowyn was surprised early in the trip when he asked her what it was and she showed him the title: *Antiquity of Cainwen*. She was full of surprises.

At his comment she marked the page and put the book in her lap. She pulled the curtain back and leaned over to look up at the sky. "It shouldn't be that much longer. Ser Rhein assured me they would have the tent up quickly. Like previous nights, we will take a short walk until we can move into the tent for the remainder of the night."

Rowyn had noticed that Casandra had been spending a lot of time talking with the leader of their escort, the Shield Rhein, whenever they stopped. It irritated Rowyn, but he wasn't sure exactly why.

"I hope so," Rowyn responded, but he wasn't very confident. So far, Casandra had managed to handle everything better than he had expected. Even when they stopped for a privy break she escorted him away from the carriage and the eyes of the guardsmen. She would stop once they were out of eyesight and keep talking loudly, about absolutely nothing, as if she were carrying on a conversation with Willoe. This gave Rowyn the chance to move a little farther away from her so he could have a moment of privacy.

As if on cue the coachman pulled in the reins and the carriage came to a halt. Rowyn could hear a horse trot up next to the carriage and then a knock on the carriage door.

Casandra opened the door enough to address the Shield without exposing Rowyn sitting across from her, and spoke for them, though Rowyn could see part of the Shield's face. "Yes, Ser Rhein?"

Ser Rhein was tall even for a Cainwen and Rowyn had seen him in the morning before he had put on his jerkin – strength seemed to flow from the Shield. Rhein's dark blond hair hung down just above his shoulders. It was thick like Rowyn's, but straight, split down the middle, the ends curving around his face. He was clean shaven, and big brown eyes stared out from a strong face. Rowyn realized that the Shield was everything Rowyn was not. Rowyn wasn't one normally to compare – he had rarely cared about such things in the past – but he suddenly felt different; even though he couldn't be seen, he sank down into the seat, suddenly feeling smallish.

Ser Rhein bowed and looked off to the right, pointing. "There is a sheltered meadow off to the east up ahead near the river. I think it would be best to make camp there for the night. We may not find a better location for another couple of turns. If you and Princess Willoe would care to step out, we will pull the carriage into the meadow so we can unload and set up your tent." He looked back at Casandra and Rowyn thought he could see the Shield straighten, the perfect example of a professional soldier.

"That would be fine. Give us a few moments." Casandra closed the carriage door and moved to the bench where Rowyn sat. Looking at Rowyn as if analyzing a piece of artwork, she reached out and pulled the hood of his cloak up over his head. "Just like last night. Keep the hood up and don't look directly at anyone. When you step out turn your head to the left and start walking up the road. He will probably expect it, but I will tell Ser Rhein we are going for our nightly walk."

Rowyn nodded his head and sucked in his breath.

Casandra leaned forward and lifted the curtain over the window.

She turned back to look at Rowyn as they waited for the last guardsman to move away from the carriage. "I know what was said in Wil's apartment, but I have still wondered why you agreed to this switch." She peeked out the window again and then back to Rowyn. "I know why Wil is doing it, but why you?"

Rowyn just stared ahead and wondered for the hundredth time himself. Then he answered slowly. "Willoe has filled the role of mother for me over the years." He turned his face to Casandra. "I didn't think that would shock you." He sighed. "Not that she ever pampered me, just looked out for me. I don't... I don't do well around most people." He smiled. "I've always wished I could do something for her."

Rowyn lifted the curtain this time. "I think we can go now." Dilys opened the door, then Casandra stepped out and Rowyn followed. As instructed, Rowyn stepped down to the wooden step the coachman had placed by the door, then to the ground. He immediately turned his head to the left. Casandra stood to his left and began to talk as they headed up the road. This would give Rowyn a reason to keep looking to his left and not at the guardsmen.

"Ser Rhein," Casandra called over her shoulder, flashing her teeth in the most innocent smile. "Princess Willoe would like to take in more of the countryside, seeing as she rarely travels this far north. Please let us know when the tent is ready." Her smile widened.

She turned back to the road, locked her arm in Rowyn's and led them away, pointing to something in the field to their left. They walked for a short distance, the small stones and seashells of the road crunching under their feet.

"You are utterly astonishing, cousin," Rowyn complimented Casandra as they walked arm in arm. "You must have nerves like iron. And the way you can weave a story while smiling innocently the whole time. You almost had *me* convinced I was Willoe."

"You are not a woman, cousin." She smiled at him. "It comes with the territory."

He smiled back. "Did I mention that you scare me more than the Shadows?"

"Ah… then you are learning." She laughed and held his arm tighter.

They walked a bit farther up the road at a slow pace, talking about past exploits, their expectations of the next few moons at Highkeep, wondering how it was going with Willoe and Aeron, and just about anything that came to mind. Rowyn was surprised when Casandra looked over her shoulder and told him that they could return now. She said the tent was up and what baggage they needed for the night appeared to have been moved in. Dilys had headed over to the guardsmen to oversee the tent setup and the transfer of the contents the ladies would need for the night.

Rowyn was a solitary fellow; as Aeron would enjoy saying, a lone wolf. He smiled to himself. *I guess that is why he does most of the talking.* He looked forward to the times when he and Casandra were alone and could talk in private, like this. It gave him a warm feeling. In fact, he was amazed at how warm he currently felt, considering how cool the weather had turned. He could even feel a few drops of sweat on the back of his neck. He wondered if he should change to a lighter cloak for tomorrow.

They turned and started walking back to camp. It was a short walk. When moving away from the camp they had stopped every few minutes to gaze out at the landscape while they talked.

As they neared the camp, a screech drowned out everything else. The sound was like a bird of prey, similar to the red-tailed hawks that Rowyn was familiar with from numerous hunts, but ten times louder. It caused Rowyn to bend over, holding his hands to his ears. He turned his head toward the camp and saw that even tied to the picket line as they were, the horses tried to bolt at the frightening sound. If not for the competence of the coachman and one of the guardsmen, the horses would have injured themselves or wreaked havoc in the camp. The other guardsmen dropped whatever they were doing and pulled their swords and grabbed lances.

Rowyn recovered as Ser Rhein and two guardsmen ran up to the road to encircle Rowyn and Casandra. Rowyn had worn loose pants and a vest that would roughly pass for Willoe's riding garments, but even so, he lowered his head to keep his face hidden when they approached. Rowyn doubted any of the guardsmen would be able to tell him and Willoe apart, but he didn't want to take any chances. The penetrating screech did not repeat and Casandra persuaded the Shield that there wasn't any danger. The bodyguards walked back to the meadow, Ser Rhein turning constantly to make sure there wasn't any threat.

Casandra watched as they left and smiled at the Shield to assure him. Still looking at the retreating guardsmen, Casandra spoke to Rowyn in hushed tones. "We will give them a few more minutes and then head for the tent."

While they waited, Rowyn turned to look out across the fields, waiting for the Shield and guardsmen to clear, when he thought he glimpsed something over the forest. Something large that glinted in the fading sun. He only saw it for a moment before it was gone. He was turning to ask Casandra whether she had seen it when a sudden burning sensation flared down his back.

His body jerked and he fell into Casandra before collapsing to the ground, dragging her down diagonally across him. She lifted her head, just inches from his face, and looked into his eyes. Rowyn could hear her yelling for the Shield, but could not make out what she was saying. The fire disappeared, yet he couldn't move and just stared up at Casandra, trying to say something, anything, but his mind and throat just weren't working together.

This close he noticed that Casandra smelled like a flower. *Primrose, I think.* His mind found this funny considering his body wouldn't obey him. The sensation of heat began to rise and fall through his veins again, dragging his mind back to reality.

Not again. This hadn't happened since he was nine, and then again at twelve. Feared gripped his mind, but not for himself... he thought suddenly of his sister. The thought was short-lived as the heat spiked again, and his mind was consumed with the searing pain that went through every muscle and nerve in his body. He lay there, sure that his body was engulfed in flames and not able to do anything about it. Tears flooded his eyes as the colors on the edge of his vision faded and then it all disappeared in a black void.

14

Lor Cian

Casandra wiped the sweat off Rowyn's forehead. She had never trained with a healer, but once when the horse she was riding kicked one of the stable boys in the leg, she knew which bone had been fractured. Cleric Yoan had shown up and confirmed her diagnosis, though when he questioned her she couldn't explain to him how she knew. She had just touched the boy and could feel where the pain was coming from.

Cleric Yoan had only lifted an eyebrow. "Interesting… very interesting."

She put the back of her hand on her cousin's cheek. *He's still on fire.* As her hand rested on his cheek she sensed some manner of extreme heat, deeper and more intense than what she felt on his skin. She considered telling Ser Rhein that they should turn back in the morning and transport Rowyn to Cleric Yoan. But then the whole charade would be exposed and she couldn't fathom what would happen to Rowyn and Willoe when the king found out.

Yet Rowyn was not responding to anything she could think to do. She fretted that she might be putting Rowyn's life at risk even now by waiting until morning, but Dilys had convinced her to wait. The old maidservant was unusually calm, which baffled and somewhat angered Casandra, but Dilys wouldn't tell her why she felt it best to wait. Casandra was torn and wished that Rowyn would just wake up, but he just lay there, his breath shallow and his face damp with sweat.

Casandra let her hand linger for a moment and a sigh escaped her lips as she closed her eyes and thought of possible futures. She had grown up with Rowyn, but lately she had felt… she didn't know what. Her eyes popped open and she quickly pulled her hand back, then turned away from Rowyn as the tent flap was pushed back and Dilys entered. She carried two bowls of soup, the aroma making Casandra's mouth water. Casandra had no idea whether the guardsmen were any good at guarding, but she did know that at least one of them was a great cook. After Rowyn had been settled she had left him with Dilys and had gone to the privy. On her return she had seen the cook sizzling chunks of meat on a spit just above the campfire.

Dilys set the bowls down on the little fold-up table that had been packed as part of the tent's standard furnishings. Dilys was like an aunt to both Willoe and Casandra, being the only older woman at Castle Westhedge that the girls truly trusted. Casandra's mother would spend as much time as she could at Westhedge, but her first duty was at Castle Mount Somerled with Casandra's father.

"Come and eat, lassie." Dilys beckoned Casandra to sit. "Supper has come and gone. The boy be not helped by starving yourself." She looked over at Rowyn and said with confidence. "He be fine." As hard as she had tried, Casandra had never been able to find out where Dilys originated from, but from the servant's accent — so similar to Protector Dougal's — it sounded as if she had grown up along the northern borders.

"How can we know?" she snapped at the older woman. "You said your-self you did not know what to do." She hated the feeling of being out of control.

Dilys' constant smile gave Casandra some comfort. The maid finished setting up the spoon and cloth for Casandra to use. "Ye listen, but not hear. I nev'r said I did not know what to do..." She poured a goblet of fruit wine and put it next to the bowl. "I said I could not do anything." She patted the cushioned wooden chair to indicate for Casandra to come over.

Casandra stood up and started to say something, but felt a slight cramp in her right leg from sitting by Rowyn's cot. At least she had changed clothes earlier, donning riding pants and a long overshirt, belted at her waist, to replace the cumbersome and confining traveling dress she had worn during the day. The riding outfit gave her a little more flexibility and was more comfortable. She rubbed the cramp out and moved over to sit at the table. She inhaled deeply and just sat enjoying the aroma for a few mo-ments. The cook had thrown in some of the meat chunks along with sof-tened vegetables like onions. "But I do not see a difference," she said final-ly. She was still confused, but the stew smelled so good she picked up the silver spoon and scooped up a little.

As she sipped on the warm liquid, Dilys nodded her approval. "Oh, but there be, lassie. Quite a bit, as ye be seeing."

Dilys stepped behind her and stroked Casandra's head, just like her mother used to do. It made Casandra relax a little and the Burning Lady knew, she had been through enough today.

After a moment Dilys stepped back around and looked down at the ta-ble before her smile turned into a frown. "I be getting old as an Elf. I forgot the brown rolls. That guardsman do wonders with wholemeal and a little cinnamon."

She left the tent before Casandra could ask any further questions.

Casandra savored the simple meal and wondered why Dilys used such an allegory. The Elfs, if they still existed, were reported to be extremely old, but Casandra had never heard anyone compare their age to one. Dilys was surely one of the strangest people Casandra had ever met, but maybe that was some of why they all loved her so much.

She was getting used to the plain meals they ate on the trip. The Shield acted as if he had committed an offense against the kingdom, but he also took full blame for it, even though Casandra knew that one of the food trunks had been left behind by the guardsmen. Casandra didn't mind; she relished a change from the lush castle fare. She also appreciated the way the new Shield was always so very polite and attentive. Not to mention handsome, if one cared for a muscular body and a chiseled chin. She smiled as she pictured him.

Casandra dipped the spoon in several more times and as good as the stew was, her mind drifted back to the Shield. The spoon hung from her fingers as she rested her elbows on the table and propped her head on her hands. Looking over at Rowyn lying on the cot, she considered his features. He wasn't tall and handsome like Ser Rhein. He wasn't what one would call imposing, and nothing about him was even memorable. *Well, other than the hair and eyes*, she reminded herself. He wasn't witty like Aeron. In fact, he rarely talked, and when he did he was so serious. Except when he was with Aeron. Something about her brother and cousin's relationship brought out the little boy in Rowyn, and she found the impish side of him appealing. *Quit being a muddle-headed little farm girl*, she told herself as she shook her head. She needed to figure out how to help Rowyn, not waste time on whimsical dreams.

The sound of the tent flap being opened behind her interrupted her thoughts. Her mixed feelings momentarily forgotten, Casandra took another sip and commented with lightness in her voice, "The soup is delicious, Dilys. Come try it." When Dilys didn't answer, Casandra turned in her chair and saw standing in the tent entrance a man in dark blue robes. He stepped forward into the tent and she realized her mistake. It wasn't a man. He was a good head taller than any of the guardsmen, and the light of the tent's lanterns reflected off bright silver hair that hung down below his waist. But the eyes... To look in those eyes made Casandra feel as if she were looking into the chronicles of history itself. The most telling feature, however, had to be the long barbed ears protruding through his hair.

She had never met an Elf, and hadn't even been sure if they still existed. She had only seen a few drawings in old books which spoke of how the Elfs lived long lives and kept a youthful appearance. In contrast, this one had jowls that drooped a little and creases around his eyes. But what the books hadn't told her was the feeling of power that emanated from the older Elf. It wasn't overwhelming, but more akin to sitting near a warm fire on a cold night when you hadn't realized that it had become chilly.

Her chair fell back as she stood. She wasn't sure if she should yell for help, grab the knife strapped to her arm under her sleeve — something she had learned from Willoe — or curtsy to her mythical guest. Her mind was muddled with worry over Rowyn and the shock of meeting a creature she thought might only exist in the stories of old people and bards. *What exactly does one do when encountering an Elf?*

"Lady Casandra." His voice had a piercing, deep-toned sound which was in total contrast to what she associated with an older person… well, an older Elf. It resonated with authority. Then, to her surprise, he smiled — a big, open smile. He looked over at Rowyn. "Ah, this must be the young Prince." He walked over to the cot, his floor-length robe swirling as he walked. He looked down at the prone body. Without looking back, he asked, "How long has he been like this?" There wasn't any concern or worry in his voice.

"Ahh—" *Why was she even talking to this strange… this Elf?* "A few turns," she heard herself answer without thought. She walked over to stand behind the Elf, who did not take his eyes off Rowyn. "He just collapsed and has had a high fever ever since."

The Elf leaned over and touched Rowyn's forehead. His lips twisted and he stood back up. "I wonder."

Wonder what? She stared at his back as if she could will an answer from him, but he didn't say anything more.

The question on her lips was interrupted when Dilys entered with the rolls. Casandra turned to Dilys as the servant looked up and saw the Elf.

Dilys looked past Casandra as if she didn't exist and said, "Lor Cian".

He turned and smiled that smile again. "Oh, Lady Dilys," he said in a matter-of-fact tone, addressing her as an old friend. "I am pleased to see you again."

"And I as well ye," was all Willoe's maid said, confirming the familiarity.

"Dilys, you will continue to Highkeep. You will need glimmers." He turned back to Rowyn. "Like before."

"I had a mind to," Dilys answered and then turned to the table, righting the chair and straightening the bowls and spoons as if someone were still sitting there eating.

Casandra turned to glare at Dilys. Willoe's servant had the same outward appearance that Casandra had grown so accustomed to over the years, but Casandra could now sense something different about Dilys. Something like what she felt with the Elf. And why did the Elf call her 'Lady Dilys'? It all just added more questions to her befuddled mind. Then she realized what the Elf had told Dilys and she swung back around to face the Elf. "Glimmers? Excuse me… Lor Cian." So many questions were running through her mind. "Who is going where?" She looked at Dilys. "You know this… this Elf?" Casandra still couldn't believe this was all happening.

Dilys looked up from straightening and only nodded her head.

"How?"

Before Dilys could answer, Cian spoke. "Cian will do. Lor is a bit formal. Especially considering how close the three of us will become." The Elf turned back to Rowyn and bent down, putting his hands on either side of Rowyn's face.

Cian closed his eyes and Casandra noticed a slight tremble in the Elf's arm. After a few moments he removed his hands and slowly opened his eyes. Rowyn's body jerked once and in contrast to Cian's, Rowyn's eyes popped wide open. The center of the eye was bloodred, the rest of the eye filled with black.

Casandra, still slightly behind the Elf, started forward but Cian held up his hand without looking at her. She automatically froze, not sure why, but she didn't question the elderly Elf's authority.

Rowyn stared at the roof of the tent with balls of red and just as quickly as his eyes had opened, they closed.

Casandra was afraid he had gone back into the feverish sleep, but then he slowly re-opened his eyes and they were back to a bright green and looking normal again.

"Ah, good." Cian said softly and rubbed his hands together with pleasure. "Well, then—" He turned to look at Casandra. "We should be off."

Baffled, she stammered out several false starts and finally managed to say, "Are you just going to walk in here and then just leave us without any further explanation?"

Cian looked at her, his forehead wrinkled, and he responded with a slight annoyance in his voice. "No. Of course not. We are all going. Prince Rowyn, you, and I. We have a long way to go tonight and must get started." Casandra was still perplexed and, fabled Elf or not, she was starting to get angry and gritted her teeth. "We cannot go anywhere. He has a high fever." She was quickly regretting that she hadn't called for Ser Rhein the moment the Elf had entered.

Cian stepped aside and indicated Rowyn with his hand.

Suspicious, she stepped past the Elf — staring up at him as she went — and reached down to put the back of her hand on Rowyn's forehead, still keeping her eyes on the Elf.

Her head spun to look down at her cousin as she pulled her hand away like she had been stung. It was not at all what she expected. She put her hand back on his forehead and then ran it down both cheeks. *What has happened?* He was no longer feverish. She focused for a moment and no longer had a sense of something boiling inside, though there remained a consistent warmth of sorts within. She couldn't explain exactly what it was, but she sensed it was not a comforting warmth. Instead, she felt a simmering warmth that seemed as if it could bubble over at any moment. While she was still uneasy about the Elf, she had to admit it was a significant improvement from earlier.

Casandra heard Cian speak to Dilys.

"I will come by after we are settled in. If you need me before then I will look for your messenger." Giving up on trying to figure out the relationship between Dilys and the Elf, for now, Casandra, in a mocking tone, said, "Please do not take offense to my words, Lor Cian, but where do you plan to take us? The Prince is in no condition to go anywhere. A few moments ago he was burning up. He needs rest."

The Elf gave a slight chuckle and looked at Rowyn. "He's fine now."

As if on command, Rowyn started to sit up in his cot. He seemed a little wobbly at first, but then he stood up and stretched his arms like he had just risen from a long sleep.

"What happened?" He leaned his head to the right and then to the left, and twisted back and forth, stretching his neck.

"You collapsed in the middle of the road and your skin was so hot. It felt like you were on fire." She stepped nearer, looking at his face and into his bright green eyes to see if she could determine his condition. "We brought you into the tent." She still couldn't believe he had cooled off as much as he had in such a short time. "Then he — the Elf, that is — came in." She pointed an incriminating finger at Cian. "He says we are going somewhere with him, though he has not bothered to tell me where."

Rowyn stepped protectively between Casandra and Cian. She assumed he had never met an Elf before either, but there was no mistaking Cian for anything but an Elf.

His tone somewhat edgy, Rowyn asked bluntly, "Who are you?"

The Elf bowed slightly and said formally, "I am Cian, First Lor of the Shandelon." This meant exactly nothing to Casandra and, from Rowyn's expression, neither did it mean anything to him. "Prince Rowyn, we must go now," Cian said firmly, but respectfully.

Casandra had not thought about it before, but as he addressed Rowyn now she realized that the Elf had known it was Rowyn since entering the tent. He hadn't shown any hesitation or surprise. "How did you know he was Prince Rowyn and not Princess Willoe?"

He turned to Casandra, his eyes narrowed and spoke in the same annoyed tone he had used earlier, all the formality gone. "I am First Lor!" He turned back to Rowyn as if that had answered the question. "Now, if you will follow me—"

"Wait!" Rowyn nearly shouted. "We are not going anywhere with you, or anyone else." He squeezed his eyes shut several times, evidently still trying to clear his head and comprehend the situation. He continued in a commanding voice, so contrary to how she normally saw him that it surprised her. "I do not know who you are, but you will explain yourself or I shall call Shield Rhein and his troops to get to the truth of this."

Casandra wondered why the Shield hadn't already inquired what was going on with all the noise coming from the tent.

"Your escort will not be bothering us, but we really need to be on our way." The Elf was becoming adamant and irritated.

Casandra pictured the Shield and his guardsmen lying around the camp, butchered by hidden compatriots of Cian's. She gasped. "What did you do to them?"

Cian sighed deeply and murmured to himself before answering over his shoulder to her. "They are fine. Let's just say they will not miss this time." Cian reached out and touched Rowyn on the shoulder.

The Elf leaned in and whispered into Rowyn's ear, then pulled away, still touching Rowyn's shoulder.

Rowyn's eyes still appeared glazed, but his body seemed relaxed and his expression lax.

Cian leaned in and whispered again. This time, when he pulled away, Rowyn was staring ahead as if his mind were elsewhere.

"We are going with the Elf," Rowyn stated, his voice sounding strained, as he stared at Casandra.

Casandra looked at him in disbelief. *How could he have changed his mind so quickly and why is he so willing to go now?*

Cian turned and headed for the tent flaps with Rowyn following obediently like a little pup.

As Cian walked past Casandra she reached out and grabbed his arm. She was not about to go without more information and wasn't going to let Rowyn leave either, regardless of his abrupt change of mind. As she touched the Elf's arm she felt a soothing warmth flood her body, along with a sense of calm and wellbeing. She yanked back her hand and looked at it, turning it over. The feeling began to subside, but some residue remained.

Cian stopped and turned to her. "I mean you and Prince Rowyn no harm, Casandra Cadwal. There is no time to explain now. You must trust me."

Her eyes closed and she thought, *Even if he is an Elf, how can I trust someone I just met?* Every thought passing through her head said no. She opened her eyes, realized she had been holding her breath, let it out and looked directly into his deep eyes. Against everything logic said, her gut, her instincts, her feminine intuition told her to trust. "I will go with you, Elf," she said sternly. "But I still expect answers… soon."

His lips turned up in a smile. "You are truly everything I have been led to believe." Then he lifted the tent flap and stepped outside.

Now what did he mean? Who do I know who could have told the Elf anything about me? And what was it that he had been led to believe? This was just so confusing. She grabbed Rowyn's cloak, then started to follow them outside. At the last moment she picked up the book Uncle Brom had given her for Rowyn.

She stomped down the porch steps, putting the book into the pocket of her jacket, but at the foot of the steps she stopped short, coming face-to-face with Ser Rhein. He was at the bottom of the hastily constructed steps and was apparently ready to step up the stairs.

She had almost slammed into his chest. "Oh, sorry—" she started to apologize, but then realized he was staring right past her, up to the tent entrance. She followed his gaze, saw nothing, and turned back, finally noticing that he had not moved. She waved a hand in front of his face and he didn't even blink, though she could feel his breath on her hand. It was as if he were frozen in place. Looking past him she saw that the guardsmen were not asleep nor injured, as she had thought a possibility, but were all about the camp in different states, frozen in the dark of the night. Two were out on the perimeter as if walking sentry, the cook was wiping out a pot, and a couple of other guardsmen were at the horse line. She noticed that even the horses were also suspended in place. Other guardsmen were in the midst of some ordinary function, frozen in mid-step. She looked at Cian, who had stopped and turned back to face her when she stopped. Her face must have shown the confusion she felt.

"They are fine. When we leave they will continue as if no time has passed," Cian assured her.

"But what happens when they find out we are gone?" This was beyond anything she could conceive.

Dilys stepped out of the tent and onto the small temporary porch, closed both eyes tightly, made a sweeping circle with both arms and finished by bringing both hands together in a clap in the air. The air next to Dilys shimmered and then an image of Casandra and Willoe appeared.

"Glimmers," Cian said without further explanation.

Dilys pulled back the tent flap and the glimmers entered. She nodded, then entered the tent herself, dropping the flap.

Casandra stared at the tent, her mouth open. She turned back to see Cian and Rowyn already on the road headed north. She watched Cian and Rowyn's retreating backs and then looked once again at the tent. *Willoe and Aeron will never believe this*, she thought as she spun and ran after Cian and Rowyn, catching up with them on the road as the mist settled in. A light wind blew over her skin as she glanced over her shoulder at the camp, the late-night breeze ruffling the edges of the tent. She put Rowyn's cloak over his shoulders, then the other one over her own. She walked next to him as they headed toward a clump of trees at a bend in the road. She wondered if she would ever see her brother and Willoe again, and if she did, she didn't even know what she would tell them – as she had no idea where she was going and what she would be doing. It only reminded her that their fate was in the hands of the Elf, and he had not shown her a reason to trust him. She was resolved to keep a keen eye on Cian, and at the first sign he may be a threat to them, she would do what she must to protect Rowyn, Elf or no.

15

Kata-heni

The Shield, Rhein, couldn't remember why he had stopped at the bottom of the stairs. He was on his way to see if Princess Willoe's condition had changed. He planned to suggest to Lady Casandra that they turn back to Castle Westhedge in the morning. At the same time he couldn't keep his mind off the young Lady Casandra. It wasn't just her beauty, though he had to admit she was one of the most stunning women he had ever met; he was more impressed with how she handled herself. Formidable and adept. When Princess Willoe fainted on the road, Lady Casandra didn't wither and fall apart like many women he knew would have. Instead, she gave orders like a veteran sergeant.

The only word that came to Rhein's mind, when he thought of her, was *intoxicating*. He even just now imagined he had been only inches from her face and his mind even conjured up her scent. *Primroses*, he thought. But that was impossible. He reminded himself that she was a noble, and not just any noble, but the daughter of the First Duke, and he just a newly initiated Shield. Berating himself for such foolish thoughts, he stood a little taller and walked up to the porch. "Lady Casandra?" he called into the tent.

Dilys lifted the flap and stepped out. "Ser Rhein. Can we help you?"

"I desire to talk with Lady Casandra. I would ask how Princess Willoe is faring. Is there anything Lady Casandra requires?"

"Everything be well," Dilys assured him. "Princess Willoe has fully recovered. She nae be use to such a long ride in the carriage. The excitement of the journey be a wee bit draining." Dilys smiled. "You know how it be with young women sometimes."

Rhein did not. But he was also afraid that the next couple of days' ride would be just as long and tiring. How would the Princess fare?

In answer to the unasked question, Dilys added with a widening smile, "She be fine the rest of the trip."

"Then if there is nothing else you require—" He wanted to make sure they did not want for anything.

"No, we be settled in for the night." She held the flap back a little and Rhein could see the two women seated around the table sipping from cups. Princess Willoe turned her head and smiled at him, then quickly turned back to her cup. "We be ready at daybreak. Princess Willoe be anxious to get to Highkeep." Dilys dropped the tent flap, dismissing Rhein.

The Shield nodded to the tent cover and turned to walk back down the steps. Everything seemed fine, he thought, but he had a strange feeling. He had advanced in the king's personal guard not only because of his skill with weapons and his leadership ability, but the fact that he relied on his gut more often than not, often with remarkable results. Nothing was out of place, but he decided to keep his eyes open for something, anything, out of the ordinary.

The dense clump of trees — the remainder of the forest that once covered the entire land, including the fields — effectively hid any view of the camp. Once around the bend, Cian stopped and turned toward the trees. A rustle in the brush soon approached and three large creatures stepped out. They reminded Casandra of mountain lions, even down to the black spots over the eyes, but the biggest mountain lions she had ever seen would be like cubs to these creatures. They were enormous. Two were a light brown and the third one red. They sauntered out of the trees toward the three of them. Casandra and Rowyn, even in his stupor, pulled back at their approach.

The lead one walked straight up to Cian. Casandra could see the powerful muscles ripple under the thick fur. Unable to move, she could only watch as the creature moved to within an arms length of Cian and then, to her surprise, it leaned its head down and nuzzled against Cian's head. Cian reached up and scratched it behind the ear.

"Please mount the Kata-heni." Cian indicated the other two creatures. "We have a long hard ride to reach safety."

It was then that Casandra noticed that each animal had a light blanket laid across its back with a small leather saddle and stirrups. The two beasts came over toward them, the red one to Rowyn and the last one to Casandra. As it neared her it let out a low growl that made her jump back.

"Lydenna!" Cian chided the creature. "We don't have time for such foolishness."

The beast, Lydenna, turned to look back at Cian and then back to Casandra. She could swear the animal had a smile on its face. It circled around Casandra so she could get a good look, as if it were showing off for her. It was a little shorter at the shoulders than the palfrey she normally rode, but it was bulkier, with muscles that surged and flowed as it sauntered around her. It came to a stop sideways in front of Casandra and lowered to the ground on its stomach with paws folded under.

Cian explained that they should straddle the small saddle and without a pommel or reins Cian told them to just hold onto the thick fur on the back of the neck.

Hesitantly, she threw a leg over, grabbed a handful of skin and fur, and pulled herself up into the saddle. Lydenna began to rise and Casandra had to hold on and shift her weight to stay upright as the animal's upper body rose first, followed by the rear. The strange creature began to move around in a circle again, stopped, and then a voice popped into Casandra's head. She knew it wasn't just her imagination as the strange voice even sounded different. It had a raw feeling to it. *Move back—legs. Blocked.*

Baffled, she finally noticed Lydenna looking back at her. A voice that was her own said, *This is crazy.* Regardless, she scooted back just a little and realized she could now put her feet in the stirrups more comfortably. Was it her imagination again or did Lydenna smile?

Before Casandra could consider what her mind tried to tell her, the creature turned its head forward and started to follow Cian as he moved slowly down the road on his Kata-heni. Casandra tried to adjust to the strange movement of Lydenna, as it differed from what she was use to with a horse. She quickly realized why she had needed to move back. Unlike her normal mare, Lydenna was more muscular. Casandra could easily see now that where her knees had originally been located would impair the movement of the creature's front shoulder blades when it was moving at more than a walk.

"Are you ready?" Cian called back to Casandra and Rowyn.

"Since you will not tell me where we are going…" she called up to him. "Can you at least tell me why?"

Cian turned to look back at her with a wide smile, one that she was becoming accustomed to. "Why, I thought you would have gathered that by now."

She stared at him, a little perplexed.

"To train me." Rowyn's voice behind her was a surprise, seeing as he had still been sluggish when she had looked in his direction last.

She glanced back and he was seated on the third Kata-heni, staring at her.

"Is he going to make you into a wizard?" she asked aloud.

Cian laughed for the first time and she turned back to the Elf. "No, no. He isn't a wizard at all."

Again she was stunned. *If not a wizard, then what?*

"He is so much more than a wizard." Cian's laughter faded, but the smile remained. He said something to his mount that spurred it to take off at a comfortable run. Holding on to Lydenna's fur, Casandra quickly felt the rhythm of the creature's loping stride and leaned forward as Lydenna took off after Cian's mount.

As they began to pick up more speed, Cian turned to look over his shoulder and with a hearty laugh yelled back to her, "You, on the other hand, are going to make a most delightful wizard." Then all three mounts raced down the road faster than any horse she had ever ridden. Casandra held on tightly, her mind reeling.

16

Man-at-Arms

Only four days on the road and Willoe had already learned that the life of a man-at-arms didn't quite live up to the glamorous world she had envisioned. Even without the hulking armor, the lighter gambeson and surcoat, the hefty leather belt, heavy cotton cloak, and other gear were a lot heavier than her normal raiment. Most of the dresses she usually wore, even in layers, were made of lightweight fabrics like silk or linen. Even in the winter, the heavier combed wool dresses and furred capes were worn for short times when she would need to be outside, which was seldom.

But she had never had to wear any of her dresses in the saddle from nearly dawn to dusk.

She shifted in her saddle and Aeron leaned over. "What's wrong?"

"Nothing." But even though she denied it she couldn't sit still.

"Tell me what's going on." Aeron moved his horse closer so he could whisper.

"My thighs." She hated to have to explain, but she was at straws end. "They are chapped. From all the riding."

"That is strange." Aeron looked thoughtful. "The breeks should prevent that from happening."

"The breeks?" Willoe snapped her head and glanced over. "They were too thick and baggy."

Aeron roared with laughter, which only made Willoe angry.

She had tried on Rowyn's breeks before leaving Westhedge, but they were heavy and hung to her knees. She much preferred her tighter cotton undergarments. She had figured no one would see what she wore under her leggings so it made no difference.

In between burst of laughter he told her, "They are baggy and thick for a reason." Aeron shook his head. "The breeks are loose so they adjust as you move with the rhythm of the horse, and they are thick to pad your thighs to help prevent chapping."

Willoe mumbled unhappily – defeated by her own logic.

"Here, try these on." They were in their tent and Aeron was handing her a pair of his breeks. She wasn't thoroughly convinced, but the rash was becoming unbearable.

She took the breeks, holding them out with both hands and crunching up her nose. Then, still holding the breeks, she motioned for him to turn around. "Don't look."

"Don't worry, I won't." He turned his back to her.

"I know, you only have eyes for a certain raven-haired lady." Willoe smirked.

"I do not—" Aeron began to turn back.

"Aeron!" she screamed.

He stopped and turned away. "I find her entertaining, but I have no interest in her."

"Why then, every time Captain Harte calls for a break, during the day, you happen to find yourself by her carriage? And where do you disappear to after supper?"

"I—" he began to disagree, then changed the subject. "Are you ready?"

"Yes."

"Follow me." He turned and lifted the tent flap, then walked out.

She tagged along behind him as they approached the supply tent. Supply Sergeant Trystan stood in the light of a lamp, going through a crate.

"Sergeant Trystan." Aeron spoke as they came up to the sergeant. "I was wondering if you had any of that ointment for rashes?"

"That I do, Lord Aeron." The sergeant started to go through another crate.

"Do we really need the ointment?" Willoe whispered from behind Aeron.

"Do you want to get rid of the rash?"

She nodded, even though she knew he couldn't see.

"Here you go." The sergeant pulled a small jar out of the crate he had been rummaging through. "Just what you are looking for. Marigold petals prepared with clarified fat. My mother's own recipe."

He handed it to Aeron, who thanked the sergeant and headed back to the tent.

That night, when Aeron went off after supper, Willoe applied the ointment. She sighed as soon as she put it on. She was glad she had listened to him about the balm. Grudgingly she admitted to herself that in some things he was just wiser than she, but when it came to the Franchon woman, she was sure he had lost his senses. What was going to happen if Mael found out?

Willoe couldn't sleep and woke early. Aeron still slept and it wouldn't help her to wake him. After a week she had gotten accustomed to riding all day and Sergeant Trystan's ointment had made it almost enjoyable, but she still had trouble sleeping at night, even though worn from the long days in the saddle. The Burning Lady's words still haunted Willoe. She had not yet discovered anything about the promise her ancestors had made and was worried she wouldn't know when the time was right to find the Lady in the Woods, or where to find her. *No wonder sleep doesn't come*, she thought, shaking her head. The thoughts just wouldn't settle.

She dressed and lifted the tent flap, stepping outside into the cold morning air. She pulled up the hood of her cloak and strode to the nearest campfire.

"I will get food." The page Tomos handed her a cup of warmed, spiced wine, then excused himself and headed off to the supply tent where the cooks would have something to break the soldiers' fast.

Willoe stood there sipping at the wine, holding the mug in both hands. The simmer in her body kept her from being too cold, but the heat and spicy taste of the wine gave her a different kind of warmth.

She scanned the camp, watching the servants and many of the guardsmen prepare to break camp.

She turned around and nearly dropped her wine when three naked wet men ran toward her. They were laughing and came at the campfire. Her first thought was to run, but before she could convince her body to move, the men had arrived and stood with their backs to the fire. She tried to keep her eyes cast down at the ground. She lifted one eye, having never seen a man's buttocks, and realized it wasn't much different than a woman's, though she wondered if they were all as hairy as these.

One of the men turned around and Willoe put her head fully down.

"Sorry, my lord." The man was still chuckling. "We thought a quick dip in the stream might take some of the grime off. Obliged you sharing your fire."

She kept her eyes down and could see the man's feet as he stepped closer.

"Are you well, lord?"

One of the things Aeron had taught her was that a gentleman, one of a noble birth, would always look someone in the eyes, whether an equal or someone from a lower class. To do otherwise would be considered dishonorable.

Squeezing the cup tightly with both hands, she looked up into the man's eyes. She recognized him as one of Captain Harte's guardsmen.

"Prince Rowyn." The guardsman was a little taken aback. "I... I mean, we—"

"The road has been hard on us all, Guardsman." She hoped her cheeks were not turning red; her face felt flushed. Not from the fire inside, but the embarrassment.

"We only meant to cleanse the filth." The guardsman seemed both flustered and startled.

"I wish more would follow your lead." She tried to smile, but didn't think it came off well. "The horses are beginning to smell better than the men."

"That's the truth, your Highness." The man laughed. The other two men had turned around and Willoe took a deep breath, keeping her eyes straight ahead.

"If it please your Highness, we need to get dressed and make report to our sergeant." The man continued to smile.

"Do not let it be said that I kept the Captain's guardsmen from their duty."

"Thank you, your Highness." All three guardsmen saluted, fist to chest, then ran off toward another part of the camp.

Willoe couldn't help but watch. She had a strange feeling in her stomach and wondered if her noble husband would look as good. The thought only brought back what awaited her upon her return to Westhedge and she frowned when she saw the page returning with a full platter. It was only day four. Suddenly, food did not appeal to her.

17

Blood Stalkers

They had ridden all night and through much of the next day, heading north. Eventually they slowed and Cian led them off the main road until they reached a small clearing in a wooded area near a stream. Rowyn slid off his over-sized mountain lion, the one Cian called Moya, and stomped over to the Elf, who had already dismounted. The only thing that had kept Rowyn from grabbing Casandra and turning back to the camp was Cian's whispered comment 'I have been sent to train you... by your uncle.' That, and the fact that jumping off a racing Kata-heni would have been like taking a fall from a galloping horse... off a high cliff. Rowyn had been going over and over it in his mind during the long night's ride, and while he would do almost anything to avoid confrontations, he was determined to find out from Cian exactly what the Elf intended and how he knew Uncle Brom.

Rowyn approached Cian just as the Elf was turning from his Kata-heni.

Rowyn held up a finger to start making his point when Cian said first, "Well, I believe we evaded them. I think we should eat something while the Katas water. We have another long ride ahead of us before we reach my home." He grinned and the corner of his eyes creased as he continued, "I know you probably have a lot of questions, but they are best answered when we reach Fayhaven." Cian turned back to the Kata-heni, untied a bag of food from the back of the saddle and then walked over to drop it in the middle of the clearing. Once released, the Kata-heni loped off after Rowyn's.

"Evade who?" Rowyn was startled by Cian's comment.

Cian casually commented, "The Blood Stalkers, of course."

"Blood Stalkers?"

"Yes." Cian turned back to Rowyn as he placed the bag on the ground,

137

pursed his lips and shook his head. "Very nasty creatures. They are small." He held out his hand level with his waist. "It is easy to identify a Blood Stalker. They have blazing red eyes and a long white beard."

"I know a Tink. Drel Donlin. He may be irritating, but I wouldn't think of him as a threat." Drel Donlin was about the same height as the Elf indicated.

"Some folks mistake Blood Stalkers for Waljantinks, but they are nothing alike. Drel Donlin. Yes, quite an interesting Waljantink. Did you know that he once faced a mountain troll—" He stopped and seemed to consider something, then continued. "Maybe for another time."

Of course he would know the Tink if he knows Uncle Brom. The thought reminded Rowyn of the reason he had wanted to question Cian to begin with. He wanted some answers, but Cian kept talking, leaving Rowyn no chance to speak.

"We were talking about Blood Stalkers, were we not? I said people mistook them for Waljantinks, but that could be the last mistake they made. Blood Stalkers wear boots made from iron, but it does not slow them down. They are nearly as quick as a Waljantinks." Cian pulled an assortment of cold meats, breads, and other foods out of the bag. It seemed like it was much more than could have fit into the bag, and he was still pulling out more bits of food.

Rowyn had to think for a moment before he remembered Uncle Brom using the name Waljantink once instead of Tinks, like everyone else. "They have claws for hands, like an eagle, that they use to rend flesh. They also have large teeth, more like fangs that they can use along with the claws. But they normally don't use those until after they bring down their victim with a pikestaff. The claws are long and wrap around the stick as if designed for the pikestaff." He smiled with a soft laugh. "Nature is funny that way. But the main reason they are called Blood Stalkers is that they hunt their victims like hounds. Once they get the scent they are hard to avoid. Did I mention that they stain their hats with the blood of their victims? Very interesting, if rather a crude habit."

"No, you did not." Rowyn tried unsuccessfully to keep his voice from rising.

He tried to control the fear in his voice. "Why are they after us and how do you know they are not nearby?"

"Oh, they are not chasing after *us*. They just want you."

Rowyn froze. Casandra walked up, her own Kata-heni already gone off looking for water like the others. She looked past Rowyn at the Elf, then back at Rowyn. "What do you think?" Traveling as Willoe, Rowyn had no weapons with him and the vision of a short white-bearded man with blood dripping from claws and fangs seemed like a fairly reasonable deterrent. Rowyn also had no idea what the Elf might do if they tried to leave. At the same time, Rowyn's curiosity was piqued by what Cian had said.

"I am not sure we have much choice at the moment," he told Casandra with a frown. "We do not know where we are. We have no supplies, and no way of returning to camp. Did you hear what he said about the Blood Stalkers?"

She twisted her lips as if in thought and finally said, "Have you ever seen a Blood Stalker or even heard of them before?"

Rowyn couldn't say he had. Was the old Elf just trying to scare them into staying with him? Rowyn had to smile to himself as he had to admit that it had worked, at least on him.

Casandra seemed to take it all in stride and seemed to have made some sort of decision. "But you are right about the other things. And who knows, he might not be lying. In that case, let us eat. Do you see all the food he is pulling out of that bag? Marvelous!" She gave him a big smile and shrugged — he had not noticed before that she shared her brother's habit — and then she walked toward Cian saying, "I am starved." She sat down next to Cian and started talking politely with the Elf as she picked at the food in front of them.

Rowyn sat next to Casandra, but looked at Cian. "How do you know—"

"Try this fruit…" Cian held out something wrapped in a cloth.

Rowyn's stomach growled and he took the bundle, then unwrapped it and saw three unblemished plums huddled in the bottom of the cloth.

"The season is over for these. How did you get them?" Rowyn picked up and bit into a ruby red fruit. A trickle of juice ran down his chin.

"Row." Casandra reached over and wiped his chin with a cloth she had tucked into her sleeve. "You should spend more time with Steward Robat."

"It is from Fayhaven." Cian just smiled as Rowyn took another bite.

Rowyn finished one and picked up another. He didn't know where Fayhaven was, but the plums were delicious; not overly sweet, but juicy the way he liked them. At least he could now put a name to where they were headed, but he still had quite a few additional questions for the Elf.

He let the last plum sit while he turned so he could face Cian. He straightened his back and clenched his jaw, then leaned forward and wagged his finger toward the Elf. He wasn't going to move from this spot until he got his answers. His mouth opened, but before any words could come out a loud squeal resounded from somewhere in the forest. It was like that of a pig, but low-pitched, deep and chilling.

Cian leapt to his feet, the food on his lap flying off, a roll hitting Rowyn on the forehead and some sort of sauce splashing onto his cloak.

"Are you mad?" Rowyn rose quickly and looked down at the stain, brushing at it with one hand. He looked back up to continue his rebuke, but the Elf was already ten paces away toward the stream.

"Lydenna, Moya, Anyon," Cian called out to the Kata-henis. He spun around to Rowyn and Casandra, who had also stood up. "We need to mount and make haste."

Rowyn looked to Casandra; she stared at Cian, her frightful expression turning his spine to ice.

"What's wrong?" she demanded.

Instead of answering, he hastily reached out and pointed a hand at Rowyn and Casandra. Blue light bolted from his fingertips, flying between Rowyn and Casandra. They both dove to the side, away from the bolt, landing on the ground, Rowyn on his back.

"Auggg!" A deep voice came from behind them.

Rowyn rolled over to stare at the soles of steel boots, not five paces away. He got to his knees and stood.

Casandra was scrambling to her feet and looking back at the smoldering man lying on the ground. *No*, Rowyn thought, as his eyes took in the short creature with claws and fangs... and a red hat. It was a Blood Stalker.

The wail of many squeals flooded the air.

The Kata-henis raced into the clearing, each heading toward its rider. The animals did not take time to lower; Cian leapt onto his Kata-heni's back and Casandra, a much better rider than Rowyn, scurried up into her saddle. Rowyn tried to jump and grab the upper edge of Moya's saddle, but missed and he fell back to the ground.

He started to rise when a harsh grunt sounded right behind him. He turned and ducked as the blade of a pikestaff swung just above his head. He move to the side, away from his Kata-heni and the Blood Stalker. The Blood Stalker brought the pikestaff around in a circle again and Rowyn had to fall on his back to avoid being opened at the chest.

Rowyn was so scared he could feel the bile rising in his throat. He and the Blood Stalker were separated from the Elf — and his power — by the Kata-heni.

The half-sized man raised the blade to bring it down in a chopping motion. The Blood Stalker was too close for Rowyn to roll away and he had no weapon with which to defend himself. Then something flared. Like on the road to Highkeep, but this time it didn't paralyze him. A voice... no, not a voice, but a sensation, cried out urgently in his mind 'Give yourself over to us.' He did.

Both of Rowyn's hands suddenly pointed up at the Blood Stalker and the creature flew through the air to bounce off of Rowyn's Kata-heni. The animal dropped its head and bit at the Blood Stalker's neck. Red spurted as the half-sized man screamed. The Kana-heni clawed at the Blood Stalker until he stopped moving.

Struggling, Rowyn climbed to his feet and stared at his hands. He still felt a warmth in his blood, but the fire waned.

"Row." The pressing tone of Casandra's voice broke through his stupor.

"Hurry, Cian says more are coming."

He move quickly toward Moya, jumping over the chewed and shredded body of the Blood Stalker. This time he was able to pull himself into the saddle and dig his fingers into the skin of Moya's neck as he had been taught.

The animal turned and all three Kata-henis raced out of the clearing, through a clump of trees, and emerged into a large field. They didn't stop but picked up speed as they dashed across broken fields of dirt and brush. Twice they passed through small woods, each time coming out into more fields. They had been at it for several turns of the glass; Rowyn was barely able to stay on his Kata-heni as they leapt across crevices and over rocky outcroppings.

Every time Rowyn could safely glance over his shoulder — which was seldom — he could see splotches of red in the distance. He looked again and he could actually make out more than a dozen of the Blood Stalkers closing in on them, with more behind.

"They're gaining!" Rowyn yelled up to Cian just ahead, with Casandra between them. He could feel the bile rising again, but he swallowed hard, forcing it back down.

"Just a little farther," Cian shouted back. "The forest is just ahead." He pointed to a large forest on the horizon that stretched far to their left and right.

How could more trees help them? They had passed through them twice and it did not seem to have slowed down the vile creatures. The squealing was getting louder and Rowyn was afraid to turn around. It was well into dusk and as he looked once more over his shoulder, he could barely make out any of their pursuers. The sounds pursuing them, however, assured him the Blood Stalkers were right on their heels.

"Hurry, we are almost there!" Cian shouted without turning around.

Rowyn lifted his head and saw the edge of the forest in front of them. It was lit up with a thousand lights, like the lights in the sky.

The harsh squeals sounded as if they were right behind Rowyn. He leaned forward over Moya's neck, willing the creature to move faster.

Cian disappeared through an opening in the trees that Rowyn had not even seen until the Elf vanished into the lighted path. Casandra was next and then Rowyn followed, the branches and wide leaves slapping at him as he entered. He realized the light was coming from shining trees scattered throughout the woods.

As he rode through the bright leafy screen, his Kata-heni slid to a halt, nearly dislodging Rowyn. Cian and Casandra sat motionless, their Kata-henis facing him.

"Why did you stop? They're right behind me!" Rowyn yelled, wondering whether they had lost their minds. He looked over his shoulder as the two frontmost of the Blood Stalkers neared the entrance to the path. He slammed his feet into Moya's sides, but the Kata-heni just turned so that Rowyn was facing the oncoming Blood Stalkers.

Rowyn's eyes went wide and he called loudly over his shoulder, "Cian!"

"Watch," was all Cian said.

In the light of the trees Rowyn watched the two eager Blood Stalkers race into the pathway, their pikestaffs held in front of them as they charged forward. Rowyn cringed; he could make out their fangs and the gnashing of their teeth, glinting sharply in the light of the shimmering woods. He could swear he saw blood dripping from their long, funnel-shaped hats.

He closed one eye and turned his head to watch from the side. He kicked Moya again and pulled at the skin on her neck, but she only growled angrily.

The first of the short killers was less than a dozen paces from Rowyn, the creature's feet moved at an incredible speed. Rowyn lifted out of the saddle, turning to leap off, but paused again, not sure what he would do once on the ground.

A scream made him turn back. The first of the Blood Stalkers was hanging in the air, several branches poking through its body, blood dripping from the wounds. As Rowyn watched, another branch dropped down from the forest canopy and wrapped around the second Blood Stalker's neck. He was lifted off the ground as he struggled to break free. The newly lifted Blood Stalker clawed at the branches. One of the large boughs swung out of the forest and slammed into the creature. When it swung back, the Blood Stalker swayed limply from the branch. Blood dripped from dozens of little punctures and Rowyn couldn't even make out its face. A lone fang dropped to the ground.

"This is the Greenwald Forest." Cian's voice came from behind.

Rowyn turned to Cian and Casandra. "I don't understand." Then he realized where he was. The homeland of the Elfs.

"No one enters Greenwald without the permission of the Elfs." Cian grinned. He started to turn his Kana-heni around. "No rush now. We can stop up ahead, eat and rest, then make Fayhaven by morning."

"Wait." Rowyn was starved and the thought of resting sounded wonderful, but he had to know at least one thing first. "I thought you said we had evaded them?" He failed to keep outright anger from his tone.

Cian looked over his shoulder, his grin broadening. "I guess I was wrong." Then he turned; his Kata-heni leaped a fallen tree in the path, and he continued down the trail.

Casandra laughed, a hearty opened-mouth laugh. She shook her head, then smiled before turning to follow Cian. "Let's go, Lydenna. Please go around the tree." She didn't spur the animal or make any other movement that Rowyn could see, but her Kata-heni started forward and walked carefully around the edge of the fallen tree.

Rowyn spurred Moya, who loped ahead and instead of following Casandra, jumped the tree, bouncing Rowyn in the saddle with a grunt. He groaned and then heard his Kata-heni make a new rumbling sound. Certainly it was impossible, but the sound was akin to what he imagined a laugh would sound like if filtered through a growl.

18

Fayhaven

The Kata-henis slowed when Cian called out, "My home is ahead."

It was daybreak of another day and even with the short rest, Rowyn was worn thin. "My back feels as I have been stretched on the Rack," he complained to his cousin as he twisted in his saddle, lifting and wiggling his shoulders.

"Maybe you need to talk to Moya about that," Casandra suggested. "Maybe she can help you with your balance."

"What?"

"Send thoughts to your Kata-heni. That's what I do with Lydenna."

"They wouldn't understand. They're just animals. And even if they did, I can't send my thoughts through the air. They are in my mind, not something I can transfer outside of my head." He wished Casandra would try to be serious.

Moya changed step and Rowyn bounced forward, groaning as he hit against the Kata-heni's neck. The rumbling sound could be heard coming from the big cat as before.

Was Casey just being silly? How could he send his thoughts to another creature? A smirk crossed his face. She must be jesting. 'What do you think Moya? Does she take me for an idiot?' He formed the thoughts clearly in his mind, but felt silly doing so. Rowyn leaned back a little in the saddle and laughed until a voice entered his mind, not of his making. 'You are.'

He almost fell out of the saddle, his heart stopping for a moment as he stared down at the Kata-Heni. "You talked."

'No.' The voice came again. 'Spirit-link.'

"Spirit-link?"

"Yes," Casandra answered to his spoken words. "If you have the talent you can talk with some of the more perceptive creatures. It makes sense. Both we and the Kata-henis are children of the Burning Lady's Spirit, so why shouldn't we be able to communicate through our common link?"

His mind reeled. He just stared at her back. She had said it like it was an everyday occurrence. Talking with animals. It seemed like everything he had thought was turned upside down.

'Slide back,' Moya told him.

He did and found that he was in rhythm with the Kata-heni's movements and he didn't bounce as often, providing a smoother ride.

'Why didn't you tell me about this before?' He still thought it strange to be talking to his mount, particular one that could devour him if it desired.

The animal just rumbled its strange laughter again and continued its loping stride.

Cian edged back to just in front of them, turning to talk over his shoulder as his Kata-heni glided along the path. "My home is around the bend." Rowyn was picturing a small hut secluded amongst the trees. Elfs were all about nature, after all. Weren't they? *Probably a little hovel we will have to share with an assortment of small forest creatures.*

Not known for being forceful, Rowyn nevertheless was determined to find out what had happened to him back at the camp. And again with the Blood Stalker. He could still remember the fever-like sensation that had flooded his body. The power that had surged through his muscles. And the voice. He suddenly tied that to what Casandra had said and what he had just experienced with Moya. Had someone, or something, Spirit-linked with him? He was used to analyzing the mysterious until he came up with a rational answer, but he needed information first, and Cian seemed to be the only available source.

Cian continued on the tree-lined path. "You need to learn control."

What was it that he needed to control? Rowyn was sure it was related to what had happened to him, but since he didn't know what had happened, he had even less of an idea of what controlling it entailed. But what was it Cian had said to Casandra? *You are going to make a most delightful wizard.* That was just as strange to Rowyn as his own situation, if not more. Casandra had never shown any magical talents, nor even any interest in the Spirit world, at least that he was aware of. Though when he thought of it, neither had he.

As Rowyn considered all these contradictions, Cian said, "Welcome to my home, Fayhaven."

They passed through a leafy screen, and found themselves on a small rise where both Casandra and Rowyn could only stare, dumbfounded, as their Kata-heni continued to walk slowly toward the Elf's home.

Below them stood a vast valley that stretched for several miles to either side and disappeared over a small hill a few miles ahead of them. Near them was a house. That was not right. It was more like a manor. Cian's home had three levels, but it was unlike any manor Rowyn had ever seen. To either side were rows of great oak trees that marched from front to back.

"Look at the trees. Have you ever seen anything like that before?" What drew Rowyn's attention wasn't that the trees towered over the three levels, but the hundreds of large intertwining branches spreading out from the trees all across the front of the manor, like the wooden braces used at the castle. "And the stones. They look like marble." Along with the branches there were different stones inlaid into the wall giving it a colorful appearance. It looked to be marble with streaks of orange, blue, rose, yellow and dozens of other colors lined on the bright white background. "So many colors." He had to remember to breathe.

The wood appeared as if it had grown into shapes to meet the needs of the building. In place of the protective arrow slits and guarded window casements that were common for most manors in Cainwen, multiple branches snaked along, leaving massive openings across the upper levels of the building's front. These openings held large sheets of colored glass with some tilted open to add to the airy feeling. Rowyn couldn't see, but imagined the sides of the manor were similarly constructed. The blending of wood, marble, and glass, with the airy construction, made it seem like it had one day all of sudden decided to raise itself up from the ground as part of the landscape.

"It is beautiful," Casandra commented next to him. He could hear her gasp as he imagined she noticed one piece after another of the manor's strange construction, as he had.

There weren't any surrounding protective walls, just a manicured grassy carpet that stretched from the forest's edge to the front of the main house and disappeared around the sides. Large weepy trees bordered a path that ran down the middle toward the manor's entrance and extended outward to create a small grove. The visual effect was stunning.

"The flowers," she said and he looked over to see her smiling brightly.

Outside the manor's green skirt, the rest of the meadow contained wild flowers, planted fields, and assorted clumps of trees. To the side of the manor Rowyn could see other smaller houses that he assumed were a cook house, barn, and other common structures. Beyond the manor, leading down into the valley, were also many smaller houses that were each encircled in a lush green framework similar to the manor house. All of them had trees on either side of the houses with marble accents and open airy architecture. The trees varied in size depending on the size of the structure as if they grew to meet the needs of each house.

They reached the edge of the groomed area and all three Kata-heni lowered to the ground so Cian, Casandra and Rowyn could dismount. Three Drel Donlin look-alikes came up and bowed to Cian. They gave him some type of formal greeting that Cian returned, and then the Elf said, "Ah, Drel Firil, thank you." Without a word the Tinks removed the small saddles and, with a nod from Cian, the Kata-heni loped off around the corner of the manor to wherever they called home.

Cian signaled for Casandra and Rowyn to follow, then he started to stroll down the path toward the manor's entrance.

Rowyn cringed as he stretched his legs from all the riding, but then Casandra linked her arm in his and started walking after the retreating Cian. This surprised Rowyn and he felt a strange tingle. They picked up their pace, as the Elf's stride was a lot longer than theirs.

"Did you know this was here?" Casandra asked, looking from side-to-side.

"Not in the least." He was just as bewildered as his cousin. "Cian said we have entered Greenwald Forest, which might explain why no one knows about this," he said, indicating the valley around them.

The weeping tree leaves fluttered, the sun creating a patchwork of light on the three of them. Rowyn breathed in deeply. The fragrant sweet smell of the leaves wafted over him and it had a freshness that he hadn't experienced for some time.

Looking past the trees Rowyn noticed several other Elfs around the manor and out working at various tasks.

"Members of my family," Cian answered in response to Rowyn's thoughts. He continued walking without looking back. "And a few visitors from Ealhdun."

"The Elfish Kingdom!" Casandra said.

"The same," Cian acknowledged casually as they approached the entrance.

It made sense to Rowyn; they were in the Greenwald Forest and Ealhdun was reportedly in the same forest, though no one he knew could confirm its existence. Elfs, however, were not a subject that came up often, and it had never occurred to him to ask Uncle Brom.

"What was that you did to the Blood Stalker?" Casandra asked as they walked under the shade of the trees.

"I don't know. It was… it was like how I felt back on the road, but not as strong. I was lying there, the Blood Stalker was coming at me." A chill went down his spine as he remembered the drool dripping off the creature's fangs. "Then a fire sprang into my body." Speaking it brought back memories he had long forgotten. At nine and twelve. But the voice was new, he thought. What was going on with him?

"Well, whatever it was, what you did was impressive. I thought the Burning Lady was coming for." Casandra turned and smiled at him, seemingly relieved. "Maybe it has something to do with what Cian said about control?" she added, raising an eyebrow.

"Maybe." He thought it was possible, but it appeared anything was, judging by his experiences over the last couple of days.

As they continued toward the manor, Rowyn noticed an assortment of strange creatures he had somehow missed upon their initial approach.

They stopped at the steps leading to an archway entrance into the manor proper so Cian could talk to a creature that Rowyn had never seen or heard of before. It was furry, except around the face and hands. It had long ears like a rabbit, a face with human characteristics, but with a small button nose. The eyes particularly reflected a strong intelligence. It had hind legs bowed backwards like an animal, which it walked on, making it nearly as tall as Rowyn. The front legs, or arms, were shorter, and the creature used them like human hands. When the creature approached Cian it brought both its hand-paws up to its mouth and then lowered them so they opened toward Cian. The Elf returned the gesture. This was similar to what Drel Firil had done earlier. They talked in a strange language that neither Rowyn nor Casandra recognized.

"What is it, Row?" Casandra whispered, her head tilted toward the creature.

"I do not know." Rowyn held up his hand to cover his mouth as he whispered back. "Maybe some type of giant rabbit or something."

The creature turned and stared directly at Rowyn, its ears twitching, then it said in a low-pitched voice, "I am certainly not a rabbit any more than you are an ice giant, Prince Brynmor." The creature emphasized Rowyn's title in a way that definitely lacked any deference. Lifting its head proudly, the creature wiggled its ears back and forth. "These are very sensitive." It smiled — at least, Rowyn thought it did — and walked away, having finishing its conversation with Cian.

"Inkinds are a bit touchy about being compared to a common rabbit," Cian said as Rowyn watched the creature as it headed away from the manor.

Rowyn could swear that it hopped slightly, but was not inclined to comment.

"They are disposed to scholarly fields and very good at it," Cian whispered as he headed up the marble steps toward the archway, "But they are also an overly proud race. As with everything in the world, the Spirits trade one thing for another."

Even though a good distance away, Rowyn could hear the Inkind say in a disapproving tone, "Well."

Cian smirked and passed through the archway that acted as the entrance. There were no doors to the entrance, as if welcoming anyone that found their way to the manor itself.

As they started through the opening, Rowyn touched the surrounding wood that made up the arch. The wood was not cut, but intertwined limbs that he assumed had wound their way from the nearby trees. What did surprise him was the warmth of the wood. Not as if heated by the sun, but heat that was generated from the inside.

A tug on his arm and Casandra pulled him away from the opening. "Look at this place," she said as she scanned the entire area.

The archway led into a large courtyard filled with more strange creatures and Elfs that were busy in one way or another. Sprouting out of the ground all over the yard were wooden and marble seats, tables, troughs, overhangs, and a wide variety of small functional structures. Around the courtyard were three levels of the building that faced inward, with a gallery on the second and third level similar to what Rowyn was used to in Castle Westhedge. But again, the wood and colorful marble construction gave a warm and welcoming feel that he had not felt at the many castles he had visited in the past.

Cian had stopped in the middle of the courtyard near another large tree. As Rowyn and Casandra joined him, another Elf walked up, smiling.

The Elf brought both hands to its mouth like the Inkind and the Tink had, then bowed slightly and opened the hands level with the ground facing Cian. "Trichetara-orala ehwe yaba ia imthie yorthre-ara."

Cian returned the gesture as he had with the Inkind, though Rowyn noticed he didn't bow as deeply as the other Elf or the Inkind had. Cian repeated the salutation, then turned to face Rowyn and Casandra. "This is my grandson Saraid. He will be assisting with your training, along with Helel."

Saraid turned toward them and gave them the same greeting. "Trichetara-orala ehwe yaba ia imthie yorthre-ara." Then he added in common Taran, "May the Spirits grant you a life worth living."

Rowyn brought his hands up in a rough emulation of what he had seen before and said, "And you also."

Casandra gave Rowyn a look that he always ended up regretting, then she rolled her eyes. She turned to Saraid and brought her hands to her mouth matching the Elfs' actions exactly and said, "May the Spirits grant you a life worth living."

What bothered Rowyn was the look on Casandra's face as she greeted Cian's grandson. Her eyes were alight and he didn't remember if he had ever seen her smile so engagingly before. *Though maybe with Ser Rhein,* he thought sourly. But the more he thought about it, he realized he hadn't paid much attention to her in the past to begin with, so he really wasn't sure.

Cian's grandson was nearly as tall as Cian himself and Rowyn noticed the muscular build under the Elfs light blue tunic. His hair was light brown, maybe more blond, and hung down to his waist. The Elfs ears stuck through the sides of the hair. His features were soft, with high cheekbones and no facial hair. Suddenly, Rowyn realized how a woman might find Saraid attractive, though he had never spent much time in the past thinking about what a woman might think. Not that he didn't care, he had just never considered it.

"I look forward to working with you over the next few months," Saraid said, his eyes as bright as his smile. "From what Grandfather has told me, I am excited to see what you can accomplish." One of the creatures, in a squeaky high voice, called to Saraid from across the courtyard, and he excused himself to walk away briskly. His body moved so smoothly it gave the impression that he was gliding over the ground.

Rowyn glanced out of the corner of his eye to see Casandra's gaze intently following the receding Elf.

"Drel Corklin will take you to your rooms, as I am sure you would enjoy a respite after the long ride. It has been a long and eventful day." He grinned at Rowyn. "Supper will be brought up to your room. When you wake tomorrow we will start. There is a lot to cover in a short period of time." Just then, another Drel Donlin look-alike, who Rowyn assumed was Drel Corklin, walked up as if he had waited off to the side until called.

"I will see you in the morning." Cian smiled, then walked toward a large archway to their right.

Drel Corklin stepped up quickly and bowed, taking Cian's place, then said in a voice that sounded like wagons rolling over a cobblestone road, "Please follow me." He turned and started toward another archway to their left.

Casandra started after the Tink and left Rowyn with little choice but to follow. Before leaving he called out to the old Elf with one of the main questions that had weighed on his mind. "How did Uncle Brom know Willoe and I switched?"

Cian stopped and looked over his shoulder, and he smiled, the face creasing grin Rowyn had already come to expect. "I never mentioned it was your uncle Brom."

"Then who?" Confusion had been Rowyn's steady companion over the last few days.

"Your other uncle, of course." The old Elf laughed and entered the archway, disappearing.

19

Interference

The arrival at Highkeep had been uneventful, but Rhein still had a nagging feeling that would not give him rest. The carriage came to a halt in front of the manor and Dilys stepped down, followed by the ladies.

Rhein started to intercept the ladies to ask how they had fared that day, but Dilys stepped in front of him. "It be best if ye set up camp while the Princess and Lady settle in." She looked over her shoulder as the two ladies entered the door that led up the stairs to their room. She turned back to Rhein with a sweet smile. "It be a day or two for them to rest then we see what we see."

Rhein frowned, as he had already planned to set up camp first; and he didn't need to be told by the Princess' servant. Rules and a hierarchy of command had guided his life for the last ten years, and in just the last couple of days of travel, this woman was wreaking havoc with the protocols that Rhein lived by. Yet he would never belittle anyone because of their station in life, as his own beginnings were not something he shared readily. He nodded and decided he would take the situation up with the Princess in a couple of days after she had recovered from the trip.

"Sergeant Crowley, if you wouldn't mind," Rhein called over his second-in-command.

The sergeant came over and they began a tour of the manor while the men set up camp. It was a rather small house with only two stories and no towers. Traditionally constructed with stone walls, wood doors and floors, and no great hall to speak of, it was modest by royal standards.

They stood staring at the front of the house and Rhein thought he would question the sergeant discreetly about that night. "Do you remember anything… strange the other night?"

"Which night do you mean, Ser?" Sergeant Crowley kept looking at the framework of the manor.

"Two nights ago." Rhein had only recently earned his spurs and been inducted into the Order of Coel. Even though the sergeant had served with Rhein, when Rhein was a lieutenant fighting against the Tonn tribes, he didn't want to seem foolish or anxious about anything. "Did you notice anything... different?"

The sergeant turned his head toward Rhein, his eyebrows knitted. "Not that comes to mind."

Rhein twisted his lips and wondered if he was just letting wild thoughts run away with his mind.

Then the sergeant added as if an afterthought, "I did have a strange feeling right after dinner. A little unsettled, off balance. I gave Cook a difficult time about it."

An uneasy feeling overcame Rhein and he wanted to ask more, but thought better of it, for now.

Rhein pointed to windows along the lower level. "There is a library, small dining area, servant quarters, and two small guest rooms on the ground floor with two large chambers on the second floor, one on each side of the manor. The maid, Dilys, tells me that the ladies will be eating their meals in their room. Something about maintaining their meditation." This seemed strange to Rhein, but he had spent most of his time in the field so didn't know if this was common or not. The grounds had only three out-buildings: a cook house, stable, and a large one for storage. They passed a small garden that appeared to be lying fallow, waiting for the spring planting. He assumed it provided vegetables for the small staff as the Royals would undoubtedly bring much of their own food with them when they visited, which he had been told was rarely. That, and what they gathered from hunting.

"The men will set up their tents to the east as you ordered." The old veteran sergeant pointed to one side of the large clearing at the front of the manor.

Rhein nodded his approval. They kept walking as he considered his orders from Captain Harte. They were not that specific, other than to keep guard over the Princess and Lady Casandra. No threats were identified, but as a member of the royal family Princess Willoe, or even Lady Casandra, as the First Duke's daughter, would require sort of special escort. He was surprised that Protector Dougal was not along, but Rhein smiled as he thought that traveling to the Franchon capital would probably be considered a great deal more dangerous than a few moons away at Highkeep.

Rhein and Sergeant Crowley continued around to circle the manor noting possible areas of concern, until they reached the north side of the manor. "This could be a problem." He pointed to the small forest that bordered the manor on that side. Rhein had been told by one of the servants that it provided for excellent hunting, which was one reason why Royals and their guests frequented Highkeep a couple of times a year. "The woods come up to just a stone's throw from the manor. Someone could work their way up here and we would not see them until they were nearly upon us."

"Aye, but the growth is thick all along the front except here, where this path comes down. Looks like a hunting trail." The sergeant pointed at an opening in the dense woods where the hard-packed dirt trail began. "But it thins out to the front of the manor." He turned, looking to his right at the front of the manor.

Rhein turned with the sergeant. He had already considered the danger the woods to the front presented. The road led underneath a cover of tree limbs and emptied out into the clearing. At least the clearing provided a lot of open ground between the tree line and the manor, another reason Rhein had set up camp there. He turned back to look at the eastern woods. With his limited men he would do his best.

According to his map, beyond the forest were open fields for several miles until one reached the edge of the dreaded Greymoor Forest. Just the name gave Rhein a slight shiver that he kept to himself. It was rumored that an entire column of soldiers had entered the forest chasing wild Tonn warriors, and had never returned. He would not have given it much credence except that one of the soldiers had been an old friend of his father's, and his father was oft the teller of this particular tale.

They walked over looking into the northern woods and checked to make sure no other paths led to the manor before making their way back around to the front.

"A wee bit to cover with half a Lance, Ser." Sergeant Crowley was merely stating Rhein's own thoughts.

With a full Lance of twenty-five men Rhein would have placed a guard on each side of the house with two more roaming on an intermittent schedule. "I agree, Sergeant, but we have to make do with what we have. Set up a rotation of three guards, one on each side and one in the back of manor, on three separate shifts. That will leave the cook, horse master, you and me to take care of everything else." He smiled to reassure the Sergeant, though he didn't feel reassured himself. He imagined the remoteness of the manor had something to do with the small escort. When he had received his orders he had figured that his greatest duty was to keep Princess Willoe out of trouble. He had heard enough rumors of her exploits, and Captain Harte had specifically told Rhein to keep a close eye on her. Rhein wasn't sure whether his real assignment was to protect the Princess from others or from herself. It didn't appear as though the Princess would be causing too many problems, so Rhein expected his most difficult task would be to keep his men focused on their work and prevent boredom from creeping in among their ranks.

"The boys are just 'bout ready, Ser," the sergeant told Rhein.

They finished discussing who would take guard first and Sergeant Crowley turned to set up the first shift. He looked back over his shoulder before heading over to assign the men. "You're doing fine, Ser. The men are already taking to your command." Then he walked over toward the fire the cook had already started.

They had been at Highkeep Manor for nearly a week and Rhein had yet to talk with Lady Casandra or Princess Willoe. Not that he hadn't tried, but Dilys had thwarted his attempts at every turn. Whenever he tried to approach them in their rooms, Dilys was there, answering his knock and making one excuse after another for why they were not available. They rarely left their rooms.

Rhein was a patient man. Patience, along with careful consideration of all the information available, had more than once saved him and his men against the Tonn. That, and several years of working his way through the ranks, establishing himself as a sound leader, had put him on that river as lieutenant. The one that earned him his spurs. But after a week, even his patience had worn thin and he was tiring of Dilys' interference. He had a duty and had no intention of guarding them from a distance. He entered the western wing of the manor and took the steps two at a time up to the second level. There was only the single apartment, normally reserved for the highest ranking guest. As he held up his fist to knock on the door, it opened and the diminutive Dilys stood there.

"What be bringing ye to our door, Ser Rhein?" she greeted him, staring up into his face.

He straightened and brought his arm back down. He had that strange feeling again, the one he had had that misty night on the road. Like something was missing. "I request an audience with Princess Willoe," he told her firmly. "We have yet to exchange a word since our arrival and I wish to find out if the Princess has any requirements of me or my men."

"She not be disturbed, Shield." Dilys smiled sweetly, but just as firmly rejected his request.

"I must insist." He was amazed at how a short, dumpy woman could have a presence that filled an entire room, but he was not going to let a servant, even a highly respected one like Dilys, stand between him and his duty. "I must find out what her plans are. If there are any special needs.

What are her expectations? Not that I don't trust you, but I am responsible for her safety and so I must check on her to verify it."

A small sigh escaped Dilys' lips and for a moment her eyes narrowed and gazed past him as if concentrating, then she focused back on Rhein. "I will take your request to Princess Willoe. Please wait." She opened the door farther and Rhein could see Princess Willoe sitting by the hearth, her back toward him, but angled to the door so he could see a book in her hand. Lady Casandra was off to the side pouring a dark liquid from what looked like a teapot, the steam rising as the stream ran into the mug.

Leaving the Shield in the doorway, Dilys walked to Princess Willoe's side and leaned over talking to the Princess, but was far enough away that Rhein could not hear what was said. The Princess turned her head back to look at Rhein and smiled. He bowed in return. She spoke in a whisper to Dilys, nodded once to Rhein and then turned back to face the hearth.

Dilys walked back over and shook her head slightly. "As I told ye before, Princess Willoe has asked she not be disturbed. The Princess wants time spent in reflection on her upcoming marriage bond. The Princess has taken a vow of purity to cleanse her thoughts. This includes any contact with men." Her mouth pouted slightly. "It be a sorry thing, but ye will not be able to talk with the Princess during our stay at Highkeep. Princess Willoe has asked that ye pass any request through me."

"Then perhaps Lady Casandra?" He said it bluntly and looked in the lady's direction, trying to keep his frustration from surfacing.

"Ahh—" Dilys bit her bottom lip and looked over to Lady Casandra, then quickly snapped back to look at Rhein with the smile planted once again. "In a show of support Lady Casandra has taken a similar vow."

Lady Casandra glanced up from the mug held in both hands and he saw just the hint of a smile before Dilys closed the door and stepped out into the hallway. Again the feeling of something missing pressed upon him. He was about to ask Dilys why he had not been told about this before when she grabbed his elbow and directed him toward the stairs. She asked in a friendly tone, "Rumors say ye recently be anointed a Shield?"

"Yes, just a few months ago." Rhein was still getting used to the title, but also took his responsibility as a Shield seriously.

"No offense, but ye be not from a noble house if what I heard be the truth." She was leading him down the stairs as they talked.

He took great pleasure in the fact that he had not been granted his Shield by reason of birth, but had earned it through his deeds. His answer rang with the pride he felt, though normally he avoided the topic. "That is true. My father was a weaponsmith, he was my first teacher of the sword, but he passed when I was a young man. My mother worked with a noble lady to teach the lady's children and so my mother taught me."

"But how did ye be a Shield? It not be an easy thing for one not born to the nobility to rise so high." Dilys showed a real interest in Rhein's story and though he rarely shared it, something about her voice drew him out.

"After my father passed, my uncle, who was in the City Guard, took over my training. His sergeant thought I had some skill and I was given the opportunity to join the City Guard. Later I applied for the King's Guard and was accepted after passing all the tests." The countless and harsh tests came back as if he had gone through them just yesterday. "There were many times I thought I would fail for sure." For some reason, talking with Dilys seemed natural and he felt no embarrassment in sharing his commoner past nor the difficulty he'd had in becoming a guardsman.

They had reached the bottom of the stairs and exited the manor into the clearing. "Ye be young." She looked up into his eyes and he felt so relaxed. "I say no more than twenty summers."

"Twenty-two." He smiled back at her.

"If ye don't mind me asking, how did ye become a Shield?"

"A year after coming to the King's Guard I was sent to the field to track down bandits, and was shortly promoted to Sergeant and then Senior Sergeant. I was leading a patrol along the northern border with a small contingent of mounted guardsmen, along with a band of archers and pikemen." They had stopped in the clearing and he looked out across the fields to the west, the memory as strong as the day it had happened. The heavy feeling weighed on his chest as it had that day a year before. "The patrol had been routine until we stumbled across a large group of warriors from one of the Tonn tribes, from the Open Lands, who were ransacking a small river village."

"The Tonn?" she asked with interest. "I have not been with any of their tribes for many a time."

Rhein couldn't imagine the smallish woman having any sort of contact with the savage Tonn, but he continued his story nonetheless. "From time to time they wander into either the Cainwen or Franchon – and, I have heard, Haldane – lands, stealing stock and killing anyone who tries to stop them. The villagers resented the Tonn taking their cattle and sheep, with the expected results. We routed the Tonn." He stopped the tale and his eyes gazed into the past again, his thoughts torn as the scene of battle flashed into his memory. He could feel the excitement of riding into the fray once again, but also the horror of men dying under his sword. He heard himself saying, "I can still smell the blood. It's like wet iron or copper. It fills my nostrils whenever I remember them. Not many of my men, but over a hundred of the savages. Their bodies torn and dying."

"Savages they be not." The bitter tone of Dilys' voice cut through the mental image of the village and the battle.

"Pardon me." Rhein turned to her.

Dilys gripped his arm tighter, a frown crossing her face, but she let it slide back into a smile. "Nothing. There be more that I hear in your voice?"

He recounted it almost as if he were telling someone else's story. "I had split my smaller force in two, some would say a dangerous strategy. I sent half the archers and all the pikemen in a circle around the Tonn to the other side of the river. I had the remaining archers move around the edge of the village and let two flights fly into the massed warriors. Luck was on our side. The Tonn had not seen our approach and were taken by surprise. In the ensuing havoc I led the mounted Guard directly into the heart of the Tonn ravagers. The attack was so brutal and unexpected that they must have thought we were a much larger force. They fled toward the river and while crossing they were caught on the opposite shore by the archers and pikemen I had sent around earlier. We killed many and dispersed the remaining. We suffered few casualties in return." He stopped and realized he had been breathing heavily as he relayed the tale. But he also felt better than he had in months. He had not told anyone, even Captain Harte, about how he'd felt during the battle and afterward. It felt like a burden had been lifted. A heavy burden. He finished the story. "As I said, upon our return to Castle Westhedge, word had gone before and I received my spurs."

"Be it King Einion himself who bestowed it on ye?" Dilys asked, looking up at him again.

"Yes," he replied, the grateful tone of his voice sweeping through. "This is my first assignment as a Shield."

Dilys patted him on the arm like a doting grandmother. "And ye are doing a fine job. Princess Willoe be extremely satisfied with your actions. Let me know if ye have anything to tell the Princess." She finished with that reassuring smile she always seemed to show and turned away to head back into the manor.

Rhein stared after her for a moment and a smile also creased his face. He couldn't understand why he had been so suspicious of her. He still had the nagging feeling that something wasn't as it should be, but the feeling of relief he was now feeling helped to push it further to the back of his mind.

The Guard cook calling to him made Rhein shake his head, as if it were filled with cobwebs, and he turned to see the cook standing near one of the tents. *Was it supper already?* he thought. He turned back to watch as Dilys entered the manor and then he headed over to follow the cook. He had not felt so hungry in a long time.

20

Rumors

The Great Crossway was quiet this time of year. With most people involved bringing in the harvest, few people had time to travel between Westhedge and White Cliffs.

Protector Dougal would drop back to ride with Willoe and Aeron several times a day, but Aeron's gift for conversation engaged the Protector and kept Willoe from having to speak very often. To their benefit Protector Dougal spent much of his time with Captain Harte, though never far away. Willoe knew that guarding the convoy was also guarding Prince Rowyn.

On their sixth day out of Westhedge, Protector Dougal came by Aeron's and her campfire at a time when Aeron was off talking with Captain Harte.

"Are ye feeling well?" the Protector said as he sat down next to her. "Ye be distant since we took our leave of Westhedge."

"An adjustment. A lot of riding." She tried to keep her words short and hoped he would see Rowyn's sullen tone.

"That it be," he responded, staring at the fire.

Willoe also looked into the fire and kept her cloak pulled up, though with the heat of the campfire and the strange warmth that simmered throughout her body, she felt like it was a sweltering summer day. While she sweated a little, she was grateful that the searing fire had not returned, the one inside, but the subtle warmth coursing through her veins was a constant reminder it could return at any moment.

Protector Dougal leaned a little closer, still looking down at the fire, and counseled her. "I noticed some of the guardsmen have welcomed you."

Her friendly banter with the naked guardsmen had evidently spread and while the guardsmen weren't overly friendly, they were not avoiding her on purpose any longer.

"But I have watched and I nay see you talking with the Shields." He indicated the other campfires. Willoe could tell that he was trying to be honest and provide good advice to whom he thought was Rowyn. Men shivered when facing the large Protector, but he hesitated as he took a deep breath, then looked at Willoe with a sincere expression. "It is important that you develop relationships with men like these. They be at your side and serve under you in the future."

So far Willoe had tried to keep her speech to a minimum or let Aeron do the talking, but now it was just the two of them.

She turned her face a little toward him so as not to raise suspicions. "I haven't had many chances to talk with them. We're in the saddle all day and at night it's supper and then sleep. I'm not used to a journey of this length and I'm easily tired."

The Protector didn't say anything and just turned his gaze toward her. She was going to say something else, but he turned back to the fire and spoke first. "Make an effort. It be important to make you one with your peers."

"I will try." And she was determined to do it, if for no other reason than she had been thinking about it and understood that what she did now would fall upon Rowyn later. "I promise to make more of an effort."

"Ye must think of your future." He picked up a stick to stir up the embers. "I be not always there for ye."

"I know you care for me."

"I am your Protector," He said brusquely, but she could hear his voice crack and knew it was more than that.

Maybe it had been the trials and exhaustion of the road, she thought, but at that moment a surge of emotions filled her. He had always been there and she never questioned that he would give his life for her, but in this rare sign of affection, she suddenly grasped that she loved the old Protector as much as she did her own father. He had been the first father she had known, though she remembered very little at age three. He was also one of only two people she knew who had met her mother. "You knew my mother?" Her voice was hesitant, as much a statement as a question. She was unsure what prompted the question, but once out she was glad she asked it.

Protector Dougal kept stirring the campfire, but didn't say anything else.

"There are many stories, but the most common one is that you rode right past the king's guard into my father's camp." Her heart pounded, but she couldn't stop.

He remained silent, pushing a log that had fallen away back into the others. Then, without looking over at her, he started to tell the tale.

"Crown Prince Beynon and your two brothers, Prince Mael, nine, and Hafgan, seven, be on a hunting trip." He stopped to stir the fire alive again.

"It be just after nightfall when I rode into their camp. I presented ye to your father, as promised, and he accepted the both of ye."

"Whom did you promise?" she asked and held her breath.

"Someone special." A sadness was behind his words.

Aeron walked back into the firelight and Protector Dougal stood, then threw his stick into the fire. He looked down at Willoe and said in his steady, deep voice, "Think well on your peers and future alliances, my Prince." Then he left the campfire, heading back to join Captain Harte at the next fire.

"What did he say?" Areon asked as he sat down next to her.

She stared at the Protector's retreating back. "It is what he didn't say. He started to tell me about when we first came to Westhedge."

"Rumor has it that, if not for Captain Harte, the Protector would have been killed on the spot." Aeron's said it as if a well-known story.

"Why?" She snapped her head toward him. She had never heard this before, though she rarely paid attention to rumors. She was too often the brunt of many herself.

"The captain of your father's personal guard took it as a disgrace that the strange warrior had not been stopped by the captain's guards. It was Captain Harte, just a lieutenant at the time, who stepped in... Let me see..." Aeron's mouth twisted and he shut his eyes in thought before opening them again. "As it was told to me, Captain Harte told your father 'The major families of Haldane are represented by different color, the exception being the royal family, who have multiple colors.' Then he walked over and held a torch up near the warrior, who wore a cloak woven of crossed blue, green, and yellow colors."

Willoe was shocked. She should have been told. "Protector Dougal is Haldane royalty?"

"No, though I understand the Crown Prince asked the same question." Aeron laughed. "Captain Harte pointed to the warrior's shield. It had crossed curved swords over a dragon intertwined around a heart."

"Protector Dougal's shield." Willoe was like a child sitting at Dilys' knee, listening to a most exciting tale.

"'The same.' The Captain pointed at the shield 'The other exception being a Protector. The Protector is here to protect you,' Captain Harte proclaimed to the king."

"That isn't true." Willoe was shocked and angry. *He is playing with me.*

Aeron chuckled. "Ah, but he was wrong. Protector Dougal opened his cloak and had the two of you sitting in front of him. He told the Crown Prince that you were his children and..." He faltered.

Willoe gritted her teeth and glared at him in the firelight.

He lowered his head. "And that your mother had died. I understand there was a lot of argument before your father announced that you were his children."

Willoe hunched over, looking into the flickering light. This tale answered questions she had always had, but never asked. Yet she wondered if it were true. Then another question rose in her mind. "Why would father accept us on just the Protector's word?"

Aeron smiled. "My father told me that Protector Dougal had dismounted with the children and left them in Harte's care while he took the Crown Prince aside for several minutes. Then the two of them came back to you and Rowyn, the king holding a torch so he could see you. After a few moments your father was heard to say 'Just like her.'"

Tears welled in Willoe's eyes as she leaned her head forward and put her forehead on folded hands.

Aeron reached over and put a hand on her back.

She sniffled, sat back, sighed, and tried to smile. "I hope we get to White Cliffs soon."

Aeron patted her and smiled back. "I am sure the worst is over."

21

Ken Mud

When Casandra woke that first morning in Fayhaven, she went across the hall to Rowyn's room and knocked several times. After receiving no answer, she wandered out into the manor's courtyard looking for both him and Cian. The expansive courtyard still amazed her with the interwoven tree branches and marble walls. She also noticed another substance with a reddish-brown hue that ran in-between the tree branches and the stone. She thought it might be like daub when it is first applied. She had seen such a clay mixture used generously at Castle Westhedge to plaster walls and fill in gaps between wood and stone.

She strolled over to one wall and noticed that it not only filled the gaps between the branches and the stone, but also ran between many of the stones. Stepping up to look closer, she could see that the material looked pliable, and it also sparkled like a gem. She ran her fingers over the glistening material and pressed her fingers against it. It indeed was pliable. It gave way easily and her fingers slipped into a large patch of it between one branch and the stone above it. At first it felt a little sticky and was warmer than she had expected, though not an unpleasant feeling, like a jar of honey. Then, unexpectedly, she felt a tremor, like a thumping beat.

She yanked her hand off the wall with a sucking sound as her fingers pulled out of the warm material. She stepped back and nearly tripped over Drel Corklin, who had come up behind her. She turned and looked down at the Tink, who stared back up at her. She hadn't heard him come up behind her, but the Tink's smile was infectious and she had to smile back.

"Have you not seen calei before?" His voice was still gravelly, like yesterday, but it didn't come off as harsh.

"Calei?" She wasn't sure what he meant.

He pointed at the wall. "The material you were looking at. You acted surprised."

"Oh—" She twisted her head to glance at the wall and thought she saw the material pulsating slightly. *But that is impossible*, she thought. "No, I have not seen it before. It looked like something I am familiar with, but it is warm and it almost felt like... like a heartbeat." She laughed as she thought about how silly that must sound. Then she turned her head, but the Tink was gone.

"Very good observation. It be." Drel Corklin's voice came from back behind her, between her and the wall. She turned around to see him standing near the wall, the same friendly smile still shining through his close-cropped beard.

"It is what?" Casandra twisted again as she spoke and then back to look at the elusive creature. How could he move around her without her notice? And so quickly?

As incredible as it was, she thought his smile had grown larger. "The calei. It be alive." He put his hand on a section of the material and sunk his fingers into it. She could see the back of his hand actually move slightly as the material underneath pulsed. He continued, "It be what keeps the trees and stone together. It also controls much of the manor and the other structures in Fayhaven. It knows where everything should go and it grows as the valley and everything in it grows. But it be more." He stepped over to another section of the wall and motioned for her to join him.

When she got there he took her hand and held it up to a different section of the material, about a hand's width high, which ran along the entire wall. She flinched, but he just continued to smile and nodded for her to put her hand on the wall. She grimaced but laid her hand on the material and pushed four fingers into the soft mud, like she had seen Drel Corklin do. Immediately she felt the warm pulsating beat inside the material.

"What do you wish of the calei?" the Tink asked her.

"What do you mean?" She didn't understand, but left her fingers sunk into the wall. The warm pulsating sensation made her feel relaxed.

"What do you need?" Drel Corklin put one of his fat little hands on her arm. "Try to clear your mind."

She closed her eyes and found that she was suddenly able to empty her mind of any thoughts except the wall. She was startled at first as she felt a warmth spreading through her body, but she held steady. She was amazed at how easy it was to remove any random thoughts and settle into the warm glow flowing through her.

"Good," the Tink said as if he could tell when she had accomplished the feat. "Now focus on what you want and direct the thought to the calei."

"What I want?" She opened her eyes and stared at Drel Corklin.

The Tink did not show any frustration and continued to instruct her.

"What do you want to know right now?"

"I was looking for my cousin."

"Ask the calei."

She felt a little foolish, but the Tink seemed so sincere and insistent. She closed her eyes and thought, *Where is Rowyn?* But, as she expected, nothing happened. She wondered if the Tink was teasing her, seeing as the wall only pulsed as before.

She could hear Drel Corklin giggle, though it came out more like a soft growl with his graveled voice, and then he said, "To obtain what you need, you have to recognize the calei for what it be. A living creature much like yourself. Think of communication with it as a conversation with a friend. Picture in your mind the calei as an entity, and then focus your mind on conversing with that entity."

She cleared her throat and then her mind again. She tried to personalize the material, calling it Afanen, as the red pocketed material reminded her of the color of raspberries. It was very hard, but she tried to give the material a physical structure. At first she could only visualize a hazy form, neither man nor woman, but with concentration it slowly changed into an image of her mother. Someone whom she would talk with late into the night when she had a problem. Satisfied, she thought, *Hello Afanen.*

To her shock, she heard a voice that centered in her mind. *Good morrow, Casandra Cadwal. I am pleased at your presence.*

"That's fine. Now ask your question." Drel Corklin's words came from outside, unlike the voice of the calei.

She tried to remain calm and kept her fingers in the pulsating clay. She finally regained a relaxed attitude and focused her thought again. *Afanen, can you tell me where I can find my cousin Rowyn?*

Casandra still held the image of her mother standing in front of her, with a smile on her face. The one that her mother always gave her when they had sat and talked about almost anything under the sun. It gave Casandra a comforting feeling that was only heightened by the warmth and slow beat that came to her through the clay. The image said, *You will find Rowyn Brynmor on a hilltop, next to the manor, under the Learning Tree.* The voice even sounded like her mother. Casandra continued to stand there, unable to move, the image of her mother emblazoned in her mind.

From behind her, Drel Corklin said, "Good. You be doing well." Then he pulled her hand off the wall, the fingers reluctant to release her mother.

As her hand pulled loose, the image faded and Casandra wiped a single tear away with her other hand.

The helpful Tink led her to the door that Casandra thought led into the manor's Great Hall. He spoke as he walked. "Before you join the men you need to break morning fast. Saraid and your cousin ate at daybreak and will be waiting for you to join them."

"But the wall—" It really was alive, but was even more than that. It was sentient.

She kept trying to turn her head to look at the spot on the wall she had touched, as Drel Corklin led her away.

"The calei be all around you if you know where to look. It be another form of the *il fennore*, the Spirit world. Most just call it Cennan Mud," the Tink informed her as he continued to lead her toward the Great Hall.

Casandra recognized the word from something Uncle Brom had once said. The word was old… ancient. She tried to think what it was called now. *Ken*, she remembered. To know. No, it was more like to have knowledge and perception. To guide and teach.

Her thoughts were interrupted as Drel Corklin complimented her. "You did very well with your first lesson."

She finally turned and followed so she wouldn't stumble. "Lesson?" She felt like a bass out of water. Everything was so confusing. Then she asked, "Where is Cian?"

The Tink slowed as they approached the doorway. "Clearing the mind is critical to everything else you will learn. You managed that very quickly." He opened the door for her and the sweet, woody aroma of cinnamon greeted her. She could also smell some type of meaty stew and freshly baked bread.

As they entered, he answered her second question. "An owl arrived after midnight and Lor Cian left before dawn. His instructions were for you to start your training with Saraid and Helel." Before she could ask where, he provided, "No one knows where. He said he would be back soon." And with a little smirk he added, "Which could mean today, next week or in a moon." His expression changed and he confided to Casandra. "He seemed concerned with whatever message he received."

An owl? Ravens carry messages, not owls, Casandra thought. She went through the door and felt that leaving the sunlight to enter the darker room was akin to what the last couple of days had been like. She wondered if all this would become clear soon or if she and her cousin would continue down a path that just became darker and darker. The heavy feeling in her stomach was a poor omen indeed.

22

Il Fennore

On that first day, Saraid kept them out all day on the grassy knoll about a hundred and fifty paces from the manor. Alone on the hill sat a weeping tree, like the ones in front of the manor, but this one dwarfed the others. Saraid called it the Learning Tree. Other than the tree, much of the area was open and covered with a soft layer of grass and wild flowers. Saraid said they would train on the hilltop each day.

Casandra sat under the drooping branches with Rowyn and Saraid. He had promised to tell them why they had been brought to Fayhaven.

They sat staring at each other until Rowyn spoke up. "You said you would tell us why Cian carried us away in the middle of the night."

"Yes, that." Saraid looked thoughtful. "Only Cian can answer that."

Rowyn raised a finger to object, but Saraid went on, "I can tell you, though, why you are here. Cian says you both have special abilities, but you do not have the knowledge to use those abilities."

Rowyn lowered his hand, but frowned.

"I unfortunately do not have the gift to manipulate the Spirit world, the *il fennore.*" The look on Saraid's face as he said it told Casandra that it was a sore subject with him. "My gift is the ability to recognize the Spirit in the world around us. This is why I am your teacher." He turned slightly to take in them both. "What my gift tells me is that you both are powerful." He glanced from her to Rowyn. "More powerful than any man or Elf I have met in the past. This is why I believe my grandfather has brought you here."

Rowyn still seemed bitter about Cian's disappearance, and it showed in his tight lips and hunched shoulders. "What special abilities do we have?" He glanced over at her and she could see that he found Saraid's explanation

169

hard to believe. She wondered if it was because he had already said that he had no gift, or that he couldn't believe that she might have one.

"That is what we need to find out." Saraid's smile was ever-present.

His legs were crossed, but now his shoulders relaxed and he settled down, his long, muscular arms placed gently on his knees. "To determine this, over the next couple of days we will appraise your talents and determine where they lie."

"What do you mean when you say 'where they lie'?" Casandra asked.

"How are you going to appraise us?" Rowyn chimed in.

"I will explain." Saraid held up a hand and laughed. He put his hand back in his lap and looked at Casandra. "Not all wizards have the same skills. Some can make plants, flowers, and other objects grow. Some connect to the elements and impact the weather or control water and fire. A few are able to create power from the very air and use it as a weapon."

"Cian did that when he killed the Blood Stalker." Casandra was excited to begin understanding how wizards like Cian did what they did.

"Yes, I heard about that." Saraid nodded.

"It would have slaughtered us if Cian hadn't used the… the—" Casandra did not know what Cian had actually done.

"A Spirit Ball," Saraid provided before continuing, "And of course there are Clerics. Most people in the south do not see them as wizards, but that they are. Most wizards can perform some healing, mend small wounds, but Clerics have a unique ability to scry and locate the obscure traces of disease, while treating the entire body and performing intricate operations."

"If you are willing, there are some tests we can perform to see what type of wizard you may be." Saraid stood. "Rowyn, can you step over here?" He motioned for Rowyn to follow him as he walked over to the Learning Tree. "Put your had on the trunk."

Rowyn looked at Casandra, his mouth twisted as if uncertain, but he stood and moved over to Cian's grandson. He put his hand on the tree. "I can feel something throbbing. Reminds me of a heartbeat."

It suddenly came to Casandra. "Ken Mud."

Saraid looked at her with one eyebrow raised.

"Calei," she corrected.

He smiled and turned back to Rowyn. "Now dig your feet into the soil between the roots."

Casandra looked at Rowyn's feet. She had not noticed the tops of the roots that ran out from the Learning Tree and down the hillside. The dirt looked loose around the base of the tree.

Rowyn had already taken off his boots when they sat down, and he put one bare foot on each side of a large root and wiggled them from side-to-side, pushing his toes into the soil to dig even deeper.

"I feel it in the ground as well." Rowyn closed his eyes.

"What do you see with your mind's eye?"

"A thousand thoughts," Rowyn reported.

"Empty your mind and try to picture a Spiro. They don't have a body as we think of it, but are nearly transparent. Try to imagine strands, like cobwebs, that are strung together and move with purpose." Saraid spoke softly to Rowyn as if guiding him through a passage.

"Everything is obscure. Darker than a moonless night." Rowyn wrinkled his nose, which Casandra knew was a sign of his frustration.

"Look for a point of light."

It was several moments before Rowyn reported, "I see a small pinpoint of light."

"Good," Saraid complimented Rowyn "Now move toward it."

"Move toward it?" Rowyn wrinkled his nose, but then he smiled. "If I focus on the light I can see it starting to grow. There are strands of lights to either side that seem to be coming from the dot." He was quiet for a moment, then, "I broke through the dot and I'm surrounded by a bright white light, like a hundred suns." His voice trembled.

"You have crossed over. What you are seeing is natural, nothing to fear." The silky tone of Saraid's voice seemed to have an impact on Rowyn.

Casandra could see a serene look overtaking Rowyn's face and his shoulders lowered, his hands, a moment earlier balled into fists, had relaxed.

"Use your mind. Scan the horizon; look for a twinkle or any movement in the light. The Spiro might appear as a fine mist with a constantly changing shape."

"I see something." Rowyn's voice rose with excitement. "It's coming toward me."

"Good. That is a Spiro."

"It's coming closer. It is rushing in my direction." There was a tightness in Rowyn's words, an apprehension. "It is coming right at me."

"Do not be afraid." Saraid looked at Casandra, a worried expression covering his face.

"No, stop." Rowyn threw up his other arm in front of his face as he yelled. "Go away!"

"Rowyn!" Saraid grabbed Rowyn's hand on the tree and pulled him free.

Rowyn dropped to his knees and his eyes came open. Casandra could see tears.

Saraid dropped to his knees next to Rowyn. "What happened? I could feel the Spiro approach and then it was if a blaze flared and the Spiro fled."

"I don't know." Rowyn was breathing heavily, and sweat beaded on his forehead. "I saw it coming at me. It sped up as it approached and then, as you said, a flame engulfed the air between us and it fled."

"I have never heard of this before." The Elf helped Rowyn to his feet and they walked over so he could sit down next to Casandra again. Rowyn was still shaking, the color drained from his face, but he seemed to have calmed down a little.

"I could barely feel the Spiro through you, but it seemed scared." The look on Saraid's face bothered Casandra.

"I could also feel something from the Spiro," Rowyn admitted, the shakes nearly gone.

"What was it?" Casandra interrupted.

Rowyn turned toward her, his eyes sharp. "Fear."

All three sat for a little, while Rowyn recovered. The color eventually returned to his face.

"Cian said I would be a wizard. What type will I be?" After Rowyn's experience Casandra was hesitant even to ask, but she was torn. Ever since leaving the camp, on the way to Highkeep, the idea of wielding the power of a wizard had excited her. Four days ago she was destined to a life as the loyal wife of some Cainwen noble, but now... it was the farthest thing from her mind. Yet, she stared at Rowyn, who looked like he hadn't slept for a week, and she felt her own fear rising.

Saraid only nodded and walked back over to the Learning Tree.

She stood and slowly made her way to the tree. She placed a hand on the trunk. The bark was soft and pliant, a light gray with scaly crisscross ridges. It was unexpectedly warm to the touch and she could feel the bark throb under her touch. It was similar to when she had put her fingers into the Ken Mud. She pushed her fingers in between the ridges.

Without being asked she dug her bare feet into the soil around the roots. The ground under her feet throbbed like the tree and she closed her eyes, letting the rhythm flow from her feet to her hand.

"Good. You can feel it. Focus on the rising and falling of the pulse." Saraid guided her in a soft and soothing voice.

Casandra focused on the pulse and shortly her own heartbeat matched the cadence of the tree and ground.

"What do you see?" The Elf's voice became faint. She could still hear his words clearly, but at a whisper, as if a fog had settled into her head.

She started to open her eyes.

"Keep them closed," Saraid told her. "See with your Spirit. Stretch out to the Spirit world of the Burning Lady, the *il fennore*. The essence of the Burning Lady, the Spirit, co-exists with the physical world."

Saraid continued with his explanation of the *il fennore* and how wizards performed what appeared to many as magic. The words came slowly, but she understood them. "Spiros can freely roam the *il fennore*, and when merged with a wizard, in the physical world, they can influence the Spirit in objects that impact the physical world. This manipulation is only possible because there is a connection from the object's Spirit, in the Spirit world, and the object's physical presence in our world. Spiros have no connection to the physical world of their own. They cannot... feel. Though 'feel' is not the correct word."

His words ran through her head as she crossed over, just as Rowyn had, and then scanned the horizon. Even though she had heard Saraid explain to Rowyn, she did not know what to expect. "I don't—" she started to say, but then bright gossamer beings floated in the light, their presence only noticeable by the shimmering of their form against the background and the silky-looking strands that sometimes were visible. The transparent Spiros moved around her and at first she was scared, especially after Rowyn's experience. Eventually all but one of the beings disappeared. The lone Spiro floated off to the side as a small doe, with an injured leg, came into her mind's view. It solidified and she could see it clearly.

"Casandra." The cloud in her mind diminished and the sound of Saraid's soft tone was as clear as the peal of a bell.

She opened her eyes and standing in front of her was the doe she had just pictured. It took a couple of steps forward, limping. Without thinking she knelt and reached out to place a hand on the injured animal. A sensation filled her and she lost her breath as she realized that the lone Spiro was merging.

She started breathing again, but it was in quick spurts and the air burned in her throat. It was flooding through her body, the very core of her. She wanted to scream, but she resisted, fascinated by the sensation. It was not what she had expected. It made her feel warm and her skin tingled, but it was also not an unpleasant feeling. She relaxed and breathed deeply.

"Is she shining?" Rowyn sounded worried.

"She has merged," Saraid explained. "I didn't expect this."

"Expected what?" Rowyn asked, his tone concerned, but challenging.

"I did not expect her to merge so quickly."

"Casey, are you all right?" She could feel Rowyn's presence to her right.

She didn't answer, but instead focused on the doe. She closed her eyes again and could see underneath the animal's skin, down to the bone.

"She is scrying," Saraid whispered to Rowyn.

There was a rip in the tendons of the knee. She wasn't sure what to do, but fixed her attention on the rip. Around the tendon she could actually see thin strands that she knew was part of the doe's Spirit. She willed the rip to seal and as she watched the strands came together, as though woven, mended by an expert seamstress.

She suddenly felt tired and opened her eyes. The animal was running off toward with the woods. It no longer limped.

"I feel tired." She sat back and leaned forward, looking up at Saraid and Rowyn.

"A Spiro remains only as long as the wizard is performing a task. It becomes an extension of the wizard; this is how the wizard is able to manipulate another object's Spirit." Saraid's smile faded and his expression became serious. "To perform a task with the Spiro, the wizard must give up some of his or her own spiritual energy, though it is replenished with time so the wizard is returned to normal. In most cases, the wizard rarely knows that they have lost any energy. Even if it is a demanding task, the wizard quickly recovers with rest. As I said, the task is normally simple and the wizard feels nothing."

Casandra was already starting to feel better.

Rowyn appeared to grasp upon something that Casandra had not caught, because he narrowed his eyes and asked, "What if it is not so simple? What if it is a very demanding task?"

"The greater the task, the longer the Spiro would co-exist with the conjurer and the more energy it would consume."

"And—" Rowyn began as he stared intently at the Elf.

"If the task is too great then the Spiro could consume all of the wizard's Spirit essence."

"And—" Casandra spoke this time. She knew there was something more that Saraid was hesitant to tell them.

"It is very rare, but possible, that a Spiro will consume all the wizard's Spirit essence and… the wizard would cease to exist."

Casandra had known what he was going to say, but it still came as a shock to actually hear it.

"Let me say that I have only heard of a couple of instances of this in the history of the Elfs. A very long history, I remind you. Death is extremely rare."

Rowyn sat back with a satisfied smirk on his face. "But it is possible."

"Yes, it is."

Saraid's acknowledgment shook Casandra and she lowered her head to stare at her feet. He had to be mistaken. The Spiro had made her feel better, not worse – and not as if it were stealing her essence. But he would have no reason to lie to her. And she did feel tired after healing the doe. To know that it could kill her made her wonder if she would ever do it again. Then the memory returned, of the power to heal the injured animal and the sensation of pleasure that had filled her body, and she knew she would. Casandra smiled weakly. She would just have to be careful.

Casandra walked into her room and came to a stop.

"Hello, Casandra." The light-blond Elfen sat in the chair across the room, with a smile that filled the room.

"Hello," Casandra said uncertainly.

The female Elf — which Casandra had been told by Saraid was called an Elfen — stood and came up to Casandra, then wrapped her arms around Casandra and squeezed tightly. She finally let go and stepped back, holding Casandra's shoulders in her hands. "You must be overwhelmed with every-thing that has happened."

Before Casandra could think of an answer the Elfen turned and picked up a cup off the table. "Please, sit." She glanced at the chair across the table from her. "I had Drel Corklin brew this fresh."

Casandra sat and lifted the cup. She held it for a moment, not sure if she should drink it or not. But if the Elfs had wanted to poison her, they'd al-ready had more than a sufficient number of chances to do so. She sipped at the cup and was startled. She had only tasted it once before while visiting her father and mother at Castle Mount Somerled. Tea was not well-known and her mother had once obtained some from a traveling merchant. *There's honey in this*, she thought, pleasantly surprised again. It made quite a differ-ence from the last time she had tried the drink. But such thoughts were dis-tracting her. She didn't even know who the Elfen was.

"I am Helel, Saraid's cousin," the Elfen told Casandra, as if reading her thoughts.

"Ah, he mentioned you would be coming." It now made sense to Casandra, but at Westhedge it would have been a serious breach of eti-quette. One of the first things she had learned at Fayhaven, however, had been that privacy was not something that concerned many of the valley's inhabitants.

Casandra tried not to stare at Helel. The Elfen had high cheekbones, as seemed to be common among the Elfs, but her eyes were upturned, natu-rally lifted at the outer corners and set close together. They were striking, but only one of the many things that made her oddly beautiful.

"Come with me." Helel stood and headed for the open door.

Casandra took one last quick sip of the tea and put the cup down. She stood and looked down at the cup, hoping that there would be more later. Then she followed Helel out of the room and out of the manor. They walked along a path that ran around the side of the manor and down to a cluster of houses a hundred paces away.

"Were you able to bring changes of clothes with you?" Helel asked as they strolled down the path.

"I didn't have time." Casandra pulled at the riding clothes she still wore. "Cian— I mean, Lor Cian rushed us and I—"

"Just like a man." Helel shook her head. "You would think that a First Lor would know better." She continued toward one of the two story houses along the path. "And don't bother with Lor. I'm sure Uncle Cian would prefer just Cian. He only uses Lor when he wants to impress someone or when he has to perform official duties."

The house they approached was along the same design as the manor, tree limbs weaving through rock and marble, but on a much smaller scale. A fenced corral ran from around the side to and around the back of the house. Helel walked straight up to the door and opened it, entering without announcing herself.

It didn't feel right, but Casandra had to remind herself that she was in Fayhaven.

As they entered an older Elfen greeted them.

"Helel. Casandra. Trichetara-orala ehwe yaba ia imthie yorthre-ara."

"Trichetara-orala ehwe yaba ia imthie yorthre-ara. Zellar," Helel repeated.

"Trichetara-orala ehwe yaba imthe yorfre-are," Casandra stated, bowing.

Both the Elfens laughed softly.

"Did I say something wrong?"

"Someday I will tell you." Zellar put a hand over her mouth, and then cleared her throat and smiled. "It takes time to learn Alfar."

Casandra turned to Helel with a question in her eyes.

"The speech of the Elfs," Helel provided, then continued into another room, through it, and out a back door.

When Casandra came out of the house she was greeted by a small group. Six were Elfen, all as beautiful as Helel, but the remaining five were... odd. One was short, coming up to under Casandra's chin, and was covered head to paw in scales, except for the face and paws; one was as tall as the Elfen, but covered in a light blue fur; the third she recognized as one of the Inkind; and the last two were Tinks.

"I thought you might want to meet some of the neighbors." Helel introduced each of them in turn and Casandra was surprised to find out they were all females. Especially the Tinks, as they looked just like Drel Donlin and Drel Corklin, except with softer hair.

"We thought you might require a few more things to wear." Zellar brought two big bundles out of the house.

"We took some of our things and altered them to fit you," one of the other Elfen added.

"Not all contributed apparel." The Inkind rubbed an ear absentmindedly. "Though all altered."

Casandra took one of the dresses and held it up. She had never seen anything so exquisite. She suddenly felt overwhelmed. Not like when the Blood Stalkers were chasing them, but like the first time she saw her mother again after taking up residence at Castle Westhedge. She smiled and tried to keep the tears away. Whether Elfen, Tink, or Inkind, she had found new friends.

23

Groom

Willoe felt much better, even after eight days on the Great Crossway and all the emotional turmoil she had gone through. They had crossed the Lower Saltrock River earlier in the day and she was looking forward to supper.

She dismounted and pulled her pack off the horse as the groom, Doy, took Willoe's and Aeron's horses. He walked them into a nearby field to cool them down before returning. He tied Aeron's horse on the picket line and walked Willoe's a short distance away and started to wipe it down with a cloth. Willoe watched Doy until the page, Tomos, came up.

"Your tent will be ready in half a turn." Tomos held out a hand, offering to take her pack.

"What do you know about that groom?" she asked, trying to sound just mildly interested.

The page turned his head to follow her gaze. "He was already at Westhedge when Sion and I first arrived. I had thought he had started as a youth, like most of the others, but found out he only became a groom less than three years ago. I have also heard he is one of the Horse Marshall's favorites."

"Have you ever talked with him?"

"He was one of the first people we met." Tomos became excited, his dimpled smile melting Willoe's heart. "Castle Westhedge is so much grander than our home, we were..." He hesitated. "Ill-prepared. The groom, his name is Doy," Tomos provided. "He took our horses and I fear we must have had a dazed look, as he guided us through the main parts of the castle that first day. He treated us like nobles."

"You are nobles, or will soon be," Willoe corrected the young man.

His smile widened. "We didn't feel like it. At the end of the day he told us where we could find Steward Robat and what to say when we found him. He also told us if we had any questions we could come ask him." His eyes lowered. "I think he knew we were a bit scared to ask questions of the nobles and castle officers."

"Did you?"

Tomos looked back up and bit his lip, seemingly reluctant to tell her, but he finally decided to go ahead. "Many times. He knows a lot about the castle and the city."

"Thank you for your honesty, Tomos." She looked back over toward Doy as he wiped down her horse. "Strange, for a groom."

Tomos just looked at her, his head tilted a little.

"Please put this in the tent." She handed him the pack. He had accidentally opened the smaller bag a few days into the trip and Willoe had told him the cotton was in case of wounds. The boy had looked confused, but accepted her explanation.

He took the pack, bowed, and then headed over to Aeron, who was helping the Lady Emeline out of her carriage.

Willoe put her shoulders back, took a deep breath, and slowly walked over to the horse line. She scratched Rowyn's horse behind the ear and ran her hand down the neck. She looked over the horse at Doy, who was using a brush down the hair on the horse's side. "She's not used to such a long trip. Make sure to feed her extra oats and lots of water."

Doy stopped brushing and looked back over the horse's back at her. His expression was stern and he did not say anything.

She started to tell him to check the animal's hooves when he smiled and said, "Yes, my lord." Then he bent over and continued brushing.

Finally she couldn't keep her curiosity at bay. "I—" She caught herself and quickly changed her words. "My sister told me once of a cutpurse that she came across. I think it was four years ago."

The groom kept brushing, but did not lift his gaze to look at her. Instead he said, "There are many cutpurses in the city, my lord. There are some that find themselves in circumstances beyond their control."

She was taken aback. His words were not that of one who had lived on the streets. Maybe she was wrong, but no... the scar.

He rose to brush the rear of the horse.

"She described a scar." Willoe traced an imaginary one on her own face that matched his.

Doy stopped brushing and stared at her. "I remember."

"How did you become a groom? A royal groom?" She knew she should not be prying, but his secrets intrigued her. His transformation had been sitting, like a pebble in a shoe, in the back of her mind most of the trip. At least, those times when she wasn't trying to unravel the Burning Lady's words, or worrying about being discovered for her own secrets.

He put his head down and shook it, then lifted it again, taking a long breath. "There was a time. A time when I had no one that cared about me, and I felt the same."

"What happened?" Her voice had risen — she had forgotten for a moment that she was supposed to be Rowyn — and she had to quickly correct it. "I mean, how did you end up like that? What about your parents?"

His eyes shut for a moment and he shook his head again. He opened them to stare at Willoe. "Is this necessary, my lord? Have I not performed my duties to your satisfaction?"

"No, you have done well." She wanted to ask so much more, but could not find any justification for doing so. "The Horse Marshall seems to have confidence in your abilities. I won't question you any further."

He nodded, turned his eyes from her and went back to his brushing.

She started away as the Horse Marshall approached her.

"Is something amiss, Prince Rowyn?" He stopped to talk with her more than a dozen paces away from the groom. "Is Doy not taking care of your horse properly?" He glanced over her shoulder in the direction of the horses and the groom.

"No. Nothing is amiss. I haven't found any flaws with his work."

"Good." The Horse Marshall grinned. "Doy is a good boy. I ran into him when I was walking home one night from—" He bit his lip and thought for a moment before continuing. "From meeting friends. I heard a sound from a narrow passage off the street. I would have ignored it, but the sound pulled at my heart. The cries hurt just to hear them. I pulled my blade and edged down the passage." He drew his sword and hunched over to demonstrate. "I couldn't find anyone at first. Then, buried under a pile of rotting food and cast off stones, I found that one." He nodded toward Doy. "He was near dead. Had more cuts and bruises than a loser in the Lifts. Don't know why, but I pulled him out and threw him over my shoulder. Brought him home to me mistress and she patched him up." His grin widened. "Took about a month to get him back on his feet. He tried to run off before he could even walk, but I just asked him, 'What you have got to go back to?'"

Willoe was familiar with the Horse Marshall's tendency to turn every conversation into a story, but this time she listened willingly.

"He saw the right of it and said he wanted to pay me back for what me and the wife had done. But he admitted all his money had been stolen. I told him he could help out in the stables if he felt the need." The man shook his head as if amazed. "He has become the best groom in the stable. Has a way with animals, that one does. Never seen the likes of it."

"Do you know where he came from?"

"Not sure, though I have seen him a time or two playing with one of the guardsmen's swords. Doy has a way of making friends." The Horse Marshall chuckled, possibly thinking back over some event before continuing. "Alls I know is he has a natural skill with weapons that didn't come from running the streets." One of the other grooms called out to the Horse Master to help with a horse he was having difficulty with, and the man excused himself to go lend a hand.

Willoe turned to find her tent, but was lost in thought as she walked. There was something about Doy's story that just didn't fit. How could a cutpurse have learned how to use a guardsman's sword? At least, in the short time he had been a groomsman. She knew the greatswords were difficult to wield by even experienced swordsmen. If he had learned before becoming a cutpurse, what had he been and why did he become a cutpurse? And the scar?

24

A Ride Too Far

Pulling Windsinger's reins to the right, Willoe brought her horse off the road to let the two carriages pass. It had been two days since they had crossed the Saltrock River into Franchon. Word had been passed that they would be stopping at the Raven's Head Inn in Prestonford. Aeron had told Willoe that it was a very large tavern and that he and Willoe would most likely get their own room. Captain Harte called for a short break to give everyone a respite before the final push to Prestonford only three turns of the glass ahead. From there it was only four more days to White Cliffs. Once there, Mael would have few expectations of his sibling until the return journey. Without any responsibilities to hinder them, Aeron and Willoe could wander about Lealacité, the city surrounding Castle White Cliffs and one of the largest on Taran.

Willoe sat her horse and watched as the carriages and supply wagons moved toward the side of the road. The journey had not been as exciting as she had imagined. She had spent most of the trip breathing the dust of the carriages, with the occasional change where she rode in front, as she had today. Even Aeron had a break from the monotony every so often and rode ahead with the outriders or hunted with the escort's two huntsmen and several of the guardsmen who had a knack for tracking. But not Willoe. Protector Dougal and Captain Harte kept her close to the main escort.

Captain Harte was riding back to the rear, while the carriages and wagons were still pulling off. Even after nearly a week and a half of riding, he still looked every part the commander. Even with graying hair she knew he was about Protector Dougal's age and, like Protector Dougal, looked as fit as a guardsman half his age. It did not surprise Willoe. She knew he had been a young Shield and part of the guard when the Protector rode into her father's camp with the three-year-old Rowyn and herself. She easily believed the story since the two of them spent much of their spare time together. Whenever she needed to find the Protector within the bounds of the castle, she could expect to find the Captain and Protector Dougal talking over some ale or, more likely, pushing themselves to their limits on the training grounds.

An idea suddenly came to Willoe and she turned her horse back up to the road to head off Captain Harte. She rode up to him, her lips parting to allow for a big smile when she remembered Aeron's training. A smile had always accompanied her request with her father, grandfather, and Protector Dougal, but it would not be what two men-at-arms would do. She quickly thinned her lips and tried to look serious. "Captain Harte."

He pulled back on his reins and came to halt facing her. "Prince Rowyn," he said formally.

Her instinct was to smile to soften the hardened soldier, but she fought the impulse and kept her face placid. "The advance party will be heading out in a moment." It was a statement more than a question, seeing as it had been the daily routine. "I would like to join this evening."

"Too dangerous," the stern captain shot back, as if that would end the conversation.

Willoe wasn't about to let the stringent captain deter her from her plan. "It is about three turns of the glass down the road and it would give me a chance to function as part of the escort." She pressed her argument and hoped she didn't sound like she was whining or complaining. "Is not that the king's desire? Why am I a member of the escort?"

"Well—"

Captain Harte's hesitation was the opening Willoe had hoped for. "How can we accomplish the king's purpose if I am never allowed to perform the duties of an escort member?" She pushed again. "Protector Dougal has told me that it is important for me to become more engaged with the other Shields and guardsmen. He told me that the king would want you to provide opportunities to experience the life of a man-at-arms." It was sort of the truth, she thought.

"That is true," Captain Harte said to himself as he looked back up the road at Protector Dougal, who was heading off into the woods. The captain swung his head back to Willoe, staring intently at her, and asked, "Protector Dougal said you should join the outriders?"

She almost faltered, but pulled her shoulders back and stared right back at the captain. "Does me participating in the advance party not further the king's desires?" Again, almost true.

"Hmmm, that it would." Once the decision was made, his natural disposition took over and she knew he would be committed. He looked back up the road once again and called out, "Ser Tanguy, are you ready to move out?"

"Ser Tanguy?" Willoe's heart dropped. Tanguy was the champion Mael used most often to torment Rowyn, as he had the day of the banquet, in the Pell.

"Yes, Captain Harte." Tanguy had been talking with a Franchon Shield while a Cainwen and a Franchon guardsman sat to the side waiting. "We were preparing to depart."

Captain Harte pointed back to Willoe. "Prince Rowyn will be joining you."

Tanguy sneered. "He will now, will he?"

"Look after him," the captain commanded sharply, then turned from Ser Tanguy back to Willoe. "It goes without further instructions that you are to follow Ser Tanguy's command as if it were my own. Protector Dougal is correct. Take advantage of this time and learn from a tried and trusted Shield." She noticed his posture change as if he were shifting his focus to one of the myriad details he had to deal with. Willoe gently pushed with her heels and pulled the horse's head to the left with her reins to move around Captain Harte, but as she pulled away she heard him say almost absentmindedly to himself, "At least you don't have your sister's disposition for getting into trouble."

Willoe almost began to quarrel with him, but held her tongue. She had no intention of becoming friendly with the massive Shield or learning anything from him. Instead she just wanted to enjoy the freedom away from the main escort.

As she rode toward Ser Tanguy, he watched her. He was bigger than most men and reminded Willoe of a fighter she once saw at the Harvest Festival before Protector Dougal had dragged her away from the crowd. The Shield had the same solid face with a forehead that pushed out over his eyes, giving him a deadly look. He had a narrow mouth with a big nose that twisted several times, which Willoe thought must have been broken more than once. A couple of scars dotted the right side of his face.

She had not run across the Shield often, even back at Westhedge. Not like Rowyn and Aeron. From the way they talked about the man she expected him to be slovenly or slipshod, even though she knew he was a three time champion of the levies. Maybe his size was what had won the day. She could easily see, however, that his chain mail was well maintained, even after days of riding on the dusty road. His head was cleanly shaven. It was said he had beautiful hair, but it was also rumored he had shaved his head so it would not interfere with his ability to fight. Nothing about the man suggested he was anything but a professional. She had to wonder why he was part of Mael's group of comrades.

Ser Tanguy's eyes followed Willoe as she approached, his thin lips arching into a smile. "So, young Prince Rowyn is going to venture forth with us lowly warriors." He didn't wait for Willoe to answer, but turned his horse up the road and called the others forward. The Franchon guardsman took the lead, followed by Tanguy and the Franchon Shield. Willoe pressed her knees against the palfrey's side and it moved out at a steady pace. The Cainwen guardsman followed behind at a short distance. The cool weather of fall seemed colder after the Shield's welcome.

After a full turn on the road, the ride had been unexceptional. The same open fields broken only by a few small farms grouped together and set back at a distance from the road. It wasn't much different from riding with the carriages, only a little less dusty. As Willoe looked down the road, she could see it wind its way into a small forest. The array of the season's colors gave the dense woods a beautiful and peaceful impression. Finally, a change of scenery. Willoe rode by herself with the two Shields in front of her, both of them talking about a wide range of topics. The lead guardsman entered the forest and disappeared, as even the edge of the forest seemed to be thick with brush and knitted trees. Willoe could even smell the musk of the forest before she reached it. It had a dampness that was missing from the dusty road and open fields.

The two Shields followed the guardsman and then Willoe entered underneath the leafy canopy herself. She pulled the edges of her cloak tighter as the thick overhanging branches had kept the sun at bay, the forest path retaining the cold of the season. The forest's charm was somewhat tarnished when seen from the inside. The road had narrowed, though still wide enough for the wagons and carriages to maneuver between the trees. The scarred bark of the oak trees closed in from either side, interwoven with clumps of silver birch. A breeze caused the weepy leaves of the birch trees to flutter lively in contrast to the peeling bark, which looked diseased. The brush was very thick along the sides, filling in any open space.

At first she thought the sudden change in scenery was the cause of her discomfort, but she soon became aware of something else. Her skin tingled and she could almost feel the trees to either side. She also realized that there were fewer sounds than she would have expected along the road. She couldn't hear a single bird chirping and there should have been the rustle of small animals crashing through the underbrush, fleeing from the riders invading their territory. Even the pounding of the horses' hooves was silenced by the soft surface of the path. The only sound was the tinkling of chainmail and the snorts of the horses as they rode through the forest.

Then the warmth running through her veins began to heat up.

25

Fire and Blood

Willoe's body tensed with dread at the memory of the burn she had felt leaving Westhedge. She shuddered as the fire inside flourished and filled her body.

A veil settled over her mind and she tried to clear her head by blinking and shaking it from side to side. The haze was still there. Looking up, she thought it had become worse because the men in front of her had a pale reddish glow to them. *What is happening to me?* She couldn't focus. The heat was overbearing and the blurred eyesight made guiding her horse difficult. It made no sense.

She shook her head again, but the glow did not disappear. Looking around, she noticed the trees and brush spread out all around her, iridescent colors fluctuating from tan to a dark green. Everything living seemed to glow, which highlighted that a snake, off to the side of the road, was the only animal in the immediate area.

Willoe was still trying to make some sense out of it when she heard the Franchon guardsman's warning.

"Ambush. Bandits."

She saw him galloping back toward them. He had only come a few horse-lengths when three men rushed out of the dense woods between the guardsman and the two Shields. Two of the men had long sticks that looked like homemade spears and one a long knife a little shorter than an arming sword. They wore pieces of armor, mostly just leather or heavy layered cotton, and their weapons were rusty. The road was too narrow for the guardsman to get around the men, so he rode straight into them. He drove closer to the spear and knife wielder on the right, forcing both men to fall backwards.

At the same time the man on the left thrust his spear toward the guardsman's chest. It looked as if the Franchon had anticipated this, as he leaned forward to avoid the thrust. Unfortunately, the horse reacted to the collision with the two men on its right by jerking to the left, bringing the guardsman closer to the thrusting spearman. The spearhead reached the guardsman sooner than both he and the spearman had judged. The wrought iron head of the spear caught the guardsman in the soft area of neck and plunged all the way through, wrenching the spear out of the surprised spearman's hands and knocking him to the ground.

Before the horror could set in, shouting farther up the road drew her attention. Another eight or nine men, dressed similarly to the bandits, came running as the three men who had been knocked down started to regain their feet. Most of their weapons were a mix of different styles and types, from polearms to plain spears to a couple of short swords. Most wore a mix of farm clothing and a few pieces of some type of armor. Some wore just threadbare peasant clothes. One of the bandits wore a leather tunic covered with iron rings and on his head was an iron cap with a nose guard. A great deal more protection than his comrades, though still something shed by Shields possibly forty or fifty years ago. His sword was also far superior to the weapons of the others.

Ser Tanguy dismounted and drew his greatsword. He glanced back quickly at Willoe and the remaining guardsman, his expression fierce with determination. "Take Prince Rowyn," he shouted before turning back to face the oncoming ragtag group of men, both his hands raising the greatsword straight up over his right shoulder so he could swing it down in an arc in front of himself. The Franchon Shield remained mounted and pulled his shorter arming sword.

A bandit was no match for an experienced Shield or guardsman, but a dozen bandits, even poorly armed as these were, could be a problem for the two Shields and the remaining guardsman. Tanguy evidently considered his royal charge more of a disadvantage than an asset.

Willoe just stared at Ser Tanguy, rooted in her saddle even as her veins began to burn. The rear guardsman raced forward and wasted no time in grabbing the reins from her hand. He turned them both quickly, almost dislodging Willoe. Before they turned, Willoe noticed the glow around the two Shields brighten, and she saw that the charging men also emitted a strange light, some just barely while others bright like the Shields. But all she could glimpse before wildly grabbing for the saddle's pommel were hues of a variety of dark colors around the attacking men. Then she felt the fading sensation that came with the heat. It was as if another's memories were trying to push her own thoughts aside. She imagined it as another Spirit.

After a moment she broke temporarily through the fog and noticed she was being led away at a gallop from the two Shields who were covering her escape at their own peril. She tried to reach for the reins to turn back but they were stretched between her horse and the guardsman's hand ahead where she couldn't reach them. A light red glow covered his body. They rounded one bend in the road and were approaching another one. She leaned forward to try to grab the bridle again, still trying to fight off the Spirit of the heat that wanted control, but jerked back as she caught sight of half a dozen men running around the second corner, cutting off their retreat.

The guardsman managed to draw his greatsword before he and the bandits nearly collided. The guardsman's horse skidded to a stop, rearing as one of the men thrust a spear in the guardsman's direction. The horse's body was between the spearman and the guardsman, so the spear was driven into the chest of the horse. The spear must have punctured the heart because a gush of blood spurted out and soaked the front of the horse. The force of the thrust threw the horse to the side, dumping the guardsman to the ground head first.

He lay there crumpled on the ground, the rump of his fallen horse trapping his left leg as the horse jerked twice in death throes. Willoe could see he was still breathing and a glow still covered his body.

The attacking men had jumped back to avoid the thrashing horse. Each of them was encircled by a glow. The colors ranged from white-yellow to an ebony black. They were dressed similarly to the other bandits. A torn leather vest on one, a home-made shield held by another. Most of them, however, barely had any protection other than a heavy cotton jerkin, except for one man who wore a leather and iron ring hauberk and iron cap like that worn by one of the swordsmen who had originally attacked their party. Most of the weapons were old and in many cases rusted, but dull and rusted or not, they could still kill — the dead Franchon guardsman and the skewered horse were proof enough. Again, the only exception was the short sword carried by the man with the better armor. It matched the one carried by the man in the ring armor from the first group. It did not take a lot of thought to know he was the leader of this new group.

The fire in Willoe's veins had been building as the danger had increased, but now an inferno filled her. Something in her head spoke as if from the bottom of a well. 'Give thyself to us.'

She shook her head again, trying to clear the fog that had settled in and she found herself wondering whether the distress of her situation was causing her to lose her sanity, which only increased her apprehension.

'Ye be one of us. Give thyself to us.' This time she heard several voices, and they were stronger.

The fear swelled until she sensed that the voices were coming from a dark, forgotten corner of her own mind.

Once the dying animal settled down, the leader shouted encouragement to the others and started toward the horse and the downed guardsman.

'Now,' the voices commanded.

The fire flared, but not like the other times when her skin had felt like it was on fire. This time it was contained. Directed. Filling every part of her body with an intense heat that strengthened and heightened the awareness of her body. The fog, in her mind, was at once consumed by the fire. She felt more acutely aware of her surroundings. She felt alert. She felt agile. She felt alive as she never had before.

She almost flew from the horse, landed just behind and above the injured guardsman, her feet spread in the defensive position that Protector Dougal had shown her. She drew the arming sword, the only weapon she had been carrying, and reached down to snatch the greatsword's hilt from the guardsman's hand. Somewhere in the back of her mind she knew she should not be able to lift the heavy two-handed weapon, but the voices, now filling her head, spoke again.

'We be the strength of many.'

She held the greatsword out in front of her with just one hand. Willoe swung it once in front of her body and was surprised to find that it seemed to weigh no more than a riding crop. The fear had fled as the voices took control. Standing firm, she glared at the men, her teeth gritted.

The charging men stopped just on the other side of the horse and stared at her for a moment. Their look told her that they had not expected opposition.

She glanced down. The Cainwen guardsman was not moving, but she could see a faint glow around his body. He was still alive. She flipped her gaze back up to stare at the men, her teeth gritted. She heard a loud growl and then realized it was coming from her.

The men looked questioningly at each other until the leader yelled at them. "Get him! Remember, take him alive." He started around the horse, but held back a little while the others charged toward Willoe.

She started to hold the swords in the primary defensive position Protector Dougal had taught her, but her arms and legs shifted into a stance she had never seen. It felt natural, like something she had done a thousand times before. It dawned on her that the new stance was not to defend, but to attack.

One brave soul with a spear raced over the horse ahead of the leader and threatened Willoe. The fire inside guided her and following her strange new instincts, she drove the greatsword into the ground and used her free hand to reach around and grab the shaft just behind the iron head of the spear. She yanked it toward herself, the tip missing her head by a couple of inches.

The spearman held onto the shaft, as the voices had told her he would, and his momentum kept him running directly at Willoe. She merely stepped aside and brought the shorter arming sword up with her left hand and the man ran directly into it, his grunt more surprised than pained. As blood ran down the blade she flipped it to the side, gutting and tossing the man to her left. The weight slid off the blade as the spearman fell sideways, his hands grabbing for the intestines that were spilling out. She only looked at him for a second; the only thing that registered was the steam rising from the opening in his stomach as the warm entrails spilled out onto the cold road. Another man, one with a long gray beard, carried an old war hammer that had seen better days. He looked over at the leader.

Willoe watched both men at the same time.

The leader seemed to think for a moment, then yelled over to Old War Hammer, "Disarm him if he won't give up!"

A sneer crossed Old War Hammer's face and he brought his weapon back to swing it at Willoe.

'At your legs.'

He let the hammer fly in a wide arc angled down toward her legs, a strap keeping the hammer connected to his wrist, but out of range of the greatsword.

Willoe jumped almost as high as the man himself and the hammer flew under her legs, the man losing his balance as the strap pulled tight and he fell into Willoe.

She grabbed him by the neck to stop him and held him there.

His eyes bulged as she tightened her grip on his throat. A desire to choke him lifeless filled her, but the leader's scream stopped that thought.

"Kill him!" the leader snapped at the remaining men and she didn't need to look to see they were charging.

Acting quickly, she brought Old War Hammer's face close to hers and drove the arming sword up through his chin with her other hand. She felt the tip of the blade slice through the soft tissue as his eyes grew wide and the life faded from them. She was only a few inches from his face and his rank breath blew out on her. The shocked look in his wide eyes almost froze her, like when the ambushers had first attacked. But then the fire commanded her onward. Willoe pulled the sword down and pushed the dead body away from her, then wiped the blood off her hand onto her chest and grabbed the two-handed sword again. She stepped forward to meet the remaining four men.

Two were almost on her, but the world around her had slowed. The men took several moments for each step to complete. Their cheeks grew drawn in and then bulged out as she watched each of their heavy breaths being sucked in and pushed back out.

The one closest had a blade that looked homemade and was sized between a dagger and a short sword. Next to him was another ancient war hammer. It was funny that in the midst of all this her mind, almost separate from her actions, noticed how dirty the remaining men looked. The stench of ale and urine assaulted her nose. Somewhere in her mind the thought formed: *As bad as when Grandfather made us rake the pigsty.* She also noticed the one with the war hammer resembled Old War Hammer, but younger.

Willoe was startled as a sound between a shout and a roar screamed around her. She recognized, through the raging howl, that it had come forth from herself. She jumped the short distance between her and the two men. Their faces were filled with terror but both tried to defend themselves. In one motion, Willoe charged into them, the greatsword in her right hand shoving forward to skewer Long Knife in the chest, while with the arming sword she sliced upward to open a gash in Young War Hammer. The strength flowed through her bones and muscles, the blade nearly cutting Young War Hammer in half from waist to shoulder. The grating of the sword as it cut through bone and sinew rang in her ears.

The greatsword met little resistance as it plunged through ribs and lungs, exiting Long Knife's back. Young War Hammer crumpled to the ground, twitching.

Long Knife stood, his hands wrapped around the blade that kept him from falling. He tried to say something, but only gurgled up blood that poured from his mouth.

Willoe felt a minor strain on her muscles, but easily kept the blade upright even with the weight of the limp body pulling on it. Staring at the man, the fire seemed satisfied by the blood spilled, but in the back of her mind she wondered if he had a family or if he even cared whether he died or not. This close she noticed he had the same nose and eyes as Old War Hammer. The voices pushed her thoughts further into the hollow where her mind waited. She pulled the blade back while pushing on the body and Long Knife dropped next to his comrades.

The only two left were the leader and behind him another man — not much more than a boy — who stood with a homemade variation of a spear. The leader's lips pursed as if he were making a judgment. With some decision made, he yelled, pulled out a long knife with his other hand, and charged forward, the sword and knife both held to attack.

'He be one of some skill.' The voices of the fire filled her mind with the information.

His movements were slow, as had been the others, while her own flowed quickly and effortlessly. She easily blocked his sword with the greatsword and his knife with her own arming sword, then swung the light sword back to slice across the leader's chest. Even at a slowed speed he managed to jump back using his own short sword to deflect Willoe's blow. Her killing stroke missed, but a slash ran across the leader's hauberk, leaving the bottom barely attached by a few strands, and a line of blood seeping through the cloth jerkin he wore under the hauberk. The leader shut his eyes tight for just a moment and gritted his teeth, but then he stepped forward with a deep breath, once again trying to feint with the knife and instead brought the short sword around to stab straight at Willoe's neck.

A part of her felt like laughing at the man's effort, but that was the fire. From the hollow, the other part of her wanted to stop the attacker without killing him, but that part was not in control.

She barely bothered with the leader's knife, as that was just a diversion. Instead she used the arming sword to knock the bandit's sword to the side and spun around, bringing the greatsword in a crosscut that took him at the neck, severing his head from his body in one swing. A burst of red spurted ten feet behind him to splatter the boy, who barely held on to the spear in his hands.

She stood covered with the blood and gore of the five men she had just executed. The remaining boy, without a single piece of armor on his body, stared blankly. Willoe's mind took a moment to notice that the glow around the boy was a pale white-yellow with a hint of black. He stared at her in horror as if she were a mythical monster, then turned to run back down the road.

Willoe stood, lifting her head and roaring loud enough to make the retreating spearman stumble, tripping over his own feet and falling onto the narrow road at her ferocious roar. It wasn't a human sound.

From the ground he looked up as Willoe stared down at him. He was shaking and tears began to flood his eyes. It took two tries to get on his feet, and he finally backed away from her, holding his spear as if it were his last connection to life. In the back of Willoe's mind she could only imagine what she must look like. Both swords covered with blood to the hilts, *dripping* blood, and she could feel her teeth clamped together with lips pulled back in a savage snarl. She took a step toward the spearman. He screamed once and turned to run away, nearly tripping again as he rounded the corner of the road.

The fire urged her to follow and take payment.

26

No Witnesses

The fire said *chase*. It said *enemy*. It told her kill. But as the spearman disappeared, with the last of the ambushers in retreat, a part of her — something other than the Spirits in control — fought for balance, and the fire began to subside. She just stood, panting, and stared at the turn in the road as if expecting the spearman to come running back with more bandits. She stood like that for many heartbeats, her swords held ready for action, but when no new ambushers came her arms started to lower and the fire continued to fade. Finally she turned back to face the battle scene. The horse's blood, mixed with that of the downed men, had spread out to provide a red blanket under the entire scene. She noticed that the horse and four of the downed attackers had no aura, and as she watched, the aura around the fifth, Young War Hammer, faded away as he twitched one last time. The glow vanished entirely. The fallen guardsman, however, still had one. Even though he had not moved from the start. It was weak, but it was there.

This reminded her of the Shields stopping to confront the men who had originally ambushed them at the other end of the road. She started to head in that direction to give what assistance she could, but the burning sensation was fading and she felt so tired. Her arms were like lumps of lead. She thought she might even drop the greatsword as it seemed to have gained tremendous weight in just a few steps. The sound of hoofbeats on the dirt-packed road stopped her and she dropped the arming sword so she could hold the greatsword with both hands.

Riding around the corner at full speed came the champion Shield, Tanguy, closely followed by the Franchon Shield. The fading fire still enabled Willoe to focus on the details of the two warriors. Tanguy had multiple scrapes on his chainmail and gauntlets with a small cut on his right upper leg. Blood stained parts of him and his horse, though little of it appeared to be his. The Franchon Shield had similar marks on his armor and red splotches but also had taken a more serious wound on his left shoulder; the broken shaft of an arrow dangled from the break in chainmail between the shoulder and arm. In his right hand he still held his shorter arming sword, but his greatsword was nowhere in sight.

They slowed as they approached Willoe and both lowered their swords, finally coming to a standstill in front of her. Their eyes went wide as they scanned the carnage behind her. Tanguy looked down at Willoe, her gambeson and surcoat coated in blood, some already drying. "What did— How did you—" If she hadn't felt so worn, and if she wasn't focused on the aura fading around the two Shields as the fire in her veins dimmed into the warm simmer again, she probably would have been amused by the usually stalwart Shield's stuttering.

She put the point of the greatsword on the ground and rested her left hand on the pommel. "Guardsman Frenlin is still alive." She pointed over her shoulder. Tanguy looked in the direction she indicated, where the guardsman was now starting to stir. The Shield, his face still uncomprehending, dismounted and walked past Willoe. He stared at her as he passed. The Franchon Shield walked his horse past her too, never taking his eyes off her. She could see him as he touched his forehead, lips and then heart in the sign of the Burning Lady, followed by a protective oath.

Once past he dismounted and between his one good arm and Tanguy's efforts they were able to nudge the dead horse off the guardsman and pull the guardsman away from the soaked ground. By this time her body had returned to normal, a slow warmth circulated throughout her veins, but no burning.

After watching the two Shields drag the guardsman away, she looked back at the horse with the dead men piled around it. She took in the scene for a few moments. It seemed as a dream to her, but her mind was not foolish enough to think someone else had caused these deaths. A rumbling began in her stomach, accompanied by a pain in her chest, causing her to drop to her knees as she emptied her stomach into the middle of the road. She continued, leaning forward, until only dry heaves wracked her body.

Tanguy walked over and helped her to her feet. "First time can make the stomach weak," he said in a comforting tone that greatly surprised her. Before she could respond, the sound of many horses came from the direction that the lone ambusher had fled.

She forced her body to stand and tried to prepare herself for another attack when the horses rounded the corner and in the lead she could see Captain Harte, with Protector Dougal at his side, followed by a Shield and three mounted guardsmen, all in Cainwen green and gold. They came to a halt, spreading out in a semi-circle at the scene of the battle. Captain Harte and

Dougal nearly jumped from their horses before they came to a stop, a guardsman ran up to grab the hanging reins. Harte slowed to ask about the condition of Guardsman Frenlin from the Franchon Shield, but never stopped as he and Protector Dougal approached Willoe and Tanguy.

Protector Dougal ran up to Willoe and hurriedly examined her. "Where be you wounded?" he asked. She just shook her head. She heard "Hmmm" as he worked his way around to her back, checking every inch of her upper body. She thought maybe she *had* been wounded when he stopped for several moments before continuing. Evidently satisfied she had not taken any serious wounds, he stood to her right. He looked down and Willoe followed his eyes to the mess at her feet. She was mortified. He seemed to understand, though; he squeezed her shoulder and said softly, "For every life you deliver to the Spirits, there be a price. Even if it be deserved, or not of your choosing, with time it be possible to reap an impoverished soul." She had to think about this *I guess everyone, even a warrior as unflinching as Protector Dougal, has to give some of themselves to take a life*. She realized that if one gave too much, then all that would be left would be an empty husk. *An impoverished soul.*

Harte stopped in front of Tanguy. "We caught this worm. He darted right into us." He pointed to the spearman that had retreated from Willoe's swords, now held by a guardsman on either side of him, his head hanging low, his expression forlorn. "He was running down the road right at us. When he saw us he threw his spear away and dropped face first to the road and kept screaming, '*Mercy, I didn't harm anyone.*' It took no time at all to get from him what had happened. We rode as fast as we could."

"We were ambushed," Tanguy reported bluntly. "A large group attacked from the front and killed Guardsman—"

"Ernaut. Guardsman Ernaut." The Franchon Shield provided.

"I ordered Guardsman Frenlin to flee with Prince Rowyn." Tanguy glanced over at the pile of dead men and then back to Harte. "It appears they had planned for that." He continued in a matter-of-fact manner as if talking about the latest harvest. "After Prince Rowyn fled, the ambushers scarcely pressed their attack. We killed two and wounded a couple of others before they fled. We would have pursued but there was another in the woods with a bow." Tanguy pointed to the shaft protruding from the Franchon Shield's arm.

"Good judgment. Protecting Prince Rowyn was your priority." Captain Harte nodded his commendation.

Protector Dougal looked up and then back down the road. "Possibly they be only holding you."

"What do you mean?" Tanguy spun around and looked quizzically at Protector Dougal.

"Some tie you two in knots, knowing the first thing you would do be get

Prince Rowyn away from the fight. Once out of sight, and belief be the Prince be on his way to safety, the other bandits attack the Prince. Only one guardsman to protect him." His forehead crinkled in thought and he added, "They knew Prince Rowyn be with the advance party."

Willoe swallowed to make sure nothing would come up before speaking. "The leader." She pointed to the headless body. "He said they wanted to take me alive."

Turning to the pile of bodies, Harte asked, "What happened here? Guardsman Frenlin?"

Tanguy's voice suddenly changed, the excitement creeping in and trying to force its way to the surface. "Not at all. It appears Guardsman Frenlin was trapped under his horse and unconscious until we arrived." He indicated the Franchon Shield and himself then turned to face Willoe. "This is all Prince Rowyn." He emphasized the title in a different way this time, and it held both awe and fear. "When we came back here thinking the Prince and Guardsman Frenlin would have already reached you, we found this!" He indicated the dead men once again.

Master Gwron, whom Willoe had not seen in the back of the pack, walked closer, taking in the entire scene. "How?"

Willoe was still sweating from the heaving and the burning sensation. She tried to think of an answer, but there was no good answer to his question. Gwron would have been intimately aware of Rowyn's skill level from their time in the Pell.

She was saved from answering when Protector Dougal spoke up. "The Prince has been training with me in his spare time. I asked him not to tell anyone as I wanted him to be judged less than he was in case he needed to face a deadly opponent."

What? Willoe almost turned toward Protector Dougal in shock, but recovered her composure and stared straight ahead. She knew Rowyn had never spent a single minute of training with their Protector, so why was he covering for her?

"Well, it seemed to have worked." Gwron walked closer to examine the details of the wounds like a master carpenter appraising another artisan's work. Walking away and toward Protector Dougal, he said "In the future I would appreciate if you conducted your training in the Pell." He smiled with just the hint of a laugh. "And since you are so set on improving on my work, you can share a little of that training by working with some of the other young nobles who think swordplay is nothing more than dancing around waving a sharp stick in the air." He ended a couple of feet from Protector Dougal, his smile broadening. "I am sure the king will agree with me when we get back."

"Yes, I be sure he will," was Protector Dougal's only reply.

They were interrupted as Mael and a large party of riders arrived.

Among them was Bat-Uul and Aeron. Mael naturally took charge and rode up to them, peering at the bodies as he passed them. "Harte?" he demanded.

Captain Harte relayed everything that had been reported up until now. Mael turned in his saddle to look back at the dead bodies and then at Willoe. He stared at her for a moment and shook his head slightly in disbelief. He turned his horse sideways and commanded the two guardsmen to bring the dejected ambusher forward. Bat-Uul walked his horse up a little behind Mael. He never took his eyes off of Willoe, a frown creasing his face as if annoyed.

"Why did you attack my men?" Mael demanded of the bandit.

Willoe noticed just how dirty the boy was. His pants and shirt were so threadbare she wondered how they stayed on. He did not look very dangerous now. He just stood there with his head hung low. The guardsmen were evidently holding him up or he would likely have fallen.

"I asked you a question, whoreson," Mael bellowed. He gestured to one of the guardsmen, who grabbed the boy by the hair and pulled his head up so he was looking at Mael.

"Why did you attack my men?"

The boy gulped, his fear-filled eyes wide as he cringed from Mael. "We... we were paid for it."

"By whom and for what reason?" Mael was angry, which Willoe knew would not have a good outcome.

"I don't know. I sorry as a worn rope, Lord. I mean no harm." Tears rolled down the boy's cheeks.

Mael moved his horse forward to stand right in front of the boy, causing the younger man to try to move back, but the guardsman held him in place. "Who? *Who* would dare to attack my men?" Mael leaned down and towered menacingly over the boy.

The boy began to whimper. "Randin." He pointed to the decapitated body. "He and his brother Janen — at Raven's Head Inn — he offered us more than I can'na make farming in two seaons. We been working ahead for days until just a while ago, when Randin and Janen led us into the woods."

Mael's gaze followed the boy's finger and he sniffed in disgust. "He does not look like he would have that sort of gold."

"I see som'on." The boy spoke rapidly. "They didn't see me. I see the two of them talking to som'on out by the stable. He pass Randin a bag. A money bag."

"What did this someone look like?" Mael ordered the young man to answer.

"I'm not sure. It was gettin dark and they were across the yard." The boy became more frightened.

Mael leaned closer and screamed, "Tell me!"

"He had a dark skin. That's all I see. I can'na see his face. He had a hood. But the odor. Even from where I was there was a smell—" The boy gagged and put his hands up to his throat. His eyes popped and he appeared to be choking for no apparent reason.

Mael looked at the guardsmen. "What's wrong with him?"

Both guardsmen looked confused and let go of the bandit, stepping away. The ragtag boy dropped to the ground and squirmed, continuing to claw at his throat. His dirty fingernails ripped at his skin, causing runlets of blood as he tried to open his own throat and breathe. No one moved. No one knew what to do. The boy squirmed another moment, turning a bluish color, and finally his hands dropped and he ceased to move, his eyes wide open.

"What in the name of the Shadows happened?" Mael screamed.

Gwron knelt down and checked the boy. "Strangled." He indicated marks around the dead boy's neck, ones that were not from the boy himself.

"How?" Mael demanded.

No one had an answer. Mael turned his horse toward Willoe and glared at her suspiciously while speaking to the assembly in general. "Why would they want to capture Prince Rowyn?" He turned around in a circle to look at Harte, Protector Dougal, and Tanguy, his face contorted in rage.

No one answered that question either. Willoe glanced at Protector Dougal, who was staring absentmindedly into the distance.

She turned back to stare at her older sibling, then heard the Protector whisper to himself, "And how did they know she was even in the advance party?"

She flinched and stifled a gasp as she lowered her head. She hoped her shocked expression had not caught anyone's attention. She tried to calm her breathing for raising her head and staring straight ahead. *By the Shadows, he knows I'm not Rowyn!*

27

A Hint at the Truth

The leaves swirled around Casandra as she focused her attention on the small whirlwind she had created with little instruction. Just a few turns of the glass. "Rowyn," she yelled out in her excitement, but he just sat under the Learning Tree with a sour look on his face. He had tried four more times over as many days, yet it ended without Rowyn being able to merge with a Spiro, or even come close to one. They fled whenever he came near. All Saraid could do was rub his chin and frown. His best advice was to keep trying until Cian returned. Casandra had to commend her cousin's efforts, though. He did not give up and kept trying different ways of interacting with the Spiros, as directed by Saraid.

As difficult as it was, she pushed thoughts of Rowyn aside, instead choosing to enjoy all the colors the fall leaves created. It reminded Casandra of one of her mother's tapestries back at Castle Mount Somerled, and how much her mother loved bright colors. Casandra felt a moment of longing for home, but only momentarily, as she knew she only needed to insert her fingers into the Ken Mud and see her mother at any time.

The wind spinning along the outside churned up everything in its path, but the inside of the circle was barely affected. Her long hair flowed straight up in the wind's draft, the tips twirling and spinning around each other. She knew it would take half the night to untangle it, but for now she enjoyed the freedom of the chaos. She wasn't being tossed about, but she was glad she had worn the belted tunic over the breeches, both given to her by Helel and her other new friends.

As she slowed the whirlwind and the leaves settled to the ground, she said the words Helel had taught her to thank the particular Spiro that had helped her.

Casandra strolled over and sat down under the tree next to Rowyn, who was looking at the ground while pulling apart a blade of grass. Casandra didn't know what to say to him so she looked over to the two Elfs and felt content in the afterglow of her merging. "That was so refreshing." She remembered that the two could not merge and was ashamed that she was flaunting the way she felt. "I am sorry that you cannot experience what it feels like. "Do not feel ashamed," Saraid said cheerfully.

Casandra had forgotten that the two Elfs could feel her embarrassment, which simply served to sharpen the feeling.

"We could not feel the Spiro itself, but we could feel your joy at the merging," Helel added, her tone very sympathetic and assuring. "How do you feel?"

"Not tired like before." Casandra had had to rest up for a couple of turns after merging with a Spiro the first few times, but she required less and less time to recover. Helel had said Casandra was growing accustomed to the merging and her body was learning how to ration her Spirit essence so that the Spiro couldn't deplete it so quickly.

"That is good. Your skills as a wizard are developing quickly," Saraid said. He turned his head to look at Helel. "Have you conducted more tests of her ability to heal?"

"Not necessary. Over the last two days a host of animals have appeared along with a Stromworth and a Culrant."

The Stromworths had shocked Casandra at first. Humanoid in appearance but half the size of an Elf with red skin and two horns on their head — it took all her courage to approach it even after Helel had told Casandra the Stromworth was as intelligent as Casandra herself. And then there was the Culrant, which reminded Casandra of a large porcupine the size of a donkey.

"All with problems that Casey diagnosed and healed quickly." Helel smiled at her student.

Casandra smiled at the compliment. She wondered what the ladies at Castle Westhedge would think if they knew that Casandra was not only a wizard, but a Healer. Her smile turned into a grin.

The wind blew gently through Rowyn's hair and he concentrated again like Saraid had instructed him. After a few moments his mind wandered and he knew he was going to fail once again. After the first three attempts, Spiros never came close enough for the flame to come between Rowyn and them.

He leaned his head back and inhaled deeply, then brought his head back and opened his eyes. "I do not know how many times I must repeat myself. I do not have the gift." His voice was harsher than he meant it to be, but he was getting tired of people telling him he could do something that he knew he could not.

Saraid crinkled his lips, then said in an encouraging tone, "You do have the gift. I can sense it in you."

"You sound like my uncle." Rowyn tried to keep the irritation out of his voice. He had come to like the Elf, even though Saraid kept pushing him to try to merge — something which he knew he could not do.

Rowyn just wanted to stop all this. He had been at it all week and he didn't see where continued attempts would have different results. No matter how hard he tried, if he didn't have the gift he could wander the *il fennore* forever without ever achieving what Saraid and the others wanted him to do.

He started to argue the point for the fifth time in as many turns of the glass when he suddenly collapsed to the ground as if his bones had dissolved. He lay there, on his side in the grass, his thoughts jumbled. He stared, the blades of grass blocking much of his view. He could hear Saraid yelling in the background as the green blades faded and were replaced with tall clumps of willowing grass. He lay there for several moments, unable to move, and then the world disappeared again into utter darkness.

Rowyn came awake as he was rolled over, unable to resist, and stared up into the Elf's face. A strange thought poked at his mind. *I didn't know that Elfs had beards.* Then he realized that everything was fuzzy, not just Saraid's face.

"What happened? Rowyn, can you hear me?" Saraid shouted.

Not able to answer, Rowyn just looked up and blinked, trying to clear his vision. He felt like he had just ridden for a week straight without any sleep. He was having trouble keeping his eyes open, but he strained not to close them.

Finally things became clearer just as Casandra and Helel's faces came into view. His cousin's mouth was wide open as she stared down at him.

"What happened to him?" Helel asked quickly.

"He was just sitting there talking, then he keeled over."

"What's wrong with him?" Casandra's tone held the panic that Rowyn felt himself.

Saraid shook his head. "I don't know. He was fine, then—" He pointed toward Rowyn's prone body.

Rowyn lay there for a while, long enough for Drel Corklin to run up, look down at Rowyn's face, then disappear again. Saraid and Helel traded possibilities back-and-forth as to what had happened to Rowyn while they found flaws in each other's diagnosis. Casandra kept talking to Rowyn in a soft and pleasant voice. He didn't know if she were trying to calm him or herself. Probably both.

After a bit longer the fog began to clear from Rowyn's mind. "I... I think I am feeling better." And he was. He could sense his arms and legs again. He was no longer paralyzed though he still felt very weak, as if he had been squeezed like a lemon.

"Are you sure?" Casandra leaned closer and Rowyn could smell primroses. It must be something about her, as he thought she didn't have time to bring any fragrances with her when Cian had taken them away from the camp.

"I think so." He was regaining a little strength, but still could not sit up. In the back of his mind an image flashed just for a moment. It was Willoe, but not the twin he knew. This image was feral like a beast, wild and crazed. It was covered with blood and if not for the eyes Rowyn would not have recognized her. But it was Willoe. He knew without a doubt.

His thoughts were interrupted as a deep voice boomed from off to Rowyn's left. "What has happened?"

He could feel the vibration through the ground as someone approached and then Cian was looking down at him. Cian twisted his head from side to side, inspecting Rowyn from different angles.

The others all spoke up telling Cian what they knew.

The old Elf only listened for a few moments, then shushed them to silence. He bent down and used a finger to hold open one of Rowyn's eyes, and then the other, while he inspected them.

"What did you see?" Cian commanded in a no-nonsense manner.

How could he know I saw something? The implications of that stunned Rowyn.

"Tell me. What did you see?" Cian's tone demanded an immediate response.

"Willoe." Rowyn's voice was dry. "It was Willoe. But I barely recognized her."

Cian stood as Saraid helped Rowyn to sit. The old Elf looked up at the sky as if looking for guidance, then he spoke in a saddened voice. "It has begun." He scanned the sky and Rowyn couldn't tell if the Elf was questioning or proclaiming as he continued. "He is the weak one. The sacrifice."

28

Payment

They moved away from the ambush, the forest fighting them all the way and Janen cursing the entire time. Another thorn snagged his jacket and he had to pull it loose, creating one more rip. He would have to replace his jacket and pants after they got back to Rain Hollow. But five Gold Stags would buy a lot of jackets. It wasn't like he and Rankin were going to share any of that with the other men. Well, they would have to give something to Jurdurl. They would need him to help with the others. After all, this wouldn't be the first time that the brothers have had to reduce the number of shares to be distributed. The crossbowman had been invaluable in the past. To make it even better, Jurdurl was not overly greedy and didn't seem to flinch at any task, no matter how gruesome, a fact that had fit into the brothers' plans very nicely more than once.

As they approached the agreed-upon meeting spot, Janen sent Jurdurl out to the side with his crossbow. He told the others it was to cover them, just in case. Janen had lost the farm boy and the drunkard to the Shields. He couldn't remember the boy's or the drunk's name, but he didn't really care; the diversion was needed to separate the Prince from the Shields. It just meant two fewer to deal with after they met up with Rankin and his men.

His mind wandered as he pushed his way through the thick underbrush. *Let's get this over with and get out of here.* There was a particular blonde in Rain Hollow he had plans to spend at least a week with, along with a never-ending supply of the tavern's best ale. By the Spirits, he could spend an entire moon. After paying off the crossbowman, he and Rankin would have more than two Goldens each. He could live like a king for a couple of moons and still have plenty left over.

Pushing branches aside, they forced their way through one last barrier and came into the clearing, but Rankin was nowhere in sight. Instead they found Red Robe, the money man, with an exotic-looking warrior next to him. Janen wasn't sure if he was the same Red Robe who had handed over the Goldens. He wore the same priest-like robes. But, like before, Janen wondered who the man was. Every priest he had seen wore either white, brown, green or black robes, whereas the man standing across the opening stood out clearly in blood red edged in golden thread. Janen didn't know, but he figured the trim alone would cost a small fortune.

Just like when they had been paid, the red hood was pulled up over the priest's head so only a dark slit was visible to Janen. In fact, the only thing that showed were the priest's hands. They were dark on top, though not dirty, and lighter underneath, with spindle fingers that stuck out like crooked branches. The priest wore a gold ring with a large blue stone that sparkled with the setting sun. Janen recognized the ring from before. *It must be the same one, but what is he doing here?* Whether it was the same or not, Janen did not like this change in plans. Any change in plans made him nervous. Janen and his men walked out into the clearing. A smirk passed Janen's lips. *Maybe putting Jurdurl out there was a fortunate accident.*

As they strode out into the small meadow, Janen got a good look at the guard. He was definitely not a Taran, though he did look a little like the one Haldanen he had seen, but shorter. In fact, the guard was a good three fingers shorter than even Janen, who was not a tall man. He wore a strange helmet covered with what looked like some type of hair sticking out of its pointed top. The guard wore a vest of metal strips strung together with leather straps. He had loose-fitting trousers and knee-high leather boots. He wore a coat that hung to his knees with sleeves that seemed too long, as they were rolled back. His skin color was much darker than a Taran, more like the robed man standing across from Janen, and while he had a long mustache his chin was cleanly shaven.

Very strange, but if it came down to it Janen was certain a bolt would easily take out the strange guard and he had no doubt he could deal with the smaller hooded man. Janen walked to the middle of the small meadow and stood, his hands on his hips and his chest out in a defiant manner. The other six men spread out behind him. Most were just common thugs or farmers fallen on hard times. He was not counting on them if things went sour.

"So, did you come to check on your money?" Even with his husky voice, Janen's sarcastic remark came through clearly. A couple of his men laughed; the others barely squawked, not sure what to think. The robed figure and his guard did not move. "We were going to deliver the boy to you back in Rain Hollow, but if you want to take him now that would be even better." He looked around, wondering what was delaying his younger brother. The longer they waited, the more nervous Janen became. He frowned as he thought, *Rankin should be here any moment and we can finish this.*

"Rankin will be here soon, so we—" Janen began.

"He will not be coming." The voice was higher than Janen remembered and it definitely had a foreign lilt to it.

He didn't know what sort of game Red Robe was playing at, but he would trust his brother with his life. And if Rankin said he would be here, he would be here. Unless—

"He's dead," Red Robe finished the thought for him. The blunt statement was spoken with no signs of feeling.

Gritting his teeth, Janen stomped toward Red Robe. The guard stepped forward, his sword flashing into his hand so quickly Janen never saw his hand move. Janen stopped short of the guard's reach and stared warily at the long, curved sword pointing at his throat. Janen's hand wavered just above his own sword, but as much as his anger urged him to pull it, part of his mind cautioned. Instead he looked over at Red Robe and demanded, "How do you know that?"

"He and all his men." He paused and Janen could see the robe shake just slightly, and then Red Robe continued. "Yes... all of them are dead."

Janen stepped back to put a little more distance between himself and the guard, who stepped back next to Red Robe, his expression never changing. The sound of a couple of his men stepping up behind him made Janen feel a bit more confident. He drew his own sword and, smiling, he yelled, "Jurdurl. If Red Robe here or his fancy guard takes one step in any direction, kill them." He waved the end of his sword around, taunting Red Robe and his man. "Now we will find out the truth about these lies you are telling." He started forward again, determined to wring the truth out of the lying priest.

Red Robe reached out one hand, his scrawny fingers pointing at Janen, and spoke words Janen couldn't decipher.

"Esotati yulli."

As the last word ended Janen froze in place. His sword was pointed toward Red Robe but he couldn't move it. Fear gripped him as he realized he couldn't move any of his limbs. He stood there, one foot planted forward, his hand reaching out with the sword. He couldn't grasp what was going on and began to panic. His vision was fixed forward on Red Robe. He couldn't even glance left or right. But he found his voice worked and he yelled Jurdurl's name feverishly, hoping the crossbowman would come to his aid.

As he watched, another guard like the one next to Red Robe stepped into his line of vision. The warrior threw a body at Red Robe's feet. Janen's stomach turned over as he saw the hand of the body and the mark that Jurdurl said his father had burned into him as a child, for fun. Thoughts ran rampant through Janen's mind, but as hard as he tried his mind couldn't comprehend what was happening to him. He couldn't hear any of his men and finally realized they were most likely frozen like him.

Red Robe leaned down to look at the body at his feet and then stepped over the body to approach Janen. Even when he stopped a finger's breadth beyond Janen's outstretched sword, Janen's gaze still could not penetrate the depth of Red Robe's hood.

The priest pushed Janen's sword to the side effortlessly and stepped a little closer. "You are a pitiful man, are you not?" The words took Janen by surprise. The tone reminded him of his father when the old man used the rope on Rankin and him, which had happened often. "Your brother failed to take the boy and died in the attempt. *Esotele yulla.*"

Janen's concern for his brother disappeared as Janen contemplated his own possible death. "Even if Rankin failed," — he still wasn't sure that it was the case — "we can still get the boy for you," Janen pleaded, his voice hopeful.

The red hood shook slightly. "But you were supposed to fail."

This confused Janen all the more. Why had they been paid to fail?

The familiar swish of metal sounded behind him, followed by a dull sound like the slap of a butcher cutting up a cow — also an all-too-familiar sound. His breath started coming quicker as the same sound was rapidly repeated seven more times. The smell of fresh blood contrasted with the spicy nut odor he was now picking up from the man in front of him. "I'll give back the money."

"The money is unimportant." Red Robe gestured with his hand and spoke quickly, "*Esotati yulli.*"

Though he couldn't understand the words, part of his mind — the part that wasn't petrified with fear — wondered where this priest had come from. The other part of his mind, the one concerned with his survival, tried to continue bargaining for his life, but his lips wouldn't move. They suddenly froze with the rest of his body.

"Do not feel your efforts were in vain," the priest told him in the same lecturing tone. "You did succeed. The test was very successful... very successful indeed." The priest turned his back on Janen and nodded to the guard who had been standing several steps behind Red Robe. Janen stared as Red Robe walked away and the guard stepped calmly to Janen's left out of Janen's field of vision. He would have cried out, if he were able, as he heard the familiar swish once again.

It had been hard for Bat-Uul to get away from camp. Everyone was on edge after the incident with Prince Rowyn. It had come as a shock when Bat-Uul had ridden into the blood-filled scene. He was baffled like the others. What he had seen and been told about Prince Rowyn had made Ser Tanguy's tale anything but believable. Then there was that farm boy. Luck had been with Bat-Uul as he was mounted to the side of the main group. He was sure no one had seen him when the gift had been sucked out of him. What Dimah-Uul had done to Bat-Uul was unconscionable.

As the priest pushed through the thick branches he did not feel the spiteful undergrowth that whipped his arms and legs. He could sense the other Uul's presence just ahead. He broke through the brush and tree limbs onto a worn footpath that ran through the dense forest. Approaching from up ahead was Dimah-Uul, followed by three warriors. Their helmets were made from iron with a pointed top and a tail of horse hair coming out and hanging down in the back. Leather hung down the neck and the fur ear flaps were folded up and secured to the iron helmet.

Steppe warriors, Bat-Uul thought, feeling a foul taste form in his mouth. It was seldom one saw Jidig warriors outside of the great plains in the far eastern kingdoms. They must have come with the new Uul that Dimah-Uul had mentioned in his letter. Why would this Chuluun-Uul need to bring the savage prairie warriors to Taran? Many questions battered Bat-Uul's mind, but right now he only had one for his superior.

"What did you do to me?" Bat-Uul shouted at the approaching Uul, who had just noticed the raging priest in his path.

"Is there a problem?" Dimah-Uul stopped and the skin around his eyes tightened as he glared at his assistant. "Shouldn't you be at the camp?"

Bat-Uul had never before been violated as he had with the farm boy and the pent-up hate he had for his superior came out in a flood. "You know exactly what the problem is. You used my Spirit. You drew upon my gift to kill that boy."

"You are strong for one so young. I knew it would not harm you. I could not afford to be drained." Dimah-Uul treated the incident as if it had been nothing more than a walk through woods instead of the defilement it had been.

The casual way his superior addressed Bat-Uul's concerns only infuriated him even more. "I would never have given you permission." Bat-Uul could still feel the perverted Uul's presence in his Spirit and Bat-Uul wondered if the slimy feeling would ever leave him. "You had no right—"

"I had every right!" The older priest's red hood flew back as he stepped up to within a few fingers of Bat-Uul's face. "I am on a mission from Chuluun-Uul. He is one of the Gai-Ten."

Bat-Uul was stunned. He did not know how many Uul belonged to the Master's inner circle, but it was said that they could be counted on two hands. What could possibly have brought one of the Gai-Ten to Taran?

"Gai-Ten?"

"Yes, he will lead us in the Master's will." The look on Dimah-Uul's face was one Bat-Uul had rarely seen, except when the old priest had returned from one of his 'private' visits to the dungeons, the ones he did not discuss with Bat-Uul, and that Bat-Uul never asked about.

The thought that their mission was important enough to warrant a Gai-Ten momentarily distracted Bat-Uul and he felt a sense of pride. He shook his head, trying to clear the thought that was contrary to the Shin-il Way. "You Shifted my Spirit!" The fury had not completely died and Bat-Uul wanted answers.

"Whatever has happened has happened for a reason. Your strength is to be commended. It would have killed a lesser priest. Though I felt hesitancy in your Spirit to do my will." Dimah-Uul looked steadily into Bat-Uul's eyes.

Bat-Uul rarely crossed into the *il fennore*. His past ventures into the Spirit world had been pleasant. His mentor in Avanis, Poojan-Uul, had shown him how to attract Spiros and merge.

But this time he had been directed. Directed by Dimah-Uul to do something tainted, something wicked. Something Bat-Uul had never experienced before. His mentor had mentioned the Shift, but his mentor had never mentioned how it would leave Bat-Uul. The feeling was coarse, like being scrubbed with unpolished rocks. He still felt queasy from the contact, as if he had been soaked in a foul liquid and had swallowed much of it. Dimah-Uul had used Bat-Uul's Spirit to pull the Spirit out of the young bandit. Bat-Uul was stunned and confused. He had never considered that anyone would use the Shift to do such a thing... especially a Uul.

"And the boy...?"

Dimah-Uul stepped back with a sneer. "Just make sure both Prince Rowyn and Prince Mael make it to White Cliffs safely." Dimah-Uul paused and added with an ominous smile, "Your failure in bringing Princess Willoe has been noted by the Gai-Ten."

"King Einion disagreed." Surely the Gai-Ten would understand that Bat-Uul could not force the Cainwen king to send his granddaughter.

"You should be returning to camp before you are missed." The older, bent-over priest dismissed his junior.

Dimah-Uul pushed past Bat-Uul to continue down the path.

As a final thought, Bat-Uul grabbed his superior's arm and asked, "And the bandits?"

Dimah-Uul stopped and looked at the hand on his arm. The smile had vanished and been replaced with another sneer. The feelings between the two were mutual. Bat-Uul knew the older priest would just as soon feed Bat-Uul to the dogs as talk to him. But the sneer soon widened into a grisly smile, giving Bat-Uul a sick feeling, and then the old priest spoke once more before continuing on his way with the guards in tow. "The plan required it."

Bat-Uul stared after the retreating priest and his Jidig warrior escort. He could still see the young bandit's eyes bulging as he gasped for breath. He turned to head back to camp and noticed a figure standing back in the trees that ran along the path. "Caspar-Jin?" Bat-Uul wasn't sure if it was his aide or not.

"I did not mean to disturb you." The aide bowed with folded hands. "When I went looking for you, no one knew of your whereabouts."

"I had to get away." It was true in one sense.

"May I accompany you back to camp? You must be exhausted." Caspar-Jin stepped to the side to expose a path that Bat-Uul assumed led back to camp.

"Yes, that would be good. I am really tired." Bat-Uul started down the path with his aide close behind. He knew it was not really his fault, but Bat-Uul still felt a sense of responsibility for the young bandit's death. Dimah-Uul did not know how close Bat-Uul actually was to giving up his own Spirit. It had taken all of Bat-Uul's inner strength to keep the Shifting from draining his Spirit in the process and he stumbled as he struggled to make it back to camp.

"Let me help you." Caspar-Jin stepped up and held Bat-Uul's arm as they walked.

Bat-Uul wondered if Dimah-Uul would try again and if the Gai-Ten knew that the older priest could Shift. Regardless, Bat-Uul was determined that it would never happen again, though he did not know how to prevent it. Yet.

"You may want to rest after your ordeal," The Jin priest suggested.

It was kind of his aide to be so concerned for his well-being, Bat-Uul thought. Dimah-Uul's foul seizure of Bat-Uul's Spirit had truly drained Bat-Uul. Only then did it occur to Bat-Uul to wonder what Caspar-Jin would know of his ordeal. Did he know what Dimah-Uul had done? Or even that Dimah-Uul was here? And how had his aide, his companion, and advisor found him so easily?

29

In the Darkest of Woods

They had passed a greater number of farms and several large villages over the last couple of days, which Aeron had said could only mean they were getting close to the city of Lealacité and Castle White Cliffs. Captain Harte confirmed this to Willoe as they headed off the road to set up camp for the night. Two more days and they would see White Cliffs sitting along the Wailing Straights.

Ser Tanguy drifted back next to Willoe when Aeron was out with one of the hunters, something he seemed to enjoy greatly.

"How do you fare today, my Prince?" Tanguy actually wore the hint of a smile.

"I will be glad to see the white walls of Lealacité." She smiled gently in return. This had not been the first time the Shield had started a conversation with her. Many of the Shields had now begun to talk with her in passing and even shared a jest or two. She could only imagine that, after the ambush, the Shields' gradual acceptance of her was because some type of brotherhood now existed between them and her. The guardsmen were even friendly, more so than after the incident with the stream bathers.

"I will not argue with that."

They rode in silence for a few moments before curiosity got the better of Willoe. It had not really bothered her, but it was one of those things that wouldn't leave her alone. "Why do you do my brother's bidding?"

"Your brother?" He looked a bit confused.

"Mael." She pointed to the front of the column.

Tanguy smiled again. "We have history." She must have had a strange look, because he laughed. "Ten years ago I was accompanying the Crown Prince, hunting south of Westhedge. You were but a babe, so we only had

Prince Mael and a small escort with us. Mael was still yet a man, had not earned his spurs yet." He looked as if remembering the time as though it were yesterday.

"Ser Tanguy." A guardsman came riding from the front. "His Highness commands your presence."

The Shield did not seem disturbed by the blunt order. Instead he looked at Willoe. "To shorten a long tale, I was riding alone, scouting out an area for the next day's hunt. A foolish thing to do on my own. My only excuse is that I was young and inexperienced. My horse was spooked by a mountain lion and I was thrown to the ground, breaking my leg. The horse ran off with my sword still in its scabbard. I tried to move away, but the lion had other ideas. It moved slowly toward me and I pulled my arming sword, though I had little hope it would save me."

Willoe was caught up in the tale, leaning forward, holding her breath.

"The lion leaped and I held up my sword, but a spear came from behind and to my side, taking the lion in the chest and knocking it to the ground next to me. Next thing I know your brother, the heir apparent, not even a man yet, jumped over me and with his sword, half the size of my greatsword, stabbed the lion four more times until it quit moving."

Willoe finally let out her breath. She had never heard the story and was amazed at Mael's bravery.

"That, my Prince, is why I do your brother's bidding." He laughed again. "And gladly." He spurred his horse and galloped toward the front.

One of the carriages had broken down earlier in the day, and after the ambush they traveled only as fast as the slowest part of convoy could move. Mael was not happy because this had put them two days behind schedule. It had taken half the morning to get the carriage moving again, which meant the plan to stop at the village ahead had been abandoned in favor of pulling off into a nearby field. The field was near a stream for water and surrounded by a forest that would provide firewood.

"Prince Rowyn." The page Tomos came up as Willoe dismounted, a routine he had established.

"Yes, Tomos?" She lowered her voice to match Rowyn's.

The boy's smile was infectious. He always seemed to be enjoying whatever he was doing no matter the task, even emptying Mael's chamber pot. Both he and his brother treated Willoe with the same respect they did all the other nobles. Even after the ambush he did not hold back in the friendly banter she had encouraged with him.

She couldn't say the same about many of the servants whom she would catch glancing her way when they thought she wasn't looking. At least the Shields and guardsmen had accepted her, to a certain extent. She only wished Mael felt the same, but he seemed bent on ignoring her as if she were a blemish on his personal honor.

"Lord Aeron's and your Lordship's tent is ready." He pointed over to a spot near the edge of the forest.

"Tomos." Willoe narrowed her eyes and shook her head.

At first he frowned and then smiled again. "Aeron's and your tent is ready."

She had told him to speak informally with her and Aeron when others were not around.

"You will not be a page forever. Someday you will be a Shield and a Baron. Maybe even a noble of greater rank. It is good to practice being a man with equals." She started to reach out her hand to cup his face, but then just put it on his shoulder at the last moment. It took a constant effort to be Rowyn.

"Thank you, Lo—" He stumbled over the word, but the grin remained. "Rowyn," he finished. He paused and she could see he wanted to say something, but hesitated.

"Was there something else, Tomos?"

"I was just wondering if you are feeling alright." He said it slowly. "They say that you weren't yourself. You know… when—"

"I'm fine, Tomos." She tried to smile to put the boy at ease. "Thank you for asking."

He smiled, making his eyes narrow.

She handed him her pack, then unhooked the scabbard and greatsword from the horse. The weight of the weapon was substantial. She pulled the sword from the scabbard and held it out with both hands to look down the blade. It was like the one she had used in training with Protector Dougal back at Westhedge. He had given it to her the day after the ambush, when they stopped for the night.

"Come with me." The Protector had drawn the sword and handed it to her, then led her away from camp to a small clearing separated from the camp by tall oak trees. He stopped her on one side of the clearing and then walked across to the other side, turned back to face her, and pulled another greatsword from a scabbard he had been carrying. With knees bent he told her, "We see how ye be improved." He held the sword out with both hands tilted toward her, his eyes steadily watching her.

"I am tired. Now is not a good time." She held the hilt of the sword with both hands, with the tip of the sword resting on the ground in front of her. She knew Rowyn had trained with the greatsword; it was one of the weapons Master Gwron insisted all the young nobles learn. But she also knew he was not very adept with the greatsword... or any weapon, for that matter. Not that she was an expert, but at least she knew the basic movements.

Protector Dougal took two steps forward and swung his sword down at an angle toward her shoulder, his movements quick and decisive.

A blaze burst forth from her chest, like a pine cone erupting in a campfire, and filled her arms and legs. The world slowed and she could see the Protector's sword falling toward her, but as if looking at his movements from faraway through a spyglass. The part of her that was the old Willoe settled in as an observer.

Her arms easily lifted the sword, bringing it up and catching the Protector's plunging strike well away from her body. Her sword pushed his up and to her side, then her body continued to spin around with the momentum of her sword. He was recovering from her block as she spun back to face him, just bringing his sword back from his side. But in her current state, his movements were too slow and her sword reached for his side.

Her thoughts jumped forward through the spyglass and slammed into her mind. It felt as if she had bounced off a wall. Her hand jerked up and the sword missed the Protector's body, slicing across his forearm. She dropped the sword as the fire died and she stared at the cut in his arm, putting both hands over her mouth.

He stared down at the wound, inspecting it without so much as a grunt. "Nay, but a scratch." He looked back at her, his head tilted a little and he rubbed his chin with the wounded arm. "It be well enough." He turned and picked up the scabbard of the greatsword he still held. Then he came back to her and picked up her greatsword, handing it back to her with the hint of a smile. "Ye need to take more care with ye weapons." Then he strode past her back toward the camp.

"Rowyn. Are you sure you are okay?" Tomos' worrisome tone interrupted her reflection.

"Yes. I am fine. I really am." She sheathed the greatsword and handed it to him to take to her tent. "Off with you now. I can find my way to the tent on my own."

Tomos nodded and headed off with the pack and scabbard.

Once the page had left, Willoe's shoulders nearly collapsed as the horror filled her mind for the hundredth time. She tried to keep a cheerful face to the world... well, as cheerful as Rowyn was known for being, which meant she didn't have to try too hard. Between the constant fear of her deception being exposed and the fire, she spent a great deal of her time tense and feeling worn. At least the incident with Protector Dougal had proved that even if she couldn't control the fire, she could possibly influence it. She didn't know if she could do it again, though.

Aeron walked up. "Supper should be ready soon. Protector Dougal tells me we are starting early tomorrow to make up for today's delay. I would expect it to be an early night for everyone."

She only nodded, her head lowered.

"Are you well?" He tilted his headed to look at her face. "Is it the dreams again?"

The night of the ambush she had told Aeron what had happened; the fire and the voices, leaving nothing out. He hadn't seemed to accept her explanation completely, yet, as he had himself said, 'You couldn't have done it yourself.' In spite of that, he had tried to talk her out of the mood almost as many times as it had come over her.

"I thought you agreed that there was nothing you could do?" He pulled her head up to look in his eyes, then let go before anyone could see. "Didn't you say the fire took over and you could only observe, not control your arms and legs?"

She nodded again, but this time stared into his face.

"Then crying over something you had no control over is a waste of your time." He smiled at her and winked.

"I'm not crying." She lifted her head and wiped at a tear.

"Whatever you say." He laughed.

"Prince Rowyn," an authoritative voice called out and Willoe turned to see Count Idwal approaching.

She had not had much time to talk with the count, but his reputation preceded him. Her father had told her he was one of the most loyal retainers supporting the family. The count's family went back nearly as far as the Brynmor lineage. The man knew everything there was to know about the nobility and maintained a clear sense of right and wrong regarding the classes. He was also respected as a man who treated his castle staff and the peasant farmers well, ensuring that the ill, elderly, and those struck with misfortune were cared for. Willoe wondered whether, if slavery had not been banned in ancient times, if he would have treated his slaves the same way.

"Count Idwal." She cleared her throat to make sure she spoke with Rowyn's voice.

"Your presence is required in the command tent." He pointed to the largest tent in the camp, the one Mael used as his sleeping quarters and also for nightly meetings with the Cainwen leaders of the envoy. Willoe had never been invited before.

"It would be my pleasure." Finally she would be included in some of the command decisions. After all, Rowyn was a Prince and should be at the meetings.

Count Idwal turned toward the tent, then stopped and twisted halfway back to look at Willoe. "It will only take a moment. It is important that you know what to expect when we are received by King Benoit. I believe you have little experience with such matters." He said it without any malice, more as the fact it was. "There is little you will need to do, but it is important that your actions be appropriate for a member of the royal family." He turned back and continued toward the meeting. "Lord Aeron, you are expected as usual."

"Wil," Aeron whispered to her.

"No, it's alright." She held up a hand and fought to keep herself under control. She wanted to scream in anger and cry at the same time, but it was something Rowyn would not do. He probably wouldn't even understand the slight for what it was. "I understand him," she went on. "I don't think he can help it. He is of pure noble blood and my father tells me that even though the count has tried, he has never been able to make peace with the fact that we are bastards." She stepped forward to follow the nobleman to the tent, and found herself wondering whether the powerful count would ever turn his loyalties to her or her twin.

Willoe rolled around on her cot. She had drifted off quickly, as she had most nights after riding all day, but then had woken a short time ago and couldn't get back to sleep. Men covered in blood with her standing over them howling were her nightly visitors now. The lump in her chest never seemed to disappear. But tonight it was different. In her nightmare she gazed out on an endless field of bodies, torn and bleeding. Men, horses, and creatures she had never seen or even imagined. She continued to roll back and forth, the bed constraining her. In the midst of the battlefield a bright light bleached the scene and then a blackness filled her mind. A sudden urge to get out of the tent came over her like an itch that couldn't be scratched. She closed her eyes tightly and tried to go back to sleep, but a bit more of rolling back-and-forth forced her to get up and put on a cloak over her pants and shirt. The itch had gotten worse, which led her to walk past Aeron's cot, raise the flap and wander outside. There was a campfire still burning at either end of the camp for the guards, but only the fading light of embers were visible from the many other campfires throughout the rest of the camp.

Aeron's and her tent was near the western campfire, so she made her way toward it. Something in the back of her mind seemed to pull her in that direction. She reached the fire and stood near it, rubbing her hands over it, then crossed her arms to warm them with her hands. Two guards, probably getting ready to go on duty, sat by the fire and nodded at her as she stood there, but they didn't say anything, which was as she expected considering the rumors that had spread through the camp. She nodded back, and after a few moments headed past the fire toward the inner guard position. She didn't realize it at first, but she had not thought to leave the camp.

As she approached the guard she nodded to him and said, "Visiting the privy."

He just nodded his acknowledgment, as she had hoped he would, and continued the short route he followed around his section of the camp. The path to the privy wound around the camp in a half-circle, cutting through the forest. Mounted guards would be posted farther out, along a trail that ran from the road through and around the forest, so she felt safe heading off down the path on her own.

She was a quarter of the way down the path when she felt a powerful tug on her mind, a stronger feeling like the urge she had felt in camp. It seemed to be edging its way into her thoughts. She turned in response toward the forest and spotted a narrow path branching off the footpath, one she probably would not have noticed even in the daylight. A hunter's trail. She felt as if a rope were tied around her, pulling her toward the trail. She could see no reason to follow the trail so she turned back to the main path, but every step she took increased the headache that had suddenly come upon her. She stopped and took two steps backward. The pain decreased. She walked all the way back to the trail and the headache disappeared, replaced by the thought urging her to step into the woods. Taking two steps back down the trail toward camp, she winced as the headache returned.

It became a choice between following the trail or having her head burst open from pain. She pulled the short knife she carried in her boot — the swords left in the tent — and pushed the brush aside to follow the trail. She followed it for several moments and thought that she would surely come across the mounted guard. After a few more steps she still had not passed the path the guards rode and had not passed any clearing, path or otherwise.

This is insane. Anyone could be out here. I need to go back.

Her next step brought her into an almost perfectly circular clearing. The branches shone in the moonlight, their shadows creating an eerie effect along the clearing's edge. It looked like tentacles reaching out from the surrounding forest, waiting to grab her.

She quickly walked out into the center, away from the shadows, and turned around in a circle, ready to run back down the trail at the first sign of an attacker. A light wind whirled in the clearing and she pulled the cloak tighter against the cool fall night. Standing there, she realized that the urge had faded and her mind was empty of all except her own thoughts. A rustle from back along the way she had come made her crouch and step away from the trail head, backing up across the clearing. She kept checking over her shoulder to make sure nothing was waiting behind her.

The noise stopped and she waited a moment before she realized she had been holding her breath. She had to laugh and stood up, relaxing, but then something pushed out of the trail head. It was hidden in the shadows and Willoe jumped back, the knife held out in front of her. "Keep back," she ordered the intruder.

"Why?" She recognized Aeron's voice.

She let out a big sigh and let her arm fall to her side. "What are you doing out here?" Her tone was harsh and she felt every right to it, seeing as he had scared the breeks off her.

"I could ask you the same thing." His voice did not hold the same anger hers had.

"Sorry." She started across the clearing when a loud sound came from overhead and a bright light lit the middle of the clearing. *Not again*, she thought as she threw up an arm in front of her eyes.

The light settled, still bright, but ebbed enough that she could lower her arm. The golden dragon stood in the middle of the clearing between Willoe and Aeron. This time it was riderless.

The dragon wound its neck and head around its folded wings to face Willoe without shifting its body. The ears flared back, framing the triangular face. In Willoe's mind she heard a rich, deep voice tell her, "Thou hast taken life, Willoe Brynmor."

The picture of the dead bandits flashed in her mind and she shivered. She wondered if the dragon had come to take retribution.

"Many more will follow," the voice told her without any emotion.

Her breathing caught in her chest as the dragon confirmed her most recent nightmare. Letting the breath out, she wanted to tell the dragon it was a mistake. She had not wanted to kill those men.

She never had a chance to speak before the dragon swung its head closer to her. The ball of the dragon's eyes were a lighter shade of the golden scales that covered much of its body. In the center of the eye was a vertical slit that bored into Willoe as it moved its head closer. The golden eyelids blinked once, then the voice told her, "Many will give their lives so that thou canst live. Tens of thousands will die at thy word."

Willoe almost fell to the ground as the dragon's pronouncement hit her like the end of a lance. "It must be a mistake. I would never give any such commands, and who would even follow such orders?"

The dragon did not respond and instead, while she tried to recover, it turned its head toward Aeron and she could see that he was awestruck, but she was impressed that he did not show any fear. She stood there, not sure of what to do until the dragon finally turned its head back to her.

"The Lady of the Woods is waiting. Go to her." The command in the dragon's voice was unmistakable.

She finally got up the courage to speak, though her voice trembled. "I do not know how to find the Lady you speak of."

"The one who cares for thee will lead thee. But not until thou hast need of them."

A riddle was the last thing she needed at the moment, but before she could speak again the glow around the dragon began to intensify and she had to put her arm back up.

Before the dragon vanished, its voice flashed in her mind. "The Lady of the Woods. Thy life, and the lives of those thou lovest art at peril."

The light grew so bright that Willoe could still see it even with her eyes closed and both arms now up and blocking her view. Then it vanished as quickly as it had come, leaving her and her cousin alone in the clearing.

"What was that?" Aeron asked after the dragon had disappeared.

"I have only seen it once—"

"You have seen the dragon before? Why did you not say anything?"

The disbelief in his voice made her feel a little guilty for not telling him and Rowyn earlier. She went on to describe the night of the first visitation. "I swear on the Burning Lady's favor that I did not know the dragon would appear again."

"Well, the Burning Lady is right. How could you not say anything?" She could tell he was getting over his anger though he still was not happy with her and his sister.

"I am sorry. Can we just go back to camp?"

"Fine. But first, have you tried to find this Lady in the Woods?"

"Rowyn tried to find out something from Uncle Brom, but he knew nothing."

"Rowyn knew?" Aeron's anger was returning.

"No. I didn't tell him about the dragon or the Burning Lady. I just asked him to see if Uncle Brom knew anything about the Lady in the Woods." She pleaded, trying to make him understand. She couldn't afford for him to be angry at her. Without him, she didn't think she could make it all the way to White Cliffs.

"Oh."

"According to the dragon I am not meant to find the Lady until I have a need. Though I also don't know what the need will be or who it is that will lead me to the Lady."

"It's late. We can discuss it tomorrow on the road." He stepped aside so she could make her way back down the trail.

As she stepped up to him she asked, "How did you get here? Did you follow me?"

He hesitated for a moment, then with the anger all but gone from his tone, answered, "I did not know I would find you here. I just couldn't sleep and went for a walk then something urged me to follow this trail."

She didn't say anything else other than to nod, and then led the way back to their tent.

She lay there, her face turned away from Aeron. She knew she wouldn't be able to sleep the rest of the night, but did not want to let Aeron know. The tears soaked the cot and the only thing that kept going through her mind was the dragon's words. The dragon, who was a messenger from the Burning Lady herself. Thousands would die because of her.

Aeron could hear Willoe's quiet sniffling across the tent. She had refused to tell him, on the walk back, what the dragon had said to her. But he couldn't bemoan her a secret. After all, he had his own. He had told Willoe that the dragon had not spoken to him, but it had. He lay there with his back to Willoe as he ran the words through his mind. The dragon's voice had shocked him at first; he had never experienced anything like it, but when the dragon called him by name and then told him his future, he had no choice but to accept the reality of it. The only issue for him was how the dragon's deadly omen would come about.

Be brave, Aeron Cadwal, thy life shall not be spent for naught. Thou shalt be the harbinger of fire that consumes the world. War shall be thy legacy.

30

White Cliffs

From the top of the rise they could see the high walls of Castle White Cliffs in the distance. The fortress squatted on a hill overlooking the lesser walls around the Franchon capital of Lealacité.

"You can even see the Wailing Straights beyond." Aeron pointed out the silver shimmer of the Straights.

"I heard that they were called the Wailing Straights because of all the death wrought when the Franchons crossed over to spread onto Taran," Willoe said as she pulled up next to Aeron.

"My father told me that it had to do with the winds. He said voyagers reported the moan of the winds that blew between Taran and the mainland of Kieran. It reminded them of a mournful song, like a thousand Spirits calling out in pain." Aeron had never traveled to the mainland, so could neither confirm nor deny the claims.

"Both sound accurate." Willoe snickered. It was the first humorous words from her since the ambush.

Aeron smiled and hoped it was not the last. He put the thought behind him and guessed they would probably arrive at the gates by early evening. The road curved down the hill and ran fairly straight through the harvested fields surrounding the castle.

"It is all white," Tomos said in awe as he rode up just in front of Willoe and Aeron, who had stopped to take in the entire valley below.

Both Aeron and Willoe smiled where the page couldn't see. This was all part of the boy's training to take over his father's barony.

"The castle and much of the city is constructed of limestone from the cliffs that run along the Straights. The limestone contains quartz, but also flint and a chalky white substance that give the cliffs their color." Aeron

221

educated the page without embarrassing the young boy. "It also gave the castle its name."

Tomos smiled at Aeron and nodded. The boy seemed to hang on every word that Willoe or Aeron said. The cousins had come to care about the brothers. They had not had a chance to be spoiled by the clamor and intrigue of the castle. Their father's land was on the outer reaches of Cainwen and had not been poisoned by the royal court.

As they rode down the hill Aeron glanced over at his cousin riding next to him. He had to admit he was impressed with the way she had held up since the ambush and the night with the golden dragon. He still had trouble sleeping as the dragon's words stuck in his mind.

Riding through the harvested fields toward the gates into Lealacité, Aeron was surprised by the lack of workers. Even with the harvest in there should still be lots of work clearing and preparing the ground. Only about a quarter of the workable area was turned over.

As they approached the Western Gate the party slowed and one of the Shields, the captain of the Franchon escort, rode forward to talk with the guards. Only a few travelers were coming and going, which was even more surprising than the empty fields. The capital of the kingdom should have had a constant flow of people passing through the gates as night approached. He had also noticed there were very few wagons on the road for the past two days. Another curiosity. By the time the rest of the caravan reached the gate the few travelers moved aside and the delegation rode through under the gate's Watch Tower. As they rode through he looked up at the decorative markings on the ceiling. He studied them closely and saw what he had expected. The decorations hid the true purpose: The slits — the murder holes — that defenders could use to shoot arrows or pour boiling water down upon attackers who would be caught between the latticed grilles at either end of the tunnel.

Upon leaving the tunnel they entered a large bailey with buildings all around the square. They were led to one end of the bailey and funneled into a wide thoroughfare of two story buildings, mostly royal buildings and a few trade shops. These quickly gave way to smaller avenues that branched out to channel traffic to different parts of the city.

The riders headed up the middle street, the clatter of wagons and hoofs on cobblestones rebounding off the walls of the houses to either side. The envoy followed the street and wound their way through the city.

"Lealacité feels bigger than Faywynne," Tomos commented as they rode along the thoroughfare.

"It is, but not by much," Aeron informed the page. "Look at the architecture. You can see that it is of a newer design. The Franchon capital is quite a bit younger than Cainwen's."

Tomos stared at the buildings they passed, but Aeron didn't think that the boy had spent much time considering architecture. He would, with time.

Aeron tried to remember what he knew about the city. The spot on which White Castle sat had once been a Cainwen fort, Motte Whitehill, that had guarded the fishing villages along the coast until the Franchons had invaded. Over the seven hundred years the old fort had been replaced piece by piece until it had grown into a match for the much older Castle Westhedge. The city around it had grown quickly with new commerce from the Franchon homeland across the Straights.

"It feels different," Tomos said, still looking at the buildings.

He was learning quicker than Aeron had expected.

"The difference between the two capitals is like the difference between our peoples. Cainwens have an ancient history with traditions that go back thousands of years. The Franchons have always reminded me of a child grasping for everything within its reach. Impatient and throwing out the old for anything new." Aeron may not have paid enough attention to Uncle Brom's instruction, but when it came to the Franchon and Haldane kingdoms, Aeron consumed everything Uncle Brom had to say.

"Didn't they come from the mainland, Kieran?"

"Yes, the Franchon homeland is due east of Sur Terre Harbor." Aeron traced the expansion of the Franchon Empire in his mind. "They sit along the coast of Kieran and had expanded north, south, and east, taking the lands of their neighbors. Then they crossed the Wailing Straights to Taran and came up against our forebears who stopped them at the Saltrock River. They tried to go north and were confronted by the Haldanen."

Talking about the differences with the page brought back memories of when he had first arrived at Castle Westhedge. The castle and the city of Faywynne were older than anyone could remember. Parts had been torn down and rebuilt so many times that it had become a patchwork of different architectures. Aeron always felt comfortable with the hotchpotch construction. He could go from one part of the castle to another and follow a history of Cainwen in the building styles he saw. His family's castle, Mount Somerled, was younger than Westhedge but older than White Cliffs. It originally had been built to control traffic along the Saltrock River, but after Legendre's Folly, Mount Somerled became the northern buffer against the Franchons. It was able to both defend the border and provide a secure base for trade in the eastern provinces of the newly defined Cainwen. In just over six hundred years it had grown to be nearly as large as Westhedge, and Aeron's family's position had grown with it. A recent ancestor of Aeron's was eventually granted a dukedom and then the title of First Duke.

Moving past the city walls, the inner curtain, they worked their way up to White Cliffs' outer walls. Aeron noticed about twice as many soldiers on the wall as there would have been at Westhedge. At the same time he noticed just a trickle of people on the streets.

Shadows were growing as dusk settled in, and many of the shops had already closed. Entering the castle's bailey, they rode up to the steps that led to the Great Hall, where they dismounted. Servants and groomsmen came to fetch the horses and to show the visiting guardsmen and servants where they would bunk. Supply Sergeant Trystan could be heard ordering the Franchon servants along with his own party, not trusting the care of the wagons and supplies to anyone else. Mael and the Franchon count led the way up the stairs and the rest of them followed.

The Great Hall was of the same architecture as the rest of the castle and city. Everything felt foreign to Aeron. The tapestry, the rugs, the furniture — everything about the Great Hall spoke of Kieran and the Franchon homeland. A dozen guards lined each side of the Hall, duplicates of the ones that had journeyed with them from Westhedge. At the end of the Hall was a large platform with a richly ornamental throne on it. The man sitting on the throne wore a red robe, not something Aeron would expect of King Benoit or his Chancellor Hamond.

To either side of the man stood a guard unlike anything Aeron had ever seen before. They were shorter but stockier than the Franchon guards. Their skin color, their eyes, everything about them foreign even more so than the Franchons themselves, who at least resembled the Cainwens somewhat. They carried curved swords like Protector Dougal, though shorter. There was no consistency in the clothing of the two, other than a lot of leather and a strange form of chainmail.

Standing to the sides and behind the guards were a dozen Franchon nobles. Aeron had seen at least one of them visiting Westhedge in the past. The man on the throne wore a robe that Aeron decided looked nearly identical to the one that the priest Bat-Uul always wore, a loose garment with flaring sleeves which draped over the sides of the finely carved throne. While the throne itself was lined and trimmed with gold and a variety of jewels, the man occupying it wore no embellishments other than a large pendant around his neck, a black oval with a red stone in the middle that matched his robe. His face was narrow, with high cheekbones that highlighted his bronze skin. His features were similar to that of the strange warriors, but yet still foreign to even them. A thin layer of hair graced his chin. Black hair — almost blue — hung down to below his shoulders. But what drew his attention most was the man's piercing eyes. They were a dark blue that matched the color of his hair. As the man watched the new arrivals cross the Hall, Aeron felt as if those eyes peered into the depths of his soul. He suddenly felt unclean.

Ten paces from the foot of the throne's pedestal they stopped, the count and Emeline seemingly a bit confused and unable to speak.

Bat-Uul bowed to the man on the throne.

With the Franchon count speechless, Mael stepped forward to address the robed man. "I presume that you are not King Benoit Gautier?"

The seated man didn't answer immediately, but instead shifted in the seat, looked from side to side and then pulled the robes off the arms and settled them neatly in his lap. Aeron expected to see smoke rising from Mael as the Prince stood there being ignored. Mael opened his mouth to speak again, but the man seated above them spoke first. "You are correct."

Again, after a short delay Mael asked in a sharp tone, his posture stiff, "Then may we inquire as to your title and name, and as to King Benoit's absence? At the king's request we have journeyed to this fine city and we had an expectation that King Beniot would welcome us with his royal personage." Aeron could feel Mael's anger permeating the entire Hall as this was a complete affront to court protocol.

The man paused again before responding. He didn't show any deference to Mael as he stared directly at the visiting Prince. "His Majesty is away from Castle White Cliffs at the moment. I sent a messenger as soon as I was informed that Your Highness would be arriving, but it might be some time before he can return." The voice was calming, but Aeron felt anything but soothed. The foreigner continued. "I am known as Chuluun-Uul. I am…" He looked around at the two guards and the other nobles to either side, then back at Mael. "I am what you might call King Benoit's advisor. His Majesty has asked that I take over the duties of the court while he is absent." He paused yet again. "And I humbly accepted."

Aeron doubted that Chuluun-Uul ever did anything humbly. Mael's shoulders relaxed and he looked back at his entourage. A small laugh escaped him and he faced the throne again, crossing his arms as he leaned a little backwards. "May I ask why Chancellor Hamond is not receiving our envoy?" Aeron had personally met the man who ran the kingdom in the king's absence two years before, when he had visited with the nobleman Aeron recognized.

Chuluun-Uul picked from a bowl of berries next to the throne. His face showed no expression. "Chancellor Hamond has been ill and is resting at his manor to the north. I am sure when he regains his health he will return to his duties." Picking another berry, he held it up to his mouth, then seemed to decide against it. Instead he looked beyond Mael, staring directly at Willoe. Aeron suddenly felt a strange sensation flow over him, like a flood completely covering his skin with little pinpricks, an irritation that he felt to his bones. It passed as quickly as it came. Aeron noticed Mael flinch at the same moment and could feel Willoe shuffle her feet to his side.

The king's new advisor snapped his head to look at Aeron for a second, a grimace forming on his lips, then turned his attention back to Willoe. He sat back thoughtfully and then said to no one in particular, "Yes, it makes sense." His expression changed with a sly smile. "You must be Prince

Rowyn." It was more a statement than a question. He stood and walked down the three steps, waving gently for Willoe to step forward. Seemingly unsure of what to do, she stepped up next to Mael, whose body language showed him to be dealing with an inner struggle. "We have heard so much of you." Aeron thought Chuluun-Uul turned his head toward Willoe as he said this, but then he looked over the entire party. "Please, you must be worn from your travels. We will have plenty of time to talk after you are rested, while we wait for King Benoit's return."

He clapped twice and servants, dressed as foreign as the two guards, appeared from several directions and offered to lead the men off to their rooms. He looked around at all the Cainwens. "We have had your accommodations prepared and ready for you. Please do take advantage of them. Supper is being delivered to your rooms." He looked back to Mael. "Perhaps tomorrow we can meet in a less spacious setting and discuss your business in more detail."

Mael began to protest, but the robed advisor held up his hand, a gesture that only inflamed Mael that much more. "Please, Prince Mael. We have a lot to talk about and it is getting late. Tomorrow will be a fresh new day." He glanced about as if making a proclamation. He turned and headed out of the Hall, his robes flowing behind him. He was followed by his guards, the Franchon nobles, the count and Lady Emeline, who glanced back at Aeron with an unreadable expression that made Aeron faintly uncomfortable.

None of the Cainwens moved as Mael stood there, his body shaking visibly. The obvious dismissal by one of King Benoit's underlings would have had immediate repercussions in Westhedge, but for all Mael's faults, Aeron knew he put his family and kingdom ahead of his own feelings. After a few heartbeats his body stilled and he simply stood staring. Aeron was impressed with his control; he was sure that no one had ever stood up to the Prince like that in his life. Mael turned to the nearest servant and politely asked to be shown to their rooms. Then he turned back to the Cainwens with a smile.

Aeron could tell by the way Mael's right eye narrowed that under the surface, a storm raged in the Prince as violently as winter in the Wailing Straights. "It appears our hosts have plans for us. Let us rest after our journey and then see what we can do about making our own." The smile widened and Mael's right eye nearly closed.

Mael had sent word for the senior members of the delegation to meet in his rooms after their evening meal. Willoe and Aeron were there along with Protector Dougal, Captain Harte, Cleric Yoan, Count Idwal, Master Gwron, and Mael's three Shields, including Tanguy. The Tybalt boys moved among the men performing their duties as pages, one with a flagon of wine and the other with a platter of various cheeses and meats. The remaining Shields were absent, checking on the rest of the escort. Mael's apartment was large, as was his due, with plenty of chairs. Mael asked the men to sit at a round table in the middle of the room, with the three Shields lounging on various furniture scattered around the apartment. He then started to talk about mundane subjects that Aeron thought could have waited until the morrow. "Sergeant Trystan tells me that everything is stored and he will be providing a complete inventory within a day." Again Aeron could not imagine Mael bothering with a supply inventory.

Facing Willoe, Mael asked with knitted eyebrows, "Are you well, brother? You do not look like yourself."

Willoe straightened in her chair and Aeron could feel himself flinch. Has Willoe been uncovered? Aeron searched for the words to distract Mael.

"It be a hard time on us all," Protector Dougal answered for Willoe.

Mael nodded and then turned to Tanguy, smiling at his friend and supporter. "Why not provide us a little entertainment? I noticed you brought your lute."

It never failed to impress Aeron how the Prince managed to exude his arrogance in even something as simple as a request.

Mael's closest friend reached over and picked up the pear-shaped instrument. "Any requests?" he asked of the assembled group.

Mael answered quickly. "Something energetic. It would go well with the wine."

Tanguy nodded and started strumming a loud, robust song about soldiers long out in the field. The other two Shields joined in singing the chorus boisterously to accompany their friend and fellow Shield.

Aeron was surprised. It was the first time he had heard the fierce Shield play the instrument. The song was coarse, but he handled the lute as expertly as he did a lance.

As he plucked at the strings and the volume increased, Mael leaned forward, motioning for the remaining men to lean in. The smile faded and he addressed them in a low voice. "We need to develop a plan, but keep your voices low." He glanced from side to side.

Aeron understood, but evidently Willoe took a moment to grasp it before her expression changed. "You mean that someone is listening?"

Mael looked at her and his eyes shut for a moment, then he looked around at the group again and went on as if she had not spoken. "I am sure we all realize that this is all very strange." Again, Aeron looked over at Willoe, who seemed to be somewhat lost.

"The walls and entrances are heavily guarded," Aeron said. "Well beyond what one would expect."

Captain Harte added his observations. "Most of these are recent additions. Their uniforms are new and they are too stiff. Regular guardsmen would be more relaxed with the constant routine."

"The streets were nearly empty. And I saw only women and children," Count Idwal pointed out. "The only men I saw were either old, peddlers from the countryside, or traders from outside Lealacité. And few of them at that."

They all nodded their heads. They had all noticed the same thing.

Cleric Yoan cleared his throat.

"Yes?" Mael asked.

"Well, for years, whenever I left or entered Faywynne, I would look to the walls and say a prayer to the Burning Lady for the poor criminals mounted on the wall. I know their crimes were the cause of their demise, but the Burning Lady takes pity on all her children." Mael's look could easily be interpreted; and he wanted the old cleric to get to his point. Yoan put his hands together on the table and leaned a little closer almost whispering. "When we came through the gates today, I saw many more heads mounted on spikes atop the wall than I have ever seen at Faywynne."

"There could be many reasons for that," Master Gwron interjected.

Cleric Yoan continued. "I was here two years ago with another envoy and spent a great deal of time among the people of the court."

"Yes." Mael inhaled and let out a breath, not trying to hide his impatience.

The Cleric looked around, causing everyone else to scan the room, and then he leaned in almost to the center of the table. "It was partially rotted, but one of the heads, I believe, was Chancellor Hamond. I recognized him from my many meetings with him."

They all sat back a little to absorb what Yoan had just shared. Mael finally leaned forward again and spoke. "I do not want any of the guards roaming the streets by themselves. I want the servants kept close and if they need go out, for whatever reason, I want them escorted by at least two guards." He looked around the table. "We need to get more information. I imagine I will be watched constantly, as will most of you. Some less than others." He looked over at Aeron and Willoe, before glancing at the rest of them around the table. "We need to find the answers to the questions raised here. Pass information back through Captain Harte. We need to gather the truth about this Chuluun-Uul and find out what has transpired here at White Cliffs." He ended by nodding to Cleric Yoan.

Mael leaned back and smiled, took a drink from his goblet and then started joining in with the song in a loud voice. The others followed his lead.

Aeron sang with the rest of them, but turned his head a little to see Wil-loe out of the corner of his eye. She wasn't singing, but was deep in thought. He wondered if her mind was far away like his, thinking about Casandra and Rowyn. He said a little prayer of thanks that they were not here and were safe enjoying their quiet time away at Manor Highkeep. He just hoped that he would see the both of them again.

31

Secrets

After receiving the Cainwen envoy, Chuluun-Uul motioned for Dimah-Uul and Bat-Uul to follow him up to the set of rooms he had taken over as his own. When they reached the rooms he dismissed the guards and minor priests. Bat-Uul glanced at the Jin priests and tried to remember when he had been one of their number — known then as Gened-Jin, *the surprise gift*. He had to remind himself that it had been less than two years ago.

The last of the Jin priests exited, closing the door behind them and leaving the three Uuls to themselves. With the sound of the door fitting into its frame the Gai-Ten's smile dropped and he whipped around to glare at Bat-Uul, his face contorted with fury.

"You were ordered to bring both Prince Rowyn and Princess Willoe!" Chuluun-Uul yelled, then paced across the room, shaking his head as he stared back at Bat-Uul every couple of steps. "Why did you not comply with your orders?"

"I asked the count to request both to return with the envoy. King Einion thought otherwise." Surely the Gai-Ten would understand Bat-Uul could only influence, not command. It was not the Shin-il Way.

"Regardless, you have failed in your duties. Unacceptable." Chuluun-Uul had stopped in front of Bat-Uul and stared directly into his eyes.

Bat-Uul had a hard time keeping eye contact with the older and more senior Uul. He had never met a Gai-Ten and was still somewhat awed by one of the inner circle.

"However, all is not lost." Chuluun-Uul walked over to the table in the middle of the room and sat. "Arrangements have been made for the girl."

"Why are the royal twins necessary? King Benoit is prepared to convert. A marriage bond between his niece and the Cainwen heir, Prince Mael, will surely make spreading the Shin-il Way to Cainwen a foregone conclusion. This leaves only Haldane." Bat-Uul had been raised in the way of the Master, the Shin-il Way. His mind brought up the canon he had known his entire life. *The Body does not destroy itself. Conflict is brought about by differences. Eliminate differences and conflict is eliminated. When all are as one Body, peace and harmony shall ensue.* Then the final line of the doctrine came to him. *Peace and harmony are a choice each must make on their own.* This was why the priests never resorted to force. Gentle influence and persuasion had succeeded in converting much of the known world from one end of Kieran to the other. That was the Master's plan. At least, that is what Bat-Uul had been told. The kingdom of Avanis had always been under the Shin-il Way and Bat-Uul knew no other system of belief.

"You question the Master?" Dimah-Uul nearly shouted, his face contorted at his deputy's arguing.

"No, never." Bat-Uul cast his eyes down. He knew it was not within his power to question his seniors. Other priests would not. It was not the Shin-il Way. Yet again the subtle differences surfaced.

But those differences were what he knew deep down was the reason he had been lifted to Uul and sent to Taran. He had never known any place other than Avanis. He was too young to remember his parents; they had died when he had been just a baby and he had been given over to the temple. All he knew was that they were from the western shores of Kieran, his features a testament to his far west heritage. He had been told he would blend with the Taran culture more readily and could assist in converting the three kingdoms of this isle. He had been excited to finally spread the Master's words, but while he was close to the Tarans in appearance, culturally he was as ignorant as Chuluun-Uul and Dimah-Uul. He was still baffled by many of the Tarans' actions and reactions. Maybe this is what led them into the current situation.

"Pour us some wine and then sit." Chuluun-Uul smiled at Bat-Uul.

Dimah-Uul sat while Bat-Uul poured a goblet for each of them, then took a chair himself.

Once seated, Chuluun-Uul leaned forward and looked at Bat-Uul. "The Cainwens are familiar with you. Keep engaging them and make them believe you are passing information to King Benoit. And continue to use the Lady Emeline. I am told that she has developed a relationship with one of the senior Cainwens. We may be able to use that." Then he turned toward Dimah-Uul. "Is the guard firmly under your control?"

"Their captain is a man of many — how should I say? — *unusual* tastes. Ones he would rather not become public. He is more than willing to do our bidding. He has replaced most of the veterans with our new recruits. They are still bewildered at their sudden promotion and will eagerly do anything the captain commands." Bat-Uul could hear the undercurrent of laughter in

Dimah-Uul's answer.

"Fine. When we find the girl we will coordinate the capture of Prince Mael and Prince Rowyn." Chuluun-Uul sat back as if satisfied.

"Are you sure that it is necessary?" Bat-Uul asked earnestly. He still felt it would only lead to unnecessary trouble. "It is not part of the plan."

Chuluun-Uul looked at him, his eyes narrowing. "The Master agreed."

Bat-Uul could not offer an argument. The Master could not be wrong. Everything he had ever read, been told, and experienced reinforced the belief.

When Bat-Uul did not say anything else, Chuluun-Uul's smile returned. "Good." He reached across the table and put a hand on Bat-Uul's forearm. "It is all part of the Master's plan." He then finished the wine and leaned back in his chair. "I have a busy schedule." He looked at Bat-Uul as he said it, and then waited.

It was obvious Bat-Uul had been dismissed. He stood and bowed to the Gai-Ten. Then he turned and, as much as it was against his nature, bowed to the twisted Dimah-Uul, who had remained seated.

Bat-Uul let himself out but left the door ajar. He scolded himself, but still lingered near the door, casually leaning toward the crack. He couldn't hear anything at first, but then he heard Dimah-Uul's voice, the nasal sound unmistakable.

"He is going to be trouble."

"It is nothing that we cannot manage," Chuluun-Uul answered.

"He should never have been lifted to a Uul. He is as foolish as the sheep we herd," Dimah-Uul argued.

"He has a role to fulfill," the Gai-Ten stated as easily as if he were ordering another goblet of wine. "When he has done his duty we will see what lies ahead for our young friend."

32

In Control

While the speaker went on and on — something about fishing rights — Grioral Malbery, Earl of Greenmerrow, waded his way through the nobles. He made his way to King Einion's right, just off the dais, and stood next to Prince Hafgan. Malbery took a deep breath, straightened his vest and composed himself. With shoulders back, a bright smile on his face, and an unwavering stare, he knew he captured the perfect image of nobility. His berry vest over a light shirt and a dark blue cape proudly reflected the Greenmerrow colors. Standing next to the dais, he provided quite a contrast to the uninspiring Prince on his left.

Not that the Prince wasn't handsome. After all, he was the son of Crown Prince Beynon, whom many of the castle women whispered was one of the most attractive men in the kingdom. But the Prince just did not exude the same charisma as his father, nor that of his older brother or even his grandfather. He had freckles on his cheeks along with the high cheekbones and light eyes not uncommon among Cainwens. The dark brown hair with a blond, nearly gold streak from front to back on the left side was a unique characteristic shared by all in his family, except for the twins.

Yet his posture was slumped, his hair unkempt and his cape was heavily creased even though he had a roomful of servants waiting upon his every command. Instead of reflecting a look of royal confidence, his eyes darted around the room as if constantly spying some threat, and he had a bad habit of running his finger under his nose as if it itched constantly. It could have been attributed to the stubble of a mustache he had been trying to grow for some time, but Grioral had known him since he was a child and he had done it even then.

Malbery put a hand on Hafgan's shoulder. "Calm, my Prince. The king is watching." And, true enough, King Einion had looked over at the fidgeting Prince with a frown as the speaker droned on. Hafgan straightened, but stared down at the floor rather than into his grandfather's eyes. The king sighed, and refocused on the petition being placed before him.

It was obvious that the king had been ill, as reported by all the castle gossips. He looked drawn and barely kept his attention on the man standing before him. His beard was unusually thin and as close as Malbery was he could make out the heavily chapped lips with some cuts in them, and the bloodshot eyes that looked much older than the king's actual age.

The petitioner finished and rolled up the scroll he had been reading from, then bowed to the king. He stood there waiting patiently, with some hope, for the king's decision. King Einion sat there staring out across the room as if he were the only one there. After several minutes of silence, Chancellor Liam whispered into the king's ear. Einion blinked several times, then looked at the man at the bottom of the dais in front of him. "Yes, of course." He seemed a little lost. "Fishing rights. Yes." He cleared his throat twice. "We will take your petition under consideration and give Our answer on the morrow." The man looked disappointed, but bowed as required and stepped back until he reached the gathering of people standing in a semi-circle around the dais.

The chancellor stepped forward and banged the floor twice with a staff taller than the man himself. It had an elaborate set of designs covering it, from the winged dragon on the top to the carved tree around the bottom. There were no jewels set in it nor any such garish embellishment, and no one knew how old it was. Stories had it at thousands of years. Some of the writing on it was undecipherable, which supported the stories. It was a scepter representing the royal family, but had become more of a fixture associated with the position of the Chancellor for over a thousand years now. "The Court is retired for the day." The shoulders of several men who had waited all day to make their petitions drooped as they realized it would mean waiting another long day to put their wants and needs before the king.

Everyone curtsied or bowed, including Malbery and Hafgan, as the king was helped from his throne and down the back of the dais by two pages. They entered the smaller chamber, in the rear of the hall, where most of the kingdom's business was conducted. As everyone else filed out the Earl and Prince Hafgan followed the king into the chamber, followed by several other nobles. It was a much smaller version of the throne room with a less decorative but more comfortable chair for the king at one end and a long table made of highly polished cherry wood that glistened like glass. Around it were chairs intricately carved of the same rich cherry and seats padded with a rich fabric and stuffed with goose feathers.

Crown Prince Beynon sat next to the king, and next to Beynon sat Morcar Priddy, the Royal Treasurer and also trusted advisor. The remaining men took their seats according to rank. Malbery, as Earl of Greenmerrow, sat at the table next to Prince Hafgan, a preferred spot from the Earl's perspective. Once the men were seated King Einion spoke, his voice grating. "We have received word from my grandson, Prince Mael." He pointed to the Chancellor.

"A falcon arrived today from Prince Mael." He unrolled a transcribed copy of the message. "My Lord, King Einion—" the king flipped his hand, telling the Chancellor to skip the perfunctory introduction. The Chancellor cleared his throat and looked down to where the actual report began. "We have yet to be brought in front of the person of King Benoit. A foreigner, a Chuluun-Uul, has replaced Chancellor Hamond and does nothing but delay any attempts for meaningful discussions."

"Is not this man associated with the fellow that was here with that Franchon count recently?" the king interrupted.

"Bat-Uul, Your Majesty," Chancellor Liam provided.

"Damn fool name. What is an Uul, anyways?" The king muttered something else inaudible and then waved for Liam to continue.

Chancellor Liam bent back down to the scroll. "Our local spies have reported that a large number of sellswords from the Franchon homeland on Kieran have been brought ashore and our own eyes tell us that many of the young men of the surrounding area have been conscripted."

"Benoit is either planning a campaign or is dealing with some internal conflict that requires a large army." Crown Prince Beynon stated the obvious from the side of the king.

Across from Malbery an old warrior, Owein Manus, spoke up. He was the Baron of Winterpass, broad-shouldered with a near bald head and a long salt and pepper beard. "We have had no reports of rebellion inside Franchon borders." He turned to the man next to him and said, "Though with the way Benoit has doubled taxes and put the collar on his people, it is no wonder."

"Maybe the Tonn," Morcar Priddy suggested. The nomadic Tonn tribes had been a nuisance to all three major kingdoms as long as anyone could remember.

"Not enough to warrant sellswords," Manus countered.

"Very true," Beynon agreed, shaking his head along with all the other men around the table.

"Then a campaign," King Einion stated, the words dragging out of him like a heavy stone. "The question is when and where."

Again all the men nodded their agreement.

Turning to his son, the king spoke not with the authority the nobles were used to for these many years, but as a tired old man. "Beynon, I will leave preparations in your hands, along with Morcar and Manus." With that he rose and all the men in the room stood and bowed as the king slowly left for his chambers.

Once alone, Prince Beynon turned to the Chancellor. "Liam, send a falcon to Mount Somerled with a copy of Prince Mael's message. I believe the First Duke is still there. He will deduce what we have here."

Beynon looked across at Malbery. "Malbery, how are your provisions?"

"The harvest this year was plentiful. Our warehouses are full," Earl Malbery replied confidently.

"Good, good." Beynon smiled. "With Mount Somerled to the northeast and you to the southeast, we have a strong defense if the Franchons try to cross the Saltrock River."

As the barrier between the kingdom and all invaders along the southern end of the Saltrock, Greenmerrow commanded more troops than any other noble in Cainwen other than the Duke of Pembroke and Castle Westhedge itself.

"Have the healers discovered the cause of the king's ailment yet, sire?" one of the other men asked.

The Prince became solemn. "No. They are at a loss. They are still working on a course of action, but the king is strong and we believe he will recover soon." His response was met with immediate agreement from everyone. Their king had weathered near-fatal battle injuries, the death of wife and daughter-in-law, and everything else the world had thrown at him. They were sure he would return to his strong decisive ways in no time at all. In Cainwen's oldest dialects, Einion meant "Anvil" and he had always lived up to that name.

"Manus, can we get a message through to Princes Mael and Rowyn?" Beynon looked at the older man. Grioral noticed the stress lines in Beynon's face as he turned his attention to the matter of his sons.

Baron Manus turned to a man behind him and asked another question, stroking his beard as he listened to the response. "Aye," he said, turning back. "We have a way." Winterpass was a small domain, but controlled the only pass through the Kingdom's Gate Mountains, and had a commanding look over Northurst, a trading town that was located at the intersection of Cainwen, Franchon and Haldane along the Saltrock River. The town was part of Manus' barony and not only provided much of the Baron's income, but also made the Baron the obvious choice for spymaster for Cainwen, a role he fulfilled skillfully.

"The cost of conflict will be great, my Prince." The intent of Morcar Priddy's words sounded to Malbery, as usual, laden with an intricate maze of meanings.

"Your concern is well noted, Lord Priddy." The bitterness between the Crown Prince and the advisor was well-known, though few knew the reason why. Malbery was one of the few. Priddy's estates had grown considerably over the last twenty years, since taking over the royal treasury, and the king would not hear any of it from the Crown Prince. Priddy was one of the king's oldest childhood friends.

Prince Beynon's smile returned as he nodded at Manus. "I know you will give him whatever support is necessary." Then he scanned the table. "If there are no other questions, we will adjourn until Manus can provide more information." He nodded in the Spymaster's direction again.

Grioral was amazed at the man's control and command of everything around him. He looked, sounded, and acted like a leader. And Malbery hated him.

The Earl of Greenmerrow and his escort rode along the little-used road, then turned sharply into the edge of the forest, pushing aside branches that partially hid the entrance, and then turned again down a path toward an abandoned watermill sitting on a dry creek. Brown, gold, and red leaves covered the path as the weather began to chill. Next to him rode the nervous Prince Hafgan with two of Malbery's personal guardsmen riding behind. Guardsmen Royce and Tavin had been assigned to Malbery when he was yet a youth. As Malbery grew into manhood he had realized that the two soldiers were pliable and of questionable scruples, something that Malbery found a great asset in his dealings with his vassals and many others.

Their party approached the ruins of a small watermill. Broken stones crumbled from one wall and a fence stretched out from the wall, but only two sections still stood before the rails ended haphazardly in the ground. A sellsword stepped out from bushes across from the watermill and strode forward, taking both Malbery's and Hafgan's bridles while they dismounted. Four other sellswords appeared from the bushes and from behind the watermill. They strolled over to the fence and leaned up against it, their hands hovering not far from the hilts of their swords. The scowl on the mounted guardsmen's faces spoke of the hatred between legitimate soldiers of the kingdom and those that sold their sword to the highest bidder. The returned sneers from the sellswords told of their own feelings toward those that had rejected them.

"Come, my Prince." Malbery started for the doorway, knowing that the Prince would follow like a hungry puppy. He had spent the last eighteen years preparing for this time. At first he had coddled and pampered the young Prince, while Hafgan's older sibling Mael took the limelight as the heir apparent, relegating Hafgan to the role of 'the other son.' Hafgan might be in line for dukedom, but more likely it would be a minor role at Court. The boy needed a friend and Malbery provided both that and a mentor. As the boy grew, Malbery had made sure that no one came between them, and with the burden of the court consuming much of the Crown Prince's time, Malbery had become more a father than the boy's own father. Hafgan spent as much time at Malbery's Castle Clanmor as he did with his family at Castle Westhedge.

Malbery looked over at the sellswords as he entered the relic of a building. The Earl looked more like the sellswords than the Prince tagging along behind on his heels. With long black hair and blue eyes, Malbery could easily be mistaken for a Franchon. Considering many of Greenmerrow's citizens were of Franchon descent, it was not that unusual. A tall, grassy marshland ran from the Saltrock River westward several miles toward Castle Clanmor, the center of the Earl's territory, and south toward Howell's Shallows, creating a natural barrier that protected the territory to the east and south. The rest of the Earl's domain was farmland and forest, but the soil was hard and the forest paled in comparison to the northern forests around the Shadows' Gate Mountains or along Crystal Bay.

His father had held the land with pride. For years the name Malbery held a favored place in the Cainwen noble hierarchy, as his father had reminded Grioral often. Malbery's father had boasted that Greenmerrow was the tip of the spear for his beloved King Einion. But all Malbery saw was that his family's funds went for the training and upkeep of soldiers to defend the borders, while other nobles spent their resources on the upkeep of their castles and the many luxuries that was their right. The reward? Nothing more than the county of Greenmerrow with a neglected castle and miserly vassals that whined about his tax leverage. All these thoughts flashed through his mind as he considered his own heritage.

It took a moment for Malbery's eyes to adjust to the dim interior after he entered through the empty doorway. Once they did, he spotted the black-robed figure in the corner holding a child's doll.

The figure held up the doll by the rope hair as he inspected it. "An interesting plaything." His hood was back and Malbery could see the strange-looking tattoos on the dark skin of his bald head. Even without the body decorations his accent easily identified him as a foreigner to Taran. "But..." He fumbled for the right word and his eyes lit up as he found it. "Worthless. Makes a child soft." He smiled and casually tossed the doll across the room onto a heap of rubble.

As the foreigner approached them, the Prince cringed a little and stepped behind his mentor.

"Earl." The priest bowed slightly and Malbery bowed in return.

"Besut-Jin."

"I was sent. Events near time." His flat eyes pierced Malbery.

In response, the Earl shifted his eyes to look around at the crumbling walls and debris that littered the floor. "Disgusting," he commented.

Besut-Jin's inked head followed Malbery's eyes and he made no comment. A slight shrug of his shoulders, however, made Malbery believe that the foreign priest had seen worse. Much worse.

Prince Hafgan crept closer to Malbery's back, but Malbery ignored the young Prince as he addressed the shorter priest. "Do you have the potion?" The sooner he finished this the better.

The priest's lips tightened and, without a word, he pulled a small vial out of his robe and held it out to the Earl. It was half full of a blue liquid, and had a stopper tied on tight with a red ribbon.

Malbery reached out and took it, holding the vial up to what little light broke through the remains of the roof. "Will it be enough?"

"Yes. The Obeah promise."

Malbery had no idea what or who an Obeah was, but the three previous potions the little priest had given him before had more than met his expectations. King Einion had steadily deteriorated and the Court healers had no leads on what might be the cause. The Earl smiled.

"Are you sure this is the right thing to do, Grioral?" an unsteady voice behind him asked. Malbery was surprised that the Prince had the guts to speak up. He would have to do something about that… soon.

He put the vial in his belt purse and turned, taking hold of the Prince by both arms. He stared into the frightened eyes and spoke as calmly as he could. "We have talked about this, my Prince. They do not understand you." Then he added in the fatherly voice he had learned to adopt when explaining to his protégé. "Who has taken care of you?"

"You have," The Prince said, his voice remaining low.

"Have I ever lied to you?"

"No."

"Have I ever mistreated you like Mael or your father or your grandfather?" In reality, Malbery had never seen or heard that they had ever abused Hafgan, but being ignored alongside the rigors of having to live up to royal family standards was easily twisted and exploited. By now, Hafgan saw himself as a victim of overbearing and cruel elders.

"No."

"Then do you feel justified in questioning me now?" The guilt factor placed at the right time was more powerful than any reprimand he could give the young man. Malbery let go of the Prince and let his shoulders sag as if he had been struck with a weapon.

"I am sorry Grioral," the Prince said quickly. "I only thought—" His voice trailed off as he turned his head to look away from his mentor.

Malbery turned back to the priest. "We will be ready."

The priest bowed again and Malbery bowed in return. He wished he had known these priests when Hafgan's mother had died. It would have made it so much easier. The tragedy with her horse had nearly gone awry. The death of the groomsman had been unexpected, but necessary. He wondered what he would have done without Royce and Tavin. He had to smile as he thought, *A conscience can be fatal, it seems.*

33

Paired Sensibility

It had been almost three weeks since arriving at Fayhaven and Rowyn had made little progress other than wandering around the *il fennore*, which still amazed Cian, Saraid, and Helel. They had told Rowyn that all other wizards crossed into the *il fennore* but could only call out to a Spiro. They had to wait until a Spiro approached them. They had no explanation as to how Rowyn could move around within the *il fennore*.

Rowyn focused his concentration on the point of light that would give him entrance into the ethereal world and its gossamer beings.

"Continue to focus." The sound of Saraid's voice cut through Rowyn's thoughts.

"I am," Rowyn answered sharply. This is a waste of time, he thought.

His mind was blank and he took a couple of deep breaths, then he centered his thoughts on a point in the center of the darkness. It was as if dozens of lights, like strings, came from all over his mind and ended at the central point, creating a cone-shaped image from the back to the front of his mind. The lights became brighter as the darkness faded and then it was as if Rowyn were rushing toward the point. The shining lights streaked past until he reached the dot and he crossed over.

It took his eyes a few moments to adjust to the light, but where black had filled his mind's eye, an intense milky white was all that he could now see. He couldn't feel or see any part of his body, but he knew he drifted in the murky void. A twinkle to his right made him shift in that direction. He started to move by thought alone, without knowing exactly how.

He could see it in the distance and sped up. It was only a flutter, more of a shifting of the light, but he recognized it as one of the *il fennore* inhabitants, a Spiro. He was racing toward it when a burst of flames shot up between Rowyn and the translucent Spiro. The fire died down, but the Spiro was already fleeing, its silky strands floating behind it. Rowyn reflected that his time had not been totally wasted, as he had discovered a side effect of delving into the *il fennore*: He'd found he could sense the Spirit around him and solidify it in his mind's eye.

Not that wizards couldn't also sense the essence of the Burning Lady's Spirit around them, but according to Saraid and Helel, it required them to first Merge with a Spiro, and the wizard had to have visual contact with an object to see the essence. Furthermore, an object's essence was usually seen through the Spiro's view, giving the wizard a hazy, obscure form of the object's true appearance.

Rowyn thought it strange that he could see the essence without the ability to Merge, but wanted to explore this newfound ability more, on his own, before bringing it to Saraid's attention. He had already figured out that with practice he could clear away the haze and actually form an accurate picture of the object in his mind. Sitting on the grassy knoll behind the manor, under the Learning Tree, Rowyn could sense a hundred different essences in the trees, river, animals, and the others with him.

He concentrated harder and he could feel his perception expanding. At first a picture formed of the Tink, Krel Monlor. It shook Rowyn momentarily as the form took shape. The Tink was on the other side of the manor outside of Rowyn's physical view. The young Tink, with just the beginning of a blond beard starting to cover his chin, faced the two-wheeled cart that he used to make his daily trip around the valley. Over the weeks Rowyn had seen the Tink take goods from one home to another and even out to the more distant farms. The Tink pulled on the rope, trying to get his hairy Borlender, Swift, to move. It was not difficult for Rowyn to create a picture of the bear-like creature with brown and blond stripes, long floppy ears and a flat face, just sitting on its haunches, not budging. Rowyn could see in his mind Krel Monlor yelling, cajoling, and threatening his long-time cart-mate to no avail. Rowyn could even feel the annoyance swelling up in the small Tink, yet there was also a sense of humor underlying the exasperation. Rowyn was also sensitive to the sensations and impressions of the creature Swift as it sat enjoying the situation. In this state Rowyn could simultaneously capture the image of a hundred similar encounters going on around the valley as he sat in the shade of the weepy branches. He noticed that the farther his mind wandered the weaker his mind-seeing became until he could only sense dim shadows.

Rowyn didn't need this new sense to hear Casandra, Saraid, and Helel nearby. He focused his thoughts for a few moments on Helel. Possibly it was his lack of experience with women, but he found her the most beautiful woman he had ever met. Even among the Elfs she stood out above the others. He had asked Casandra about this once, and she had only taken a deep breath and stomped off, leaving him confused.

"He looks like he is in pain," Helel commented, her voice a little concerned.

"As well he should be." Casandra's tone sounded harsh and hurt at the same time.

He wished he could fix whatever had made her mad at him, but she avoided him whenever possible and he didn't want to ask either of the Elfs what to do.

"He claims he feels no pain," Saraid answered the Elfen. "He is focusing on the *il fennore*."

Rowyn still had his eyes closed, and said, "I found another one, but like the others it is pulling away from me."

"We can try again tomorrow." Though the Elf was trying, Rowyn could still hear the disappointment in Saraid's voice.

"I can try to catch it if you want." Rowyn opened his eyes and stared at his teacher. "I can still feel the presence, but it is moving away quickly."

"Are you still in the *il fennore*?" Saraid's eyes were wide as he looked at Rowyn. The Elf's face had tightened, and his voice was just as tight.

Rowyn looked around and noticed that he was indeed fully back in his body — he could feel his body, his hands, his legs, and he was speaking — yet he could also see the Spirit world as clearly as he saw the manor and the valley beyond. It was a strange new sensation but it also felt innately natural once he accepted both worlds as one.

He could see the Learning Tree. The actual physical appearance of the tree was as usual, but he also could see the essence of the Spirit *in* the tree. He turned to see bright shining spots, which he associated with the Spirit, in all the trees along the forest's edge, but the trees themselves looked as they would when he was not in the *il fennore*. This was not mind-seeing, but his actual physical body looking at the trees. He shifted his gaze to the nearby stream and could see the essence flowing under the ripple of the water. A fox peeked out from some brambles under the trees and Rowyn could see the spark at its center. He could even see a thread of the essence running in lines under the surface of the ground. He turned back to Saraid and saw the brightest spark in the Elf's chest.

"Yes, but I see it and the physical world together. The *il fennore* no longer feels murky. I can see everything around me, but I can also see the essence of the Burning Lady in everything."

"That is impossible. You have not Merged." Saraid stood and began to pace. "Even if you had Merged with a Spiro, you should only see the essence through the Spiro and not both worlds blended, as you state."

"But I can." It didn't seem like a good time for Rowyn to tell his trainer that he had been able to see the essence without a Spiro for some time now, though this blending of worlds was something new to him.

Saraid stopped and stared at Rowyn; the Elf's body had become tense and he gasped, seemingly stunned.

"If you can see the physical and the essence together, can you touch the Spirit in an object without Merging?" Saraid asked.

Rowyn reached out to the essence he felt as much as saw in a loaf of bread that Drel Corklin had brought up and had put on the blanket between the trainers and trainees. It surprised him that the loaf would even have a Spirit, but as Saraid had explained, the bread was made from wheat and other ingredients. These all had been alive at one time and had the essence within them. Why would they not have it after being brought together into a new form?

Saraid's words came to Rowyn. *The essence is not like the physical world. It is not a solid object that retains one form from birth until death. It flows and ebbs like the Forever Waters to the west of Taran.* Saraid went on to tell Rowyn, *If you die, your essence doesn't disappear. It just becomes one with the* il fennore *again.* This had been a little difficult for Rowyn to accept, but without any information to counter Saraid's statement, he had left it for later investigation.

His mind touched the bread and Rowyn told Saraid, "I can touch the bread."

Saraid looked at the bread and then back at Rowyn. "But can you wield it?"

Rowyn responded by imagining the bread being lifted into the air, and it did just that. Then it broke into two pieces, his mind seeing it just a breath before the loaf actually came apart.

The Elf stood quickly and looked at the two pieces of bread hanging in the air. "How did you do that?" he asked, in awe.

"I just did what you told me to do. I reached and lifted the bread."

"You should not be able to do that." Saraid reached out and tried to grab one of the hunks of bread, but Rowyn forced the Spirit to move and snatched it away at the last moment. The Elf tried twice more and Rowyn pulled it away each time.

Rowyn smiled up at his teacher as the Elf frowned and finally looked back down at Rowyn, his lips tight with disapproval and his arms crossed. Rowyn let the two pieces of the loaf drop back down onto the blanket.

Saraid stared for a few more moments, then burst out laughing. "Grandfather is going to be very surprised when I tell him about this." First Helel and then Casandra began to laugh and then, for the first time since arriving at Fayhaven, Rowyn joined them.

Rowyn laughed so hard that tears began to roll down his cheeks. He wiped them away with the backs of his hands and looked at the wetness of the tears. Cian's words continued to haunt him. 'He is the weak one.' He suddenly wondered how long it would be before they became tears of mourning.

34

A New Threat

Since arriving at White Cliffs, they had intentionally avoided any major gathering of the Cainwen senior members, instead working through Captain Harte to pass on any information or receive orders from Mael. This weighed on Willoe's thoughts as she and Aeron made their way up the circular stairs, along the inside wall of the tower where the heir apparent had been assigned an apartment, to the unexpected meeting Mael had called.

A little over two weeks had passed in White Cliffs and they had yet to get an audience with King Benoit. The Shin-il priest Bat-Uul had been accommodating at every turn, assuring Mael, as the head of the envoy, that he had relayed all of the Cainwens' requests to his superior, the king's advisor, Chuluun-Uul. But, other than three short meetings with the senior priest, their efforts had been blunted at every turn. Mael had agreed to discuss the border skirmishes with Chuluun-Uul, but even that was diverted to a minor noble, a Baron that, it was agreed upon by the Cainwens, could barely find his way to the room set aside for the meetings. After two meetings with the incompetent Baron, Mael had elected to wait until they could meet with King Benoit upon his return, whenever that might be, which was something no one could tell them.

Captain Harte, Count Idwal, Master Gwron, Cleric Yoan, and the rest of the senior staff, were seated around the table they had sat at the first night. Mael was pacing at one end of the room and talking with Ser Tanguy. Willoe and Aeron were the last to arrive and Willoe could tell that the atmosphere of those seated was moody at best. They sat across from the empty chair where Mael would probably sit.

After finishing his discussion with Ser Tanguy, Mael sat and the Shield left the room on whatever mission the Prince had sent him. Knowing her sibling, Willoe could see from his posture that he was tense.

"I am pleased all could accept my invitation." Mael smiled and looked around the table.

Willoe could see the others were as confused as she, except for Captain Harte and Count Idwal. Captain Harte even had a little smirk, but Count Idwal was all business, as usual.

"We have had little time to break bread together." Mael waved to the two pages, who brought a platter of meat and bread, along with a decanter to serve wine.

Willoe picked up the goblet after Sion had filled it and sipped, not sure what to make of the festive welcome. She had only seen Mael fuming ever since they had arrived, but now he picked up his goblet and saluted those at the table.

The creak of the door opening behind Willoe turned her head. She had thought the senior staff was all present. Ser Tanguy was entering, and after closing the door, nodded to Mael.

"I understand you have not been able to find your associates? The ones you came to discuss mining operations with?" Mael put his goblet down, and the smile disappeared as he addressed Count Idwal.

"No, my liege." The count shook his head with a frown. "I have searched all of Lealacité and cannot find them within the walls. It is as if they have disappeared."

Mael turned to Cleric Yoan. "You were going to contact the leading Clerics and find out what news they might have?"

"I have not been able to find any of the senior Clerics." Yoan seemed distraught. "The few minor Clerics I came across would not talk with me, giving no excuse for their lack of grace."

The room was quiet for several moments until Mael finally spoke. "I have received word through Baron Manus."

"Should we be discussing this here?" Cleric Yoan said as he looked around the room.

"We are safe for the moment. I am rarely in my room this time of day and there is only one set of ears. Those ears have mysteriously gone missing," Mael said with a smile.

Willoe now understood where Ser Tanguy had gone.

"We only have a short time before his presence is missed and another takes his place."

Everyone nodded their understanding.

"Cuthbert, you can come out now," Mael called to the doorway leading to the bed chamber.

A man came out and approached the table. Willoe didn't know him and doubted she would recognize him if she met him on the street after this. He looked... the best she could come up with was, *common*. There was nothing about his features that made him stand out or that one would remember. He was of average height and his hair was a dark brown, almost black, like many Franchons. His eyes, nose, chin — everything about him was no different than she could find if she walked out of the castle and picked a dozen men walking past at random. She smiled to herself. If this man was bringing a message from Manus, he must be one of the spymaster's agents. If so, his common look made perfect sense.

"The message, if you will," Mael ordered as the man took up position just behind the Prince.

The man smiled at everyone seated, scanning each one individually. She almost felt as if he were taking in each person at the table and categorizing them in some fashion.

"Baron Manus sends his most honored wishes to Prince Mael, Prince Rowyn, and Count Idwal. He has a message from Crown Prince Beynon for his oldest son, his Lordship Prince Mael."

"Mael, we received your report with a saddened heart. Information gathered by Baron Manus supports your observations. The Franchons have hired sellswords and conscripted a large number of their own population, and are massing an army to the north of White Cliffs. All signs point to a campaign, though where is uncertain. However, considering winter is nigh upon us, it is unlikely the Franchons will be moving against the northern kingdom of Haldane."

Even Willoe was astute enough to know that only left Cainwen.

The nondescript agent continued. "We do not know King Benoit's intentions nor the provocation for his actions, but we believe your position may be at risk. Take whatever action you and your advisors deem necessary to protect yourself and your company."

He stopped and Mael asked, "Is there more?"

The man cleared his throat. "Baron Manus added a verbal message to the Crown Prince's message."

"Yes, what is it?" Mael had never been a patient man.

The messenger nodded his head and stood straighter. "The fen-sucking, dog-hearted whoresons be planning ye harm. I can'na tell you what they be set to do, but it has the smell of a rotting swine. Keep your eyes open and be prepared."

The Baron's words had everyone laughing, something that few of them had done in quite a while.

Even Mael was laughing and, as he finished, he asked with a smile, "Is that all?"

"Yes, Your Lordship." The man bowed, having finished his task.

"Is there anything you can add to your master's message?"

The man looked around the table once again as if considering his options, then spoke. "In my dealings," the man left the interpretation of what he meant to each of them, "I have confirmed the Crown Prince's assessment. A large army has been gathering fifty miles northwest of the city."

"That explains the lack of menfolk in and around the city," Count Idwal interjected.

"That is correct, Lord Idwal. That is also why you saw little traffic as you entered the city. Much of the harvests from the surrounding farms and the catches from the fishing villages have been diverted to feed the troops north of here."

"Why wasn't this reported earlier?" Mael's right eye narrowed ever so slightly.

"My Prince, the troops only recently came together. Smaller contingents were based throughout the kingdom while they were being trained." The agent, Cuthbert, spoke quickly, almost nervously. "It was only recently that they were brought together under a single command."

"Any idea of what our hosts have planned for us?" Captain Harte asked of the man.

"I have been unable to uncover what is intended. King Benoit has not been seen since the day before your envoy arrived. The Shin-il priest Chuluun-Uul appears to have unbridled authority over the castle. His subordinate, Dimah-Uul, is running the City Guard, and little happens without the priests' permission. My personal opinion—" he held up giving his thoughts. Willoe supposed it was one thing to report facts to two Princes and a count, but the agent providing his personal thoughts might have been considered overstepping his bounds.

"Finish, for the Lady's sake, man." Count Idwal waved a hand at the man to continue.

The agent cleared his throat. "In my opinion, King Benoit is either dead or being held somewhere away from the castle. I believe this Chuluun-Uul is behind the recent actions."

Captain Harte spoke up again. "How could he take over the entire Franchon army?"

"I can't answer that with complete confidence, but the sellswords were brought over with money from the priests. Many among the general staff have been replaced with those favoring the priests and quite a few of the Shin-il priests are matched with these new leaders. These are called Jin priests. I have been told they are subordinate to Chuluun-Uul, who, I have discovered, is a member of a higher caste within their religious hierarchy."

As he finished, it was quiet for a moment, until Mael asked, "What about the priest Bat-Uul, the one that traveled with our envoy and meets with us daily? What do you know of him?"

The man showed the first expression Willoe had seen since he had entered the room. It was as if he was deep in thought, but he did not speak until he had worked out whatever was going through his mind.

"He doesn't look like the other priests or their strangely outfitted guards. He has the features of a Franchon, but acts as if he is new to our island. Many of the servants and even quite a few of the castle staff and nobles have little good to say about the other priests, but no one speaks ill of Bat-Uul. Everyone reports he is kind and does not demand more than what he absolutely requires. He is a mystery."

Willoe could see that the agent did not like mysteries.

"How are the people reacting to these priests?" Count Idwal asked. The question made sense to Willoe as she had also wondered whether they would find any allies among the civilian population.

"More kindly than you would believe. Several ships have arrived loaded with the lower-caste Jin priests who are all over the city talking with shop owners and even stopping at houses to talk with the women. They talk of their Shin-il Way and promise many things. Their words are like honey and people are flocking to their standard. Hundreds have become what the priests call acolytes, trainees for the priesthood, though I think some joined just to avoid the army's recruitment squads."

"What about the Clerics? They must be counseling people about these foreign beliefs?" Cleric Yoan looked worried.

"I am afraid that any who spoke out have disappeared." The agent shook his head sadly and it was evident he did not like speaking of it to Cleric Yoan. "Some were vocal at first, but since they went missing, the others have kept to healing and not much else."

Cleric Yoan could only nod his head in return. Willoe would have bet that the Cleric would have been one of the vocal ones regardless of the consequences.

The agent nodded in return as if to apologize.

"Where has the Franchon nobility been during all this?" Count Idwal's face was tight and his voice firm. "If this were Cainwen, the nobles would have risen in opposition to these priests long ago."

Cuthbert addressed the count and from the slow and deliberate way he spoke, Willoe got the impression he was choosing his words carefully. "When Chancellor Hamond and King Benoit disappeared several counts and Duke Dufort, the First Duke of Franchon, confronted Chuluun-Uul."

Count Idwal nodded his approval.

"They have since disappeared as well."

Several of the men whispered their disbelief.

"What about others? Surely these priests couldn't silence all the nobles?" Count Idwal was reddening.

"Some, mainly those with domains to the south and far from White Cliffs, have declared their resistance to the new hierarchy, though none have made any effort to come to White Cliffs and confront the priests. Un-like the south, which seems content with waiting to see what happens next, the Franchon territories to the north of White Cliffs, where the First Duke and most of the counts that supported him held sway, have rebelled. The priests have deployed many of their sellswords to keep a tight rein on the people and remaining northern nobles. "

"I find it hard to believe that no one has come to King Benoit's aid," Captain Harte argued.

Cuthbert turned to Captain Harte. "In truth, the Shin-il priests still claim they are carrying out the orders of King Benoit. Though few believe it, the southern nobles have given credence to the fact. Too few northern nobles with power remain to be of any help."

Looking back to Count Idwal, the agent continued. "There was one who opposed the influence of the priests even before King Benoit disappeared. It was more than a handful of moons ago. He, with a following of nobles from the north and around White Cliffs, pleaded with King Benoit to throw the priests out."

"What happened?" Willoe heard herself asking.

"I am sorry to say, Prince Rowyn, that the priest Dimah-Uul produced evidence, witnesses and documents proving that the noble was planning treason against the crown. The noble, and those supporting him, had to fight their way out of the castle."

Count Idwal seemed pleased at this new information. "At least someone had the spine to face these vile priests. Where is this nobleman now?"

"He is rumored to be in the north, just inside the Open Lands. Some-how he managed to get past Tierran's Wall and cause havoc throughout the north, stirring up the villagers and recruiting other nobles to join his re-sistance." Cuthbert smiled for the first time since he had started his report. "They call him the Black Falcon."

Mael looked at the agent questioningly.

"Beg my pardon, my Prince." Cuthbert bowed. "He is reported to be dressed in all black from head to foot, and he attacks in one place and then another so quickly that they say he must fly from one to the other. It is whispered in the taverns that he is bringing a message to the priests that Franchon will not be taken easily."

Some of the men snorted, while others smiled, at the image of a falcon, a noble's messenger. Willoe had learned that under great stress many men would bait each other or jest in the face of danger. Not something she was familiar with in the small circle of women she knew at Westhedge. In her mind, the situation was anything but mirthful. She was personally fright-ened and worried about their future. Some things about men she thought she might never understand.

Even Count Idwal had a grin. "That is the kind of man I would like to meet. Who is he?"

"No one knows for sure," Cuthbert had to admit, though Willoe got the impression it bothered the agent that he didn't know. "I have heard that he is a high ranking noble, from around White Cliffs, but with so many nobles missing or in hiding, it is hard to say for sure who it could be."

"Any further questions? Our time is short." Mael addressed those around the table, his tone suggesting that they needed to continue with other business.

"Your report is appreciated," Mael told the agent when no one spoke. "Contact Captain Harte if any new information becomes available."

Dismissed, Cuthbert bowed and left the solar.

After the door had closed, Mael leaned forward with hands folded on the tabletop. "I do not see any hope for our mission."

All at the table nodded.

"The question becomes: what do we do next? I do not believe sitting and waiting for the Franchons to act would be in our best interest."

The men agreed.

Mael looked over at Captain Harte, who nodded twice to Mael and then took over the meeting. "Prince Mael, Count Idwal and I have discussed our options and have come up with a plan."

It did not take much on Willoe's part to notice that she — or rather, Rowyn — had been excluded from the discussions, even though as a Prince her ranking in the envoy should have been just under Mael.

The Captain put a goblet to his right, and then another to his left, and then one directly across from himself and a fourth between the one across and the goblet to his left. "The city has few means to get out. Castle White Cliffs sits at the northern tip." He put his hand on the goblet to his right. "Bruyant's Walk comes down the western edge, along the Straights, to Windfell Quad and the Southern Gate." He ran his hand along the edge of the table from the goblet on his right to the one on his left. "There is Hernaudin's Gate." He tapped the goblet directly across from him. "And the smaller Durie's Gate, the one we entered on arrival." He finished by pointing at the goblet between the one to his left and the one directly across from himself. "A canal from the north runs around the entire city and empties into Sur Terre Harbor to the south. If we made it over the canal, to either the Southern or Durie's gates, there is nothing but farms and open fields. It would be easy to track anyone going that way and we would never be able to outrace any pursuit." Aeron scratched his cheek and stared at the goblets as if he were studying a map.

"True." Captain Harte smiled at Aeron's keen observation. "That leaves Hernaudin's Gate. Once across the bridge, the land is hilly with groves of trees spread north and northwest. We could make our way between toward Pembroke. We would have to avoid the Great Crossway, and if we stay north of that and south of the Franchon army, there should be lots of cover. We will send riders ahead to Castle Mount Somerled and command an escort."

"Of first order is to determine a line of escape if the need should arise; which seems likely. We will send out groups of three and four taking different routes through the city. They will observe and report back on guard placements, their movements, which avenues are open and which are closed, along with any other details that can help to identify an escape route."

Mael sat back and added to the Captain's plan, "Make sure those under you are ready at a moment's notice." He turned to look at Captain Harte again. "Inform Sergeant Trystan. He will take the longest to prepare."

The captain's eyebrows lowered and his lips pursed, as if considering something. He only did this for a moment before his expression returned to normal and he nodded his agreement to Prince Mael.

Mael stood and glanced around the table. "I do not anticipate that we will be able to meet like this again until we are ready to move. As before, talk with Captain Harte. He will put together the patrols and the paths they are to follow. Any questions?"

No one had any, so Mael dismissed the assembled men and Willoe.

Aeron and Willoe had already stood to leave when Captain Harte called Aeron over for a private talk.

"I will meet you in your room. I am not sure what this is about or how long it will take." Aeron's look told her he would clear up the mystery later.

Aeron walked over to the corner of the room Captain Harte had moved to. Some of the others slowly made their way out of the room, talking as they went.

"We have a special task for you." The captain kept his voice low. "You are friendly with the Lady Emeline." It was a statement rather than a question.

It was true that Aeron had spent some time with Emeline over the last moon, but it had always been in a public setting such as the market or in one of the castle courtyards. Even though no marriage vow had been made between her and Mael, he was very aware of not appearing as if he were interested in the lady. They would just walk and talk, always with Willoe or Emeline's servant along.

His expression must have reflected his concern as Captain Harte smiled. "Do not worry. The Prince is not accusing you of any misconduct. In fact, we need you to deepen your relationship with the woman. She is the king's niece and is seen regularly with Bat-Uul. She could be a fount of information if she could be convinced to share what she hears and sees in the castle."

"But Mael. Prince Mael and her—"

"That seems rather irrelevant now, would you not say?" His smile broadened. "If truth be told, I doubt our Prince had any intention of marrying the young woman. Ever since leaving Westhedge he has been trying to find a way to avoid the lady. One night he even talked about how Prince Hafgan or even Prince Rowyn might be a better suitor for the lady's hand."

"I will do whatever is required of me." Aeron had to keep from smiling as he agreed to the Captain's and Mael's plan.

"Fine. Report to me anything she says. Anything. You never know what might be important." The captain clasped Aeron's forearm and Aeron clasped the captain's with that hand. Then the captain walked over to talk with Mael and Ser Tanguy, who had returned.

Aeron left the solar to go meet with Willoe as promised. He had to think about the captain's words. He already knew that if things went as he hoped, he would likely not report everything that the beautiful lady said to him.

The only issue now was what to tell Willoe. She would not be happy with this, he knew, but the fluttering of excitement in his stomach wouldn't cease as he thought about the chance to spend more time with Lady Emeline.

35

Secrets Shared

It was still early evening and Bat-Uul stared out the tower window down at the lights that would soon blanket the city below. Most were just simple candles in houses or a tradesman shop working late, barely visible as more than a speck. The brighter lights of lanterns could be seen from taverns or a successful merchant's home. What galled him, though, were the street torches. Brackets hung on street corners with pitch that barely lit the corner yet managed to put out an exorbitant amount of smoke. He couldn't help but think again how backwards these people were.

Over a year in White Cliffs and he was still not used to the Franchon lifestyle. His first duty, five years in the kingdom of Avanis, had not prepared him for the culture shock of western Kieran, and especially the far western island lands of Taran.

He rubbed a finger across his chin in thought and the stubble scratched his hand. He made a mental note to shave it clean before going to bed. It was another reminder of the differences between him and the other Uul and Jin priests. He had tried to make those differences disappear, but one could not help their birth. He knew having to wait in Chuluun-Uul's solar was part of the reason for his unproductive thoughts, so he looked out over the edge and glanced down at the stone wall of the castle's inner curtain to give his mind something to focus on.

The wind, particularly strong at that height, whipped at his robe. He let his eyes follow the high wall as it stretched from the tower itself to his right, crossing in front of the inner courtyard until it met the southeast tower. Because of the window's location he could only visualize the wall continuing to the southwest tower and finally to the royal family's quarters in the northwest tower.

His gaze returned to below the window and he watched two guards walking along the walkway atop the wall until they reached the battlement, which projected out to protect one of the two gates to the inner courtyard. The guards turned and marched back toward the tower. A mind-numbing duty, but one that Bat-Uul sometimes envied.

The door opened to let Chuluun-Uul and the ghoulish Dimah-Uul enter. Several minor priests, all of the lower-level Jin sect, followed the two Uuls and closed the door behind them before continuing to another room in the apartment.

The black-robed priests shut the door to the neighboring room, leaving the three Uuls alone in the well-lit solar. Chuluun-Uul and Dimah-Uul sat at the small round table in the middle of the room.

"Dear brother, wine and then please join us." Chuluun-Uul waved to the table against the wall, indicating to Bat-Uul the expensive decanter and several clean goblets. Chuluun-Uul had that drawn look each time he communed with the Master, a private task that the two older Uuls undertook without Bat-Uul's assistance. Bat-Uul knew not how the communication was performed other than it required the despised Obeah priests. From the look of the Gai-Ten, Bat-Uul was not anxious to participate.

He thought that the Obeah priests would use their herbs and incantations on Chuluun-Uul to allow him to commune somehow with the Master. Like most of the Shin-il priests, Bat-Uul despised the silent Islanders and their detestable potions.

In contrast, Dimah-Uul had a sickly smile creasing his already heavily wrinkled face. From working under him for over a year, Bat-Uul had become aware of the priest's grisly taste, which gave him pause to wonder again about the communication process.

After pouring three goblets, Bat-Uul set them on the table, then sat down.

Chuluun-Uul lifted his goblet and took a strong draw, then set it back down with a loud thump. He took a deep breath and turned to Bat-Uul. "The Master is extremely happy with our progress." He smiled at that. "Though we have had some setbacks, the plan is still achievable." He stared at Bat-Uul as he made the statement.

Bat-Uul tried not to think of the conversation between the other two Uuls the day the Cainwens had arrived, but it was always in the back of his mind. He couldn't get rid of it. All he could do was his best, and he had done everything expected of him that was in his power to accomplish.

"Have the Jin been sent for the girl?" Chuluun-Uul asked Dimah-Uul.

"Princess Willoe has been located?" Bat-Uul interrupted. He had not heard of this yet. For some reason he felt a little saddened by the news.

Dimah-Uul snarled at Bat-Uul's question as he sat forward to lean on the table. "She has. An unnecessary effort, if you had completed your task."

Holding up both hands, Chuluun-Uul stopped Dimah-Uul's accusations. "Enough. Fighting amongst ourselves will not further the plan."

The twisted Dimah-Uul curled his gnarled fingers into a fist, but sat back in his chair. His previous supervisor had shown a level of hatred toward Bat-Uul — ever since Chuluun-Uul had arrived — that Bat-Uul could not explain. He thought that possibly Dimah-Uul did not want to share Chuluun-Uul's attention, or maybe the repulsive little priest was afraid that Bat-Uul would somehow usurp Dimah-Uul's role on the mission.

A wicked smile appeared on Dimah-Uul's face as he turned from Bat-Uul to the Gai-Ten. "Three of our best Jins left two days ago for the west. They will be met by troops from our friend."

Bat-Uul's ears picked up at the word *friend*. He realized that he might not be aware of the entire plan after all.

"Fine. They understand they must reach the girl at the time of the new moon?" Chuluun-Uul's question to Dimah-Uul sounded more like a command.

"Yes," Dimah-Uul responded, nodding his head. "The timing will be in harmony with our plans here."

The full moon had recently passed, so Bat-Uul knew that whatever the Uul's plan entailed, it would happen in little less than two weeks. Much was not being said and Bat-Uul thought that maybe his initial resistance to the plan had caused the others to hold back information. The other priests' conversation about him surged back into his mind and he had to wonder whether he was ever intended to fully understand the true details of the plan.

"Fine." Chuluun-Uul repeated.

"The king. Something has come up." Dimah-Uul looked from Chuluun-Uul to Bat-Uul.

This was something Bat-Uul had wanted to ask - since King Benoit had been in residence when Bat-Uul had left for Westhedge — but he had resisted, considering his footing with the other two Uuls.

"Yes, I understand." Chuluun-Uul nodded and turned his gaze on Bat-Uul and told him, "You may leave now, Brother. I asked you here because I wanted to remind you that the Lady Emeline is an important link to the Cainwens. But you must also remember that a tool can be used against you, if not handled properly. She has spent a lot of time with the son of the Cainwen duke. She may have uncovered something of use."

Bat-Uul stiffened at the mention of Lord Aeron. The young lordling annoyed Bat-Uul on several levels, but the priest despised himself even more because he felt a stab of envy at the thought of the young Shield.

They had been walking for more than a turn and Bat-Uul felt as if he could continue that way the rest of the afternoon. Lady Emeline smiled at each of his remarks and giggled twice at his poor attempts to make a joke, but he felt that she was only being pleasant.

"I am grateful that you are taking time to walk with me," Bat-Uul told her.

"How could I not? You have done so much for me." She smiled and Bat-Uul felt a pounding in his chest.

He knew she saw him as a jailer on their trip to Westhedge, but with time had come also understanding. For the both of them. Upon returning to White Cliffs he had not violated his superior's orders, but had tried to help her in little ways, like passing on news about her parents, who had fled to the mainland. She had come to rely on him when she had nowhere else to turn and he relished those times.

As they turned a corner they came to Bat-Uul's favorite courtyard. It was quite bare with only one tree, a small bench and a pool of water under the tree, while much of the ground was sand and crushed rock with only a little greenery to the side. A couple of big rocks had been placed in the middle of the courtyard or had been left, too heavy for the designers to bother with moving. He knew it would look desolate to most of the castle's inhabitants — a tiny, neglected space — but it reminded him of his adopted home, Avanis, with its calming deserts and beautiful oases.

Bat-Uul indicated the bench and Lady Emeline sat. He sat next to her and stared out at the courtyard. If he focused his eyes on the rocks he could imagine the little canyon where he had spent many days in solitary reflection. It was hidden deep in the mountains behind the temple where he had spent a happy childhood under the supervision of gentle Poojan-Uul. Bat-Uul wondered how the elderly teacher was faring.

The clearing of Lady Emeline's throat made Bat-Uul end his reflection and turn toward her, smiling. "What do you think of my little retreat?"

The smile on her small mouth didn't waver as she glanced around the bare space. "It certainly leaves one with little to distract from their contemplation."

Bat-Uul found himself smiling. "A polite, diplomatic response." His smile broadened with laughter.

He could see in her eyes that his comment had struck at the heart of her response. "I apologize if I—"

Bat-Uul put a hand on her arm, something he would never have done before coming to this island country. But constant contact with the alluring niece of King Benoit had muddled his thinking — something he had spent many turns of the glass in prayer trying to figure out. "You have nothing to atone for. I would be surprised if you thought otherwise."

He left his hand on her arm for a few moments, then pulled it back, feeling a little flushed. He turned to look back out at the courtyard. "It reminds me of where I spent much of my childhood as a young initiate."

He could see her out of the corner of his eye as she turned toward him and her smile faded, replaced with a small frown of concern.

"Was it difficult?" Her tone was reflective of her expression.

Bat-Uul tried not to laugh again. "No, not at all. As you said, few distractions. I spent much of the time in meditation."

"Oh." She turned away again and he could see she was deep in thought.

He didn't think she understood, but the fact that she didn't smirk at his feelings was one of the reasons he had come to enjoy spending time with her.

They sat in silence like that for several moments, both looking straight ahead into the barren yet restful courtyard. Bat-Uul's mind was anything but calm, his thoughts racing.

He could feel his legs shaking under his robe. He spoke, trying to keep his voice from trembling. "You need to stay away from the Cainwens."

"You must be mistaken." Her eyes opened wide as she turned to him. He could see the fear in those eyes.

"It is well known." He shook his head. "You have been followed."

Her expression shifted from fear to anger. "You have had someone spying on me?"

"Not I. Others." He did not wish her mad with him, only to make sure she was not caught up in what was to come. "Anyone with them may come to the same end."

"What do you mean?" She was still angry, but a tinge of panic was evident in her tone.

He had already said too much, but he couldn't watch her in such distress. "I have said more than I should. I do not want to see you endangered when—"

She grabbed his arm and leaned toward him. "When what? What is going to happen?"

He quickly stood and put his hand over hers. He gently removed her hand, though he longed for it to remain. "I cannot tell you more. I just beg of you to stay away from the Cainwens. It is not safe."

She stared up at him and the confusion on her face hurt him, but he had done everything he could to try to protect her. She began to plead, with tears appearing, but he couldn't stay. He spun away and walked hastily from the courtyard. Bat-Uul knew he would never return to the cloistered enclosure. The memories of his childhood would be overshadowed by the image of the tearful woman. None of it would matter, in any case, if his superiors were to discover what he had done; he and Emeline both would find themselves begging for mercy before the day was done, and would be together in death the way they never could in life.

36

A Mistress

"Lady Emeline." The man in the blue overcoat with the elegantly feathered hat nodded deeply to her as they passed on the street. The wide variety of different inexpensive jewels quickly told her he must be a minor noble or a successful merchant, though she had no idea who he was. It was disconcerting that he quickly recognized her. She had gone to a lot of trouble to borrow a plain brown dress with a matching cloak from her servant and even wore her hair pulled back in a commoner's style.

She pulled the cloak's hood up and hurried down Tradesman Way and turned left as she passed a goldsmith's shop, into a narrow alley. She wanted to run, but forced herself to walk quickly between the white-washed two and three story houses that bounded the narrow passage. She took the alley, cutting across two other streets and coming out on Bruyant's Walk, which ran from the castle and curved along the cliffs. It eventually spilled out, along with several other streets, into Windfell Quad, giving them all access to the gate leading south along the coast.

She cursed herself for the fourth time since leaving the castle. *How did I let this happen?* She was only supposed to entice Prince Mael; that was the bargain she had struck with Dimah-Uul, the one her uncle, the king, had forced upon her. He had assured her that she would not actually have to marry the Prince, though she did not truly trust the crooked priest. He had never done anything to encourage such confidence. Why she was to attract the Cainwen heir, she had no idea, but she did not question when the king commanded her to do it. Especially under the ever-watchful eyes of the priests. She had a lot at stake personally and couldn't afford to be seen as uncooperative. Well, at least that had been the plan until the ambush. The day after, Bat-Uul had told her it was no longer necessary. No explanation.

No other directions. Just sit in the carriage and be quiet.

But no, I couldn't just do as I was told and leave it at that. I had to fall in love. If anyone found out, it would be the end of her. She kept near the buildings as she slowed her steps and headed down the Walk. This time of year few strolled along the street, with the strong winds swirling and sometimes blowing in from the Straights. It wasn't long before she found the Storming Cove, the tavern they had agreed upon. It wasn't a place she would ever enter under different circumstances, but it also wasn't one where she was likely to run into anyone she knew. It catered mostly to visitors from outside the city and a few sailors waiting to ship out again. It had been selected as the tavern keeper was accustomed to unfamiliar faces.

She pushed open the door and stepped through into an expansive room with a large hearth on the opposite wall, the crackling fire providing light and some warmth. With the cooler weather the doors and windows were closed, and smoke floated across the room from wall lanterns scattered around the chamber. Along with the hearth they provided adequate lighting, yet dim compared to the brilliance of what she was use to at the castle.

Beyond the smoky smell and the stench of people from different districts and occupations in one room, she could catch the aroma of meaty stew and freshly baked bread. Though she had no real appetite it still made her mouth water. A bar and over a dozen tables covered much of the floor. Many of the tables were filled with strangers, rubbing shoulders and talking animatedly or sullenly staring into their mugs of ale. Most were villagers or farmhands looking to make their fortunes inside the city's walls. Some of the latter sat focused intently on the hot meal in front of them while others chatted with neighbors to still the loneliness. With minor variations they wore nondescript cloaks or overcoats with cotton shirts and pants in an assortment of colors and styles depending upon their homeland and social status.

A couple of the tables were taken by different merchants come to sell their wares in the city, their hired men sitting with them, and one table to her right was surrounded by ship's officers. Only a few tables had open spaces, but she spotted one in a back corner where the light from the lanterns barely reached.

Around the table sat three men. One appeared to be a conservatively dressed merchant, the other two in moderately well kept overcoats, but with the tips of sword scabbards sticking out underneath like the scabbards of the hired hands that sat at other tables. But she could recognize the man that held her heart in any light or in any clothes. She pulled the hood a little more forward and made her way slowly toward the table. Heads turned as she went by, but just as quickly turned back. No one wanted trouble with a merchant's wife or, even worse, a lover.

She sat in the empty chair next to the merchant, one of the hired men to her right and the other to the merchant's left. In the darkened corner she slid her hood back and smiled for the first time since leaving the castle. She put her left hand on the table and he reached over and put his hand on top of hers. The two men to either side faced out into the room, but leaned in toward each other, making it even more difficult for anyone to view the couple. Her smile faded and as her face tensed she started to speak, but he put his finger to her lips. She breathed in deeply, her eyes closed, trying to wash away all her thoughts.

He let his finger sit on her lips for several heartbeats, feeling the softness, then pulled it away and pulled back his own hood, returning the smile. "Humor me and let me bathe in the allure of your presence for just a moment." Aeron breathed deeply, inhaling the familiar scent. Captain Harte's orders had only legitimized what he had been doing on his own. Whether he had intended it to happen or not, he had come to love this Franchon woman. He found her intelligent, modest, and very thoughtful.

He still did not understand why she acted as she had at Westhedge. From what he had ascertained she had no more interest in Mael than the Prince evidently had in her. All Aeron knew was that it was some type of threat from her uncle. She wouldn't give him details other than to say she had her duty.

Her smile returned at his comment and she stared into his eyes, showing a hint of the seductress he first took her for, but he knew this time it was genuine and it made the blood rush in his cheeks.

A serving girl came up to the table to find out if the newcomer required anything, but the two men turned her away politely but firmly. This only confirmed the idea of a mistress for the few that noticed the table at all.

Finally she closed her eyes and sighed in what he hoped was contentment. Then the smile disappeared and her mouth was set tightly.

His smile faded slightly in response, then he said in a low voice, "Let me introduce my compatriots. This is Guardsman Llyr. And I believe you already know Shield Tanguy." He indicated the two men sitting with them. The older gray-haired guardsman nodded and Tanguy just said, "My Lady." Both turned back to face the rest of the room.

"Shield. Guardsman," she responded, recognizing both. She quickly scanned the tavern and then leaned in closer to Aeron, whispering, "You are in trouble."

He smiled again and stated with a little quip to his voice, "Whatever I did to offend the Lady, I will gladly die a thousand times to reconcile my crimes."

Her lips slid in and out of a smile as she pushed on his shoulder. "No, I am serious." Her mouth tightened again as she continued. "They are going to do something. I do not know what it is but it will endanger you. All of you."

"What?" Aeron was taken back and his voice rose. Among all the possibilities it was the last thing he would have considered. Lowering his tone once again he questioned her. "King Benoit would not dare to harm an envoy, would he?"

"Not my uncle. The priest, Chuluun-Uul." She looked around nervously to make sure Aeron's outburst had not drawn unwanted attention. "All I know is that he is planning to move against all of you." She was breathing a little heavier thinking of Aeron in the dungeons.

He scratched his jaw, near his ear, and thought about what she was saying. "Did he say when?" His mind was spinning with the political implications that such a move would have.

"I do not know, but it would be soon." She was trying to remember everything she had heard.

"How long ago did you hear Chuluun-Uul say all this?"

"I did not hear it from him. I heard it from Bat-Uul."

Aeron's dislike of the foreigner rose quickly and he wanted to beat the man for no apparent reason. Well, other than he seemed to have some type of control over the woman Aeron cared for deeply.

She quickly followed up with, "It is my duty. I have to… have to attend with him at functions. Chuluun-Uul wants a show of alliance between the royal family and the foreigners. Many believe the strangers have too great an influence over the king and his court." She said the last part sadly as if there were more she wanted to say. She struggled through whatever it was that had come to mind and finished her story. "I think he was trying to warn you."

Aeron doubted the foreigner would do anything to help the Cainwens. Tanguy tapped the table with his fingers and turned as if saying something to Guardsman Llyr. Both Aeron and Emeline stopped talking and looked at the doorway. Five soldiers in gray — emblazoned with the Franchon Red Lion — had entered, immediately quieting the room. The commander nodded and two guards started walking along the wall around the right side of tavern and the other two around the left, leaving the commander standing in the doorway. A serving girl brought a steaming tankard, probably mead, up to the leader, who took and drank while scrutinizing each table. Aeron wasn't sure how often the patrol visited the tavern, but he was pretty sure that the sergeant had never paid for a single tankard.

It was unlikely that any of the guard would know her, but Emeline pulled her hood back up and leaned her head down just in case. One of the city guard stopped in front of their table and stared directly at Aeron, who looked directly back at the city guardsman before remembering his role. He turned his eyes down in a compliant manner like he had seen some of the other merchants do.

After a quick turn around the tavern the four guards went back to the front. The commander finished the tankard, put it on the table by the door and then all five headed back out into the wind and cold.

After a few moments the noise level rose considerably, the chatter and clatter of the tavern returning to normal. The anxiety level also dropped appreciably.

Emeline lifted her head but left the hood up. "I have to get back. If Chuluun-Uul found out I had told you any of this my—" She stopped suddenly, the words left hanging as if a great secret were about to be revealed, but something she could not divulge. At least not yet.

Aeron hated that something threatened her that she couldn't talk about, but he understood duty and respected her secrecy. He put his hand back on top of hers and squeezed it gently. "If there is anything…"

"No, there is nothing you can do." She choked on the words. "But I must leave."

He looked into her eyes and he could see a deep sorrow there that pained him more than he had expected.

"I will send word soon." He gripped her wrist, not tightly, but he wanted to accent the importance of her being there. He let go and took her hand in his, raised it to his lips and softly kissed it.

She nodded without saying anything. Once he let go of her hand she pulled the hood further over her face, stood, and left the tavern. Moments later Tanguy threw four silvers on the table and they left, going the opposite direction than the lady would have taken.

Standing in a doorway farther north, the page Tomos watched as Lady Emeline walked briskly up from the Storming Cove and turned back into the same alley she had exited from just a short time ago. He waited just inside the doorway, removing his hat so he could peek around the door jamb and watch as the agent slipped out of a doorway just south of the tavern and followed the lady at a distance. Just as Captain Harte predicted. Tomos waited several heartbeats as the Captain had instructed and then quickly dropped off the stoop and kept close to the wall, heading around the corner into the alley with the agent still in sight.

Bat-Uul was having trouble focusing at prayers. It had nothing to do with the makeshift temple that had been set up in one of the towers at Castle White Cliffs. Draped in dark red cloth and surrounded by colorful tapestry all the way from Tsagaan, it wasn't as grand as the prayer room he had grown up in at the temple in Avanis, but appearance wasn't what made a prayer room. Kneeling, he leaned forward three times, beads held between his clasped hands as he prayed to Koke Tengri, the name his people used for the god of all things. Since arriving in Taran he had learned of the Burning Lady and often wondered about the similarities. He asked for forgiveness, as anything that distracted him from his duties was a sin and he had been on the hard floor for many turns asking Koke Tengri to cleanse him of his desires. The tap on his shoulder made him flinch.

"We must talk." Even had he not recognized the voice, the heavy Tsagaan accent would have told him the command was from his superior, Chuluun-Uul.

Finishing up his prayer, holding both hands to his heart and bowing, Bat-Uul stood. He followed the higher priest out of the temple so they wouldn't disturb lesser priests and acolytes who had come since Bat-Uul had started his attempt at redemption. After walking a short distance away they stepped into a small alcove away from any prying eyes.

"I received a report tonight that Lady Emeline has met secretly with the Cainwens." Chuluun-Uul's lips narrowed. "Should we be worried?"

Bat-Uul's mind raced as he thought of the other day in the courtyard. He had spoken of things told to him in private... by his superior. Not the Shin-il Way. "She knows nothing." He tried not to show the tension he felt. He would not believe that she had taken the information to the Cainwens. At the same time he wondered what else would prompt her to continue to meet with the Cainwens after his warning.

"Good." Chuluun-Uul smiled, his eyes lightening. He turned and walked away, leaving Bat-Uul alone in the alcove.

After a few moments Bat-Uul returned to the makeshift temple and dropped to his knees again, pulling the string of blessed stones from the sleeve of his robe. He began the ritual again, but was still unable to concentrate. Too many thoughts forced their way into the serenity he tried to cultivate. Why couldn't he take his mind off of her? A feeling deep inside gnawed at his Spirit, like huge fangs trying to force their way out. A battle raged inside him and he felt as if he was powerless to intervene. He wondered if it would ever be won and, if so, which side would be victorious.

37

Battle Plan

Beynon Brynmor, Crown Prince to the western kingdom of Cainwen, stood over a map that was spread out on the long, polished cherrywood table in the main council chamber. The map was of the entire island of Taran and oriented so the southern end was nearest him, with the Kingdom of Haldane at the other end of the table. He was at the head of the table with several lords and senior officers to either side, including his middle son Hafgan.

It tugged at Beynon's mind that his father, King Einion, was not in attendance. The elderly king's health had been failing steadily and baffled the healers that had tried everything in their power, all for naught. When the healers performed a Seeing they reported that it was as if his body was attacking itself. There was an unknown poison spreading throughout all the limbs and major organs, and all the potions and *il fennore* they could conjure did little more than slow the progression. He could not focus on that at the moment, however, as the war council all looked to him for direction.

Reaching out, he traced a line just to the west of the Saltrock River with his finger and stopped a little north of halfway between Pembroke and Greenmerrow.

"If the Franchon army is as large as our reports say, then the only place to cross an army of that size is here at Daere Mawr." Several of the men around the table started talking about the terrain around the hills running up to the river.

It was still early enough in the day that the windows along the one side of the intimate room provided enough light without the use of any of the sconces mounted along the other walls. A servant stood at either end of the room, each next to a table holding platters of fruit and roasted meat along

271

with several decanters of wine that were barely touched as the nobles and Shields focused on the map. The decorative chairs normally used for such meetings were all pushed back from the table as every man stood to get the best view. Amidst the intense focus on the map, one of the servants reached out and grabbed two slices of a roasted pork and slipped them into his coat pocket.

The Prince smiled to himself and wondered what the young boy would have thought if he knew that his Crown Prince noticed everything, even in the midst of all the chatter. Beynon had a few moments while the other men discussed options before any real decisions could be made and plans developed. He considered the servant boy again. It wasn't good for the boy to think he could steal, even something small like a slice of pork. It would only lead to more villainous acts that another noble might not take so lightly.

The Prince made a mental note to talk with Steward Robat and see that the boy was gently reprimanded. Beynon could count on Robat to handle it without any physical enforcement. The Steward was as strict and as hard as they came, but Beynon knew that all the servants saw him as a firm but fair father figure. Robat also understood how the Prince felt about his servants. They were like children to him, even those twice his age. He demanded their service, but would treat them as best as he could considering their difference in station.

"Sire, might I ask why not up at Snake Ridge?" A young nobleman standing to the Crown Prince's right intruded on his thoughts and Beynon looked down to where the young man was pointing — a set of wavy lines that ran west-to-east a little farther north. The boy was still fresh to the council of his elders and still clung to the formality that most of the others had learned to forgo behind the closed doors of this assembly.

"Lord Sulyen brings up a valid point, sire." Morcar Priddy stood next to the young nobleman. Sulyen smiled at the older man's compliment.

Beynon glared at the slim advisor. He wore an ornate robe and a gold-trimmed doublet, with a jewel-studded hilt hanging at his side, though Beynon doubted the man had ever drawn it other than to have a servant clean it. The man had no hair on the top of his head, but shoulder-length hair hung from the sides, which he wore like a mantle along with his clean-shaven face. His bushy eyebrows covered narrow eyes that always made Beynon uneasy.

Yet the Crown Prince kept hold of his tongue, seeing as the man was Father's friend. The advisor had been at the king's side for weeks, rarely leaving the king's chamber, even taking his meals with Beynon's father. But the man's presence still unsettled Beynon. If the king had not forbidden it, the Crown Prince would have personally led a troop to the Treasurer's estates and gone through every paper until he had the proof he needed. *One day*, Beynon thought.

Across from the young nobleman, one of the seasoned members of the council, General Gavyn Rees, a noble himself, had been absentmindedly cleaning his nails with a small knife. He snorted at the nobleman's question and Priddy's comment, then glanced at Beynon.

Beynon knew that for the boy Sulyen to become a true member of the council he had to learn how to fit in with the more senior nobles. The Prince nodded to the general.

General Rees glanced the Treasurer. "No disrespect to Lord Priddy's far-reaching battle experience." Beynon smiled, but had to stifle his laughter. "If they crossed here," the general shifted his eyes to the young Sulyen, then reached across the table and used the knife, moving it over the map back-and-forth along the river in front of the Ridge, which also happened to be the shortest distance across the river for many miles, "which, may I add, is the only place where they could reasonably get the wagons across, they would have to break into multiple columns to get through the ridges."

The younger nobleman took a harder stance and questioned the veteran without the formality he had shown the Prince. "But once they massed their forces beyond the Snake they could make their way down to the Great Crossway." He pointed to the main east-to-west road that connected Castle Westhedge to Castle White Cliffs. "From there they could follow it all the way to the walls of Faywynne."

Prince Beynon glanced to his left and saw his closest friend Drem, the First Duke, smiling. He had to keep from smirking himself at the young nobleman's question. The boy, Sulyen, was the heir to the dukedom of Wellingford and had recently arrived from Morien Castle. The Prince needed the boy's grandfather's full commitment of troops to the army. Of course he would be required to assist in the defense of Cainwen regardless, but there were always valid reasons and excuses that could be raised for not providing the full royal levy.

General Rees sighed, but tried to be somewhat polite to the young Sulyen and continued to explain. "They could only move in small numbers through the canyons, making them easy targets from the Ridge, and as they crossed the Saltrock they would get backed up at the crossing itself. As they waited for the troops that had already crossed to move forward, the army would be caught on both sides of the river. The ones on the western bank would be chewed up before those on the eastern side could cross. Any guardsman could tell you that the Franchon army would be slaughtered, with their troops spread out in different canyons, unable to support each other."

He moved his knife down to the area the Prince had originally indicated and drew an imaginary circle with the end of the knife. "They could cross here with not much more difficulty, but once they got across they could move en masse either south or north around Daere Mawr and then up to the Great Crossway and not have to expose their troops to the same vulnerabilities that they would at Snake Ridge."

"Our task will be to make sure they don't cross in great numbers," the First Duke added.

Prince Beynon was impressed that the young man didn't try to argue the point any further. Instead, Sulyen just studied the two positions and nodded his head slowly in recognition of the veterans' wisdom.

"I must admit I am not familiar with the eastern border." Sulyen's confession made Prince Beynon smile even more. The boy showed good sense. "Aren't there other places where they may try to cross?"

"Not in such numbers." General Rees ran his knife up and down the Lower Saltrock River. "The river is too deep except at Snake Ridge and Daere Mawr." He moved the knife north of Snake Ridge and then below Daere Mawr. "Farther north the First Duke's Mount Somerled can safely repel any forces that cross." The general nodded to the First Duke, who returned the acknowledgment. "South is Greenmerrow and Castle Clanmor. Even without Clanmor, the Franchons have not forgotten Legendre's Folly. The marshes have only gotten worse over time."

No one else spoke and Duke Cadwal leaned forward over the table. He pushed back his flowing brown mane to keep it from falling forward. The gray streaks on the sides matched the ones in his trimmed beard. Like his son Aeron he was tall and very muscular, commanding attention and respect whenever he entered a room. "If we can block them to the north and south, and take away the Daere road," as he spoke he indicated the road between the Daere Mawr and the river, moving his finger north and south around the heights, "they would be forced to come up to the heights of the Mawr, giving us a significant advantage." He ran his finger west from the river across the low mountain. "Again, the plan is to prevent them from moving a big enough force across the river to overrun the heights."

The Duke of Wellingford's grandson started to speak, but Duke Cadwal cut him off, already anticipating the young man's question. "The roads running along the river to either end of the Mawr are not very wide. A small force to both the north and south could easily hold those roads for moons. With the ends clipped, the Franchons would be forced to stack up at the crossing, and if they did manage to get a good-sized force across they would still be forced to come straight at our forces up a steep slope, giving us the advantage of both height and the Franchons' having poor footing. It is mostly loose dirt and jagged rocks that have tumbled from the top of the slope."

The young nobleman nodded again and Prince Beynon could tell that the young man was smart enough to know that the duke had saved him another embarrassing question. *If he is like his father, he will learn the ways of war quick enough,* Beynon thought as he watched the young heir of Wellingford. The young man's father had been a good friend to Beynon and he missed the man's council. He still remembered the pain he felt when news of the accident came by raven.

"Then we are agreed," Beynon concluded. "Drem, detail a force to cover the northern route with the rest of your men placed on the heights." Duke Cadwal nodded his understanding. "And send a few men up to Snake Ridge. It never hurts to make sure all possibilities are covered." Wellingford's grandson looked up and smiled at the Prince, who gave him a little smile back.

"Greenmerrow can cover the southern route with a small force. The remainder of the Earl's men will be stationed at the back of the Mawr to provide reinforcements to either road or to the heights as needed." Beynon looked across the table at Chancellor Liam, who stood at the other end. "Was a raven sent to Earl Malbery?"

"Yes, Sire," the Chancellor answered in his soft voice. "A message was returned that the Earl was not at Castle Clanmor and it would take some time to reach him. The First Duke," he nodded to Duke Cadwal, "was already at Westhedge, as were most of the others here." The council meeting had been called on short notice and it was not surprising that more were not present.

"It seems rather strange that Malbery could not be reached," the duke commented.

The Chancellor bowed and responded in the same unemotional voice that had become his trademark. "I cannot speak to that, my Lord."

Beynon just nodded in acceptance. "Make sure all the plans are sent by raven." He knew he did not need to add that two should be sent to ensure the message was received. "Then another to Winterpass. I am sure that Manus will have his hands full with Franchons himself, so we won't expect any help from there. But he should be aware of the plans nonetheless."

The Chancellor had already been given directions to issue the levy a week before. All nobles would respond, from those with small manors who could only offer up a dozen Shields to the larger territories that could provide a hundred Shields and more than a thousand footmen and archers. The only exceptions would be those located along the border. Most would need what few men they had to guard their own people as they evacuated their small villages and hamlets from roaming troops and bandits that took advantage of trying times like these. This would naturally not include Pembroke or Greenmerrow. They existed primarily to protect the borders and trade. They would provide nearly half the army at Daere Mawr while still leaving enough forces to protect their own castles. The young Sulyen's grandfather and a few others would be excepted. They were too far west to arrive in time, so Beynon had ordered that Westhedge would be stripped of most of its garrison to make up the bulk of the Prince's own forces. Wellingford and other western provinces would send troops to protect Westhedge, if needed.

"We will meet here." The Prince put his finger on Meadowmoor, a large trading town where major roads from both the north and south intersected with the Great Crossway. "In a week's time."

The Chancellor's eyes narrowed and the Prince added, "I know it is not much time, but we must be up in the heights before King Benoit reaches the river." All the men, even young Sulyen whose grandfather's territory sat along the Forever Waters farthest to the west, nodded in agreement. The Chancellor also nodded, though he bore a slight frown.

Beynon knew that the old man would have to deal with all the complaints that would quickly be flying in on black wings. He only wished he could foretell what news they would bring. It all hinged on gathering the necessary troops in time. He knew Drem would do whatever it took, he only hoped Malbery would be as diligent.

38

Olcas Mogwai

Cian sat at the head of the main table in the Great Hall with Rowyn seated to his right. Saraid sat on his grandfather's left.

Rowyn wasn't sure why Cian had interrupted Rowyn's training, but there were many things that had not been answered to Rowyn's satisfaction. "When you first came to take Casandra and me away, you said my uncle had sent you. But later when I asked you said that it wasn't my Uncle Brom, but my other uncle." With all the training, Rowyn had had little time to think about it, but it tugged at the back of his mind nonetheless.

"Yes, I did." The old Elf had an ancient tome in front of him on the table. It was so large it would require two hands to pick up, and even then it must have weighed as much as a small fawn. He didn't say anything else, but just stared at it and ran his finger along a design that was engraved in the leather binding.

"Who is—"

"You heard what I said when you were struck with the fire?" Cian's words cut off any further questions from Rowyn. The fire was constantly on his mind. He could hardly forget it. It haunted his thoughts every day. *He is the weak one. The sacrifice.* Rowyn nodded his head.

Opening the book, Cian flipped through it until he came to a page he had marked with a feather. He turned the book so Rowyn could see it.

At first Rowyn couldn't read anything on the page, but then he realized the ancient runes were similar to the ones he had been trying to decipher during his limited free time, in the book Uncle Brom had mistakenly given him, thinking he was Willoe.

Rowyn focused harder on the runes and began to make out a few of the words. He read them out loud. "*King. Golden.* I think that word is *agreed.*"

"The word is *covenant*." Cian turned the book back so it was in front of him again. "I came across this and was surprised by its condition when I realized its age. It had a preservation spell on it. It outdates any other tome I have come across. I believe it is from the time of the original Dragon King."

"The one that made the covenant?" Saraid asked, sitting up straight.

"Yes, the same."

What covenant were they speaking of? Rowyn wanted to ask, but Cian continued reading.

"A great evil plagued the world and many suffered for the sake of the few. The forces of the evil ones came from the east and Taran was wounded deeply, the blood of its people covering the land."

As Cian read, Rowyn realized that the Elf was translating the words into a context that Rowyn could understand rather than the original ancient form, which would likely have been difficult for Rowyn to easily grasp.

"A king rose among the people to bring the tribes together, but dark creatures battled the king and his people, and they could not drive the dark evil from the lands." Turning the page, the Elf continued. "The king and his people fought the evil creatures and would not submit to the rule of the great evil. Then, from the Shadows rose a host of Shades to devour the king and his people. The king was desperate for hope and begged the Lady of the Spirit to come to their aid."

"The Burning Lady?" Rowyn interrupted.

Cian nodded and kept reading. "A Golden Dragon appeared to the king. It was the greatest of all the dragons, the king of the dragons. And it proclaimed to the king that it had come to deliver his people from the evil."

Rowyn remembered the tapestry at the end of the Hall of History and wondered if it was the same king. What did Uncle Brom call the king in the image? He struggled to remember, then said out loud, "King Cormac."

Cian smiled. "The same."

Rowyn nodded. He had never considered the story as fact. He had never read anything about King Cormac in Uncle Brom's library, but he also supposed that most tales had some truth at their base.

Cian turned the page again and Rowyn wanted to tell him to hurry. It reminded Rowyn of when Uncle Brom used to read him stories about ancient warriors and their deeds of heroism.

"The dragon would save the people, but there would be a sacrifice. The dragon would have to die to save the people."

Rowyn was stunned. How could that be? That was never part of the tale that Uncle Brom told.

The old Elf turned the page one more time and before reading, looked up at Rowyn, a frown filling his entire face. "Then I came across this." He started to read again.

"In great need the dragons will call the ones filled with the King's seed
The ones called by the dragons will be filled with the dragon's breath"

"It's talking about the fire I feel," Rowyn said, quickly grasping what the words meant.

"The seed of the ancestors shall come alive and guide the ones called
The dragon's breath shall consume the life of one and gift it to the other"

"And the sacrifice," Saraid added quietly.

All three sat for several moments before Rowyn spoke.

"Does it say what the great evil is?"

Shaking his head, Cian answered, "It only gives it the name *Olcas Mogwai*. It appears the dragon knew the evil would return and the king had to promise to confront the evil. To defeat it." Cian paused. "From my reading, the dragon declared that the king's descendants would be the shield against the evil, the weapons that went into the den of the evil to defeat it. The dragon told the king that every generation would bear two that would be alike."

Rowyn thought about it and realized the tale was referring to twins.

"These two would be blessed by the dragons and given special abilities. When the time came and the great evil rose again, those of that generation would be called by the dragons. They would be the Dragon-Called." Cian stared at Rowyn as he spoke.

"The Dragon-Called," Rowyn said, running the words through his head. As he did, he felt the fire respond: a momentary flare that settled quickly. Rowyn looked at Cian with knitted eyebrows.

"What about this sacrifice?" Rowyn was eager to understand everything he could about this covenant.

Gently closing the book, Cian stared at Rowyn so intently that it made Rowyn feel uncomfortable. "If I am correct, the power of each of the chosen, the Dragon-Called, by itself is not enough to defeat the *Olcas Mogwai*. It requires both powers be brought into one of the Dragon-Called and then that one will be strong enough to face the forces of the evil ones."

Rowyn thought for a moment and was confused. "How can that happen? If both of the Dragon-Called have the power, how can one have the power of both?"

Saraid sat back in his chair, the look on his face scaring Rowyn, as if all the air had been taken out of the room.

Rowyn looked from Saraid to Cian, not sure what he had missed, but it had to be important to get the reaction it did from Saraid.

The younger Elf continued to sit as if he had lost his muscles, but then he spoke with an unbelieving tone to his voice. "It is the Gnawing."

"Gnawing?"

Saraid explained, still not himself. "A wizard can draw the Spirit out of another."

"Without a Spirit, the person would die!" Rowyn blurted.

"Yes." The old Elf nodded slowly. "It is rare and only used when no other choice is given."

"I have never heard of that." Rowyn had to admit, though, that he knew very little about the Spirit, other than what Cleric Yoan and what he had learned about the *il fennore* from his uncle.

"It is rare," Cian answered. "It consumes, eats away at the Spirit... from both the wizard and the one the wizard is attacking. The wizard does not survive."

"Then—" Rowyn started to ask.

"That is why it is so rare. But it is possible," Saraid answered again.

"How does this—"

Cian answered Rowyn's question before he could finish asking. "From what I have read, the Spirit of the twins are more powerful than even the Spiros and, using this, one of the Dragon-Called can use their Spirit to pull the power out of their twin and multiply their own power ten-fold. With this they can confront the great evil." He patted the book. "It is the only way."

"And the twins...?" Rowyn asked cautiously, looking at Cian for any sign of confirmation.

The Elf stared at him and Rowyn could tell from the look in his eyes that he had guessed correctly. "Unlike the Gnawing, when the stronger twin draws the power from the other it increases the power of the stronger one. And I believe it also does not drain the Spirit from the more powerful twin. In this way I believe it differs from the Gnawing."

"What about the twin's Spirit that is being drawn out by the more powerful one?" Rowyn asked, but he already guessed the answer.

"In that it is like the Gnawing. The giver would be left without Spirit. I have thought through what you are experiencing when you cross over to the *il fennore* and it fits what I have read." He tapped the cover of the book. "I think Spiros avoid you because you already have a Spirit that would overpower and consume them."

What Cian said made sense to Rowyn. It explained a lot.

"I believe you and your sister are the descendants of King Cormac. And a great evil has infected our world. According to this text, the signs of the

Dragon-Called are the blood of the dragon, the ability to become as a Spiro — one with the *il fennore,* and the ability to transcend the ages to become a medium for the greatest warriors and wizards ever to walk Taran."

Rowyn leaned back like Saraid and sat quietly mulling over what he had just heard. The blood of the dragon. The fire that flared in him and still resided there, simmering. The ability to become one with the *il fennore.* He could exist and move in the Spirit world, manipulating the Spirit in other objects, like a Spiro. A medium for ancient warriors did not mean anything to him until he realized that Willoe seemed to have the skill of a warrior, and that he knew nothing of what she was going through.

He turned to look at the old Elf and hoped he was wrong. "You said, 'He is the weak one. The sacrifice.' Do you think that Willoe will perform this — what did you call it? Gnawing? Or something akin to it — to take my powers and my Spirit?"

"I am not as sure as I had once been. Have there been times when something happened to your twin and you? I am not sure what it might be. Did you have a connection with her?"

Rowyn had wondered, but he had never approached Willoe about this. It had always seemed like a subject that she wanted to avoid and he had never had justification to force the subject. Only his suspicions. "There were," he answered nonetheless.

"We do not know what the truth is yet." Cian stood and came around to Rowyn, putting a hand on Rowyn's shoulder. "You have not had training. We do not know the extent of your power."

"But if I am the powerful one, that means that Willoe would die." The logic came to him like a lightning strike. He could not — he would not! — kill his sister. Then he thought of another question. "Have there been other Dragon-Called?"

"I do not know. I have never read of this other than here." The old Elf laid his hand on the book cover. "The tale of King Cormac and a dragon exists in many forms, but only here have I read of the covenant." Cian stared into Rowyn's eyes.

Quiet filled the room again as both Elfs continued to look at Rowyn with thin-lipped expressions. He couldn't look them directly in the eyes. He was itching to ask more questions, but none came to mind. Maybe after he'd had time to think about it he might come up with some, but for now he could do little more than continue to train and wait to talk with Willoe upon her return from White Cliffs. He wondered what she would say when he told her they were Dragon-Called. But what consumed most of his thoughts was what form the great evil had taken. *Olcas Mogwai.* What was it?

39

Gharzith

Willoe walked next to Aeron, with Protector Dougal and Ser Tanguy two steps behind. The page Sion trailed a few spaces behind, providing additional space between them and the Franchon guards cloaked in gray and red that followed a dozen paces behind. With Aeron's help, and with more than a moon to practice, Willoe no longer walked or had the mannerisms of a woman and she would even have fooled him if he didn't know better. She had had lots of time to practice. They had not had much to do since arriving at White Cliffs and still had not met with King Benoit. The priest Chuluun-Uul continued to put them off with one excuse after another.

The five Cainwens made no attempt to hide that they were from the western kingdom, proudly wearing green cloaks over their pants and vests. The tips of their scabbards pushed the hem of their mantles up, and provided the only sign that they were more than common travelers. Protector Dougal wore the colorful mantle of a Protector pushed back off his shoulders. It was not surprising that occasionally someone, most likely a visitor to the city, would stop and stare at his fur-trimmed studded vest with curved swords crossed on his back, studded wrist bands, and leather breeches. His cloak was green, as the others, but it had a multi-colored trim. It was pulled back, exposing his arms and shoulders, even with the approaching cold.

"Why do you think the delay?" Aeron asked Protector Dougal as they continued the long walk down one of the main avenues winding its way from the castle, on the northwestern edge of the city's walls, to the large bailey just inside the Western Gate. Willoe wasn't sure if he meant their ability to meet with King Benoit or the information that Emeline had given Aeron.

Protector Dougal ran his hand along a house wall and looked down at the white powder on his palm. They had learned much about the castle and city while waiting. Like the castle, many of the buildings in the city were mainly constructed of limestone from the cliffs. "That be the question," he answered bluntly as they continued down the slight decline, working their way away from the many richly adorned merchant and noble houses that surrounded the castle's outer walls.

"There is little we can do as long as the priest is the gatekeeper," Ser Tanguy added as they walked along the cobblestone road and passed row upon row of shops that spread out along the western and north sides of the city. If they continued on that path they would eventually run into the stables and inns that surrounded the bailey at the Western Gate. No one said what they all knew — diplomacy was no longer an option for getting them out of White Cliffs.

"Aye," Protector Dougal agreed.

Ser Tanguy lifted his head. "Smell that?"

Both Willoe and Aeron took in a deep breath and the faint odor of burnt sulfur, salt, tanning solvents, and many other smells drifted over from farther east in the city. The Shield informed them, "Most of the craftsmen and artisans have their workshops between here and the taverns that run along the eastern edge by the cliffs. They mingle with stables, coopers, saddlers, and harness makers. The workshops run upward to the Western Gate where more inns, stables, and craftsmen circle the bailey there."

On a different day Willoe might think the Shield was making idle chatter, but she knew it was important information he was imparting to them. The smell was strong and could easily hide the odor of a large number of horses moving through this part of the city.

They had seen much of the north end of the city near the castle itself and had recently explored the western approaches. Willoe took in the words and used it to help fill in a picture of the remainder of the city.

"It would be so simple if we could just leave and go back to Westhedge." Aeron blew out a large breath in frustration that created a small cloud, as it had turned colder.

"And leave the Lady Emeline?" Willoe smiled at her own joke.

Aeron only grimaced and punched Willoe in the arm like he would have Rowyn, though not as hard. Little actions like that had continued to build the charade over time. His relationship with the lady was not well known, but the information she shared was invaluable to the Cainwens.

Thinking of how Aeron had talked constantly about the Franchon woman on the trip out from Westhedge brought back other memories of the trip. Specifically, the short battle in the forest and the fire that slowly burned inside of her. It had not flared since, but she knew it was still there, simmering and just waiting. The fear and thrill of those few moments still haunted her.

Protector Dougal indicated they should turn down another main avenue heading due west toward the gates.

They passed the Ravished Sister, which brought back memories of when they had first arrived at White Cliffs. She had tried to follow the Protector's advice and spent more time with Shields and guardsmen, the ones who didn't know Rowyn very well. It went well until she, Aeron, and three guardsmen staggered out of the Cask and Larder. Instead of heading back to the castle one of the guardsmen had led them to the house of whores.

"The girls here are from all over Taran, even a couple from Kieran." The guardsman was pleased with himself as he walked up the steps to the door.

Willoe stepped back, bumping into Aeron. "I can't—"

He grabbed her by the arms. "Don't act shocked," Aeron whispered.

"I think we will pass tonight. Too much wine," Aeron said, laughing.

"Come on now, are you going to let us poor guardsmen have all the fun?" A guardsman behind Aeron slapped him on the shoulder, something he would not do during the day. "Don't tell me that lords such as yourself have never visited such a place?"

"My name is known around Faywynne," Aeron said, laughing a little louder.

"And the Prince?" One of the other guardsmen had quit smiling and looked at Willoe. "The young Prince likes women, does he not?" The guardsman's expression posed the question even more than his words had.

If Willoe did not go in the whorehouse, then the men would think her either a eunuch or one who preferred boys. It wasn't something she – or rather, Rowyn — could afford to live with.

She swallowed hard, her throat feeling as if it were closing, then smiled and took a step forward.

"Prince Rowyn," Protector Dougal's voice called to her.

She turned to see the Protector and Captain Harte approaching from across the street.

"May I have a word with ye?"

"Yes. Of course." Willoe turned to the guardsman that had questioned her. "Go without us. Sadly, duty calls." She tried to make her expression appear disappointed, but it was hard to keep the relief out off her face.

The guardsman smiled. "Maybe next time, my Prince." He bowed, put his arms around the shoulders of the other two guardsmen and all three entered the house.

Aeron and Willoe met the Protector and Captain Harte in the middle of the street.

Before Willoe could ask what the Protector wanted, he interrupted. "It be an ill time for ye to be out." He lifted his head toward the whorehouse.

"It be a fine thing for ye to know the men, but ye need be more attentive with what ye do."

He turned to Aeron. "Lord Aeron, be ye companion to the Prince?"

"By all means." Aeron sounded insulted.

"Then ye go 'bout it poorly." Protector Dougal's tone was harsh.

Aeron started to speak, but apparently decided to hold his tongue. He glanced over at Willoe, biting his lower lip.

"We shall escort you back to the castle," Captain Harte offered.

Willoe and Aeron followed a couple paces behind and Protector Dougal didn't look back once all the way to the castle gates.

But that had been weeks ago. The Protector had not rebuked them again. However, anytime Willoe did something out of character, in the Protector's presence, he would give Aeron a hard look.

Continuing through a couple of more turns they slowly worked their way in the direction of the bailey. To any casual observer, and hopefully the guard detachment as well, they were just stopping at one shop or another, occasionally purchasing some small item. At one intersection Aeron said, "I will be right back." He entered a corner shop and spent some time looking over a table of expensive gems with an excited shopkeeper going on about how each gem was specifically cut for the shopkeeper.

The other four stood outside the shop as had been the routine each time they stopped: one or two would go inside and the others would stand outside waiting in idle chatter. This also gave them the opportunity to take in the surrounding buildings, streets that ran into the intersection, and the number of guards on each street, along with the timing and direction of their patrols.

As they stood there waiting for Aeron, Willoe said in a low voice, "Could there really be over forty thousand troops to the north of the city? Where could Franchon find such an army?" The man who had first brought the message from her father had evidently been active, as the Cainwens had a good idea of what was happening with the Franchon army, if not what was planned by the priests.

Protector Dougal didn't answer right away and she thought she had whispered too softly, but then the Protector spoke in a dry, low voice. "Look about you." He indicated the people in the street. "We now know where the young men have gone. Also, we have the reports about the sellswords. The number may even be greater than what our spies know."

Aeron came out placing a small package in his belt purse and Willoe gave him a questioning look. Aeron just shrugged innocently and walked off, obviously not wanting to talk about it. They reached the western bailey as the sunlight began to fail and dusk approached. Like the southern bailey, stables, taverns and more shops catering to travelers ran all the way around the bailey, working their way down the city walls to meet with similar buildings running up from the Southern Gate. They selected a tavern directly across from the gate and sat down at one of the small wooden tables placed outside the entrance along the tavern's wall. Their talk was light as they watched the guard detail change and only six Franchon guardsmen replaced the twelve that had stood guard in the afternoon. After a short meal they headed back up the hill at a much quicker pace, as they had memorized the fastest route and only needed to count the number of night guards and their locations along the way.

As they entered the castle, their following Franchon guard left them and the four of them headed to meet with Captain Harte at a tavern, as previously arranged. A night of drinking and singing commenced shortly thereafter while Ser Tanguy and Protector Dougal reported on their mission.

After the Franchon guardsman gave his report, he left and the young acolyte followed him out, closing the door behind the both of them. Chuluun-Uul turned back to face the two Uuls seated around the all-too-familiar table in the Counselor's solar. "It appears the Cainwens are not enthralled with our delays." He focused his attention on the younger Uul. "It would seem they do, however, have a taste for seeing the sights."

"They have been all over the city." Dimah-Uul commented.

"But it has been different groups. They are probably giving each group a chance to get out of their cramped quarters." Bat-Uul had come to hate the leather-skinned priest, for which he had been spending many turns of the glass on his knees in prayer.

Chuluun-Uul cut off any further discussion. "I believe you are correct." He looked toward Bat-Uul. "I do not see any mystery in their actions." He smiled as he continued to look at Bat-Uul. "It appears that your young woman is just foolishly in love and our plans remain just among ourselves." He leaned back and flicked a hand in the air to wave off the thought.

Bat-Uul fought to hold his bland expression while his fist tightened under the table.

Rubbing the bare space on his chin between the hanging sides of his mustache, Chuluun-Uul stared off as if thinking. "With her brother's offenses, if she were found to be undecided on her loyalties — well, I would hate to think of what might happen even to the niece of the king."

Bat-Uul's gaze lifted before he could stop it. Had Chuluun-Uul guessed?

"But what business is it of mine what the lady does with her life?" Chuluun-Uul's smile faded.

"We are ready to move on the girl," Dimah-Uul informed Chuluun-Uul, taking the superior's focus off Bat-Uul.

Glad for the diversion, Bat-Uul turned his attention to the older priest. Dimah-Uul had been there many years, a representative from the Franchon kin on Kieran, slowly wheedling his way into King Benoit's graces. His red robes hung on his too-thin body and his skin, darkened from years as a child in the deserts, looked as if he was covered in well-worn leather. Bat-Uul was amazed at how the old Uul had managed to keep his perversions hidden for so long.

Chuluun-Uul's pause indicated he was considering the news. "Soon. Very soon. We must take her and her twin at the same time."

Dimah-Uul had the same questioning look on his face.

"We cannot afford any mistakes. The powers available to them are not perfectly understood, even among the Gai-Ten. If we take one, the other might know, and then we may lose that one." Chuluun-Uul's words didn't help Bat-Uul's understanding. "We must also be prepared to move on the Cainwens as soon as the twins are ours. A Tumen Tenth of Jidig will be arriving within days. They will join the army and then we can take the twins."

Even in the small peaceful kingdom of Avanis, they had heard about the murderous horse-warriors feared across the empire. What purpose was there in bringing over a hundred of the Jidig warriors to Taran?

"They will be bringing Gharzith."

Dimah-Uul grinned, but Bat-Uul found himself speechless. He had never seen one, but the stories were enough to make Bat-Uul wonder what Chuluun-Uul could be planning. What would cause his superior to import the Dog-men? And a better question in Bat-Uul's mind was, what would Chuluun-Uul do with them?

40

A Flicker in the Air

Ser Rhein walked around the manor talking with each of the three guards he had posted and then settled down at the campfire with the remaining guardsmen. Sergeant Crowley tried to engage him, but his mind wasn't open to deep conversation and the sergeant moved on to other discussions, leaving him to his solitude. He stared into the fire mesmerized by the flickering yellow fingers that reached upwards into blue tips. The bottoms of the logs sparkled like gemstones as wood turned to embers and the sturdy branches became ash. Everything around him disappeared as he inhaled the smoke and only the tunnel of flames remained.

His mind cleared of his duties as his thoughts drifted to the Lady Casandra. He had only caught glimpses of her over the previous weeks and had never had an opportunity to talk with her. More than once Dilys had reminded him of the oath Casandra had taken in support of her cousin, the Princess Willoe. But knowing that did not make it any easier. He knew she was the daughter of the First Duke, would most likely marry another Cainwen noble, and Rhein would never even be considered an acceptable choice. If nothing else, the truth about his background would see to that. But even so, in his dreams they found a way to share a life. They rode through open fields and swam naked in a cool river, drying off on the grassy river bank under a warm summer sun. Her hair unraveled and stretched out above and around her head, framing her fine features. He could almost feel the touch of her soft fingers on his face.

A pine cone burst in the flames, sending sparks into the air, and he jerked out of his musing; the fantasy dissolved as the crack of the burnt cone faded. Dilys stood there staring at him with a queer look on her face. He felt like she knew something about him. Something personal.

He smiled up at her and offered her a seat next to him. It had been the custom for Dilys to join the guardsmen around their campfire after dinner each night. Rhein had come to like the Princess' servant, but even if he hadn't, she was the only source of information he had on the Lady Casandra and he couldn't get enough.

He had not grown up around the castle and only spent a short time with the guardsmen there before being sent to the northern border. Most of what he knew of the lady came from castle gossip. Unlike most high-born, she was known as a gentle and compassionate noble lady. Always had time to answer a question or help someone in distress regardless of their station. She was even reported to have spent quite a bit of time in the kitchens because she said she wanted to know how to feed herself. Rhein couldn't even fathom the wonders that made Lady Casandra so unique, but he nonetheless always found himself wanting to know more.

"Aye, she did that. She still visits with the cook each month to help prepare a meal, though her father and the king be horrified if they knew," Dilys said as she nibbled on one of the rolls Guardsman Rhodri had made earlier. She added, "I don't think I have ever heard her say an unkind word 'bout anyone."

Rhein had to take a moment to understand what Dilys was saying. He wondered if he had been speaking his thoughts out loud. He could only imagine that he had done just that.

Dilys smiled at him as she took another roll from the pan.

His mood improved and he asked Dilys a few more questions. He sucked up everything she said and asked for more. After weeks of evening talks with Dilys he felt like he had known the Lady Casandra his entire life, for all he had not talked with her more than a handful of times on their trip out from Castle Westhedge.

Dilys had commandeered two camp chairs from the manor shortly after arrival. Rhein and she sat in them at the side of the fire facing each other, while the guardsmen sat on cut logs that had been placed around the fire pit.

After a turn of the glass he pushed his dark blond hair back behind his ears and rubbed his palms against his eyes, then blinked to clear them. It had been a long day and he was tired. He was going to ask another question when Dilys held up her hand, closed her eyes for a hand of heartbeats, then said in a hushed tone, "They be coming."

He looked from side to side and then looked directly at her. "Who's coming?" He couldn't see anyone.

"They be coming down the main road." She had her back to the road facing the manor, but he had a perfect view of the road. He started to stand to look, but she grabbed his wrist and pulled him back down. "Don't show ye know," she chided.

He wasn't sure what she was talking about, but he had come to trust her in their long stay together at the manor. He stared over her shoulder but couldn't see anyone or anything coming down the road. "Are you sure? I don't see anyone."

Her voice was tight, but controlled. "Look directly down the middle of the road." He did as instructed. "I know it be getting dark, but keep looking down the road. Look for a flicker, a shimmering in the air."

He narrowed his eyes as he focused on the road in the dwindling light. He wasn't sure what he was looking for but kept looking nonetheless.

"See it?" she asked in a hurried tone.

"No, nothing." He grimaced leaning a little forward. "Wait!" He'd caught something. Then he saw it again. It was like the air flickered. "I see it."

She leaned toward him so they were only a couple of hands apart and whispered, "They be heavily armed. They be shielded and be waiting for something."

He had no idea what was going on, but he was smart enough to focus closely on what Dilys was telling him. He was already shifting into the mindset that had gotten him his Shield and was running alternatives through his mind even as he asked her, "Shielded?"

"It be a form of glimmering," she said, and added, "Like what I did with the ladies."

It struck him then. "The ladies!" He stood quickly, but she stood with him.

Her face was gravely serious. "Don't, they be not here."

His mind sped up as he considered Dilys' statement. How could that be? He had seen the ladies earlier in the day. Had those approaching in the night, whoever they were, taken Willoe and Casandra somehow?

Before he could say anything more, Dilys said hurriedly, "They be nev'r here. They be just glimmers. Illusions."

He held his face and posture stiff, but inside he was in total shock. He could only wonder. Had he been fooled all this time? He was personally responsible for Princess Willoe and the Lady Casandra. Had he failed in his duty? "What do you mean they are just illusions?"

"Later." The ladies' servant continued quickly, "We need to act now. Ye must trust me. They be safe with friends." The soft servant's face had disappeared, to be replaced with one used to wielding authority.

He wanted more answers, but if she was telling the truth, he would have to make an immediate decision. He met her gaze, something he felt was the gateway to a person's true intentions. He stared into her gray eyes and they looked the same as they had ever since arriving at Highkeep, but he focused now and saw a depth that he had not noticed before. A depth that spoke of knowledge and history. He couldn't say how, but it gave him the reassurance he needed. He nodded twice.

She tipped her head toward the guardsmen around the fire. "Have your men prepare, but quietly. I'm going over to the servants' quarters and will have them ready to move. In a couple of moments I will break the shielding and ye will be able to see them. They be all across the front of ye, coming slowly toward the house."

"What about the sides and back?" His mind was starting to overcome its shock.

"Only a couple in the back and one to the left. Two others be making their way through the woods to the north."

That made sense to him, as there was little cover in the back and left side. And if they could move unseen against them in the front there wasn't much need to have more men on the left side. They were probably waiting for these two to get in place before attacking. "Be ready to move toward the woods," he told Dilys.

She started to walk past him, but he asked quickly, "How many?"

She hesitated and finally said reluctantly, "Forty, maybe fifty. I'm not sure." She then headed at a brisk walk to the servants' entrance on the ground floor near the right side of the manor.

At least three times their own number, but there was nothing that could be done about that now. If his people could reach the woods there was a chance. Sergeant Crowley had been watching the exchange, but Rhein doubted the sergeant had heard what Dilys had said. The sergeant leaned over the fire, stoking it with a stick and looking sideways at Rhein, but did not say anything. Rhein was impressed by the sergeant's perception that something was wrong. As the stick moved one of the logs around, spewing sparks into the air, Rhein sat back down and turned to face the fire. Leaning in a little himself, he turned his head away from the road as if looking toward the manor and the sergeant. "Sergeant, there are armed men spread across the road."

Still turning over logs, the sergeant casually turned his head and peered down the road, squinting. Again, Rhein wondered how the veteran had learned to be so calm, even in a situation as strange as confronted them now.

"You cannot see them," Rhein said, though it seemed unbelievable to him even as he said it.

Thankfully Sergeant Crowley didn't question Rhein and instead turned his head back toward the fire and lifted his eyes to his commander as if waiting for further instructions.

Still looking away from the main road, Rhein continued in a low, steady voice. "Make your way around the perimeter and collect Hartha and Owain. There are men out there also, but I think they are there just in case we try to escape that way. When you reach Clairfield, wait until it starts here. There are two more in the woods near Clairfield. I imagine they will be near the path leading to the creek. You need to take them quickly, then send someone ahead to make sure the path stays clear." He leaned his head in Dilys' direction as she headed toward the doorway. "The servants should get to you first. Send them on. We will cover as long as we can before following."

The expression on the sergeant's face must have echoed Rhein's when he was told. "What about the ladies?" the concerned sergeant asked.

Rhein started to tell him what Dilys said, but thought the better of it. Unseen assailants were enough to deal with at one time. "They will be safe."

Sergeant Crowley's mouth twisted as if he were thinking it over, but his military training took over and he nodded.

"Tell the men, but quietly."

The old campaigner had rarely run from a fight, so had to ask one more question. "Numbers?"

"Maybe forty." Rhein said, trying to keep a show of confidence.

The sergeant nodded again, the look in his eyes letting Rhein know he understood. Rhein and the others would only be able to hold them for a few moments before they were overcome or had to make for the woods themselves.

He put the stick down, rolled his shoulders back like he was stretching muscles, exchanged light words with a couple of the men near him and then headed toward the left side of the manor. To anyone watching he was just letting them know he was going to check on the guards on duty. As he walked away the men leaned over and started campside conversations among themselves. But, as they did, all the men slowly — and quietly — brought their swords a little closer. Two had bows they were able to reach without making any obvious movements.

Rhein looked around and swore to himself. His greatsword was a good six or seven steps away, leaning up against a small tree in front of the fire where he had put it earlier. He looked around as if taking in the surroundings, but he wanted to get another quick glance at the shimmering air. The early evening light had faded and all he could see were shadows of trees and outhouses from the light of the fire. At least it was a full moon, so when Dilys broke the shield it would help his men see their attackers. For now he couldn't see the gleaming air he had seen before. He tried to pinpoint where he had seen it earlier and estimated that it couldn't be more than a dozen or so paces to that spot. The question was, could he get to the sword before the hidden attackers reached him?

He looked back over to where Dilys stood in the open doorway, casually looking his way. He couldn't see anyone else there, but had to assume she had gathered the servants and was ready to go. When she had his attention she closed her eyes and he thought he could see a little light outline her, and not from the campfire or the moon.

He turned back to the men and whispered loud enough for them to hear. "Get ready." He brought his right foot back a little and planted it in the ground to push off toward his greatsword. He heard Dilys shout some words he couldn't discern, but the results were immediately evident.

A loud pop battered his ears and flashes of light filled the air in front of them like the sparks Crowley had stirred up in the campfire earlier. The light was nearly blinding, but his guardsmen reacted well, showing their training in spite of the bright lights. They stood and drew swords, and as Rhein pushed off he could hear the *twang* of two arrows being released.

He was almost to his greatsword when he caught the glint of the fading light off steel in the corner of his eye. He dove to his right and could actually feel the air stir as the attacker's sword swiped over him, missing his shoulder by no more than the width of a couple of fingers. He rolled to his right and came back up on his feet to face his attacker. The man was already charging again with sword raised high. The weapon came flying down at an angle intended to cut Rhein open from shoulder to waist. A better swordsman might have succeeded, but Rhein grabbed one of the larger sticks set aside for the fire and was able to get it up in time to deflect the blade. His hand stung as the stick flew from his grip.

The attacker roared and turned again to face Rhein. The man had black hair sticking out from underneath his helmet, with a scraggly beard and heavy eyebrows showing beneath the headgear. He wasn't heavy, but a good three fingers taller than Rhein. His leather vest and wrist bands were studded with iron rivets. They were plain, no emblem announcing the man's loyalties. The man wielded his one-handed smallsword in his left hand, which Rhein quickly realized he could use to his own advantage.

With another roar the fighter charged forward again, this time with his sword pointing at Rhein's chest. Rhein started to his left, which the man had expected. The man turned his sword across his body to his right, but Rhein shifted his weight back to his right at the last moment and the attacker's sword slid past him. Expecting to skewer Rhein, the man's own motion was carrying him past when Rhein reached across and knocked the assailant's left forearm upward and backward with his own forearm. The attacker's arm and sword came up in front of the fighter's chest and sliced into his neck. It wouldn't have cut too deep except that Rhein had kept pressure on the man's arm and as the man's momentum carried him past Rhein, the blood spurting out like a fountain told Rhein that this opponent was no longer a problem.

Rhein reached down and grabbed the hilt of his own sword, but before he could pull it out of the scabbard another fighter dressed like the first one was upon him. He blocked the man's downward swing with the tip of the scabbard and then swung the hilt end up to catch the man on the chin with the guard of the greatsword. The satisfying crunch of bone as the man fell let Rhein shift his attention long enough to draw his greatsword. Pulling it out in a quick motion, he dropped the scabbard in time to hear pounding footsteps behind him. He put his other hand on the handle and swung it around in a circle, slicing the man rushing him from behind in the waist, just below his half chainmail vest, almost severing the surprised attacker in half.

He stood up and looked for another attacker, but none were in reach. The sound of metal on metal drew his attention back toward the manor where his men were being pressed by the attackers. At least three of the Cainwen men were already down and others were bleeding, some from multiple wounds. Rhein felt a certain pride when he noted that, among the enemies' ranks, more than three times their number were down as well.

He glanced over to the manor and saw Dilys and the servants as they ran between the manor and the woods. He wondered why they had not already reached the trees when he noticed one of the attackers on the ground, unmoving, behind the fleeing servants. Dilys was halfway to the trail, where Sergeant Crowley waited, when two of the attackers came out of the woods to their right. The men were closer to the servants than Sergeant Crowley would be.

Rhein started to yell, but Dilys stepped forward and met the charging men. Her hand moved so quick Rhein barely saw it, but she drew her arm back, holding a long kitchen knife, and swung it in front of her, catching the first man by surprise and opening his throat. The other man slid to a halt and stabbed at the old woman. Dilys danced around the blade, spinning to the man's side and driving the now-bloody kitchen knife into his side, just below the arm where there wasn't any chainmail. The man fell and Dilys ran to catch up with the servants that had run past during the fight.

Rhein stood stunned as he watched the strange woman disappear around the corner of the manor. It almost spelled his ending, as he heard the footsteps behind him only at the last moment. He dropped to his knees and rolled, bringing his sword around and catching the man behind him at the knees. The bottom of the man's right leg separated and he fell sideways, screaming and clutching his bleeding stump.

Rhein stood, and above the bleeding man's shrieking and crying, Rhein yelled to one of his men, "Gerallt." The guardsman was pulling his sword out of his opponent's stomach and looked over. Rhein flipped his head toward the woods. The blood-covered guardsman nodded and yelled orders to the remaining men. Two men with more serious wounds disengaged from the battle and ran as fast as their wounds would allow toward the trail in the woods. Gerallt was fighting back to back with two other men, one of them the cook, Guardsman Rhodri. That one was swinging a smallsword, in one hand, and backing off one attacker while skewering another with the spit he had used earlier to roast a hare. They were fighting off twice as many of the mysterious attackers. On a command from Gerallt they turned and ran after the wounded guardsmen. Rhein cut down another of the enemy as he raced to catch up with Gerallt and the others.

As he neared the path, he met Crowley and Guardsman Owain, who stood with swords ready, Dilys at their side. Gerallt and the other two guardsmen were disappearing down the path as Rhein reached the edge of the woods. He turned around to face the manor, intending to help the two guardsmen meet their attackers and to give the others time, but no one was behind them. He was bewildered. *They must know that we can't hold them off for long.*

"They be trying to break into the ladies' room," Dilys said at his elbow.

A momentary shock filled him until he remembered what Dilys had said earlier. How she knew they were at the ladies' door was another mystery. He ordered the sergeant and guardsman, "We need to move before they realize that the ladies aren't here." He was rewarded with a strange look from the sergeant.

"We need to head north," Dilys told him without a moment's hesitation.

The Shield frowned at her. "But Castle Westhedge is south."

Dilys' look left no doubt in Ser Rhein's mind and he nodded. "North it is then. But where to?"

"Just head north. They be through the door shortly and then headed our way." All four of them started running down the path away from the manor until they reached a small opening in the overhanging oak and elm branches. Dilys came to a stop, closed her eyes again and in just a few moments a large owl flew through the opening above them, its wings flapping as it landed on a tree branch just above her head. Its weight caused the branch to bend. All three of the guardsmen flinched at the sudden appearance.

Dilys opened her eyes and whistled a quick song at the blinking owl and when she finished it launched back through the canopy. The whole exchange only lasted a few moments. Dilys smiled, which Rhein thought rather strange. "Help is on its way," she assured him.

She turned back to the trail and closed her eyes once again. Rhein heard her whispering something and then she pointed her hands back down the path. Nothing happened at first, but then a flame sprang up, cutting across the path into the woods on either side.

Both Rhein and the sergeant jumped back.

"It be another glimmer. An illusion," she told them.

"But I can feel the heat." Sergeant Crowley leaned away from the rising flames.

She smiled at them. "It be a good illusion." Then she hiked up her skirt and started running down the dirt path toward the creek.

Rhein and Sergeant Crowley, looked at the flame one more time, then turned to watch Dilys running north. Rhein hadn't noticed before that her dress was wet and sticky with blood.

Crowley, standing at his side watching her, said in an unbelieving voice, "Three of them. Fully armed and armored. There's more to her than just a lady's maid." His voice held a certain appreciation.

Rhein would have laughed at the understatement if it weren't for the fact that they were all probably going to die before the night was out. But a smile did crease his face and he said, "North." Then they followed her at a quick run, Rhein already wondering how he would get a group of servants and wounded guardsmen through the northern wilderness with no supplies.

41

Meadowmoor

Drem Cadwal, the First Duke, stood next to where General Eryls' tent had sat moments earlier, while servants finished packing it away. Waiting for his general to arrive, he scanned the camps to either side of the Great Crossway, just east of the trading town Meadowmoor, as soldiers were breaking camp, the camp followers, mostly women and children, busy making final preparations for whatever soldier they had latched onto, while servants scurried about carrying out their masters' orders. Merchants and other hangers-on made their last offers of wares before the northern army pulled out of Meadowmoor, leaving all the civilians in their wake.

"Duke Cadwal, I had not expected to see you today." General Eryls walked up with his senior staff around him. The general had been making a tour of the camp before forming up the army.

"I left early this morning and rode out ahead of the main Western Army. They are about half a day behind. I wanted to go over the deployment one more time." Drem clamped hand to arm with the general as he smiled.

The general returned the smile and called out to his page, "Bring the map."

The page pulled a rolled scroll from a leather case and spread it out on a table that a servant had quickly set up.

Drem talked as he pointed to a narrow flat area running along the ridge of Daere Mawr. "The main body will be deployed along here. Mostly archers supported with pike and guardsmen." Then he moved his finger to the bottom of the western slope. "Reserves will be camped here. Until the Greenmerrows arrive, troops will need to be deployed at the southern and northern gaps." He stroked his finger perpendicular to the north and south of Daere Mawr.

"If they arrive," General Eryls scoffed. There was no love lost between the northern and southern nobles, a sentiment felt all the way down to the soldiers and citizens of Pembroke.

"The possibility exists."

"How many?" Drem asked as he turned and looked at the activity spreading throughout the camps.

"We split our troops in half. Coming south, Counts and Earls Colle, Began, Neacal, Pierce, Blethen, along with nearly a dozen of your barons, joined the army, delivering an assortment of Shields, pike, archers, and sundry foot. A few more barons and small groups of Shields with their men continue to arrive." The general lifted his head as if in thought. "At last count, ten thousand. That leaves four thousand to defend Castle Mount Somerled and our side of the river from north of Snake Ridge to Northurst. The Franchons still hold sway on their side of the river and Tierran's Wall."

Drem nodded his approval. He knew Baron Manus, at Fort Winterpass, and the vassals between the Greymoor Forest and Kingdom's Gate Mountains would hold the north in case the Tonn took advantage of the war, and also to support Mount Somerled, if needed.

"Were the sappers successful?" If they weren't then it would put the entire plan at risk.

"Word just arrived this morning." The general held out a hand to his side and the page placed a scroll in it. The general unrolled it and read. "Destruction of bridge was completed at dawn. Franchon advance guard ambushed with few losses. Western side blocked and fortified."

Drem welcomed the brevity of military communications.

The general rolled the scroll back up and held it out for the page as he continued. "The messenger told me that over a hundred Franchons had come upon the sappers before they had completed the destruction of the bridge. The escort for the sappers had planned for such and set a trap. Not a single Franchon escaped, and the two ferries south of the bridge have been burned."

"Who was leading the escort?"

"Lieutenant Wogan."

"After this is over, see that he is recommended for his spurs."

The general smiled, then his eyes narrowed as he changed the subject. "The Western Army?"

"The Crown Prince was able to field close to three thousand troops from around Westhedge and the castle itself, mostly guardsmen and archers." Drem had cautioned the Prince that drawing most of the troops away from Westhedge could be dangerous, but Beynon had already sent word to vassals farther west to send troops for the defence of the capital. "The western vassals will reinforce Westhedge and Faywynne."

General Eryls gave Drem another questioning look.

"They will not be able to reach Castle Westhedge before the Western Army marched."

The general nodded his understanding.

"Every day vassals answered the call with their forces and before I rode out this morning, I estimate another six or seven thousand troops have joined the main army en route to Meadowmoor." Drem had hoped for nearly twice that number, but without the western forces… he only hoped Malbery could bring a full contingent.

After discussing the final strategy from the meetings back at Westhedge, the bulk of the northern army left to prepare the sites at Daere Mawr for the remainder of the Cainwen army.

Drem sat in the saddle waiting at the entrance to Meadowmoor. Winter was starting to show its unkinder side and he was wrapped in a black Gorlin fur cloak. It had been a close thing, the winter before last, when he had killed the Gorlin in the mountains north of Castle Mount Somerled. Two of the Gorlin's foot-long claws had dug into the duke's left chest after he had driven the spear up under the Gorlin's chin and into the brain. It passed right through and the powerful creature fell forward, its one paw reaching out to snag Drem and pulling him down. Even now as Drem thought about it he still felt a tightness from the scars on his chest, but this made him prouder of the cloak he now wore and he pulled its warmth tighter against the light wind.

"The army comes," a Shield called out.

Drem sat up in his saddle and looked down the road. The first sign that the Western Army approached was the dust cloud out past the small woods that lined the road for many miles westward. The duke called for a page to bring up a drink. Anything wet and Drem knew it would not be strong drink. The duke was not one to keep others from filling their goblets when feasts were held at Mount Somerled, though most tempered their consumption as one never knew — but the duke himself always kept a clear head even when visiting Westhedge. He wished his son Aeron followed his example a bit more in this area, but Aeron was his own man and Drem was proud of that.

"My lord." The page came running back with a small platter that held flowered wine, so watered down that it could not really be considered intoxicating. The platter also held some cheese and a hunk of bread. Drem kept an eye on the road as he absentmindedly reached down while the page held the platter up so the duke could easily take up the goblet or some of the food. Drem looked up at the sun, which was high in the sky, but did not warm the air significantly.

Then the familiar clink from thousands of chainmail-clad soldiers along with the hoofbeats of more than a thousand warhorses floated to Drem on the wind. Moments later he could see banners fluttering in the air. He signaled for the page to take away the platter and he focused his attention on the oncoming army.

A score of the duke's personal guard and several of the senior nobles were saddled behind him on the road. The nobles pulled off to the side while the guard formed up into two columns. The duke straightened and wished once again that he wouldn't have to wear the small, golden, jeweled circlet on his head. He didn't care how decorative it appeared or how regal it made him look; the air was cold and a piece of cold metal on his head made little sense to him. But one had to keep to formality at times like this. Once they were back on the road to Daere Mawr he could replace the circlet with a nicely furred hat.

He could spy the leading guard and beyond that the banner signifying the Crown Prince himself. The column of troops wound well back out of the duke's vision, lost in the trees that lined the road, but he could make out a variety of banners representing the different noble holdings between Castle Westhedge and Meadowmoor. Drem might never see the entire army until they reached Daere Mawr.

A shadow had grown long next to Drem, as the sun had left its apex, before the forward guard rode up and spread out to either side of the road, providing a clear road for the Prince and some of the major nobles that rode with him to come up and meet the duke. Drem was surprised to see the Crown Prince's brother, Lord Brom, riding next to the Prince. The older brother was bundled up under so many layers that Drem had trouble recognizing him at first. Drem had never paid much attention to the Prince's brother. He never involved himself with court politics. He had definitely never taken an interest nor participated in any warlike activities, so his presence baffled Drem at best.

The Crown Prince evidently saw the look in his old friend's eyes as he said with a smile, "Yes, it is my dear brother. For some reason he insisted on joining the campaign. Why, I cannot imagine."

Beynon was clothed similarly to Drem, the fur cloak coming from a creature that Beynon had killed on a hunt with Drem just last year. Beynon also wore a circlet on his head, but he also had a fox collar that helped to keep his neck and head warm. Drem made a note to have one added to the collar of his Gorlin cloak. Both men wore leather vests, but when they reached Daere Mawr they would have to don the full set of chainmail trappings and Drem was not looking forward to all that extra weight, especially as it would be a lot colder up on the ridge.

The duke bowed to the Crown Prince's brother as befitted his rank, but when Lord Brom tried to acknowledge the duke with a little bow he was so bundled that it came off as barely leaning forward in the saddle.

Beynon had shown an innate ability as a leader, but Drem wondered how Brom would have fared if, when barely a man, Beynon's older brother had not abdicated the crown. The two Princes were very close as brothers even though their interests varied widely.

Beynon's children carried these same differences in character. Prince Mael was a mirror both in looks and personality of his father, while Prince Rowyn plainly bore his uncle's distaste for weapons and love of academia. Princess Willoe a strong character like her father, but also showed a wealth of compassion and love for her people, something most thought Prince Mael lacked. The middle child, Prince Hafgan, seemed to have missed inheriting the traits from either of the king's sons.

Beynon slapped his brother on the back and laughed. "What are you going to do when the wind blows on the ridge and the cold bites into you like a starving wolf?"

Lord Brom managed a small smile and said in a sarcastic but brotherly tone, "Probably freeze to death."

Beynon's laughter bellowed across the road and Drem joined him as he had always enjoyed the Lord's biting humor. Brom often said things that Drem wished he could say himself. In that the Lord was a much braver man.

After they settled back down Beynon gave the reins a light slap and his courser stepped forward in a slow gait that his retinue started to follow. Drem turned his horse and came up next to his friend, the duke's guard split with half joining the leading elements and the remainder falling back in a single column next to the two columns of the Crown Prince's larger guard.

As Drem pulled in next to Beynon he saw a pack horse tied to Brom's horse and had to look twice before he realized that on one side of the pack horse was bundled gear, probably Brom's, but on the other side was what appeared to be a tub of sorts. A narrow metal tub tied to the horse's side, like the bundle on the opposite side. A heavy blanket was laid between the tub and the horse's side to protect it from rubbing.

What made him look twice was what sat inside the tub. The Tink, Drel Donlin, was leaning back in the tub facing forwards and was sipping on a flask with one hand and holding a small loaf of brownish bread in the other. As Drem watched the Tink put the bread down and pulled a fur hat off its head, then tipped it toward the duke. He put the hat back on and took another sip. Drem had to smile at the little creature. Drel Donlin seemed perfectly comfortable in the little carrier, but Drem thought the Tink must be awfully cold in the metal pot.

As if to dispel the duke's concerns the Tink reached out a finger and touched the edge of the tub. An orange tint ran through the gray metal and Drem could tell that the Tink had just warmed the metal slightly. He realized the blanket served a dual purpose. Drem was sure the Tink would not want for warmth even up on the heights of Daere Mawr. And, for that matter, he thought Lord Brom would have no difficulty with the cold up on the ridge either.

They rode on in silence for a while until Beynon turned in his saddle and faced Drem. "Have you received word from Greenmerrow?"

"No word yet. I sent riders south but they have yet to return." Drem looked to the south hoping that one of his riders might be approaching even now. The duke considered the worst case and said as such. "It would take Malbery time to call in his vassals. Greenmerrow is not like Pembroke. Between the marshes and all the shoreline estates it would take more time to gather his troops. I sent messages to Mount Somerled after our first meeting, so they had more time to prepare and even with that they only arrived last night."

Beynon turned back to the road and rode on for a few more minutes, then offered, "I suppose you are correct." He turned back to one of his officers and told the man to send three additional riders south on the road to Castle Clanmor with extra horses. He wanted a report by the time the army broke camp in the morning.

Shortly after that Beynon and some of the leading nobles pulled off the road with their guards, pages, and other members of their escort. Two servants set up a large table and spread out food and drink, though they had to use knives to hold down some of the lighter items against the rising wind.

Drem dismounted, handing his reins to a groom, then moved over toward the table pulling his cloak tighter. Beynon and General Gavyn Rees, the commander of the Western Army, along with some of the vassals, approached the table as well. Drem was surprised to see the young Lord Sulyen, grandson of the Duke Wellingford, at the general's side. It seemed that the General had taken the boy under his wing.

As Drem approached, Lord Brom strolled up and casually looked at the table. Drem had to keep down a chuckle as the Crown Prince's brother licked his lips.

"It has been a long morning," Lord Brom said as he reached for a goblet of wine and a cold slab of salted boar.

As the rest nibbled on the small feast, Beynon spoke. "We need to have a plan for temporarily redistributing our troops if Malbery is late. I am sure King Benoit will not be so kind as to wait until the Earl's men arrive. Yet I think stout-hearted Cainwen soldiers can hold against the likes of the Franchons for a little while." He laughed as he said it. Most of the others laughed with the Crown Prince, except Drem and Lord Brom.

Even if the Crown Prince wasn't worried, Drem knew that without the troops from Greenmerrow it would be impossible to hold the gaps for very long.

The discussion went on for a short time, with everyone providing ideas on how to deploy the troops, until Lord Brom asked, "What if the Earl of Greenmerrow doesn't show at all?"

Beynon stopped looking at the map and glared at his brother. "Malbery will show." He commanded it as if that alone would make it happen.

He pointed a finger at his brother and appeared to want to say more, but pounding of hoofs interrupted as a rider came down the road at a gallop. The rider reached the guardsmen blocking the road. After words passed between the guard captain and the rider, the captain directed the rider to the group around the table. As the rider approached he dismounted and Drem could see that he was in the dark green and blue uniform of Greenmerrow. The rider strode quickly up to the Crown Prince and knelt, head down.

Beynon told him to rise. "Do you bring word from your earl?"

"Yes, Sire." He held out a scroll with the Earl of Greenmerrow's insignia stamped on it in wax.

Unfolding the document, Beynon read it and then handed it to Drem. The message said:

His Majesty Crown Prince Beynon,

Sire, I was away at the Baron Poyner's estates when your message arrived at Castle Clanmor.

Your summons made its way into my hands and I immediately sent word to my vassals to make arrangements for travel back to Castle Clanmor and then Meadowmoor.

I regret to report that I have not gathered the forces I had wished to bring to you at Meadowmoor in support of this great campaign.

Even with our reduced number the men of Greenmerrow will not fail our lord and liege. I will be leaving tomorrow with a force of two thousand five hundred mounted troops consisting of lance and bow. We should arrive at Daere Mawr three days hence. Another three thousand foot will arrive two days after.

May the Burning Lady look over you until then.

Your Servant, Grioral Malbery, Earl of Greenmerrow.

Below his signature the Earl had also written

Death to those that dare raise arms against Cainwen and the Brynmor family.

Drem passed it on to the General.

"Well, as I said, Malbery will be there." Beynon looked at his brother and smirked. He then signaled the servants to clear the food. He put his gloves back on and slapped his hands together, a smile on his face.

Brom addressed the Greenmerrow messenger. "You should have passed our riders. They were headed south on the same road you came up."

The messenger stood there silent for a few moments then without changing his expression he answered. "I did not see any other riders on the road, Your Lordship."

Drem noticed that Lord Brom did not seem appeased by the messenger's answer. "Half a dozen riders and you did not see a single one of them?"

The young Sulyen nodded in agreement to the side.

The messenger shifted his feet slightly but stared straight ahead, not looking at any of the men around him. "I cannot say, my Lordship. Many things can happen on the road to a lone rider." He barely flinched at the brother of the Crown Prince's questioning.

Lord Brom moved closer to the messenger so the man had no chance but look directly at the Lord. "That seems rather peculiar, out of six riders not a single—"

Beynon interrupted his brother, obviously irritated. "Many things could have diverted them as the man states. A break off the road, bandits, a slew of unexpected obstacles." Beynon waved his hands in circles, dismissing his brother's line of questioning.

Drem thought that Brom had a point and would have liked to question the messenger further, but the Crown Prince's words ended any chance of continuing.

Addressing the messenger, Beynon said, "Tell the Earl that we look forward to his arrival."

The messenger bowed and without even taking a drink or food, mounted his horse and trotted back down the road he had come up not half a turn ago.

"Let us move on." Beynon looked up at the gathering clouds. "I want to reach Daere Mawr by tomorrow before the weather turns."

Calling for his courser, the Crown Prince gestured for everyone to mount. Before the mount arrived another rider came galloping down the northern road from Castle Mount Somerled; the man in the saddle looked well worn and hardly able to keep in the saddle. He rode right up to the guards who barely stopped him from charging past them.

The man wore the mantle of Pembroke, Drem's Duchy. He called to the guards to let the man through. The guards let him through and the rider raced forward, sliding to a halt on the road just above the gathered nobles. The rider slid from the horse and, breathing hard, bowed as he handed a scroll to Drem. The seal was from Drem's wife.

"Get this man some food and drink," Beynon commanded a servant standing off to the side. The rider nodded his gratefulness and started to head over to the servant.

Drem quickly unraveled the scroll and read it, but instead of handing it over he rolled it back up and looked at Beynon. "Manus sent a message through Mount Somerled. His man in White Cliffs reports that all information points to King Benoit being either dead or held hostage."

Beynon took the scroll, unrolled it, and read it himself.

"They be in great danger," General Rees added.

Lord Brom didn't speak, but was rubbing his face, seemingly in deep thought.

"If the king is not ruling, then who?" Sulyen asked.

"The priests. The one who Mael said was the king's advisor. Chuluun-Uul," Lord Brom pronounced.

"Why?" This time General Rees asked.

Brom did not offer an answer.

Drem's mind ran rampant with questions of his own, but he knew there were no answers without more information. He could only do what he could do... his duty.

A page brought up the Crown Prince's courser and stood to the side holding the reins.

Stiffening his back, Beynon stood higher and took the reins from the page. He mounted and looked over at his brother and Drem. "We have a battle to win." He kicked his horse into a trot leaving his guards to quickly mount and gallop to catch up.

Drem mounted and sat in the saddle for a moment as he stared after his friend and Prince. He finally spurred his horse forward as his thoughts whirled. He was not worried about himself, he had lived a good life, but he feared that even if he survived he might not see his son again.

42

At the Heart of the Matter

Mael, Count Idwal and Captain Harte just stared across the table at Aeron. They were in a small inn off the castle grounds. Several guardsmen sat at tables around them so that no one else could get close.

"I see no point in bringing her along," Count Idwal said for the tenth time in the last turn of the glass.

"We can't just leave her." Aeron's head felt like it was going to explode. Why couldn't they understand?

"We have already been over this, Lord Aeron," Captain Harte spoke up. "There is too great a risk."

"Without her information we wouldn't know about the priests' plans." He wouldn't give up. "You know as well as I that when we escape, that monster Dimah-Uul will make her pay a high price for helping us."

"We do not know that." Mael's face was set and he seemed more annoyed than usual.

Aeron stared at the heir apparent. He had to make his point before the Prince's right eye closed entirely.

"If King Benoit is dead, who would that leave as next in line for the throne?" He had just thought of this line of reasoning and hoped it worked.

"That would be his brother, Lord Mayne," Count Idwal stated. His knowledge of the peerage of both kingdoms was well known.

"And after him?"

"His firstborn son, Remi."

"Do we know if they are still alive? No one has heard from them." Aeron hoped the men would come to the conclusions he wanted.

"That would leave the Lady Emeline." Count Idwal sat back with a smile.

"Since we don't know of the whereabouts of King Benoit, his brother, or the Lord Remi, the Lady Emeline might possibly be the heir to the kingdom of Franchon."

Mael started to say something, but Aeron kept on. He needed to finish his argument before they dismissed him. "If we take the Lady Emeline with us when we escape, we are likely taking the next ruler of Franchon. She would be indebted to us for saving her. It could mean an unrivaled opportunity for peace between Franchon and Cainwen."

"If we survive our current circumstances," Captain Harte added glumly.

"Notwithstanding, we would have Lady Emeline and can put her back on the throne, or we have a valuable bargaining tool if the king or her father or brother are still alive."

The three men sat there just looking at Aeron.

"There may be merit to what the Lord Aeron suggests." Count Idwal was nodding thoughtfully.

"The risk…" Captain Harte did not seem to be satisfied.

"If the Lady Emeline is truly the last direct member of the family…" Mael looked up as if pondering deeply, before looking back at Aeron. "Then my marriage to her would put both kingdoms under one throne."

Aeron was shocked. He had not thought of that. Mael had no more interest in the Lady Emeline than Aeron had in Willoe.

Mael smiled at Aeron. "You have our permission to bring her when we escape." He rose after making his proclamation, asking Count Idwal to join him. They walked out of the inn with a levy of guardsmen that walked in front and behind the two.

"You did not expect that?" Captain Harte stared at Aeron and shook his head.

"He doesn't even care for her."

"You should know Prince Mael sees everything as a tool to be used to further the kingdom's prosperity. How could he not take this opportunity? This possibility was discussed. You will be in Count Idwal's group, the last before Prince Mael and the rearguard make their escape. Get word to the lady to meet you tomorrow night under the southwestern tower. It is the least guarded and is not far from the gate you will need to use."

"Prince Rowyn will want to come along." Aeron already anticipated Willoe's demands.

Captain Harte didn't answer at first, then said with a sigh, "Last time I let the Prince go off on a task, we know what happened." He stared at Aeron for a moment more. "But he handled himself well." Then he stood. "Tanguy and a guardsmen will go with you and the Prince. Then you can join up with Count Idwal. Talk with the count for where to muster." Before walking away the captain looked down at Aeron. "If this should go awry, Lord Aeron…" He let the words trail off.

Willoe stood underneath the southwestern tower with Aeron at her side. The hoods of their cloaks were pulled forward and they tried to appear as small as possible against the wall surrounding the bailey. The moon had risen in the sky and they hid in the shadow cast against the tower. Aeron had promised Willoe that Emeline would be there and the woman was already half-a-turn late. Willoe had been there when the page Sion had said he had delivered the message. Willoe could still picture the boy in her mind as he pushed the brown locks out of his eyes, something he and his brother both seemed to have a problem with. She had nearly laughed as his dimples deepened at being able to play a role in the intrigue. As if it were a game to be won.

The young page had grown on both Willoe and her cousin. Not as easy-going and friendly as his bigger brother, Tomos, he nonetheless had latched onto Aeron and Willoe, willing to do whatever they needed. Many of the Shields had accepted Willoe and during their time at White Cliffs the rest of the Cainwen retinue had slowly accepted her into their company, though her opinion was still rarely considered, if it was even requested at all. The events of the ambush had become more a legendary story than a reality and the event had become fainter in their minds over time. But the two brothers, the pages Tomos and Sion, had always gone out of their way to be friendly to Willoe and Aeron even back when the servants and guardsmen had isolated them and made them feel like they had the plague. Maybe it was the naivety of their youth, but Willoe liked to think that they just had such big hearts. Both boys had also grown while at White Cliffs, with their Naming Days only several days apart. Tomos was now thirteen and Sion twelve.

"Where is she?" Willoe asked in frustration as her eyes darted upward to scan the top of the wall. She expected to be discovered by the guards walking behind the parapet at any moment. She pulled the dark gray cloak tighter around her body and grasped the pommel of her sword for the hundredth time. The entire escape plan hinged on none of the Cainwen groups being discovered until they had made it out the Western Gate of the city. It was unlikely that anyone would notice small groups of six or fewer travelers in gray Franchon cloaks, making their way through the city at night.

"She will be here shortly," Aeron tried to reassure her.

Willoe looked up as the cloud cover Cleric Yoan had predicted started to settle in. If the smell of moisture in the air was any indication, they could expect rain, also as the Cleric had predicted. "How do you think he knew?" she asked in a whisper, eyeing those clouds.

Aeron had been facing away and now turned to look at her and asked in response, "Who?"

"Cleric Yoan." She moved closer so they wouldn't be overheard. "How did he know it was going to rain? And specifically, how did he know it would be shortly after dark?"

Biting his lower lip in thought, Aeron replied, "The Clerics are the messengers of the Burning Lady, so that means they must have some connection with the Spirits. The way I look at it, they are the closest thing to a wizard in the lands south of the Greenwald Forest."

"Uncle Brom," she added with a light smirk.

She could make out the hint of Aeron's smile in the wraps of his hood. "An abnormality." He smiled awkwardly and let out a quiet snort.

"So you think they ask the White Lady about things like the weather?"

"Maybe they ask the Spirits," he responded and looked around again to see if Emeline was coming yet. Looking away from Willoe he added, "I am just glad we have them." He turned back, his lips thin and eyes wide. "Can you imagine what it would be like if we didn't have Clerics to close sores or fix broken bones?" Then he smiled again and opened his mouth to laugh, but shut it just as quickly, looking up at the wall above them.

She automatically reached up under her hood and touched the scar on the back of her neck as she considered the ramifications of life without healers.

The slap of boots on the cobblestone edge of the courtyard made them sink closer to the wall. The familiar figure of the page Sion came along the wall to where they were standing. They moved a little out from the wall as he approached, the gathering clouds providing as much cover as the shadow would allow. The boy stopped and leaned forward, putting his hands on his knees and panting to try to catch his breath. Like them, he wore a gray Franchon cloak. He pulled his hood back, strands of wet hair clinging to his forehead and along his jawline. Finally he looked up at them and, between breaths, told them, "She will be here in a few minutes." He inhaled deeply and straightened. "But she has someone with her." His expression reflected their own worry over this unexpected turn.

"Who is it?" Willoe asked as she absentmindedly opened her cloak and reached in to put her hand on the pommel of her sword again.

Sion shook his head and squished his nose in frustration before answering. "I do not know. That one is cloaked like the lady, but they are not much bigger than I am."

Aeron and Willoe shared a worried look. She could see in his expression that he didn't have any idea either.

The sound of voices could be heard across the yard and all three of them turned as two figures in matching dark gray cloaks came out into the bailey and made their way toward the southern tower. As the newcomers reached the Cainwens, Aeron pulled back his hood to give them a large smile. The gray-hooded newcomer in front pulled back the hood and Lady Emeline's teeth and bright eyes shone in the fading moonlight. She took two quick steps and fell into Aeron's waiting arms. They hugged for several moments until Willoe tried to bring them back to reality, her voice harsh as she still had not reconciled her feelings about Aeron's love interest.

"Who is this?" She pointed to the other gray hood with one hand while still keeping her hand resting on the sword inside her cloak.

Emeline reluctantly pulled away from Aeron and turned back to look at her companion. With a smile she said, "This is Josiane, my maid." The other figure pulled its hood back to expose a young girl, maybe fourteen, who had her eyes downcast and shifted from foot to foot. She had the same Franchon hair and features as her mistress, but without the fine lines and robust curves.

Willoe remembered her from the few times she had escorted Emeline when Aeron and Emeline had gone for their walks.

Willoe was infuriated. She hadn't wanted to take the Lady Emeline with them in the first place. Now Aeron's feelings for the niece of the Franchon king was jeopardizing them even further by involving this young girl.

Willoe's anger must have been evident as Emeline gave her a hard stare of defiance before turning to Aeron, her lower lip rising into a pout. "You can't expect me to just leave her," she protested with a huff as if Willoe's accusation was a stain on her honor.

Ser Tanguy and Guardsman Llyr ran up from the same direction as Emeline and her maid. Willoe could see Aeron's shoulders physically relax as their approach changed the focus. The guardsman was cleaning off his knife with a cloth as Tanguy spoke. "There were two of them. Cloaked."

"I already said I could not leave her. I would trust her with my life." Emeline became defensive, apparently believing Tanguy was talking about her and her maid.

"He meant that you were being followed," Aeron told Emeline. "By two men."

Guardsman Llyr only grinned as he continued to clean his knife from what Willoe could now tell was drying blood.

Understanding finally dawned on Emeline. "You killed my uncle's guardsmen?" Her eyes widened and her voice started to rise.

Aeron put his finger to his lips to quiet her while Tanguy told the shocked lady, "They were only sellswords."

This seemed to calm the woman and when she turned back to Aeron, Tanguy looked over her back at Willoe, his eyebrows raised as he shrugged his shoulders. She suddenly found herself wondering about something. *How would he know if the men were Sellswords or not?*

The moon was almost totally hidden by the clouds now and a slight drizzle started to fall on them. Aeron shaded his eyes to keep the drizzle out and looked up at the sky, then scanned the courtyard to make sure they were still alone. "We had better go."

Willoe started to object. The issue of the unexpected maid was still unresolved in her mind, but Sion took off to scout ahead while Aeron took hold of Emeline's arm and, with her maid following, headed off after Sion. Willoe stood there for a moment and snorted her frustration. Nothing could be done at the moment, however, so she strode off after them with Tanguy and Llyr bringing up the rear, looking to either side, searching for threats as they followed at a fast walk into the darkness that was the city of Lealacité.

Aeron pulled Emeline along, not roughly but he was still vexed with her bringing the maid along. This was not part of the plan and he was not looking forward to telling Mael, or to when Willoe cornered him alone. The look on Willoe's face alone was enough to turn his blood to ice.

They walked a short distance and exited through a well-hidden postern gate in the castle wall that Emeline had told them about. It was similar to the small gates the other eight parties had taken, and to another that Mael would take with the last and largest group to leave. The passageway through the wall was narrow and they had to walk in single file to reach the wooden gate.

Once outside the white stone wall, they walked briskly along it until they neared the main gate between the southwestern and southeastern towers. Aeron hoped the drizzle would drown out the sound of their footsteps as they came under the battlement protruding over the top of the gate. At least, that was the plan. In fact, the entire plan hinged on the cold drizzle keeping the guards in the battlement instead of on the wall. Or at least so bundled up they wouldn't pay much attention to anything below the walls. They cut across the front of the closed gate and waited, pressed up tightly against the wall.

Aeron could feel Emeline shivering but he didn't know whether it was from the dampness or the fact that they might get caught. Probably both, he thought. They were pressed up against the wall, the rugged stones pushing against his back as they waited for Sion to give them the all clear. The water running down the wall didn't help, as it drenched their backs. The page had gone ahead into the merchant's sector, so he could get a visual at the top of the wall and let them know if the guards were out or not. If they were then he would signal when the guards turned at the end of their route and headed back to either tower.

The trill of a loon sounded three times in succession, telling them that they could move.

"Go quickly." Aeron pulled Emeline away from the wall and guided her across the yard. She followed blindly, running through puddles, trying not to slip on the wet cobblestones. They crossed the yard into the safety of a street nestled in amongst the large merchant houses that encircled the bailey outside the main gate. Once away from the looming outer wall they made better time, but still tried not to run, though the temptation was great. After dark, and with the sky spitting on them, few people would be on the street. They didn't need to draw more attention to themselves, however, by racing through the streets.

They worked their way along the route agreed upon for more than a turn and came out where the trade sector came in from the eastern part of the city to merge with the lower merchant houses at one of the three main thoroughfares. They hugged the wall of a tanner's shop, their clothes dripping from the light rain, as Aeron looked out into the intersection. *They wouldn't have left without us, would they?* He looked through the haze down each of the smaller streets that ran into the crossway, but the drizzle was turning into rain drops and kept him from seeing clearly. He cursed the Shadows for making them late, trying not to blame the raven-haired girl at his side.

He leaned over to confer with Ser Tanguy to determine whether they should head onward to the gate and try to catch up with the others or wait a little longer in case the others had been delayed. The soaked young page tugged on Aeron's cloak. Looking up, Aeron wiped the rain out of his eyes and followed the boy's pointing finger to the other side of the intersection leading away to the Western Gate. Aeron could make out a horse, a bay stallion, and astride it was Protector Dougal wrapped in a black fur cloak. He held his hand up and signaled for them to come.

Aeron pointed out the Protector to the others and they crossed the major intersection looking around to make sure no one was coming down one of the side streets. He half expected to see a troop of Franchon guardsmen standing in one of the narrow streets just waiting for his little group to cross the main road. Reaching the other side they found one of the groups waiting for them. Count Idwal was among the seven, from the other party, and from his expression Aeron could tell he was fuming.

"We are late," he said gruffly, the rain dripping off his soaked beard and making him look like a wild street dog. The count was from an old family and his loyalty to the royal family was beyond reproach. While he respected the Prince, the same did not necessarily apply to Willoe or Rowyn personally, yet it was enough to keep him from saying what he really seemed to want to say.

Three guardsmen held six horses ready for them to mount. The fact that there was an additional rider only delayed them momentarily. Josiane was saddled behind one of the guardsmen and when Protector Dougal gave Aeron a questioning look, all Aeron could do was mouth, *Later.*

They rode at a walk until they were near the bailey at the Western Gate. The rain kept up, but had not increased in intensity. Even so, it was still early in the rainy season and the cobblestones were slick. It took a steady hand to keep the horses moving forward without a misstep.

They came to a corner just outside of the bailey and two hooded men, with swords drawn, stepped out from a doorway. One walked over to the count and pulled back his hood. Aeron recognized him as one of Captain Harte's guardsmen. "They're waiting at the gate," he told them and then he and the other guardsman moved aside so the riders could pass.

The riders continued around the corner, entering the courtyard. As the guardsmen had reported, Captain Harte, Cleric Yoan, Supply Sergeant Trystan, several guardsmen, the Horse Marshall, and a dozen servants waited to the side of the large wood-and-iron gate. Enough horses for the entire party were tied up at a stable on the opposite side of the yard from the gatehouse. Several additional ones were loaded down with supplies as they could not safely get the wagons out of the castle without raising an alarm.

As they rode up, Captain Harte approached. "What delayed you?" he asked more out of concern than anger. Willoe pointed to Emeline and her maid. The Captain just made an *Oh* with his mouth and gave Aeron a questioning look.

43

An Owl for Supper

They were all seated around the table in Cian's Hall for a late night feast. The Hall could hold more than sixty at any one time, and often did, but tonight all the other tables were empty and it was only the cousins and their Elven friends — Cian, Saraid, and Helel — at one of the tables. Cian did not believe in having a head table so all seven dinner tables were identical. Only a few of the sconces on the walls were lit and two lanterns hanging right above the table gave it a very intimate but casual feel. Yet their host had told them to dress up for the night, hinting at some news.

"Fine evening to you," Casandra greeted Rowyn, Cian, and Saraid as she entered and walked up to the table.

"That it is." Cian was friendlier than normal, which made Casandra wonder even more about what was behind the formal feast. The other two men nodded with a smile, something she had not seen from Rowyn since Cian had told her cousin about the Covenant.

Maybe tonight will be enjoyable after all, she thought, after the constant testing and practice both she and Rowyn had been doing over more than a full moon.

Casandra wore one of the dresses the Elfen had given her. It was made of a form-fitting fabric that she supposed was wrought from linen and had a softness she had only felt in the finest of material, yet what no Cainwen dressmaker could accomplish was the unique attributes of the material. Helel told her that even though feather-light, all the outfits would keep her either cool or warm depending upon the surrounding weather.

The red dress she wore tonight was trimmed with a gold brocade and finished off with a twisted gold belt around her waist. The neckline plunged in what had become a fashionable style. The only jewelry she wore was a

317

narrow chain hung around her neck supporting her family's crest. She had always been fond of the silver wolfhead pendant with the small ruby eyes that appeared to glow in the soft light from the sconces.

Helel and the other Elfs assured her the dress was very becoming on her. And from Rowyn's and Saraid's occasional glances in her direction she was sure it was. Helel was similarly dressed in a pale blue robe that only emphasized her golden hair. Casandra had smiled when she caught Rowyn looking her way, but then his eyes shifted back to Helel. She wondered how a man could stay true to the same horse for years, the way their eyes wandered to the brightest object in their view.

The men had also dressed up for the evening. All three of them were in bright tunics of a similar material worn over breeches, each in a different color. She was surprised at how well Rowyn cleaned up. His hair had grown out just enough, over the time they had been in Fayhaven, that he had been able to pull it together and band it in the back like the Elfs. She found she liked the look.

The normal kitchen staff did not wait on them and instead both Drel Corklin and Krel Monlor carted various foods and drinks from the side tables. When everyone had a full plate and goblet, Cian waved his goblet to catch Drel Corklin's attention before indicating the table. The head Tink nodded and came over to put a decanter in the middle of the feasters, then gestured to his junior. They both filled plates to overflowing, and each picked up another full decanter, then sat down at the other end of the table. They didn't join the conversation but instead focused on their plates and especially the decanter. Casandra had learned without being told that Tinks, at least all the ones she had met, consumed an extensive amount of both food and wine, ale, or any other type of fermented drink.

Rowyn laughed as he watched the Tinks' single-minded focus. It had been a while since Casandra had heard that sound. Not that Rowyn had laughed a lot before they started the trip from Westhedge, but when he had before it had filled her like a deep breath on a summer day; full of warmth and a fresh feeling of beautiful days to come. But there had been none of that since Cian told Rowyn of the Covenant.

The others joined in and Krel Monlor looked up, but only for a moment. He shrugged and dove right back into his meal, filling his goblet a second time. Drel Corklin tapped his junior's arm with a friendly snarl and Krel Monlor poured another for the older Tink as well.

The Cainwens and Elfs settled in, enjoying the small feast, all of them smiling and laughing from time to time as the talk was light and cheerful.

As the last few bites were going down, Cian stood. "Saraid and Helel," he nodded to each in turn, "tell me that you both have made significant progress. I thought it was time we broke from your demanding routine for a day or two and take some time to refresh your Spirits."

Casandra sighed. Yes, a couple of days' rest would be welcomed.

Rowyn opened his mouth to ask further when a loud squawking noise cut him off. They all turned to one of the open windows as a large feathered beast flew through it and landed, barely stopping on their table. The two Tinks jumped back to avoid being hit by the worn bird. The owl turned its head around to look at each of them and finally centered on Cian, shifting its body to line up with the head. It started to make a series of hooting sounds with a barely discernible difference in tones and pitches. Cian stood, hands leaning forward on the table, and whistled back a couple of times. The owl responded with more hoots. After a few moments of this back-and-forth exchange the owl launched from the table, flapping its large wings and taking one turn around the room before flying out of the window it had come in.

He sat back down with a worried look on his face. He rubbed his chin, a habit he shared with his grandson, and seemed lost in some private thought.

They waited patiently for a few moments before Rowyn spoke up to break the silence. "What did the owl say?" From the look on his face this question must have sounded as strange to Rowyn as it did to Casandra.

"Oh." Cian looked around as if seeing the rest of them for the first time. "Highkeep has been attacked."

Both Rowyn and Casandra stood up in shock, their questions tumbling over each other.

Cian held up his hand to silence them. Once quiet, he continued. "The servants, Dilys, and some of the guardsmen got away. And also the Shield."

Casandra could picture the young, tall, muscular, blond Shield in her mind. It brought a strangely comforting smile to her face which she quickly shook off, but not before she caught Rowyn looking at her with a frown on his face.

Cian stood again and paced back and forth. "The manor was attacked yesterday at around dusk."

"By whom?" Rowyn asked.

"Dilys could not tell. They were unmarked."

Dilys again. Casandra was definitely planning on cornering the old maid-servant at the first opportunity.

"But they were *shielded*," Cian added.

This made Saraid and Helel look at each other, obviously concerned.

"Which means a strong influence on the *il fennore* to perform such a task." Saraid frowned as he stated what was obvious to Cian, Helel, and he.

"Or Shadow conjuring," Helel added, her expression darkening at the words.

"Where are they now?" Casandra was more interested in what was happening with them *now* than what had happened.

"They escaped, but are being chased. With the servants and a few wounded it will be difficult for them to avoid their pursuers for long." The lines in the old Elf's forehead deepened as he thought. Then he looked back at the other end of the table. The Tinks had not sat back down since the owl flew off. "Krel Monlor. We are leaving tonight." He turned to look at the older Tink and ordered, "Wake the Kata-henis and have them ready in a turn."

Drel Corklin nodded and then added, "I'm going along."

As the Tink turned to leave the Hall, Cian stopped him. "Krel Monlor will be enough," he stated as if that ended the discussion, but the little Tink stood with legs apart and arms crossed over his chest.

"If Lady Dilys be in trouble, I am coming."

Cian sighed and nodded his head at which both the Tinks turned and left to get everything ready for a quick departure.

Cian started around the table and put a hand on Rowyn's shoulder. "This could be very dangerous. I don't know how many of the attackers are following them and the evidence of possible Shadow influence is not a good sign. The two of you can wait here if you wish."

Rowyn didn't even wait a heartbeat. "I am not sure what I can do with my limited abilities, but Wil would never forgive me if I let something happen to Dilys."

Cian looked across the table at Casandra. She took a deep breath and found herself saying in a strangely humorous tone, "I am not letting a bunch of Elfs and an inexperienced Dragon-Called run off into the wild without me. Who is going keep you from getting into trouble?" Casandra considered the absurdity of how events can change at a moment's notice.

Smiling, Cian patted Rowyn on the shoulder and winked at Casandra. "I was hoping you would say that. It will make it easier. If we ride through the remainder of the night and keep a steady pace for a couple of days we should be able to come in above them and meet them as they come out of the forest." His bushy eyebrows lowered and came together as he added softly, "If they make it through the forest."

"Where are they headed?" Saraid asked, apparently trying to figure out Cian's comment.

"There was only one way for Dilys to take them that might give them enough time for us to catch up, so they are headed north," he said as he gazed out the window as if he could see all the way to Highkeep. He breathed deeply and exhaled before adding, "Right into the heart of the Greymoor Forest."

44

Brother and Sister

Willoe dismounted, looking directly at Doy as he took her reins, but he only returned the smile that had haunted her. She walked over and joined the other senior officers and nobles as Captain Harte was speaking to the count and Protector Dougal. "We have the guards locked up in the gatehouse and two men posted on each of the main streets," he said, looking around at the growing group around them. "Prince Mael and the rest of the guardsmen should arrive within a few moments."

They had broken up into smaller groups leaving the castle a half-a-turn apart so as not to raise any suspicions.

"The servants and the spies?" Count Idwal's question carried his authority.

Master Gwron's group had been responsible for ensuring the spies in the walls of Mael's room and the Franchon servants couldn't raise an alarm. "Cleric Yoan's potion worked as he stated. They are all safely locked up in the stable where the wagons are stored. I believe they're still sleeping." He smiled to emphasize.

"Sergeant Trystan is going to miss those wagons." Captain Harte's grin was shared as they all looked over at the supply sergeant, who was ordering some of his servants to some task.

Master Gwron added, "There weren't enough horses in the stables, but some of the servants should be able to ride on the pack horses."

The seaward wind had shifted and it started to blow the rain at them rather than down on them. As the storm intensified the servants crowded into the tunnel between the two portcullises to wait in the relative dryness of the gateway.

The Cainwens waited more than a quarter of a turn past when Prince

Mael and his group was to arrive and Willoe could feel the anxious mood of those around her as they paced or kept looking at the avenue Mael had planned to take. The longer they waited the greater the chance of discovery.

Count Idwal took a couple of steps out into the bailey and shielded his face with his arm to stare up the avenue where Prince Mael was supposed to come down. Willoe had heard tales of Count Idwal's exploits, but she had thought of the count as just a spent old noble who played at being a warrior. Watching him stand like a rock in the sleeting rain, it was easy to see where his reputation had come from and why he had been added to the escort as Mael's second. Just the way he held his body, as if he held sway over the downpour, exhibited a determination that bolstered Willoe's own confidence.

Sopping, the count turned back and walked toward the group, shaking his head. He walked under the gate and shook his shoulders, flapping the ends of the cloak as water flew to the ground around him in a circle. The count gathered the other leaders together to discuss their options.

"The guard will be changing shortly and that will create a whole new set of issues." He stated the obvious, but evidently he wanted to make sure everyone was clear on their situation. Running his hands down the side of his beard he scraped off the excess water. "We can assume Prince Mael has run into some difficulty that has delayed him." He looked back up into the sky. "Which is understandable. If it is just the weather then he may show shortly. In that case we either proceed as planned and head west, hoping that he will catch up with us," his eyes narrowed as he spoke, "or we wait and set a trap for the guards that will be showing up shortly. If, however, he has been captured or killed and will not be showing-"

Willoe started to object to that idea, but the count held up his hand, cutting her off. "When we planned this we discussed the possibility and Prince Mael knew the risk of riding with the rear guard," he said firmly. "It is well past time and if we sit here waiting, we will most likely be captured or killed ourselves." He pointed to Willoe. "If — and I repeat, *if* — Prince Mael is not coming then we have a responsibility to get Prince Rowyn to safety." The count's fealty was his life.

His words sunk in and Willoe began to truly worry that her brother Mael may have been captured or killed. She wanted to strangle him more often than not, but while he treated Rowyn and her with little respect, he always protected the family and the kingdom above all else. And his leadership at White Cliffs had won her respect.

Willoe knew she should be in charge — or rather, Rowyn should — as a member of the royal family, but just like in Westhedge no one really considered either her or her brother worth asking for advice. Under other circumstances she would speak out, but in this case it would only draw unwanted attention to herself. Aeron would someday be a duke, but for now he was just the son of a duke. With her holding her tongue, Count Idwal became the unquestionable leader.

Cleric Yoan spoke up. "I think our duty is to get the Prince to safety." He added to clarify, "Prince Rowyn, that is. Whether Prince Mael shows soon or is not going to show up at all, waiting for more armed guards to show up does not seem a prudent course of action."

The men all nodded in agreement.

Willoe wasn't about to allow them to sacrifice Mael for her sake and she started to say so when Aeron grabbed her wrist, out of sight of the others, and jerked her arm, pulling her backwards away from the circle of the Cainwen leaders.

"Leave me, Aeron," she snarled at him, barely above a whisper.

"Fine, that is settled then." Count Idwal turned to Captain Harte. "Call in your guardsmen and have everyone mount."

Before Willoe could step forward, Captain Harte sent runners to get the guardsmen who had been standing lookout on each of the major avenues.

"You can't change their minds." Aeron kept a tight hold of her arm.

She could feel the heat growing, but it faded just as quickly when she stopped and Aeron let go of her arm.

Captain Harte told the Horse Marshall to ready the mounts and called over to Supply Sergeant Trystan to get the supply horses and servants ready to move. The sergeant yelled for the servants and directed them out into the rain where they started to pull the pack horses away from the stable and toward the gate. The Horse Marshall and grooms readied the senior Cainwens' horses, while the guardsmen pulled their own horses away from the stables.

With the gate's guards as prisoners, there was no one to stop several servants who took to the wheel to lower the bridge over the moat. Willoe cringed as the *click-clack* of the wheel's cogs and the clanking of the chain being fed through the holes above the gate could easily be heard above the sound of the wind and rain. Two guardsmen went to each gate to pull them open.

The nobles and warriors were already getting on their horses as the rest of the servants began to climb up on the pack horses or, for those who had a horse not laden down with supplies, into their saddles.

With half the party ready, the procession began to gather, with guardsmen in front followed by some of the senior Cainwens, then the servants and pack horses. More guardsmen came up leading their horses and would fall in behind the servants. Willoe, Protector Dougal, Aeron, and Tomos prepared to mount as their horses were brought up. More guardsmen would bring up the rear.

Doy helped Willoe into the saddle as he held her reins. The sound of hoofs and the clink of metal on metal sounded across the bailey from one of the avenues. Along with everyone else, Willoe turned in her saddle and tried to see through the pouring rain. She could barely make out three horses racing down the avenue where Mael was expected, heading into the courtyard.

Following them were three more horses and she recognized Mael on the middle horse of the second group, his sword out and swinging at the rider to his right. They crossed swords two, three times as they came down the avenue and on a backhanded stroke Mael finally cut under the other's swing and he brought the blade up to catch the Franchon guardsman across the chest. The man jerked upright, then he fell forward between the two horses. She couldn't tell what happened, but the rider's horse suddenly pulled to the left and charged into Mael's mount. Pushed sideways, Mael's horse skidded on the slick cobblestones, a front leg folding and bringing both the animal and Mael down hard onto the cobblestone avenue.

The rain was coming harder, but it looked to Willoe as if Mael wasn't moving, trapped under the animal's body. She kicked her horse to move it around, but Doy still held her reins and she could only face sideways to the oncoming riders.

"Give me the reins," she yelled, trying to pull the leather straps away from the groom. Mael needed help! But Doy was stronger and held the horse steady.

"Hold him." Protector Dougal had looked back, between Willoe and Mael.

She tried to kick out at Doy to get him to drop the reins, but he just stepped aside. Then she tried to spur the horse forward and break his hold.

"Hold Windsinger." The groom planted his feet and held the horse in place, stroking its forehead speaking calmly to it. Windsinger only moved from side to side, but would not follow Willoe's commands.

"You Burning Bastard." She pounded her fist on her leg, but gave up trying to break free. All she could do was watch the events unfold in the courtyard as guardsmen, Captain Harte and the others came back to her and the others.

Running water flowed over Mael and the horse as it jerked, trying unsuccessfully to get up. It probably had a broken leg. When the horse jerked it made Mael flinch and she noted with relief that he was still alive. He finally leaned up and reached out touching the horse's saddle as if he could stop the horse from moving. The Cainwen guardsman on Mael's left had already ridden past, but stopped his horse, jumped down, and ran back to help his Prince. Ser Tanguy and two guardsmen charged out from the group near the gate and headed for Mael. The other three riders of Mael's party must not have seen the Prince fall as they pulled in their mounts nearly at the gate when Ser Tanguy and the others raced past them. Willoe noticed one of them was Master Gwron.

It was getting harder to see through the pouring rain, but she could still see Mael as the Cainwen guardsman, who had dismounted, reached Mael and was trying to help him out from underneath the horse. He was pushing on the horse as Mael pulled on his leg. When Ser Tanguy was about halfway to them, Mael finally pulled his leg free and tried to stand.

The guardsman helping Mael was stepping over to assist the heir apparent when a bolt hit the guardsman in the head and knocked him to the ground. A handful of bolts flashed past Mael and three found their mark, striking Ser Tanguy and the two guardsmen rushing to Mael's aid. One of the guardsmen was struck somewhere in the upper body or head and was thrown from his horse, while another bolt must have passed completely through the edge of Ser Tanguy's leg, because Willoe could see red freely flowing from beneath the Shield's armor. The hardened Shield continued to maintain control of his horse and rein it in. Willoe could see a bolt sticking out of the back of another guardsman's arm, but he still sat his horse, leaning forward over the mount's neck as soon as the animal came to a halt. Beyond Mael a mass of Franchon soldiers were running down the avenue toward him. She couldn't make out the precise number as a turn in the avenue hid some of their company.

Still balancing primarily on one leg, Mael bent over and picked up his sword to face the oncoming Franchons.

Others started to spur their horses to aid Mael when another volley of bolts came from the back of the onrushing Franchon soldiers. Most missed, but Willoe's head whipped back and she screamed as a searing pain ripped through her chest. Breathing raggedly, she looked down and saw that a bolt had penetrated her chainmail and embedded itself just above her breast. She wanted to scream again, but the pain flared at the mere thought, so she settled for deep, easing breaths. It took everything she could muster to stay in her saddle.

More bolts flew around her and she could hear at least one other voice yell out in shock as a bolt must have found its mark. As she leaned a little forward her eyes squeezed tight as she could feel the bolt inside her and the pain was so sharp she had trouble catching her breath.

"Hold on!" Doy's voice came through the fog of pain and she could feel his hand on her arm, helping to keep her in the saddle.

She opened her eyes to see one of the pages — she couldn't tell through the tears in her eyes which one — position himself between her and the threat of the bolts. She tried to sit up and saw Aeron, Captain Harte and others with longbows returning fire at the crossbowmen.

The fire spread through her veins and the pain diminished. She sat up to see Protector Dougal move back and join the page in creating a barrier for her. Her thoughts were cordoned off from the fire and her mind, but this time the world was clear and she could see with a clarity like when she was fighting the bandits. She could see, through the deluge, Mael twisting back toward the gate waving off Ser Tanguy and the others.

"Get him to safety!" he yelled before swiveling back with sword in hand to face the oncoming enemy. The men, including Count Idwal, who had started out from the gate, stopped at the command. With blood running from his leg, Ser Tanguy spurred his horse toward his Prince. The guardsman with Ser Tanguy turned his horse toward the gate, doing his utmost to stay in the saddle. Mael must have heard the Shield's horse because he turned back away from the charging Franchons as a bolt missed his head by a finger's width.

Though he didn't say it loudly, Willoe could hear Mael plainly.

"Get the Prince to safety…" Her sibling stared directly at Ser Tanguy. "Now!"

Ser Tanguy stopped and sat his horse for a moment with Mael staring at him, then bowed in the saddle and turned his horse, spurring it into a gallop toward the gate. Gone was the man's fierce posture and eagerness of before; the figure of Tanguy making his way back was a mere shadow of the man who had been willing to rush headlong into the fray to save Mael. He was suddenly bent low in his saddle, his face locked in a grimace. It occurred to Willoe that obeying that order may have been the most painful decision Tanguy had had to make in his entire life.

Mael nodded at the retreating Tanguy and then shifted to look at Willoe. The storm was even more vicious and he looked like he was standing under a waterfall. Even with her oddly enhanced vision, his image was becoming somewhat dimmed through the downpour. He swayed slightly, but then straightened, brought his arm up over his forehead and pushed the clinging hair up off his face. He put his fist on his chest then held it straight out at her, the salute given to royalty.

She nodded and he grinned, then turned back toward the oncoming Franchons who were nearly upon him. The sound of the rain was deafening, but she heard him scream a challenge that she couldn't make out and then he quickly dispatched the first two soldiers that reached him with a slash to the right and then back across his body to stab the second soldier. He pulled the blade out as the man fell and, hopping on one foot, yelled again at the Franchons.

Willoe's tears of pain were replaced with tears of respect as Mael was quickly encircled, and the only sound coming from the melee was the clash of blades, with her brother no longer even visible. The fire continued to flare and before it took her completely over she realized, at that moment, that Mael may not have loved her, but his love of family and the royal creed were things he held at his core.

In the back of her mind she could hear Captain Harte bellowing orders for the guardsmen to open the gate and shouting at Supply Sergeant

Trystan to get the supply horses and servants moving. She inhaled deeply and flinched from a sharp pain around the bolt, the fire quickly smothering the spasm. While she had watched Mael, guardsmen had worked their way around her with their shields up to protect her from more bolts. Aeron was still firing at the Franchons along with some of the other guardsmen and Shields. She reached out to the page to tell him to get behind her, but before she could touch him a bolt struck him in the chest, coming in over the shields of the guardsmen. It drove completely through his little body, the tip sticking out his upper back. A fountain of blood came through with the tip; it must have struck the heart. He was thrown backwards and bounced off her horse to land on the ground, his arms and legs flailing wildly.

She tried to reach down, but her horse jumped back and she heard Count Idwal's curse. "Damn them to Ifrinn! Guardsmen to the front!"

In the back of her mind she agreed that they were most assuredly in the third level of the Shadows, but she glanced to the left toward the gate to see what new threat had arrived.

She could see the gates open and the bridge lowered, but coming up the bridge was another company of Franchons. The fire told her it had been a trap all along. She realized that it had only been moments since she had been struck with the bolt, everything slowing down around her as the fire neared boiling and she faded further into the back of her mind. An angry woman's voice followed by a scream drew her attention over to the wall beside the gate. She saw Emeline reach out and slap Josiane a second time. "You stupid bitch!" she snarled at the younger woman.

Josiane jerked back from the slap and started screaming in between tears. "I didn't have a choice. I had to tell my parents. I couldn't... I couldn't leave without them knowing." She broke down crying. "They went to Dimah-Uul," she added between sobs. "But he said he would protect you and me." Her plea was a desperate attempt to appease her mistress.

Emeline pulled a knife from her sleeve, which gave Willoe a new appreciation for the lady. The woman held it up as if to strike her maid. "You betrayed us. We will all die because of you." She held back, but the knife shook in her hand and it was obviously a strain to keep from slashing out at the girl.

The young servant girl seemed to take it as a real threat and shrieked as she rounded her horse and darted past the startled guardsmen that were placed facing the oncoming Franchons in the courtyard. The maid headed right toward the Franchons and only managed to cover a handful of paces before a bolt took her. She flew off the back of the horse as if a rope had been tying her to the gate and had suddenly come to its length.

Emeline screamed. "Josiane!" The knife fell to her side as she slumped forward, steadying herself to keep from falling.

The scene before Willoe was drowned out as the fire reached a peak.

She felt as if her skin were ablaze, but it only strengthened her rather than caused additional pain. She could still see the bolt in her chest, but the pain had disappeared, leaving a burning, yet soothing sensation throughout her entire body. She yanked the reins still held by Doy and they ripped out of his hands. She turned her horse toward the gate, spurring it into action, then dropped the reins and reached down with both hands to snap the ash shaft of the bolt.

The nobles and officers were trying to form up two defensive lines. One faced the Franchons moving across the bailey. Between the rain and the mass of Franchons rushing toward the gate, somewhere in the thinking part of Willoe's mind she could only guess at Mael's fate. A second line was trying to form facing the other group of Franchons coming in across the bridge, but the odds were not in their favor. At least Aeron and a few others had kept the crossbowmen in the courtyard at a distance with their longbows so that only an occasional bolt flew into their midst; those were easily knocked aside by the guardsmen's shields now that they knew to expect them. With only about twenty-five battle-capable guardsmen, plus the nobles and a dozen servants, they couldn't force their way past the men on the bridge, as it would leave their backs exposed. The force coming across the bailey was slowed only by the longbows. It was only a matter of time before they would overwhelm the Cainwen force.

45

Greymoor Forest

Rhein was surprised they had kept ahead of their mysterious pursuers. He was still angry that he had lost one of the wounded guardsmen while crossing the fields between the woods around Highkeep Manor and the feared Greymoor Forest that first night. A shallow grave and a pile of rocks didn't seem a fitting burial, but he had the living to deal with.

Evening was setting in on their second night and it was slow going along the narrow trail they followed. Luckily it was just as slow for their pursuers. The forest was alive with sounds. The howls, screeches and caws let them know it was feeding time for many of the denizens of the forest. They were deep down the path when Guardsman Gerallt called out.

"We have a problem back here, Ser."

"Rest!" Rhein called a halt and worked his way back to the guardsman.

A young girl, whom Rhein recognized as the daughter of the cook, sat on a fallen tree and cried as her father tried to coax her into getting up.

"Please Lilia, we have to keep up with the rest or we'll be left behind."

The girl's tears streamed down her face as she sat awkwardly on the log. "I can'na father, I can'na." She dropped her head into her hands and started to bawl louder.

The father tried to pull the girl by the arm, but she yanked her arm free, turning away from her father and leaning over the tree facing the forest.

"Lilia, you have to get up. The Shield is coming." He looked up at Rhein; the cook's eyes implored Rhein to help.

Another loud screech from the forest, where the girl faced — just one of many — made the girl scream and jump up from the tree. She look out in the direction of the recent shrill howl, screamed again and bolted from her father's grasp to flee into the forest on the other side of the path.

"Lilia!" the cook yelled after her.

"Gerallt, Hartha," Rhein ordered the two closest guardsmen.

Both pulled their swords and ran into the woods after the girl.

The cook cried out his daughter's name again while Rhein held him by the arm. Rhein did not need another civilian running around in the brush.

It was nearly half a turn before the guardsmen returned. Gerallt glanced at Rhein and shook his head with a frown.

"Lilia!" The cook cried out again. "Is she—"

"Dead." Gerallt cut him off.

Dilys had come to the back when the girl first went missing and she now put an arm around the cook as he dropped onto the same downed tree, placed his face in his hands and cried, while the two guardsmen and Rhein stood by. Many of the others were watching from ahead, none wanting to interrupt. After a moment Dilys helped him to stand and walked him toward the main group. The senior maid and another woman came up on either side of the man and took his arms, relieving Dilys and escorting the shocked cook up the path.

Gerallt spoke quietly. "There was a large snake-like creature, over forty paces long and as big around as a wild boar. It was covered with a smooth fur. Never seen anything like it. It was wrapped around her body. We killed it, though not easily."

"The body?" Rhein assumed they would have brought it back for the cook's sake.

"A pretty thing," Hartha said, twisting his lips. "Crushed. Nothing but blood and bones. She burst like an overripe melon."

Rhein cringed.

The lady's maid came back to Rhein and the guardsmen, close enough that no one else could hear. "I sense as many as a hundred behind us."

Rhein was shocked. He thought no more than thirty remained from the initial attack. They must have had reinforcements nearby that joined them before they entered the forest.

"If you can sense our pursuers, why not the snake that got the cook's daughter?" Rhein did not understand what Dilys did or how she did it.

Dilys made a sour face then shook her head. "The ones behind are not creatures of Greymoor," she said flatly and headed back to join the servants starting up the trail.

Gerallt and Hartha came up the path to Rhein.

"We cut some meat from the beast and have it wrapped in our cloaks just behind that bush." Gerallt tilted his head to the side of the path. "It was a big snake."

"Good thinking. The meat will be welcomed over the next few days." Rhein put a hand on the guardsman's arm. Dilys said the trail wound through the forest and at their pace it would take them another four days to reach the other side.

"We dug a shallow trench, but had no rocks to stack on it." Gerallt shook his head. "They'll have her before the moon comes up." He tilted his head again, but this time toward the unseen creatures in the forest.

Rhein just nodded. Better the cook remember her as she was. Rhein had seen death poured out on the innocent and guilty alike over the last few years. And not just men. He had seen too many women and children butchered to believe otherwise. But he choked up watching the old cook as he bawled, trying not to stumble up the path.

Ser Rhein looked up through the branches to try to judge the time. The limbs were so intertwined that the only thing he could do was determine that the sun had gone down as the grayish outlines of the surrounding trees and brush faded in the darkening forest. It was hard to imagine that just three days ago they had been sitting around the supper fire talking about heading back to the castle in less than a moon. But that was then. Now it was time to get the survivors on their feet and moving again.

While guardsmen and servants rested he signaled for Sergeant Crowley and Dilys to join him at the front of the trail. He spoke in a quiet voice. "How far?" It was not necessary to clarify what he meant.

Dilys closed her eyes and raised her head as if looking up into the dark branches overhead. The ritual had become a common occurrence during their flight and he waited patiently for her scrying. After just a moment she lowered her head and opened her eyes, saying, "They be on the path again. But a little further back."

"How do they know?" Frustration was only one of the many feelings running through his head. "Every time we come to a fork in the path they find the right branch. Your spells have covered our tracks completely. I checked our backtrail myself."

"They be touching the *il fennore*," she stated bluntly. "My illusions delay them for a short while. Then I feel a surge in the *il fennore* and they be on our track again. It be something dark."

Sergeant Crowley grunted before commenting. "At least it buys us time." He looked behind them at the remaining six guardsmen and nine servants. "We can't outrun them and we can't stand against them…" He looked around at the close-knit trees on either side of the narrow path. "At least, not here."

Rhein knew he was right. Dilys' manipulation of the Spirits was the only thing keeping them ahead of the attackers. Her glimmering masked their trail from time-to-time; she told him that she was shielding them as well so that whoever was following couldn't pinpoint their exact location. But they were not without losses even so. "How is the cook doing?" he asked Dilys, who had taken over command of the servants.

She looked over at the plump man sitting near the back of the group, his head down in his hands. "Not well, as ye can imagine. She be his only daughter."

Rhein followed her gaze to look over at the man. The Shield didn't have any children of his own, but he felt for the man. The girl had not been un-attractive — there had been a certain something different about her — but her constant whining had not helped the morale of the survivors. She had been crying nearly the entire run through the night. They had made their way through the small woods and across the open fields that first night be-fore finally reaching the Greymoor Forest.

"Take the lead, Sergeant," Rhein ordered and waited until most of the group had gone by before stepping along the path. He heard laughter ahead and saw Guardsman Clairfield talking over his shoulder to a young maid walking behind him.

After the grim affair of the cook's daughter's death it made Rhein smile to see the young guardsman dallying with the girl. Rhein could hear the end of a lewd tale as the girl laughed out loud, then turned her head to the side.

Rhein could see her blushing. The girl turned back as she continued up the path and Clairfield walked backwards using his hands to embellish a new tale he was starting. They were moving single file, about the only way to travel on this narrow part of the path.

Out of the forest, a black creature leaped across the path, taking Clair-field with it into the bush on the other side. The girl's giggle turned into a horrified scream. Rhein only got the briefest of looks as it passed; the beast resembled a giant cat of some sort, bigger than anything Rhein had ever seen, and black as night, with teeth that hung down below its jaw.

"Gerallt! With me!" Rhein yelled for the guardsman who was behind him on the trail, and then jumped into the forest using his sword to try to fight his way through the dense foliage and thick branches. Both of them searched a half a hundred paces into the forest until finally Rhein admitted defeat. "He's gone." He jammed his sword into the scabbard and turned back toward the path. "Time is against us."

They came out on to the path where Dilys and Sergeant Crowley waited. Rhein shook his head and asked, "How are the others?"

"The girl be upset, but be not holding us back," Dilys told him.

"The men are awaiting orders, Ser." Sergeant Crowley stared up the path at the guardsmen and servants sitting to rest. "Even Guardsman Myrick. His wounds were not as serious," he reminded his commander. "From what the stable boy behind the girl was able to tell us of the beast, we thought it might end this way."

Rhein nodded with a sigh. "Get them up and moving, Sergeant. If we can stay ahead I estimate we will reach the mountains in two days."

The sergeant nodded and started rousing the others; a couple had even fallen asleep. They had been on their feet for almost three days with only minor breaks, and once for a couple of turns when Dilys said their pursuers had stopped. How long they could keep this up was a question Rhein constantly asked himself. Along with what they would do once they got through the forest, if they did.

He looked over at Dilys, who had begun to look pale and drawn. She had told Sergeant Crowley that it was the constant use of *il fennore* for the shield and occasional glimmers. Evidently, every time she dipped into the *il fennore*, as she liked to say, it drained some of the Spirit in her, and without extended rest she couldn't fully recover. She was looking back at him now as if she knew his thoughts. She turned to look up the path and then back at him again with an encouraging smile. "Another day and we be there. They should be there also."

He still had no idea who she meant, but he had trusted her this far. And, if not for her, they would never even have made it to the forest to begin with.

Everyone was on their feet, some barely, but each of them, even the servants, had a determined look that spurred his own confidence. He motioned his head up the path for Guardsmen Hartha and Owain to start off in the lead. They just needed to keep going. That's all they had to do… keep moving.

It took them several turns to load up the Borlender with supplies for the four-day ride Cian told them they needed to make to catch up with Dilys.

"It will be a hard ride," Cian told Rowyn, Casandra, and the two younger Elfs as they all mounted their Kata-henis. "We will only be able to stop to feed and water our mounts. The Waljantinks will provide food for us as we ride." His voice lowered with a serious tone. "You will have to rest in the saddle. There are straps on the saddles to keep you from falling."

Rowyn checked and found leather straps at the back of the saddle that he wrapped around his waist. He was glad he had as they raced across the valley entering the forest heading east.

After riding all day through the forest they reached open fields and sped up, continuing northeast into the night. Rowyn was exhausted but the anxiety would not allow him rest. It was compounded by the fear that increased as the heat grew, but the panic diminished as the fire finally settled to a simmer. With Moya's help he kept in rhythm and while a bit sore, his back and shoulders were holding up better than when he had arrived at Fayhaven.

They rode on through the dark; it was almost the new moon and the only light came from the pinpoints in the night sky. He was near the rear of the column, just in front of Saraid and the Borlender. The Tinks rode on Swift, except for when they fed the other riders. Then they would drop from the Borlender, run alongside each of the riders and leap up behind the rider with a bundle of food and a flask. Then they would jump down, back to the Borlender and repeat the process with another rider. Rowyn couldn't believe the Tinks kept up with the Kata-henis, but they had no trouble, easily racing from Borlender to Kata-heni.

He was stretching his shoulders when he suddenly fell forward, as the ever-present fire flared and leapt through his body. His breath came quickly and his vision faded.

He opened his eyes and stared up at the tall grass drifting back and forth in a light wind. After a few moments he was able to breathe steadily and got to his knees. He turned his head, scanning the horizon and seeing nothing but more of the tall grass until he noticed a thicket of trees, their limbs drooping as if weeping. He started to rise from his knees when a searing pain hit every muscle in his body and he saw the ground rising to meet him before the light was lost once more.

'Where have you been?' A voice wormed into his mind that Rowyn recognized as Moya's Spirit-link.

Rowyn pushed on the saddle and straightened. His eyes were only half open and he felt dazed. He couldn't remember ever feeling more drained. The rapid back and forth motion under him told him Moya was still bounding over the fields. His thoughts were as worn as his body, the fire having died down, but his body still tingled from the effect.

"The straps really work." Saraid's voice came from behind. "You would have been on the ground by now if you had dropped off like that without the leather."

"What? Yes." Rowyn's head was starting to clear, but his body was like a flag in the wind; he jerked to the front and then to the back.

'Rhythm.'

Rowyn focused his mind and shortly was back in balance with the flow of the Kata-heni as they darted over breaks in the ground and around knots of heavy brush.

"It is good to get rest when you can." The Elf's voice came again from behind. "I imagine we will have quite a time when we reach them."

Just getting there might be a challenge in itself, Rowyn thought, with the memory of the blistering fire still fresh in his mind. And if the fire visited him, then… what had happened to Willoe?

46

Fire on the Bridge

Willoe looked around and couldn't see how they would survive as the two arms of the ambush tightened, but then the fire took over all thought and pushed her conscious mind to the back. Picking her reins up, she kicked her spurs into the Franchon warhorse, one of the ones stolen from the stables. She bolted toward the bridge leaving those guarding her, including Protector Dougal, still facing the bailey. Riding hard, she charged past the still-forming line of defending Cainwens facing the bridge. She steered her mount past the two guardsmen at the gates and pulled her greatsword with one hand and the short sword with the other. The warhorse was trained to charge with the reins lax and the enraged Willoe continued to spur it on toward the Franchons coming up the bridge. She let out a blood-curling growl from somewhere deep inside and charged right into the advancing Franchons.

On a cold, rainy night, the sight of a lone warrior charging at them and roaring like a feral animal, with water flowing off her like a water sprite, must have shocked and confused the Franchons, as the first two men she encountered never even lifted a sword while she cut them down. She sliced to the right with the greatsword, cutting the man from his right shoulder across the chest to the waist and stabbing to the left to drive the short sword down into the other man's chest. The dying scream of the shocked man on her left only drove the fire to greater heights. As the men around her began to realize that they were actually being attacked by this lone warrior, she cut down two more, using her legs to steer her horse to the left, forcing three more men off the bridge into the moat where they would sink to the bottom under the weight of their chainmail. At the same time she swung wide with the long sword, decapitating another man who probably thought he had escaped being pushed off the bridge. Blood spurted over the men behind the headless body and held them in place for a few extra moments.

As she reined the warhorse right again it reared, and as close together as the guardsmen were, two of them were unable to get away; the horse's powerful hoofs caved in the skull of one with a sickening crunch, while the other fell backwards as the warhorse's hoof crashed into his breast, the guardsman's chainmail unable to prevent his chest from caving in. The tumbling men in turn knocked a couple more of the enemy soldiers off their feet. With a little room, Willoe swung her longsword across her body to her left, wounding two more men while she dropped the reins and stabbed out at a third to her rear with the short sword. The fire had no concern for defense and she wielded her swords mercilessly without fear of being wounded or killed. Those closest to her backed away as if they had a demon in their midst, which is how it must have appeared to them. As the men backed away they forced the ones behind them farther out where they could not bring their swords to bear on the crazed fighter restricting those that could reach her.

She had already worked her way more than halfway into the pack of troops coming up the bridge and killed or rendered useless more than a quarter of the dazed Franchon guardsmen. The large courser moved left and right nimbly, keeping the men jumping back. Its nose foamed as it tried to kick out and kill another of its rider's enemies. The ferocity of the horse encouraged the fire in Willoe even more and her mind reeled, looking for the closest enemy to attack. As she struck out once again at an unlucky man, she heard the Cainwen warcry and the *chink* of blade on chainmail. She found herself momentarily without a foe in reach and looked around to see Protector Dougal working his way to her left and Aeron to her right, both chopping at the enemy and widening the circle around Willoe. In her frenzy she almost swung the greatsword at Aeron, but he yelled "Willoe!" and somewhere in the depths of her mind she realized who he was. With allies at her sides the fire began to subside. As her mind began to return, somewhere in the back of it she wondered whether Protector Dougal had heard Aeron's call.

Her mind began to clear and she saw Captain Harte, several of the Shields, and most of the guardsmen engage the Franchons, forcing them back down the bridge. The ones that didn't retreat were forced over the side of the bridge by the power of the Cainwens' horses and sent to the depths of the moat. Count Idwal was at the forefront of the fighting, both hands around the hilt of his greatsword, cleaving a path through any Franchon guardsmen unfortunate enough to get in his way. In a matter of moments they had cleared the bridge, with the few Franchons that had not been killed or wounded fleeing along the bank of the moat to either side of the bridge.

Captain Harte yelled commands and two hands of guardsmen along with Count Idwal and Cleric Yoan led the way off the bridge. They were quickly followed by the servants, their supply horses, and Lady Emeline. As the rear guard came out of the gate, shooting a final flight of arrows at the Franchons chasing them, they met up with Captain Harte and headed down the bridge.

With the way clear Protector Dougal grabbed the reins out of Willoe's hands. "Sheathe your swords," he commanded loudly and with authority. She put her swords back in their scabbards and with Aeron on her other side keeping pace, they led her off the bridge at a gallop and down the road, heading for the small hill that would put them out of crossbow range. They topped the rise and started down the knoll heading west away from the castle. By the time they reached the bottom of the hillock with a long flat path ahead of them, the fire had abated and the pain had returned. Her eyelids started to fall as she rode. Finally she couldn't hang on any longer and leaned forward over the horn of the saddle and shoved her feet further into the stirrups to attempt to keep her balance. As her lids started to close the last thing she saw was her cousin reaching over to grab her arm and steady her, then her eyelids fluttered and she lost the world around her.

Bat-Uul rushed from the bailey and out the gate with the Franchon guardsmen. He could see his superior, Dimah-Uul, yelling at the crossbowmen, waving frantically at them as he started to run through the bunched guardsmen. Bat-Uul peered through the rain, struggling to capture everything that was going on. What was the crazy fool doing now? The servants had already disappeared but many of the Cainwens were still making their way over the hill, including what looked like Prince Rowyn. "Kill them, kill them!" Dimah-Uul shouted almost hysterically. The crossbowmen ran to the front, most of them having to stop and crank back the string on the crossbow so they could load a bolt. Less than half had already loaded and knelt, releasing a handful of bolts. One Cainwen in the rear took a bolt in the arm, but he kept riding.

Bat-Uul ran up in front of the crossbowmen and held up his hands, waving them frantically. "Stop!" he shouted as loudly as he could. "Do not shoot." He ran back-and-forth in front of the men, continuing to yell for them to put down their crossbows.

Dimah-Uul ran up, his eyes nearly bulging as he pushed Bat-Uul aside and nearly knocked him off balance. "What are you doing?" he yelled at the other priest. "They're getting away!" He started to yell at the crossbowmen to fire again when Bat-Uul grabbed him and spun him around, taking hold of Dimah-Uul by the neck of the older priest's robes and one arm.

He spoke with his face only a few fingers from Dimah-Uul's, trying to keep his voice down, but his jowls tightened and he hoped he had made his expression stern enough. "You could hit the Prince!" Dimah-Uul, the smaller man between the two, tried to pull out of Bat-Uul's grip, but Bat-Uul only tightened it. Dimah-Uul started to yell at his subordinate, but Bat-Uul cut him off, shaking the other man by the arms. "Do you want to tell Chuluun-Uul you killed the Prince?"

Bat-Uul could see his superior cringe. The older priest was going to have enough of a problem explaining to the Gai-Ten that the Cainwens had escaped. He would be lucky to escape himself with no more than a whipping for his failure. Dimah-Uul shook his head in agreement, keeping his gaze down. Bat-Uul had learned that the priest had an ego that was nearly insatiable, and to admit that Bat-Uul was correct must have rankled. Bat-Uul had been trying to be careful, but now he would have to watch every step he made around the monstrous man.

Turning back to the confused guardsmen, who were standing and kneeling as they waited for a command, Dimah-Uul yelled out angrily, "Put the crossbows away!" He looked toward the rear of the guardsmen and called out with his jaw clenched. "Bring him here."

The troops parted as two guardsmen half walked, half dragged Prince Mael up to the two priests. The Cainwen Prince stumbled between the guardsmen. He was bleeding from the same leg that he had hurt under his fallen horse. There were several other cuts on both arms, though they seemed minor compared to the wound on the leg.

Prince Mael regained his feet and stood in front of the two priests, balancing on one leg. He could obviously see the last of his men going over the rise. He turned back to look at Dimah-Uul and smiled, his face covered with the blood of those he had killed or wounded before he took the leg wound and was captured. "What happened? Did your trap go awry?"

Bat-Uul could see Dimah-Uul tense like a snake ready to strike and was not surprised when the diminutive priest balled up his fist and struck the Prince across the chin, knocking the younger man to the ground as the surprised guards lost their handle on their prisoner.

His mouth bloody, Prince Mael looked up at the priest who had attacked him. He wiped the blood away and smiled again, but in a voice that sent shivers up Bat-Uul's spine he said, "You will die for that, Priest."

Dimah-Uul flinched at the threat but quickly recovered and ordered the guards to take the Prince to Chuluun-Uul's tower.

Bat-Uul looked at the empty hilltop. Chuluun-Uul would probably send out a priest and troops first thing in the morning to hunt down the Cainwens. He wasn't too worried about success. *After all, where can they go? The entire army has moved and is now between the Cainwens and their homeland.*

47

A Deadly Business

It was a little after supper and Cuthbert walked along as if he was one of the many tradesmen who frequented Castle White Cliffs' Steward and the Head Cook. Which was the truth. He had spent the last ten years working his way into the confidence of the two men and their many subordinates. His face was well known among the servants and lower guardsmen, even though there was nothing particularly memorable about it, which he thought was one of the reasons he had been picked for this assignment. He had virtually free run of the lower regions of the castle. A quick change of clothes and he could travel the city docks down on the shore without leaving a lasting impression. Another change and he fit in with the stablemen beside one of the city's gates.

All this had helped him provide critical information to the Cainwen delegation so they could make their escape. He knew there were others like him throughout White Cliffs and the surrounding Lealacité, but Baron Manus of Winterpass was shrewd and very good at what he did. Cuthbert had no idea who these others were. He even received his orders delivered by a different street urchin each and every time.

But this day Cuthbert strained to keep a friendly smile on his face as he moved along the stone walls of the cooking level. Even with the main kitchen behind him, the heat from a dozen ovens kept the hallway warm even though the weather had become quite a bit colder over the last four days. It was as if the weather had changed in response to the Cainwens' flight. He could feel the sweat on the back of his neck, but it wasn't from the kitchen.

It had been a full day before he heard rumors that the Cainwen Prince had been taken and another night, along with several tankards of ale for

Guardsman Richer, to find out that Prince Mael had been captured and was being held in the lower regions of the castle. Guardsman Richer had said proudly — as if he had had something to do with the Prince's capture — that he'd been there when the Prince had been brought in.

While hosting Guardsman Richer again last night, the young under-trained guardsman had complained with a slight slur, as he slopped ale onto his uniform, that the older guard would sneak out after supper each night to bed one of the scullery maids and then would stop by and take some of the food left over from the noble's table. Richer's complaint wasn't that the other guard was dipping his wick in some young maid barely old enough to perform the act, but that the older, more experienced guard would only bring the younger guard some bread and, if lucky, one small slab of beef or pork. This as much as anything demonstrated the boy's youth and inno-cence.

The rest of the plan had been a bit more difficult for Cuthbert to bring together. In the past weeks, through Richer, Cuthbert had come to know one of the torturers. A sullen man with a distinctive hump who never had anything good to say about anything or anyone. Cuthbert detested the man, but over time Cuthbert had uncovered the man's love of gambling, which was evidently not something the loathsome little man was very good or lucky at. At least, that's what Cuthbert gathered from the way he whined about his losses. It had cost Cuthbert three golden dragons to get the man's attention and ensure the hunchback would find business elsewhere when Cuthbert needed to execute his plan.

Listening to Richer's immature slurred grumbling paid off last night when Cuthbert found out that the next night the young guard would be on duty with his older wandering companion and the torturer would be alone watching Prince Mael. Cuthbert wasn't sure what value would be gained by cultivating contacts like the young guard and the torturer, but he had made a habit of finding a connection to almost every corner of the castle. This time the investment would pay off considerably more than Cuthbert could have ever imagined. He had put his hurried plans into action.

As he ducked into a stairway leading down into the dungeon area, far below the castle proper, Cuthbert considered the young guardsman. He shook his head and frowned as he pictured the young man and thought he looked more boy than man. He barely had fuzz on his chin, but his lack of experience and his trusting nature was exactly why Cuthbert had singled him out and had been cultivating the boy's trust for weeks. With the more experienced guardsmen called away to fill out the army aimed at Cainwen, more untried troops like Richer and the older less trustworthy guardsman had been put into positions they were never meant to fill.

As he rounded the last corner leading to the chamber where the tortur-ers worked, he put his right hand on the hilt of the small knife concealed underneath his vest.

"Richer," Cuthbert yelled out to the young guard as he approached the boy standing beside the cell door.

"Cuthbert?" Guardsman Richer called back with a confused look crossing his face, but his bewilderment disappeared quickly and his dimples appeared as he smiled at his friend. He pushed the straggling hair out of his face and his smile widened as he saw a flask in Cuthbert's left hand.

"A gift for my friend on a cold night." Cuthbert smiled back and wondered in the back of his mind how a boy this naive could end up a guardsman in the first place. The rawest soldier knew drinking while on guard duty was a quick trip to the headsman's block. That is if the officer in charge didn't just skewer the guard on the spot. But Cuthbert had counted on the boy's innocence in his plans.

As Cuthbert was still moving toward the boy and an arm's length away, he held out the flask, but not too far in front of himself.

"Thanks Cuthbert. Wait until I tell you what happened tonight. But first—" The boy's eyes were focused on the flask and he leaned the heavy spear against the wall and stepped forward, reaching out for the flask, grabbing it in one hand and uncorking it with the other.

The boy's eyes popped and he hunched forward, the flask fell from his hand and clattered as it hit the floor, the alcohol spilling out. His body jerked three times as Cuthbert shoved the knife upward through the young guardsman's stomach into his heart and lungs. Cuthbert held the boy up for a moment. The look of utter shock in the boy's face told Cuthbert he still didn't understand what had just happened. With blood running down his chin Richer tried to speak, but Cuthbert just reached down at Richer's waist to unhook the keys and then dropped the dying boy's body to the cold stone floor.

Without another look Cuthbert tried several keys until he found the one that fit. As the door opened he was surprised at the severe darkness beyond. Stepping back into the hallway he grabbed one of the torches out of its holder on the wall and then stepped into the cell. He noticed how thick the walls were as he went through the doorway. He imagined it was to keep the screams from upsetting the castle's guests up above.

The door opened to the left and he turned to his right, holding the torch out. At the far end of the light he saw a small cage hanging from the ceiling. He stepped closer and as the light spread upwards he could see his Prince between the cage's bars. It was very cold and damp in the cell. Prince Mael was edged up against the back end of the cage, naked and shivering. The cage was only about a score of hands high and maybe twice that to either side. It would be impossible for the Prince to sit up or even lie down. The best the tortured Prince could do was the half crouched position he was in.

Cuthbert had met the Prince just the day before the rest of the Cainwens had escaped and seeing him now in this condition Cuthbert's eyes began to water. Prince Mael tried to speak, but only a harsh dry sound came out. Cuthbert moved closer, trying to hear. As the torchlight shone brighter on the Prince, Cuthbert could see not only the wounds the Prince had earned before capture, but also a slew of criss-crossed burns on his legs and arms and even several along the groin. As hardened a spy as Cuthbert was, he cringed as he stared at the damage the Prince's body had taken.

The cage swayed gently as the Prince leaned left to right and tried in vain to speak.

"Don't worry, my Prince." Cuthbert spoke softly with deep respect for the Heir Apparent. "I will have you out of that cage shortly and I have a place we can hide out until you are well enough to ride."

The Prince banged his head repeatedly on the bars as if frustrated.

Cuthbert reached over through the bars and gripped the Prince's arm. "Please, Prince Mael, you will only injure yourself more."

Prince Mael slapped Cuthbert's hands away, surprising the spy, and he became angry before realizing that maybe even under these circumstances the Prince considered it inappropriate for someone less than nobility to touch a royal family member. Cuthbert let it go quickly as he had a lot to do and he didn't know for sure when the other guard would return.

He started to turn from the Prince when the tortured man finally got out in a barely audible voice, "There!" He was pointing to Cuthbert's left.

Cuthbert turned and moved forward carefully around a table that seemed to be covered with fresh blood. A lot of it. As he moved toward the cell wall he noticed a body hanging loosely on the wall, its wrist cuffed with chains hanging from two hooks in the stone wall. Cuthbert nearly vomited as he moved the torch from side to side to get a better view. The skin on the man's chest, legs and parts of the face had been flayed, leaving exposed muscle and in some cases the gray-white of bone. Cuthbert wondered what the man could possibly have done to deserve this sort of treatment.

"Cuthbert?" A strange, hushed voice squeaked from the direction of the body, the word almost unintelligible, and Cuthbert realized that the poor man was still alive. Trying to keep his supper down he stepped a little closer. He could see that the man's eyelids had been removed and his nose along with part of the upper lip had been cut out. Blood streamed from all the cuts and Cuthbert wondered how it was possible that the man still lived.

He approached and the man managed a grotesque half smile from a mouth with only a few teeth. It repeated, "Cuthbert." Then the appalling figure began to laugh. A soft, barely discernible but still hideous cackle. Cuthbert stepped away squinting in disgust. As he backed away the man's head fell forward as he continued to mock Cuthbert. It was then that Cuthbert saw the flayed hump on the little man's back.

Shadows and Shades, Cuthbert thought quickly and turned to come face to face with a yellow-hooded figure who shoved his hand at Cuthbert. The robed figure must not have had a blade, as Cuthbert only felt a small pinch from the stranger's finger. Raising his hand to knock the robed figure's hand away, Cuthbert then reached with the same hand for his knife. But his hand never made it to the hilt. Halfway there his arm froze as if the bones and muscles had suddenly coalesced, like water turning to ice. Cuthbert tried to move his other arm and nothing happened. It was held out at an angle, still holding the torch.

He couldn't feel a thing. He tried to move, but his legs wouldn't budge. Somehow he was held in place; he had no control over his body. Cuthbert couldn't see inside the dark of the hood, even with the light of the torch flickering between them. A dark hand reached out from the yellow sleeve and came toward Cuthbert. He couldn't look down, so saw the hand disappear as it came close to his body. Suddenly the pinch disappeared and the dark hand pulled away from Cuthbert's body holding a very thin needle that had to be maybe a hand long.

Though his body was frozen his mind was completely aware of his surroundings. He had no idea what sort of poison the yellow-robed man had used, but Cuthbert recognized the effect. He had used something similar once before, but it had not worked nearly as quickly. He wondered what the poison was and how he could acquire it. He would have smiled, if his face muscles would have obeyed, as he considered how ridiculous the idea was. *Once a spy, always a spy*, he thought.

He did curse himself, though, for being so careless. He shouldn't have killed the boy so quickly. Maybe what the innocent guardsman was going to tell him was that the hunchbacked torturer had been seized and tortured himself. Cuthbert realized what a fool he had been. He couldn't turn his head, but he did see Prince Mael in his peripheral vision, crouched in his cage, looking toward Cuthbert, his body pressed to the floor of the cage as much as it could. Cuthbert knew this was always a possibility. It was part of the game. His only regret was that he could not save his Prince and now Prince Mael looked even more defeated than he had when Cuthbert had entered.

Another yellow-robed man came into Cuthbert's view, and Cuthbert couldn't tell which one was the first one and which the second. They appeared the same in their flowing yellow robes; the only things showing were their identical dark hands. They lay a heavy cloth on the bloody table and between the two of them they spread out an assortment of blades of different sizes and shapes with the greatest care, before unwrapping a variety of crushed leaves and herbs. They never said a word. They finished and, as if on cue, the cell door opened. Because Cuthbert was frozen facing in that direction, he could see the gnarly Dimah-Uul step in. Cuthbert could just see a corner of the open door and caught sight of a guardsman bending over to pick up one end of something, which Cuthbert casually assumed was the body of the foolish boy.

Dimah-Uul stepped over to the table and Cuthbert thought it interesting, the look of distaste on the priest's face as he looked first at the yellow-robed men. But then Dimah-Uul's expression changed to one of delight as he looked down at the table. The old priest seemed to shake with excitement and his face took on the same expression Cuthbert had seen on men leaving a whore house. Turning his head to look at Cuthbert for the first time, Dimah-Uul started to giggle in a sickly manner.

Cuthbert couldn't move a muscle and watched helplessly as Dimah-Uul rolled up the sleeves of his red robe and started to lift one blade after another, inspecting them like a skilled craftsman. Cuthbert wondered how the priest would react when he discovered that this whole exercise was going to be a waste of time. Cuthbert knew nothing. He wouldn't have thought it possible, but a funny thought passed through his mind as he waited for the perverted priest to make up his mind. Baron Manus really knew what he was doing.

48

Rise of the Prince

Willoe's eyelids fluttered and she heard a familiar voice. "There now, open those eyes so I can look at you." It took her a minute to recognize the voice as that of Cleric Yoan. She could feel a small rock dig into her back and realized she was lying on the ground. He wiped a damp cloth across her eyes to remove the build-up of scum that had settled there and she blinked to help clear her vision. Finally she was able to get them to stay open and able to see the Cleric's smiling face.

He had been her healer and gateway to understanding the Burning Lady since she could remember. In her mind he hadn't aged since she was a child; he had always had a receding white hairline, which – as a child — she had thought had been because it had fallen down on his chin, giving him a long, flowing white beard. His genial face, creased and crumpled with age, gave her a sense of security, until she remembered the battle at the bridge, the crossbow bolt she had taken and that Mael was probably dead.

Looking around as best she could from the ground she noticed they were under a tent cover that appeared to be strung up between some trees. She tried to sit up quickly but her head swirled and a sharp pain shot through her chest and left shoulder.

"Gently. Not so quick, Princess," he said and helped support her with a hand behind her back. "Try sitting up slowly." He pushed gently with his hand as he brought the other hand around to her shoulder, the one that wasn't screaming at her in pain, to let her sit up without exerting muscles in her shoulder and chest. "There you go." With his help, she managed to rise into a sitting position. "Now how does that feel?" he said.

As she looked at him he stared intently into her eyes and gave a satisfied nod.

She tried to roll the shoulder on the injured side and was rewarded with a streaking pain, but not as sharp as it had been when she tried to sit up without his help. "It hurts."

He smiled, his teeth showing through the bushy beard and mustache. "I would be greatly surprised if it did not." He put two fingers to the left side of her chest. "You had a pretty nasty bolt in there, in addition to a score of other cuts and bruises." With that he frowned, which she had come to know from years of broken bones and other minor injuries, as a sign of disapproval. "When are you going to learn that you cannot do everything a man can?" He didn't say it as a condemnation, like her grandfather the king would have, but stated it more as a plea out of concern for her. "At least do not charge forty armed soldiers by yourself again." He smiled again.

"I can do anything that a—" She took up the same argument they had every time she showed up in his rooms with a new injury and realized with a shock that he had called her Princess earlier. "How did you—? Who told—? Who else—?" So many questions flooded her mind she couldn't get them out in any sort of coherent manner.

"Just calm yourself," he reassured her. "No one else has been told, though your cousin evidently was aware as he did not even blink when I discovered who you really are." One eyebrow went up as he looked at her.

"How did you know?" she managed to get out.

A little smiled creased his beard. "Well, it was rather obvious when I had to cut your shirt back to get to the wound."

She felt a little flushed, but nothing like when the fire overcame her. Cleric Yoan, as her healer, had seen every part of her body more than once, but while she had known her cousin for many years and trusted him with her life, she had never been exposed before his eyes.

She realized she must have been blushing because the old man laughed and told her, "Do not worry. When I noticed the cloth wrapped around your chest I made him leave and I put up a screen before I removed the cloth." Looking past him she saw that another cover had indeed been hung from one side of the makeshift tent.

He continued to probe with his fingers and she felt a pang as he came close to where she imagined the bolt had been. He pulled his fingers back. "It will be sufficient for now," he reassured her again, but then the smile faded and his lips flattened out in a serious expression. "I must give you a warning. I was able to remove the bolt and stop the bleeding, and I did lay a healing spell over the wound." He continued. "But something is preventing the healing spell from fulfilling its purpose." He looked at her suspiciously as if she might provide some answers.

She only shook her head, her eyes raised in innocence.

"I have never encountered this before. If we were back at Castle Wes-thedge..." He twisted his lips and his nose wrinkled. "I have some other devices that I could use to possibly seal it properly."

"What is the worst that could happen?" she asked directly, as he had always been totally honest with her in the past.

He twisted his lips and wrinkled his nose. "Without knowing what is stopping the healing spell from working properly I do not have an answer. My main concern is that there is the chance that the temporary seal could rupture and you could bleed internally. More likely the healing spell will not keep the blood clean. I just do not know." His voice sounded frustrated. "If we could only get to Westhedge."

"I thought that was where we were headed." She was confused. She sat up a little straighter and winced, but it was feeling a bit better now that she had moved a little and had worked some of the stiffness out of her shoulder. She could hear the sound of men moving around on the other side of the curtain, of a horse being moved and even the sound of a blade being sharpened on a whetstone, along with the murmur of voices through the canvas covering.

Before the Cleric could answer, Aeron came around the side of the curtain and smiled. "Ah, I thought you were going to sleep until the Burning Lady's feast."

"How long?" she asked, ignoring his jab. They didn't celebrate the goddess' blessings until spring.

"After we escaped White Cliffs we spent the next day and night evading Franchon search parties," Aeron told her as he knelt down on one knee next to her.

"So I have been out for an entire day?" Her voice rose a little in amazement. Then she thought what that implied. "Why did we stop?"

"Actually two. After we put enough miles between ourselves and White Cliffs we stopped so Cleric Yoan could patch you up. You were not in any condition to ride. We cobbled together a pallet and put you between two horses." Aeron nodded his head toward the Cleric. "We headed north for a while longer and when it looked like we had lost our pursuers, he told Captain Harte that if we did not stop and remove the bolt you would most likely die." His voice trailed off as if a stressful memory had invaded his thoughts. "That was yesterday."

His description of their flight was a total blur to her; all she remembered were flashes of riding and, now that he mentioned it, once waking on her back with horses to either side of her. But that had only lasted for a couple of heartbeats before she had fallen back into a fitful sleep. "North? I thought we were heading west toward Westhedge. Why are we going north?"

"Oh," Aeron said as if he were surprised. "I forgot you have been taking a nap," he added with a little snicker again. "We headed west at first, just like Mael had planned."

The sound of his name made her heart sink.

Aeron must have noticed because the grin faded and his tone became more serious. "By mid-day that first day, our scouts reported that the Franchon army was right in our path. Their numbers flowed down the road heading west like a river. More than we imagined. Many more."

"I thought they were to the north of White Cliffs."

"That is what we thought." He shifted on his knee and put one forearm down on it as he leaned a little forward. "But they had evidently moved over the last few days before we escaped. Count Idwal and Captain Harte believe they are preparing to move on Cainwen. Count Idwal said that a force that large could only have one objective — Cainwen."

"What about going around—" she started, but he cut her off, shaking his head side to side.

"The scouts report large groups of Franchons as far north and south of the road as the scouts could go in a half day."

She couldn't believe that the Franchons would be so reckless as to attack her kingdom. What did they have to gain? But she realized that was a foolish question as Franchon had always envied the plentiful Cainwen coal mines in the northwestern mountains.

Her thoughts were interrupted as Aeron continued. "The count and the rest are out there right now trying to decide on our course of action. Count Idwal and the Shields want to break into smaller groups and try to make a way through the Franchon lines to Cainwen ahead of the Franchon army."

"What about Protector Dougal and Captain Harte?" she asked, noting that he had not mentioned them.

He shrugged his shoulders. "Protector Dougal believes trying to sneak through the Franchon lines will put you at great risk. He wants to continue heading north. He says we can possibly make it to Winterpass or, if the Franchons already have it besieged, which seems likely, that we could continue into Haldane. At least that would keep us out of the Franchons' reach. Captain Harte would like to try for Westhedge, but agrees with Protector Dougal that it is too dangerous. He is trying to work out a plan with everyone now as he is also worried about staying too long in any one place. Even here." He looked around at the surrounding glade.

She noticed for the first time that they were encircled by a thick cover of firs and pines, and that the glade was sunken below the surrounding brush. She thought it would be difficult for anyone to know they were here unless they passed very close along the tree-line.

She tried to rise to her feet and Aeron helped her on one side, rising himself, while Cleric Yoan helped on the other. Once she was standing the Cleric began to gather up some of his tools. He reached over and took down the curtain, she could see the small group of men in heated discussion a short distance away while the guardsmen and servants were busy at different tasks. Count Idwal was facing her and his face was contorted in frustration as he argued with the Captain and Protector.

As she watched a thought ran through her mind and she knew what they needed to do. She strode determinedly over to the group and Aeron kept up next to her in case she stumbled. Her shoulder spasmed a little and her chest felt as if she had been butted with the end of a fighting stick, but the pain was considerably less than she remembered from after they escaped White Cliffs. Cleric Yoan's healing spells must have had some effect.

Still wincing, she approached the group.

"I see you are up and about," Count Idwal called to her as she approached. All the men turned toward her, Captain Harte seeming almost relieved to have a break in the discussion.

Captain Harte asked, "How are you feeling, Sire?"

"The rest did me well. Cleric Yoan can work wonders." She tried to smile but her nose wrinkled as she felt another little jab of pain and the looks on the men's faces told her that her expression must have come across as somewhat peculiar. Even so, all the men nodded their heads in agreement.

She faced Count Idwal. "Lord Aeron has told me about the Franchon army and of your plans."

Count Idwal spoke with the authority of one who was used to being in command. "We were just coming to an agreement." Captain Harte's mouth opened to argue, but Count Idwal continued as if it was a settled discussion. "I will take a small force of guardsmen and one of the Shields out first to clear a way and then Sers Erwood and Bithel will bring along the second group later." He indicated two of the Shields. "After a way has been cleared, Captain Harte will lead the rest of you a few turns later." He started to direct the men to get the camp ready, ignoring Captain Harte's protest. He finally turned back to the captain and his posture was that of a stone mountain. "I am senior, *Captain*, and I have decided."

"I would have to disagree," Willoe said with a tinge of command that came from somewhere deep inside her. "There is one senior to you." She had come to a conclusion and had no intention of being bullied into something else.

The count pushed out his chest, a frown marking his face. His hands went to his hips and he stood glaring at Willoe. Without the usual formality he demanded of himself and those around him, he sucked in his breath and then asked in the command voice, "You may not remember, but Prince Mael did not make it out of Castle White Cliffs, whether he be alive or dead."

Willoe could tell the count was moved by the loss of Mael, and few thought of her and her twin as truly members of the royal family, but she had to make a stand now or subject herself to the count's decisions from that point forward. She could see a thought pass through Captain Harte's eyes as he cracked a slight smile. She hoped either he or Protector Dougal would catch her meaning without her saying anything more. It would have a greater impact if it came from either of them.

The Captain turned toward Count Idwal and spoke without a hint of smugness. "I do believe a member of the royal family has authority over any of our number."

"If the Prince were here I would gladly bow to his counsel."

"But the Prince is," Aeron said.

Count Idwal's head tilted slightly as he looked first at Captain Harte and then at Aeron with his eyebrows knitted in confusion. He finally realized what they were alluding to and began to sputter. "You cannot mean the bas—" He cut off his own derogatory yet commonly used reference for the twins and instead looked at Willoe. "You mean Rowyn?"

Aeron stepped up slightly in front of Willoe. "Do you mean *Prince* Rowyn?"

"Yes, yes, of course," the count said, stuttering slightly, his impregnable demeanor fractured. "While we appreciate Prince Rowyn's efforts on the bridge, you cannot seriously mean—"

"You mean when he broke the Franchons and saved us all." Aeron squared his shoulders and stood staunchly facing the count. As the future First Duke, she knew he was not beyond confronting almost anyone in the kingdom if he felt someone were being mistreated.

Willoe spoke up quickly, not wanting to allow the count to recapture his composure or an argument break out between Aeron and the count. "That is exactly what they mean. Since my brother, heir apparent to the throne, is no longer with us…" Her heart ached thinking about it, but she didn't let it show. She let her words settle with them and took the time to muster all the strength she had so as not to fold under the stare of the count and the Shields. "Leadership of the envoy falls to me."

"I am sure the king never meant for you to take on such responsibility."

"I am sure my grandfather never intended for Mael to be…" she began harshly, but then stopped herself from saying it. She still held out hope. "Become a prisoner of the Franchons," she finished more moderately.

"True." The count sighed and rubbed a hand up and down the side of his face.

"If we attempt to break through the Franchon lines, the leading force will most surely be captured or killed, even if the rest of us did make it through." She admired the count's valor, but it was misplaced.

The count pulled himself up proudly. "That is quite possible, but if we can clear a path or at least draw off enough of the Franchons to let the rest of you through, then Your Person would have a better chance of making it to Westhedge." He used 'Your Person' to assert her royal lineage, though he might not personally have agreed. If nothing else, Willoe thought the man no coward. Yet the chance his plan would work was slim.

"Courageous, yet unwise." She was not going to sacrifice these men just to save herself. The golden dragon's words still hung fresh in her mind.

"I suppose you want to follow Protector Dougal's plan to try to make Winterpass?"

"No, that is just as likely to get us all killed or captured," she answered bluntly.

Aeron turned his head over to look at her, a slight frown creasing his forehead.

She felt a momentary pain followed by a throbbing in her left shoulder, a reminder of Cleric Yoan's concerns over the healing spell. Then the voices spoke to her.

'You have a way.'

They spoke, but the fire did not flare. Surprised, Willoe lost her balance and stumbled to her right, where Aeron caught her.

"Are you well, Prince?" Count Idwal also reached forward to steady her. "You should rest longer."

"I am fine." She regained her footing, shaking her head. "I was off my feet a long time."

The voices came from the back, while she still maintained control of her own mind.

'The one who cares for you will lead you.'

She shook her head again, and suddenly it dawned on her. She walked over to Protector Dougal and addressed him with her back to the other men, her voice lowered so only he could hear. "You are going to take us to the Lady in the Woods. She is the only one that can help me." She didn't know how or why, but she realized at that moment that her statement held several meanings to it, as did the dragon's riddle. Who had taken care of both Rowyn and her as toddlers, risking everything to bring them to Cainwen and giving up a life of their own to protect them? Who cared for them more than their Protector?

Protector Dougal's mouth moved but nothing came out. She thought it was the first time she had ever seen him surprised.

Captain Harte spoke up from behind her. "Who is the Lady in the Woods?"

Right on his heels Count Idwal asked, "And where is she?"

"I do not have the answer to either question," Willoe answered without hesitation. "But he does." She continued to stare at her Protector.

After a moment he sighed, his large muscular body shrinking in defeat. "As you wish, my Prince."

"It is foolish to go racing around the countryside looking for some person only the Burning Lady and her Spirits know where," the count argued, his face getting red.

Willoe turned back to the group. "He knows."

"This is insanity, we cannot do it." The count stood straighter, pulling his shoulders back. "We will not do it."

Willoe knew that the count was only thinking of her safety. There was no greater supporter of the Brynmor line than the count, but this time she felt his loyalty would get in the way of her plans.

Aeron stepped back next to Willoe and said defiantly, "I am following my Prince."

Captain Harte followed and stepped over to the other side of her. "I also will follow my Prince."

To everyone's surprise, Ser Tanguy stepped out from behind the count and walked over to stand next to Captain Harte. He put both hands on the hilt of his sword. "I will follow Prince Mael's kin wherever he leads." He scanned the remaining Shields and stopped his gaze directly on Count Idwal. "Who else will follow Prince Rowyn?" Then, with a note of finality he added, "Our Prince?"

Ser Tanguy's unexpected show of loyalty finalized the decision. Count Idwal's will dwindled as he realized he had no choice. To his credit, after a few moments it looked to Willoe as if he had returned to his normal sense of unswerving duty and unrelenting devotion to the Cainwen royal family. He stared past the other men, his eyes confronting Protector Dougal, his voice filling with the noble tone they were all familiar with as he spoke. "Protector Dougal, how long will it take to get to this Lady or these Woods?"

Protector Dougal thought for a moment before answering. "Three days. It is in the Blackburn Mountains."

The declaration sent a bit of a shock through the group, including Willoe. The Blackburn Mountains were a source of rumors about strange creatures and even stranger occurrences.

Count Idwal impressed Willoe; he seemed taken aback by their destination as was the rest of them, but he recovered before the others and started directing the Shields and even Captain Harte and Aeron to break up the camp, send out scouts, and attending to other details so they could move out quickly. He turned back to Willoe and spoke without a hint of sarcasm or disrespect. "If this meets with your pleasure, Prince Rowyn."

She had to catch her own breath for a moment. Everything had turned around so quickly. One minute she was the bastard child of the Crown Prince that was barely tolerated by even the lower nobility of the castle and now a count and a number of well-known Shields were bowing to her will. Finally she acknowledged his words. "It is good, Count Idwal. I will always respect your opinion when it comes to the command of our forces. Your experience and judgment does you credit and I depend upon your counsel."

This seemed to mollify the noble and he smiled at her for the first time. Still smiling, he headed off, yelling another command to Supply Sergeant Trystan, who started ordering his staff around before the count even finished. She felt she could get to like the count given enough time.

With everyone carrying out their orders it left Protector Dougal and Willoe by themselves. She studied him for a moment. His body language had returned to the forceful determined Protector she had grown up with. They started to walk to their mounts that the groom Doy had brought up.

She felt a rush of adrenaline that was just now starting to fade. Nothing like the fire she had felt before — nothing really, compared to that — but it still made her feel energized and she barely felt the pain in her chest and shoulder. She realized that, with all the news she had to try to quickly assimilate, along with the stress of the confrontation, she hadn't thought to ask. "When we were back in the bailey yard. Before—"

"Before ye risked your life," he said flatly.

"Well, yes." She reached toward the back of her neck to place a clasp to hold back her hair but the stiffness and pain kept her from going that far. She would have to get Aeron to do it until her muscles loosened up and the pain subsided. "Before I tried to goad our troops into clearing the bridge," she worded it differently, laying the groundwork for her defense when he cornered her later. "I saw one of the pages. I could not recognize him. He was struck by a bolt. Did he survive?" She had come to love the boys.

Protector Dougal stalled, then answered to the point. "The bolt drove through his heart. The boy be dead before you reached the bridge."

She stopped and lost her breath, almost breaking down in tears. She had known the answer without asking, but hearing it made it all too real. She fought against the feelings welling up within her. "Which one?" she asked, not really wanting to know.

"The boy Tomos."

Tomos. The unrestrained one, full of life. The big brother. Her eyes burned, but she held back the tears. She couldn't let the others see any weakness.

Her Protector pointed ahead of them and as she followed his finger she saw Sion, the little brother, standing next to Doy. The strapping groomsman had a protective arm around the small boy's shoulders and seemed to be providing the page additional strength. Even at this distance she could see the boy's red and swollen eyes. Her feet were frozen in place. How could she face him after his brother had died for her?

Anticipating her reaction, Protector Dougal put a hand on her unwounded shoulder and gave it a gentle squeeze. "We all have a duty to perform. And we give all we have to perform that duty."

His words struck her like the edge of a sword. She had never thought about it, but since Mael's last command, shouted before he was overwhelmed by the Franchon guardsmen, all of them — every one of the

Shields and guardsmen, the count and Captain — every single one of them would die to protect her. It was almost unbearable to have that responsibility, but she knew she had to go to the Blackburn Mountains. She had been commanded, twice, and for whatever reason she felt in her gut that she had to comply.

"It was very confusing on the bridge. People yelling. Swords and shields. The horses. I could barely understand what anyone said." She gave a sideways glance at Protector Dougal to see if she could judge what he knew from his response. She could feel her strength failing and wondered how long she would be able to sit a horse. He kept walking.

She thought that maybe he had not heard Aeron and started to breathe a little easier when he suddenly spoke again, still staring ahead of them, his expression unchanged. "It could be as you said, my *Prince*."

49

Woods and Rocks

Just a few more moments, Ser Rhein thought as Sergeant Crowley gently shook him. "It's time to move on, Ser." Rhein opened his eyes and took a deep breath to clear his head from not enough sleep. He rolled over to his side then pushed himself up on his knees and finally stood. He looked at the remaining members of their party as those not on guard duty slowly rose and started to collect what little belongings and supplies they had. The snake meat was just about gone, but if Dilys was correct they were almost at the end of the forest. Though that did not guarantee they would find food or that the mysterious help Dilys assured him of would actually be there.

He hoped she was right as they had lost another servant, the stable boy, last night during one of the short breaks. No one saw him disappear and he made no sound. They stopped to rest for about fifteen minutes and when they started up again he was simply missing. A quick search only turned up a bloody rock where someone had remembered the boy sitting when they had stopped. A trail of blood ran away through the thick brush behind the rock, into the forest. The morale of the group had dropped even more after the boy's disappearance.

That was one reason Rhein was more than happy to call another break so soon after the earlier one. He had found over the last six days that even a few moments' rest did wonders for the group, though everyone's nerves were fraying with every turn they spent in the cursed forest. The sound of two servants arguing over who would have to carry the boy's pack only emphasized the stress they were under.

He nibbled sourly on the last of the snake Sergeant Crowley had handed him. Everyone was on their feet and, though grumbling, were forming up into a line again. The forest had thinned slightly and they could walk two abreast without difficulty.

A chilling scream came from behind them, causing most of the servants and even a couple of guardsmen to cringe down protectively. Everyone turned to look at their neighbors to make sure no one else was missing.

"Another one," Sergeant Crowley stated next to Rhein.

"I would assume," Rhein answered. "Have you kept count?"

The sergeant thought for a moment. "Seven that I could hear. I don't know how many more that I couldn't."

The sound of one of their pursuers screaming in surprise and pain had become a periodic occurrence ever since entering Greymoor Forest. The fact that the pursuers had lost more than twice as many as his own little party did little to comfort him. Once, during a breach in the shield hiding their pursuers, Dilys had noted that they had more than doubled their original numbers, so a loss of seven had little impact on the force that could be brought to bear on Rhein and his people.

"That was rather close," Sergeant Crowley commented uneasily.

"We need to get everyone going quickly," Rhein agreed. "Dilys says a couple more turns of the glass and we are out."

Sergeant Crowley responded flatly. "Then what?" He turned and headed to the front of the column, not waiting for an answer.

For the first time in days Rhein could actually feel the warmth of sunlight on his face as the path opened up in front of them. He could see, over the people and the sparse branches hanging down over the trail in front of him, an open space beyond the forest and a steep slope that blocked his view of anything beyond.

Guardsmen Hartha and Owain spread out to either side of the small clearing and took up positions, scanning the slope and the edges of the forest behind them. Rhein came out with Dilys right behind him. He stopped and looked to the left where the forest met the clearing, then slowly turned his head to the right until his eyes met the forest again. What he saw did nothing to reduce his anxiety. The forest's edge ended like it had been cut off with a knife. Between the forest and the mountainside ahead was a layer of sparse grass and low brush.

Dilys stood next to him and her eyes took the same tour of the surrounding area. She looked ten years older than when they had started fleeing from Highkeep. "The mountain butts up right against the forest," she commented, staring straight ahead at the rocks and boulders embedded in the slope rising at a sharp incline.

"That is what I see," Rhein answered without excitement as he also stared straight at the wall of rocks, sand and pebbles that blocked their way.

"The mountain goes all the way around the clearing," she added.

"Again, true," Rhein answered in a monotone voice, both of them staring at the mountain in front of them.

"How do we get up there?" She turned her head to look up the steep slope.

He turned his head toward her. "I do not know."

The rest of their company had come out of the forest and were standing around in the clearing, looking up at the rubble of stones dotted with large boulders. The mountain rose steeply for at least a hundred feet in front and to either side of the clearing before a more stable-looking, tree-lined ridge hid the rest of the mountain higher up.

Rhein did not have a lot of experience with mountain terrain, but it was obvious to him that the wall of scree would shift under a person's feet and make it very difficult to climb the steep incline. Getting up to the forest line would be difficult at best, even if they had had the proper gear and experience to get everyone safely up over the shifting rocks and large boulders. But they had neither. Another shrill scream from the forest reminded him of how precious time was at the moment.

Sergeant Crowley strode over, his back to most of the other survivors, and leaned in a little closer toward Rhein. "Ser. We'll never scale that in time."

Rhein just nodded his agreement, but then a thought started to develop. "Can we get everyone up there?" He pointed to a group of large boulders that stretched twenty feet across and sat maybe halfway up the slope.

The sergeant turned to assess the boulders Rhein had indicated. After only a moment he turned back. "Yes. It will take a little while, but I think we can make it." He turned back again to look around a little more and then pointed to a smaller set of boulders stacked a little to the left. "We can place Gerallt and Hartha up there. Dilys brought two bows with her." He smiled at the little woman still standing next to his commander. "Though I have no idea where she got them or how she even thought to bring them."

Rhein nodded his approval at the sergeant's suggestion.

"But we only have a score of arrows between the two of them." The sergeant frowned as he gave Rhein the news.

Rhein knew with maybe close to eighty or ninety armed men close behind, that many arrows would only slow them down a little. At least the forest was too dense around the clearing and the trail limited their pursuers to only entering the open space two or three at a time. Until the arrows ran out.

"Get everyone up there as quick as you can. Leave anything in the clearing that cannot be used as a weapon," Rhein ordered, still thinking of a plan.

But the plan depended on one thing. He turned back to the woman that had become a friend and confidant during the many nights around the fire and on their trek from Highkeep. She had lost most of the color in her face and looked like she could barely keep her feet under her, so even as he asked he hated himself for doing so. "Can you create one of your glimmers that will stall them long enough to get everyone up there?"

"How long?" she asked in a tired voice.

"Ten, maybe fifteen minutes at most."

She seemed to sag, but nodded her head in affirmation. Without another word she trudged over toward Sergeant Crowley, who was organizing the refugees into an orderly group while a boy — Rhein thought the son of one of the maids — was climbing and sliding his way up the mountain creating a small rockslide as he went. He had one of the two ropes Dilys had brought with them draped over his left shoulder and head as he scampered up the rocks like a young mountain goat. At the same time Guardsman Gerallt was moving much slower up the left slope toward the stacked boulders with one end of the other rope tied around his waist and the other end trailing behind him down to Guardsman Hartha, who waited at the bottom with the two bows and the single quiver of arrows.

The boy disappeared over the top of the grouping of boulders and then, after a short delay, one end of the rope flew back over the boulder to land at Sergeant Crowley's feet. A muscular servant, who served as part blacksmith and part woodcutter, grabbed the rope and started to pull himself up the rocks, his feet sliding but still moving upward. Once at the top he turned around to look down at the others. He spit on his hands and got a good hold on the rope, then braced his feet against the boulders, ready to start helping pull up the remainder of the party.

Dilys stepped up next and the sergeant tied the rope around her waist while she took a feeble grip on the rope above her. On signal the blacksmith-woodcutter started to pull her up.

Rhein wondered if he was asking too much, if he was killing the poor woman. But they all depended upon her abilities. He watched as Dilys half-walked and was half-dragged up the sliding rock and dirt slope, and thought, *Just a little more, Dilys. Just a little more.*

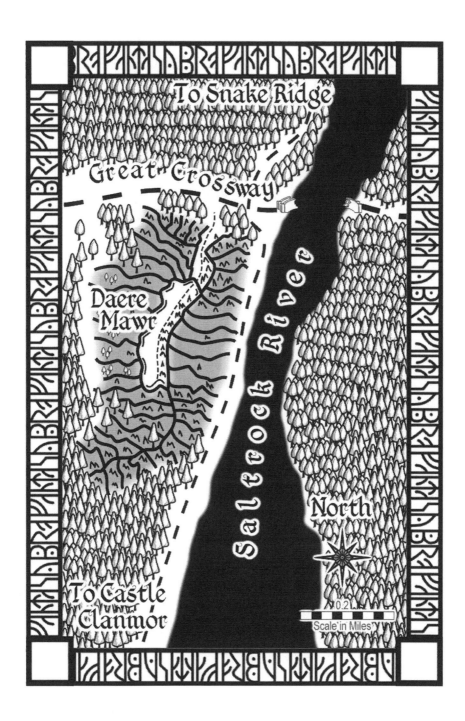

50

Daere Mawr

Drem stood on the top of the rock wall with a spyglass and looked to where the ridge ran up nearly to the river, a small gap where the road ran south of Daere Mawr. At one time, long before Drem's grandfather's time, the Saltrock River had been higher, running right up to the ridge line. Over time, as the river level had dropped, a road had been built between the ridge and the river to provide a more direct north to south route along the river.

He turned his spyglass to the southern gap, now littered with Franchon bodies. He did not need to look north to know it was the same at the northern barricade. For two days now the Franchon army had been swimming over the Saltrock, leaving their heavy armor behind, and tried first the northern gap and then the southern.

After more than half a dozen attempts on the gaps the Franchons had only managed, at a great cost of life, to put up a half-dozen cobbled together wooden overhangs, at the bottom of the slope, to protect against Cainwen arrows. A sheet of iron placed on top of each protected well against Cainwen fire arrows. In the end the Franchons had settled into a stalemate with the Cainwen defenders. The bulk of the Franchon army still waited on the other side of the Saltrock under the thick woods that stretched eastward.

"They cannot stay that way for long." Standing on the other side of General Rees, the young Sulyen, heir to the Dukedom of Wellingford, stated what was obvious to Drem and the general. Then the young man asked a question any veteran guardsman could have answered. "Do you think they might turn back to White Cliffs?"

General Rees' graveled voice answered solemnly. "They won't be turning back." The general was on the other side of Sulyen and had kept the boy near him in what Drem would say was protective custody.

"The guard reports the construction sounds stopped earlier this morning." Sulyen spoke what they all knew, a nervous habit Drem had witnessed more than once from young men in their first battle.

The noises had been disturbing for the Cainwen command seeing as none of the scouts they had sent out to see what the Franchons were building had returned.

The previous day, just before daybreak, a small contingent of Franchons had tried to cross at the Snake, but as General Rees had predicted the few Cainwen troops that had been sent north had easily blocked the Franchons' passage. After more than half of the Franchon contingent had fallen in the gamble, no further attempts had been made. Whatever it was the Franchons had been building, it would be something they thought they needed to make a frontal attack the ridge.

Drem lifted the spyglass to look across the river, whatever the Franchon general had been building was evidently ready and that worried Drem. He looked down the hill to take in the rising slope. "They will come up the slope, but it would not be easy even if we were not in their way. We can only hope we make it that much more difficult."

Daere Mawr itself rose like a sea wave over the lowland area. It was a very large free-standing mound, what Drem's people called a tor, rising over one hundred and fifty feet above the ground, with the ridge facing east mostly covered in rocks that had been shoved up by the gently rolling land around it in another era. On the western side of the ridge, at the top of Daere Mawr was a small flat area that ran the length of the ridge.

"What is to stop them from flanking us?" the young Sulyen asked, concerned as he stared to the side of slope in front.

Rees laughed gruffly and pointed to their right, to where jagged rocks could be seen peeking up before the rough slopes fell away southward. "Have you seen the southern slopes? It be more than hard climbing for anyone trying to make their way up on that side. Those Franchon dogs be paying a high price in blood if they be brave enough to try it. Ye can'na see it from here, but the northern slope be the same."

Sulyen looked behind them to the west. Drem followed his gaze. The western slope gently rose with deciduous trees at the foot giving way to heather shrubs that reached to the rocky summit. Beyond the trees, westward, the ground spread out in wide open rolling fields with woods to the south and small clumps of trees sporadically breaking up the grassy fields to the west and north. He looked down the line of troops that stood along the rocky ridge at the top of the eastern slope, creating a barrier between the steep incline and flatter top of the tor.

Sulyen turned back to the east, Drem following the young man's gaze. "We have a natural wall from which to defend and from our position we can easily maneuver and reinforce whichever front may require it." The young noble tried to sound confident, but he cleared his throat twice, nervously, showing his hesitancy.

Drem knew that if the Franchons could get around the ridges of Daere Mawr, there was little to stop them from moving on either his Castle Mount Somerled or directly against the city and castle of Westhedge. Castle Clanmor to the south still had its marshes as another line of defense.

"Good. Good." General Rees smiled. He pointed down the eastern slope facing the river and instructed his young charge. "You can see this be a steeper incline, as if the eastern side be cut away by the river at one time. I be told by Lord Brom that it be the case. With the jagged barriers north and south, the Franchons be coming up along this thousand-foot-wide stretch. Bare dirt covered with broken rocks and loose stones – I be pitying the Franchon general, if I did not wish him be gone to the Shadows."

The three men worked their way back down from the ridge to the Crown Prince's encampment. It was placed in a rare level area about three-fourths of the way up the western side of the tor. As they worked their way down the rocky ridge Drem saw his old friend, the Crown Prince Beynon, walking toward them from the command tent. The three men reached the encampment about the same time that Beynon reached them.

Beynon put a hand on Drem's shoulder as he turned to walk back toward the command tent. In war, many of the formalities of the court were set aside. As they walked Beynon simply asked, "How soon?"

"Soon, very soon. They have completed whatever they were building," Drem answered.

From behind them General Rees added, "Supplies be an issue. I would imagine before sunset, maybe just after mid-day."

Drem nodded his agreement.

They reached the table where nobles and senior Shields waited, looking over a map of Daere Mawr and the surrounding area. The men moved to either side, leaving a space in the center for the Prince, Duke, and General, though Sulyen had to move down to the end of the table to find a spot between two younger Shields.

Beynon stared down at the map for several moments. Carved stone replicas of horses, archers, and footmen were placed on the map for both the Franchon and Cainwen armies. He questioned one of the Cainwen commanders who stood opposite the Prince. "What do we have left in reserve?"

The commander reached out with a straight stick, stripped of bark so it could be used as a pointer. He pointed to a small number of stone figures that looked like bowmen at the base of the western slope to the north. "Archers are camped here." Then he moved the pointer a little farther south along the foot of the tor to some stone riders. "A thousand mounted guardsmen and a score of Shields are camped here." He moved the pointer to the farthest point south. "And here." Then, between the two locations, he pointed to another area that had stone men with pikes held in the air. "Foot with about half pike."

Beynon seemed to be thinking for a short time, then asked the same commander, "Is that all we have?"

General Rees spoke up and the commander's shoulders dropped, seemingly relieved. "Without Greenmerrow we be forced to replenish the troops at both the northern and southern gaps." He pointed to the grouping of carved archers, foot, and horse at both ends of the river road. "With the Earl's men we could hold out until the Burning Lady herself visited us. Without them—" He let the unfinished sentence speak for itself as he looked at the stone figures of the promised troops still sitting off to the side of the map.

"Malbery!" Beynon slammed a hand on the table, knocking over several of the stone figures. "Where is he?"

Drem could see that Beynon was trying to come to some decision and the Prince finally let out a deep breath and addressed all the men at the table. "Duke Cadwal and General Rees believe we can expect an attack before dusk. Split the mounted reserve to each of the gaps." He moved some of the horse and rider figures around to the southern gap and the remainder to the northern. "If the Franchons force the ridge," he moved the carved pikemen and guardsmen, representing the Franchon army, up the slope to the edge of the ridge, "then we may need the northern and southern guard to strike their flank to break the assault." He pushed the mounted guardsmen figures from the gaps into the side of the Franchon figures to emphasize his words. He moved the archer and pike figures to the center of the base of the tor. "Centralize the footmen outside the tree line so they can be moved up the ridge or to either gap as needed."

The commander held his fist up to his heart and bowed, then turned and, followed by four of his subordinates, headed off to see that the Prince's orders were put into operation.

The Prince turned to five other officers and directed them to the ridge line on the map. "Make sure that archers are to the front with pike behind ready to move up if the Franchons force the ridge." He moved the archers and pike stone figures at the top of the ridge into two lines. Then he took all the guardsmen figures on the ridge and placed them in a block in the middle behind the pike figures. "The guardsmen will remain here so they can move to support whichever flank is forced."

Drem looked at the map and the placement of troops. He automatically recounted the numbers in his mind. Roughly twenty thousand troops in all. What reports they had gotten from scouts confirmed that the Franchons numbered over thirty thousand, but under the cover of the trees the number could be off by as much as five thousand or more. The

Lord Brom had been standing quietly at one end of the table and when the last of the Shields departed it left just the Prince, Drem, Sulyen, General Rees, and Lord Brom. The Prince's brother stood there softly stroking the stubble on his chin as he stared down at the map.

Beynon looked at his brother with a frown on his face and was about to speak when Lord Brom spoke without looking up.

"Do you think it wise to move the mounted guard? It leaves us little protection against a mounted attack from the west."

Beynon only shook his head with a sigh. "The enemy is in front of us, Brom, not behind." He swept his hand up and down the Saltrock River on the map. He then pointed to the two gaps. "We will need the guardsmen to break the attack on the eastern slope if the Franchons are able to reach the ridge."

"I understand the logic, I am only thinking that even the outside chance that—" Lord Brom started to present his rationale when Beynon cut him off.

"Damn the Four Shadows, Brom. You gave up your claim years ago," Beynon nearly shouted. "I know not why you wanted to come along on this campaign."

Lord Brom just looked back at Beynon with his all-too-familiar friendly smile. "I did not mean to belittle your decision, dear Brother. I only meant to point out all the possibilities so as to ensure our success." He bowed and Drem could tell that there was no sarcasm in his actions.

Beynon leaned his head forward for a few moments, then lifted it again, staring at his brother. "I know, Brom. I know you would not disrespect me." He turned and looked out at the eastern fields. "Without Malbery's troops there are a dozen different ways that the battle could go awry. I cannot cover every possibly so I must focus on the most likely ones. When he shows up we can redistribute the troops."

"I understand." Lord Brom nodded, though the frown did not disappear.

"Good." Beynon turned back to his brother. "I appreciate your support." Then Beynon turned again to look up at the ridge. "How long, General?"

General Rees looked up at the sun as it passed its pinnacle and stroked his beard. "It be no more than a few turns, at best. Then we be seeing what the dogs be up to. If they've found a way to cross the Saltrock, we be in for a rough night."

51

Just a Rock

The last servant was starting up to the boulder when Rhein heard the rustle of trees down the path they had used to exit the cursed forest. There were still two more guardsmen and himself in the clearing. They would never get up before the men following them reached the clearing. He drew his two-handed greatsword and looked up to the boulders. He could see Sergeant Crowley, whom Rhein had made go up earlier, just in case.

The sergeant and three guardsmen looked down into the clearing, a worried expression on each of their faces. At a call from Sergeant Crowley, Dilys' head popped up next to the sergeant. She looked down at Rhein. He just nodded back at her.

Rhein couldn't hear her but could see her take a long breath, that looked more like a deep sigh, and close her eyes.

The sudden appearance of flames leaping up in the forest path caused Rhein and the two guardsmen to jump back, until Rhein realized that it was Dilys' glimmer. He had to admit that the flames seemed incredibly real. He could even hear the crackle from the wall of fire.

He pointed to one of the guardsmen, who sheathed his sword and took a hold of the rope, beginning his climb toward the boulders. Rhein could now hear shouts on the other side of the fire though he couldn't see anyone. He waited just a few moments before he nodded to the other guardsman as he moved away from the fire toward the rope. The guardsman had just started up when a handful of arrows came flying through the fire into the clearing. They didn't seem to be targeted at anything in particular seeing as half landed in the other side of the clearing. As the guardsman scrambled up the mountain, dust and small rocks rained down on Rhein. While he waited for the guardsman to get halfway to the boulder he sheathed his own sword and prepared to start the climb.

As Rhein started up the rope he heard a noise behind him and turned to see two armed men charge through the fire into the clearing. They both looked down to make sure they were truly unburnt, but never looked up again before both were struck by arrows and fell to the ground. Rhein didn't wait to see if other men would come through as there was no doubt in his mind. He continued to pull himself up hand over fist, looking up at the boulders. The muscular servant and a guardsman were pulling the rope up at the same time making his progress that much faster, but it made it harder for him to keep his footing on the slippery gravel, sand, and chunks of crushed rock.

The sound of an arrow striking the stones to his right made him jerk left away from the sound. He looked over to see that it had been less than a hand from his head, yet he couldn't do anything except keep climbing.

The rope suddenly went slack and he fell onto jagged stones, the sharp rocks slicing into his left cheek. It was immediately followed by a scream from above and the rope became taut again, but it did not start pulling at him like before.

He got to his knees and looked up to see the blacksmith-woodsman on his knees holding the shaft of an arrow that was protruding from his left arm. The guardsman was still holding on to the rope and leaning back, trying to keep it taut. Rhein knew they would have tied it around a smaller boulder behind the large one Rhein was working toward, or he would probably have fallen halfway back down the slope yet it still needed the guardsman to keep the hemp rope from rubbing on the rocks and shredding.

Rhein was impressed as he watched the burly servant break the end of the arrow off, then reach down with his right hand to grab the rope and start pulling again with his good arm. Between him and the guardsman they were able to start pulling on the rope once again. Rhein staggered to his feet and started scaling the sheer slope again.

A couple more arrows came at Rhein and he couldn't do anything to avoid them. One struck the back of his studded and ringed leather vest but didn't penetrate, dangling from the rings. He finally reached the boulder and the muscular servant reached down with his good hand, grabbed Rhein by the cuff of the neck and pulled him roughly up over the top. The Shield fell down into a small gulley, as wide as a man is high, that ran between the large boulder Rhein had just tumbled over and the boulder that sat behind it. The servant dropped down next to him, a grimace on the man's face as he held his right hand around the broken shaft in his left arm.

Rhein looked over at him and thanked him between deep breaths. The wounded servant looked back, gritting his teeth, and only nodded.

After taking a couple of breaths to settle his heartbeat, Rhein crawled forward up next to Sergeant Crowley and looked down over the boulder, avoiding another flight of arrows that went over their heads. He quickly scanned the clearing below. The fire was gone and a dozen or so bodies littered the clearing, a couple of them having more than one arrow sticking out of them. The remaining men were under the cover of the forest. He could see several of them stepping out just long enough to shoot an arrow and then ducking back under the cover of the trees. As he watched, one man stepped out, but an arrow from Rhein's right sped down and caught the man in the head. The man dropped his bow as he collapsed to the ground and a pool of blood spread out from under the archer's body.

Rhein estimated there were about eighteen arrows in the twelve men, which meant Guardsmen Gerallt and Hartha would only have one or two left. They were evidently saving these for the archers. He checked those around him. Two of the guardsmen had spears that they had had with them from guard duty at Highkeep, the remaining three and Sergeant Crowley had their swords drawn. The cook who had lost his daughter stood with the guardsmen, a large butcher's knife in his hands. Another servant held a sword taken from the fallen guardsman they had covered with rocks in the open fields. Several servant women stood behind the men with various sharp implements they had brought from the manor. The boy — Rhein thought he was maybe thirteen — stood with the women. Dilys was sitting against the boulders that backed up to their little trench. She looked barely awake and her face was so drawn he was worried she might not survive.

He could feel his face tighten, causing it to sting from when he had fallen. He wanted to help her, but couldn't turn his attention from the armed men at the edge of the forest. He looked back down into the clearing. No other archers were stepping out and it appeared to be a stand-off for the moment. It was more than he had hoped for. The temperature had been steadily dropping during their flight through the forest as the landscape had risen, right up until they had reached the foot of the mountain. Even with the hint of winter in the air, sweat made his linen shirt cling to his body under the leather vest.

An all-too-familiar sound of a frantic scream came from near the forest edge. He looked back over the large rock, but whatever had caused the piercing cry was hidden by the canopy of branches. The victim's shriek continued, but faded as whatever had taken the man could be heard quickly departing the area around the clearing. Rhein felt sorry for the man and wondered what sort of monster had dragged him off into the forest.

Sergeant Crowley looked over at Rhein and smiled. "One less."

Rhein agreed, but his face didn't express it. He turned and leaned back against the boulder pointing out an important fact to the sergeant. "One less, but how long do you think they will let themselves be picked off one at a time?"

The sergeant seemed to consider what his commander had said, then his smile faded and he stated the obvious. "They'll come in force shortly."

Rhein just nodded. Even though the men in the forest didn't know how many arrows the Cainwen guardsmen had left, they had to know that there were only two archers against them and that if they concentrated enough arrows of their own, they could keep the defending archers from being a major factor. With the threat of Rhein's archers essentially eliminated the men in the forest would feel confident that they could rush the boulder and overwhelm Rhein's small party. Unfortunately, they were correct. More archers and quivers, or even another dozen guardsmen, and he believed he could have held them off. They would be coming up the loose rocks at them and the advantage of position would be his. But without the archers or additional guardsmen, even he had to admit to himself it was hopeless.

He looked over at the determined, but frightened, servants who stood behind the too few guardsmen, waiting. They had no choice. He had little hope that the men in the forest, and whatever power was guiding them, would give any of them mercy. At least, from what he had seen at the man-or.

Rolling back over, he slid up on the boulder next to Sergeant Crowley and peered over the edge. There was a lot of rustling along the tree line. Rhein assumed it was the troops moving together rather than spread out along the forest's edge as they had been earlier. Grouped together they would make an easier target for his archers, but they would also be able to approach the boulder en masse. That was what Rhein would do.

They didn't have to wait long before loud shouting came from the forest and men burst from the path yelling war cries to bolster their own courage. It took just a moment to realize that the war cry was one he was familiar with from a few years ago when he was assigned along Crystal Bay in the south. It was a war cry common among soldiers of Greenmerrow.

As the armed men raced across the clearing, two fell at the front to arrows from Gerallt and Hartha. Both guardsmen rose and took down two more attackers. Rhein wasn't sure where they had found more arrows, but imagined they were using the ones shot at them by the attackers. Six or seven archers came out to the side of the charging men and were firing steadily at the boulder where the two guardsmen had taken up position to flank the clearing, pinning them down.

Unhindered, seventy armed men charged across the clearing and started up the mountain toward Rhein. Grouping as they were may not have been the best plan because when one of the men slipped on the moving rocks and fell he would take down one or more behind him. It didn't take long before the massive rush broke down into small groups struggling to make their way up to the boulder.

As the first small group reached the boulder and started to climb over, Rhein and his men came over the top and cut them down before the attackers could get up to a point where they could easily fight. The attackers fell back, but quickly pressed the attack again. Rhein and his men came back over again with the same result, only one of his men taking a wound on the leg. The next time they went over and fought then jumped back behind the boulder to catch their breath, he saw that the cook had taken the wounded guardsman's place. The cook looked over at him and smiled as he took long, deep breaths, holding up his long butcher's knife — coated with blood — for Rhein to see. Rhein nodded at the man with a small smile of his own, but he could hear the rumble of loose rocks and turned, still out of breath, to jump back over the boulder again with his men.

Rhein could barely catch his breath. They had managed to cut down maybe twelve or fifteen of the attackers, but that left more than enough to overwhelm Rhein's position. Creeping up so that he could just barely peer over the boulder, he noticed that the men on the slope had held up. The ones at the top, maybe two-thirds the way up the slope between the clearing and Rhein's boulder, waited for the others to catch up so they could rush the boulder in large numbers rather than the smaller groups that had failed so miserably.

This would probably be an all or nothing attempt on their part and Rhein knew they would be successful. With the sound of sliding rocks and pebbles Rhein jumped up to the top of the boulder as an arrow shot past him. The attacking leader had also shifted his archers to their position and Sergeant Crowley took an arrow in the chest, falling back down into the small gully they had been hiding in. Rhein cut down the man in front of him and dodged another arrow as he saw that the other servant with the wounded guardsman's sword had jumped over the boulder also. As Rhein parried the blow of the man in front of him and then ran his own sword through the man's stomach, he saw from the corner of his eye that two others had jumped into the fray. The young boy slashed out with Sergeant Crowley's sword and a large woman had grabbed a fallen sword from the ground and swung it with both hands, cutting into a shocked attacker. The din of metal on metal and the occasional scream filled the air.

The sliding rocks and pebbles were still a problem for the attackers and they had trouble getting too many men in the front of their lines at one time. Rhein cut one man across the chest and a second slipped and fell away, taking the two men behind him. The breather was short-lived as two more men started up at him, but he did have time to look to his right and saw that Guardsman Gerallt had joined the battle. He couldn't see the other archer, Guardsman Hartha. The only good thing was that with so many men in front of them the archers at the bottom couldn't get a decent shot at Rhein and his fighters.

Stepping back and almost slipping on the shifting rocks himself, he barely got his sword up in time to block a two-handed stroke from one of the men attacking him. The other man came at Rhein from the right, sword raised to strike down at him. The Shield tried to rise while swinging his own sword at the man, but missed as his foot slipped a second time. He tried to bring his sword back again, but knew it would be too late. As the attacker's sword came down it kept going over Rhein along with the man himself as the attacker tumbled down the slope.

Rhein looked at the man slide past, then back to where the man had been. With a grin on his face, the cook held out his knife as fresh blood dripped from it. He stared down at Rhein and said, still grinning, "For Lilia."

The grin turned to wide-eyed shock when the cook stared down at his stomach to see the tip of a bloody spear poking through. His look was so surprised that Rhein realized that the man never thought that he could actually die in this battle. In contrast, a professional guardsman always thought that he probably would and was surprised when he didn't. The cook fell sideways down into another group of attackers, his last act being to pull down several armed men who had just made their way into the battle.

As Rhein pushed to his feet he stabbed upward, impaling the attacker that had just put his spear into the cook. The man's grunt was quickly drowned out by another sound directly above Rhein on the boulder. He looked up to see Dilys standing on top of the boulder above the battle, still as white as a snowy mountain top, with her hands next to each other pointing down into the still considerable mass of attackers. Wherever she pointed a whitish blue light shot out of her hands and to Rhein it looked like lightning he had only ever seen at a distance. Wherever it struck, rocks, dirt and bodies flew into the air. Each time a blue light flared her body sunk a little more as if it was draining what little life force remained.

Rhein heard rather than saw the attacker coming at his back and he swung around, his sword flashing in a wide arc that caught the attacker right above the neck slicing through the man's face just below the eyes. Rhein was already covered in blood, some his own but most from the men he had faced.

Even Dilys' use of *il fennore* only dented the number of oncoming attackers. It was as if they were more afraid of what was behind them then the defenders in front of them. But the last blue flash had cleared a small space in front of Rhein.

He took two quick breaths and heard a voice shout, "Lady Dilys!"

He looked back at the boulder to see that a man had jumped up and was propping Dilys up. No, not a man, a Tink. Rhein had seen the Tink that roomed with the Crown Prince's brother, Lord Brom, once. The diminutive creature looked like Lord Brom's Tink, but different enough that Rhein knew it was not the same one. Dilys finally seemed to notice the Tink and, as recognition dawned on her face, she actually flashed a little smile. "My dear Drel Corklin."

An attacker had climbed up on the boulder and was charging toward them; Rhein could see that Dilys was so weak that she didn't even notice she was under attack. The Tink stepped around the woman and put himself between her and the attacker. He raised both hands above his head and the charging man went flying into the air well above the battle to land halfway down the slope, disappearing into a group of his fellow attackers.

Rhein was nearly blinded when a red flash struck the Tink, who was momentarily outlined in red and as the flash disappeared the Tink was left standing there motionless, his body smoking. He folded a moment later and toppled to the rocks at the bottom of the boulder. Dilys stared at the fallen body and then dropped to her knees, screaming.

Rhein turned to look back at the clearing and saw three black-robed men standing at the edge of the forest. One had his hands outstretched toward where the Tink had stood. The one who had just sent the lightning-like bolt at the Tink had his hands still poised at Dilys' location when a blue bolt struck him and threw him backward into the trees, trailing a ribbon of blood. Nearly everyone on the slope watched as the bolts flew back and forth over their heads. Rhein turned back to where the Tink had been and a tall man in a dark blue robe stood there, his hands pointing to the clearing where the black-robed man had been standing. The man was very tall and equally thin, with long white hair. Then Rhein saw something he never thought he would see: A pointed ear stuck out through the hair. *It's an Elf!*

His thoughts shifted as more arrows landed on the slope. At first he thought the attacking archers had launched another volley, but the arrows were coming from above and definitely falling onto the attackers and not the defenders. A handful of the attackers were already down.

Then two more of the Elfs, both dressed in green vests and pants, dropped down next to Rhein. They dropped their bows and drew long curved swords in one motion. The one closest didn't look over at Rhein, but with a smile on his face, yelled, "Well met, Shield. Can we be of help?" Then, with swords gleaming of silver and gold, the Elfs jumped forward into the attackers and laid four of them out before the men even knew they were being attacked. The Elfs moved forward, pushing the shocked attackers back.

Another red flash flew up from the clearing, striking the boulder right above Rhein's head and just below Dilys and the older Elf. Shards of rock flew out across the battlefield, raining down on defender and attacker alike. Rhein covered his head with an arm and felt something cut across his forearm. Looking back up, he saw that a big chunk of the boulder was gone. There was no trace of Dilys or the Elf.

The Elfs and Tink had barely registered in Rhein's mind when Prince

Rowyn stepped up on the boulder. *Wasn't he at White Cliffs?* Rhein thought; his mind was having trouble making sense of the last few moments. A wild thought crossed his mind. Could this be another of Dilys' glimmers? The Elfs forced the attackers back, a good thing for Rhein as he otherwise would have been an easy target as he stood, the sword slack in his hand, amazed at the events of the last couple of moments. He turned to see the Elfs wading into the attackers. He gripped the sword, his mind trying to push the confusion to the background. He brought the sword up and took a step forward when a deafening sound pierced his ears and he was thrown to his back. He felt a sharp sting at the back of his head. His eyes blurred, he couldn't focus, and his stomach felt queasy. He felt a rumbling through the ground and heard a sound as if the fabric of the mountain itself was being torn apart, and then even that faded as he lost contact with the world.

52

The Lady in the Woods

It had been four days since leaving White Cliffs and Aeron couldn't keep his mind off of Willoe. Ever since his cousin had woken and made the decision to head toward the Blackburn Mountains, she quickly weakened and they had to put her back on the pallet within a day. Cleric Yoan acknowledged that he had managed to remove the bolt and put a seal on the wound, but that an infection had set in and he was not able to cleanse it.

The Cleric had spoken to the command group when they put Willoe back on the pallet, frustration swelling in his aged voice. "There is something about the Prin— Prince's blood that keeps my healing from taking hold and flushing out the infection." He seemed somewhat bewildered as he went on. "I have never come across this type of resistance before. It is almost as if the blood is fighting my use of the *il fennore*. It has put up a shield, with which I am unfamiliar, to protect itself. This shield is preventing me from cleansing the blood. I can feel the Spirit behind the shield, but cannot access it. Unfortunately, I can tell the Spirit is fading."

Later the next day, with Willoe slipping in and out of consciousness, Count Idwal felt they should try for Winterpass, but Protector Dougal insisted that they continue into the Blackburn Mountains.

An argument followed and while Count Idwal outranked Captain Harte, the Captain remained resolute. "As long as Prince Rowyn lives I am duty-bound to follow his commands. And unless I am mistaken, the last command I received from the Prince was to follow Protector Dougal into the Blackburn Mountains."

Count Idwal countered quickly. "That is exactly why we should turn toward Winterpass. With the Prince's infection worsening we need to get to a proper castle with better-equipped healers." He glanced sideways at Cleric

Yoan.

The Cleric glared at the count. "I can assure you, Count Idwal, that I am more than qualified to treat the Prince." He looked over at the Prince lying unconscious on the wooden pallet strung between two packhorses and stroked his long beard with a frown before adding, "As well as any healer can."

Protector Dougal had kept quiet during most of the argument but finally spoke up. "Winterpass be another three days' hard ride. We be a day on the current path." He pointed toward the looming Blackburn Mountains ahead of them.

The Protector scratched behind his neck under the vest and then under the vest again by the arm. By the time they had left behind any search parties they had already passed beyond anything larger than a trickle of a stream. Without any water to spare for bathing, they all had trouble keeping vermin from under their clothing. Even old, hardened veterans like the count were becoming increasingly disgruntled over the miserable conditions. The best any of them could do was to wipe leaves covered with urine under their leather and chainmail, which only heightened the stink and subsequently dampened the morale of the entire company.

Focusing again, Protector Dougal spoke frankly as he looked over at Willoe. "Healers be not a help to yon Prince."

Aeron had looked at the Protector along with the others in the small command group. Was the Protector telling them that Willoe was going to die? If the Healers couldn't help, then what was left?

The Protector looked to the northeast, away from Winterpass, toward the Blackburn Mountains which were visible on the horizon. He narrowed his eyes as if he could peer all the way there. "Only the Lady in the Woods be able to help the Prince," he told them before turning back to face them. "If we continue to argue, the risk be greater." He let the words drop like a weighty stone.

Captain Harte would not stand for any more arguments and immediately ordered the men to move out toward the Blackburn Mountains. Aeron looked to the northeast and tried to imagine he could see their destination. With a sigh he glanced over at the pallet where Willoe's body jerked once and she rolled from side to side restlessly.

Would they be in time?

Many of the men would never admit to being superstitious, but Aeron noticed more than one putting their thumb and two fingers against head, lips, and heart as they rode through the foothills, continuing farther into the mysterious mountains.

Protector Dougal had told them there were no traveled paths, but led them steadily through the forest. They were surrounded by large evergreen trees with a heavy underbrush, though it didn't delay their passage. The Protector had ridden ahead saying he needed to scout out their route, as it had been many years. Aeron could see him coming down through the trees toward them, reining his horse to the left, then back again, around some large stumps and downed trees, broken limbs, leaves and small rocks tumbling down along with him.

He rode past the two guardsmen in the lead and came up to Captain Harte and Count Idwal. Aeron couldn't hear what he was saying, but as the Protector turned his horse to take the lead again, Captain Harte turned in his saddle and called back to Aeron and the others behind. "Just over the ridge. Another two or three turns of the glass."

They rode on, following Protector Dougal over the ridge into a small wooded canyon with a large winding stream running through the middle that was visible from the top of the ridge. They could also see a large wooden structure in a glade that sat along the stream.

They worked their way down from the ridge, reaching the glade in just over a turn. They rode into the clearing and spread out around the front of a cottage made from logs stacked sideways, the gaps filled with some sort of daub. The roof was covered with slate tiles and smoke streamed from a small stone chimney at the top. Aeron could see part of a garden off to one side that disappeared around to the back. They waited several minutes and no one appeared.

Master Gwron shifted in his saddle next to Aeron and spoke, breaking the silence. "I would think someone would have seen us coming."

The count started to respond when the cottage door opened and a woman appeared. She was in a simple green linen dress, but with a gold and red hem on the bottom, sleeves, and around the plunging neckline. The first thing that came to Aeron's mind was that she was beautiful. She was of average height, but the well-fitting dress draped nicely around her breasts and hips. Then Aeron realized what really stood out, and knew that he should have realized it immediately: the woman had long, flowing red hair, and the eyes... They captured you. He couldn't look away. They were green, like Willoe's and Rowyn's, but brighter, and pulled you in like falling into a well. A deep well.

Lady Emeline forced her horse over, to her left, jostling Aeron's horse, which made Aeron look at her. She was glaring at him, then cleared her throat. He just shrugged, unable to fathom her actions.

Turning back toward the cottage he saw that the strange lady had walked up to Protector Dougal. Aeron had not noticed at first, but now saw that she was older than he originally thought, though he had never been good at guessing women's ages and had learned not even to try.

As the woman walked up to Protector Dougal she reached up to take hold of the horse's reins. She gave him a wide smile that only seemed to make her more graceful and alluring. Looking up, she spoke in a lilting voice. "Dougal." Aeron could feel the love in her tone.

Aeron was surprised when the Protector smiled in return and said softly, "Kerye."

They stayed like that, smiling at each other, while the entire clearing filled with men and Lady Emeline waited. It felt to Aeron — and, he assumed, most everyone else — that they were invading a private moment and he didn't quite know what to do. It was even more uncomfortable considering one of them was Protector Dougal.

After what seemed like multiple turns of the glass, but was actually only a few moments, the green-dressed lady turned away and walked over to where Willoe lay on the pallet strung between the packhorses. Reaching down, the lady stroked Willoe's head and Aeron saw her whisper something, but could not make out what it was. The lady turned from Willoe to look right at Aeron and said in a commanding voice, "Aeron, Dougal, bring in the pallet. Cleric Yoan, you be also needed. And Lady Emeline, you may join if you desire."

Aeron could see the Cleric was as stunned as Aeron himself. *How does she know the Cleric's and my name?* Aeron dismounted and handed his reins over to Master Gwron.

Two guardsmen helped Protector Dougal and Aeron unstrap the pallet, then Protector Dougal took the front and Aeron grabbed the rear poles. As they started toward the cottage the lady spoke to Captain Harte, her voice filled with authority. "Captain Harte, send out a couple of your best hunters and they should find easy game. You may billet your people in the front." She pointed to an area next to the cottage near the wood-line. "And near the stream. There be plenty of water for cooking and..." she paused and sniffed, "washing."

She strode up to the cottage door and turned back one more time before entering. She looked squarely at the Count. "I be answering some of your questions later, Count Idwal." She emphasized the word *some*. "I must now attend to the Prince." She entered the cottage.

Aeron looked around before entering and saw the men looking at each other in confusion before Captain Harte started yelling out orders to set up camp.

Once inside the lady directed Aeron and Protector Dougal to put the pallet across a table in the middle of the room. After placing it softly on the table, Aeron stood and stretched after the long ride and the exertion of carrying in the heavy pallet. He looked around and was surprised by the main room.

It was decorated in what he could only think of as a simple fashion, but also elegant, with almost a noble feel to it. It was evidently a room primarily used by a woman as there were small finely woven tapestries hung on the walls and light from one of the several windows glistened off a fine glass decanter that sat on another smaller table across the room under another window.

Two chairs were placed on either side of the table and Aeron thought it would be a nice place to sit in the morning's sun. A small cupboard sat in the corner beside the fireplace, with a pewter jug and a couple of cups on the shelf in front of the two upper doors. The smell of dried sweet herbs hung over the cooking fire and permeated the room. In contrast to all the finery, the hides of a couple of beasts that Aeron did not recognize hung on either side of the fireplace and a few more were folded on a large chest at the opposite end of the room. Considering how cold Aeron thought it might get up in these mountains, they would come in handy.

There was even glass in the windows and he had seen thick shutters on the outside. There were two doors leading out of the room, at least one presumed a bedroom as nothing in the current room would indicate it was used for sleeping.

While the lady, whom Protector Dougal had called Kerye, rummaged through one of the chests, Aeron dropped into a large wooden chair, in the corner, that had fabric cushions placed on the seat. Looking around, he wondered how all this could have made its way up into the secluded canyon. It would require no small effort to build something this large, but then all the fine furnishings would have had to follow. *How did it all get up here in the first place?*

Emeline stood next to his chair and when he looked up she was staring down at him with an icy glare. For some reason she was angry with him and he really had no idea what he had done. He was relieved when their hostess came back to the table and called them over. "I need all of you here. Though not you, Lady Emeline. I be needing you later, but I thought it best you found out now."

"Found out what?" Emeline's question was not very friendly, but it also held a hint of curiosity. It was a question Aeron wanted to ask himself.

Kerye's eyes narrowed and the look quickly took the wind out of Emeline's anger. "You be finding out soon enough."

After calling over Cleric Yoan, Kerye started giving him directions. "Her blood has been Dragon-Called. It be trying to ward itself from any Spirit attacks, which be how it be perceiving your healing spell. But because of your healing spell, the ward also prevented her own body from healing itself, which it would have done if not for the ward."

Cleric Yoan listened intently, but with wide eyes. "How do you know this?"

Her voice was patient. "The explanation is long, but you must trust my word until later. I need you to remove the spell so I can release the ward."

"I didn't know— I only thought—" the Cleric stuttered and he seemed confused that his healing spell might actually have caused the problem.

"You did well, Cleric." She put a hand on his shoulder in a comforting gesture. "Removing the bolt saved her life. And you be having no way of knowing about the Dragon-Called blood." She turned back to Willoe and ran a hand over the girl's hair again, pushing it to lie above Willoe's head on the pallet. "It is a blessing and a curse that Willoe be having to learn to control."

The Cleric nodded with some relief, though still looked confused.

Kerye's words explained a lot in Aeron's mind. The strange flying beast Willoe had seen in the distance when they had left Westhedge, the fire taking over her body, the golden dragon in the clearing. He could finally put some of it together and at least had a name to put to it… Dragon-Called. Then he quickly stood as he realized Kerye had said 'her' and even called Willoe by her true name. "How did you know?" he asked, still somewhat shocked.

Emeline stepped closer to Aeron and looked from him to Kerye. "How did she know what?" Her voice was becoming strained, but Aeron ignored her as he waited for Kerye to answer.

Kerye ran a finger gently across Willoe's forehead, moving a few loose strands off Willoe's face, and said to Protector Dougal, "She looks just like her mother. And, I imagine, me at sixteen."

"Aye, that she does, Kerye," Protector Dougal said and nodded.

Even with the red hair and green eyes, Aeron had not really made the connection. But once Kerye had made the comment it became obvious. The hair and eyes aside, Willoe had the same body shape and many of the same features as the older woman. He tried to picture Kerye about twenty years younger and cursed himself for not seeing it.

Looking back at Aeron, Kerye spoke without any fanfare. "Do you think I would not be able to recognize my own niece, even after all these years?"

Aeron plopped back down in the chair as Emeline started and pointed at the table. "Willoe! This is Princess Willoe, not Prince Rowyn?" She flipped her head back and forth between Aeron and Kerye as if she couldn't determine whom to question. "How could that be?" She finally decided to focus on Aeron. "You knew this and did not tell me?"

"You are a Franchon," Aeron snapped back, and regretted it even before he had finished saying it.

Emeline's eyes flew open and she sucked in her breath sharply, then stomped over to the other side of the table to stand next to Protector Dougal. Her lips were pursed so hard Aeron was worried she might break her teeth from gritting them so tightly.

There was little Aeron could do about it now. He only hoped he could smooth things over with her later. He stood once again and came up to the side of the table, looking across at Protector Dougal who had not blinked an eye at Kerye's statement. Aeron spoke, more a statement than a question. "And you knew also."

"The day leaving Westhedge," Protector Dougal said, not taking his eyes off of Willoe.

"I wish I had known," Aeron said with a frown.

"Neither ye nor Princess Willoe found it necessary to speak of this. There be no reason to acknowledge the attempts to hide her identity. It fit what be foretold."

What was foretold? Aeron wondered, but before he could ask, the conversation was interrupted as Kerye started instructing the Cleric on what to do once again. "I need you to start withdrawing the spell and when you have it fully removed I be able to release the ward and put a new healing spell upon her," she told Cleric Yoan as she felt around the sides of the wound.

The Cleric closed his eyes tightly and Aeron could see him straining. After a few moments he let out a breath, opened his eyes and nodded to Kerye.

She stood at the end of the table and put a hand on each of Willoe's shoulders. Kerye closed her eyes like the Cleric and Aeron watched as she stiffened. Her breath came quickly as if she was battling some unseen foe, then her chest began to slow down until she was finally able to draw air in deeply, her body relaxing. After several more moments she took one final long breath and opened her eyes. She lifted her hands and rubbed them together, her face cringing, then relaxing.

She walked to the side of the table, looking down at Willoe. "I was able to cleanse the infection from her blood. Her Spirit is still strong and the ward should heal the internal damage itself."

Everyone at the table let out a sigh of relief.

"We just need to keep the wound itself clean and help her regain her physical strength." As she talked she opened Willoe's vest and took a knife she had put at the head of the table. She cut the linen shirt underneath, then took the same knife and carefully cut away the chest wrap that the Cleric had put back on Willoe. It had continued to hide Willoe's identity while doubling as a way to secure the bandage Cleric Yoan had put over the wound. When Kerye finished cutting the wrap she pulled it to either side, exposing Willoe's small breasts and the blood-soaked linen placed below the left breast.

As Kerye removed the bloody bandage the stench from the wound made Aeron step back, but only for a second. He stepped up to the table and it was obvious that the skin around the wound was still infected. What surprised Aeron was that Emeline was leaning forward over the table, inspecting the wound. She did not seem in the least bit put off by the wound or the odor.

Kerye was already working on cleaning the wound with a cloth that had been soaking in a bowl over the fire in the hearth. Aeron wondered how she had known they were coming, to have all this ready when they arrived.

After cleaning the external area of the wound she dropped the cloth back into the bowl and put a salve of some sort directly on the open wound. "That should help to heal the outside. With the ward released the healing spell can mend the inside. She should be up within a day or two."

The tense mood filling the room seemed to lessen as everyone physically relaxed at the pronouncement. Aeron could see even Cleric Yoan and Kerye smiling with relief.

Emeline looked over at Aeron, her demeanor slightly less angry with the tension removed. "I still think you should have told me about—"

The slamming down of both Kerye's hands on the open wound, her eyes closed with a tense frown on her face, quickly ended any conversation and brought back an atmosphere of tension to the room. Everyone looked at her anxiously.

Finally Cleric Yoan asked, "What is it?"

"The Spirit, it be fleeing her," Kerye said through clenched teeth, eyes still closed. "I cannot will it to stay."

"How can that be?" Aeron heard himself ask, his voice losing control.

"I don't know. It be as if it be drawn away. I can't stop it." Her eyes opened, but swelled as she added, "Nothing I am trying be making a difference. If the Spirit continues to flee—"

The words hung in the air. They all understood that nothing existed without the Spirit.

53

An Old Friend Indeed

Casandra just finished calling a Spiro and started a healing on Sergeant Crowley when both Dilys and Cian bounced off the boulder behind her. They crumpled to the ground next to her. She reached down and touched Cian on the chest, using the Spiro to perform a Seeing. With a sigh of relief she quickly determined he was just knocked out and only sustained a few bruises. Dilys, on the other hand, was barely alive. Not so much from being thrown off the top of the boulder by whatever had caused such a loud noise and sent bits of rocks flying into the air, but her life's Spirit was fading quickly nevertheless.

Dilys' breathing was shallow as Casandra put both hands on the woman's chest. A streak of fear went through Casandra when she realized she could not bring back the brave little woman. It required more than she, even with the help of the Spiro, could do. "Come on, woman. Live!" Casandra yelled at the prone Dilys in front of her even as she unsuccessfully tried to inflame the spark of Spirit that was fading quickly in Dilys' chest. *What more can I do?* she thought frantically as the spark was almost gone. Casandra wanted to cry, but fought off the feeling.

Then she remembered what Drel Corklin had told her that first morning at Fayhaven. *The calei is all around you if you know where to look.* Casandra looked at the ground to her left and right. It all looked gray and beige like the rocks and dirt. There were specks of black and other colors, but it all looked the same. She focused her mind and directed the Spiro to enhance her vision.

And there it was. A reddish-brown sparkling streak that ran along the bottom of the boulder near her. She reached out, but it was too far away. She grabbed Dilys' arm and dragged her toward the boulder. She could sense Dilys' Spirit fading faster.

Reaching the boulder, she put one hand on Dilys' chest and drove the fingers of her other hand into what she hoped was the Ken Mud, the calei. The warmth met her as she sunk her fingers in and the heartbeat greeted her like an old friend. *Afanen*, she screamed in her mind.

Good morrow, Casandra Cadwal, the familiar voice came to her. *I feel your agony.* Her mother's image floated in front of her, wearing the same expression as when her mother would console her as a child.

Afanen, I need help. She is dying. Casandra could feel the tears running down her cheeks. What did she expect of the calei? She needed something that would help her bring Dilys' Spirit back.

The heat around her fingers increased and the heartbeat pounded in sync with her own. A power ebbed up her arm, through her heart like it was a water wheel and down her other arm, into her hand. She lifted her head to the sky as the power surged through her body. The pulse on her hand increased and the Spiro in her seemed to grow ten-fold. She felt as if she could reach out and grab the spark of Dilys' Spirit. Then she did. Once in her grip she pulled it back to Dilys and held it in place until it took hold like the roots of a tree.

Nothing happened at first but then slowly it started to grow like a flower budding in spring. The spark began to spread out from Dilys' heart to the rest of her body.

As the healing took over Dilys' body, Casandra thanked the calei and pulled her fingers out of the clay. The surge of power disappeared and she released the Spiro that had come to her calling.

Once she was able to focus again she noticed Rowyn standing a few paces away, staring down at Cian and Dilys. He looked around at the huddled women who remained in the gully and also down at the arrow still sticking out of the Sergeant and the other wounded guardsman, both of whom were unconscious. With a small part of her she could sense a firestorm building in her cousin.

Casandra stood and started toward Rowyn, but froze. He was glowing slightly, like something was sitting just below his skin and radiating to the surface. His face was barely recognizable as his green eyes gleamed brightly. There were several cuts across his face from the flying rock, but his face was contorted like he was suffering some great pain other than the raining shards of rock. Before she could take another step he was up on the boulder; she never even saw him jump.

He spread his arms and screamed, an inhuman sound somewhere between the howl of a gray wolf and the screech of a large hawk, but at several times the volume of either. The sound was so deafening Casandra had to put her hands to her ears and even then it penetrated the depths of her skull.

54

Sanctuary

The fire had a hold of him, but Rowyn did not care as he stood in the gully looking at the injured around him. He had just seen the little Tink, the gruff but lovable caretaker of Cian's manor brought down by a mysterious flash. And then Cian and Dilys were flung off the boulder by some powerful force. The fire filled him and he suffered his blood to boil, almost welcoming it. He wanted to be on top of the boulder and then he was. He looked down at the few guardsmen fighting right below him and the mass of attackers still charging up the slope toward them. He also saw two black-robed men standing below in the clearing. They had to be the leaders.

Rowyn had always found bloodshed abhorrent. He even detested hunting and would only participate if forced by his father. But there was a part of him, the part coming to life through the fire, that had no such reservation. Drawing on something from deep inside. Something that was raw and savage. Something that he felt, inexplicably, was from an ancient kindred Spirit.

A host of voices filled his mind and he spread his arms, daring anyone or anything to attack him. He let loose a challenge, a threat, proclaiming his – their – presence. The sound brought nearly everyone on the slope to their knees, cringing and covering their ears.

One of the black-robed men was the first to recover and held his hands forward, pointing up at Rowyn. Sneering, Rowyn could feel the *il fennore* build as the man began to cast a destructive spell. Almost laughing, Rowyn looked at the man and the fire within called upon the Spirit directly. It pulled the Spirit of the air down between Rowyn's hands, one top and one underneath as if holding a ball, and heated the air. As the ball of air warmed, the fire within, the dragon's breath, injected itself into the whirling air until it became a burning swirl of flame.

With the ball of fire held in his hands, Rowyn reached back with one hand, then cast the fireball into the clearing. The ball struck the black-robed man at the waist and chest before the man could even finish building his own spell. As Rowyn watched, the flames roared up around the man, and he screamed in what Rowyn could only imagine was excruciating pain.

The man on fire was nearest to the path and his robed accomplice ran over to try to put the fire out, but he quickly realized it was hopeless. It was not just fire. It was made from the Spirits themselves and would burn until what it consumed was nothing but ash. After staring back up at Rowyn for a mere moment, the remaining black-robed man turned and ran back down the path before Rowyn could send more of the Spirit fire down upon him.

The soldiers below Rowyn were starting to regain their feet. The fire still strong in him, Rowyn focused on the Spirit of the ground under the slope itself and the hill began to tremble. His Spirit strained as he pulled at the ground. He was too newly come to his abilities and had not developed the strength yet that he needed. Nevertheless he still latched onto the essence of the layers, under the ground, with the fire that ran through his body. He closed his eyes as the fire demanded more power.

The world around him disappeared and he found himself on a grassy plain that stretched as far as his vision would allow. The grass came up to his waist, but no animals could be seen, not even birds. A ways off he saw a clump of trees, the only ones on the entire plain. He knew it was the same plain in which he had found himself in the past. He walked toward the trees, letting his hands brush the top of the grass that swayed back and forth, expecting a searing pain at any moment, though he did not feel any fear.

The fields of grass reminded him of the one time he had visited the western shores. He had stood on the cliffs looking out on the Forever Waters that stretched from the shores of Taran to the furthest horizon. What had struck him the most was the flowing waves that crisscrossed the water. The only thing he knew with which to compare were ripples, like when one threw a stone in a lake, but when he tried to make the connection with the waves, it didn't fit and he just stared out over the blue water.

He approached the trees and realized they were weeping trees similar to those in Fayhaven, but fuller, and they were swaying in a light breeze. Once through the trees he found a pool of water the length and width of five men. He walked over to the pool and looked into the water. It was crystal clear, though he could not see the bottom. The breeze caused a slight ripple, which again reminded him of waves, but it calmed enough that it reflected his body as a mirror image.

He stood there staring at the pool and wondered how he had come to this place and where it was. As he looked at his reflection something or someone demanded his attention. He remembered the fire that had run through his body and he sensed the fire calling him to its demands. It wanted more. It pounded at his brain, demanding that he give more. He tried to deny it, but that only made it more insistent. It needed more power.

He stared down into the pool and tried to think of where he might find the power to sate the fire. The fire filled his mind and compelled him to focus his mind on obtaining more power.

As he continued to look at his reflection in the pool, his thoughts filling with the fire's craving, a familiar face came up next to his, gazing down at the two reflections that looked back up at them.

She smiled. It was Willoe.

He could sense the fire's pleasure as it growled out its approval.

"I am glad to see you, Wil," Rowyn told her while staring out into the water.

She had woken in a plain, covered in tall green grass, to Rowyn's summons. The horizon was only broken by a copse of trees. She found him there standing next to a pond and she came up next to him.

"And you, Row." She stared into the water at their joint reflection. "You need me," she said.

"I do. I need you as you have needed me."

"I understand." She was surprised at how calm her voice remained.

She could sense something pulling at her. She grabbed her twin's arm to keep from falling as she suddenly felt weak and dizzy.

Rowyn continued to stare into the water, but the concentration on his face caused lines to form across his forehead and his eyes bulged as if his entire body were tearing from the inside out.

She held on to his arm as she dropped to her knees. She looked one last time at their reflection in the water and saw her own body crumbling in on itself, drawn tight, merely skin and bones. Then the world disappeared.

55

Fog

With the wall and safety of the rocks behind them, Drem stood with Prince Beynon and General Rees at the top of the eastern slope with spyglasses, looking down at the opposite shoreline of the Saltrock. They had been called up when the ridge commander reported loud noises across the river near the remains of the stone bridge the Cainwen sappers had destroyed to cut the road that provided access from east to west. The sky had clouded over and Drem prayed to the Burning Lady for rain. He scanned the gray clouds overhead and then looked down at the slope. *If they make it across we will need the Spirits to give us rain. The Franchons would have to slog their way all the way up.*

"What do you think they are moving toward the river?" Drem asked the Prince.

Beynon only shrugged as he continued to scan the shore near the broken bridge.

A few moments later soldiers appeared from a path that ran between the road and the forest. They carried logs, each the length of five men, tied together side by side and wide enough for half a dozen men to stand on. After coming out they halted at the river's edge.

As the soldiers exited the forest, they turned the hewn bridge sideways and moved it down the shoreline until they reached a spot about two-thirds the distance of the tor, where the river started to widen again after passing through the narrowest portion of the Lower Saltrock. Drem frowned. The logs looked as if they would barely stretch the distance between the eastern and western shore. Five more times soldiers came out of the forest carrying sets of bound logs, moving along the river so that the bridges were laid parallel to the river, evenly spaced along the shore from one end of the narrow to the other.

Drem lowered his spyglass and Beynon followed suit.

"Now we know what they were building," Beynon commented.

"Archers to wall!" General Rees yelled off to his right and then his left at the officers commanding each side.

There was no need to use the spyglass anymore. They watched helplessly as the edges of the six bridges were angled out over the river. Franchon soldiers stripped naked and then dropped into the water.

Drem shuddered; he knew the water must be cold, though two months from now and it would be unbearable.

The soldiers took hold of thick ropes attached to the end of the bridges, and began to swim across the river. A few arrows flew from the ridge, but fell short of the eastern shore and only stuck into or clattered off the wooden canopies on the western shore. Though a couple of swimmers never made it to the other side, their places were quickly taken by others.

Once the swimmers were across and safely under the wooden overhangs, the ropes were pulled taut and the makeshift bridges started to edge their way out into the river and across it. All Drem and Beynon could do was watch the bridges as they moved one jerk at a time across the river, finally coming to rest with one end on the west side of the river and the other on the east. Drem estimated it wouldn't hold out the day with armored men running across it, but it wouldn't need to.

"Ready archers," General Rees, standing on the other side of Beynon, called out to the two commanders on either side. The commanders called out, "Archers, pull!" The command was repeated a dozen times as other Shields repeated the order on the left and right, all the way down the line. The archers stood ready in three rows with two rows behind the rocky wall and one on top. The sound of fifteen hundred archers, spread out along the entire ridge, nocking arrows and pulling back the bowstrings on their longbows, had an almost musical quality to Drem. A few hundred guardsmen drew their bows also to add to the volley, as they would not need swords unless the enemy breached the ridge.

A light rain began to fall.

As soon as the bridges were secured on both sides, a loud roar could be heard as men came charging out of the forest with pike and sword. The General raised his arm straight up, but waited until all the bridges were completely full of men racing across. They came four to six across, bunched up, anxious to get to the other side. Once the bridges nearest to the forest path were packed, the General brought his arm down and the commanders to the left and right yelled, "Loose!"

A flight of arrows rose out from the ridge and was followed by others down the line, while the second and third rows loosed their arrows at counts of ten and twenty. The sky blackened as if three lopsided, wedge-shaped flocks of birds had taken flight off the ridge and would continue off to the east. These birds, however, only continued on their path for a moment before diving to fall onto those crossing the bridges. The arrows fell on the bridges nearest to the path first, the rest falling in succession on the other bridges. The men on the bridges held their shields up, but that still left a lot of room between shields and with over five hundred arrows falling on them, quite a few managed to find their targets.

As the next wave of soldiers were more than halfway across the bridge the second flight of arrows fell upon them, with the same results striking the third wave, who probably had thought themselves safe.

"Pitch," General Rees called out to his commanders.

Every third archer on the wall reached down for arrows with tips that had been coated in pitch and placed near the designated archers. Soldiers pulled torches from waiting fires in front of the archer's line and ran along the line, lighting the tips as they went.

"Pull," the command was given once again.

As another wave of soldiers raced onto the bridge, pushing their dead companions off to the sides, Drem could hear the commanders shouting "Loose." The second flock fell, killing and wounding most of the Franchons on the bridge and setting small fires scattered from one end to the other.

The sky seemed to open then, letting the rain fall heavily on the good and bad below.

Soldiers ran out from the Franchon lines with buckets of water to douse many of the flames, though not all.

"Pitch." The archers reached for another round of coated arrows.

Drem could see that some of the fires down below had been soaked in the rain and not all the arrows were yet lit when the third wave moved forward, pushed by those waiting on the shore. Another flight of arrows went up with many finding their mark, but few fires broke out and those were quickly extinguished by the rain.

Drem stared up at the sky and wondered if this is what his mother had meant by being careful what you asked of the Burning Lady.

When the soldiers stopped their mad rush and kept back, huddled on the eastern side of the bridges, Drem estimated that over six hundred dead littered the bridges and could be seen stacking up under the surface of the river as the soldiers sunk to the bottom in their heavy armor. The river flowing south was tinted with the blood of those who had not made it over. Looking down on the bridges, the only movement Drem could see was the jerks of those who were in the process of dying, along with those who stumbled or dragged themselves to one end or the other of the death-filled bridges. The archer line had nocked another arrow and stood ready to pull and release on command, most of the fires along the wall now quenched by the rain. They waited, but nothing was happening on the river. The bridges remained empty, but Drem knew that more than half the crossing troops had managed to get across and to safety under the wooden hangings on the western side of the Saltrock.

It was becoming hard to see through the sleeting rain.

"They would not be giving up so soon," General Rees stated as he held up his spyglass again. After a moment he pointed to the edge of the woods near one of the center bridges. They all watched as a dozen brown-robed figures came out from under the tree branches, followed by four of the black-hooded priests, and spread out along the river bank from one side of the southern most bridge up to beyond the northern most. The larger group of men in dung-colored robes stood along the river bank with the four black-robed men spaced evenly behind them. A single red-robed man stepped out behind them. He was short and slightly bent over. He yelled something to the black-clad men, though Drem couldn't understand what he said.

"What in the Four Shadows be they doing?" General Rees asked.

A few arrows flew from nervous archers, but they fell into the river, well short of the opposing riverbank.

Neither Beynon nor Drem had an answer. All they could do was watch through the rain as the black-robed men held their arms out and the bodies of the men in front of them instantly became stiff. Soon the river started to bubble. The red-robed man held up his arms straight up in the air and the four black-robed men straightened, but did not become rigid like the men in the dung-colored robes.

Another arrow flew from the ridge and struck one of the dung-colored men, the man falling forward into the river and his body floating away with the current. The black-robed man behind him staggered for just a moment before he regained his footing and once again stood straight. A cheer went up from the Cainwens on the ridge, but it was only temporary.

The river continued to bubble and something akin to steam started to rise off the water's surface. The steam looked almost like a fog and it continued to grow and thicken. The rain seemed to have little effect on it, which was bothersome by itself, but it wasn't long before the fog had grown to cover the bottom of the bridges and started to spread its way up the western riverbank toward the wooden overhangs.

General Rees turned to one of the commanders. "Have your archers ready. Once that cursed fog rises enough to cover up the bridges, they be crossing again."

The commander stared at the developing fog. "If we cannot see the bridge, how can we hit anything on it?"

"Aim now while you be able to see it!" General Rees stormed at the commander, but then calmed. "We can get at least one flight off. After that

I think we be too busy on this side of the river."

The command "Pull!" was heard all along the ridge and, as the General had predicted, the fog rose up out of the river and totally covered the bridges. It also covered the wooden hangings and started to move up the slope.

The sound of war cries rose out of the fog and General Rees put his arm in the air again. Drem could see the General's mouth move as he counted off silently to ten, then he dropped his arm and the command "Loose!" ran down either side of the line. Again three flocks of birds seemed to fly in the air and as they fell upon the river the screams of those struck could be heard up on the ridge. But not nearly as many as before.

The fog continued to rise and seemed to settle in at about two-thirds of the way up the slope. After the last of the wounded cries faded the Cainwens stood, ready, but the silence was deafening. Without any visual points of reference the Cainwens could only guess at the Franchons' next move. Most likely they would come up the slope, but if they decided to use the extra troops to force one of the gaps, the reserves at the bottom of the western slope would have to be rerouted quickly to support one or the other of the gaps.

Three lines of archers and guardsmen stood, weapons ready, as the silence continued louder than a roaring river.

56

Unleashed

Saraid's and Helel's arrows had thrown the attackers into confusion, allowing the two of them to jump down from the boulder into the conflict. Saraid's decades of training kicked in as his and Helel's swords cut into the front ranks of the attackers. Not true wizards, the Elfs were nonetheless excellent teachers with their gifts for observing Spirits. The wielding of *il fennore* was better left to Cian and others, leaving the two Elfs with the bow and sword as their primary weapons. This suited Saraid just fine. The hard feel of steel or wood in his hands gave him something he could grasp.

Standing between Helel and the Shield, Saraid fought using every trick and skill he had learned, but then a flash above his head sent shards of rock showering down on his head, one catching him across an ear and another striking his shoulder. As he staggered to recover, the attackers began to push forward again with reinforcements starting to join the attack and Saraid felt they would shortly turn the tide against the defenders.

He planted his feet, flexed his knees, and prepared to meet the charge when a ferocious noise from above caused him to fall backward, bouncing a shoulder off of the boulder and flipping to the side so he was facing uphill. He looked over and saw the Shield lying on his back, blood seeping from under the soldier's head, but Saraid breathed a sigh of relief as he could still feel the Spirit strong in the man. Saraid found his sword in the rubble next to him and started to rise, using the boulder as a brace. He stood and looked up to see that the roar had come from Rowyn standing atop what was left of the boulder, his arms spread as if offering a challenge to all comers.

The Prince's body was glowing and his face was contorted in a sneer that shook Saraid. The Elf turned to look back down the slope where he could see that nearly all the fifty or so remaining attackers had been brought to their knees along with most of the defenders. They all held their hands over their ears, blood leaking from the ears of more than a few. Though more sensitive than a man's, Saraid was thankful that Elf ears also contained an extra layer of protection inside the ear canal.

Saraid watched as one of the black-robed men in the clearing went up in flames. Wizard fire. Something the Elf had rarely seen done, and then only by the strongest wizards like Cian. Saraid looked back up at Rowyn and could sense something building in him. The Prince was pulling at the essence of the Spirit all over the slope. The Elf couldn't define it, but it felt to Saraid as if Rowyn were focusing the Spirit at a single point on the slope.

He was starting to send a thread of his Spirit toward Rowyn to see if he could sense exactly what the Prince was doing when the ground under his feet shook so violently that his feet began to slip, rocks and pebbles bouncing wildly down the slope. The mountain itself began to ripple and pulse. Before Saraid fell to his knees he saw Rowyn growl, and Saraid felt a sudden surge in the *il fennore*.

The surge of power flowed out across the slope like a windstorm and Saraid could sense the essence of the ground itself as it shuddered. Still lying on the ground, he twisted over to look down the hill and saw the ground parting right in the midst of the attackers. The split widened quickly, swallowing more than a dozen men that had the misfortune to be standing on top of the crack that ran across the slope. The opening pushed up the slope further and another dozen or more slipped from the edges and into the void.

Saraid and Helel both rose and took advantage of the confusion. Together they attacked the men on the uphill side of the split. Most of the soldiers were still in shock and the two Elfs, with the help of the guardsmen and servants still standing, killed the attacking soldiers outright or forced them to fall into the deep fracture just below their position. The word that came to Saraid's mind was *slaughter*, but his mind also reminded him that when one picked up a weapon, one accepted the consequences of one's actions. The remaining men, lucky enough to be farther down the slope — just a little over two handfuls — turned and ran toward the forest.

After the last of the attackers fled down the path under the cover of the trees, Saraid could hear a scream a little ways further into the forest.

He turned to look at the ruined bodies scattered across the slope. His heart was heavy with the knowledge that many had died by his own hands, though he did not doubt that they had earned their early deaths. As a rule Elfs took no pleasure in killing, as seemed to be man's passion. But what saddened him more was that he knew it would not be the end. In the midst of the power surge on the killing field he had sensed the Dragon-Called Prince's Spirit. It was as if it had grown and encompassed everything on the slope. The power it wielded was staggering, and it was filled with rage that had not yet been satisfied, even after it wrought the carnage that surrounded him now. No, this was not the end. If Cian was correct it was merely the beginning of a struggle long foretold, a struggle Saraid would have been content to avoid if at all possible. His instincts, however, along with his long years of study, told him that avoiding it would no longer be an option.

Rhein had come to his senses; someone had propped him up on a large piece of rock, broken off from the boulder. He looked down the slope but could see no attackers. He rose to his knees, turned to look back up at the main portion of the boulder and could see a body collapsed on top, limp and unmoving. Rhein staggered up onto the boulder. He recognized Prince Rowyn, then remembered seeing the Prince aglow just before he lost consciousness. The Prince looked as white as a Great Hall table cover, his face so drawn that Rhein could see the edges of Prince Rowyn's cheekbones pushing up against the skin.

"Move aside, Shield," a deep voice told him.

He turned toward the voice to see Lady Casandra and the old Elf Rhein had first seen standing on the boulder earlier, crawling up toward him. He first thought that it might be one of Dilys' glimmers, but the Lady Casandra pushed past him close enough that he could both feel and smell her. He wasn't sure, though, if such things were possible with a glimmer or not, as Rhein remembered feeling the heat from the illusions of fire that Dilys had used during their flight from Highkeep.

As both the lady and Elf took up positions on either side of the Prince, the Lady Casandra said to the Elf, "I need to do a Seeing."

The old Elf just nodded and backed away from the Prince's body as she placed one hand over the Prince's heart and the other on his head.

Rhein slid off the boulder and dropped down to sit a little farther away, resting up against smaller remains of the boulder.

After a few moments she started to stand. "I need to get him to the ground."

"Why the ground?" The Elf seemed confused.

"Calei." She pointed behind the boulder. "Over there."

The Elf's gaze followed her hand, then he turned back to her, his eyes narrowing. "Saraid," he yelled down to someone and one of the younger Elfs — Rhein believed him to be the one that had fought next to him — quickly came up to join the other two on top of the boulder. "We need to get the Prince off the boulder." He started to pull the Prince by his shoulders while the younger Elf took Prince Rowyn's feet. They carefully lowered the Prince down out of sight.

Rhein made his way up to the top of the boulder, his joints stiff and his movements slow. He looked down into the gulley where the Prince was laid out, his body next to the second boulder that created the small channel Rhein and his people had used for their protection.

"Ser Rhein," Guardsman Gerallt's voice called out to him. Rhein turned his head to see the surviving servants and guardsmen at one end of the gulley.

Right below him the lady was hovered over the prone body of the Prince. She had one hand on his chest, her eyes closed. As Rhein watched, he was surprised to see her push her fingers into the ground and then her body became taut and a light glow settled over her.

Three Elfs stood around her. Sergeant Crowley and Dilys were both stretched out at the other end where a Tink seemed to be tending to them. The image of a Tink falling, its body heavily burned, came to mind, but Rhein pushed it to the back as he turned his attention back to the Prince and Lady Casandra.

Like the others, he watched helplessly as Lady Casandra's back jerked twice, while he could hear her sucking in air loudly several times. After more than a full turn of the glass she finally sat back, lifting her hand off the Prince's chest and pulling her fingers out of the soft ground.

The old Elf helped her over to the boulder, poured something into a bowl and made her drink. Shortly after, the Prince began to stir and the two young Elfs helped him to sit up and drink.

Rhein was relieved that they had apparently defeated their attackers, though he was not sure how, and he felt a certain pride that many of his people had survived. There was little comfort as he looked down at Prince Rowyn, Lady Casandra, and the Elfs. He had been through a lot, but his concern now centered on more pressing thoughts: Where had Lady Casandra been? Where had the Elfs come from? And if Prince Rowyn was here, where was Princess Willoe?

57

Reinforcements

Beynon could see many of the archers shifting from side to side. A soldier didn't have much time to think in the midst of battle and only had to listen for the next command. But this was different. The worse part of battle was knowing something was going to happen, but not exactly what, and worse, exactly when.

He, General Rees, and his friend, the First Duke, stood behind the rock wall on a platform built so they could get a clear view of the slope.

The sound of boots on wood could be heard along with the clatter of armor. Then a new sound echoed up the slope. It rose as a rumble at first, then grew louder, the rain not dampening the regular cadence of metal banging on metal, a sound that reminded him of swords on shields, interchanged with a pounding of the ground that rebounded all the way to the ridge. Beynon could feel the tension of the men along the ridge as the measured sound of the approaching Franchon soldiers echoed through the fog laden afternoon. Beynon squinted, trying to catch sight of the Franchons through the rainstorm.

The raindrops came faster, making it even harder to see.

General Rees yelled, "Archers forward!" The order was repeated down the line. The first row of archers stepped up and over the ridge to stand right in front of the rocks that created a barrier. The second row stepped up on top of the rocky ridge. The commanders called out "Pull!" without waiting for the General's orders. The General raised his arm once again. Beynon looked down the line of archers waiting impatiently as the sound came faster and louder, weighing on his and their nerves in equal measure. One archer released and an arrow flew into the fog, followed by a scream as it hit its hidden target.

Just after that a wall of armed men burst from the fog, stretching the entire width of the slope. The Franchons finally let loose with war cries as they broke ranks and charged the wall.

"Hold!" General Rees yelled out as loud as he could.

The enemy had covered about half the distance between the fog and the ridge when General Rees dropped his arm and the call came from the commanders. "Loose!" A solid curtain of arrows flashed straight down the slope at the stumbling and sliding soldiers trying to make their way up to the muddy ridge. Many of the Franchons held up their shields, but the distance was close, and most of the first few rows flew back as if struck by a giant fist. Their companions, pushed by those behind, had no choice but to step over or on their fallen comrades as they moved further up the slope.

This scene was repeated twice more and Beynon estimated a thousand or more soldiers had fallen coming up the slope already. *The Franchons must have a lot more men than was reported*, Beynon thought as he stared at the slaughter happening below him. Even so, he wondered how any commander could waste their men this way.

Arrows flew over the front rows and dropped into the fog. As planned, the third row of Cainwen archers stayed behind the ridge and fired into the fog behind the front line as observers looked down over the ridge to direct their flight.

It wasn't long before arrows started flying back up the slope with some scoring hits on the Cainwen archers, who fell forward down the slope or backward off the ridge.

"The archers are holding well," Beynon remarked to General Rees while he continued to watch the oncoming soldiers.

"Aye, that they be."

If an archer on the front row went down the archer behind him in the second row would step down to take his place. If an archer on the second row stepped forward or was himself wounded, the archer behind him in the third row would step up onto the rocky ridge.

They stepped off the platform, Beynon wanting to meet with the other senior staff, seeing as the Franchons seemed to be faltering under the onslaught of the archers. As he turned around he was met by Sulyen, whom Beynon knew the General had specifically ordered to stay back at the command camp and his brother, Brom, with the Tink Drel Donlin in tow.

"What are you doing up here?" Beynon asked his brother.

"What be ye doing here?" General Rees almost yelled at the young Sulyen at the same time.

Brom was about the last person Beynon expected or wanted to see at the moment. Brom had been a good swordsman in his youth — he had even showed Beynon most of what the Crown Prince knew — but that was many years in the past. A couple of arrows passed over their heads as if to stress Beynon's and the General's surprise.

Brom's ever-present smile made Beynon shake his head, but he had to smile nevertheless. In a calm voice his older brother said, "I thought I might be of help. Besides, you have been very fruitful, dear brother. If something happened to the both of us I am sure there is someone who would welcome such a weighty crown."

This garnered a chuckle from Beynon as another arrow flew over their heads, but the humor was quickly lost as Beynon thought of the last report regarding Mael and Rowyn. If something had happened to them it would leave Willoe and Hafgan. *Willoe is more of a man than Hafgan will ever be*, he thought. Protector Dougal's reports on her private training confirmed this. He could only imagine what the king would say if he knew. The image made Beynon's smile widen.

"They're forcing the ridge!" A messenger from the wall commander hurried down from the rocks.

Beynon looked at Drem, his forehead furrowed. He felt torn. Should he call on the horse to move against the Franchon flanks? If he misjudged and called upon them too early, it would leave both barriers vulnerable and increase the possibility either one could be overrun if the Franchons shifted their attack from the ridge. His thoughts were interrupted as he heard General Rees shout, "Pike to the front!"

"Signal," Beynon called over a signal man. "Stand nearby."

The sound of the pikemen's armor as they moved up to just behind the ridge drew Beynon's attention. Unlike archers, the pikemen required more discipline, and Beynon was pleased to see them move as one, forming up in rows behind the wall. The archers from rows one and two bolted back over the ridge to join the third row behind the protection of the pikemen.

The archer commanders lined up their men in two rows with two-thirds in the front and the remaining third in the back row. The front row put their bows behind them and pulled a short sword that they carried for close-in fighting. The second row nocked and pulled the bowstrings back, aiming just above the pikemen's heads.

The rain poured down on them and many of the archers were having trouble maintaining a solid footing.

Screams came from the other side of the rock barrier. Beynon could picture in his mind the Franchons reaching the ridge only to be quickly speared by pikemen reaching over and down from the rock wall. What a waste of men! As Beynon stared up at the wall, a few of the Franchons managed to get up on the rocks, but these were skewered by the back row of archers, who quickly nocked another arrow and let fly without command. Those that didn't take arrows were pierced by the pikemen.

"They're falling back," one of the pikemen called out and the news was reported all down the line.

Beynon rushed up to the platform to see for himself as several of his personal guard trailed behind.

He looked over and saw that the loose dirt on the slope had become a muddy pit that was sucking at the feet of the Franchon soldiers. They were falling back toward the fog, which had come a little further up the slope.

General Rees came up next to him as a new sound echoed up the slope. It sounded like a hundred packs of wolves howling and growling over fallen prey. As the Franchon soldiers staggered back down the slope, a group of large four-legged creatures, muscles rippling along hairless bodies with long fangs and claws, rushed out of the wall of fog, past the retreating Franchons, and up the slope toward the wall. Some of the dog-like creatures attacked even the retreating Franchons.

The creatures were fast and quickly covered the ground between the fog and the rock wall. They leapt up the wall at the stunned defenders.

Beynon jumped off the platform, followed by the general, both pulling their swords along with the few guardsmen around them.

A few of the pikemen appeared to have recovered in time to spear a fair number of the creatures, but most of the beasts came up and over the wall into the middle of the surprised soldiers. The creatures snapped out with fangs and claws, ripping into the men, who couldn't bring their pikes to bear at such close range. The lines of pikemen were ravaged, hundreds screaming as skin, muscle, and bones were ripped and torn by the creatures.

"Guardsmen!" Beynon yelled, a moment ahead of General Rees and Drem who both called out the same command.

The first line of archers bravely jumped forward into the fray, quickly followed by the reserve guardsmen and Shields. Too many of the Cainwens died, but amidst a flurry of swords and claws the beasts were being killed one at a time. Beynon saw four pikemen corner one of the beasts and skewer it. Even after it fell to the ground the pikemen continued to stab it over and over again.

One such beast broke through the line and charged toward Drem, Brom, and Sulyen. Two guardsmen jumped in front of the beast, but it raked one of the guardsmen with its claws and bit into the shoulder of the other before loping toward Brom and the others. All three men already had their swords out and stood their ground as the creature let out something between a growl and a bark. When it was a few paces from them, a pike took it in the side. A Shield, two pikemen and one of the sword-wielding archers came at the beast from above, by the wall. The creature was momentarily thrown to the side, but jumped back up and started snapping at Sulyen. Drem shoved his sword straight into the vicious creature's mouth and up into its head. Brom's blade momentarily flashed a brilliant white that lit up the scene, even in the downpour, then Beynon's heavyset brother brought his sword down across the creature's neck and severed it. The head rolled a few paces down the hill, Drem's blade still jammed up into and sticking out the back of the head. The Shield and soldiers reached them, ready to attack the unnatural beast, but it was already down. The Shield stepped up and drove his sword down into the creature's chest. One of the pikemen pulled his long wooden pike out of the heavy body.

Drem nodded to the pikeman. "Well thrown, soldier."

The man grinned at the praise.

Scanning the ridge, Beynon couldn't see any more of the creatures alive, but the surviving soldiers continued to stab the beasts. No new Franchon soldiers were coming over the wall and the spotters, on the wall, were not shouting out any warnings.

Beynon knelt next to the head and examined it along with the separated body. It was larger than a wolf, with padded feet and long claws. But it was hairless and at the end of its severed neck was a human head. On closer inspection Beynon decided that it might have once been human, but no longer. It was larger and its nose flatter.

"Look at those teeth." Drem knelt down next to him.

The ears were longer and curved, the teeth sharpened like spikes with two fangs on the bottom and two longer ones that hung over the bottom lips. But the eyes. Even in death Beynon could see that they were human, as was the overall structure of the face.

Standing back up, Beynon turned to his brother, who was sheathing his sword.

"How did you do that?" Beynon grabbed the hilt and pulled it back out to look at the blade.

"What?"

"You cut the beast's head off with one stroke. How did you do that?" Beynon held the sword out. looking down the length of the blade.

"The *il fennore*." Brom grinned and took the sword, slipping it back into its sheath.

Beynon watched as the surviving pikemen, along with the archers, dragged the heavy carcasses and the dead Cainwens off to the side while the guardsmen and Shields manned the wall.

The messenger from earlier came down at an easier pace than before, and this time bowed to Beynon. "My Prince, all spotters report no activity and no sounds from the fog."

The moans and screams for help from the dying Franchon soldiers was enough noise for Beynon. Better the Franchons than his own men, but he would have preferred none die today.

Everyone was soaked, Beynon's own cloak having gained twice its weight in the last half a turn of glass, though the skin had kept him drier than probably most of the footmen.

"What are those?" Sulyen's voice was shaky as he stared at the heap of dead creatures stacked away from the wall and out of the way of the soldiers.

Brom had been examining one of the heaps, and was shaking his head as he returned to the command group. "Beast that should not exist."

Everyone looked at him, all confused.

"They are called Gharzith. Creatures from the far ends of the world. Dark and evil creatures. Part man, part wolf." His nose wrinkled as just the thought seemed to give him a bad taste in his mouth.

Beynon had never heard of such a creature, but from what he had seen of the one, he could agree with Brom's description. "How did they get here?"

Before his brother could answer Sulyen yelled out, "Look!" and pointed west.

They all turned to see a large body of dark-cloaked riders coming from the south and just turning east to head toward Daere Mawr. It was hard to judge numbers as the riders were moving at a gallop, but it looked to be the twenty-five hundred that Malbery had promised.

"It must be Malbery," Sulyen cried out with a grin on his face.

"Finally," Beynon said and let out a sigh of relief.

The riders were still a bit off and Beynon couldn't make out any details, the rain making it impossible to see clearly, but Greenmerrow colors were a dark blue so it had to be Malbery's men.

"I can'na make them out." General Rees wiped off the spyglass he held and tried again, but shook his head as he brought the spyglass down, holding it in his right hand.

Beynon turned to one of the pages. "Get down there quickly and have the horse split half to the north half to the south. On your way, tell the reserve commander to send his troops up to the ridge. If the Franchons make another attempt on the ridge I want the Greenmerrow horse to attack the flanks."

The page mounted a horse and started to make his way down the slope.

The rain continued, but it had ceased to pour as heavily as before.

A commander on the wall yelled back to General Rees. "Here they come!"

Beynon turned back to the rest of the command group, rubbing his hands together. "We will squeeze them at the bottom and with the reserves we will drive them back down the slope and back across the river. They would be foolish to keep up the fight."

Most of the command group turned to the rock barrier. Beynon kept scanning the plain that spread out to the west. As he watched, nearly a third of the riders peeled off and headed right toward the southern gap. "Some are headed south. Good, Malbery must have perceived our plan."

General Rees and Brom both turned back for a moment, then the General looked back to the wall while Brom came to stand next to his brother.

Why weren't the remaining troops turning north? he wondered as the riders proceeded toward the base of the western slope.

"What do you think—" Beynon turned to ask his brother if he thought it strange, but Brom had his eyes closed and looked as if in deep thought. *What good is a scholar on a battlefield?* Beynon frowned. He reached out a hand to shake Brom by the shoulder, but before he could touch his brother, Brom's eyes popped open.

"These are not Greenmerrow." Brom took two quick steps up to General Rees and snatched the spyglass from the general's hand.

The general looked around at Brom and frowned, but then turned his attention back to the wall.

Brom put the glass up to his eye and stared for a moment, then without putting the glass down informed Beynon. "Their uniforms are black and the insignia on the chest is a white boar."

The general snapped around and grabbed the spyglass out of Brom's hand to take a look himself. Beynon held up a hand over his eyes trying to see through the lessening rain.

"Razorbacks!" the general yelled, his voice tight with alarm. "Those be sellswords from Kieran."

58

Fleeting Survivors

Rhein sat down next to Sergeant Crowley and propped his back against the boulder. He leaned his head back and winced as the bandage brushed against the boulder. Rhein noticed the older man seemed to be recovering steadily. He gently squeezed the older man's shoulder and smiled. "What say, Sergeant, it looks as if the Burning Lady has no room for two damaged soldiers as we."

The sergeant nodded, returning the smile with only about half his teeth visible. "I knew we could take them. I wasn't worried one bit." They both knew it was only bravado. The sergeant held up a flask for Rhein, who shook his head politely. The sergeant sipped from the flask and then continued to eat some dried meat the Elfs had brought with them. "What I don't understand is how they got here?" He pointed to the strange mix of Elfs, Prince Rowyn, Lady Casandra, and the small Tink. "I didn't know there was a way in here except through the bloody forest or over the mountains."

Rhein had been asking himself the same thing, along with a host of other questions. As a Shield and leader he was used to dealing with facts, not mysteries.

The sergeant continued. "I know the Princess— I mean, Prince, told you them mountain lions and that big beast were safe, but I'm keeping me eye on them." The Sergeant held his flask out to point at the riding animals the Elfs called Kata-henis and the huge bear-like Borlender that carried most of the Elfs' supplies.

"I could not agree more, Sergeant. Those fangs don't look very friendly." The sergeant's remarks only reminded Rhein of the problem still facing him. He had left Castle Westhedge with Princess Willoe, who had somehow turned into Prince Rowyn. He had been going over his orders, trying to sort out exactly what this meant to him and his men. It was not something one normally encountered. At least he understood how he had been misled. The old Elf, the one Dilys called Lor Cian, had explained to Rhein that it had been Prince Rowyn in the carriage when they had left the castle and that Cian had taken the Prince and lady away.

"I know you said that the Princess and lady was only — I forget — I think you said glimmers, but why did the Elf take them away?" The Sergeant was starting to slur slightly, but Rhein let him enjoy the feeling of still being alive, something neither thought they would feel again.

"I am not sure." The Shield already grasped the idea of the glimmers and explained it to the sergeant, comparing them to the illusions Dilys had used to baffle their pursuers and keep them alive. He didn't try to explain what the Elf had told him about the *il fennore*. Cian had told how he had come in the night and taken the Prince and lady, which finally explained the strange feelings Rhein had had that night. But the Elf had waved away the question when Rhein asked why he had led away the Prince and lady only saying 'control.' It was one of those mysteries the Shield had yet to unravel.

But what confused him the most was Prince Rowyn and what he had done. The wound in the ground was still there and impossible to ignore. He watched as Lady Casandra went from each of the wounded and put her hands on them. She would close her eyes then open them back up with a cheerful smile. He could hear her say to one person, "Healing nicely." And to another, "It will only be sore for a couple of days." Nearly everyone had at least some type of minor wound, and several had much more serious wounds from either the attackers or the shower of shards.

Rhein stood back up as the Elf, Saraid, and Guardsman Gerallt walked over to him. Amazing as it was, the Guardsman only had one small cut on the back of his neck from the flying rock.

Guardsman Gerallt spoke with a saddened voice as he reported. "Of the guard, it's just myself, Guardsman Rhodri — who seems to be recovering rather well from the leg wound — Sergeant Crowley, and yourself, Ser."

Rhein hadn't been sure all the others had been killed at first, but guessed as much. Gerallt had already told him that Guardsman Hartha had been struck with an arrow as he and Gerallt had bounded over their boulder to join the battle. Rhein had seen two others fall himself.

Of the servants he had found the manor's cook just above the crack in the slope right after the battle. The man was just barely alive when Rhein knelt down next to him. The body of the manor's cook was covered with blood, much of it seeping from the man's own wounds. As Rhein tried to lift his head and give him some water the cook coughed and then grinned. The man's broken body became stiff, he grabbed the sleeve of Rhein's shirt and tried to speak, coughing again. Finally, with blood trickling from his mouth, he asked, "We got them Shield? We got them?"

Rhein nodded. "Yes we did. We routed them."

The cook let go of Rhein's sleeve and his body seemed to relax. The grin stayed on the his face as Rhein lay him back down and when he spoke again, Rhein realized the cook wasn't talking to him anymore. "I got them, Lilia. I got them, my little flower." Then the man's eyes just stared blankly up into the sky. Rhein had seen a lot of tragedy and more than his share of killing during his short life, but the cook's final declaration to his daughter caused tears to well up in the young Shield's eyes.

The memory still fresh, Rhein nodded to Gerallt. "What about the boy?"

The veteran guardsman seemed to delay for a moment, his voice a little choked as he said, "I found the head. The body must have fallen into the pit." This was what the survivors had taken to calling the crack in the slope. "The other man, the one that helped out with the maintenance of the manor and the gardens? I couldn't find him anywhere. He must have fallen in while fighting, or else his body slid into it afterward. I saw a couple of others do that while the earth was still shaking right after—"

"The woman?" Rhein asked without having to specify which one.

Guardsman Gerallt finally smiled. "She is a tough one. I saw her kill two myself. With one she stepped right into the sweep of his sword and then blocked the back swing while driving her sword cleanly through him." He turned and pointed over to a tall, slightly plump woman who had streaks of blood running down the front of her dress.

She saw them and smiled, waving to them with the bloody sword still in her hand.

Gerallt turned back with a bigger smile. "She says her grandfather was a weaponsmith and she spent a lot of time at the furnaces and practicing with his wares."

"Quite a woman," Rhein commented.

"Yes... quite a woman," Gerallt responded, turning to look back at the woman who, seeing him, smiled shyly and turned away. A much different picture than what Rhein remembered when he last saw the woman on the battlefield. Her face had been set with determination and she had wielded her sword without hesitation.

"The Tink that tried to help Dilys—?" Rhein asked, trying to remember the name of the Tink he had been told.

The Elf cleared his throat, apparently unsettled. "Drel Corklin." He finally said and then added, "He was a close friend to me for over sixty years and to Dilys and my family for much longer than that."

Rhein knew that Elfs lived a long time, but the Elf standing in front of him looked more like twenty than sixty. And if Saraid was over sixty, then how old was Lor Cian? And Dilys?

"He will be greatly missed," Saraid finished, his eyes cast down.

Rhein could only nod his head in agreement as he had never met the Tink, but knew enough of his bravery and thanked him silently for defending Rhein's ever more mysterious friend Dilys. Thinking about Dilys, he thanked Saraid and Gerallt before excusing himself to walk over to Dilys, who was leaning up against one of the other boulders as another Tink helped her drink from a cup.

"How are you faring?" Rhein asked as he slid down next to her.

She sipped from the cup and then signaled the Tink, who had arrived after the battle, to take it away. She winced as she sat up a little more. "I be fine shortly, thanks to the Lady Casandra." She tilted her head to the lady farther up the gully checking on the injured blacksmith.

Rhein smiled at the mention of her name.

"Saraid told me, but be it true 'bout Drel Corklin?" Rhein figured she already knew the answer but her question showed that she hoped beyond hope the Elf had been wrong.

Unable to look her directly in the eyes, he bowed his head forward.

"No answer be needed." A sigh escaped her lips.

He raised his head to look at the tears in her eyes.

"He be my friend. Did you know that?" she asked softly.

"Saraid told me. I am sorry." Rhein knew how to tell a man that he would probably die in an upcoming fight, but not how to console a woman whom he had begun to think of as a loving aunt. A very strange and eccentric one, but still family. "I heard him call you 'Lady Dilys?' " He asked, not sure why other than it had struck him as curious.

She smiled a little as if remembering something pleasant. "The Tinks. We have a long history together. Ye might say my abilities and theirs have certain... how shall we say... similarities. There are few of my people left—"

"Your people?" Rhein interrupted, confused by her statement. He thought she was talking about their small group and he spread his hand and arm out, taking in the group resting in the gully. "We are still here."

Her smile broadened. "Your people, not mine." She twisted her head from side to side as if stretching long unused muscles. "My people are an old race. We lived to the far north with the Tinks and others of old Taranona."

Rhein tried to comprehend what she was saying. Where was Taranona? Maybe she meant Taran? His mind swirled and he felt it might just stop working altogether.

Before he could ask another question a different voice spoke up.

"Lady Dilys be worshiped by my people." The Tink had come back over to them and stood, his head even with Rhein even though Rhein was sitting. Rhein had not known there was a second one of the little people until the Tink arrived with the Kata-henis and the large bear-like creature.

Dilys shifted uncomfortably and then introduced the Tink. "This be Krel Monlor." She grimaced with a small wince as she pointed over to the end of the gully. "That hairy beast over there that looks like a cross between a bear and a large hound, be Swift. He be a Borlender. If you need to go somewhere and need to take a lot of supplies with you, a Borlender be indispensable."

The flat face of the creature grinned, literally ear to ear, at hearing Dilys' comments.

Then she corrected the Tink's statement. "I want no one worshiping me."

The Tink looked at Dilys almost scoldingly. "That be your choice, me lady." He then tried to help her sit more comfortably and continued to explain. "My people, the Waljantinks, and Lady Dilys' people," he glanced at Dilys, "the Cradoe, have lived in harmony long before men came to our shores."

Rhein's head twisted from side to side as he looked at both the Tink and Dilys, finally focusing on Krel Monlor. He wasn't sure he had heard the Tink correctly. "Before men came to Taran? I don't understand."

Krel Monlor looked at Rhein, the little creature's thick eyebrows knitted at being interrupted. "It be called Taranona in ancient days. But that be before your people came. Ye have only been on this land for a few thousand years."

Rhein leaned back, the implications of what the Tink said staggering. He turned back to Dilys. "Is this what you meant? Your people are not men?" He waved his arm at the others and then realized there were Elfs among them as well. "I mean, besides the Elfs and the Little People." He indicated Krel Monlor as he said this.

Krel Monlor sucked in his breath and, with a strained look, snapped back, "I am not one of the Little People."

Dilys put a hand on the Tink's arm and told him gently, "Please calm down, my friend. The young Shield has evidently never met a Piskey." She patted Krel Monlor on the shoulder and smiled at the Tink, then looked back at Rhein. "Just know that Tinks have brown or blond hair and once they reach maturity have a small beard." She scratched Krel Monlor's, and he looked amused. She stopped. "Even the women."

Krel Monlor laughed. "I know several women with chin hair that almost feels like silk. And sometimes scented. Nothing more comforting on a long winter night. Softness and the aroma of flowers. Like laying down in a meadow." He closed his eyes and inhaled deeply. The little Tink's face looked as if he were drawing upon a familiar memory.

Dilys stifled a laugh then leaned a little toward Rhein to whisper, "He be quite the lady's man. Travels a lot." She leaned back against the rock.

Dilys and the Tink's discussion didn't help Rhein much, but he tried to understand as best he could. He addressed the Tink. "You said that your people the Tinks… I mean the Waljantinks, and Dilys' people, the Cradoe, were the only peoples in Taran?"

"And the Elfs. They be here before even our ancient peoples." The Tink continued with his story. "The Waljantinks and the Cradoe were ruled jointly by the royal families of both our people." He reached into a pocket and brought out a jeweled flask. He pulled the top off and handed it to Dilys. "Lady Dilys be the last of her family line."

Dilys took a long swig of the flask and smacked her lips. "Almost as good as Lady Casandra's healing." She took another swig and reluctantly returned it to Krel Monlor.

Rhein had too many thoughts flowing through his mind. "If you are royalty, why are you—?"

"Enough, Shield. Can't you just let an old woman be?" she gently chided him and lay back, closing her eyes.

He shook his head and knew she was just cutting the conversation off to avoid answering any more questions, something he had grown used to with her, but he could not refuse her wish.

Krel Monlor sat down protectively next to Dilys and watched her slowly breathe.

Rhein nodded to the Tink, then he stood and walked over to the old Elf, who had a bandage on his head where he had fallen against the rear boulder. Prince Rowyn, looking better than he had right after the battle, was talking with Cian.

"Ah, Shield. Fine, just fine. We were finalizing plans."

Rhein breathed a small sigh of relief, as he had been wondering himself where to go from here. They were stuck between the killer forest and the sheer cliffs of the mountain. Either way held little promise in his mind.

Cian continued. "There is a small path along the lower ridges of the mountain that will bring us out at a small trading village called Peltbush. This is how we came. From there you can take the servants and make your way back to Westhedge. I don't believe you will have any difficulty."

"The Lady Casandra and Prince Rowyn?" Rhein asked, concerned with what he thought he had just been told.

Up close Rhein could see that the Prince still looked a little drawn and weak. Saraid had given Rhein a long explanation and said it had something to do with the expending of Spirit energy, but the explanation didn't really register with Rhein. He knew what using the *il fennore* had done to Dilys so he just figured it was similar for the Prince. He'd never thought of the Prince as a wizard. Then again, he had never thought of Lady Casandra as one either.

The Prince answered. "We will be going with the Elfs and the Tink. And

Dilys will be coming along also."

"I and my men will also be joining you." The confusion about his orders disappeared in that instant, and Rhein spoke flatly.

Cian spoke to Rhein in an authoritative tone similar to what Rhein was used to. "We do not need your assistance. It is best if you return to Westhedge. We do not know where our path will lead."

But Rhein still had his duty and the Elf had no authority over him. "I have my duty to protect Lady Casandra and Princess— I mean, Prince Rowyn. We will not be returning to Westhedge unless the Prince and lady are returning with us."

Prince Rowyn turned to Rhein and told him in an angry tone, "I am commanding you, Shield, to return to the castle."

Rhein wanted to comply, as a Shield was well below a Prince, but he would not be deterred and straightened his back before answering. "I beg your pardon, my Lord, but my orders come from your father, the Crown Prince, and he personally told me that I am not to leave either Lady Casandra or the Princess. I am interpreting this to also mean your Lordship. I am to guard you with my life. This goes for my men as well." He pulled back his shoulders, hoping he could keep up the bravado long enough. "Either we all go on this quest or we all go back to the castle."

The old Elf frowned and no one said anything for a moment, but Rhein could see that the Prince was not taking this well. Finally the Elf spoke. "If it is the Burning Lady's will, then it shall be. A few extra weapons may come in handy since we know not where we travel." He looked over at the sun setting over the mountain peak. "We will take the servants to the village and then we will begin our search. It will be dark soon. We will leave in the morning. The injured will be well enough to travel by then."

Rhein had no idea what they were searching for, but he was relieved to see that with a decision made the Prince seemed to relax.

The Elf walked off to talk with Saraid and Dilys.

The Prince stayed behind and stared at Rhein for a moment as if trying to make up his mind about something. Rhein stood completely still as if on parade and waited for the Prince to speak.

Finally the Prince's lips turned slightly upward and he laughed softly without opening his mouth. Then he put his finger on Rhein's chest. "If you are coming with us then it is Rowyn — not Prince, not my Lord, or any other title. And tell your men. I have enough to worry about without having to try to act like royalty just to make you feel better."

With that shocking statement the Prince walked off, heading over toward Casandra.

Rhein stood there and wished he were back in Castle Westhedge. At least there he knew what to do and how to act. Here it was if the entire world had gone crazy. Elfs, Tinks, Dilys the ruler of an ancient unknown people, Casandra and Rowyn powerful wizards. Now off on some strange quest for something, and Rhein not knowing what it was or why they were searching for it. His days as a lieutenant, riding in the bitter cold along the northern border and fighting Tonns, seemed like a pleasant memory. He only hoped that the future would not lead to the last few days becoming one of his more pleasant memories.

59

Bone Fang

While the General had been identifying the riders, Drem and the others watched as the page Beynon had sent rode out and brought his horse to a halt, waiting for the oncoming riders. The page must have realized the riders weren't from Greenmerrow because he turned his horse and spurred it into a gallop back toward the slope, but before he could get more than a couple of lengths, the charging riders overtook him, one rider reaching out with a sword to cut the page down from behind, leaving the horse to run ahead of the small horde, riderless.

"No!" Beynon yelled, seeing his page be murdered.

Beynon called out to a signal man to warn the Cainwen reinforcements still making their way up the slope, but before the soldier could do anything the riders lowered their lances and charged into the archers and pike that had not already started up the slope. They ran right over the unsuspecting soldiers, spearing them as they tried to run, and then continued under the trees. They were riding up the slope now, running down the reserve pike and archers, most of whom most likely didn't even know they were being attacked.

A call from the senior commander on the wall drew the command group's attention. "They are coming in force. We need reinforcements!"

General Rees turned back to face Beynon and the others, his face blood red with rage. He ordered the commander of the personal guard. "We are lost. Take the Prince down the ridge to the northern gap."

Beynon grabbed the General's arm. "I am not deserting the men." The Prince's face was firm with determination.

The General stared into Beynon's face for a long moment, the rain spattering on his helmet, then said, "We all go north. The path narrows and the

Franchons, they have to come at us in small groups."

Drem looked down at the sellswords making their way up the slope. They would have to dismount before they reached the Cainwen lines.

General Rees followed Drem's gaze and added, "If we can a reach the northern gap and the bastards have not routed our men there be a chance we can reach Duke Cadwal's lands and even, the Spirits willing, Castle Mount Somerled."

Beynon gripped the General's arm tighter and Drem could see the frustration and hate in Beynon's expression. Not at the General, but at the turn of events.

The General added, "We have to move quickly or we lose the freedom to make a decision." He looked back down at the sellswords. "It be made for us."

After another moment Beynon nodded and let go of the General's arm.

The General turned back to the wall and yelled up to a few of the commanders along the wall. "Pull off every second man and send them down the northern trail." He called to one of the commanders in particular. "I want two squads as a rear guard."

Sulyen, his young face filled with fear and still not truly understanding, asked, "What about the southern gap and all the men we just sent there?"

There was no time for niceties, but Drem did not want to be too hard on the boy. Sulyen reminded him somewhat of his own son a few years ago, though Aeron was an astute student of strategy and would have realized the truth already. The boy needed to learn about the realities of war, and quickly. Drem said bluntly, but gently, "All lost. Between the Franchons on the slope and the sellswords coming from the south they are already dead. Our only hope is that they can buy us time to reach the northern gap."

The boy was soaked and Drem couldn't tell if young Sulyen was wiping away the rain or tears. Drem had to remember that he was only around fourteen, not much older than the average page. Like the one that had just died on the open fields. Drem pulled the boy tighter and then let him go, gently pushing him toward Lord Brom. "Master Sulyen, if you could assist Lord Brom it would be a big help as we move north."

With a task to keep him busy the boy wiped his eyes and put his head back, standing straighter. Lord Brom looked over at Drem with a frown, but didn't say anything.

The personal guard started heading out in front, down the northern path. The Crown Prince followed with the guard commander. Lord Brom started after them with the boy Sulyen at his side. As he watched, Drel Donlin was suddenly right behind them. Drem had never even seen the Tink among them until his startling appearance. Lord Brom's companion turned and waved to Drem with a smirk.

Drem stayed with General Rees and several of his commanders as they started to curve the ends of their southern line around, building a half circle at the end of the path. The few foot that had made it up the slope joined the retreating troops. Most of the men, already worn from the battle on the ridge, ran or stumbled down the path, following the command staff. In a matter of moments the entire path was filled with Cainwen troops running toward the northern gap.

Drem and the General ran ahead of a small group of pike and guardsmen who would stop every so often and push back the pursuing Franchons, then they would turn and run again, keeping a forced gap between themselves and the retreating troops. It was a full turn of stop and fight then turn and run, but finally the end of the path was in sight. The remaining rear guard turned one last time and pushed back the pursuers before following Drem and General Rees. The path was bounded by sharp ragged rocks the entire way, but now these started to give way to a dense wall of trees that ran the rest of the way to the end of the path where it would come out just a few paces from the Great Crossway.

As the general and Drem reached the end of the path, Drem heard screaming from behind and turned to see the path filled with dying Franchons punctured with arrows. Someone had had the keen sense to set archers to ambush the Franchons as they pursued the rear guard. The path was clear of living Franchons for at least a hundred feet up to a turn in the path around large boulders. A few Franchons came out around the corner and were immediately covered with a dozen arrows each. At least it would keep the Franchons at bay for a short time.

Drem and the general walked over to the barrier where the command staff was looking at a map unfolded on a flat rock. A clear cover was over the map, but it was hard to see with the rain pounding on it. As they approached, Beynon was talking to one of Drem's senior Shields, second in command to General Eryls. A sense of relief filled Drem, but he was still hoping the general also survived.

"Good to see you, Drem, General." Beynon nodded as they walked up.

"If we stay along this route," the Shield continued as he pointed to a route that stayed just west of the forest's edge, "we can lessen contact with the Franchon horse."

"I have already sent the bulk of the army on their way." Beynon looked over at General Rees. "You will start out after them and take command. You will make for Mount Somerled."

"It be taking us five days on foot." General Rees studied the map.

The Shield nodded his agreement, then looked at a dozen Shields off to the side. "Half the horse will ride with the army."

"Not nearly enough." Beynon looked worn, his face drawn into a constant frown. The loss of life weighed heavily on Drem and he could only imagine how the Crown Prince must feel. They had lost more than half of the horse and the reserve troops that had been sent to the northern gap. The southern troops were considered wholly lost. Most of the other mounted guardsmen were now afoot, their horses taken by Shields to replace the ones thought safe at the bottom of the western slope, but now lost to the sellswords. All told, a loss of over two thousand horses and a resounding defeat.

"We can fall back into the woods if attacked and can set ambushes if the Franchons try to come cross the tree line, while the horse harass the Franchons and split their attention."

"There is more than twenty miles of open fields between the end of the forest and Mount Somerled." Coming late, Drem wanted to make sure they considered all possibilities.

"I will be leading the command staff," General Eryls spoke as he turned from talking with a Shield. Drem was glad to see the commander of his forces and only hoped many of his guardsmen had survived. "The command staff will ride with a hundred Shields, each man taking a second horse to switch along the way." He ran his finger along the edge of the forest and tapped the spot indicating Drem's castle. "With hard riding we should reach Mount Somerled in under two days. Once there we can put out a call to rally more troops and then bring the guardsmen from the castle to the aid of General Rees. This should be as the army comes out of the forest a day's march from the castle."

Drem thought the plan would work and nodded his agreement. It was clear they could not confront the Franchons head-on, but if they could get the army to Mount Somerled, then they could reinforce from the western and northern vassals. With fresh troops they could make plans for how they could push the Franchons out of Cainwen.

"I believe I should remain with the army." Beynon shook his head after hearing General Eryls' plan.

"It is important you get to safety, my Prince." Drem knew how stubborn his friend could be.

"I am the—" Beynon started to argue, but Drem was prepared.

"The Prince. Yes." Drem had to cut this off quickly or Beynon would get himself wound up so that it would be impossible to convince him otherwise. "And as the Crown Prince you are needed to rally our people to push these bastards back to White Cliffs."

Heads nodded around the table until an arrow shot past the command staff and hit a tree nearby. Drem tried to look back toward the path and through the sheeting rain could see that a Franchon archer had gotten up on top of one of the boulders at the turn and was shooting down the path. The archer got off one more shot before he was struck by an arrow himself and rolled off the boulder. It was clear for the moment, but Drem could imagine the boulder would be crawling with archers shortly.

The senior Shield rolled up the map as General Eryls started shouting orders. Most of the hundred mounted Shields had already ridden ahead to ensure the path clear for the command staff, leaving only a dozen Shields to ride with the staff themselves.

Sixty archers and guardsmen would remain behind to man the northern barrier with one side facing the road south, the other side looking east across the river and the remains of the stone bridge. They would give the command staff a half-a-glass lead and then they would pull back slowly, providing a rearguard. Drem knew that it was unlikely half would make it to his castle. He was also sure that they knew this, but would fulfill their duty nevertheless.

General Eryls saluted with his fist over his heart and then headed off to catch up with the front of the column.

The remaining command staff grabbed a quick bite and checked out their mounts. They were saddling up when a loud rumbling noise, like a small avalanche, assaulted their ears.

Lord Brom began to shout a warning. "Get down—" But then they were all thrown to the ground by a great force. It was followed by flying splinters of wood and rock chips, some of which scored Drem's arms and face. His head was swirling as he tried to stand, but his ears still rang and he had trouble balancing as he stood. His eyes cleared and he looked down the road at the tree and rock barricade that had been built when the Cainwens first arrived. A large gap in the barricade had appeared and bodies of the soldiers, torn and ripped apart, lay scattered around the hole. Other soldiers were trying to stand up clumsily and get their bearings.

Drem looked through the smoke that filled the gap and as it dissipated he could see a man dressed like the one that had visited from White Cliffs. This priest, however, looked like the one that had been at the river shoreline. He was shorter than Bat-Uul and his back was bent. In front of him were a hand full of black-robed men who looked as if chiseled from rock. They were frozen in place. The red-robed priest had his hands out in front of him and Drem assumed that he was somehow responsible for the gap in the barrier.

The duke only had a moment to think on it before the gap was suddenly filled with Franchon warriors charging through the opening and cutting down the still-woozy Cainwen soldiers. Beynon and the others were still struggling to their feet and unaware of the Franchons. Drem stepped over and grabbed Beynon by the arm, pulling him toward the forest along the river's edge. The Prince staggered as if he was not sure of where they were going or what exactly was going on. General Rees, Lord Brom, and Lord Sulyen followed along with five of the personal guard who careened from side to side behind them. Bringing up the rear, Drem saw the Tink waving his hands in the air. A moment later the wind suddenly picked up and scattered debris stirred. A wall of debris flew into the air in a spinning whirl-wind of lethal shards. The spinning death grew and flew toward the oncoming Franchons.

The small group of survivors crashed through the woods. Drem led them upriver, still under the cover of the dense tree line. Behind them the screams of the Franchons rose above the sound of the wind.

60

Ancestors

Willoe could see them clearly. Men — at least, she thought they were men — in red robes, but their forms constantly shifting as if in a haze. Dark, almost burnt hands, boney fingers with long black fingernails, pointing directly at her. A green dragon impatiently padding back and forth as if it were waiting for something. Another image of the red robes, in a circle around her, fire spouting from each finger pointing to her that combined to encircle her with flames, yet she didn't burn. The dragon once more, roaring, and the sound should have frightened her, but instead she felt filled with warmth and power.

The images had come between bouts of semi-consciousness when she was being jostled on the pallet. She felt drained and hot, the pain in her chest had increased. She remembered Cleric Yoan's face over her letting her know they were heading up into the mountains and covering her with another blanket.

Then a strange dream where she was with Rowyn. Beside a pond in a big open plain. He needed her and she gave willingly. She could still see her sunken skin as she folded up on the shore of the pond. The dream was so real. Then Rowyn reached down and pulled her up. He put one hand behind her to keep her upright and then put the other hand on her chest, above her heart. She grabbed hold of his forearm.

He stared into her eyes. She had seen that gaze before. The same eyes from when she had first seen the dragon and the Burning Lady. Small flames of red and orange flickered where the color should be. Then a voice, not Rowyn's, spoke to her. "It not be time, child. Return to the living. The time for choosing the sacrificial one has not come." The eyes in Rowyn's face continued to stare into hers. "All is not lost. To save thyself and thy

425

twin ye must find the sword and the staff."

Then the entity that was somehow Rowyn opened its mouth and blew a breath of air toward Willoe. But the air didn't stop; instead it grew in volume like on a windy day. The wind continued to become stronger and Willoe's eyes blinked rapidly as she felt her loose skin start to drag back against her face. She couldn't pull her arms free as the wind pushed her head back. She couldn't keep her eyes open any longer, and as she closed them the world returned to darkness, the silence deafening.

A voice drifted into her mind. "Ah, there. That be better."

She didn't recognize it — at least, she didn't think so — but there was something familiar about it. Her eyes fluttered and she tried to open them, but they were stuck together and would only partially open. She reached up and started to wipe when a soft hand pulled hers away and she felt a warm, wet cloth wiping her eyes. She blinked several times and slowly opened her eyes. She was on her back again and felt like she had done this before. Everything was a little blurry but as it started to clear she found herself staring into a mirror.

Then her image moved while she had not. The image became more vivid and she noticed the bare outlines of crow's feet at the corners of the eyes, the hair color that was a shade darker. The shape of the lips was just a little off and the cheeks a little fuller. Willoe was not one to sit in front of her own image endlessly but, unlike a man, she knew every detail of her body and the image she saw was not hers.

The image leaned down and softly spoke to her in a comforting voice. "You be resting for a bit longer, but I think you be up and back to normal by tomorrow." The image smiled. "Maybe not normal, but yourself at least."

The image turned away and Emeline came into view. "I have some stew for you, Princess Willoe." She helped Willoe sit up. Willoe was lying on a thick mattress and a thick warm white cover was pulled up to her chest. As she scooted up to lean against the headboard of the bed, she saw that she was in a small windowed room with bright wall decorations and two small chairs in addition to a wardrobe and a small rectangular table next to the bed.

When she was comfortable Emeline sat in a chair next to the bed and took a pewter bowl off the table. She dipped a spoon in and held it out toward Willoe to eat. "Lady Kerye said this would help you to regain your strength."

Willoe took a spoonful of the stew; it warmed her as it went down. Before Emeline could offer another spoonful Willoe asked hesitantly, "You know who I am?"

Emeline smiled. "Yes."

Willoe reached out a hand and put it on the other woman's arm. "How many others?" Willoe asked while still holding on tightly to Emeline's arm.

Emeline's smile brightened. "Just myself, Aeron, Cleric Yoan, Protector Dougal." She put the spoon in the bowl and left it there, putting her hand on top of Willoe's. "And, of course, your aunt."

Willoe's eyes and mouth opened wide and she inhaled deeply at the news. Her face must have registered her shock to the utmost degree because Emeline gripped her hand and asked in a worried tone, "Are you failing again, Princess?"

It took a moment but Willoe relaxed her body and let go of Emeline's arm. "I am fine. I just did not know I had an aunt." Frowning in concentration, she fixed her gaze on Emeline as the implications ran rampant through her mind. "Are you sure?"

As she spooned another helping of the stew out of the bowl, Emeline spoke cheerfully and with kindness, as if she and Willoe were childhood friends. "Oh yes. Lady Kerye is your aunt. At least, she says she is and Protector Dougal seems to know her. Here, try another spoonful."

Willoe swallowed the spoonful of stew and a few more until the bowl was nearly empty. "What about the others? Captain Harte and Count Idwal?"

Emeline shook her head. "No one else knows. Your aunt said it was best if we continued the deception for now." Emeline stood up and took the bowl off the table. "Protector Dougal agreed. He said as long as they still think you are Prince Rowyn, they will follow your orders." She reached down and patted Willoe on the shoulder. "I will be back in a little while."

The Franchon woman walked across the room and out the door as the woman she had seen earlier came in.

The woman almost seemed to float over to the bed and sat in the chair Emeline had vacated. Willoe had seen many women of grace and this lady exemplified all the characteristics she had seen in those other women. There was no doubt in Willoe's mind that this woman was a lady born to great nobility. As the woman sat she put a hand on Willoe's chest and closed her eyes. Willoe could feel the woman's presence as it wound its way through Willoe's body.

After a moment the lady, her aunt, opened her eyes and smiled. "Very good. You be healing well. You be coming back just fine from your brush with death."

This shocked Willoe again. She knew she had been sick, but not to the extent her aunt recounted. She realized that she had no idea how long she had even been asleep so was not a judge of her condition during that time. "I almost died? I did not think the wounds that serious."

"It not be your wounds. Cleric Yoan did a fine job getting you here and then I be able to cleanse the wound. It was healing well."

"Then why did I come close to death?"

Her aunt looked a little embarrassed and finally said, "I don't know. You be healing fine when the Spirit fled your body. I thought you would perish, but then as suddenly as it fled, it returned, stronger than before. I have never seen such a thing."

Willoe thought back to her dream, but did not mention it to her aunt. Instead she shifted the conversation. "The Lady Emeline tells me that you are my aunt."

"That be true," the woman answered as she straightened the covers. "But you must call me Kerye. I insist."

"Lady— I mean Kerye, my mother—" She couldn't get the words out, but if anyone would know, it had to be this woman.

A sad look came over Kerye as she reached out and put a hand on the covers over Willoe's leg. "She passed when you were but a wee babe."

Willoe could feel a dampness at her eyes, and her lip quivered. "How?"

Kerye hesitated and Willoe could see it was not easy for her to speak. Finally she took a deep breath and said, "You and Rowyn had just entered your second year."

Looking at Willoe, Kerye's eyes were filled with a sadness that pulled at Willoe's heart.

"She sent a message saying that she had to get the children to me. Why, I don't know. I think she scried it was going to happen."

"Scried?" Willoe didn't want to interrupt, but felt she might miss something if she didn't know what exactly Kerye meant.

A light smile peeked out from Kerye's strained face. "She was the best there was. It was because of the blood, the blood we all have. Most people with the ability to scry can only see events happening within a few miles of their location. But your mother—" Kerye smiled wider and Willoe thought her aunt straightened a little with pride. "She could see people and events almost anywhere, given enough desire and with enough focus. That be how she be able to save your father."

A dozen questions ran through Willoe's mind. *What about the blood? How did she save my father?* But Kerye kept talking and Willoe wanted to hear the answer to the question that had scraped at the back of her mind since she was a child. *What had happened to my mother?*

"But Alina… that be her name." Kerye smiled as she said it.

Willoe took the name and consumed it, imprinted it in her mind.

Kerye's smile faded. She patted Willoe's leg again, a little pride still remaining in her voice. "Alina could do what no other scryer could do. She could not only scry distance, but to a lesser degree time. She could see images a wee bit into the future." Kerye's eyes were ablaze as she talked about her sister. "But I had only ever known her to look a turn or so at the most. In her note she said she saw something. Something to come." Her voice changed and Willoe could hear regret. "She never said what it be. I think it be something much further in the future than a turn or two, because she said she needed to get the children to me before… before it happened."

"She did not tell you later?" Willoe was almost scared to ask.

The grip on Willoe's leg told her that Kerye's next words would stick with Willoe for her entire life.

"I never saw her again. I be responding to her when Dougal arrived with the two of you, three days after I received the note. He told me that Alina be attacked and killed."

Willoe was shocked. She had expected an illness or accident, but to be intentionally killed. "How—? Who did it?" Willoe blurted out.

"We don't know. I mean, we don't know who." She moved to sit on the edge of the bed and put a hand on Willoe's head. "She be in the gardens with the two of you and three ladies-in-waiting. One of the companions said Alina had just looked out at the woods along the road that led to the manor, and said, 'I was wrong. They have arrived too soon.' Your mother told the women to take you children and run for the manor house. The lady be confused, but your mother ordered her in a tone, the lady said, that left no excuse but to move quickly. The other lady told of five men who came out of the woods, near the manor house, and tried to rush after the lady and the children who had just entered the manor."

Kerye had to stop for a moment to catch her breath. The retelling seemed to drain her, but she continued regardless. "The men cut down the third lady before the women could even react, but then Alina…" She stopped again. "Your mother be a brave woman. She stood between the men and you children. We had both learned to keep a knife strapped to our arms, under any dress." This made Willoe smile to herself at the thought of her mother and the knife. It was a little something they shared. Her aunt's eyes were swollen. "She killed two of the men with that knife, but took several deep wounds herself. The other three men made it past her and be headed for the manor. Alina be never much of a wizard. Besides scrying, she could do little else. But I imagine when she saw the men heading for you children she must have reached down inside herself and called upon her own Spirit to take the life of the three attackers."

Willoe did not know a lot about what Rowyn called the *il fennore*, but it was well known that a wizard couldn't draw the Spirit out of another person, otherwise wizards would be hunted down and killed out of fear. "I thought that was not possible."

"That's what most people think. But a wizard can call a Spiro to themselves and make the Spiro reach into the body of another and pull the Spirit out. It be called Spirit Void."

"That is terrible!" Willoe was horrified. "Why have I not heard of this?"

Kerye shook her head. "Because it almost never happens. You know that when a wizard calls upon the *il fennore* it drains some of the wizard's

Spirit."

"For a wizard to draw the Spirit out of another, the Spiro will use the wizard's own Spirit. It will drain one for one from both the victim and the wizard."

"But if the Spirit is totally drained, will not the wizard die?"

"Yes." Kerye nodded. "That be why you rarely hear of it." "My mother—?"

"She must have pulled the Spirit from all three of the attackers. They found all three stretched out on the path leading to the manor. The lady-in-waiting said they just collapsed as if their bones had been removed. One after another." Kerye had tears in her eyes. "But your mother, my sister, collapsed only after the last of the attackers fell to the ground. When the lady reached Alina she be already gone, but the lady told Dougal later that your mother had a smile on her face."

Kerye lay down next to Willoe, put her arm over Willoe's head and put the other arm over Willoe. "I think what she saw was the attack. And saw that the only way to stop it be to sacrifice herself. She had written Dougal, telling him he needed to bring you to me. This be before the attack. She made him promise to protect the both of you. From what, she did not say. Dougal arrived to save your mother the day after the attack."

Willoe rubbed her aunt's arm that lay across Willoe. Then she asked, "Did they ever find out who the attackers were?"

"They were sellswords. Why they wanted you children, no one knows."

They lay like that for a while before Willoe spoke with another tear starting to run down her nose as she sniffed. "Why did you send us away? You are our aunt."

Kerye stiffened as if struck by an arrow, then relaxed again. She sat back up, her back to Willoe. "There be reasons." She hesitated. "Life with me would not have been for the best." Kerye's voice faded with the memory. She turned her head to look over her shoulder at Willoe, her lips trembling. "I am… I have had to live in isolation." She raised her hand indicating the cottage around them.

"Why?" Willoe could tell there was a lot of pain behind her Aunt's words, but she felt there was something missing. Something important.

"I— we are different." Kerye stood and walked across the room before turning to look back at Willoe.

Willoe was afraid, but could see her questions were a strain on Kerye, so she tried to move on and resolved to ask more about her aunt's reason later. "You look a lot like me. Did my mother— do I look like her also?"

The hint of a smile crossed Kerye's face. "Yes. You look just like she did at your age. We be twins like you and Rowyn. But, like the both of you, we be different." She moved back to stand behind the chair and wiped away a tear from her cheek. As her smile grew she said in a more cheerful voice,

"But now you be here and we be together again." Kerye paused as if considering something. "Have you ever heard the words 'Dragon-Called?'" Kerye asked, her face drawn, though Willoe couldn't tell whether from fear or sadness.

Willoe shook her head.

Kerye sat down in the chair next to the bed. "There are old, ancient stories told of how dragons be the guardians of the world, the Burning Lady's emissaries to the world of men, Elfs, and all the other creatures under the Burning Lady's care."

Willoe could attest to this herself, but held back from telling her aunt about the golden dragon.

"There be one story told of a time when men first ventured onto these lands. There was a king, as much Elf as man, who created a pact with the dragons. As the story goes, the dragons had saved this halfling king's people from destruction by Spirits of the Dark. Spirits not of the Burning Lady, but sent from the Dark Lord himself. In return this king swore to give his blood, and the blood of his descendants, if and when the dragons required the king's assistance. Those summoned by the dragons would be known as the Dragon-Called."

She went on to tell Willoe how twins were born in each generation of descendants that had special abilities and waited to be called by the dragons, called once again to fight against the dark Spirits.

Willoe thought of the fire beneath her skin and the blood she had borne on her hands. *Could that be me?*

Before she could ask, Kerye answered. "My dear sister, your mother, had the ancient blood flowing through her veins, as do you and Rowyn."

"Did her blood feel like it was boiling?" Willoe asked quickly, a little excited to think that maybe what she felt was not all that strange, but her excitement quickly diminished as Kerye shook her head, wearing a frown.

Kerye stood up and walked to the end of the bed and then strode back and forth, wringing her hands as she appeared to be looking up at the ceiling to avoid looking directly at the bed. Willoe's eyes followed her aunt as Kerye went from one end of the bed to the other and back again. Finally Kerye stopped and looked down at Willoe, her expression drawn with tension.

"No, she did not. Only those that are Dragon-Called have this feeling."

Willoe finally had a name for the fire, but did not understand why her mother had not felt the fire this way. "I thought you said she was Dragon-Called?"

"I said she could be Dragon-Called, not that she be." Kerye sat back down next to the bed and reached out, taking one of Willoe's hands in both of her own. She stared into Willoe's eyes and said very slowly, "The twins in our family carry the blood of the ancient halfling king. And we all have special abilities such as your mother's scrying. But the feeling you describe, the heating of the blood, only happens if the twins be called by the dragons to fulfill the covenant." She paused and lowered her head, then raised it once again to look into Willoe's eyes with a sadness that Willoe didn't understand.

Willoe had a sense that there was something more that she needed to know. "What are you not telling me?" It took several moments for Kerye to say anything and then, when she did, it was barely a whisper. "Only a few times in these thousands of years have the dragons invoked the covenant. But in all cases, to defeat the evil, one of the descendant twins be sacrificed. Either you or Rowyn will die so the other can face the dark Spirits."

The flaming eyes sprang back into Willoe's mind and she could hear again the voice at the pond. *To save thyself, and thy twin, ye must find the sword and the staff.* Following her instincts, Willoe asked, "Where is the sword and the staff?"

Kerye sat back, her eyes wide, then she shook her head. "Where did you hear that?"

"Please just tell me you know." Willoe's heart started to sink as she realized it might really just have been a dream.

"I don't know for sure." Kerye stared off as if deep in thought. "The story does not say anything 'bout them, but other stories, ones that came after, tell of a Sword and a Staff that the dragons made for the Dragon-Called."

"Do the stories say where they can be found?" The hope flooded back.

A smile started to work its way onto her aunt's face. "They do, but they may only be rumors. A bard enhancing the original tale."

Willoe almost jumped out of her bed as she latched onto this thread of hope.

"There are tales of a Sword and a Staff made by the dragons, but not why they were created." The smile faded as Kerye seemed to remember something. "The tales also say that the Sword and the Staff can be found... found in the Hoarfrost Mountains."

The Hoarfrost Mountains, Willoe thought as she slumped back down into the bed. The most northern tip of Taran. A place where no man lived. Or, if they did venture there, they would not live for long. Her eyes started to swell as she realized that this sword and staff – the only things that could save her and Rowyn – were hidden away amidst and most likely guarded by the ferocious legendary Ice Giants.

61

Eastward

They had stumbled and dragged themselves upriver for what Drem thought was a few turns of the glass. The sun had set and darkness had closed in around them. He had pushed them until they finally dropped from fatigue. When they stopped, all sat around trying to catch their breath, every one of them dripping blood from various wounds on arms, legs, and head. Lord Brom went from man to man, followed by Drel Donlin, starting with the Crown Prince. Lord Brom and the Tink put their hands on Beynon as the two of them closed their eyes. Beynon closed his own eyes, as if he were napping, and then he woke. As Lord Brom stood, Beynon had quit bleeding and the color started to return to his face. Lord Brom and the Tink moved around the circle to each of the men, each falling asleep and wakening with their cuts healing.

The Lord knelt next to Drem and put his hands on Drem's left shoulder. His small companion reached out and put his hands on Drem's right one. Drem felt a warmth spread through his body and he closed his eyes, nearly forgetting where he was. When he opened them he felt, if not rested, at least refreshed. He looked up and Lord Brom smiled down at him. Drem put his hand up to his cheek and could feel where the wound was already beginning to seal.

After they had rested the command staff sat and talked while the guardsmen watched for any pursuit.

The Prince spoke first. "We are most likely on our own. If anyone came back to look for us they would only find the Franchons and assume we were either dead or captured."

Everyone nodded and Drem asked, "What are our chances of joining up with the main army or of making our own way to Mount Somerled?" He looked to General Rees who seemed to be familiar with this area more than any of the others.

The General thought for a moment. "It be we could'a find the army, but they be ahead and to the west. We be just as likely run into Franchon patrols. If we follow the river north we be able cut west toward Somerled. Again, Franchon patrols to contend with."

They had started to discuss the options then Lord Brom spoke up. "The most likely case is that we will run into Franchon patrols. They will be scouring all the routes north and west, looking for stragglers."

Again everyone nodded.

Lord Brom continued. "I believe our best chance is to the east."

All of them, even Sulyen, started to argue with him.

He stood and walked around behind his brother and put his hands on the back of Beynon's shoulders. "I think we can find help if we head to the Blackburn Mountains."

Beynon's head snapped up to look at his brother and the rest of them just stared at the Prince's strange reaction.

"Do you think—" Beynon started, but Lord Brom interrupted him.

"Yes," was all Lord Brom said.

None of the rest of them spoke, everyone seeming a little confused until Beynon stood.

"We are going east."

"We be going right into the lion's lair."

Lord Brom walked back around the circle. "Where they would not be looking for us."

"Why the Blackburn?" Sulyen asked.

"Friends," was all Lord Brom would say.

"We can cross at Snake Ridge." Drem pictured the river winding up toward his castle.

At General Rees' command, two guardsmen started north, through the heavy underbrush, toward Snake Ridge where they could still cross the Saltrock without too much difficulty. Drem wasn't sure where they were going, after they crossed into Franchon, or why, but he was bound to follow his friend and Prince.

62

A Lonely Choice

Bat-Uul looked over at Prince Mael, who wore a plain simple robe, tied at the waist, the hood pulled up even though the rain was starting to subside. The Prince sat on his horse with Bat-Uul on one side and the Franchon general on the other. They were escorted by large sturdy warriors, the ones Bat-Uul had only heard of, but had never seen before this campaign: the deadly Jidig. Bat-Uul had seen them defeat three times their number in practice, since their arrival at White Cliffs, and he had no reason to believe they would perform any differently in battle.

Their small group sat mounted on the north side of the barrier the Cainwen defenders had built and that now lay in ruins. Smoke drifted on the air from the broken and burning logs.

Dimah-Uul had not shown the Cainwen defenders any mercy. Not a single one lived, though he had questioned a few of the wounded before putting them to the sword. Mael cringed every time one of his countrymen dropped to the ground, blood draining from the cut across their neck.

The twisted older priest mounted his horse after personally slitting the throat of the last tied-up prisoner. He rode back to their group and commanded the General. "Their army is headed north, toward the Pembroke castle."

The General nodded his head and said, "Castle Mount Somerled."

"Their mounted units have been mostly destroyed, thanks to the sellswords." The look on Dimah-Uul's face as he said it made Bat-Uul sick.

Bat-Uul's mind revisited the scene of the slaughter, at the southern gap, and it turned his stomach, but the perverted little priest had seemed to enjoy it, even relished in the death and destruction.

Dimah-Uul reined his horse so he could look north and pointed. "The foot will be making their way along the edge of the forest. I understand there is a large field a several miles north of here to move the troops. There is a village and quite a few farms just west of the field where you can get whatever supplies you need." He added with stern voice, "Leave nothing."

The General's eyebrows lifting was the only sign Bat-Uul could see that the man disagreed with Dimah-Uul's command. The grim fate of the man's predecessor was cause enough for the General to hold his tongue. The General turned his head and spoke to an aide, who rode off toward a group of commanders and other Shields who seemed to be keeping their distance from the Uuls and the foreign warriors.

Bat-Uul could hear some of the commanders calling out orders to their troops nearby, while others rode back past the group to start getting their own soldiers moving.

"We will rest tonight and then, in the morning, you should not have a problem running down the cowards." Dimah-Uul started forward behind the first group of soldiers heading north when Mael called out, though timidly.

"My father?"

Dimah-Uul turned his horse and rode back to stop right next to the Prince, their legs touching.

Mael's shoulders hunched and he leaned a little away from the priest.

He didn't know why, but Bat-Uul nudged his horse closer to Mael, giving the young Prince whatever support he could. It did not surprise Bat-Uul that the Cainwen Prince shrank from Dimah-Uul. Bat-Uul did not know what had happened between the two, but after the Cainwens' escape, he had not seen Prince Mael for several days. When he had next seen the young man, the Prince was nothing like the man who had threatened Di-mah-Uul at the bridge. He cowered at even the slightest movement by Di-mah-Uul. It reminded Bat-Uul of the cat that roamed the temple in Avanis. It kept watching everything, in all directions, and was always ready to jump away at the remotest hint of a threat. But it wasn't just Dimah-Uul. Prince Mael reacted the same way to both Bat-Uul and Chuluun-Uul. Anyone wearing a red robe, in fact.

Leveraging the Prince's trepidation, Dimah-Uul reached a finger out toward Mael's face.

The Prince flinched and turned his head away, his eyes squinted.

"Don't worry, my Prince." Dimah-Uul snorted. "We have not found his body yet. But we will." He pulled back his hand. "Your grandfather may already be gone and you will soon enough be on the throne." His expression shifted, a menacing tone filling his voice. "Unless you would rather have another lesson."

The Prince hunched even more at the priest's threat.

Dimah-Uul snickered. "In that case, we always have your sniveling younger brother." He laughed loudly, turned his horse and spurred it north.

Hundreds of campfires dotted the fields on both sides of the road as Bat-Uul walked away from the nobles' pavilions and the thousands of the tents, though tent was probably too generous a word. Many of the common soldiers slept in what they called a canvas lluest. Two sticks, crossed at the top, in the front and back, with another stick laid at the top, front to back, and a canvas cover draped over the top. It wasn't much, but kept the wind at bay.

His heart moaned at noticing just how many more of the lights had dotted the army's camp just a few days ago. So many dead, on both sides. Bat-Uul walked farther away from the main camp along the road. He needed to get away from the others. *No*, he corrected himself. He needed to get away from his superior, Dimah-Uul.

He finally came to a stop and turned his face upwards. The clouds had cleared and he looked up into a sky filled with specks of light. "Is this your will, Master? Where is the Shin-il Way in all this blood?" He knew his words only floated on the air, but the burden on his Spirit was tearing at the very fabric of who he was. How could he reconcile his own faith with the events of the last few weeks? His last view of the battlefield was of blood flowing freely, like the Saltrock itself. And all in the name of the Shin-il Way.

Tears came as he continued to look up and prayed to something, he knew not what, for some guidance; some insight from the flickering lights, but nothing came. A sudden thought came to him. Something he had been told by his old teacher, Poojan-Uul, at the temple. *"The truth can be found in your own heart. When you encounter that which you question, but your mind cannot settle, look to the canon and your own heart… the truth will become clear."*

He had nearly forgotten the serenity he had always felt as an acolyte and a Jin priest. He thought of the canon.

"The body does not destroy itself." But does it destroy others? he wondered.

"Conflict is brought about by differences." True, he thought.

"Eliminate differences and conflict is eliminated." Again true, but at what expense?

"When all are as one body, peace and harmony shall ensue." Again, at what expense? his mind argued.

"Peace and harmony are a choice each must make on their own."

The last sentence sat with him as he focused on the final words. *"A choice each must make on their own."* He had to make a choice. He looked down and closed his eyes as he considered what he would do. Opening his eyes, he turned back to the camp and walked back with purpose.

He passed several patrols as he walked directly toward Dimah-Uul's pavilion. It was easy to find as it was largest of the all the noble lodgings, and was located toward the rear of the camp. Bat-Uul grimaced as he thought how it was just another example of how the twisted priest rejected the basic tenets of the Shin-il Way. *One must lead from the bottom so not only the top will benefit.* Poojan-Uul had taught him that a priest must think little of himself and only of others. His words floated to Bat-Uul on the wind. *"Ego was the root that drove priests from the Way; wealth and power the signs of their transgressions."*

He approached the pavilion entrance and his mind noticed vaguely that no guards were visible as he pushed through the flap. He stumbled over the bodies of the two guards just inside the pavilion entrance, but regained his footing. They lay crumpled one on top of the other with blood running out in a puddle under them. He heard a grunt and looked up to see, at the back of the large tent, Prince Mael holding Dimah-Uul by the collar of his nightrobe. They were chest to chest which only confused Bat-Uul more. Dimah-Uul turned his head toward Bat-Uul, his eyes wide, and he opened his mouth to say something, but only blood leaked down his lips.

Prince Mael stepped back and let Dimah-Uul drop, the priest trying to grab hold of the Prince as he slid to the ground. The long hilt of a knife stuck out from the nightrobe, just below the ribs.

The Prince looked down on the body, the skin on the Prince's face pulled taut with a tenseness Bat-Uul could only imagine. Through gritted teeth the young Prince said, "I keep my promises, Priest." He finished by spitting on the priest's limp body.

Bat-Uul remembered the Prince's words as clearly as it had just happened. *You will die for that, Priest.*

The Prince turned toward Bat-Uul as if he had just noticed the priest had entered.

Bat-Uul thought to run or at least call for help, but he saw the pain in the tormented Prince's eyes and held his voice.

"He deserved to die," the Prince said.

Bat-Uul heard a voice — his own — say, "I know."

At that the Prince seemed to fold up on himself. He dropped to his knees, his head hanging forward.

Bat-Uul ran over to the Prince and kept him from falling over. He noticed the blood blotting the front of the Prince's robe. The priest looked around for something else and grabbed a cotton cover that was at the foot of the dead priest's bed. He wrapped the cover around the Prince and up over his head, then he made the Prince stand.

He did not know why he was doing what was running through his mind, but he told the Prince, "Keep your head down and say nothing. I am going to walk you to your tent."

The Prince raised an arm to push himself away, but Bat-Uul grabbed the weak young man and spoke as calmly as he could, considering what he had planned. "I am going to walk you back to your tent and you are going to pretend you know nothing of what happened here tonight."

The look the Prince gave him was one of wonder and relief.

"Walk. I will be right next to you." He started the Prince moving toward the pavilion flap.

They exited the pavilion and Bat-Uul breathed a sigh of relief that no one saw them come out. They walked past several pavilions without anyone stopping them or even looking in their direction. It must have just looked like the priest walking with someone, maybe even a woman, judging from the way the Prince was wrapped. Bat-Uul thought it said something about the dead priest that no one would notice a priest alone with a woman.

As they passed one of the smaller pavilions, Bat-Uul told the Prince to stop. Hanging off the side of the pavilion were several over-shirts that had been hung out earlier to dry and had been forgotten. Bat-Uul pulled the Prince over and grabbed one of the light over-shirts. "Take off the cover and robe." He pulled the cotton cover off the Prince and helped him to get the bloody robe over his head. "Put this on." He looked around them to make sure no one saw them as the Prince slid the shirt over his head. It reached down to his knees. Luckily no blood had gotten on the Prince's leggings. "It's a little big, but it will do. Now to your tent."

They walked, this time with Bat-Uul behind as if the Prince were his prisoner. It wasn't much farther before Bat-Uul spotted the small pavilion where the Prince was being held.

As they walked up two of the Jidig stepped forward to intercept them, their curved swords out and ready. The warriors wore their traditional leather vests with leather shoulder-pads, layered leather padding down the arms and separate leather strips on the forearms. Metal plates were sewn into the leather vest. Bat-Uul had seen how the layers of leather, and the metal-embedded leather vest could deflect a weapon like chainmail.

The warriors' faces expressed their confusion and one began to babble in his native tongue.

Bat-Uul held up a hand and answered in what little he knew of the language spoken by the steppe warriors. "Return after talk."

The warrior's eyebrows knotted and then he asked another question. Bat-Uul couldn't understand everything the warrior said, but he grasped that the warrior was insistent that the Prince should not be out of the tent.

"Before. Other guards." Bat-Uul knew that earlier in the day Franchon soldiers had held guard until additional Jidig guards could be brought up to the camp. He hoped that lack of contact between the Franchon and Jidig would keep any questions from being asked.

The warrior was silent for a moment. Finally grasping what Bat-Uul meant, he said something Bat-Uul didn't understand, but the warrior grabbed a hold of Prince Mael's arm and led him toward the pavilion.

The Prince turned his head to look back at Bat-Uul and, in the flicker of the fire, Bat-Uul could see the Prince bow his head before the warrior pushed him through the flap and into the pavilion.

Walking back toward his own small pavilion — not much more than a space for him and Caspar-Jin and a few supplies — Bat-Uul wondered what the Franchon General would think when Dimah-Uul's body was found. He didn't have long to wait because just then an alarm was sounded, guards yelling and feet pounding across the back of the camp.

"My Uul." Caspar-Jin came running up to him, out of breath. He stopped, leaned forward, and put his hands on his knees. "You were not in your tent."

It was dark and Bat-Uul had trouble making out his aide's face, but from what he could see it looked as accusing as the tone in Caspar-Jin's voice.

"I went for a walk." He kept his voice calm, though the pounding in his chest said otherwise. "What is the noise for?"

"Dimah-Uul." The aide pointed across the camp. "He has been murdered."

Bat-Uul offered what he hoped was a shocked expression as he thought that 'murdered' was probably the wrong word. 'Payment' seemed more fitting.

"Lead the way." Bat-Uul followed his aide, who kept looking back at Bat-Uul as they wove their way around tents toward the largest pavilion. There would be a lot of shouting and accusations, but in the end they would all turn to Bat-Uul. With Dimah-Uul dead, the officers would assume Bat-Uul would take command. He was already thinking of his rationale for not pursuing the Cainwens. He would spread out half the army along the river, holding what they had already fought and died for, possibly even placing troops around Mount Somerled. Spread out, they could also forage for their own food without putting too great a strain on any of the locals that still lived. The other half he would send back to White Cliffs. Bat-Uul had no doubt General Lozon would not present much of an argument. The man did not seem to relish continuing the fight any more than Bat-Uul himself.

Bat-Uul would return to White Cliffs and he would take the Prince with him, though he knew not what to do with him. Or even why he had helped the Cainwen Prince.

He would tell the Gai-Ten that they had stretched their supply line as far as they could safely go. Sending half the army back to White Cliffs lessened the supply burden and also provided extra security if the Haldanes took the opportunity, with much of the Franchon army away, to move across the northern border. Chuluun-Uul would see the soundness of that. It was something Bat-Uul was sure the Gai-Ten would do himself. Bat-Uul had been in Taran long enough to know the Haldanes would never start a campaign with winter approaching. Chuluun-Uul would most likely believe Bat-Uul. After all, the only other Uul who would know such information was Dimah-Uul, and he couldn't say anything. Bat-Uul approached the turmoil encircling the dead priest's pavilion, his mind reciting the last line of the cannon. *"Peace and harmony are a choice each must make on their own."* There had been enough death for one day.

63

No Safe Haven

It had been three days since Willoe, dressed again as Rowyn, had been out and about the makeshift camp. She could see that the men were as restless as she was herself. Tents, brought along from White Cliffs, were set up to the front of the house with a few between the house and the stream. But what had grown since her arrival was the number of makeshift lean-tos that had sprung up around the rest of the cottage and into the woods. Many were fugitives from Lealacité that had wandered into the mountains and been brought to the small valley. In a matter of days their numbers had grown to three times that of the Cainwen company. It made for a strange mixture of Cainwen and Franchon loyalists, which was what the refugees called themselves.

The crackle of campfires, even in the middle of the day, had become a common sound as the weather had continued to grow colder. She strode over to one of the fires and rubbed her hands together, holding them out over the flames for warmth.

Willoe caught sight of Aeron hurrying to come up to the command tent, buckling his belt as he half-walked, half-ran. Willoe looked back to where he had come from and saw Emeline exiting from a tent stuck back away behind some of the others. Emeline straightened her dress and turned her head from side to side, scanning the tents around her. She pulled her shoulders back and took a step, then glanced over and saw Willoe looking in her direction. Blushing, Emeline smiled at Willoe and held a hand up to her mouth to stifle a laugh before continuing to walk back across the camp toward the cottage. Willoe looked at Aeron, who had noticed the exchange. He only grinned sheepishly and Willoe just shook her head and fought to keep a smile off her face.

Willoe stepped around the fire toward the table where Captain Harte, Count Idwal, Master Gwron, several Shields and Protector Dougal stood pointing at a map while in deep discussion. Looking down at the map she saw that it was hand-drawn and roughly depicted the northern lands of Franchon, the southern edge of Haldane, the western tip of the Blackburn Mountains that ran along the edge of them both, and Tierran's Wall that ran from the Blackburn Mountains to the Bay of Lost Spirits.

Count Idwal looked up at Willoe's approach. "Prince Rowyn. You are looking better every day." He smiled and made room for Willoe next to him at the table. Moving up next to the table she put both hands down and leaned over, looking at the map. "Any word yet?"

Count Idwal answered, "Lady Kerye tells us that a Cainwen army was defeated two days ago along the Saltrock. How she knows this is unknown, but it makes sense. Last we saw the Franchon army, they were moving west. We have reports of troops moving back. Either there was a battle and the Franchons were defeated with this, the remnants running back, or, as Lady Kerye says, the Franchons won and are now redeploying their troops. Many marching north."

"I think she is correct." Willoe leaned forward on the table to look more closely at the map. "If the Franchons had lost they would be fleeing back to White Cliffs, not to the border with Haldane."

"That matched our thoughts." The other men nodded in agreement with Captain Harte.

Willoe thought about what she had just said and what that meant. She had to wonder if her father, Hafgan, and others she had known were still alive or had died defending her homeland. If a Cainwen army had been defeated, what would become of Westhedge? Her grandfather, Steward Robat and everyone else she knew? But she also couldn't dwell on that which she could not control, especially from the Blackburn Mountains. She tried to focus on what she could control.

"To what purpose, though?" Willoe questioned out loud.

Protector Dougal, who had been standing slightly back, now stepped forward. "They be intending to take Tierran's Wall before winter sets in and use it as a base to attack Haldane in the spring."

Willoe considered the idea and it seemed more and more likely Protector Dougal was correct. *But why attack Haldane?* There was little to be gained by taking the northern kingdom.

Kerye walked up and, as if she had heard Willoe's question, said, "It be not the Franchons."

Everyone looked at Kerye with the same questioning expressions.

She waited a moment before explaining. "The red-robed priest be behind these moves. They don't want just Franchon and Cainwen. They want all of Taran."

"But why?" Count Idwal asked.

"The priests leading that army do not serve the Burning Lady. They call upon the dark Spirits to do their work." Kerye spread her hands in a circle over the map. "They do not want the lands of the kingdoms. They want the Spirit of Taran."

Willoe could understand a little of what her aunt was saying. The idea that Rowyn and she had been called to fulfill a covenant with the dragons meant there was a great evil upon the land. It made sense that the foreign priests were the evil she talked about.

"We have to stop them," one of the Shields blurted out.

"Yes, we do," Kerye stated.

Willoe looked up to see her aunt staring at her across the table.

All the men nodded, their focus still on the map, but Kerye just lifted her face and peered into Willoe's eyes with a sad expression.

Walking through the woods along the stream, Willoe still wondered at the experience of having a woman for a friend. There was always Casandra, but though her cousin could be elegant and courtly, underneath she was a madcap like Willoe. She could be just as gritty and brazen as Willoe, but then the next moment turn on the charm and resemble any other noble lady.

Emeline, however, was different. She was as true a noble lady as any Willoe had met. Proper in every way. It was true that Emeline had gone against her uncle, King Benoit, and the conniving Shin-il priests, and Willoe did give the woman credit for stashing a knife up her dress, but she still wasn't Casandra.

Willoe thought that maybe it was because the woman was a couple of years older, around Aeron's age. So it amazed Willoe that she had come to like the Franchon woman so quickly. Emeline had been very helpful during Willoe's recovery and through their many talks, she had found the woman cheerful, intelligent, and someone who did not flinch at hard work. She would fetch water and boil it over the hearth herself where she could have easily requested one of the servants handle the work. Willoe now understood what her cousin Aeron saw in Emeline, besides the alluring physical attributes. Both had spoken separately to Willoe of their love for each other. A few months of being thrown together by their superiors had led to a relationship that seemed to sit well with the both of them.

It had been two weeks since Willoe had revived and she knew they couldn't stay in the valley forever. The reports continued to come in with stragglers from Lealacité that a battle had been fought at Daere Mawr, with the Cainwens routed. No word could be found on her father or Aeron's father the duke. This only heightened Willoe's desire to take some type of action, though she had no inkling as to what it should be. Count Idwal, Captain Harte, and some of the others had talked about trying to fight their way through to Winterpass, but all the discussion always led to the fact that they just didn't have the numbers.

"Do you think we will ever see White Cliffs again?" Emeline asked, picking up a stick and tossing it into the water as they strolled between the trees that ran right up to the bank of the stream.

Willoe twisted her head and looked at Emeline. The woman was looking out across the stream, almost as if she was afraid to look at Willoe.

"I do not know." Willoe said it as softly as she could, hoping to reduce the impact.

Emeline stopped and turned back to look at Willoe. "Everything is different now."

Willoe could only nod.

Emeline faced forward and they both started to walk again. Emeline picked up another stick and tossed it between two trees into the stream.

Willoe watched it as it floated away.

After a few moments Emeline spoke. "Aeron tells me that patrols have been spotted in the lower hills."

"Yes. Sellswords with Franchon guardsmen. And a few of the Shin-il's strange warriors. They have been menacing the local villages."

"I have heard many of the villagers have fled into the mountains," Emeline acknowledged and then added, "Some have joined us in the valley."

Over two hundred had made their way up to the valley. The Franchon loyalists that had fled Lealacité had stretched the Cainwens' supplies, but the guardsmen shared what they had as best they could. The hunters had killed or driven off much of the local game and the concern was that with over four hundred, the supplies would not hold out too much longer. This only enforced Willoe's decision to do something. It weighed on her mind, yet she had not come up with any plan that made sense.

Emeline shook her head and frowned. "I never thought I would see the time when my uncle would employ sellswords. He was fond of saying they were nothing but riffraff and the lowest of curs."

Willoe could see the woman's eyes swell.

"How could he do this?" Emeline demanded of the air.

Willoe shook her head, frowning, and they continued their walk in silence. The sun had passed over the mountain, the last flicker of purple, rose, blue, and green fading as dusk began to overtake them. They were almost back to the main campsite when a noise filled the air.

It was as if something were crashing through the forest. Willoe turned and looked toward the hill above the cottage. The treetops blocked much of her view but she could make out specks of light pouring down the hill and she could hear shouts of alarm. She started to run along the shoreline, cutting inland when the shore was blocked, with Emeline right behind her. From the shoreline she was able to look between the trees and could see flames spouting up ahead. She could also now hear the clink of swords and shields mingled with cries of pain.

They darted from the shoreline, around another barrier, and as branches of the trees whipped against her face and arms, Willoe burst out into the clearing around the cottage. Emeline came up next to her, breathing heavily.

"What is it?" Emeline managed to get out between breaths.

Willoe didn't answer, but looked toward the cottage that was already engulfed in flames. The sound of fighting made her turn toward the hill where, across the clearing, Cainwens were battling Franchon guardsmen and sellswords. She saw Count Idwal, his sword swinging from left to right, slicing through two guardsmen who came within his reach. Master Gwron held a weapon in each hand, one of which Willoe didn't even recognize. He was forcing back three of the attackers who seemed barely able to hold their own.

She watched as Captain Harte's young lieutenant was cut down by two men, a Franchon guardsman and a sellsword, who had backed the lieutenant up against two trees twisted together. Other Cainwens were down as were a large number of Franchons and sellswords. It was getting darker and only the light of tents on fire allowed her to see the battle. She cursed herself as she had left her sword in the cottage, an apprentice mistake. Several swords lay about where their owners had dropped them and Willoe started out toward the closest.

Willoe had taken two steps when Aeron ran from the direction of the stream, heading to her left in front of her. He held his sword out, blood soaking the edge. He only had on leggings, running bare-chested as if he had just come from a swim.

He turned his head toward her and skidded to a halt.

Willoe stopped short. She had forgotten about Emeline until the woman bumped into her from behind, almost knocking them both off their feet.

Aeron ran up to them, wet hair hanging down around his shoulders. He had a small cut on his cheek and another on his left arm. "Where have you been?" he demanded, his breath coming in spurts. "Never mind." He grabbed Willoe with his free hand and turned her toward the shoreline on the other side of the clearing, away from the main battle. "Go, go!" He pushed Willoe and then grabbed Emeline and pushed her after.

"Hurry!" he yelled as he ran behind them.

They reached the shoreline to find Ser Tanguy and a dozen guardsmen in full armor with horses, all saddled. A few servants — one of them the groomsman, Doy — stood holding the horses.

"I found them!" Aeron yelled out as they came near the waiting group.

Everyone waiting turned as Aeron, Willoe, and Emeline approached.

A moment later Protector Dougal ran up, both swords out and dripping red with their use. Captain Harte was with him, along with several guardsmen. They all looked tense and worn.

"Good. We need to get the Prince away," Captain Harte commanded.

Tanguy nodded and turned to the others of his escort. "Prepare to mount."

The guardsmen went to their horses, taking reins from the servants who had been holding them. The two that would be the forward guard mounted.

Willoe noticed several packhorses loaded with supplies.

"What is this?" Willoe was confused and stood unmoving as she scanned the escort armed and ready to rush her away from the battle.

Aeron sheathed his sword and grabbed her arm again. "A contingent has been ready to move since the day we arrived. If needed." He grabbed Emeline with his other hand and started to move them both toward the two waiting horses that groomsman Doy held for them. "If something like this happened."

"Why was I not told?" she argued, dragging her feet. "I will not leave our troops." She couldn't believe they had done this without telling her. "And Kerye."

"That is why you were not told." Aeron pulled her, his grip tightening, pushing into her muscles. "I saw Kerye run into the woods earlier. She will be fine."

Willoe wasn't going to let herself be dragged away and let more die because of her. The simmering responded and she ripped her arm loose from Aeron. She spun back to the clearing to see Count Idwal racing toward them. She was amazed the elder noble could move as fast as he was.

When the count reached them, he took a deep breath and stood tall, a feat many younger men would have trouble handling after intense sword-play and a hard run. "The hill is blocked. You will have to take the trail north." He pointed to a trail that ran along the shoreline nearest them, heading north, in the opposite direction Willoe and Emeline had gone earlier.

Protector Dougal and Captain Harte nodded together.

The count turned to Willoe. "My Prince, you must leave now. Or all this is wasted." He turned his upper body and waved his sword at the battle raging around the cottage. As he turned back, the light of multiple fires reflected off the sweat pouring down the count's face. He looked at her, bushy eyebrows and beard dripping wet, his face stern and determined, but his eyes pleaded with her.

Part of Willoe wanted to cry at the loss of life, and another part, the part that was starting to rise inside her, wanted to run into the fray. But the latter part had not grown enough to take control. She closed her eyes, nodded, then opened them again and turned to the horses.

Before she reached her horse several bolts flew into their midst. One guardsman screamed as a bolt stuck in his arm, and one of the mounted guardsmen flew from his horse, a bolt sticking out of his chest.

The guardsmen and Ser Tanguy pulled swords and turned to the northern trail, the direction from where the bolts had come. A score of sellswords and Franchon guardsmen charged out of the trail at the Cainwens.

64

Runes of Hope

It took all the next day to reach Peltbush. Rowyn didn't think the little town was much of anything, but it did have a tavern where they could get a hot meal and a room. Living in a trading town, the inhabitants were used to seeing many strange things and Rowyn guessed that Elfs also frequented the town on occasion, as Cian and the others did not draw too many stares. Krel Monlor and Swift, the massive Borlender, stayed back in the woods along with the Kata-henis. Cian apparently felt the inhabitants of Peltbush would only be so accommodating.

Two days in the town and they had not made any decisions as to their next move. They could go back to Fayhaven, but Rowyn thought they should try to get word to Willoe in White Cliffs and make arrangements to join up with her to explain about the Dragon-Called. He was curious if she had had any strange experiences. He also worried about the way fire had taken him over on that boulder. It might have been a fire-driven dream, but if he truly had called upon his twin's Spirit, he needed to find a way to control whatever was in him. If he couldn't control the fire, then he couldn't control whatever he did with the *il fennore*. The fire said Willoe lived, but if he couldn't control it, then he might kill her without even knowing it. The fire had a life of its own and he was not the master of it.

Rowyn sat in the tavern's common area, sipping on the ale. It didn't taste much better than it smelled, but the wine was even worse. He was waiting for Cian and Rhein. The old Elf and the Shield had become friends. The two of them were down at the docks assessing available riverboats. Even though they had not made definite plans, knowing what transportation they could use might be of help when they did finally decide.

He took another gulp of the ale and had to fight to keep it down. He looked around at the usual mix of farmers, boatmen, traders and locals. Nothing impressive and nothing that he had not observed over the last two days. He waited a few more moments and sighed. The boredom was starting to get to him. He leaned back in the chair and felt something press against his ribs.

He reached inside the pocket of his cloak and pulled out the ancient book of runes. He had nearly forgotten he still had it. He opened it up and started to take another drink of the ale, then stopped as the odor hit him first. He put it back down and looked down at the book. He had meant to show the book to Cian, but with everything that had happened... He licked his fingers and rapidly flipped through the book until he came to a page that had the corner turned down. He looked at each of the symbols and then came to a stop near the bottom. He read the runes there twice. *Yes, they are the same.*

The sound of the table being jostled made him look up. Cian and Ser Rhein had just sat down and were looking at him.

"What is that?" Cian asked as he tilted his head, trying to read it upside down. Rowyn held it up. "My Uncle Brom gave this to me. He found it in the midst of his collection and thought it might help me, somehow." He leaned forward, turned the book around so that it faced Cian, and pointed to the runes.

"The Sword and the Staff," Cian took the book and repeated the words slowly, then added, "It is the key to controlling the fire."

"It can be controlled?" Rowyn sat back with a thud. He had hoped, but did not think it possible.

Cian started running his finger across the page and began speaking in a mish-mash of words that Rowyn could not comprehend. The Elf flipped the page, read through it, then the other side and then flipped to another. He finally sat back. "Wonderful."

He just sat there staring at the ceiling, the way he did when he was deep in thought.

Rowyn and Rhein stared at him for a few moments until Rhein asked, "What is this Sword?"

"A Sword and a Staff," Cian responded. "It is the thing that might keep Prince Rowyn and Princess Willoe alive."

"Keep them alive?" Rhein's question was never answered as Cian came out of his thoughts.

"The book tells of devices, made by the dragons, that would allow the Dragon-Called to control the fire." Cian smiled. "It also tells the location of the instruments of the dragons."

"Dragons? Dragon-Called?" Rhein's outburst made several of the tavern occupants turn, but only for a moment.

Rowyn put a hand on Rhein's shoulder. "Yes, dragons. It must be related to the covenant."

"Covenant?"

Rowyn thought Rhein's questions were becoming annoying. "We will explain later," he told the Shield.

He turned back to Cian. "Where? Where are they?"

Cian's smile faded; his white hair hung down and framed his face as he looked at Rowyn. Without a blink he said, "In a valley deep in a mountain."

"Which mountain?" Rowyn had hoped for something, but had not really believed it.

"It does not say." Cian frowned.

Rowyn grabbed for the book and as he pulled it away a small folded paper fell out onto the table.

Rhein picked it up and unfolded it. He tilted his head as he read it, his eyebrows knitted.

"What?" Rowyn almost grabbed the paper from the Shield's hand.

Rhein looked up, still seemingly confused, and said, "Hoarfrost?"

Rowyn was speechless. He had expected the artifacts would be hidden somewhere difficult to find, but the Hoarfrost Mountains? Rowyn didn't even know exactly where they were located, other than somewhere at the northern tip of Taran. It was insane. They would have to make their way through and beyond Haldane, over the freezing peaks rumored to touch the stars, and he couldn't forget about the Ice Giants.

Rowyn, then, was just as surprised as anyone when he heard himself say, "When do we leave?"

"What does a dragon have to do with the Prince?" Rhein argued with Cian.

"It has to do with the Covenant." Prince Rowyn closed his eyes and shook his head.

Rhein was trying to understand, but he had never even heard of this King Cormac, and why would some covenant, made thousands of years in the past, cause the Prince to charge off into the dangerous northern lands?

"It is not a matter of choice." Rowyn opened his eyes and let out a deep breath. "What you need to know is that there are, or at least were, dragons at one time, and if I don't find the devices they made, either myself or Princess Willoe will surely die."

Cian nodded his agreement.

Rhein was still not convinced, but it seemed as if the Prince and the Elfs were determined to make their way to the Hoarfrost Mountains, and Lady Casandra had already told Rhein she would not return to Westhedge.

"Would it not make sense to at least get help from Fort Winterpass?" Rhein only had himself, Sergeant Crowley, and two guardsmen to escort the party, though from what he had seen of the two young Elfs' abilities they would be a blessing from the Burning Lady. He had come to grips with Dilys' illusions, but what Cian and the Prince had done was beyond his understanding. He could not argue with the results, however.

"No." Prince Rowyn shook his head adamantly. "The fewer that know we are on this quest, the better. Outside of our party, everyone believes I am at White Cliffs and I would rather keep it that way."

"I have a feeling that if certain people knew we were after the dragon-made devices, we would have to deal with a lot more trouble than we would otherwise." Cian was just as unyielding.

"What about the servants?"

"We have made arrangements for them to stay at an inn here in Peltbush. Already paid for three months. It will be a time like they have never had. I am sure they will enjoy the comfort and not speak of this," Cian explained.

Rhein could imagine what a break it would be for the servants from their normal daily toil. But it would be a difficult thing for them to contain the secret. "What if—"

"I also swore them to secrecy upon the pain of death." Prince Rowyn smiled, evidently having anticipated Rhein's argument and cut him off.

"I see." It appeared that there was no turning the Prince from his quest. "In that case there is a six man squad that arrived in Peltbush yesterday, on their way to the northern border. Their sergeant was not overly happy, but I have taken them under my command. It is not enough, but it is the best I can do, considering the constraints you have placed on me."

"We do not need any more guardsmen." The Prince shook his head again.

"We either all go or I will send word to Winterpass." Rhein stood his ground, but it felt like slippery mud.

"You dare—"

"My orders came down from the Crown Prince." He recited them, remembering Captain Harte's words. "I am to escort and do all in my power to protect you... actually it was the Princess, but it is my opinion that the orders have not changed, only the member of the royal family."

Prince Rowyn spun to Cian who only shrugged his shoulders and walked away. The Prince turned back to Rhein and huffed. "As you will." Then he followed the Elf.

"Give him a moment more, Sergeant." Rhein told his second in command as Rhein watched Guardsman Gerallt kissing the sword-wielding servant woman.

"As you wish, Ser." Sergeant Crowley smiled as he walked away from the guardsman and his new love. He saddled up next to Rhein. "Any more word on how we will go after we reach Northurst?"

"None as yet. Cian says we will leave the boat and follow the Saltrock to the Hoarfrost Mountains."

The sergeant snorted. "Did he happen to mention the Haldanes or roaming Tonn warriors? That is a far distance to travel."

"No. He didn't have an answer to the Franchon troops at Tierran's Wall, either."

The sergeant shook his head, the smile faded as he then strode toward the building where the supplies were stored.

Rhein continued to watch the guardsman until a noise from the docks distracted him. He could see the boat captain arguing with Krel Monlor as the captain pointed at the large bear-like Borlender sat on its haunches on the dock by the riverboat.

"You are not bringing that monster aboard my boat." The captain kept looking from the Tink to the brown and blond striped creature.

"I don't think you can stop him." The Tink argued back.

"It's my boat and no bear is going to come aboard."

"He's a Borlender," Krel Monlor snapped back his head as if insulted.

"I don't care what it's called." The captain stepped down the plank to the dock, blocking any access to the boat. He crossed his arms, staring at Krel Monlor. "It's not coming aboard."

"Is there a problem?" Saraid walked up from behind a building. He was leading two of the Kata-henis.

The captain staggered three steps back up the plank. "What are... what are those?"

"They're Kata-henis," Saraid said with a smile. He started to walk toward the plank.

"They're not coming aboard my—"

A roar resounded from one of the Kata-henis and the captain backed all the way up the plank.

As the boat was pulled by oxen, on the shore, Rhein lay back on a heap of supplies and stared up at the moon. He pulled his cloak tighter around his body. He had come to the back of the boat because there were few times he could be alone with his thoughts. His only company was Swift, who continued to smile at Rhein in what Krel Monlor assured Rhein was a friendly gesture. It was difficult to see anything favorable about fangs that long. At least the Kata-henis were curled up at the front of the boat.

The life of a Shield rarely allowed them to stay in one place very long. At least, a newly initiated Shield like Rhein. But his duty was taking him to the farthest reaches of their island country. His duty was to protect the Prince and lady, and if they were going to a land that would probably kill them all, his duty was to be by their side when they all died.

Rhein tried to remember everything he had heard about Ice Giants. The only thing that came to mind was that you never wanted to come up against one.

65

Unexpected

Ser Tanguy and the guardsmen rushed forward to meet the attackers. The sound of metal on metal and the flash of swords, highlighted in the illumination of the fires, engulfed all of them.

All around Willoe and Emeline men were fighting. Franchons, Cainwens, and sellswords were shouting and a few were screaming as they fell to swords or knives. A voice inside spoke to Willoe as her body heated. She reached for the sword that wasn't there and cursed herself again for her stupidity.

Protector Dougal pushed her toward the shoreline and yelled, "Go along the shore until you be around them, go north."

Two guardsmen started out ahead of her to lead the way. She stumbled, but Emeline hooked Willoe's arm and started to pull her away from the tangle of Cainwens and their attackers.

They ran, the fire within her rising until they reached the shore. She stopped and pulled her arm free from the other woman. She could feel the others, her ancestors, starting to take over as she turned back to look at those still fighting. All she could see were shadows against the light of the burning cottage. The fire told her to find a weapon, any weapon. Emeline had stopped with her. Willoe could hear Emeline shouting at her, but it seemed so far away and Emeline's words were drowned out by the beating of the fire in her veins.

The clang of sword striking sword made her whip back around toward the shore. One of the guardsmen was down and the second was just staggering away before he fell into the water's edge, lying there as his upper half floated face down, the current pulling at the body. Standing along the shore were four of the strange warriors. They looked similar to the ones that she had seen guarding the priest Chuluun-Uul at White Cliffs, complete with leather armor and strange helmets, but these were taller and bulkier. Somewhere in the back of her mind, one of the Others recognized the warriors and with the recognition came an intense sense of danger.

They stepped to the side, swords still held out, threatening Willoe and Emeline. A priest, dressed in black, his hood pulled back, stepped forward between them. The priest was bald with skin so black it was hard to tell him from the robe in the dark. Slightly behind him was one of the acolytes in their dung-colored robes. The acolyte kept his head down, subservient to the Shin-il priest.

"You come with, Prince." The priest's voice was high-pitched and his words halting as he seemed to be fighting for the right words.

Willoe looked at the swords of the fallen guardsmen, the fire urging her forward, but she knew even with the extra speed of the fire, on the muddy bank she could not reach them before the warriors would be on her. And if she lost, then Emeline would be at the mercy of the priest, his student, and the warriors. The compulsion to attack was overwhelming and her thoughts were muddled as she fought with the fire.

"Come now!" the priest yelled out to her, his voice commanding, then said something in his squeaky language and three of the warriors started toward her.

She saw little chance of surviving a fight with the warriors, but the fire surged inside and she sprang at the leading warriors. The first one on the right didn't even get his sword up before she drove her right hand into his throat. The crunch of cartilage collapsing sounded loud to her as she grabbed the sword out of the warrior's hand with her left hand. Before the warrior even started to fall, she swung the sword to her left, cutting deeply into the left arm of the warrior there. The man wrenched away from her and, with the sword lodged in bone, he ripped the weapon from her hand. The third warrior stepped forward, his sword coming down at an angle toward Willoe. She threw up her hand, catching the warrior's balled fist where it was wrapped around the hilt of the sword, and twisted the arm as it came down toward her.

She stepped sideways and let the arm continue to flow downward. As it reached the bottom of the warrior's reach, she forced it to continue around through the arc. She could hear the snap of the wrist as she brought the tip of the sword back up toward the warrior. He tried to resist Willoe and step aside at the same time, but she drove the sword upward and it sliced into his stomach and chest. The warrior fell backward and Willoe stood looking for another foe.

She spun from side to side, but didn't see anyone until she noticed the priest and the remaining warrior farther down the shoreline. The priest and his acolyte stood, the priest with his hands up and muttering in his foreign tongue. The fire inside told her that the priest was weaving some sort of spell to attack her. She stepped back to push off and charge at him when she heard Aeron's shout.

"Over here, priest!"

His sudden appearance slowed her and she looked over to the edge of the woods, where Aeron stood even with her, a sword and shield in hand. Aeron roared out another challenge to the priest. It seemed as if he were trying to draw the priest's attention away from Willoe and Emeline, who still stood a little behind Willoe, aghast.

The priest must have been surprised because he pivoted toward Aeron and his hands straightened; a ball of red light flashed from his hands and flew toward Aeron.

Aeron threw up the shield and the blazing light hit it, throwing Aeron backwards. The shield jumped out of his hand and bounced back into the woods. He appeared stunned, but started to stand, the sword still in his hand.

The priest yelled something in a language Willoe couldn't understand and then he pointed one hand at his student and the other at Aeron. Willoe could see the acolyte's back arch as if he had been struck by some unseen force.

A scream from Aeron made her turn to him again as he stood, his back arched like the acolyte, and looked as if he was being held by unseen hands. With the fire still flowing through her veins she could see the aura around Aeron quickly fading.

"No!" Somewhere in her mind she registered Emeline's scream.

Aeron let out a scream of agony before his body jerked and he crumpled to the ground.

Willoe turned back toward the priest, ready to charge at him, when two arrows struck the priest: One in the chest, the other in the throat. The priest was thrown backwards as a third arrow struck the warrior, knocking him down. The acolyte was already on the ground, his body twisted and unmoving.

Protector Dougal showed up next to her, a bow in his hand. "Princess?"

With the priest and warriors dead, the fire began to subside. She looked up at Protector Dougal, the concern written on his face. She heard a sound on the other side and turned to see the groomsman Doy, also with a bow in his hand. He had another arrow nocked and was looking down the shoreline. His teeth were gritted and his lips pulled back, his face tight and his eyes focused, but without any sign of fear in them.

A wail from Emeline brought Willoe out of the foggy state that still blanketed her mind. She turned her head back to see Emeline on her knees bent over, rocking back and forth over Aeron's body.

Willoe didn't answer Protector Dougal. Instead she raced over to

Emeline and dropped to her knees on the other side of Aeron.

Willoe shook him and screamed, "Aeron!" His limp body moved with her shaking, but he did not respond.

The fire had not completely faded and Willoe watched as the aura— a pale reddish-blue hue that encircled her cousin, her friend — waned and disappeared.

"Aeron!" She screamed again and put her head on his bare chest. Tears ran down her face as she pounded on his chest.

After just a few moments hands grabbed her and pulled her to her feet. Protector Dougal turned her around to face him. "We must go now. We be holding them, but for how long—"

She looked up into his face, her head not even coming to his chin. She thought how he had been as much a father to her as anyone. She put her head against his chest and cried. "Aeron..." she managed to get out through her tears. She could feel the Protector's arms tightening around her. It seemed like forever, but also a heartbeat, he pushed away and held her at arm's length. "We must go now, Willoe." He had never called her by name, without her title.

She wiped her eyes and turned to see Doy holding up Emeline, the bow still in his hand. Emeline sagged against him, her body shaking and her cries muffled by the fabric of his tunic.

A screech boomed across the entire clearing and all four of them crouched down. Another loud shriek flooded the air as something flew over their heads toward the clearing. It came in low and a single flap of its wings created a wind that blew the water up onto the shore. Willoe turned, her eyes following the winged creature as it glided into the clearing. It landed past the cottage towards the hill, its shrill call bouncing off the surrounding forest. Once on the ground she could finally see the creature in the light from the flames of the cottage.

It was a dragon. Like the golden dragon that had visited her twice, but this one was green. She thought it was a dark green, like the one in her dreams. It was twice the size of a man, its wingspan twice even that.

"What in the Shadows?" Doy yelled above the shrill call of the dragon.

The dragon's head swung back and forth on its long neck as if looking for something. Whatever it was searching for it must have found, because it opened its mouth and flame spewed out, landing on a group of Franchon soldiers. It swung around again, the wings flapping, the strength of their movement blowing the air and knocking down everyone nearby. The green dragon spotted another group of Franchon soldiers and sellswords, and another breath of flame landed in their midst.

Arrows flew at the dragon, a few sticking, but most harmlessly bouncing off the dragon's scales. One brave soul charged forward with a lance and stuck the dragon in the left shoulder before the beast's tail whipped around and knocked the man into the air to land somewhere in the thick woods beyond. The dragon screamed and stomped its foot, shaking the ground, until the lance fell away. This only seemed to enrage the creature as it turned and headed toward the hill spewing flames to either side.

As the dragon stomped over to the hill, Protector Dougal gripped Willow's arm again and roughly pulled her toward the stream. "Now, we go!" He led them down the shoreline until they found an opening in the trees that edged the stream. They made their way through the woods onto the northern trail and ran, though Willoe didn't remember it very well. All she could hear was Emeline's sobbing and an occasional wail, though Doy tried to keep her quiet per Protector Dougal's orders.

She realized that as long as the priests lived, there would never be a safe haven for her or any of her family. The rage built inside her, but the fire inside was kept at bay. Her anger was tempered by the confusion she felt from what she had sensed earlier. The memory of what she had felt when the dragon had arrived. The feeling lingered even as they fled her aunt's cottage. She had sensed something about the dragon's Spirit that troubled her. It had felt familiar.

66

A Party of Four

After some time — Willoe had lost track of the turns of the glass passing while they ran — they came out into another large clearing at the top of a ridge that looked down a long hill running north away from the valley.

They stopped and Willoe gasped, feeling a little light-headed. She sat on a rock as the others leaned up against a tree or sat down wheezing. It was dark and the sound of rustling trees made her jump back up and reach for the sword that was still not there. Protector Dougal jumped out between Willoe, Emeline and the noise. Doy stood next to him, the bow in his hand, an arrow nocked and pulled back.

The sound grew as it came closer. Willoe tensed, but the fire did not seem to be responding to the threat. She would have thought more about it, but whatever was making the noise had reached the clearing. Tree branches parted and two guardsmen rode through with torches, followed by Ser Tanguy. As the guardsmen rode forward and light shone on Willoe, the Shield became excited and yelled back into the woods.

More noise came from the woods behind the Shield, and a few moments later Captain Harte, Count Idwal, and a group of guardsmen with more torches rode out, followed by other guardsmen on foot and a large group of servants, villagers and Franchon loyalists. Moonlight shone down on the clearing and Willoe could see that a little over half the guardsmen had survived the battle at the cottage along with most of the civilians. Willoe wondered how the fire inside knew that there had been no threat.

The count and Captain Harte dismounted in front of Willoe. The count spoke first. "You made it. We searched along the shore and in the woods, but all we found was one of those foreign priests, feathered." He smiled. "Along with some rather large and strangely attired warriors." The smile faded.

Willoe had trouble swallowing. "And Aeron."

The look on the two men's faces was one of confusion. "We thought he might be with you." Count Idwal looked to her for an answer.

"When the priest attacked us he—" The word had trouble coming out, as if it were made of uncooked dough. "He died."

The shock on both their faces told her they had not known.

She turned away from them. The pain was so intense; how could she admit he was dead? She had seen his aura fail. Without a Spirit he could not live. She knew this and yet… she missed him so much. The irritating shrugs, the practical jokes, the way he looked after all of them.

She couldn't do anything about the heartache, but she did recognize a feeling she could do something about. It was a feeling that, at the moment, comforted her.

Anger.

An anger that was building within her. It was bolstered by the fire, but the anger was hers and hers alone. She looked over at Emeline where she was leaning against Cleric Yoan, who had come later with civilian stragglers. She had run out of tears.

She turned back to the two men. They looked as if they were staring into a raging fire; their eyes were wide and they both inhaled deeply. She couldn't imagine what she must have looked like. She could feel herself heated, not from the fire, but from her own desire for revenge.

"If they want war, then we shall oblige them." There were enough torches that, together with the moonlight, the entire clearing was lit. She looked at the civilians, well over three hundred, nearly half of them men and older boys. She walked over to stand on the stump of a tree in front of them. She called over two guards to stand on either side of her with torches. "People of the mountains and citizens of Lealacité." She made sure not to call them Franchons. "Are you tired of being trampled under the heel of King Benoit and his sellswords?" Only a few yelled aye, but she continued anyway. "Are you tired of working hard only to have it taken away by King Benoit and his sellswords, parasites on your worn backs?" More shouted aye and a few even called out their own curses on the king's minions. "Like a weed wrapped around your crops, the king sends his wag-tailed, fly-bitten foreigners, sellswords from across the Straights, to suck the life out of you. They are like a forest leech, sucking the Spirit out of you." Most of the mountainfolk were now shouting back at Willoe, calling out threats against the king's henchmen.

She saw Protector Dougal look over at her with a furrowed brow. Willoe realized he had never heard her use language like that before.

Some of the villagers were raising their hands and calling for an end to the pillaging and killing.

"Citizens!" She turned her attention to the loyalists. "Remember the days when you could walk the streets without fear?"

Many of them nodded and a few of them called out their affirmations.

"When the king, good King Hernaudin, cared for his people?"

A majority of the loyalists were agreeing now, many enthusiastically voicing their anger.

She held her hands out to them. "What has King Benoit and his foreigners brought you?"

Shouts of "Nothing!" and "They only take!" were yelled back at her.

Willoe let them shout for a few moments, then she shouted as loud as she could. "Then you will need to take the fight to them! You will have to kill the king's dogs!" She turned from the loyalists to the villagers.

Much of both crowds quieted, the noise settling into a murmur as they started talking among themselves. A few of the heartier men continued to yell obscenities until they were quieted by neighbors.

A woman near the front of the villagers finally spoke. She was broad-shouldered and Willoe guessed she was well known and commonly spoke for others. "We would fight 'em, your... your highness. But we're not soldiers. Just farmers and woodsmen. We could'na stand up to 'em."

"And we are just merchants and laborers," a man in the front row of the loyalists added to the woman's words.

Willoe had expected this and turned toward the guardsmen and Shields who had gathered to the side of two groups. Count Idwal had moved down to stand among them and look up at her. He did not looked pleased. "Weapons Master Gwron." She had spotted the old warrior when he had come in with the last of the guardsmen that had been protecting the rear of the civilians.

"My Prince." He made his way through the front row of guardsmen and stepped out from the crowd, looking up at Willoe.

She turned back to look at the villagers. She could imagine how she must look, outlined by the torches. "Do any of you know how to use a longbow?"

The villagers laughed and the broad woman answered, "We're mountainfolk. We could hold a bow 'fore we could walk. You don't live long here in the mountains if you can'na take down your own supper. That goes for us womenfolk as well." Many of the villagers around her nodded to each other.

"I can hit the eye of an owl all the way across Meryl's Glade," a man in the back shouted out, which got more laughs from many of the villagers.

Willoe had never seen Meryl's Glade so had no idea of the distance, but she laughed anyway and said, "That is a fair bit of archery. Are you sure?"

That got another round of laughter and a lot of jokes.

The man shouted back in defense, "Got the owl to prove it!" Then he laughed and everyone joined him, even the guardsmen.

"What about a sword? Anyone held a sword before?" Willoe called, looking out over the crowd.

Maybe eight or nine hands went up among the villagers, but several dozen in the group of loyalists. One of the villager men spoke up. "A few of us was with the army for a bit." He looked at those around him. "That was under old King Hernaudin."

"As were we," one of the loyalist men shouted out. "May the Burning Lady bless King Hernaudin's Spirit."

Some of the loyalists and many of the villagers put fingers together, then touched forehead, lips, and heart.

Willoe had never been superstitious and had never met King Benoit's father, but she performed the same gesture and nodded along with the villagers, which she noticed had many of the civilians smiling at her.

She turned to look down at Master Gwron. "What do you think, Master Gwron? Do these look like people that should have the right to the freedom they had under good King Hernaudin?" She swept a hand, taking in the two groups.

Master Gwron rubbed his chin and looked over at the civilians. Then he nodded and looked back up at Willoe. "Some of the best archers I have seen come from the mountain country. With a bit of training and discipline they could do well."

Then she added, "I saw many ash and beech in these woods. One could make a lot of arrows."

The Weapons Master nodded as he looked around at the nearby trees.

"And I would be willing to bet there are many a good swordsmen in this bunch," Willoe said with a smile.

"Once a soldier, always a soldier," the loyalist man who had spoken earlier shouted, which got a laugh from both groups.

Willoe could see the two groups were already merging. She jumped down from the stump and walked back and forth in front of the villagers and loyalists in the light of their torches. "People of the mountain. True and loyal citizens of Lealacité. You have a chance to stand for yourself. To send a message to King Hernaudin's son, the hound of a foreign priest, that you are not to be tread upon so lightly." She smiled to herself when she noticed some in the back trying to stand higher to get a better view of her. She stopped in the middle of the front line, between the two groups, and turned to point to the Weapons Master. "Master Gwron, who has trained Shields and kings alike, believes in you. I believe in you. Do you believe in yourself?" she ended, shouting at the top of her voice.

Only a few shouted at first, but then it quickly grew and before long the whole crowd was roaring and cheering.

Willoe walked over to Master Gwron and patted him on the shoulder as she walked past. "They're all yours, Master Gwron."

She continued back to Captain Harte and Protector Dougal.

"I notice you did not mention that they have warred with us Cainwens for hundreds of years?" Captain Harte asked with a smile.

"They have enough enemies at their door without reminding them of past feuds." She looked back over her shoulder. "Maybe it is time we put old quarrels behind us."

"Are you insane?" Count Idwal demanded as he walked up to them, then changed his tone. "Your highness." He looked past her to the civilians. "What do you expect us to do with a ragtag crowd of farmers and merchants?"

She looked him in the eye, her face hardened. "There are ten, twenty times their number roaming around these mountains. They have all been trod upon like the dirt under their feet, and drained of their resources by Benoit and his sellswords. Once you get these trained, the others will come flooding to you. The mountainfolk know these lands better than anyone. There will be a lot more coming and who better to work with Sergeant Trystan than merchants? There are blacksmiths, leathersmiths, and many other craftsmen among the loyalists. You will need them.

"And do not forget that many of the loyalists are laborers and servants, strong men and women who will lend additional strength to your ranks. With a little training, and as Master Gwron said, discipline, you and the others can take this entire mountain range, maybe others, away from Benoit and his black-hearted priest." She pulled her lips up in what must have looked like a snarl. "Do not think the lumber and farm goods will not be missed. A lot of soldiers require a lot of both."

Captain Harte narrowed his eyes. "What did you mean by 'you and the others?'"

She knew this would be the hardest part of the plan, but she was committed. "I am going north. I have to find something."

"You cannot go off to the north," Count Idwal objected.

"*Count* Idwal." She emphasized the title. "There is something that I need to find that might mean an end to this fighting. And it might also save my life."

The count was flustered, but he had no time to argue as Willoe's aunt Kerye stumbled out of the woods on the other side of the clearing. She had cuts on her face, neck and arms. A lot of dried blood covered her left arm that had run down from a bandage of torn fabric on her shoulder.

Cleric Yoan and a couple of servants ran to her and helped her over to the senior officers. They placed her so she was leaning up against a rock. Cleric Yoan started to unravel the bandage to expose a large wound. He called for his saddlebag as he began to inspect Kerye.

"You be safe." She looked up at Willoe and Protector Dougal, who had knelt next to her.

"Where have you been?" Willoe asked as she knelt next to Protector Dougal.

Kerye grimaced as Cleric Yoan inspected the area around the wound. "I had something I had to do."

Willoe wondered what could be so important.

Kerye answered a question from Cleric Yoan before looking back at Willoe. "You know what you must do."

Willoe nodded. "I am leaving as soon as I gather supplies."

Protector Dougal glanced from one woman to the other, then settled on Kerye. "Where be she going? I do not think it be wise."

"She is going to the Hoarfrost Mountains."

Protector Dougal straightened his back.

Willoe could empathize with her Protector. She still couldn't believe she was intentionally going into the land of the Ice Giants.

Kerye put a hand on Protector Dougal's wrist. "You have to go with her, then…" She paused and looked into his eyes. "Then you must take her to the Ice Queen."

His reaction stunned Willoe. She had never seen him flinch before, but he pulled back from Kerye, his eyes wide. "I cannot."

Willoe knew that her Protector would not let her go alone, even to the Hoarfrost Mountains, so his refusal must have something to do with this Ice Queen. "Who is the Ice Queen?" Willoe asked.

Kerye tried to smile at Willoe, but flinched instead as Cleric Yoan touched the wound. "The name be not normally used this far south. She be someone that can help you." She turned her gaze to the Protector. "She can help us all." Her voice was soft and gentle as something passed between the two of them.

Protector Dougal closed his eyes, breathed deeply, and then nodded once before opening them again.

She nodded back and smiled. "Now go make your plans and let the good Cleric here take care of this scratch."

"Scratch!" The Cleric huffed. "I do not know what you got yourself into, my lady, but whatever made this wound was big. Bigger than any arrow. And all these others." He was looking at her neck, face, and other arm.

"You never know what you will find in the woods." She smiled at the Cleric.

Protector Dougal helped Willoe up and they went back over to Captain Harte and Count Idwal along with Ser Tanguy, who had joined them.

Captain Harte was not smiling. "If you insist on this venture then Ser Tanguy and a squad of guardsmen are going with you."

"We have a long way to go and that large a group will only draw unnecessary attention," Willoe argued, and she sucked in her breath and straightened her back, glaring at her grandfather's captain, not willing to comply with his orders.

"We thought you would say that." Count Idwal spoke up. "Ser Tanguy will accompany you on this quest. Between him and Protector Dougal, at least one of them should be able to return and let us know of your demise." He said it with a smile, but then his face was stern again. "My liege, if you do not agree I will prevent you from leaving. Even if by force."

Willoe knew it took a lot for the count to make a threat against a member of the royal family and it showed the seriousness of his words. She thought for a moment and decided that having a champion Shield along would probably be a good idea. "Fine. Ser Tanguy can join us."

The Shield grunted as if there hadn't been any doubt.

"I'm also going," a deep voice said from behind Willoe and she turned to see the groomsman Doy standing there with a bow in his hand and a quiver thrown across his back.

Ser Tanguy let out a big breath and said harshly, "What do we need with a servant?"

"I can take care of the horses and I am a fair cook," Doy argued back, his forcefulness surprising Willoe. It took a lot of guts for a groomsman to stand up to a Shield that had killed more than his share of opponents.

Willoe wasn't sure whether she trusted the man, but she also didn't want to add to her escort. "We can take care of our own horses and I imagine we can take care of our own suppers."

Protector Dougal interrupted. "The two arrows that struck the priest be his. He feathered the priest so quickly, I had to let fly at the warrior."

She looked at the groomsman with new eyes. He grinned the same grin she remembered from all those years before. He was full of surprises and she heard herself saying, "Then we could use an extra bow. One that comes with grooming and cooking." She smiled back at him.

Ser Tanguy huffed and went over to start gathering enough horses for them to ride and a couple for carrying supplies.

As preparations were started, Willoe wondered at her strange companions. A mysterious northern warrior, a Shield whose biggest thrill seemed to be tormenting her brother, and a groomsman who had been a cutpurse and was now also an expert archer. She couldn't tell whether they would make the Hoarfrost Mountains without killing each other, but she hoped that if they did, one of them would know what to do when they ran into an Ice Giant.

67

The Truth Exposed

Malbery, Hafgan, a half-dozen Greenmerrow Shields, Guardsmen Royce and Tavin, and over a dozen more of Malbery's personal guardsmen entered the near-empty throne room. At the other end stood Chancellor Liam, Lord Morcar Priddy, while the old Duke Stockpole of Wellingford sat on a stool, his hands on a large iron staff that he held in front of his body.

Malbery and his escort walked across the chamber up to the waiting Cainwens.

"The king went to the Burning Lady before dawn," Chancellor Liam told them, his voice heavy with grief.

"Word came to us on the road this morning. We are greatly saddened by the news." Malbery lowered his head in respect and squeezed Hafgan's arm, causing the Prince also to lower his head.

Chancellor Liam walked up to Prince Hafgan, who took a step backward. "Your grandfather was a great leader."

Malbery turned his back to the others, looking past the chancellor at Hafgan. "The Prince was heartbroken. We had to stop so he could recover." He narrowed his eyes as he glared at the Prince.

"Yes. Yes, I am heartbroken," Hafgan repeated.

"The army has been routed at Daere Mawr." Priddy slid up and Malbery couldn't tell if the man was smiling or frowning. Like everything else about the advisor's words and actions, it was difficult to tell.

A loud crack made the floor tremble under Malbery's feet. He turned in time to see Duke Stockpole lift and slam his staff on the floor a second time. The blow made the floor quake. "You should have been with the army. Even the thousand guardsmen you brought here might have made the difference." The duke stepped to within a few fingers of Malbery's face.

Though old, the duke was no less commanding, just as Malbery remembered his father being. His forceful presence caused Malbery to step back and shrink slightly, but only for a moment.

Standing his ground, Malbery straightened his doublet and cleared his throat. "I had already sent archers and pike ahead. Word arrived as I was bringing the rest. It would not have accomplished anything to continue." Malbery breathed in, filling his chest. "It was more important to deliver Prince Hafgan to the capital. I brought my men to Westhedge to assist in the defense of the city."

"I brought five hundred men with me and my vassals will be sending another thousand within days," Duke Stockpole proclaimed, holding his staff to his right, his left hand resting on the hilt of his sword. "Your men are not necessary. Your time would be better spent gathering more Greenmerrow troops and moving to meet up with the remains of the army out of Mount Somerled. Together you can push these insolent invaders back across the Saltrock."

Malbery looked slowly from Duke Stockpole to Chancellor Liam and back again before saying, "I intend to remain at Westhedge."

"The Crown Prince—" the duke started.

"Is most likely dead." Malbery's muscles became rigid as he, this time, stepped toward the old duke. "And reports have it that Prince Mael is either dead or a captive of the foreign priests."

He walked past the men to Hafgan and turned back to face them. "With the death of good King Einion the right of rule falls to Crown Prince Beynon and then Prince Mael, the fates both of which are in question." He put a hand on Prince Hafgan's shoulder. "By order of birth, Prince Hafgan must be anointed with rule of the kingdom."

"The Crown Prince and his son may be alive!" the Duke screamed and pounded his staff once more.

"Prince Hafgan—" Malbery started to yell in return, but pulled back and finished in a calm tone. "Is also son of the Crown Prince and grandson of our beloved King Einion, now gone." He said the final words slowly.

"That may be too hasty. As you say, we do not know the fate of the Crown Prince and the Heir Apparent," Chancellor Liam argued.

"I believe..." Lord Priddy stepped into the middle of the clamor; he spun from one man to the other, his finger held in the air trying to make a point. "I believe history would tell us when King Morven came into his rule, his father had gone missing in the battle of Deepweard against the rebellious Count Gough. It wasn't for several moons before the death of King Morven was confirmed."

"That is more than seven hundred years in the past." Duke Stockpole shook his head at the idea.

"It is precedent," Priddy answered calmly.

The chancellor looked at Hafgan for a few moments, then at Malbery. It made Malbery feel as if the chancellor were performing a Seeing and Malbery shifted from one foot to the other under the stare.

Chancellor Liam finally turned to Duke Stockpole. "He speaks the truth. Until we confirm the fate of the Crown Prince or Prince Mael, Prince Hafgan is next in line to the throne."

"King Hafgan," Malbery corrected.

"Crown Prince Hafgan." The elderly chancellor spoke sharply. "Until we determine the whereabouts of Crown Prince Beynon and Prince Mael, Crown Prince Hafgan should rule." A sour look filled Chancellor Liam's face. "I will call the council for three days from now, after King Einion's burial, to affirm Prince Hagan as the Crown Prince until such time as we establish what has befallen Crown Prince Beynon and Prince Mael."

Malbery nodded. All had gone well. "My men and I will remain to protect the capital and the Crown Prince."

"The western vassals—" Duke Stockpole began to bring up the argument again.

"With your men and mine I believe we have sufficient forces to hold the walls." Malbery turned his back to the others and looked at Hafgan.

"No," Hafgan said hesitantly. Malbery lowered his eyebrows and stared intently at Hafgan.

"No, there are enough. The western vassals can return to their lands." Hafgan spoke more confidently, as he had been instructed on the way to Westhedge.

Malbery turned back to Duke Stockpole.

"As you wish." The duke bowed to Hafgan, but only slightly. "I will send word to the lords en route." He turned to Malbery, his eyes narrowed and his jowls firm. "I have other business in Faywynne. My men and I will stay for now." The duke bowed again to Hafgan, turned and left the chamber.

"Sire, there are matters that need to be discussed and papers that require your attention." The chancellor addressed Hafgan.

"Grioral, I mean, Earl Malbery will be my advisor. All such matters will go through him." Hafgan looked to Malbery, then smiled once his mentor had nodded approval.

"As you wish, Sire." Chancellor Liam bowed again, but his look of disapproval did not fit with the respectful gesture.

Malbery would wait until after the council met to redeploy the nine thousand Greenmerrow troops stationed around Lake Windo Bri. Stockpole and the western vassals would not be a problem for long. A smile slowly grew on Malbery's lips. Once the sniveling boy was seated on the throne, Malbery knew the first thing he was going to do. Tear down and burn the Legendre's Folly tapestry. He was Greenmerrow.

Bat-Uul looked around the king's solar and thought it was quite impressive even compared to Chuluun-Uul's old lodgings. Across the narrow table sat the Gai-Ten, shaking his head as he picked up some papers on the table and thumbed through them until he found the one he wanted.

"The fool Dimah-Uul." Chuluun-Uul scanned the paper. "I received a message while you were coming from Daere Mawr. It is from General Lozon." Chuluun-Uul lifted his eyes just enough to stare at Bat-Uul through knitted brows. "He confirms what you have said."

Bat-Uul wanted to sigh in relief, but had to keep his expression neutral.

"The attackers were never found, but the general believes Dimah-Uul had secreted Cainwen prisoners and was questioning them when events got out of hand." Chuluun-Uul lay the paper back on the stack. "He also agreed with your decision to hold just inside Cainwen and withdraw units to White Cliffs."

It had taken little to convince the general. He was more than happy to see merit in Bat-Uul's decision to hold along the Lower Saltrock. He did not seem like the kind of man who would relish sending wave after wave of his men against the high walls of Castle Mount Somerled. But what had surprised Bat-Uul was how easily the story of Cainwen prisoners was accepted. General Lozon was evidently familiar with Dimah-Uul's vicious nature and, as Bat-Uul realized later, if there were no Cainwen prisoners then the general would have a difficult time explaining the lack of security that resulted in Dimah-Uul's death.

"We can let the Cainwens stew in Mount Somerled for now." The Gai-Ten picked up another paper.

"The twins?" Bat-Uul hoped that Chuluun-Uul would raise the issue with the Master. Bat-Uul could only imagine the Gai-Ten had misunderstood, as it still made little sense to Bat-Uul.

"The twins are not your concern." Chuluun-Uul's tone became angry. "Others will take over where you have failed."

Hope died in Bat-Uul as he realized that the plan, whatever it may be, had changed.

Chuluun-Uul calmed as quickly as he had angered. He seemed to be going over something in the paper and then looked back up at Bat-Uul. "We will harvest more recruits to fill our losses and send fresh troops to General Lozon in the spring. If need be we can lay siege to Mount Somerled, seeing as we will only need to send a small force to Faywynne and Westhedge.

Though that should be a foregone conclusion by spring."

The Gai-Ten's comment confused Bat-Uul. From what little he knew, the Cainwen capital would be a formidable fortress to take.

"I have sent for three more Uuls from the mainland and ten more companies of sellswords."

"Is that necessary?" It seemed impossible that the priest would invest more and more resources into Taran. It had already exceeded more than Bat-Uul could ever imagine.

"There are three kingdoms."

That might possibly account for the Uuls.

"With many of the Franchon troops in Cainwen, the sellswords will be used to take Haldane."

Bat-Uul felt his stomach rebelling as he pictured more wounded and dead, but he retained enough of his belief that he could not bring himself to confront the Gai-Ten.

A knock on the door interrupted their conversation.

"Come."

Bat-Uul turned and was surprised to see the door open and Caspar-Jin enter.

"Beg my pardon." Bat-Uul's aide looked just as surprised, excused himself and left, closing the door.

Bat-Uul turned back to Chuluun-Uul, shaking his head. "Why would Caspar-Jin be coming to the king's solar?"

Chuluun-Uul twisted his lips, but just for a moment before answering, "He must have been looking for you."

"He did not know I was here."

The Gai-Ten stood, looking down at the table as he gathered stacks of papers. "I have others coming."

Bat-Uul knew when he was dismissed. He stood and walked to the door. As he opened the door to leave, the Gai-Ten spoke to him.

"Remember what I said about the Prince." Chuluun-Uul's voice held the same threat as earlier, the one he had used upon Bat-Uul's and Prince Mael's return to White Cliffs. When they had ridden into the castle's main bailey, Chuluun-Uul had met them and immediately ordered the Captain of the Guard to imprison Prince Mael in the Guardsman's Tower.

Against his very nature, Bat-Uul had walked up to his superior and talked to him in a low voice. "Does the plan still intend to sway Prince Mael to the Shin-il Way?"

Chuluun-Uul hesitated as if considering the question, but then nodded.

"When all are as one body, peace and harmony shall ensue." Bat-Uul quoted the fourth line of their shared canon. "There is another apartment on my floor. Leave the Prince in my care and I will win him over to our beliefs."

A slight chuckle was not what Bat-Uul had expected from the Gai-Ten, but Chuluun-Uul consented. "You may try, but he has only responded to the Obeah. And Dimah-Uul's... special talents. Familiarity will not breed the results you desire."

"Not that it was ever attempted," Bat-Uul said under his breath.

"Did you say something, Uul?" Chuluun-Uul glared at his junior.

"No, my Gai-Ten." Bat-Uul chastised himself. He would never have thought to question a senior Uul, and especially a Gai-Ten, just a few moons ago. But then, nothing that had happened recently was as expected.

"Take the Prince and do what you please with him." Chuluun-Uul had then stepped up to Bat-Uul, leaned forward next to Bat-Uul's ear and whispered, "If anything — and hear my words carefully — if *anything* happens to the Prince, I will hold you responsible." The threat in his voice had made Bat-Uul's blood chill. "And you do not want me to find you lacking."

Protector Dougal and Ser Tanguy were in the lead as they talked. Actually, Ser Tanguy was talking. The other thing he was known for besides his skill with sword and lance. It had taken two weeks to get everything settled at the makeshift camp, and get the civilians organized for training, before they could leave for the north. They had been on the road for two days and were just coming out of the Blackburn Mountains.

Willoe and Doy rode next to each other, behind the warriors, and had not said much throughout the day. Finally Doy spoke to her, but kept his gaze ahead. "I would not worry about your aunt. She will be fine."

Cleric Yoan had proclaimed Kerye would recover, though he was still puzzled by her wounds. Willoe was not overly concerned about her.

Doy continued. "The villagers adore her. They won't let anything happen to her. No noble lays claim to the mountains. The villagers see her as their mistress. Their protector."

Willoe turned to look at him. That made no sense to her. "How is she protecting them? She does not have any troops."

"An advantage of being a servant is that no one sees you, but everyone talks to you. If you were to spend some time with the lesser folks you might find out that the villagers have a lot to say." He kept looking ahead as they rode along.

Doy had infuriated her every time they talked. "There is nothing my aunt could do to protect those poor people. You must be mistaken." She stared at him, willing him to fall off the horse, but he just kept riding.

He shook his head with a short laugh. "Why do you think they call her the Dragon Lady…" he turned his head to look at her. "Princess Willoe?"

That grin again.

Captain Darcio Armel sat on the bench, his back rigid, head held high, hands folded in his lap, and he was angry. He had been elected captain of the Bloody Sun six years earlier and was not one who did well with submitting to authority, but a contract was a contract and the foreign priest, Chuluun-Uul, had paid lavishly for the sellsword company's services. The captain idly played with his belt purse as he watched the two Jidig guards that stood on either side of the door to the king's solar and inspected the details of their armor and weapons. They wore leather vests with metal strips sewn throughout. But unlike most of the other Jidig that Armel had seen since his company's arrival, these warriors had metal shoulder pads instead of leather and they had layered metal, woven into their leather padding that ran down the arm and legs, whereas other Jidig wore simple leather and heavy cotton. He had been told they were the elite of the Jidig, like Armel's own men.

He and his company had only recently arrived on the island and were still getting accustomed to the priests and their adherents. The contract was the most profitable the Bloody Sun had ever received, and it was all due to Armel. The third son of a minor noble from a small province in the Kingdom of Godelieve, he had had few choices when he reached the age of maturity. Using what little inheritance his father had given him to buy into the Bloody Sun was the best investment he had ever made. Fifteen years later and he now led seven hundred of the best known - and most successful - sellsword company in all of the west of the mainland.

The door edged open and one of the Jidig leaned his head to the opening. Armel could not understand a word that was said, but the guard nodded, then stepped over to Armel.

"Shalde cor pelel," the guard said and then shook his head, frowning, when Armel just stared at him. The guard stepped to the side and pointed to the door. When Armel didn't move, the warrior tilted his head toward the door several times and kept pointing, repeating what he had first said to Armel.

Armel understood what the guard wanted him to do, he just wanted to be difficult. He had only been in White Cliffs for a week and he already disliked the eastern warriors, though if he had to admit, he cared even less for their masters, the Shin-il priests. He had dealt with them a couple of times in the past, but only requiring a few units at any one time. This was the first time they had purchased the services of the entire company.

Finally he stood and walked to the entryway, the guard trailing behind. As he reached the door the other guard started to push it open, but the sellsword captain took two long steps and slammed his hand against the wooden planks to push the door open himself. He would enter on his own terms.

Two tens of the Jidig warriors stood against the walls around the room. He had to admit they were an intimidating sight. They were dressed as the guards, but the only thing that moved was their eyes as they watched him enter.

The self-proclaimed chancellor Chuluun-Uul stood at the back of the room reading a scroll. Armel wondered at the arrogance of the man to take the king's solar for his own. He had no idea what had happened to the Franchon king or how the priests had come to power, but as long as their gold held out he didn't really care. Shin-il acolytes, in their dung-colored robes, stood motionless in each of the corners to either side of the priest. In front of Chuluun-Uul was a desk, only about four paces wide and a couple of paces deep. It had intricate engraved symbols that ran up the legs and across the front. It was a light-colored wood that Armel was not familiar with. He thought it must be native to Taran.

Standing beside the table was a female warrior. Armel suspected it was the Jidig commander, Zaya. He had heard rumors about this particular Jidig, but this was the first time he had laid eyes on her. It was part of his makeup to find out everything he could about the competition and from what he had heard, and now confirmed with his own eyes, this commander was definitely competition.

He couldn't count the number of scars that ran across her arms and legs, with one nasty one that ran from just below the right side of the chin down across the neck to disappear under the leather vest. With long white hair tied in knots that hung down the back and several metal bands wrapped tightly around each arm, Zaya was quite an imposing figure. Armel was a big man by normal standards, but he was only on par with most of the warriors against the walls. Like her men, she didn't move, but her eyes walked with him as he came up to the desk. They were dark and reminded him of a hungry wolf he had once killed.

"Captain Armel. I have been waiting." Chuluun-Uul rolled up the scroll, walked over to the table, sat down, and put the scroll on the right side of the table along with a stack of others. He pointed to the chair across the polished table from him.

Armel sat, but did not take his eyes off of Zaya. There were few things that worried the captain, but not knowing why he had been called into this den of wolves set off his senses. The room seemed unusually cold and he felt a tingling, like something was crawling on his skin.

"Did you have trouble finding your way, Captain?" Chuluun-Uul's thin-lipped expression kept the man's intentions to himself.

Armel turned his face from the commander to the priest, but he had learned to keep his expression, and especially his eyes, unreadable. "Not at all. The king's solar was not hard to locate." Armel spoke blandly, but still managed to emphasize *king's solar*.

Chuluun-Uul frowned and Armel had to repress a smile.

"While the king is away he has graciously loaned me the use of his apartments." His words were blunt and sounded repetitive. Armel had already heard many things about the Franchon king, his men spreading out to all the usual alehouses and taverns, bringing back all they heard. If what he heard was true, gracious was not something he would associate with this king. The king's father was a different story, but not King Benoit. If the priest had taken residence in the king's apartments, the king was more likely dead or in hiding.

"I have an important mission for you, Captain. There is something of value I need retrieved from the northern lands and I need a man that can get it for me." The priest emphasized 'captain' as he reached for another scroll, unrolled the paper and glanced at it. He read it for a moment while Armel sat unaffected by Chuluun-Uul's attempts to establish his authority. He looked up from the scroll, his eyes focused on Armel's face. "Are you that man, Captain?"

"I have never defaulted on a contract, if that is what you are asking."

"That is good. Very good." Chuluun-Uul looked back down and continued to read.

Armel almost let a smirk cross his face, but kept his well-known neutral expression in place.

Chuluun-Uul finished reading and waved for one of the acolytes. "Deliver this to Donkova-Jin and let him know I am waiting for his evaluation." He handed the scroll to the initiate, who bowed deeply and left the room. He turned his attention back to Armel. "You will lead fifty of your men on a mission into Haldane." He stared intently at Armel. "You will do all in your power to keep your presence unknown."

"Who are we to bring back or kill?" Armel quickly realized there were only two reasons to conduct a covert operation with that many troops. Not that it would be his first. He was already thinking about what would be required to shift the organizational structure while he was gone and also the men he had in mind to take with him.

Chuluun-Uul smiled, evidently impressed with Armel's reasoning, as well Armel thought he should.

"You will retrieve twins that are headed for the Hoarfrost Mountains."

The captain nodded. Again he ensured his face did not betray what he thought, but under the surface he was amazed at the destination. He had only been on Taran for a week, but the land of the Ice Giants was well known and not a place one took entered lightly. Yet he prided himself on being a professional and focused on the details, pushing the concern to the back of his mind. "Are fifty men necessary?"

"The twins will not be alone. There are Elfs and others assisting them." The frown on Chuluun-Uul's face let Armel know the man was not used to being questioned, though the captain took pleasure in the priest's response. "You will not be alone. Commander Zaya…" the priest looked up at the woman standing next to his chair, "and three tens of her warriors will ride with you."

Armel inhaled, though barely noticeably, and sat back in his chair, his fingers steepled against his lips. It would not be easy to keep eighty mounted troops unseen for long and he did not relish working with the Jidig. After just a few moments Armel sat back up and looked sternly at Chuluun-Uul. "How will we find these twins?"

The priest grinned. "There is a troop of Blood Stalkers already in pursuit."

Blood Stalkers. Armel wondered if this was a name for another branch of the Jidig warriors.

"Do not worry about them for now. They may or may not play a role in this. Your guide will handle them if they are required."

The way the priest stressed the word 'guide' bothered Armel, but he filed that for later, and instead focused on getting what information he could at the moment. "Will these Blood Stalkers provide information as to the twins' whereabouts?"

"They are, shall we say, somewhat independent. But there is another source that will be your guide to the twins."

Again the priest's weight on 'guide' gave Armel an uncomfortable feeling. The captain was waiting to hear more information when he heard a door open. His hearing was acute and he could tell it was not the door leading to the hallway, but to one of the other rooms adjoining the solar.

The tingling feeling increased and his stomach started to feel queasy, something he had rarely felt since childhood, relegated as he had been to the role of an unexpected son. Out of the corner of his eye he noticed Captain Zaya flinch before regaining her composure, which piqued his curiosity. Both of the odd feelings were intensifying when Chuluun-Uul looked up, over Armel's head. The priest's grin faded, to be replaced with a mildly pained expression.

Through tight lips Chuluun-Uul told Armel, "This is Kaerabard. She is your guide and will be able to find the twins."

Armel stood and spun on his heel to look at the guide. She was taller than even the Jidig, but much thinner than Zaya. She wore a black and red cloak that covered her entire body, but from the shadows of the hood, solid green orbs shone through like beacons. A chill filled the entire room and something pulled at Armel's insides, something unnatural that made his body tense. For the first time in his adult life Armel lost control and staggered back, bumped into the edge of the table, and fell on his rear.

Chuluun-Uul spoke in a somewhat mocking tone. "I am sure you have heard of Shades... have you not, Captain?"

Epilogue

The Goddess' Hand

Aeron opened his eyes. His chest felt as if he had been hit with a lance without wearing armor. He turned his head from side to side, but all he could see was tall green grass that blocked out everything else. He sat up with a little difficulty, but the pain in his chest was starting to ease, leaving a slight burning sensation. He still couldn't see much so he forced himself to stand.

That is better, he thought as he stretched his arms and turned to take in the plains around him. As far as he could see there was nothing but the waist-high grass stretching for miles in every direction. Not even a hill or mountain. But there was *something* off in the distance. It looked like a clump of trees. He looked around once more and then started for the trees, seeing as it was the only change in the landscape.

As he made his way through the grass he wondered where he was and how he had gotten here. The last he remembered, he had been knocked down by something the black-robed priest had thrown at him. And as he stood something had grabbed him. Not on the outside, but on the inside. It had felt as if his entire inside had been pulled out. He guessed that was where the pain in his chest had come from. But he didn't remember anything after that. He was worried about Willoe and Emeline, but he couldn't do anything until he got off this plain.

As he approached the clump of trees he could hear water, like from a small waterfall. He could see a large pond through the trees, large trees with drooping branches. He pushed branches aside and thought how they felt like long fingers hanging down and stroking him.

Coming out to the pond's bank he was surprised to see a woman standing to his left, about a quarter of the way around the pond. She had red hair, like Willoe and Rowyn, which hung down to her knees. It was even curly like theirs. She wore a white full-length dress, but he couldn't see her face as she had her back to him.

He made his way around the pond until he came within five paces of her. He spoke, so as not to scare her. "Good day, my lady." He waited for her answer, but she didn't turn around. He took two steps closer and said, "Good day, my lady. Might I inquire as to where we are?"

The lady turned around and Aeron was stunned by her beauty. Then he realized she looked very much like Willoe and Kerye, but different. He had never thought of his cousin as pretty, but he could see her features in the lady, and the lady was absolutely beautiful.

"Thou might, but I have serious reservations about thine ability to grasp it." Her voice was just as radiant and lovely as her appearance.

He was unable to say anything. Everything he thought of sounded far from adequate.

She took two steps toward him so that he looked directly into her lustrous green eyes. They drew him in like the depths of a pool. He felt like he could fall into them and never come out again. Then, as he watched, the eyes changed. The bright green faded as first black filled the eye, then a small dot of a light shone out from the black. It grew until the light filled her eye sockets completely, and then it flashed brightly and was replaced by flames. The lady stepped back and Aeron could see that she no longer had red hair, but white. Her entire body was aglow with a white light that created a luminous aura, one shining brighter than he imagined possible, though it did not blind him.

He was able to see beyond her to the shining dragon, the same one that had visited Willoe and him in the woods on the way to White Cliffs. The dragon bent its long neck down to the water where it drank and then raised its head, turning its snout toward Aeron and staring at him.

He returned his gaze to the shining lady and as he stared at her his mind flew through the events of his life — from a child riding behind his father, holding on, scared beyond words yet excited at the same time, to his first intimate experience that nearly rivaled the ceremony when he passed his initiation as a Shield, to when he fought the priest on that faraway stream in the valley, with hundreds of visions in between.

His mind circled and returned to stare at the lady. She looked at him and spoke in a voice that felt far away. "Thou hast led a good life and thou hast served me well. The question now is…" She reached out a hand and put it on his bare chest.

A fire like he had never known sprang into his chest and he tried to jerk back, but he couldn't pull away from her hand as it burned into his breast.

Then she spoke again. "What to do with thee, Aeron Cadwal?" She smiled.

THE END
of the first book
of the
Dragon-Called Legend

CHARACTERS

Aeron Cadwal (ae-reon key-waol): One of two close cousins to the Brynmor twins, son of Cainwen's First Duke and heir to the Duchy of Pembroke. *See also* Casandra Cadwal, Drem Cadwal.

Darcio Armel (dar-ki-ow ahr-mel): Captain of the sellsword company Bloody Sun

Bat-Uul (bat-ul): Shin-il Priest newly ordained and assigned to the island of Taran

Benoit Gautier (ben-wah gow-tyey): Current King of Franchon

Besut-Jin (be-sot): Shin-il Priest of a lower caste assigned to work with agents in the Kingdom of Cainwen

Beynon Brynmor (bey-ih-non brihn-maor): Kingdom of Cainwen Crown Prince, father to the twins, Rowyn and Willoe

Brom Brynmor (brom): Uncle to twins and older brother of the Crown Prince, having given up his claim to the throne

Burning Lady: Goddess of the Spirit World

Calei (ca-lee) also known as Ken Mud (kin): Material of the *il fennore* (Spirit world)

Captain Harte (har-te): One of four captains that lead the King's Guard for the Kingdom of Cainwen

Casandra Cadwal (ca-ssand-ra): Aeron Cadwal's brother and twins' cousin

Caspar-Jin (cas-per): Young Shin-il priest and aide to Bat-Uul

Chancellor Liam (le-am): Chancellor for the Kingdom of Cainwen

Chuluun-Uul (ch-ay-uwln-ul): Shin-il Priest, a member of the inner circle of the Shin-il Master (one of the Gai-Ten)

Cian (key-in): Elf, First Lor, grandfather to Saraid and great uncle to Helel

Cleric Yoan (yo-ahn): Cleric (Healer & Diviner of Burning Lady) to the Court of Cainwen

Count Idwal (id-waol): Cainwen count and trusted advisor to the Brynmor family

Cuthbert (kuth-burt): Agent for spymaster Owein Manus the Baron of Winterpass in Cainwen

Dilys (dil-ys): Maid to Princess Willoe since the princess was a toddler

Dimah-Uul (dee-mah-ul): Shin-il Priest, advisor to the King of Franchon before Chuluun-Uul's arrival

Doy (doy): Cutpurse and Royal Groomsman

Drel Corklin (drel kaork-lyn): Tink living in Fayhaven – the Steward of Fayhaven Manor

Drel Donlin (daen-lyn): Tink collaborator of Brom Brynmor

Drem Cadwal (drem): First Duke of Cainwen, Duke over the Duchy of Pembroke and father to Aeron and Casandra Cadwal.

Duke Stockpole (stock-pole): Duke of Wellingford, located in the Kingdom of Cainwen

Einion Brynmor (ein-yawn): King of Cainwen, grandfather to the twins

Emeline Renier (em-a-lien): Niece to the King of Franchon

Eryls (er-ahl): General of the army of the Duchy of Pembroke out of Castle Mount Somerled

Gavyn Rees (geyn-ahn rees): General of the army of the Kingdom of Cainwen

Gerallt (ge-ralt): Cainwen guardsman in the escort to Highkeep Manor

Grioral Malbery (greer-all mal-berry): Earl of Greenmerrow and mentor to Prince Hafgan

Hafgan Brynmor (hahv-gahn): Middle son of Crown Prince Beynon

Hartha (hahr-thah): Cainwen guardsman in the escort to Highkeep Manor

Helel (he-lel): Elfen (female Elf) who trains Casandra, and is a cousin to the Elf Saraid and great niece to Cian

Janen (jan-in): Bandit Leader

Josiane (jos-e-ane): Maid to Lady Emeline

Kaerabard (kay-ra-bard): Shade

Kerye (k-rye): Lady in the Woods

Krel Monlor (mown-laor): Tink who works with Swift, the Borlender, to deliver goods throughout Fayhaven

Llyr (le-ar): Cainwen guardsman in the escort to White Cliffs

Mael Brynmor (myle): Oldest sibling to the twins and heir apparent to Kingdom of Cainwen

Master Gwron (gur-on): Weapons Master to the Court of Cainwen

Owain (o-wen): Cainwen guardsman in the escort to Highkeep Manor

Owein Manus (o-we-in man-us): Spymaster and Baron of Winterpass in Cainwen

Protector Dougal (do-gal): A warrior from the northern Kingdom of Haldane and Protector to the twins Rowyn and Willoe

Rhein (ryne): Cainwen Shield and leader of the escort to Highkeep Manor

Rhodri (rhod-ree): Cainwen guardsman and cook in the escort to Highkeep Manor

Richer (rich-er): Franchon guardsman in the dungeons of Castle White Cliffs

Steward Robat (rabb-aet): Steward of Castle Westhedge in Cainwen

Rowyn Brynmor (ro-wyn): Twin, youngest son of Crown Prince Beynon, mother unknown

Saraid (sa-rai): Elf who is training Rowyn and is the grandson of Lor Cian and cousin to Helel

Sergeant Crowley (kraw-lee): Cainwen Sergeant in the escort to Highkeep Manor

Sergeant Trystan (trist-an): Cainwen Supply Sergeant in the escort to Castle White Cliffs

Sion Tybalt (shawn tee-bolt): Royal Page to the Court of Cainwen and brother to Tomos Tybalt

Sulyen Wellingford (sil-yen): Young heir to Duchy of Wellingford in Cainwen, grandson of Duke Stockpole

Tanguy (tan-ghee): Cainwen Shield in the escort to White Cliffs, close friend of Prince Mael

Tomos Tybalt (tom-us): Royal Page to the Court of Cainwen, and brother to Sion Tybalt

Willoe Brynmor (Wil-lo): Twin, daughter of Crown Prince Beynon

Zaya (ze-yah): Commander of an elite troop of Jidig (steppe) warriors

MISCELLANEOUS INFORMATION

Uul Priest: [Red robes] Highest ranking of the Shin-il priesthood. Within the Uul's, ten are named the Gai-Ten, the inner circle to the Master, leader of the Shin-il Way.

Jin Priest: [Black robes] Shin-il priest one rank below the Uul priests.

Obeah Priest: [Yellow robes] Shin-il priest from a remote eastern island. Obeah priest are disdained by other Shin-il priest because of their use of herbs and other magical forms not of the Spirit world.

Acolytes: [Brown robes] Individuals who serve the Shin-il priest with hopes of becoming one someday themselves.

Cainwen Colors: Gold on Dark Green
Cainwen Heraldry: Dragon in Flight

Franchon Colors: Red on Dark Gray
Franchon Heraldry: Lion Roaring

Haldane Colors: White on Medium Blue
Haldane Heraldry: Hawk Attacking

READER FEEDBACK

While great care and effort have gone into making this reading experience as flawless and enjoyable as possible, there will always be improvements that could be made.

If anything about this story or the packaging and formatting it came in jumps out at you as worthy of being corrected or amended, please feel free to submit a suggestion at http://DragonCalled.com/reader-feedback/

Your feedback is valuable to the writing process, both for this book and any future stories, so we would be incredibly grateful for any suggestions!

PETER CRUIKSHANK

ABOUT THE AUTHOR

As a preteen I was introduced to Robert Heinlein's Stranger in a Strange Land by a friend's father, an author, and then later I picked up a copy of Lord of the Rings. It wasn't long before I was hooked for life.

At 18 years of age I knew I wanted to be an author, but life got in the way and my dreams were put on hold. In 2012 I turned to writing full time and now have two series in the works.

Outside of writing I obtained a MS in Information Systems and since I tend to get bored, I have worked in the private and public sectors, academia, and the ministry field. This has given me a wealth of experiences that I try to bring to my writing.

Married 30 years to a beautiful woman, with three children grown into caring and sensitive adults, I have had a wonderful and challenged life's journey. The challenged part has helped form much of my own view of the fantasy worlds that I now write about.

I believe stories are about the characters and the movement of them through some adventure or experience. That is why I focus on character development and try to show action in detail. I guess that is how I came up with my tag line: *Epic Fantasy Adventures with Character.*

COMING SOON

Dragon-Called Legend – Book 2
The Sword and the Staff (fall 2014)

Tracked by minions of the evil priest, Chuluun-Uul, the Dragon-Called twins, Rowyn and Willoe, journey on a quest to the Hoarfrost Mountains. These lands are rife with dangers, including Skoll Wolves and the fearsome Ice Giants, and may hide more than just the sought-after devices of the dragons.

Back at Westhedge, unrest stirs as it becomes clear that newly self-crowned King Hafgan will do whatever is necessary to keep his tenuous hold on the throne of Cainwen.

On the other side of Taran, the Haldane capital of Wintertide may hold a staunch new ally for the twins, but nothing comes without a price.

With time running out and fewer allies than they might have preferred, the key to opposing the Shin-il priests and taking back Taran lies in an all-out assault on Tierran's Wall – built to be impregnable. Forced to contend with Shades and even greater horrors from the deepest level of the Shadows to oppose them from without, and with foul betrayal threatening to shatter their ranks from within, Rowyn and Willoe have little hope of success.

In this, their darkest hour, is victory even possible?

And if so, at what cost?

Made in the USA
San Bernardino, CA
24 February 2014